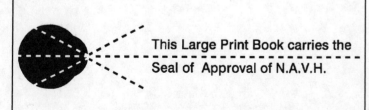

This Large Print Book carries the
Seal of Approval of N.A.V.H.

LIGHT OF THE WORLD

A DAVE ROBICHEAUX NOVEL

LIGHT OF THE WORLD

JAMES LEE BURKE

WHEELER PUBLISHING
A part of Gale, Cengage Learning

GALE
CENGAGE Learning·

Detroit • New York • San Francisco • New Haven, Conn • Waterville, Maine • London

LIBRARY OF CONGRESS CATALOGING-IN-PUBLICATION DATA

Burke, James Lee, 1936–
    Light of the world : a Dave Robicheaux novel / by James Lee Burke. — Large print edition.
        pages ; cm
        ISBN-13: 978-1-4104-5987-9 (hardcover)
        ISBN-10: 1-4104-5987-X (hardcover)
        1. Robicheaux, Dave (Fictitious character)—Fiction. 2. Good and evil—Fiction. 3. Kansas—Fiction. 4. Large type books. I. Title.
    PS3552.U723L54 2013b
    813'.54—dc23   2013022740

Published in 2013 by arrangement with Simon & Schuster, Inc.

Printed in the United States of America
1 2 3 4 5 6 7 17 16 15 14 13

Once again, to my wife, Pearl, and our children, James L. Burke III, Andree Burke Walsh, Pamala Burke, and Alafair Burke

CHAPTER 1

I was never good at solving mysteries. I don't mean the kind cops solve or the ones you read about in novels or watch on television or on a movie screen. I'm not talking about the mystery of Creation, either, or the unseen presences that reside perhaps just the other side of the physical world. I'm talking about evil, without capitalization but evil all the same, the kind whose origins sociologists and psychiatrists have trouble explaining.

Police officers keep secrets, not unlike soldiers who return from foreign battlefields with a syndrome that survivors of the Great War called the thousand-yard stare. I believe that the account of the apple taken from the forbidden tree is a metaphorical warning about looking too deeply into the darker potential of the human soul. The photographs of the inmates at Bergen-Belsen or Andersonville Prison or the bodies in the ditch at My Lai disturb us in a singular fashion because those instances of egregious human cruelty were committed for the most part by baptized Christians. At some point we close the book containing photographs of this kind and put it away and convince ourselves that the events were an aberration, the consequence of leaving soldiers too long in the field or letting a handful of misanthropes take control of a bureaucracy. It is not in our interest to extrapolate a larger meaning.

Hitler, Nero, Ted Bundy, the Bitch of Buchenwald? Their deeds are not ours.

But if these individuals are not like us, if they do not descend from the same gene pool and have the same DNA, then who were they and what turned them into monsters?

Every homicide cop lives with images he cannot rinse from his dreams; every cop who has handled investigations into child abuse has seen a side of his fellow man he never discusses with anyone, not his wife, not his colleagues, not his confessor or his bartender. There are certain burdens you do not visit on people of goodwill.

When I was in plainclothes at the NOPD, I used to deal with problems such as these in a saloon on Magazine Street, not far from the old Irish Channel. With its brass-railed bar and felt-covered bouree tables and wood-bladed fans, it became my secular church where the Louisiana of my youth, the green-gold, mossy, oak-shaded world of Bayou Teche, was only one drink away. I would start with four fingers of Jack in a thick mug, with a sweating Budweiser back, and by midnight I would be alone at the end of the bar, armed, drunk, and hunched over my glass, morally and psychologically insane.

I had come to feel loathing and disgust with the mythology that characterized the era in which I lived. I didn't "serve" in Southeast Asia; I "survived" and watched innocent people and better men than I die in large numbers while I was spared by a hand outside myself. I didn't "serve and protect" as a police officer; I witnessed the justice system's dysfunction and the government's empowerment of corporations and the exploitation of those who had no political voice. And while I brooded on all that was wrong in the world, I continued to stoke the furnace inside me with Black Jack and Smirnoff's and five-star Hennessy and, finally, two jiggers of Scotch inside a glass of milk at sunrise, constantly suppressing my desire to lock down on my enemies with the .45 automatic I had purchased in Saigon's brothel district and with which I slept as I would a woman.

My real problem wasn't the militarization of my country or any of the other problems I've mentioned. The real problem went back to a mystery that had beset me since the destruction of my natal home and family. My father, Big Aldous, was on the monkey board of an offshore drilling well when the drill bit punched into an early pay sand and a spark jumped off the wellhead and a mushroom of flaming oil and natural gas rose through the rigging like an inferno ballooning from the bottom of an elevator shaft. My mother, Alafair Mae Guillory, was seduced and blackmailed by a gambler and pimp named Mack, whom I hated more than any human being I ever knew, not because he turned her into a barroom whore but because of the Asian men I killed in his stead.

Rage and bloodlust and alcoholic blackouts became the only form of serenity I knew. From Saigon to the Philippines, from Chinatown in Los Angeles to the drunk tanks of New Orleans, the same questions haunted me and gave me no rest. Were some people made different in the womb, born without a conscience, intent on destroying everything that was good in the world? Or could a black wind blow the weather vane in the wrong direction for any of us and reshape our lives and turn us into people we no longer recognized? I knew there was an answer out there someplace, if I could only drink myself into the right frame of mind and find it.

I stayed ninety-proof for many years and got a bachelor's degree in self-immolation and a doctorate in chemically induced psychosis. When I finally entered sobriety, I thought the veil might be lifted and I would find answers to all the Byzantine riddles that had confounded me.

That was not to be the case. Instead, a man who was one of the most wicked creatures on earth made his way into our lives. This is a tale that maybe I shouldn't share. But it's not one I want to keep inside me, either.

My adopted daughter, Alafair Robicheaux, jogged up a logging road that wound through ponderosa pine and Douglas fir and cedar trees atop a ridge overlooking a two-lane highway and a swollen creek far below. The highway had been built on the exact trail that Meriwether Lewis and William Clark had followed over Lolo Pass into present-day Idaho and, eventually, to the Pacific Ocean in the year 1805. They had not been able to accomplish this feat on their own. After they and their men had sliced their moccasins to ribbons trying to make portage with their canoes through several canyons on a fork of the Columbia River, a Shoshone woman by the name of Sacagawea showed them a route that took them up a gentle slope, past the base of Lolo Peak, into the country of the Nez Perce and the spotted horses called the Appaloosa.

As Alafair jogged along the dirt road that had been graded through timber by a bulldozer, the wind blowing cool out of the trees, the western sun blazing on the fresh snow that had fallen the previous night on Lolo

Peak, she wondered at the amount of history that had been changed by one brave woman, because Sacagawea not only showed the Lewis and Clark party the way to Oregon, she saved them from starvation and being slaughtered by a rogue band of Nez Perce.

Alafair was listening to a song on her iPod when she felt a stinging sensation on her left ear. She also felt a puff of air against her cheek and the touch of a feather on her skin. Without stopping, she swatted at her hair and pressed her hand against her ear and then looked at it. There was a bright smear of blood on her palm. Above, she saw two ravens glide into the boughs of a ponderosa and begin cawing at the sky.

She continued up the logging road, her breath coming hard in her throat, until she reached the top of the ridge. Then she turned and began the descent, her knees jarring on the grade, the sun moving behind Lolo Peak, the reflected light disappearing from the surface of the creek. She touched her ear again, but the cut she believed a raven had inflicted was no longer bleeding and felt like little more than a scratch. That was when she saw the aluminum shaft of a feathered arrow embedded three inches deep in a cedar snag that had been scorched and hardened in a fire.

She slowed to a stop, her heart beating hard, and looked over her shoulder. The logging road was in shadow, the border of trees so thick she could no longer feel the wind or see where the sun was. The air smelled like snow, like the coming of winter rather than summer. She took off her earbuds and listened. She heard the crackling of limbs and rocks sliding down a slope. A big doe, a mule deer, no more than twenty yards away, jumped a pile of dirt and landed squarely in the middle of the road, its gray winter coat unchanged by spring.

"Is there a bow hunter out there?" Alafair shouted.

There was no answer.

"There's no bow season in western Montana in the spring. At least not for deer," she called out.

There was no response except the sweep of the wind in the trees, a sound like the rushing of floodwater in a dry riverbed. She ran her finger along the arrow and touched the feathers at the base. The aluminum shaft bore no trace of dirt or bird droppings or even dust. The feathers were clean and stiff when she ran the ball of her thumb along their edges.

"If you made a mistake and you're sorry, just come out and apologize," she yelled. "Who shot this arrow?"

The doe bounced away from her, almost like a kangaroo. The shadows had grown so dark inside the border of the trees that the deer was indistinguishable except for the patch of white hair under its tail. Unconsciously, Alafair pulled on her cut earlobe and studied the trees and the orange glow in the west that indicated the sun would set in the next ten minutes. She fitted both hands on the shaft of the arrow and jerked it from the cedar trunk. The arrowhead was made of steel and was bright and slick with a thin sheen of oil, and flanged and wavy on the edges, which had been honed as sharp as a razor.

She made her way back down the ridge, almost to the bottom, then walked out on a rocky point that formed a V and jutted into space and was devoid of trees and second growth. Below she saw a broad-shouldered man with a narrow waist, wearing Wranglers and a white straw hat and a bandanna tied around his neck. He had on a navy blue long-sleeved shirt buttoned at the wrists, with white stars embroidered on the shoulders and purple garters on his upper arms, the kind an exotic dancer might wear on her thighs. He was latching the door on the camper shell inserted in the bed of his pickup truck. "Hey, buddy!" Alafair said. "I want a word with you."

He turned slowly, lifting his head, a solitary ray of sunlight pooling under his hat brim. Even though the glare must have been intense, he didn't blink. He was a white man with the profile of an Indian and eyes that seemed made of glass and contained no color other than the sun's refracted brilliance. His complexion made her think of the rind on a cured ham. "Why, howdy-doody," he said, an idiot's grin painted on his mouth. "Where'd a cute little heifer like you come from?"

"Does this arrow belong to you?" she asked.

"I'll take it if you don't want it."

"Did you shoot this fucking arrow at me or not?"

"I cain't hear very good in the wind. What was that word you used?" He cupped one hand to his ear. "Want to come down here and talk?"

"Somebody almost killed me with this arrow."

He removed the thin stub of a cigar from his shirt pocket and lit it with a paper match, cupping the flame in his hands, then making a big show of shaking out the match. "There's a truck stop next to the casino. I'll buy you a Coca-Cola. They got showers there if you want one."

"Was that a bow you were putting in your camper? You owe me an answer."

"My name is Mr. Wyatt Dixon of Fort Davis, Texas. I'm a bullfighter and a handler of rough stock and a born-again Christian. What do you think of them apples? Come on down, girl. I ain't gonna bite."

"I think you need to get out of here."

"This is the home of the brave and the land of the free, and God bless you for your exercise of your First Amendment rights. But I only pretended I didn't hear what you said. Profanity does not behoove your gender. Know who said that? Thomas Jefferson did, yessiree-bobtail."

His teeth looked like they were cut out of whalebone. His whole body seemed wired with levels of energy and testicular power he could barely control. Even though his posture was relaxed, his knuckles were as hard-looking as ball bearings. "Are you deciding about my invite, or has the cat got your tongue?" he said.

She wanted to answer him, but the words wouldn't come. He removed his hat and drew a pocket comb through his silky red hair, tilting up his chin. "I'm a student of accents. You're from somewhere down south. See you down the track, sweet thing. If I was you, I'd stay out of them woods. You cain't ever tell what's roaming around in there."

He let a semi carrying a huge piece of oil machinery pass, then got in his truck and drove away. She felt a rivulet of moisture leak from her sweatband and run down her cheek. A sour odor rose from under her arms.

In the early spring Alafair and my wife, Molly, and my old partner from NOPD, Clete Purcel, had returned to western Montana with plans to spend the summer on a ranch owned by a novelist and retired English professor whose name was Albert Hollister. Albert had built a three-story house of logs and quarried rock on a knoll overlooking a railed pasture to the north and another to the south. It was a fine home, rustic but splendid in concept, a bucolic citadel where Albert could continue to wage war against the intrusions of the Industrial Age. When his beloved Asian wife died, I suspected the house she had helped design rang with an emptiness that drove him almost mad.

Albert installed Clete in a guest cabin located at the far end of the property, and the rest of us on the third floor of the house. From the balcony, we had a wonderful view of the wooded foothills that seemed to topple for miles and miles before they reached the Bitterroot Mountains, white and shining as bright as glaciers on the peaks and strung with mist at sunrise. Across from our balcony was a hillside dotted with larch and fir and pine trees and outcroppings of gray rock and traced with arroyos swollen with snowmelt and brown water and pine needles during the runoff in early April.

On a shady slope behind the house, Albert had improvised a gun range where we popped big, fat coffee cans that he propped on sticks at the foot of a trail that had been used by Chief Joseph and the Nez Perce when they tried to outrun the United States Army. Before we would begin shooting, Albert would shout out "Fire in the well!" to warn any animals grazing or sleeping among the trees. He not only posted his own property, he infuriated hunters all over the county by chain-dragging logs across public roads in order to block vehicle access to U.S. Forest Service land during big-game season. I don't know if I would call him a rabble-rouser, but I was convinced that his historical antecedent was Samuel Adams and that ten like him could have a city in flames within twenty-four hours.

The sun had set by the time Alafair returned to the house. She told me of her encounter with Wyatt Dixon.

"Did you get his tag?" I asked.

"There was mud on it. He said he was going to the casino."

"You didn't see the bow?"

"I already told you, Dave."

"I'm sorry, I wanted to get it straight. Let's take a ride."

We drove in my pickup down the dirt road to the two-lane and turned east and followed the creek into Lolo, a small service town at the gateway to the Bitterroot Mountains. The sky was purple and flecked with snow, the neon lights glowing in front of the truck stop and adjacent casino. "The orange pickup. That's his," she said.

I started to wave down a Missoula County sheriff's cruiser at the intersection, but I decided against it. So far we had nothing on Dixon. I rubbed the film off the rear window of the camper inset in his truck bed and peered inside. I could make out a lumpy duffel bag, a western saddle, a long-barrel lever-action rifle with an elevator sight, and a mud-caked truck tire and a jack. I didn't see a bow. I looked through the passenger window with the same result.

The inside of the casino was dark and refrigerated and smelled of carpet cleaner and bathroom disinfectant. A man in a white straw cowboy hat was at the bar, drinking from a soda can and eating a sandwich. A piece of paper towel was tucked like a bib into his shirt collar. He watched us in the bar mirror as we approached him.

"My name is Dave Robicheaux," I said. "This is my daughter Alafair. I'd like to have a word with you."

He bit into his sandwich and chewed, one cheek tightening into a ball, leaning forward so no crumbs fell on the bar or on his shirt or jeans. His gaze shifted sideways. "You have the look of a law dog, sir," he said.

"Have you been inside, Mr. Dixon?"

"Inside what?"

"A place where smart-asses have a way of ending up. I understand you're a rodeo man."

"What some call a rodeo clown. What we

call bullfighters. At one time I shot mustangs for a dog-food company down on the border. I don't do that no more."

"Were you hunting about five miles up Highway 12?"

"No, sir, I was changing the tire on my truck."

"You have any idea who might have shot an arrow at my daughter?"

"No, but I'm getting mighty tired of hearing about it."

"Did you see anyone on that ridge besides my daughter?"

"No, I didn't." He put down his sandwich and removed his paper bib and wiped his mouth and fingers clean. He turned on the stool. All the color seemed to be leeched out of his eyes except for the pupils, which looked like the burnt tips of wood matches. "Watch this," he said.

"Watch what?"

"This." He sprinkled salt on the bar and balanced the shaker on its edge amid the granules so it leaned at an angle like the Tower of Pisa. "Bet neither one of y'all can do that."

"Call 911," I said to Alafair.

"Can I ask you a question?" he said.

"Go ahead."

"Did somebody shoot you in the face?"

"Yeah, someone did. I was lucky. He was a bad guy, a degenerate and a sadist and a

20

stone killer."

"I bet you sent him straight to the injection table, didn't you?" he said, his eyes bulging, his mouth dropping open in mock exaltation.

"No, it didn't make the jail."

His mouth opened even wider, as though he were unable to control his level of shock. "I am completely blown away. I have traveled this great nation from coast to coast and have stood in the arena among the great heroes of our time. I am awed and humbled to be in the presence of a lawman such as yourself. Even though I am only a simple rodeo cowboy, I stand and salute you, sir."

He rose from the stool, puffing out his chest, his body rigid as though at attention, his stiffened right hand at the corner of his eyebrow. "God bless you, sir. Your kind makes me proud of the red, white, and blue, even though I am not worthy to stand in your shadow, in this lowly barroom on the backstreets of America, where men with broken hearts go and the scarlet waters flow. The likes of Colin Kelly and Audie Murphy didn't have nothing on you, kind sir."

People were staring at us, although he took no notice of them.

I said, "You called my daughter 'girl' and 'sweet thing.' You also made a veiled threat about seeing her down the track. Don't ever come near us again, Mr. Dixon."

His eyes wandered over my face. His mouth

21

was down-hooked at the corners, his skin taut as pig hide, the dimple in his chin clean-shaven and shiny, perhaps with aftershave. He glanced through the front window at a sheriff's cruiser pulling into the parking lot. The moral vacuity of his profile reminded me of a shark's when it passes close to the glass in an aquarium.

"Did you hear me?" I said.

"That 911 deputy ain't gonna find nothing in my truck, 'cause there ain't nothing to find," he said. "You asked if I was inside. I got my head lit up with amounts of electricity that make you glad for the rubber gag they put in your mouth. Before you get your nose too high in the air, Mr. Robicheaux, your daughter asked me if that 'fucking arrow' was mine. She talked to me like I was white trash."

He sat back down and began eating his sandwich again, swallowing it in large pieces without chewing or drinking from his soda, his expression reconfiguring, like that of a man who could not decide who he was.

I should have walked away. Maybe he wasn't totally to blame. Maybe Alafair had indeed spoken down to him. Regardless, he had tried to frighten her, and there are some things a father can't let slide. I touched him on the shoulder, on the pattern of white stars sewn onto the fabric. "You're not a victim, partner," I said. "I'm going to pull your jacket and see what you've been up to. I hope you've

22

been on the square with us, Mr. Dixon."

He didn't turn around, but I could see the rigidity in his back and the blood rising in his neck like the red fluid in a thermometer.

CHAPTER 2

The allure of Montana is like a commitment to a narcotic; you can never use it up or get enough of it. Its wilderness areas probably resemble the earth on the first day of creation. For me it was also a carousel, one whose song and light show never ended. The morning after Alafair's confrontation with Wyatt Dixon, we had rain, then blowing snow inside the sunshine, then sleeting snow and rain, and sunshine again and green pastures and flowers blooming in the gardens and a rainbow that arched across the mountains. All of this before nine A.M.

I walked down through the pasture, past Albert's four-stall barn, to the cabin made of split logs where Clete Purcel was staying. The cabin had been built next to a streambed shaded by cottonwoods and a solitary birch tree. The streambed carried water only in the spring and was dry and sandy the rest of the year, crisscrossed by the tracks of deer and wild turkeys and sometimes the long-footed imprints of snowshoe rabbits.

Clete's hip waders were hanging upside down from the gallery roof, rainwater slipping down their rubbery surfaces; his fly and spinning rods were propped against the gallery railing, the lines pulled tightly through the eyelets and doubled back along the length of the rods, the hooks on the lures notched into the cork handles. He had washed his canvas creel and fishnet in a bucket and had hung them and his canvas fly vest on pegs that protruded from the log wall. His restored maroon Cadillac convertible was parked behind the cabin, a tarp draped over its starched white top, the tarp speckled with the droppings of ravens and magpies.

Through the window, I could see him eating at the breakfast table, his massive upper body hunched over his food, the grate on the woodstove behind him slitted with fire. Before I could knock, he waved me in.

If space aliens ever wanted to take over the planet and wipe out the human race, they simply needed to convince the rest of us to eat the same breakfast that Clete Purcel did. With variations depending on the greasy spoon, he daily shoveled down the pipe a waffle or three pancakes soaked in syrup, or four eggs fried in butter, with toast, grits, and a bowl of milk gravy on the side; a pork chop or breakfast steak or a plate of ham and bacon; and at least three cups of café au lait.

Because he knew he had filled his digestive system with enough cholesterol and salt to clog the Suez Canal, he topped it off with a cup of stewed tomatoes or fruit cocktail, in the belief that it could neutralize a combination of grease and butter and animal fat with the viscosity of the lubricant used on train wheels.

I told him about Alafair's encounter with Wyatt Dixon and our exchange with him at the casino. Clete opened the grate to his stove and dropped two blocks of pinewood into the flames. "Dixon allowed the deputy to search his truck?" he said.

"He was completely cooperative. The only weapon in there was an old lever-action Winchester."

"Maybe he's not the guy."

"Alafair says nobody else was in the parking area or on the ridge. She's sure Dixon is the only person who could have shot the arrow."

"You think he has a jacket?"

"I called the sheriff an hour ago. Dixon has been around here for years, but nobody is sure what he is or who he is. He was mixed up with some militia people in the Bitterroot Valley who were afraid of him. When he went down for capping a rapist, Deer Lodge couldn't deal with him."

"A prison in Montana can't deal with somebody?"

26

"They sent him to electroshock."

"I didn't think they did that anymore."

"They made an exception. Dixon was kicked out of the army when he was fifteen for cutting the stripes off a black mess sergeant behind a saloon in San Antonio and stuffing them in the guy's mouth. At a rodeo he knocked a bull unconscious with his fist. He says he's born-again, and some people say he can speak in tongues. A university professor was recording a Pentecostal prayer meeting up on the rez when Wyatt Dixon got up and started testifying. The university professor claims Dixon was speaking Aramaic."

"What's Aramaic?"

"The language of Jesus."

Clete was looking at his coffee cup, his expression neutral, his little-boy haircut freshly combed and damp from his shower, his face unlined and youthful in the morning sunlight. "Dave, don't get mad at me for what I'm about to say. But we got the living shit shot out of us on the bayou. Not once but twice. Alafair went through a big trauma, just like us. I shut my eyes and I imagine things."

"Alafair's ear was cut."

"We don't know that the arrow did it. You said something about ravens fighting in a tree. Maybe it's all coincidence. Easy does it, right?"

"Alafair is nobody's fool. She doesn't go

around imagining things."

"She gets into it with people. This time it's with a wack job. The guy's truck was clean. Leave him alone and quit borrowing trouble."

"Do you know what I feel when you say something like that?" I asked.

"No, what?"

"Forget it. Have a few more slices of ham. Maybe that will help you think more clearly."

He blew out his breath. "You want to roust him?"

"He doesn't roust."

"You said he went down on a murder beef. How'd he get out?"

"A technicality of some kind."

"Okay, we'll keep an eye out, but the guy has no reason to hurt Alafair. And he doesn't add up as a guy who randomly hunts people with a bow and arrow, particularly on his home turf."

Clete was the best investigative cop I ever knew and hard to argue with. He would lay down his life for me and Alafair and Molly. He was brave and gentle and violent and self-destructive, and each morning he woke with a succubus that had fed at his heart since childhood. Whenever I spoke impatiently to him or hurt his feelings, I felt an unrelieved sense of remorse and sorrow, because I knew that Clete Purcel was one of those guys who took the heat for the rest of us. I also knew that if he were not in our midst, the world would be a much worse place.

"I guess I worry too much," I said.

"Alafair is your daughter. You're supposed to worry, noble mon," he said. "I still got some buttered toast in the skillet. Eat up."

I knew he was kidding about the buttered toast, and I hoped that our vacation was on track and that my worries about Alafair and Wyatt Dixon were unfounded. But when he poured a cup of coffee in a tin cup and pushed it across the table toward me, his green eyes not meeting mine, I knew he was thinking about something else, not about a quasi-psychotic cowboy in a casino. I also knew that whenever Clete Purcel tried to hide something, both of us were headed for trouble.

"Go ahead," I said.

"Go ahead what?"

"Say whatever it is that's bothering you."

"I was just going to update you, that's all."

"About what?"

"Gretchen just graduated from that film school in Los Angeles."

"Good," I replied, my discomfort increasing.

"She called and said she'd like to visit."

"Here?"

"Yeah, since here is where I'm staying, this is where she'd like to visit. I already talked with Albert."

I tried to keep my eyes flat, my face empty,

to clear the obstruction that was like a wishbone in my throat. He was staring into my face, expectant, wanting me to say words I couldn't.

Less than a year before, Clete discovered he had fathered a daughter out of wedlock. Her name was Gretchen Horowitz, and she had been raised in Miami by her mother, a heroin addict and a prostitute. He also found out that Gretchen had been a contract assassin for the Mafia and was known in the life as Caruso.

"Think she'll like Montana?" I said.

"Why wouldn't she?"

"It's cold country. I mean cold for a kid who grew up in the tropics."

I saw the light die in his eyes. "Sometimes you really get to me, Streak."

"I'm sorry."

"Sorry is right," he said. He picked up his dishes and dropped them loudly in the sink.

Six months ago, close to the Colorado-Kansas line, a little boy looked out the window of a house trailer not far from the intersection of a two-lane highway and a dirt road. The sky was lidded with black thunderclouds, the western rim of the landscape banded by a ribbon of cold blue light. The wind was blowing hard in the fields, lifting clouds of grit into the air, flapping the wash on the clotheslines behind the trailer. Even though the land was carpeted by miles and miles of wheat that was planted in the fall and harvested in the spring, the coldness of the season and the bitter edge in the elements made one feel this part of the world was condemned to permanent winter. It was the locale where the term "cabin fever" originated, where farm women went crazy in January and shot themselves, and a rancher had to tie a rope from the porch to the barn to find his way back to the house during a whiteout. It was a place where only the most religious and determined of people survived.

While the little boy's mother slept in front of a television screen buzzing with white noise, the boy watched a tattered man emerge from a beer joint at the crossroads and walk unsteadily down the edge of the two-lane, one hand clamped to the hat on his head, his coat whipping in the wind, his face leaning like a hatchet into the flying snow pellets that were as tiny and hard as bits of glass. Later, the boy would refer to the figure as "the scarecrow man."

A tanker truck appeared far down the wavy surface of the highway, headlights on, its weight and shimmering cylindrical shape and dedicated purpose so great and unrelenting that it seemed to move and jitter against the sun's afterglow without sound or mechanically driven power, sustained by its own momentum, as though the truck had a destiny that had been planned long ago.

From the opposite direction, a prison van with a driver and a guard in front was approaching the crossroads. The van was followed by an escort cruiser that had stopped so one of the state police officers could use the restroom. In the back of the van was a prisoner by the name of Asa Surrette, who was scheduled to testify at a murder trial in a small town on the Colorado border. His left arm had been broken by another inmate in a maximum-security unit at El Dorado, Kansas. The cast on his arm was thick and cumbersome and ran from wrist to shoulder. Because of the prisoner's history of docility in custody, his warders had not put him in a waist chain but instead had manacled his right hand to a D-ring inset in the floor, which allowed him to lie back on a perforated steel bench welded to the van wall.

The little boy saw the scarecrow man take a flat-sided amber bottle from his coat pocket and upend it against the sky, then screw down the cap and, for no apparent reason, stumble across the highway in front of the tanker truck. The boy began to make moaning sounds against the window glass. The driver of the truck hit the brakes, jackknifing the load. The tanker swung sideways across the asphalt, and the air filled with the screeching sound of torn steel, like a ship breaking apart as it sank.

The driver of the prison van probably never had a chance to react. The van crashed with such force into the truck cab that it seemed to disintegrate as the tanker rolled over it. The moment of ignition was not instantaneous. Debris rained down on the asphalt and in the ditches along the road, while a dark apron of gasoline spread from the spot where the tanker came to rest. There was a flash of light from the far side of the truck cab, followed by an explosion and a yellow-and-red ball of flame that boiled the frozen snow in the fields. The two vehicles were still burning when the volunteer fire truck arrived half an hour later.

The little boy told his mother what he had seen, and she in turn told the authorities. If a scarecrow man was the cause of the accident, there was no trace of him. Nor did anybody in the beer joint remember a drunk who had wandered down the road, perhaps with a bottle of whiskey.

An investigation resulted in the following conclusions: The two state police officers in the escort vehicle were derelict in not staying within sight of the prison van; the driver of the tanker truck should have been on the interstate but had taken a detour to visit a girlfriend; the driver of the van and the guard in the passenger seat had probably died upon impact; the little boy who had seen the scarecrow man had been diagnosed as autistic and was considered by his teachers as fanciful and uneducable in a conventional setting.

Four people were dead, the bodies burned so badly that they virtually crumbled apart when the paramedics tried to extract them from the wreckage. The centerpiece of the news story was neither the macabre nature of the accident nor the loss of innocent life but the death of the prisoner. Asa Surrette had stalked and tortured and killed eight people, including children, in the city of Wichita, and had eluded execution because the crimes to which he'd confessed had been committed before 1994, when the maximum sentence in Kansas for homicide was life imprisonment.

The news of his death went out over the wire services and was soon consigned to the category of good riddance and forgotten. Also forgotten was the account given by the autistic boy whose breath had fogged the window just before the scarecrow man silhouetted against the truck's headlights. But historical footnotes are tedious and uninteresting. Why should the little boy's tale be treated any differently?

I didn't want to be unfair to Gretchen. Her childhood had been one of neglect and abuse. No, that's not quite accurate. Her childhood had been horrific. Her body was burned with cigarettes when she was an infant. Many

34

years later, Clete Purcel caught up with the man who did it, out on the flats, on the backside of Key West. Later, a man's skin and most of his bones washed out of a sand-bar, a Bic cigarette lighter wedged in what was left of the thorax.

At age six, Gretchen was sodomized by her mother's boyfriend, a psychopath named Bix Golightly who did smash-and-grab jewel-store robberies and fenced the loot through the Dixie Mafia. Last year Gretchen took a pro bono contract on Golightly and found him sitting in his van at night in Algiers, across the river from New Orleans; she planted three rounds in his face. Clete saw it happen and called in a shots-fired but pro-tected his daughter's identity. His love for the daughter and his attempts at atonement almost cost him his life.

I liked Gretchen. She had many of her father's virtues. There was no doubt that she was fearless. There was no doubt she was intelligent. I also believed that her contrition for her former life was real. However, there is a peculiar atavistic mechanism built into each of us that doesn't always coincide with our thought processes. A tuning fork buried in the human breast develops a tremolo when we come in contact with certain kinds of people. Ask any career cop about former felons of his acquaintance who have stacked serious time in a maximum-security joint and were stand-up and took everything the system and the prison culture could throw at them and came out of it fairly intact and went to work as carpenters and welders and married decent women and started families. Every good cop is glad to witness that kind of success story. But when one of those same guys moves next door to you, or asks to come by your house, or introduces himself to your wife and children in the grocery store, a film projector clicks on in your head and you see images from this man's past that you cannot stop thinking about. As a consequence, you create an invisible moat around your castle and loved ones and subtly indicate that it is not to be crossed by the wrong people, no matter how unfair that might seem.

I was helping Albert scrub out the horse tank in the south pasture when I saw Gretchen's chopped-down hot-rod pickup coming up the dirt road from the state highway, the soft-throated rumble of the twin Hollywood mufflers echoing off the hillsides. "Albert?" I said.

"What?" he replied, obviously irritated that I had chosen to use his name as a question rather than simply ask him the question. His denim sleeves were rolled up on his arms, the exposed skin sprinkled with purple-and-blackish-brown discolorations that he refused to see a dermatologist about. Few of his university colleagues ever knew that Albert

36

had been a drifter and roustabout and migrant farmworker at age seventeen and had done six months spreading tar on a Florida road gang. The greatest contradiction about Albert lay in the antithetical mix of his egalitarian social views and work-hardened physicality with his patrician features and Southern manners, as though his creator had decided to install the soul of Sidney Lanier in the body of a hod carrier.

"Did Clete tell you very much about Miss Gretchen?" I asked.

"He said she was planning to make a documentary on shale-oil extraction."

"Did he tell you about her background?"

"He said she just finished film school."

"She got mixed up with some bad dudes in Miami."

He was bent over the rim of the tank, scrubbing a ring of dried red bacteria off its sides. I could hear him breathing above the sound of the bristles scraping against the aluminum. "What kind of bad dudes are we talking about?"

"Greaseballs from Brooklyn and Staten Island. Maybe some Cuban hitters in Little Havana."

He nodded, still moving the brush back and forth. "I never liked the term 'greaseballs.' I know you use it to characterize a state of mind and not ethnicity. Just the same, I don't like it."

"Forget political correctness. She did contract hits, Albert."

This time he stopped working. He was crouched on his knees, one arm resting on the lip of the tank. "Why isn't she in jail?"

"Clete and I looked the other way. I don't always feel real good about that."

"Is she mobbed up now?"

"No, she's done with it."

He watched Gretchen's hot rod come up the dirt road, the horses running beside it along the rail fence. "I had chains on my ankles when I was eighteen. I watched two hacks put a man on an anthill. I saw a boy locked in a corrugated tin sweatbox that almost cooked his brain. I was in a parish prison in Louisiana when a man was electrocuted twenty feet from the lockdown unit I was in. I could hear him weeping when they strapped him down."

"I had to inform you, Albert."

"Yeah, I know. If you were me, what would you do?"

I had to collect my thoughts before I spoke. "I'd ask her to leave."

"Going to Mass this Sunday?" he said.

"You know how to rub the salt in the wound."

He began hosing off the inside of the tank, tilting it sideways to force the water through the drain hole in the bottom. "We didn't have this conversation."

"Sir?"

He glanced at the sky. "It looks like more rain. We can use as much as we can get. Those goddamn oil companies are cooking the whole planet."

I resolved that one day I would ask Albert why his colleagues at the university had not shot him long ago.

Gretchen turned off the dirt road and drove under the arch above Albert's driveway and parked in front of the house. She walked across the front lawn, past the flower baskets hanging from the deck, and stopped at the pedestrian gate to the pasture where we were cleaning and refilling the horse tank. She had reddish-blond hair and Clete's clear complexion and eyes that were the color of violets and the same erect posture that made both her and Clete look taller than they were. Also like her father, she was bold and irreverent but could not be called bitter or unduly aggressive. There's a serious caveat to that. Like most individuals who have been abandoned and left to suffer at the hands of predators, Gretchen viewed the world with suspicion, analyzed every word in a conversation, considered all promises suspect, and sent storm warnings to anyone who tried to impose his way on her.

Her skin was deeply tanned, her gold neck chain and Star of David exposed on her chest, the sun shining on her hair. "I wasn't sure if I should drive down to the cabin or turn in to the drive," she said.

"Hello, Gretchen," I said, feeling both awkward and hypocritical. "This is Albert Hollister. He's our host."

"Welcome to Lolo, Montana, Ms. Horowitz," he said. "We like to say we're very humble in Lolo."

"What a wonderful place you have," she replied. "Do you own the whole valley?"

"Plum Creek owns the crown of the hill behind the house, but the rest is mine."

She gazed at the arroyo that ran from Albert's improvised gun range up to an unused logging road that traversed the top of the hill and disappeared inside stands of Douglas fir that were as fat as Christmas trees. "I saw a man up there. He must be a logger," she said.

"No, Plum Creek doesn't log up there anymore. They're selling everything off," Albert said.

"I saw a guy on that log road. He looked right at me," she said. "He was wearing a slicker with a hood. It must be wet up there."

"Did you see his face?" I asked.

"No," she said. "Having trouble with the neighbors?"

"Alafair thinks a guy farther down the ridge shot an arrow at her," I said.

"Why would someone do that?"

"We don't know," I said. I put my hands in my back pockets and gazed at the ground. I

40

felt deceitful and totally lacking in charity toward someone who'd had a horrible childhood imposed upon her. I wished I had said nothing to Albert about Gretchen's background. "I'm glad you're here."

She stared at the blue-green roll of the mountains to the south. When her eyes came back to mine, she was smiling, her cheeks full of color. The sun was bright on her face and hair and her gold chain and the tops of her breasts. She looked as though she had been caught in a camera's lens during a moment when she could only be described as absolutely stunning. "I appreciate that, Dave, more than you can know. Thanks for inviting me, Mr. Hollister," she said.

I couldn't remember when I had felt so small.

I went into the kitchen, where my wife, Molly, was slicing tomatoes on a breadboard. "Gretchen Horowitz is here," I said.

The knife slowed and stopped. "Oh," she said.

"I told Albert of her background. I told him maybe it would be better if Gretchen moved on. I actually told him to say that to her."

"Don't give yourself too much credit, Streak. Albert has two ways of doing things. There's Albert's way. Then there's Albert's way."

Molly had the shoulders and hands of a

countrywoman, and an Irish mouth and heavy arms and white skin dusted with sun freckles. Her hair was a dull red and silver on the roots; though she kept it cut short, it had a way of falling in her eyes when she worked. She was my moral compass, my navigator, my partner in everything, braver than I, more compassionate, more steadfast when the storm clouds started rolling. She had been a nun who never took vows; she worked with the Maryknolls in El Salvador and Guatemala during a time when Maryknoll women were raped and killed and the administration in Washington looked the other way. Former Sister Molly Boyle should have been running the Vatican, at least in my view.

She looked through the window at the horses grazing down the slope in the shade, their tails slashing at the insects that were starting to rise from the grass as the day warmed. I knew she was thinking about Gretchen and the violence we thought we had left behind in Louisiana.

"Gretchen saw a man looking at her from the hillside," I said. "Albert says there's no reason for anybody to be up there."

"You think it's the rodeo guy Alafair had trouble with?"

"I'm going to take a walk up there now."

"I'll come along."

"There's no need for you to. I'll be back in a few minutes."

She wiped her hands on a dish towel. "My foot," she said.

We climbed up the trail behind the house, through pine and fir and larch trees widely spaced in an arroyo that stayed in deep shade most of the day. At the top of the trail was the old Plum Creek logging road, shaped like a horseshoe and partially eroded and caved in and dotted with seedlings and heaped in places with piles of barkless and worm-eaten trees that had slid down from the bluff during the spring melt. The incline at the top of the trail was steep, and I was perspiring and breathing harder than I wanted to admit when we gained the road near the ridge. The wind was cold on my face, the sun shining through the canopy like shafts of light in a cathedral, my head reeling. When I looked back down at the valley, Albert's three-story house looked like it had been miniaturized.

"You okay, skipper?" Molly said.

"I'm fine," I said, my heart pounding. I looked in both directions on the road. I expected to see oil and brake fluid cans and lunch trash left behind by loggers, but the road was clean and the slopes below it carpeted with pine needles, the outcroppings of rock gray and striated by erosion and spotted with bird droppings.

It was an idyllic scene, one that seemed to have healed itself after years of clear-cutting and neglect. It was one of the moments when you feel that indeed the earth abideth forever, and that all the industrial abuse we've done to it will somehow disappear with time.

At the place where the logging road dead-ended in a huge pile of dirt and burned tree stumps, I saw the sunlight flash on a metallic surface. "Stay behind me," I said.

"What is it?" Molly asked.

"Probably nothing."

I walked ahead of her along the base of the bluff, through a low spot in the road where the soil was dark from the morning rain and marked by the tracks of someone wearing needle-nosed cowboy boots. The tracks were deep and sharp-edged and beaded with moisture in the center, as though the soil under the boot had been compressed only minutes earlier. Farther on, lying in the dirt next to a round boulder, were an empty potted-meat can, broken pieces of saltine crackers, and a spray of what looked like fingernail clippings.

There was no movement in the trees, no sound anywhere, not even a pinecone rolling down the hillside. A line of sweat ran from my armpit down my side. Below, I saw the wind bend the grass in Albert's pasture, then climb the hillside and sway the canopy against the sun.

"Good God, what's that smell?" Molly said.

I walked another ten yards up the road and held up my hand for her to stop. "Don't come any farther," I said.

"Tell me what it is."

"It's disgusting. Stay back."

Someone had defecated in the middle of the road and made no attempt to dig a hole or cover it up. Horseflies were swarming on the spot. Up above, behind a cluster of bushes, was an opening to a cave. I picked up a rock the size of a baseball and chunked it through the brush and heard it strike stone. "Come on out here, podna," I said.

There was only quiet. I threw a second and then a third rock with the same result. I grabbed hold of a tree trunk and pulled myself up on the slope and walked toward the cave, the ground spongy with rainwater and pine needles. I could hear Molly climbing the slope behind me. I turned and tried to signal her to stop. But that was not the way of Molly Boyle and never would be.

"Hey, buddy, we're not your enemies," I said. "We just want to know who you are. We're not going to call the cops on you."

This time when I spoke, I was close enough to the cave to create an echo and feel the cool air and smell the bat guano and pooled water inside. I took a penlight from my pocket and stepped under the overhang and shined the light on the back wall. I could see the dried skin of an animal on the floor, ribs poking through the fur, eye sockets empty.

"What's in there?" Molly said.

"A dead mountain lion. It probably got hurt or shot and went in here to die."

"You don't think a homeless person has been living there?"

"We're too far from the highway. I think the rodeo clown came back and was watching the house."

"Let's get out of here, Dave."

I turned to leave the cave; then, as an afterthought, I shone the penlight along the walls and ledges. The surface of the stone was soft with mold and lichen and bat droppings and water seepage from the surface. Close to the ceiling was a series of gashes in the lichen, a perfect canvas on which a throwback from an earlier time could leave his message. I suspected he had used a sharp stone for a stylus, trenching the letters as deep as possible, cutting through the lichen into the wall, as though savoring the alarm and injury and fear his words would inflict upon others.

I was here but you did not know me. Before there was an alpha and omega I was here. I am the one before whom every knee shall bend.

"Who *is* this guy?" Molly said.

CHAPTER 3

The sheriff's name was Elvis Bisbee. He must have been fifty and a good six and a half feet tall. He had a long face and pale blue eyes and a mustache he had let grow into ropes, the white tips hanging down from either side of his mouth. He stood with me in the shade at the foot of the arroyo at the back of the house, gazing up the slope at the bluff above the logging road. "The guy was wearing cowboy boots?" he said.

"I can show you the tracks."

"I'll take your word for it. You're pretty convinced Wyatt Dixon is stalking your daughter?" He wore a departmental uniform and a short-brim Stetson and a pistol and holster with a polished belt. His eyes seemed to see everything and nothing at the same time.

"I don't know who else would be out here," I said.

"Albert likes to stoke up things. Right now it's these heavy rigs that pass at the foot of your road on their way to Alberta."

"Oil companies don't hire deranged people to defecate on the property of a retired English professor."

"It's not Wyatt Dixon's style, either."

"What is? Killing people?"

"I grant Wyatt's got a bad history. But he's not a voyeur. He can't keep the women off him."

"Wyatt?"

"He's an unusual guy. When it comes to rodeoing, he's got a lot of admirers."

"I'm not among them."

"I can't blame you," he said, shaking a cigarette from a pack and staring up the slope. "I don't think he's your man, but I'm going to bring him in and have a talk with him. If you see him around the property, or if he tries to contact your daughter, let me know."

"There's something else. Somebody cut a message in the wall of a cave up there." I recited it and asked, "You ever see anything like that written anywhere else around here?"

"Not that I can recall. Sounds like it's from the Bible."

"Part of it, but it's screwed up."

"Meaning Dixon would be the kind of guy who'd screw up a passage from Scripture?"

"It occurred to me."

He lit his cigarette and drew in on it and turned his face aside before he blew out the smoke. "Let me confide in you," he said. "A young Indian girl went missing six days ago. She was drinking in a joint near the rez and never came home. Her foster grandfather is Love Younger."

"The oilman?"

"Some just call him the tenth wealthiest man in the United States. He has a summer home here. I'm supposed to be at his house in a half hour."

His choice of words was not good. Or maybe I misinterpreted the inference. But a county sheriff does not report to a private citizen at his home, particularly at a pre-arranged time.

"I'm not following you, Sheriff."

"You're a homicide detective, right?"

"That's correct."

"Mr. Younger is an old man. I don't like telling him his granddaughter had personal problems. I don't like telling him the girl is probably dead or close to it or in a state of mind that no seventeen-year-old girl should be in. That particular bar she went to is a hangout for ex-cons, outlaw bikers, and guys who would cut you from your liver to your lights for a package of smokes. We used to call Montana 'the last good place.' Now it's like everywhere else. A few years back somebody went into a beauty parlor just south of us and decapitated three women. I'll let you know what Dixon has to say."

He mashed out his cigarette against a tree trunk and field-stripped the paper and let the tobacco blow away in the wind.

Alafair had gone to town to buy several bottles of shampoo and baby oil and solvents to help Albert untangle the snarls and concrete-like accretions that had built up in the manes and tails of his horses. When she returned, I went upstairs to the back bedroom, where she wrote every day from early morning to midafternoon and sometimes for two or three hours in the evening. Her first novel had been published by a New York house and had done very well, and her second one was due to come out in the summer, and she was now working on a third. From her desk she had a grand view of the north pasture and the sloped roof of the barn that was limed with frost each morning and that steamed as the sun rose, and a grove of apple trees that had just gone into leaf and the velvety green treeless hills beyond it. She had a thermos of coffee on her desk, and she was staring out the window and holding a cup motionlessly to her mouth. I sat down on the bed and waited.

"Oh, hi, Dave," she said. "How long have you been there?"

"I just came in. I'm sorry for disturbing you."

"It's all right. What did the sheriff say?"

"He doesn't believe Dixon is a likely candidate."

She set down her cup and looked at it. "I think a guy was following me in town."

"Where in town?"

"He was tailgating me in a skinned-up Ford truck on the highway. He had his sun visor down, and I couldn't make out his face. At one point he was five feet from my bumper. I had to run a yellow light to get away from him. When I came out of the tack store, he was parked across the street."

"It was the same guy?"

"It was the same truck. The guy behind the wheel was smoking a pipe. I walked to the curb to get a better look, and he drove off."

"It wasn't Dixon?"

"I would have said so if it was."

"I was just asking. You couldn't see the tag?"

"No."

"Alafair, are you sure the truck parked across the street was the same one that tailgated you? You couldn't see the driver's face, right?"

I saw a light in her eyes that I had seen in the eyes of many other women who had reported stalkers or obscene callers or voyeurs or violent and dangerous men who made their lives miserable. Sometimes their complaints got lost in procedure; sometimes they were trivialized and conveniently ignored. In most homicides involving female victims,

51

there's a long paper history leading up to the woman's death. If someone feels this is an overly dour depiction, I recommend he visit a shelter for battered women.

"I wish I hadn't said anything, Dave."

"I didn't explain myself very well. A homeless or deranged man was up on the old logging road behind the house. I'm just trying to put that guy together with the guy in the skinned-up truck. The two don't fit. Why would some guy in Montana single you out as the object of his obsession?"

"I didn't say he did. I told you what happened. But it didn't sink in. So forget it."

"The sheriff is going to pick up Dixon and talk with him. I'll call him and tell him about the guy who tailgated you."

"He didn't just tailgate me. He was following me. For seven miles."

"I know."

"Then stop talking to me like I'm an idiot."

"The sheriff said a seventeen-year-old Indian girl disappeared six days ago. He thinks she may be dead. Maybe there's a very bad guy operating around here, Alafair."

She rubbed her temples and widened her eyes and closed them and opened them again, as though revisiting an experience she couldn't get out of her head. "I know who he is. I know, I know, I know."

"The abductor of the Indian girl?"

"The man who followed me today. I

thought his face was in shadow because he had his visor down. I don't think that's what I saw at all. I think he was unshaved and had a long face like a Viking's. I think I sat across a table from him three years ago and talked to him while he breathed through his mouth and tried to slip his finger on top of my hand. I remember his hair in particular. He put gel on it once so he could slick it back and impress me."

"Don't do this."

"It was him, Dave. I feel sick to my stomach."

"Asa Surrette is dead. He's not only dead, he's probably in hell."

"I knew you would say that," she replied. "I just knew it."

Three years earlier, Alafair told me of her plans to write a nonfiction book about a psychopath who for years had tortured, raped, and murdered ordinary family people in the land of Dorothy and the yellow-brick road, making his victims suffer as much as possible before he strangled or suffocated them. She told me this at the kitchen table in our home on East Main in New Iberia, on the banks of Bayou Teche, while the sun burned in a molten red orb beyond the live oaks in our yard, the moss in the limbs black against the sky. Her research would begin with an interview at the maximum-security unit east of Wichita, where the killer was kept in twenty-three-hour lockdown.

I told her what I thought of the idea.

"Why drizzle on the parade when you can pour?" she said.

She had a degree in psychology from Reed, didn't she? She was a Stanford law student who would probably clerk at the Ninth Circuit Court, wasn't she?

I told Alafair not to go near him. I told her every horrible story I could remember about the serial killers and sadists and sex predators I had known. I told her of the iniquitous light in their eyes when they tried to tantalize listeners with details about their methods in stalking victims, and the obvious pleasure they took when they suggested other bodies were out there. I told her of their inability to understand the level of suffering and despair they had imposed upon others. I told her how they picked at themselves while they talked and how their eyes reached past you and settled on someone who did not know he or she was being watched. I told her of their thespian performances when they made the big score in custody — namely, finding a defense psychiatrist who would buy into their claims of multiple personalities and other psychological complexities that gave them the dimensions of Titans.

They saw themselves as players in a Homeric epic, but what was the reality? They were terrified at the prospect of being transferred into "gen" or "main pop," where they would be shanked in the yard or the shower or lit up in their cells with a Molotov.

I compared them to the moral cowards who sat in the dock at Nuremberg. I told her that Jack the Ripper's name was used today with an almost comic-book connotation because his victims were the poorest and most desperate and vulnerable of women in London's East End. I told her I doubted Jack would have been given the sobriquet "Ripper" by the newspapers of his time if the victims were the wealthy female members of Victorian society. I told her of his final victim, an Irish prostitute who slept every night in either the workhouse or an alley. Her name was Mary Jane Kelly. The last words she spoke to a friend on the evening she died were "How do you like me jolly hat?"

"If you go inside the mind of a guy like Surrette, you'll never be the same," I told her.

"I can't handle it, but reporters from the Wichita *Eagle* can?"

"People 'handle' cancer. That doesn't mean it's pleasant to live with."

"I've already made the arrangement. I'm driving to Wichita tomorrow."

"Yeah," I said. "That's exactly what you're going to do. You will not be happy until you do just that."

"You worry too much. I'll be fine."

"Alf—"

"Stop calling me that name."

"Be careful."

"He's just a man. He's not Lucifer. Don't look at me like that. I'm not your little girl anymore."

"Don't ever say that again. *Never.*"

Wyatt Dixon saw no great puzzle at work in the universe. You got yourself squeezed out of a woman's womb; you got the hell away from home as soon as you could; and you enjoyed every pleasure the earth had to offer and busted up any man who claimed he had authority over you. You rodeoed and got bullhooked and stove in and stirrup-drug and flung into the boards and whipped like a rag doll when you tied yourself down with a suicide wrap, but you wore your scars like the Medal of Honor, and you took the women you wanted and drank whiskey like soda water and doffed your hat to no man and in effect said to hell with the rest of the human race.

Then one day, way down the line, on a morning you thought might last forever, you heard a whistle blow unexpectedly, and minutes later, against all your wishes, you climbed aboard a passing freight and sat on the spine and rode through a canyon alongside a river that had no name, wondering what lay in store on the far side of the Divide.

Was it the end of the track? Or was the party just getting started?

He didn't study on his childhood. He wasn't sure he'd had one. He knew he was born in a boxcar not far from the birthplace of Clyde Barrow. He also knew he and his family lived in a tenant shack up in Northeast Texas and picked cotton and broke corn close to the birthplace of Audie Murphy. Sometimes he had dreams about his father and would see him sitting by the window, dressed in strap overalls without a shirt, his dugs like those of a woman, drinking from a fruit jar and staring at a railroad track on which a train never passed. For the young boy, the father's silence could be like a scream. Wyatt would wake from the dream and sit for a long time on the side of the bed, waiting for the light to break in the east and burn all the shadows from the room.

He had learned long ago not to walk too far through the corridors of his soul. Whenever he allowed himself a moment of reverie, the scene was specific and controlled and always the same: He was in the bucking chute at a fairgrounds, his thighs clamped down on the horse's sides, the haze and dust from the arena iridescent in the lights blazing overhead, a Ferris wheel rotating against a salmon-colored sky, the audience in the stands waiting breathlessly for the moment when Wyatt would say, "Outside!"

Then he would be borne aloft by a horse named Bad Medicine, a piece of corkscrewing, sunfishing black lightning so wired and mean that some riders said he was one step short of a predator. In the first three seconds, Wyatt thought his buttocks would be split up the middle. A violent pain arced through his rectum into his genitals, his teeth jarred, and the discs in his spine fused into a bent iron chain that set his sciatic nerve aflame. He leaned so far back with each thud and jolt of the twelve hundred pounds between his legs that the rim of his hat touched Bad Medicine's rump. All the while Wyatt kept one hand pointed high in the air, raising his knees, slashing down his spurs, the rowels spinning and glittering like serrated dimes, his red-fringed butterfly chaps flapping, his silver-plated championship buckle biting into his navel, his scrotum tingling with the thrill of victory, the buzzer as loud in his head as a foghorn, the crowd going crazy.

He had a house and nine acres up on the Blackfoot, all of it sandwiched between the riverbank and an abandoned railway grade up on the mountain. Half of the wood house had been crushed by a winter flood and ice jam and was never repaired, but Wyatt lived comfortably in the remaining half, cooking his food either on a Dutch oven in the yard or on a woodstove inside, and fishing with worms for German browns and rainbow trout at sunset. The access to the house was by an old log road no one else used, or by a pedestrian swing bridge that was not for the faint of heart.

Wyatt liked his life. What he did not like was people messing with it. He provided rough stock at rodeos from Calgary to Cheyenne, and sometimes he still put on greasepaint and football cleats and fought the bulls for riders who had been thrown into the dirt. He paid his bills, gave witness at revivals on the rez, and filed a 1040 each year. He called it "taking care of my side of the street."

Just that afternoon, his neighbors across the river were having a party on the lawn, the stereo blaring rap music that was the equivalent of broken glass in his ears. Wyatt's solution? He waded barefoot into the stream, the cold numbing his feet, rocks cutting the soles. He cupped his hands to his mouth and shouted, "Shut up that goddamn racket before I have to come over there!"

Stereo off. People leave the yard and disappear into the house. All quiet on the Blackfoot. End of problem.

Then he got into his pickup and drove up the dirt road to the two-lane and headed for a bar called the Wigwam, on the edge of the Salish Indian reservation.

It was sunset when he arrived, and the air was cold and sweet with the smell of the Jocko River and the wheel lines blowing water

59

in a fine mist across the fields, electricity leaping inside a bank of thunderheads in the north. Rows of motorcycles were parked in front of the bar, and booted guys in leather vests and chaps, with road tans and jailhouse tats and a lot of body hair, were outside smoking and chugging beer, enjoying the breeze and the view of the Jocko Valley and the Mission Mountains rising straight up into the clouds, the rock face of each mountain so high above the floor of the valley that the waterfalls stay frozen year round.

As Wyatt stepped up on the porch and went inside, the bikers tried not to look directly at him or let their tone of voice change or their words catch in their throats. Each man was left wondering if anyone had detected the few seconds of uncontrolled fear that had gripped his heart.

Wyatt sat at a table in the back of the saloon and ordered, and soon an enormous Indian in a floppy black hat and jeans whose cuffs were stained with green manure sat down with him, his face as expressionless as a skillet. Wyatt wrote out a check and tore it loose from his checkbook and handed it to the Indian. The Indian folded the check and buttoned it into his shirt pocket and shook hands and left, hardly speaking a word. Then a second and a third Indian came to the table and sat down with Wyatt and received a check and left. When Wyatt looked up again, two large men, one in a deputy's uniform, the other in a baggy suit, were standing in his light.

"Howdy-doody, boys," he said.

"The sheriff wants to see you," the man in the suit said.

"How'd y'all know where to find me?"

"Your neighbors across the river," the uniformed deputy said, smiling. He was an auxiliary and hardly more than a boy and had a mouth like a girl's.

"I'll keep that in mind."

"Funny place to drink soda pop, Wyatt," the man in the suit said. He glanced up at the stage, where three girls were gyrating and twisting on chromed poles. "I'd think you're too old for eye candy."

"I do business with a bunch of feed growers and cutting-horse breeders up the Jocko. This is where I meet them at."

"That's interesting. We didn't know that," the man in the suit said, jotting something on a notepad. He was a plainclothes sheriff's detective by the name of Bill Pepper whose manner and way of doing business seemed to come from an earlier time. He smoked unfiltered cigarettes and wore his hair in a buzz cut and spoke with a Deep South accent, although he had been with LAPD many years and never mentioned where he'd grown up. His eyes were recessed and as dead as buckshot, his lips gray, his coat slightly askew from the lead-weighted blackjack shaped like a darning sock that he carried in the right pocket.

"Is this about that girl who says I shot an arrow at her?"

"She's not a girl. She's a grown woman. Grown women are sensitive about that these days."

"So that's what this is about?"

"What do you think?"

"I got no idea."

"I left a business card in your door. I left one in your mailbox, too."

"People stick trash in my door and mailbox every day."

"Want to sit in a cell tonight?" Pepper said.

Wyatt folded his hands on top of the table, his face tight. He blew his nose on a bandana and stuck the bandana in his pocket. "I ain't shot an arrow at nobody. I told that to your deputy. I told it to the girl and her father. Don't fuck with me."

"Lot of people say you're a mean motor scooter. Is that what you are? A mean motor scooter?"

Wyatt stared straight ahead, his pupils like small black insects frozen inside glass.

"Let me ask you another question. You come in here a lot?" Pepper said.

"When I'm of a mind to."

The plainclothes detective's pen had gone dry. He clicked the button on it several times, then took another pen from his shirt pocket. "You know what 'fortuitous' means? In this instance it means we might be looking at you in a new light. Were you in here about a week ago?"

"Maybe."

"Do you know an Indian girl by the name of Angel Deer Heart?"

"A little bitty thing, about seventeen or eighteen, her britches hanging off her seat?"

"That's the one."

"She's the granddaughter of a big oilman. Yeah, I saw her in here. A couple of times."

"You see her last Thursday night?"

"I don't remember."

"But you were here?"

"I didn't say that."

"Yeah, you did." Pepper wrote again in his notebook. "You feel protective toward young girls?"

"I don't get around them long enough to be protective."

"Seems only natural, a rodeo man like you. You see a young thing at the bar with her panties showing, and you cruise on over and buy her a drink and tell her you'll drive her home because she shouldn't be hanging in a snatch patch full of guys who'd love to tear her apart. Did something like that happen?"

"If y'all had tended to your job, she wouldn't have been drinking in here in the first place."

"Does the court still make you take those chemical cocktails?"

"I took them of my own free will."

"I hear they cause blackouts."

"Is the sheriff still at his office?"

"No, you'll see him tomorrow."

"You taking me in?"

"I'm not sure. Is it true you speak in tongues?"

"It's common up on the rez. Some do, some don't."

"Sounds to me like you need to visit the hospital at Warm Springs again, see if your batteries need charging."

"I got two other feed growers waiting on me. Hook me up or get out of my face."

"We'll see you at the courthouse at oh-eight-hundred tomorrow, Wyatt. The reason I'm not taking you in is I don't think you're worth shooting, much less wasting a cell on." The detective put away his notebook and pen and stuck an unlit cigarette in his mouth. He leaned over and raked a kitchen match across the tabletop, even though state law prohibited smoking in the bar. His coat touched Wyatt's shoulder, an odor of dried sweat wafting off his body. He blew out the match and dropped it in Wyatt's soda can. "I think we're gonna have to do something about you, boy," he said.

After Pepper had walked away, the uniformed auxiliary said, "I'm sorry about that.

He's had a bad day. Everybody has."

Wyatt looked up at him. "Y'all found that Indian girl?"

"Six hours ago," the auxiliary said. He glanced toward the front door, then at the women dancing on the runway. "Wyatt?"

"What?"

"You didn't?"

"Didn't what?"

"You know. With the girl, I mean. You didn't have anything to do with —"

"Get out of my sight," Wyatt said.

There was either a malfunction in the furnace or someone had turned up the register too high, but when Alafair stepped through the door of the interview room at the prison east of Wichita, she felt a surge of superheated air that was like damp wool on her skin; she also smelled an odor that made her think of an unventilated locker room and pipe-tobacco smoke that had soaked into someone's clothes. Asa Surrette was seated at a metal table, his wrists manacled to a waist chain, his khaki shirt buttoned at the throat. He had wide, thin shoulders, shaped a bit like a suit coat hanging on a rack, and a sharp bloodless nose that gave him the appearance of a man breathing cold or rarefied air. His eyes looked pasted on his face.

Alafair sat down at the table and placed her notebook and a pen and a recorder next to one another. Through the oblong windows in the door and the wall, she could see two correctional officers monitoring the hallway and the rooms that were usually reserved for lawyer-client meetings. "You have a degree in administration of justice?" she said.

He watched her pick up her pen. "I took writing courses, too."

"But you were a criminal science major?"

"Yes, but I never wanted to be a policeman. I thought about it, but it wasn't for me."

"You had aspirations to be a writer?" When she tried to smile, her face felt stiff and unnatural. Also, there was a pain in her chest, as though someone had pressed a thorn close to her heart. She tried not to bite the corner of her lip.

His eyes shifted sideways, the manacles tightening against the waist chain. "I studied with a professor who claimed he was a friend of Leicester Hemingway, Ernest's brother. Maybe he was just bragging. He wouldn't read one of my stories in front of the class."

"What was in the story?"

"I forget. Something that bothered him. He took it to the head of the creative writing program. I thought he was a silly guy. He said he'd published some novels. I think he was probably a fake." He stared into her face as though waiting for her to confirm or deny his perception.

"What would you like to talk about?" she said.

"I'm waiting for you to ask the question they all ask."

"I don't know what that is."

"Don't lie. You know what the question is. It's not *a* question, either. It's *the* question. It's the only reason any of you come here."

"Why did you torture and kill all those people, Mr. Surrette?"

"See?" His eyes were dark brown and contained a greasy shine, like rainwater in a wood barrel that never saw sunlight. His teeth were widely spaced, the back of his tongue visible when he breathed through his mouth.

"Are you asthmatic?" she said.

"Sometimes. I was asthmatic when I needed to get out of the navy."

"I want to clarify something. You're operating under a misconception," she said. "I have no expectation that you will ever tell me or anyone else why you tortured and killed all those innocent people. In all probability, you will never deliberately reveal your secrets. You'll refuse to tell family members where the bodies of their loved ones are buried. Your legacy will be the suffering you leave behind, and you'll leave as much of it as you can."

"Not true."

"What you don't understand, Mr. Surrette, is your deeds and your motivations are scientifically inseparable. A cause has an effect. An effect has a cause. Nothing happens in a vacuum. A physical act is the consequence of an electrical impulse in the brain. It's like watching a moth in a windstorm. The outcome is immediately demonstrable. It's not a complex idea."

His eyes seemed to dull over, as though for a few seconds he had slipped sideways in time and was no longer in the room. She could see a piece of food in his teeth and dried mucus at the corner of his mouth. "Who was it that said don't try to understand me too soon?" he asked.

She tried not to show any reaction to the confident gleam in his eye and his apparent sense of self-satisfaction.

"It was Proust," he said.

"Your first victims, or the first anyone knows about, were a mother and father and their two children south of Wichita. You strangled and/or suffocated all four of them. You saved the children for last. The little boy was nine. The girl was eleven."

"That's what they say."

"You killed the parents first. Was that because you wanted to take more time with the children? Did you feel great anger toward them?"

"I didn't know them. Why should I feel anger at them?"

"So your feelings toward them were primarily sexual? After you strangled the little girl, you ejaculated on her legs. I don't think you mentioned that in your allocution. You want to say anything about that now?"

"All I have to do is signal the CO and this is over."

"Then call him."

The heat in the room had intensified. She could smell his odor, and she remembered the correctional officer saying Surrette was allowed to shower only three times a week. His whiskers looked like emery paper. "In your letter you said your father was a police officer," he said.

"He's a sheriff's detective in Louisiana."

"That's where you learned this stuff about people with my kind of history?"

"I have a degree in psychology from Reed."

"I never heard of it."

"Why did you ejaculate on the little girl?"

His face was slanted away from her, as though a bitter wind had struck his cheek. "I can't think about that right now. I can only think about that in sessions with the counselor here. I will not talk about that now."

"Why is that? Do you think I can harm you?"

"You're trying to embarrass me. You want me to feel bad about what I am. You remind me of that creative writing professor I had at WSU. You know what I told him on the student evaluation? I said it wasn't his fault he didn't like stories about boys chewing on each other's weenies. I don't think he liked my evaluation too much."

Her stomach constricted, and she had to hold her breath and look into neutral space to hide the revulsion she felt. "Excuse me, I have hay fever," she said. She took a Kleenex from her purse and blew her nose. "In your allocution, you said you did a 'John Wayne' on another victim. He was nineteen. This was before you stabbed and strangled his wife to death. What did you mean by a 'John Wayne'?"

"I shot him. He grabbed my pistol and tried to kill me with it. He pulled the trigger twice, but it didn't fire. So I shot him."

"You were acting in self-defense at that point?"

"Yes, you could say that."

"Does that seem like a rational point of view?"

"Your face is a little red. Is it too hot in here for you?"

"You took the body of one woman to your church and posed and photographed her. You put the body back in your van and then dumped it on the roadside. No one has ever figured that out. Do you want to talk about that?"

"Why I took *her* and not somebody else to the church?"

"The question is why you would kill your victim in one place and transport her to the church where you're a parishioner. Why would you take a risk like that? Why would you photograph her in your church?"

"Maybe that's just part of my dark side. Everybody's got one."

"I can't write a book about you unless you're honest with me."

"I think you ask questions you already know the answers to. I think you ask questions that are supposed to degrade me."

"My opinions mean nothing. The publisher and the reader are interested in you, not me. A large number of people will read whatever you tell me here today."

His head was tilted on one shoulder, as though he were drowsing off or imitating a hanged man. "You're a manipulator, but that doesn't mean you're smart."

"Could be," she said.

He straightened in his chair and shouted at the door, "On the gate, boss man!"

"You took the woman to the church to mark your territory," she said. "Every animal does it."

His eyes narrowed, and she saw his nostrils whiten around the rims. When the correctional officer escorted him out of the room, his eyes were bright and hard and receded in his face and still fastened on hers.

CHAPTER 4

It was nine P.M., and rain was falling heavily on the trees and the pastures and the hillsides and cascading down Albert's roof when I got the call from the sheriff, Elvis Bisbee. "We found the missing Indian girl in a barn about two miles west of where you're at," he said. "She was tied up in the loft with a vinyl garbage bag taped around her head. The magpies probably got to her five or six days ago."

"You're talking about Love Younger's granddaughter?" I said.

"Her name was Angel Deer Heart. She would have turned eighteen next month. I just came back from her grandfather's house. That's the part of this job I never get used to."

"You've got to excuse me, Sheriff, but I'm not sure why you're calling me."

"One of our detectives interviewed Wyatt Dixon at the Wigwam, the same place the girl was drinking the night she disappeared.

Evidently, Dixon is a regular there. He didn't deny being there the night she disappeared."

"You think he might be your guy?"

"I got to thinking about that biblical message in the cave above Albert's house and Dixon's run-in with your daughter. The more I thought about it, the more I had to admit Dixon is a five-star nutcase who needs looking at real hard. Can you break down that quote for me?"

"The allusion to the bended knee refers to Christ's statement that eventually all of mankind will accept his message of peace. The alpha and omega allusion refers to Yahweh's statement in the Old Testament that He existed before the beginning of time."

"So the guy who wrote this has a little problem with ego?"

"It's called the messianic complex. It's characteristic of all narcissists."

"I want to get a forensic team up to that cave in the morning."

Through the window, I could see water pooling in the north pasture and the green-black sheen of the fir trees when lightning leaped between the clouds.

"The victim was raped?" I said.

"We don't know yet. Her jeans were pulled off. Her panties were still on. Have you worked many like this?"

"More than I want to remember."

"Dixon is supposed to come in tomorrow

at eight. If he doesn't, we'll pick him up. Does your daughter still have that arrow?"

"I'll ask her."

"If Dixon's prints are on it, I'm going to owe you and her an apology."

"No, you won't. I think you're doing a good job."

"In the last two years we've had ten sexual assaults on or near the university campus. A couple of the victims claim that university football players raped them. Sometimes I wonder if the country hasn't already gone down the drain."

I had grown up in an era when a black teen-age boy named Willie Francis was sentenced to die by electrocution in the St. Martinville Parish jail, nine miles from my home. In those days the electric chair traveled from parish to parish, along with the generators, and was nicknamed Gruesome Gertie. The first attempt at the boy's electrocution was botched by the executioners, one of whom was a trusty, because they were still drunk from the previous night. Willie Francis screamed for a full minute before the current was cut. Later, the United States Supreme Court sided with the state of Louisiana, and the governor who wrote the song "You Are My Sunshine" refused to commute the sentence. Willie Francis was strapped in the electric chair a second time and put to death.

I did not speak of these things to the sheriff,

nor do I mention them to those who pine for what they call the good old days. "See you in the morning," I said. "Be careful on our road. It looks like it's about to wash out."

The early dawn was not a good time of day for Gretchen Horowitz. That was when a man with lights on the tips of his fingers used to visit her room and touch her with a coldness that was so intense, it seared through tissue and bone into the soul, in this case the soul of a child who was hardly more than an infant.

When Gretchen woke from her first night's sleep in Montana, the rain had stopped and the cabin was filled with a blue glow that seemed to have no source, the windows smudged with fog or perhaps even the clouds, which were so low they were tangled in the trees on the hillside. She put water on her face and dressed and, while Clete was still asleep, eased open the door and got into her pickup and followed the two-lane along a swollen creek into Lolo.

At the McDonald's next to the casino she bought a breakfast to go of sausage and scrambled eggs and biscuits and scalding-hot coffee, then drove back to the ranch and walked up the hillside and spread her raincoat on a flat rock and began eating, the first glimmer of sunlight touching the tops of the trees far down the valley.

She heard sounds, up on the logging road, and only then noticed the cruiser parked behind Albert's house. Down by the south pasture, a second cruiser was coming slowly up the road, as though the driver were looking for an address. The driver turned under the archway and parked by the barn and got out. He was a heavy man who wore a suit and street shoes and a rain hat; in his left hand he carried a pair of cowboy boots. He opened the back door and pulled out a man dressed in skintight Wranglers and a long-sleeved snap-button red shirt and a straw hat. The man was barefoot, and his wrists were handcuffed behind him.

The man in the suit fitted his hand under the cowboy's arm and began to muscle him up the slope past the rock where Gretchen was sitting. The cowboy had a profile like an Indian's and a dimple in his chin and eyes that looked prosthetic rather than real. He slipped in the mud and slid down the incline, trying to stop himself with his bare feet, his clothes slathering with mud and fine gravel and pine needles.

"Get up!" said the man in the suit, grabbing him by the back of the shirt, twisting the cloth in his fingers. "Did you hear me, boy?"

The cowboy tried to get up and fell again. The man in the suit ripped the straw hat off the cowboy's head and began whipping him with it, striking him across the ears and eyes and the crown of his skull, again and again. "You want to get tased? I'll do it."

"I think you might have what they call anger-management issues," the cowboy said, squinting up from the ground. "I heered you ran into your ex at the Union Club and asked if her new boyfriend wasn't disappointed by her poor old wore-out vag, and she said, 'Soon as he got past the wore-out part, he liked it just fine, Bill.' Is that true, Detective Pepper?"

The detective dropped the boots he had been carrying and picked up the cowboy by the shirtfront and sent him crashing through the pine saplings and into a tree stump. All of this was taking place thirty feet from where Gretchen Horowitz was sitting with her Styrofoam container balanced on her knees. She pushed the tines of her plastic fork through a small piece of sausage and a bit of egg and placed them in her mouth, chewing slowly, her eyes lowered. She heard the cowboy fall again, this time grunting. When she raised her head, the cowboy was sitting with his back against a boulder, sucking wind, his mouth hanging open, his face draining as though he had been kicked in the ribs or stomach. The detective removed a Taser from his coat pocket and activated it and leaned down and touched it to the back of the cowboy's neck. The cowboy's head jerked as though he had been dropped from the end of a rope, his face contorting. The detective stepped back and turned off the Taser and glanced down the slope at Gretchen. "What are *you* looking at?" he said.

Gretchen closed the top of the Styrofoam container and set it on the rock and got up and walked up the incline toward the detective. The trees were wet and motionless in the shadows, strips of thick white cloud hanging on the crest of the ridge. "What am I looking at? Let me think. A guy in cuffs getting the shit kicked out of him?"

"You better mind your business."

"I am. I'm a guest here. I was eating breakfast. What's your name?"

"What's *my* name?"

"That's what I said."

He stared at her without answering.

"My name is Gretchen Horowitz. You don't give your name out while you're on the job?"

"*Hor*owitz?"

"It's Jewish." She picked up her gold chain and religious medal from her throat and held them in her fingers for him to see. "This is Jewish, too. It's called the Star of David."

"You're interfering with a police officer in the performance of his duty."

"Say my name again?"

"What?"

"I want to hear you pronounce my name. You accented the first syllable. You think that's funny?"

"No. You sound like you're from New York."

"Try Miami. That's in Florida. New York is north of Florida. Why not let the cowboy put on his boots?"

"Who the hell do you think you are?"

"You don't want to find out, bacon. Where's your boss?"

I had gone into Missoula with Albert early that morning to buy a fishing license, and until we pulled into the driveway, I didn't realize the forensic team was up on the hill.

"Waste of tax money," Albert said.

"What is?" I asked.

"Messing around on that ridge. Homeless people wander off the highway all the time. They camp in the woods because they don't have any other place to go. They don't kidnap girls out of biker saloons or shoot at people with hunters' bows."

"Some of them are deranged and dangerous, Albert."

"There's nothing like fearing a man with a hole in his shoe."

I didn't feel like arguing with Albert's proletarian views. "I'm going to walk up on the ridge. I'll see you inside."

"Tell that bunch I'd better not find their nasty cigarette butts on the property," he replied.

As I worked my way up the slope, I could

hear people talking on the far side of the trees. Then I saw a deputy in uniform, a second man in a baggy brown suit, a man in a checkered shirt I figured for a crime scene technician, and Wyatt Dixon, who was barefoot and hatless and sitting against the hillside, wrists manacled behind his back, clothes mud-streaked and sticking wetly to his skin. Gretchen Horowitz had just started back down the slope, her face as hot as a woodstove.

"What's wrong?" I said.

"Don't ask," she said. She went past me as though I were a wood post.

I gained the road and looked down at Dixon. His teeth were red when he grinned. "Howdy-doody, Mr. Robicheaux," he said.

"You all right, Mr. Dixon?"

The mud in his hair and the drip from the trees were running into his eyes, and he had to squint to look up at me. "Do not misinterpret the situation of this poor rodeo cowboy. I am honored to once again find myself surrounded by such noble men as yourselves. God bless America and the ground that men such as yourselves walk on."

"Where are your boots?"

He studied the bloodied tops of his feet as though seeing them for the first time. "The detective stomped my toes proper and told me I wouldn't need no foot covering for a while."

"What do you want here?" the man in the baggy suit said.

I opened my badge holder. "I'm Dave Robicheaux. I'm a homicide detective in New Iberia, Louisiana. What did y'all do to this fellow?"

"Nothing. He slipped down the slope," the man in the suit said.

"He must have slid a long way. Did you say something to Miss Gretchen?"

"What are you talking about?" he said.

"The woman who just left here. She was angry about something."

"I don't know anything about that."

"Right. What's your name?"

"Detective Bill Pepper. I told the woman not to contaminate a possible crime scene. If she got her nose bent out of shape, that's her problem."

The crime scene technician was standing in the background. "Come on up to the cave with me. I want to show you a couple of things," he said.

I grabbed hold of a pine sapling and pulled myself up on a footpath and followed the crime scene tech to the entrance of the cave. He was a rotund man with a florid face and the small ears and scar tissue of someone who might have been in the ring. He had put rubber bands around the cuffs of his cargo pants. "How you doin'?" he said.

"Better than that cowboy."

"Here's what we've got going on. The rain didn't do us any favors. There was supposed to be a bunch of scat here, but I can't find it. Same with the fingernail clippings. The boot prints are wiped out, too. Maybe somebody got here before we did."

"Is Dixon lying about getting his feet stomped?"

"Detective Pepper said he wanted Dixon's boots to be clean when he tried to match them with the tracks of the guy who was holed up in the cave. Sometimes Bill's way of doing things is a problem for the rest of us."

"Why is Dixon in cuffs? I thought he was coming in on his own."

"He didn't know the Indian girl's purse was found last night behind a hay bale in the barn where she was killed. There was a receipt in it for a bracelet she bought from Dixon. The bracelet wasn't on her body. The date on the receipt was the same day she disappeared."

"What does Dixon say?"

"He weaves bracelets out of silver and copper wire and was wearing one in the Wigwam, and she saw it and wanted to buy it. He says he sold it to her for fifty dollars."

"What was the deal with Miss Gretchen?"

"The gal who just went down the hill?"

"Down south you don't call a woman a 'gal.' I especially wouldn't do that with her."

"I want you to understand something, Detective Robicheaux. Our department treats people with respect, our current sheriff in particular. The deputy and detective out there are the exception. Frankly, they're an embarrassment."

"What happened?"

"The lady, or whatever you want to call her, Miss Gretchen, came on a little strong about Bill's treatment of Wyatt Dixon. When she was walking away, the deputy said, 'Is she butch enough for you, Bill?' Pepper goes, 'I'd probably have to tie a board across my ass so I didn't fall in.' "

"She heard them?"

"Probably. Would you tell her I apologize on behalf of the department?"

"If I were you, I'd tell your friends to do that."

"She's gonna file a complaint?"

"No, she's not given to filing complaints," I said, and looked back out the opening of the cave. "Is Dixon going to be charged?"

"Depends on what the prosecutor says. I think we've got a lot more work to do. I didn't get what you were saying. The lady is not gonna file a complaint? So what is she gonna do?"

I looked at the biblical message incised in the soft patina of lichen on the wall and wondered what kind of tangled mind was responsible for it. "It's nice meeting you," I said. "I hope to see you again. Tell those two morons out there they put their foot into the wrong Rubicon."

"Sorry?"

"Tell them to look it up."

After the first interview, Alafair waited three days in the motel for Asa Surrette's attorney to return her call. It was January, and snow was driving parallel with the ground, and the landscape was sere and stippled with weeds, and in the distance the hills looked like piles of slag raked out of a furnace.

It was a land of contradictions, settled by Populists and Mennonites but also by fanatical abolitionists under the leadership of John Brown. In spring the rivers were swollen and streaked with red sandbanks and bordered by cottonwoods that fluttered with thousands of green leaves resembling butterflies. The Russian wheat in the fields was the most disease-resistant in the world, the harvest so great that sometimes the grain had to be piled in two-story mounds by the train tracks because there was no room left in the silos.

Or the skies could blacken with dust storms or, worse, clouds of smoke rising from a peaceful town, such as Lawrence, where guerrillas under the command of William Clarke Quantrill and Bloody Bill Anderson spent an entire day systematically murdering 160 people.

Just after Alafair had given up and decided to return home the next morning, she got a call from Surrette's attorney, the same one who'd negotiated Surrette's allocution and sentence, trying to ensure that his client not be exposed to the death penalty reinstated in 1994. "Asa would like to see you again," he said.

"Why?" she asked.

There was a beat. "*Why?* To help with your project. To give his side of things."

"Your client is a narcissist. He's had no interest in helping anybody with anything. If he wants the interviews to go forward, the questions will be on my terms. He'll make an honest attempt to answer them or we're done."

"You'll have to work that out with him."

"I'll work it out with you. There will be no proscriptive areas of inquiry."

"I think you'll find Asa pretty forthcoming. He likes you."

"Are you serious?"

"If he didn't like you, he wouldn't ask you back. What did you say to him, anyway?"

"He has one reason for wanting to see me again. I bother him. I told him why he took the body of one of his victims to his church and photographed it."

There was another beat. "Ms. Robicheaux, there is one area that should not be explored in your interview. You know what it is, too."

"No, I don't," she lied.

"Asa has admitted to eight homicides committed during the 1970s and '80s. Those are the only crimes he will be discussing, because those are the only crimes he committed."

"You're sure of that?"

"I'm sure of what he told me. I'm sure the authorities, including the FBI, have never found evidence of any kind that Asa was less than truthful about any of these matters."

"The same guys who couldn't catch him for thirty years? The same people who caught him only after he contacted them and then sent them a floppy disk traceable to a computer in his workplace?"

"It's been a pleasure talking to you," the attorney said.

It was snowing the next morning, in clumps that floated softly down and broke apart and melted on the highway and were blown into a muddy spray by the trucks leaving an oil refinery whose smokestacks were red at night and streaming in the morning with gray curds of smoke that smelled like leakage from a sewage line. Asa Surrette was locked in a waist chain, waiting, when Alafair entered the interview room. Through the slitted window, she could see the snow blowing like feathers on a series of small hills that seemed to blur in the distance and then dissolve into nothingness.

"You keep looking at the hills," he said.

"The winter here is strange. It contains no light."

"I never thought of it in those terms."

"Is it true there used to be eighteen Titan missile silos ringed around the outskirts of Wichita?"

"That's right. They were all taken out."

"Nonetheless, people here lived for decades with mechanized death buried under the wheat?"

"So what?"

"Had war started with the Soviet Union, this place would have become a radioactive Grand Canyon."

"Yeah, that kind of sums it up."

"Did that enter your thinking when you committed your murders?"

He looked at her with a gleam in his eye that was between caution and hostility. "No. Why should it?"

She didn't answer.

"Why do you keep glancing out the window?" he asked.

"It's the sense of nothingness that I get when I look at the horizon. The reality is, there *is* no horizon here. The grayness seems to have no end and no purpose. Is that how you felt when you stalked your victims?"

He wrinkled his forehead, craning around, the chain on his waist tinkling. "I think that stuff you're talking about comes from Samuel Beckett. I read him in my literature class. I think his work is crap."

"What did you feel after you killed your

victims?"

"I didn't feel anything."

"Nothing?"

"What's to feel? They're dead, you're not. One day I'll be dead. So will you."

"How about the misery you caused them in their last moments? The suffering their loved ones will undergo the rest of their lives?"

"Maybe I'm sorry about that."

"You felt remorse?"

"Maybe I felt it later. I don't know. It's hard for me to think about things in sequence. People's emotions don't happen in sequence." His wrist chain clinked as he tried to raise his hands in order to make the point.

"You haven't answered the question, have you? What did you feel after you killed your victims?"

He straightened his back against the chair, breathing through his nose, his expression composed, his gaze roving over her features. He lifted his eyes toward the ceiling. "I thought about how I had stopped time and changed all the events that would have happened. I tore the hands off the clock."

She felt her eyes moisten. "Did they beg?"

"What?"

"For their lives? For the lives of their children? What did they say to you when they knew they were going to die?"

"I already talked about all that."

"No, you didn't. You told the court only

what you chose for them to hear. Do the voices of your victims visit you in your sleep?"

"I know what you're trying to do."

"No, you don't. I have no interest in statements about your behavior or your motivations. You're a psychopath, and nothing you say is reliable. That means the book I write about you will be unreliable. You've had an enormous influence on me, Mr. Surrette."

"Oh?" he said, the corner of his mouth wrinkling.

"I've always opposed capital punishment. Now I'm not so sure."

His eyes dulled over in the same way they had during the first interview, as though he had gone to a place inside himself where no one could follow. "I don't think I want to do this anymore."

"You didn't stop killing people in 1994, did you? There were other victims, in other towns or other states, weren't there?"

"No."

"People like you can't shut down the mechanism. It's always there. It's like a craving for morphine or pornography or booze or any other addiction, except much worse. How do you give up tearing the hands off the clock and changing history?"

"You're not going to write the book, are you?"

"No. You're not only untrustworthy as a source, you're too depressing a subject. I'm going to do something else, though. I'm going to publish an article or a series of articles stating my belief that you never stopped killing. That if anyone ever deserved the death penalty, it's you."

The room was sour with his smell. He was slumped in his chair, his head tilted forward, his eyes glowering under his brows. His unshaved cheeks looked smeared with soot. "You came here acting like an intellectual. You're nothing but a cunt and not worth my time. On the gate, boss man!" he said.

CHAPTER 5

It was dust in downtown Missoula when Detective Bill Pepper entered a workingman's saloon called the Union Club and ordered his first shot and beer of the evening. He knocked back the shot and drank from his mug of draft and wiped the foam off his mouth with a paper napkin, then tapped his fingernail on the lip of the shot glass for another. He was not aware that across the street, in the gloaming of the day, a young woman with a scarf wrapped around her hair had watched him enter the saloon and was now waiting for him to leave.

At eight P.M., just as the sun was setting, he emerged on the street and began walking toward the brick cottage where he lived on the opposite side of the Clark Fork of the Columbia River. In minutes he reached North Higgins and walked past the steamed windows of a Mexican restaurant filled with college kids and family people, then past an old vaudeville theater and over a long bridge, the roar of the water and its cold, heavy smell rising from far below, the sun descending in a red melt where the river fanned out and disappeared between the mountains.

On the far end of the bridge, he turned right and descended a set of steps that led down past an old train station and onto the maple-shadowed sidewalk that reminded him of the neighborhood in Mobile where he had lived as a child. He lit an unfiltered cigarette and removed a flask from his coat pocket and unscrewed the cap with his thumb and tilted the flask to his mouth, closing his eyes while a warm burn radiated through his viscera.

Down the street, a chopped-down pickup with Hollywood mufflers eased to a stop under a maple tree that blocked the light from the streetlamp. The woman in the scarf behind the wheel fitted on a pair of dark glasses and layered her mouth with lipstick, then got out and looped a tote bag over her arm. She began walking on the opposite side of the street toward a small brick bungalow set close to the river. Baskets of petunias hung from the eaves of the porch. There was a swing set in the yard and a basketball hoop nailed above the porte cochere.

She stopped under a tree directly across from the bungalow. The lights were on in the front, and she could see Bill Pepper pacing up and down in his living room while he talked on his cell phone. She removed her dark glasses and took a tiny pair of binoculars from her tote bag and adjusted the lenses on his face. There was a coarseness in his skin that reminded her of the skin around a turtle's eyes. His hands were big and knuckled, his shoulders as thick as a piano mover's. He was the kind of man who drank whiskey as casually as someone flinging an accelerant on a fire. He had probably been a brig chaser in the Corps or with CID in the army or an administrative sergeant in the air force or a land-based pencil pusher in the navy; but he was someone who knew how to make use of the system and milk it for all it was worth while staying off the firing line.

She had sworn she was through with her former life. She had seen a counselor in West Hollywood, attended Adult Children of Alcoholics meetings in the Palisades, and worked as a volunteer at a shelter in East Los Angeles to get her mind off her own problems. Unfortunately, the latter was not as therapeutic as the former. She saw women who had been raped, sodomized, burned, and beaten until they were unrecognizable. She was daily witness to the terror that never left their eyes, because each of them knew she would have to return to a home where any night a man whose children she had borne, whose problems she had shared, whose body had settled between her thighs, would rip the door out of the jamb and perhaps tear her apart. Nor could Gretchen forget their haunted look when they asked how they could change their lives, where they could work, where they could hide. She never answered their questions. If she told them what *she* would do, they would probably flee her presence.

She remembered the early lessons in the trade that she had learned from a retired button man in Hialeah whom everyone referred to as Louie, no last name. Louie had grown up in Brooklyn with Joey Gallo and claimed to be the character in *The Gang That Couldn't Shoot Straight* who walked Joey's pet lion down to the neighborhood car wash and clipped his leash to the chain that moved all the vehicles through the water jets and revolving brushes. "Don't let your feelings get mixed up in it," Louie said. "The target broke the rules or he wouldn't be the target. He made the choice, you didn't. Don't use anything bigger than a .25. You want the round to bounce around inside. One in the ear, one between the lamps. If he's a rat, the third round goes in the mouth."

Louie did not go out in a blaze of glory. He died in a lawn chair while watching a shuffleboard game at the retirement center where he lived. At his funeral, a woman in the viewing line leaned over the coffin and spat in his face. Many thought she was the widow of a victim. As it turned out, she was his landlady, and Louie had stiffed her on a winning lottery ticket they had purchased together. In death, Louie was no more dignified or intriguing than he had been in life, and all his lessons were no more than the self-serving rationale of a psychopath. The problem was that Gretchen hadn't gotten into the life for money. What she learned from Louie was a means to another end — namely, to get even for the burns that had been inflicted on an infant and for the day a man named Golightly had forever robbed her of her innocence.

Don't let your feelings get involved in it? What a laugh, she thought.

She put her dark glasses back on and dipped her hand in her tote bag and felt the can of Mace and the foamed butt of the telescopic baton she carried. She waited until a car passed, then crossed the street and stepped up on Bill Pepper's darkened porch. The bulb above the door made a loud squeak when she unscrewed it. Beyond the house, she could see the moon shining on a church steeple and hear the river humming through the willows and rocks along the riverbank.

Go home. There's still time. He's a cop. Don't throw everything away over an insult, a voice said.

Another voice replied, *Don't let anyone get over on you ever again.*

She tapped on the door with her left hand,

her breath coming hard in her chest as she stared through the glass at the detective's face approaching hers.

When he opened the door, she could smell the whiskey and cigarettes through the screen. He worked the light switch up and down, his expression puzzled. "Must have burned out a bulb," he said. "Who's that?"

Her scarf was tied down tightly on her head, the lenses in her glasses as dark as a welder's goggles. She tightened her hand around the can of Mace. On the living room wall was a framed photograph of the detective holding a little girl in a pinafore on his hip, both of them smiling. Another photograph showed him with a little boy. "You the lady from the church?" he said.

"Pardon?" she said.

"The one who called about Sarah going to Bible camp? Why are you wearing sunglasses?"

"I'm Gretchen Horowitz, and I need to talk to you about a comment you made."

His eyes went away from her. Then he smiled with recognition. "Oh yeah, I got it. Come in," he said, pushing open the screen. "I need to explain some things."

Don't do it, the voice said.

"I heard what you and your deputy said."

"I'm sorry about that. I'm expecting a phone call," he said, stepping back, motioning her in. "My granddaughter is gonna be visiting in June. I'm supposed to enroll her in Bible camp. That's why I thought —" The phone rang on a hallway table. He made a face and picked it up, leaving her in the doorway, gesturing at her to come in while he talked.

She could hear only part of the conversation, but it was obvious he was agitated and conflicted, trying to suppress his irritation and at the same time please the party on the other end of the line. "No, sir, Dixon may be a partner in the crime, but not necessarily," he said. "We have the arrow somebody shot at the Robicheaux girl. I found a salesman at Bob Ward's sporting goods who remembers a guy buying a bow and arrows of the same kind three days ago. He remembers the guy wearing a bracelet woven from metal wire . . . No, sir, the guy paid cash, so all we have on him is the salesman's description. Trust me on this, sir. I'm gonna nail the man who did this to your granddaughter."

She was standing inside the doorway when he hung up. He seemed to look at her without seeing her.

"Was that the grandfather of the Indian girl who was killed?" she asked.

"I was just doing a little outreach," he said. "Where were we? My treatment of Wyatt Dixon this morning? He's got people around here fooled, but I knew him when he was a member of a white-power group down in the

Bitterroot Valley, the same bunch at Hayden Lake over in Idaho. I saw what somebody did to that Indian girl, and this morning I went a little crazy. I lost it. I wish I hadn't."

She had taken off her glasses and placed them in her tote bag. She continued to stare at him, not speaking.

"You want a drink?" he said.

When she didn't answer, he sat down on a couch with a cheap flower-print cover. He pulled the cork from a whiskey bottle and poured into a teacup. "Let me catch my breath. Sit down, will you, please? Okay, this is what it is: I went up there on the logging road, and the deputy made a wiseacre sexist remark, and I thought I'd say something smart back. I shot off my mouth. I'm sorry I did that. Look, this doesn't excuse my behavior, but I've got a couple of problems myself, one with my prostate, the other with my daughter, who can't get her life on track."

He looked down at his teacup, then picked it up and drank it empty. "I got the Big C. I might beat it, I might not. If I had my way, I'd be down in Muscle Shoals, crabbing with my grandchildren. Except I need the income for my daughter and her kids, and I can't retire. Maybe you can help me with something here."

"I doubt it."

"Your friend the Robicheaux girl? She's

sure she didn't see who shot that arrow at her?"

"Ask her."

"Like I was saying on the phone, we got the arrow from her, but the only prints on it were hers. That means the guy who shot it wiped it down. Which means he was operating in a premeditated fashion to commit a homicide. Wyatt Dixon had no reason to target the Robicheaux girl."

"Then who was it?"

He rubbed his palms up and down on his thighs, a spark of static electricity jumping off the heel of his hand. "I got a theory. Close the door and sit down. You want a glass of wine or a Pepsi? My guess is you'd rather have a Pepsi."

"Why do you think that?"

"Because you're all business, lady. You don't mess around. I doubt you ever take guff off a man, either."

He went to the small kitchen just off the living room and opened the refrigerator and placed the ice tray and a tall glass on the counter and ripped the tab on a soda can and filled the glass, all the while talking about his grandchildren with his back to her. She was standing in the same spot when he came back into the living room. "Mind if I close this? I think it's fixing to rain again," he said, pushing the front door shut. "Dixon may not have shot at your friend, but that doesn't mean he's an innocent man. He stays viable through deception. He loved what I did to him this morning because he was center stage. I've known his kind all my life, ignorant peckerwoods always spouting from the Bible. They say they're born-again, but they'll cut your throat for a quarter and lick the cut clean for an extra dime."

"You seem to really hate him."

"What I hate is deceit. I'll tell you something I don't tell many people. My father was a brakeman on the old L and N line. He took pity on a black vagabond and fed him and let him sleep in a boxcar parked on a siding. When the guy woke up, he killed my father with a pocketknife and took his billfold and left his body on the tracks. We moved to a place on an alley in Macon, and I grew up shining shoes, and my mother and little sister did housecleaning. You learn a lot about the world looking up from a shoeshine box. How do you think that Indian girl got killed? Somebody deceived her. We know she knew Dixon because she bought a bracelet from him. Maybe her killer was Dixon's friend, maybe a partner of some kind."

She sat down in a chair across from him. "Run that by me again."

He went into a circuitous history about Dixon's background, the crimes of which he was suspected but never charged, the fact that Dixon had been a member of a separatist group in Texas and on the edge of the same circles as Timothy McVeigh. She sipped from her glass, the fatigue of the day starting to catch up with her, her concentration starting to stray. She noticed the tidy drabness of the room, the frayed carpets, the nicked furniture, like a re-creation of an impoverished working-class home from many years ago. He seemed to become frustrated with her inattention, his hands moving more rapidly, his chest swelling. He loosened his collar. "Are you listening?"

"Yes, of course."

"Why did you come here?"

"To talk."

"Then why don't you talk? Maybe you came here for something else."

"I think we've straightened it out."

"What were you going to do if that didn't happen?"

Her mouth was dry, the muscles in her chest not working right.

"Why don't you answer the question?" he said.

"What did you just say?"

"I was talking about deception. Haven't you been listening? You look a little woozy."

She set her glass on the coffee table and looked at it. She had drunk half the glass, and the ice had melted and seemed as thin as frost-coated dimes floating on top of the Pepsi. Her skin felt rubbery and dead to the touch, and her tongue was thick and her words slurred when she tried to speak.

"It's kind of like being in a slow-motion film, isn't it?" he said. "I got you, girlie."

Rohypnol, she thought.

He picked up her tote bag from the floor and pulled it open against the drawstring and lifted out the can of Mace and the expandable baton known as an ASP. "I checked you out today. Miami-Dade PD says you may have been a female badass for the Mob. This is Montana, girl. You don't do a beatdown on a Missoula County sheriff's detective. You seriously fucked yourself tonight." He got up from the couch and turned off the light in the kitchen and the table lamps in the living room. "My van is in back. But just so you know there're no hard feelings —"

He leaned down, the heat and the smell in his clothes almost suffocating her. She could taste the tobacco on his tongue when he put it in her mouth.

The accident on the state highway happened a short distance before the turnoff onto the dirt road that led to Albert Hollister's ranch. A tractor-trailer rig carrying a three-story-high piece of oil field equipment bound for Canada had blown two tires and skidded off the shoulder, toppling the load into a stand of cottonwoods by the creek. The few cars coming off the crest of Lolo Pass had come to a stop, as well as the traffic from the town. Clete and I got out of my pickup truck and started walking toward the accident. There was a trace of purple at the bottom of the sky, the evening star twinkling just above the mountains. A helicopter was hovering directly overhead. I thought it carried a news team from a local television station. I was wrong. The chopper landed on the highway, not in a field but on the highway, and one of the wealthiest men in the United States stepped out of it.

I had seen him once before, in Lafayette, right after an offshore blowout had killed eleven men on the derrick and strung miles of fecal-colored oil all over the Gulf Coast. If I ever saw a Jacksonian man, it was Love Younger. He was as rough-hewn as carved oak, with the broad forehead and wide-set eyes we associate with the Anglo-Scotch minutemen who fired the first shots at Lexington and Concord. He had grown up in a place in eastern Kentucky I visited once, a wretched community of shacks, some with dirt floors, where the residents drew their water from the same creek their privies were on. Paradoxically, he had not come to Lafayette to talk about the oil well blowout but to establish a scholarship fund based on merit and need at the University of Louisiana.

I saw Alafair standing by the side of her Honda, looking down at the massive load of

103

machinery that had toppled off the trailer into the edge of the creek, snapping all the boomer chains like string. The stand of cottonwoods it had fallen on had been crushed into the mud. "Was he speeding?" I said, looking up toward Lolo Pass.

"I heard the driver say his tires blew," she replied.

Evidently, that explanation did not work for Love Younger. He was arguing with a highway patrolman, jabbing his finger in the air, motioning at a hilltop on the far side of the highway. The patrolman kept nodding, his mouth a tight seam, raising his eyes only to nod again.

"That guy's name is Love?" Clete said.

"He claims to be a descendant of Cole Younger."

Clete wasn't impressed. "He also smeared a guy with the Silver Star and a Purple Heart."

"Have y'all heard from Gretchen?" Alafair said.

"What about her?" Clete said.

"We were going to have a drink in Missoula. She doesn't answer her cell phone."

"When's the last time you talked with her?" Clete said.

"Six."

He checked his cell phone for missed calls. "Did she say where she was going?"

"She said she had to take care of some

personal business."

Clete looked at her. "What kind of personal business?"

"The personal kind," she said. "She wouldn't tell me what it was."

"Did it have anything to do with those cops who were up on the ridge this morning?" I asked.

"Maybe. I didn't think about it at the time. I gave the arrow to a plainclothes detective named Pepper. He made me kind of queasy."

"How?" I said.

"His eyes. They look at you, but there's no light behind them."

Clete began punching a number into his cell phone with his thumb. "Direct to voice mail," he said. "What's the name of that plainclothes again?"

"Bill Pepper," I said. "Let me see how long this is going to take." I walked up to within four feet of the highway patrolman and Love Younger and two of his aides who were standing close by. None of them took any notice of me.

"My driver says he's almost sure he heard the crack of a rifle," Younger said to the patrolman.

"That's not what I heard him say, sir," the officer said.

"You calling me a liar?"

"No, sir. Your driver said he heard two popping sounds. That could have been his tires."

"Correct me if I'm wrong," Younger said. "We're two miles from the ranch of Albert Hollister. He's well known as an environmental fanatic and rabble-rouser. He and the Sierra Club have done everything in their power to stop the transportation of my equipment."

I opened my badge holder. "Would you mind if we pull out on the shoulder and work our way on up to the next turnoff?"

"Yes, sir, go right ahead," the patrolman said.

"Mr. Younger, could I have a word with you?" I said.

"Concerning what?"

"Your granddaughter."

In the illumination of emergency flares and headlights, I saw Love Younger's eyes sharpen and fix on mine. There were tiny blue and red veins in his cheeks, a bit of stubble on his throat above his collar, and a look of heated intensity in the face that usually hides either great tragedy or great anger.

"Up on that ridge just west of us, somebody shot a hunter's arrow at my daughter. It cut her ear," I said. "A half inch closer, she probably would have been killed. We think the guy who did it could be connected to the death of your granddaughter."

"What's your name?"

"Dave Robicheaux. I'm a sheriff's detective in New Iberia, Louisiana."

"Get his information," Younger said to one of his aides.

"No, sir, I'll talk to you, or we'll not talk at all."

He turned toward me, his expression neutral, and seemed to take my measure a second time. He pulled a notepad from his shirt pocket and handed it to me. "Write down your contact number. I'll call you as soon as I clean up this mess. What's your name again?"

I told him.

"You were involved in a shooting in Louisiana. I was there when it happened. You killed a man named Alexis Dupree," he said. "I knew him."

"I didn't do it, but a friend of mine did. I was there and watched it and thought my friend did the right thing. I think the world is a better place for it. I'll look forward to your call, Mr. Younger. My condolences for your loss." I walked back down the line of cars and rejoined Alafair and Clete.

"What's the haps?" Clete said.

"Jacksonian democracy is highly overrated," I replied. "Did you hear from Gretchen?"

"No, something's wrong. She always lets me know where she is, even out in California. Does a day come when you don't have to worry about your kid?"

"Never," I said.

■ ■ ■ ■

As she lay helpless in the back of the van, her wrists fastened behind her with plastic ligatures, she could see the black shapes of the mountains through the rear windows and the rain slapping against the roof and sweeping in sheets across the highway. Her muscles felt like butter, her neck so weak it could barely support the weight of her head. She estimated that the van had been on the four-lane only about ten minutes before it made a turn, and she guessed they were now on the two-lane state road that led through the old company mill town of Bonner and on up the Blackfoot River. Pepper had been silent the whole time, filling the inside of the van with the smoke from his unfiltered cigarettes.

She heard the hollow rumbling of a bridge under the van. Abruptly, the van swung off the asphalt onto a dirt surface, gravel pinging the undercarriage. Minutes later, the van climbed a steep hill and came down the other side, then turned left onto a rocky track pocked with holes and probably strewn with desiccated tree branches and twigs that snapped and splintered up into the frame.

Bill Pepper hit the brakes, tossing her against the back of his seat. When he cut the engine, she could hear the rain pattering on the roof and see the wind flattening the drops of water on the back windows. She could not remember a time in her life when the smallest of details about the natural world had seemed so important to her. Pepper continued to smoke his cigarette, leaning forward to get a better look at the heavens, like a sailor or a fisherman trying to anticipate a squall. "I like it out here," he said, staring straight ahead.

When she tried to speak, her voice box felt stuffed with cotton.

"My daddy used to take my little sister and me fishing for speckled trout south of Mobile Bay," he said. "When the rain would first dimple the water, they'd start to school up. You could smell them, just like when they're spawning."

He rolled down his window halfway and flicked his cigarette into the darkness. A balloon of yellow electricity flared and raced through the clouds overhead and disappeared without sound beyond the hills on the far side of the Blackfoot. "You brought this on your own self. You know that, don't you?" he said.

"My father is —" she began.

"Yeah, I know. Your father is going to punch my ticket. So why didn't you send him after me instead of coming to my door with Mace and an ASP in your bag?"

"Clete Purcel is my father."

"It doesn't matter who he is. It's just you

109

and me now. You came to my house to do me harm. If you do me injury, you do injury to my grandchildren, and I won't put up with that."

He got out of the van and walked to the back and opened the doors, the rain spotting his hat and leather jacket. He stepped on the back bumper and climbed inside and closed the doors behind him. He reached in his pocket and removed a small flashlight and turned it on and set it on the floor. "A vice cop in Broward County told me you pulled a train for the Florida Outlaws."

"He lied to you."

"Why would he lie?"

"Because he knew it was what you wanted to hear."

"You look like a biker girl. Except I think you have a high IQ."

His weight shifted, and she heard him remove something from his pocket. Then she heard the snap of a metallic mechanism locking into place. He fitted his left hand on her upper arm. "This same vice cop said maybe you did a couple of hits for the Mob. Was he lying then?"

"Anything I ever did was because I wanted to."

He moved his hand up the nape of her neck and slipped his fingers into her hair. "Do you think those things I did to you back there were bad? Or did you enjoy them a little?"

She craned her head and, in the corner of her eye, saw the dull-colored blade of the clasp knife and the long sliver of brightness along the bottom edge where it had been honed on a whetstone.

She straightened her arms and shoulders and closed and opened her eyes as a doll might, a pain growing in her right shoulder, her nerve endings coming alive.

"Opposites attract sometimes," he said. "I can be good to a woman and love her like a father or a husband."

She stared at the side paneling of the van and, in her mind, went to a private place where long ago she had learned to shut down her sensory system and remove herself from hands that reached down out of the dark and touched her in ways that no human being should ever be touched.

"You're an attractive girl," he said. "I may go to work for a very wealthy man. I could take care of you. Are you listening?"

"My father will get you. If he doesn't, I will."

"I wouldn't be talking like that. This could be your last night on earth."

"I'll get you anyway. I'll come back. I'd rather die than have your hands on me."

She saw his thumb slip higher on the handle of the knife, establishing a firmer grip.

"You stink and have dandruff in your hair. You're everything a woman loathes," she said.

"Even whores don't want to fuck a man like you."

"You're starting to make me angry, Gretchen."

She felt his callused fingertips go inside her shirt and move along her collarbone and settle on her carotid. He teased his thumbnail under her jaw and around her ear and spread his hand in the center of her back, pressing the heel into the muscles. "I could have been a lot harder on you," he said.

"Kill me."

"You really mean that?"

"Fuck you, asshole," she said, her hatred and level of helplessness so intense she could hardly say the words.

She heard him snapping on a pair of latex gloves; then he ran the blade of his knife down the back of her shirt and through her bra strap and through the back of her jeans and her panties. He tore the clothes off her body, even pulling off her suede boots and her socks. He opened a bottle of bleach and soaked a wad of paper towels and scrubbed her hair and skin with it, then climbed out of the van and fitted his hands under her arms and dragged her over the bumper onto the ground.

She lay in the mud, the rain falling in her face, while he went to the front of the van and removed a paper sack from behind the seat. He took out a half pint of whiskey and a

Ziploc bag of weed and splashed the whiskey in her mouth and on her face and bare breasts and over her hair, then forced weed past her lips and teeth and rubbed it into her hands and forearms and ears and nose, his chest laboring from the exertion.

He gathered up her clothes and boots and stuck them in the sack, then inserted the knife under the ligatures and sliced them loose from her wrists. "I threw your tote bag in the trees about three miles back. Write this off as a learning experience. For me it's over, in case you ever want to let bygones be bygones. Nobody is gonna believe you, Gretchen. People like me. I'm a good guy. You're shit on a stick."

He got in the van and started the engine and drove past her with the window down, lighting another cigarette, the rain slashing across the taillights.

She walked a mile and a half up the road, her skin prickling with cold, her hair matted and dripping with water and dirt and twigs. A Jeep passed her and turned in to the trees at the peak of a hill. A boy and a girl got out and stared at her. A red nylon tent with a lantern hissing inside it stood in a grove of cedar trees. Below the hill, Gretchen could see the riffle on the river gliding between giant boulders, like a long streak of black oil shining in the moonlight.

"Jesus Christ, lady, are you okay?" the boy said.

She tried to cover her breasts with her arms and discovered that nothing she could do or say would explain or change her situation or undo the damage that had been done to her, not now, not ever. The greatest injury of all was the knowledge that her own merciful tendencies had allowed this to happen.

CHAPTER 6

The phone rang at 7:14 the next morning; the caller ID was blocked. I picked up the receiver and looked out the window. The temperature had dropped during the night, and the tops of the fir trees up the slope were stiff and white with frost and bending in the wind. "Hello?" I said.

"If I give you the address, can you come up to my house now?" a voice said.

"Mr. Younger?"

"I could come out to your place, but I suspect I won't be welcomed by Albert Hollister."

"Give me your number. I'll call you back," I said.

"You'll call me back? In case you've forgotten, you approached me, Mr. Robicheaux. Do you want to talk or not?"

"I want to bring somebody with me. He's the best investigator I've ever known. His name is Clete Purcel," I said.

"I don't care who you bring with you. If

you've got information about my grand-daughter's death, I want to hear it. Otherwise, let's stop this piffle."

"Yes, sir," I said.

I put on a pair of khakis and a heavy long-sleeved shirt and brushed my teeth and shaved and went downstairs. Albert was putting a coffeepot and cups on the breakfast table. "Who was that on the phone?" he said.

"I picked up because I thought it might be Gretchen."

"She's back home. I saw her pickup by the cabin. Who were you talking to?"

"Love Younger."

His face showed no reaction.

"I'm going out to his place," I said. "I think the murder of his granddaughter might be connected to the guy who shot at Alafair."

"You watch out for Love Younger," he said, the cup in his hand rattling when he set it on a saucer. "He's a son of a bitch from his hairline to the soles of his feet."

"He donated three million dollars to a scholarship fund at the University of Louisiana."

"The devil doesn't charge his tenants for central heating, either."

"You're a closet Puritan, Albert."

"Let me start the day in peace, would you, please?" he said.

I walked down to Clete's cabin at the far end of the north pasture. Gretchen's hot rod was parked in the cottonwoods by the creek; in the east there was a blush on the underside of the clouds. Two white-tailed deer bounced through the grass and bounded over a fence railing into a stand of untended apple trees that Albert never picked, so food would always be available for the herbivores on his property. I tapped lightly on the cabin door. Clete stepped out on the gallery and eased the screen shut behind him. "Gretchen came in about three this morning," he whispered.

"Is everything okay?"

"She spent a lot of time in the shower, then went to bed with a piece under her pillow. It's an Airweight .38."

"Did she say where she'd been?"

"She told me to mind my business."

"Take a ride with me to Love Younger's home."

I could tell he didn't want me to change the subject, but I didn't believe that Clete or I or anyone else could resolve the problems of Gretchen Horowitz.

"I don't like the way that guy operates," Clete said.

"Who likes any of the people we deal with?"

"There's a difference. He hires other people to do his dirty work."

The story was political in nature and well known and, like most political stories, had already slipped into history and wasn't considered of importance by most Americans.

A United States senator got in Love Younger's way and discovered that his citations in the brown-water navy were somehow manufactured. Like many of my fellow voters, I had lost interest in taking up other people's causes. Someone had almost killed my daughter with a razor-edged hunting arrow, and I was determined to find out who it was.

"You coming or not?" I said.

"Let me check on Gretchen," Clete replied.

Younger's summer home was a ten-thousand-square-foot mansion located west of Missoula on a pinnacle high above the Clark Fork. It was beige-colored and Tudor in design, the tall windows and breezy front porch trimmed with purple rock, the lawn planted with sugar maples and blue spruce and ornamental crab apple trees that took on a sheen like melted red candy in the sunlight. There was a circular gravel driveway in front, a porte cochere on the side, and a restored Lincoln Continental parked in back. When I lifted the door knocker, electronic chimes echoed through the interior. Clete had lit a cigarette when we got out of his Caddy. "Will you get rid of that?" I said.

"No problem," he replied. He took two more puffs and flicked the butt over the porch wall onto the lawn just as a woman answered the door. Her skin was so pale it looked bloodless, to the degree that the moles on her shoulders and the one by her mouth seemed to be individually pasted on her body. Her hair had a dark luster with brown streaks, and her eyes possessed a liquescence I normally would associate with hostility or an invasive curiosity about others that bordered on disdain. I had to remind myself of the loss the Younger family had just suffered.

I introduced myself and Clete and offered our condolences, thinking that she was about to invite us in. Instead, she looked behind her, then back at us. "Who did you say you were?" she asked.

"I spoke earlier with Love Younger. He asked me to come here," I said. "This is his house, isn't it?"

"Tell them to come in, Felicity," a voice called from the hallway.

A slight man walked toward us, a vague smile on his face. He did not offer to shake hands. He was unshaved and wearing slippers and a dress shirt open at the collar. "I'm Caspian," he said. "You're a police officer?"

"Not here. In Louisiana," I said.

"You know something about Angel's death?" he said.

"Not directly, but I have some information that I feel I should share with you. I think someone tried to kill my daughter. We've also had a stalker at the place where we're staying. Can we sit down?"

"Wait here, please," he said.

119

"Like Dave says, we were invited here," Clete said. "I don't think that's getting across somehow."

"Excuse me?" Caspian said.

"We have no obligation to be here," Clete said. "We were trying to do you a favor."

"I see," said Caspian. "I know my father will be happy to see you."

The man and the woman went to the rear of the house. Clete and I waited on a leather couch by a huge fireplace filled with ash and crumpled logs that gave no heat. The windows reached almost to the ceiling and were hung with velvet curtains, the walls with oil paintings of individuals in nineteenth-century dress. The carpets were Iranian, the furniture antique, the beams in the cathedral ceiling recovered from a teardown, the wood rust-marked by iron spikes and bolts. In a side hallway, I could see a long glass-covered cabinet lined with flintlock and cap-and-ball rifles.

Clete glanced at his watch. "Do you believe these fucking people?" he said.

"Take it easy."

"They're all the same."

"I know it. You can't change them. So don't try."

I knew that the Younger family and their ingrained rudeness were not the source of Clete's discontent.

"Gretchen's never slept with a piece," he

120

said. "She's never been afraid of anything. She stayed in the shower so long that she ran all the hot water out of the tank. I saw a bruise on her neck. She said she slipped while she was hiking up the hill behind the house." He leaned forward, hands cupped on his knees. "I don't like being here, Dave. These are the same people who used to treat us like their garbage collectors."

"We'll leave in a few minutes. I promise."

"The guy was a guest at the White House. He says he's into wind energy. Does anybody buy crap like that? I say screw this."

I believed I understood Clete's resentment toward the world in which he grew up, and I didn't want to argue with him. The most telling story about his background was one he told me when he was drunk. As a boy, during the summer, he sometimes went on the milk-delivery route with his father, a brutal and childlike man who loved his children and yet was often cruel to every one of them. One day a wealthy woman in the Garden District saw Clete sitting by himself on the rear bumper of the milk truck, barefoot and wearing jeans split at the knees and eating a peanut-butter sandwich. The woman stroked his head, her eyes filling with the lights of pity and love. "You're such a beautiful little boy," she said. "Come back here at one P.M. Saturday and have ice cream and cake with me."

He put on his white suit an uncle had bought him for his confirmation and went to the woman's house one block from Audubon Park. When he knocked at the front door, a black butler answered and told him to go around to the rear. Clete walked along the flagstone path through the side yard and under a latticework arch hung with orange trumpet vine. The backyard was crowded with black children from the other side of Magazine. The woman who had stroked his hair was not there, nor did she ever show up.

That night he returned with a box of rocks and broke all the glass in her greenhouse and destroyed the flowers in her gardens.

At some point in your life, you have to give up anger or it will destroy your spirit the way cancer destroys living tissue. At least that is what I told myself, even though I was not very good at taking my own advice. I hated to see Clete suffer because of the injustice done to him by his alcoholic father. He didn't like the Love Youngers of the world, and neither did I. But why suffer because of them? I never knew one of them who didn't write his own denouement, so why not leave them to their own fate?

There was no lack of public information about Mr. Younger. He became a millionaire by buying wheat futures in the Midwest with money he borrowed from a church, when few people outside government knew the Nixon administration was about to open up new markets in Russia. Later, in a poker game, he won a 30 percent interest in an independent drilling company, one teetering on bankruptcy. He redrilled old oil fields that others had given up on, going down to a record twenty-five thousand feet, and punched into one of the biggest geological domes in Louisiana's history. Love Younger had a green thumb. Whatever he touched turned to money, huge amounts of it, millions that became billions, the kind of wealth that could buy governments or the geographic entirety of a third-world country.

The rest of his story was another matter. One son, an aviator, went down in a desert while dropping supplies to French mercenaries and died a hellish death from thirst and exposure. Another son plowed his Porsche into the side of a train in Katy, Texas. A daughter who suffered delusions and agitated depression underwent an experimental operation at a clinic in Brazil that her father had chosen for her. As promised, she awoke from the anesthesia totally free of her depression and imaginary fears. She was also a vegetable.

Felicity came back in the living room. "Follow me," she said.

"We can do that," Clete said, getting to his feet.

She turned and looked at him. She wore a peasant blouse and a thin ankle-length

123

pleated cotton skirt and white doeskin moccasins, as a flower child from the 1960s might. "I think you're here for self-serving purposes," she said.

"My daughter may be in danger," I said. "She believes a psychopath she interviewed in a Kansas prison is in this area."

"And you think this psychopath murdered Angel?"

"I'm not sure what to think."

"You're telling me that your daughter may be the reason this man is in the area and that he murdered Angel?"

"You can draw your own conclusions, Ms. Younger."

"I use my maiden name. It's Felicity Louviere. Do you want to talk to my father-in-law now, or would you prefer to leave?"

She was much smaller than Clete and I, but she looked up into my face with such animus that I almost stepped back. "I didn't mean to offend you," I said.

"We're going through a bad time right now," she replied. "You'll have to forgive me."

She walked ahead of us, past a sunlit set of French doors, her body in silhouette. "She doesn't have on any underwear. This place is a nuthouse," I heard Clete whisper.

"Will you be quiet?" I said.

"What'd I say?" he asked.

The rear windows of Love Younger's den looked onto the river and a ridge of mountains that were jagged and blue and marbled with new snow on the peaks. Younger was seated at a large worktable scattered with oily rags and bore brushes and the tiny tools of a gunsmith and the clocklike inner workings of early firearms. He looked up at me from his work on an 1851 Colt revolver, one almost unblemished by rust or wear. "Thank you for coming, gentlemen," he said. "I'm sorry I was short with you this morning, Mr. Robicheaux."

"It's all right."

"You know a sheriff's detective by the name of Bill Pepper?" he asked.

"I do. I believe he abused a man who was in his custody, a rodeo clown by the name of Wyatt Dixon."

"Abused him in what way?"

"Worked him over while his wrists were cuffed behind him."

"I've been getting feedback from Pepper, but I didn't know that about him. He says Dixon may have a partner and the partner might be the man who shot an arrow at your daughter. Pepper interviewed a salesman at a sporting goods store who sold a hunter's bow to a man wearing a bracelet like the one Dixon sold my granddaughter."

"Pepper didn't share that information with me, Mr. Younger."

"He didn't?"

"No, sir. This is Clete Purcel. He's the

friend I told you about."

"How do you do, Mr. Purcel?" Younger said. He rose slightly from his chair and shook Clete's hand. Neither his son nor his daughter-in-law had uttered a word since we entered the room, and I had the feeling they seldom spoke unless they were spoken to. "My son and daughter-in-law adopted Angel from an orphanage by the Blackfoot Reservation. I did everything I could to keep her from drinking and hanging out with bad people. She was the sweetest little girl I ever knew. Good God, what kind of man would take a teenage girl into a barn and suffocate her?"

There are times in our lives when words are of no value. This was one of them. I have never lost a child, but I know many people who have. I have also had to knock on a family's door and tell them their child was killed in an accident or by a predator. I have come to believe there is no greater sorrow than experiencing a loss of this kind, particularly when the child's life was taken to satisfy the self-centered agenda of a degenerate.

"My second wife was killed by some bad men, Mr. Younger," I said. "I didn't want people's sympathies, and I particularly resented people who felt they had to console me. At the time I had only one desire — to smoke the guys who killed my wife."

He looked up at me, waiting.

126

"I got my wish. It didn't give me any rest," I said.

"How long ago did this happen?"

"Twenty-four years ago."

"And even now you have no rest?"

"There're some things you don't get over."

The foster parents of the girl were standing behind me. Caspian, the father, stepped between me and Love Younger. His unshaved and unwashed look made me think of a man who had gone into another country, one where a person can be dissolute without penalty, only to return home and find everything he owned in ruins. "I heard you say something to Felicity about a psychopath in Kansas, a man who might be living in this area," Caspian said.

"My daughter is a writer. She had planned to write a book about a serial killer and sadist named Asa Surrette. She interviewed him two or three times but was so disgusted by the experience that she decided not to write the book. Instead, she wrote a series of articles that she hoped would expose him to the death penalty."

"Where is he?" Love Younger asked.

"The authorities in Kansas say he died in a collision involving a gasoline truck and a prison van."

His eyes searched my face. "You don't believe that?" he asked.

"Earlier this week my daughter was followed by a man in a skinned-up Ford pickup. She thinks it was Asa Surrette."

"I asked if you believe he's dead," Younger said.

"Somebody scratched a message on a cave wall on the hillside above Albert Hollister's house. It contained biblical allusions that indicate the message writer is megalomaniacal. Could Surrette have written a message of that kind? It's possible."

"Why would Angel go off with a guy like that?" Caspian said. His chin was tilted upward, his throat coated with whiskers that looked like steel filings, a hazy smile in his eyes.

"I don't know, sir," I replied.

"Be quiet, Caspian," Love Younger said.

"There's something we skipped over here, Mr. Younger," Clete said. "You mentioned this guy Pepper. Evidently, he's been reporting to you, but he didn't report the same information to Dave, whose daughter is at risk. He also told you Dixon might have a partner. For me that doesn't flush. From what I understand, Dixon's a loner, a rodeo man bikers don't mess with. A guy like that doesn't have to rely on backup. Plus, his jacket has been clean since he got out of Deer Lodge."

"His what?" Younger said.

"His record. The guy probably has Kryptonite for a brain, but count on it, he's not our guy," Clete said.

"You're saying that Pepper is trying to earn his way into my good graces by manufacturing information?" Younger said.

"It crossed my mind," Clete said.

Younger gazed out the window at the long floodplain of the Clark Fork and the great geological gorge the river flowed into. "How do we find out if Surrette is dead or alive?"

"You don't," I said.

"I don't understand."

"When is the last time any state of its own volition admitted it was wrong about anything?" I said.

Younger picked up the 1851 Colt and rubbed an oily rag across its blue-black surfaces, cocking back the hammer, locking the cylinder into place. "I made this like new," he said. "It took me six weeks, but I did it. It's like traveling back in time and somehow defying mortality. Supposedly, Wild Bill Hickok was carrying this when he got pushed into a corner by John Wesley Hardin."

I waited for him to go on, not understanding his point.

"It didn't help Hickok," he said. "Wes Hardin backed him down. It was the only time Wild Bill ever cut bait. Past or present, our best-laid plans seem to go astray, don't they?"

He set the revolver down heavily on an oilcloth, his face wan and older somehow, his hands as small as a child's.

Clete and I were both silent as we drove down the hill to catch the interstate back to Missoula. The sun was bright through the fir and pine and spruce trees lining the road, the light almost blinding when it splintered on the wet needles. The Younger enclave, with its grand vistas, seemed to validate all the basic tenets of the American Dream. Love Younger had risen from the most humble of origins and created a fortune out of virtually nothing. He had also beaten the descendants of the robber barons at their own game. I thought I understood why people were fascinated with him. If such good fortune could happen to him, it could happen to any of us, right? There were those who probably wished to touch the hem of his cloak so they could be made over in his image. But as Clete's Caddy coasted down the hillside through shadows that looked like saber points falling across the road, I felt only pity for Love Younger and his family.

"How do you read all that back there?" Clete asked.

"I don't. I've never understood the rich."

"What's to understand? They get a more expensive plot in the boneyard than the rest of us."

"Pepper is bad news. He's using the investigation for his own purposes," I said.

"So we'll have a talk with him. Did you catch the broad's accent?"

"No," I lied.

"She's from New Orleans or somewhere nearby." Clete looked sideways at me.

"Good. Now watch the road."

"I was just saying."

"I know what you were saying. You also mentioned she wasn't wearing any undergarments."

"I'm not supposed to notice something like that?"

"We're not getting personally involved with these people. You got it?"

"You know what the essential difference is between the two of us, noble mon?"

"One of us falls in love with every injured woman he sees. Then he finds out he's in the sack with the Antichrist. Sound like anyone you know?"

"No, I recognize the presence of my flopper in my life. It has X-ray vision and goes on autopilot whenever it wants. Sometimes it does the thinking for both of us. I've accepted that. I think that's a big breakthrough. You might try a little humility sometime, Streak."

"I'm not going to listen to this. I know what's coming. You can't wait to get in trouble again. I've never seen anything like it. Why don't you grow up?"

"You grow up, you grow old. Who wants to do that? Relax. Think cool thoughts and don't eat fried foods. You know who said that? Satchel Paige. Everything is very copacetic. You got my word on that."

After her last interview with Asa Surrette, Alafair published three articles about his crimes, their heinous nature, and the compulsive pattern that characterized his behavior from childhood until the day he was arrested. The thesis in each article was clinical in nature and ultimately not up for argument: A serial killer does not turn his compulsions on and off, as you do a noisy faucet. Surrette and his attorney maintained he had committed no crimes after the reinstatement of capital punishment in Kansas in 1994. Alafair believed otherwise.

The articles used direct quotations from the interview, and their arrangement created a damning portrayal of a man to whom cruelty, sexual conquest, bloodlust, and a pathological lack of remorse were a way of life.

At the time I asked if she had not become too emotionally involved in the subject.

"I have the quotes on tape. I didn't make them up. He's evil. The real question is, how could a man like this kill people in the same city for twenty years?" she said.

That was my kid.

When I returned from Love Younger's home, Alafair asked me to come upstairs. An

132

envelope and a piece of typewriter paper with a letter written on it in blue ink rested on her desk, next to her computer. "I never showed you this, Dave. Surrette wrote it to me after the articles were published," she said.

"Why didn't you want me to see it?"

"Because I thought it would make you mad. Read it."

A strange thing happened. I didn't want to touch a sheet of paper that Surrette had handled. I've known every kind of man in the world, and even held the hand of a man on the way to his electrocution in the Red Hat House at Angola. But I did not want to place my fingers on the paper that Asa Surrette had touched. I walked to her desk and looked down at his writing. His penmanship, if it could be called that, was bizarre. The paper was unlined, but every sentence, every word, every letter, was as uniform and neat and straight as the print created by a Linotype machine. Round letters were flattened and reduced to geometric slash marks, as though the penman believed forming a circle violated a principle. The greater oddity was the absence of punctuation. Surrette's sentences and phrases were set apart by dashes rather than by periods and commas, as though he could not disconnect from his own stream of consciousness, or perhaps because he believed his own thought processes had neither a beginning nor an end. This is what he wrote in his prison cell and mailed through the censor to my daughter:

Dear Alafair —
    I have read your articles and wanted to tell you how well written I think they are — I do not fault you for the way you have characterized me — I probably did not put my best foot forward during our talks — Nonetheless I believe there was a certain spark between us — One thing you did not understand about me was my origins — Some people were born before the primal dust of the world was created and have waited eons for their time to come round — Maybe you were also there before the hills and the mountains were settled — Perhaps we have much to share with each other —
    Someplace down the road I know I will see you again — Until then I will always think of you in a fond way —

As ever —
Asa

"Why'd you dig out the letter now?" I said.
"You know why."
"The line about being here before the primal dust of the world?"
"I looked it up. He lifted two or three lines from the Book of Psalms. It sounds like the stuff written on the wall in the cave."

134

"I'm going to make some calls to Kansas."

"You don't think I've already done that? The paramedics removed the carbonized remains of four individuals from the gas truck and the prison van. I called the *Eagle* in Wichita and talked to a reporter who told me an interesting story: An autistic boy may have witnessed the collision. The boy told his mother that a man walking along the edge of the highway stepped in front of the gas truck and caused the accident. If that's true, there should have been five bodies in the wreckage rather than four."

I continued to stare at Surrette's letter and wondered how I had allowed a man like this to come into our lives. "What did the cops say?"

"Forget the cops," she said. "The reporter interviewed the little boy, who said the truck didn't explode until after the collision. He said he could hear pieces of the van and truck rolling down the highway. Then he saw a great light in the sky."

"Surrette climbed out of the van and lit the spilled fuel?"

"It's the kind of thing he would do. Have you seen Gretchen?"

"What about her?"

"She's acting strange. Maybe she's still angry about those remarks the cops made up on the hillside."

"Maybe it's time we have a talk with Pep-

135

per. He told the grandfather of the murdered Indian girl that he'd found the store where a guy wearing the girl's bracelet bought a hunter's bow. Except Pepper didn't tell us that."

"You said 'we,' " she replied.

I got Bill Pepper's address from the phone book and at four-thirty P.M., we headed down the dirt road toward the two-lane. Half a mile south of Albert's ranch, we saw a bright orange pickup coming toward us, a man in a white straw cowboy hat behind the wheel. He stopped and rolled down the window. A bouquet of cut flowers wrapped in green tissue paper rested on the dashboard. "Howdy-doody. I come to see Miss Gretchen," he said.

"To my knowledge, she's not home, Mr. Dixon," I said.

"Then I'll have to talk to y'all." He shut off his engine and stepped out on the road. The sun was shining in his eyes, but he seemed to take no heed. "I heard those cops talking about the message on that cave wall."

"What about it?"

"I know what it means. I don't want to get drug into it. Not unless that's what I'm supposed to be doing."

"Drug into what? You're not making a lot of sense, partner," I said.

"The Indians on the rez have been talking about it a long time. The Bible says he'll

136

come from the sea, and you'll know him by the numbers in his name. All this countryside was under the ocean at one time. I think he's here. That was him or one of his acolytes up there in that cave."

Alafair leaned across the seat. "*Who's* here?" she said.

"Him," Dixon said. "*Him,* the one the world's been waiting on."

CHAPTER 7

The rivers were blown out by the spring runoff and the constant rains, but Clete knew a creek high up on a logging road in the Bitterroots where there was a long stretch of white water that boiled over into the trees, then above it a chain of beaver dams and deep pools and undulating riffles sliding so clear over the gravel bed that you could count each pebble five feet below the surface. He had loaded his ice chest with beer and canned fruit juice and ham-and-onion sandwiches and had put it on the backseat and his waders and fly rod and fly vest and net and creel in the trunk. He had put on his canvas coat and porkpie hat and was ready to go. There was only one problem. He couldn't get his mind off his daughter.

He went back into the cabin. "Come with me," he said.

"I have things to take care of," she said. She was sitting at the breakfast table, her food cold on her plate, her laptop open.

"What's bothering you, kid?"

"Nothing."

"I saw the Airweight under your pillow."

"I have nightmares sometimes. It's the way I am."

"Did you meet a guy last night?"

"No."

"Tell me the truth."

"I just did."

"Then what is it?"

"I have to work some things out."

He took off his hat and sat down at the table. She closed the laptop. "I'm not leaving until you tell me what it is," he said.

"I used some bad judgment."

"With a guy?"

"Not the kind you're thinking about."

"Who or what are we talking about?" he said.

"I'll handle it, Clete."

He put a hand on her arm and saw her flinch. "I'm getting a bad feeling here," he said.

"So butt out."

"Is it those cops who wised off to you?"

"Stay out of it."

"You went after them, didn't you?"

"I acted like a fool. Everything that happened to me is my own fault."

"What did they do to you?"

"I went to Bill Pepper's house. I was going to tear him up. Then I saw a swing set in his

yard and a basketball hoop over the porte cochere. When he opened the door, I saw
pictures of him with his grandchildren on the
wall. He pretended not to recognize me. He
asked if I was a church lady."

"A what?"

"He said this lady was going to enroll his
granddaughter at Bible camp. He said he
thought I was her. He's a very convincing
guy."

Clete felt a shortness in his breath, a watery
sensation in his heart. "Tell me what happened."

"I think he put Rohypnol or maybe some
sleeping pills in a glass of Pepsi he gave me."

"Go on."

"I don't remember all of it. He put his
hands on me first. Then he did some other
things."

Clete saw the blood go out of her cheeks,
the blank stare in her eyes. "Get it all out at
once," he said. "There's nothing to be
ashamed of. We're going to deal with this
together."

"He rubbed his penis on me. All over my
skin. He kept saying things with his mouth
close to my ear. I couldn't keep his breath off
my face."

Clete felt his scalp tightening, his hands
forming into fists on his knees under the
table.

"He drove me to a place on the Blackfoot,"

she said. "For a long time he let me think he was going to kill me. Then he cut my clothes off with a knife and poured whiskey and weed on me and rubbed it all over my body and left me to walk naked back to town. Two kids gave me a raincoat and took me to my truck."

The whites of her eyes had turned pink, although she had not shed any tears. Clete had to cough into his hand before he spoke. "You're not going to report him?"

"He scrubbed me with bleach. There's no DNA on me. My clothes are gone. I have nothing to prove my story."

"What were you doing on the Internet?"

"He told me he had terminal cancer. Some people I know in Miami hacked into his medical records. He was lying. I know what you're thinking. I want you to stay out of it."

"He's going down."

"I don't let other people carry my water, especially you."

"Because I wasn't there to defend you when you were a kid?"

"It's the other way around. You've been there for me in every way you could, and I'm not going to let you take my weight now."

"You've got your whole life ahead of you, kid. You've made a documentary on music, and now you're going to make one on the damage these shale-oil companies are doing. You can't throw that away because of a bum like Pepper. Leave him to me."

"That's what you don't understand, Clete. When a man molests a woman, he steals her identity. You don't know who you are anymore. You feel like you don't have an address or a mailbox or a name. You're nothing."

"Don't talk like that."

"See what I mean? You don't want to hear it. No man wants to know how painful it is. It's like a stain you can't wash out of your soul. I want to kill him, and I want to do it in pieces. I want him to suffer as much as possible."

He picked up her hand. "I don't blame you for not dime-ing him. He's probably done it before and gotten away with it. The system chews up sexual assault victims. But I'm going to get him, and when I do, it will be for both of us."

"I knew this was a mistake."

"What is?"

"Telling you. You're going to end up in prison."

He started to speak, then gave it up and stroked her hair. His head had filled with images from her account that he knew would pursue him night and day, no matter where he went or how he tried to occupy himself. As he realized the magnitude of the theft that had been perpetrated on his daughter, he felt a sensation in his stomach that was like a flame punching a hole in a sheet of paper and spreading outward until it blackened everything it touched.

A squall had just blown through Hellgate Canyon into downtown Missoula when we reached the tree-shaded neighborhood by the river where Bill Pepper lived. The limbs of the maple trees were in full leaf and shaking in great wet clusters in the wind, raindrops spotting the sidewalks, the flower baskets on Pepper's porch whipping back and forth. It was only five-thirty, but he had turned on the lights inside. I had to knock twice before I saw him appear from the kitchen, wearing a fedora, a leather jacket on his arm. He looked through the glass straight into my face, then unlocked the bolt and opened the door. "What is it?" he asked.

Fear comes in many forms, most often as a sense of apprehension that soon disappears. What I saw in the face of Bill Pepper bordered on the kind of fear I've seen only in the faces of the condemned, men who had to sit in a cell and listen to the beating of their heart while awaiting the sound of a steel door swinging open and footsteps walking down a poorly lighted corridor. I'm talking about a level of fear that turns the skin gray and leaves a man's hair soggy with sweat and his palms so stiff and dry he can't close them.

"I met with Love Younger this morning," I said. "I need to confirm a couple of things he told me."

"You're meddling in an investigation where you have no jurisdiction," Pepper said.

"That's not the case. My daughter was almost killed by an unknown assailant who's still out there. Younger says you found a sporting goods salesman who sold a hunter's bow to a guy who may have murdered Angel Deer Heart. This is information we have a right to know. Why didn't you share it with us?"

"I'm on my way out of town for the weekend. You can come to my office Monday if you want to talk."

"You nervous about something?" Alafair said.

"I'm in a rush. What right do you have to come to my house? To talk to me like that?" As though emboldened by his own rhetoric, he stepped out on the porch. Even in the wind, I could smell the alcohol on his breath.

"Our request for information is a reasonable one, Detective Pepper," I said. "I don't understand why you're upset."

"I'm fine. I don't know what you want or why you're here. We're still looking at Wyatt Dixon. To our knowledge, he's the last person to see the girl alive."

"We just ran into Dixon on the dirt road below Albert Hollister's house," I said. "He was on his way to see Gretchen Horowitz. He seemed perfectly relaxed talking to us. Does that sound like a guilty man to you?"

Pepper's eyes looked from me to Alafair and back to me. "Are they cooking up something? Maybe claiming I abused Dixon?"

This time I didn't respond. There was a tic below his left eye, a twitch by his mouth.

"Just tell us what you found out from the sporting goods salesman," Alafair said. "What did the purchaser of the hunting bow look like?"

"Middle-aged. He paid with cash. It could be anybody," he said. "Maybe it doesn't mean anything."

"That's not what you told Love Younger," Alafair said. "You told him the purchaser was wearing the kind of bracelet Dixon sold the Indian girl."

"I'm leaving now. I don't have time for this," Pepper said.

"I think your boat left the dock a little early today," I said.

"Say again?"

"You're ninety proof, partner. I used to start at lunchtime, too, particularly when I was warming up for the weekend. By Saturday morning I'd glow in the dark."

I saw a strange light come into his eyes, as though he had shifted gears inside his head and was no longer thinking about any of the things he had just said. "You're from down there. You know how they do business," he said.

"From down *where*? Who is *they*? I don't

know what you're talking about," I said.

"It's got to do with Albert Hollister and the girl. They think I'm involved. I'm out. That's what I'm saying."

"Sir, you're not making any sense," I said.

"Mr. Robicheaux?"

"What is it?"

He seemed to collect himself, like a man wanting a friend. "I'm sorry for what I did. They've got me figured out wrong. I think I'm gonna go back to Mobile. I always liked it there, living by the salt water and pole-fishing with the nigras at sunset. It's a peaceful life there on the bay."

Alafair and I stared at him. It was like watching a man disappear before our eyes. "Sorry you did what?" I asked.

"For my actions. I'd undo them if I could."

"I think you need some help," I said.

He closed the door just as the clouds broke and started to pour down, the raindrops hitting the rooftop and sidewalks as hard as hail. If there is a charnel house for souls, I believed Bill Pepper had just found it.

Albert was gone when we returned to the house. The rain had quit and the sky had turned into an ink wash, and Molly and I grilled steaks on the deck and took them inside and ate at the dining room table with Alafair and watched the moon rise above the Bitterroots. Albert came in later, holding a

146

FedEx delivery, his face ruddy from the wind. "This is for Gretchen. It was by the garage," he said. "Where is she?"

"At the cabin, I think," I replied. "Alafair and I had a talk with one of the cops who was up at the cave. Bill Pepper. Do you know him?"

"No more than I know any of them."

"He was half in the bag and scared about something. He said it had to do with you and somebody he called 'the girl.' "

Albert shook his head. "Isn't he the one who beat up the cowboy?"

"Yeah, he knocked Wyatt Dixon around."

"Why spend time talking with a man like that?" Albert said. He set the FedEx box on the table. The return address was a geological lab in Austin, Texas.

After supper, Gretchen had gone into her bedroom and lain down on top of the covers, her arm across her eyes, then turned toward the wall and fallen asleep. Clete sat at the kitchen table, a cup of coffee in front of him, and watched her sleep. He tried to think about the choices available to him. Have a quiet talk with the sheriff? Gretchen would end up shark meat. The sheriff would pull her jacket from Miami-Dade, and no credence would be given to anything she said. And the larger problem went way beyond Gretchen's background. Again and again, victims of sexual assault were put on the stand and torn apart while the perpetrator either smirked at the defense table or shook his head in feigned disbelief. Rapes were downgraded to battery; child molesters were given probation. There was another problem, too. There was a sick culture in law enforcement, particularly among vice cops, and everyone knew it, Clete in particular: the corner-of-the-mouth jokes, the smug moral superiority, the collective rush in having set up a successful sex sting, the legal proximity to a sybaritic world where you could get laid in any way you wanted by just flipping out your badge.

For a vice detective with some loose time on his hands, after-hours New Orleans may not have been the Baths of Caracalla, but it was a pretty good surrogate.

In Clete's opinion, the nation was still Puritan, at least when it came to the victimization of women. The temptress brought about her own downfall. The victim was the noun, the perpetrator an adverb. The moment Gretchen testified, she would be portrayed as a contract killer from Miami who had gone willingly to Bill Pepper's home and entered into a tryst that ended in a lurid and inconsequential denouement on the Blackfoot River. She'd be lucky if she wasn't charged with perjury.

Clete could see the curve of her hip and

the tautness of her thighs and rump against the fabric of her jeans and her back rising and falling as she slept. She had begun a spartan health regimen in California and had lost twenty pounds by dieting and working out with weights and running four miles every morning on the beach in Santa Monica. The combination of her chestnut hair and violet-colored eyes and statuesque carriage made men turn and stare as she walked by. Even more intriguing, she seemed to take no notice of the attention they paid her, as though she were a polite but temporary visitor in their midst.

It was hard for Clete to separate the daughter he was looking at now from the woman who had been called Caruso in Little Havana. Blood splatter and the curse of Cain did not rinse easily from the hands or the soul. Anyone who believed otherwise knew nothing about the makeup of human beings, he thought. Aside from psychopaths, every person who killed another human being took on a burden he carried for the rest of his life. The daylight hours allowed you to concentrate on making money and buying food and clothes and worrying about your bald automobile tires. The nocturnal hours were a little different. The gargoyles that lived in the unconscious had their own agenda and were not interested in the ebb and flow of your daily life. When you were in bed by yourself at four A.M., you could hear them slip their tethers and begin production of a horror movie in which you were the star, except you had no control of the events that were about to take place. How did you deal with it? You could try reds, four fingers of Jack, or even Nytol. Except you usually mortgaged the next day for a few hours of drugged sleep. There was another way: You could drop a solitary round in the cylinder of your .38 and pull back the hammer and, with one soft squeeze of the trigger, put the problem out of your mind forever.

Somehow Gretchen had escaped the life she had fallen into. But after she had shown mercy and trust to a rogue cop who had ridiculed her in front of other men, he had repaid the favor by drugging and binding her and torturing her with his genitalia. How did you address a situation like that? Did you hand your girl over to the system and hope she wasn't degraded again? Did you allow her to return to the criminal life she had freed herself from? Did you allow others to wad up her life like a piece of used Kleenex and throw it away?

What conclusion would any reasonable person come to?

Clete wrote a note on the back of an envelope and propped the envelope against the sugar bowl on the kitchen table. Then he pulled a duffel bag from the closet and checked its contents: a cut-down twelve-gauge Remington pump, a box of double-aught bucks and pumpkin balls that he had hand-loaded, a .25-caliber semi-auto with acid-burned serial numbers, a push-button stiletto, latex gloves, plastic ligatures, a lead-weighted blackjack that could break a two-by-four in half, handcuffs, a set of lock picks, brass knuckles, a bottle of bleach, a slim jim, nylon fishing line, and duct tape.

Restraint, reason, working within the system?

Fuck that.

He carried the duffel bag outside and put it in the trunk of the Caddy and drove away.

The note on the table read:

> Don't worry about anything, kid. I'll be back before morning. All this will be behind us.
>
> Love,
Your pop,
Cletus

One hour later, Gretchen woke and did not know where she was; nor, for the moment, did she remember the events that had occurred in the home of Bill Pepper or on the banks of the Blackfoot River. Then she realized the sleep was an illusion and the reality was the assault on her person committed by Bill Pepper. The touch of his hands and his genitalia seemed to cling to her skin like wet cobweb, and the more she rubbed her hands on herself, the more she seemed to re-create what he had done to her, as though she had become a surrogate for the man who assaulted her.

She walked to the kitchen table and read the note Clete had left. She set it down and stood for a long time under the lightbulb that hung directly over her head, trying to think of answers to her situation and his. Through the window, she saw a cinnamon cub come out of the trees on the hillside and work his way through the fence in the moonlight. Albert had sent a chain e-mail through the valley telling others that the cub had been separated from his mother and to be careful while driving down the dirt road. The cub pulled his hind foot loose from the fence, the smooth wire twanging on the posts, then disappeared into the tall grass, creating a path like a submarine gliding just below the surface of the ocean. When Gretchen stepped out on the gallery, the cub bounded across the creek and through the cottonwoods, his rump bouncing up and down in the moonlight.

Gretchen felt a tear in her eye as she watched the cub scramble under the rail fence on the far side of the pasture and head up the hill over rocks and snags into the darkness, the slag from an old geological slide rattling down the incline.

Bill Pepper had lied to her about everything except one item. He'd told the truth when he said he had thrown her tote bag in a tree by the side of the dirt road. What he had not told her was his motivation, which was probably to show his contempt for her possessions and to create a situation where he would continue to control her when she was forced to climb naked into a tree to recover what he had taken from her.

She removed her Airweight .38 from under her pillow and placed it in the bag, alongside the expandable baton and can of Mace, which were still in the bag when she plucked it out of the tree. Then she put on her scarf and her red nylon jacket, the same kind James Dean wore in *Rebel Without a Cause*. As she drove slowly under the arch onto the road in her chopped-down pickup, the subdued power of the Merc engine vibrating through the floor stick into her palm, she thought she saw the cub moving through the trees and wondered if he would find safe harbor for the night.

Bill Pepper turned his van off the two-lane highway and descended a gravel road through a grove of birch trees to the edge of Swan Lake. The moon was above the mountains, turning the lake into an oxidized mirror filled with pools of both shadow and light, the dark green sweep of the weeds as thick and undulating as wheat below the surface. He got out of his van and glanced once over his shoulder at the highway, then entered the shingled cottage at the bottom of the incline and locked the door behind him.

Bill Pepper loved his cottage. It was snug and warm during the hunting season, and in summer it was a retreat from the city and the tourists who flocked to western Montana and clogged the highways with their campers and mobile homes. This night was different; the lake and the cottage provided little comfort for the problems that had beset him. A heart-pounding fear had followed him all the way from Missoula, fouling his blood and his thoughts and his vision and any hope of restoring his self-respect. For the first time in his life, Bill Pepper wondered if he was a coward.

Couldn't he take the heat? He'd been a patrolman in South Central and Compton and what the Hispanics called East Los, and he'd taken sniper fire through his windshield on the Harbor Freeway. Pimps and dealers got off the streets when they saw him coming. Black hookers did lap dances for him in his cruiser. An unpopular Crip who had spent two years in isolation in Pelican Bay made fun of his accent and kept calling him Goober and "Bell Pepper wit' the big belly" when

Pepper tried to question him about an armed robbery. Bill smiled tolerantly and looked once over his shoulder and then smiled again just before he pinned the Crip's head against a brick wall with a baton and spat in his face and broke his windpipe. The irony was that the street people and even members of the Eighth Street Crips started yelling at his cruiser from the sidewalks, "Hey, Mr. Bill, you de motherfuckin' *man!*"

He set his Glock on the coffee table in the small living room and looked out at the vastness of the lake and the Swan Peaks rising like jagged tin in the south, and directly across from the cottage, a thickly wooded mountain that was black against a sky twinkling with stars. Just one week ago opportunities had been opening up for him right and left: He had money in the bank, a new van, and was reporting to one of the richest men in the United States. Then it all went south because of a girl named Gretchen Horowitz. An idle remark about her being butch, that's all it was, and he got a shitload of grief dropped on his head. How about the uniformed deputy who wised off first? Why didn't the girl go after *him?*

He had not turned on the lights in the cottage. He got up from the sofa and went into the kitchen and took a bottle of milk from the refrigerator, then sat back down and uncapped a pint of brandy and mixed it with milk in a jelly glass and drank it in the dark. The leafy canopy of the birch trees was swaying in the moonlight, the shadows sliding back and forth on his lawn and porch. If Bill Pepper had learned any lesson in life, it was that terrible events always had small beginnings. His father had befriended a Negro vagabond and lost his life. The Watts riot had begun not because of police beating an innocent person but because a crowd had gathered when a patrolman arrested a black taxi driver who was DWI. Within days National Guardsmen were firing .30-caliber machine guns into apartment buildings and eighty-one people were dead and flames were rising from a quarter of the city.

He could have squared the situation with the girl even after molesting her. But he'd found out today his troubles over her were just beginning. She was important to people for reasons he didn't understand. Who was she, anyway? Why were these other people coming down on him? They acted like he knew everything about her. The truth was, he knew nothing about her. If he'd known anything about her, he would have left her alone.

How had he let her get under his skin? How could he explain that to others when he couldn't explain it to himself? She was attractive, certainly. No, that wasn't the right word. She was beautiful. Her eyes were

mysterious and alluring and a little dangerous and at the same time vulnerable. She was
a young girl buried inside a body that was
every man's wet dream. He knew his thoughts
were sick, but he couldn't help desiring her.
No man could. He was only human. Maybe
his feelings were even fatherly, he told himself.

She's getting to you again, he thought. *You
know the real reason for your fascination with
her. She's not afraid. Not of you, not of anyone,
not of anything, not even death at the hands of
a man inserting a knife blade between her neck
and collar, inches from her carotid.*

He emptied his glass and filled it again, this
time not bothering to stir it, drinking the
brandy as fast as he could get it down. He
thought he heard a tree limb break and fall
into the yard. Or was that the deer coming
down to drink from the lake? He had told
that cop and his daughter from Louisiana
that he wanted to go back to Mobile. That
was still a possibility, wasn't it? His fellow
white officers at the LAPD had never understood Bill Pepper's attitude toward people of
color. He had no resentment toward them;
he felt comfortable in their midst and didn't
blame them because a deranged colored
vagabond had killed his father. The group he
couldn't abide was white trash like Wyatt
Dixon, the kind of man who visited his odium

on other Southerners, the kind of man who reminded Bill Pepper of the alleyway he lived on in Macon.

He lit a cigarette and poured more brandy in his glass and watched it swirl inside the milk. He drank the glass almost to the bottom, hoping he could stop the process taking place in his head. What did the drunks at A.A. meetings call it? Mind racing? That was it. Your head seemed to explode, like a basketball with barbed wire wrapped around it. Something even more serious was happening inside Bill Pepper's head. The world as he knew it was ending, the filmstrip ripping loose from the reel and snapping in front of the projector's light, throwing one disjointed image after another onto the screen.

Where had it all gone wrong? Secretly, he knew the answer to his question, and the problem was not the girl. Rich people did not care about people like Bill Pepper. To them, cops had the same status as yardmen. He had played the fool with Love Younger, trying to ingratiate himself, violating every protocol of his profession, believing that Younger would give him a job as a security expert or even make him a personal assistant. In fact, men like Love Younger wouldn't take the time to spit in your mouth if you were dying of thirst.

The wind was picking up outside, cutting long V's across the surface of the lake. Again he heard a sudden *crack* and a cascading sound like a limb snapping from the trunk of a birch and falling against the side of the cottage. He had never been this afraid, and worse, for the first time in his life, the booze wasn't working. His fear ate right through it, the way a hot skillet vaporizes a drop of water. He looked at his hands. They were shaking.

Write it down, a voice said. *If they get you, leave something behind that tells people you didn't deserve this. Tell them you're Bill Pepper and you were old-school at LAPD and you wronged the Horowitz girl but you're sorry and you even told her you'd like to look after her. Yes, tell them, Bill Pepper. Don't go silently into that good night.*

Where had he heard that line? Then he remembered. It came from a black prostitute who worked as an independent on South Vernon Avenue. She had cooked her head with crystal meth but was fascinated with books he had never heard of. She used to ball him for free and whisper lines of poetry to him while she spread herself on his thighs in the back of his cruiser in an alleyway behind a Vietnamese grocery. What a thing to remember, here on a lake in western Montana at the close of day. He remembered her with tenderness rather than lust and wondered if she was still alive. Or maybe it was Bill

159

Pepper who had fried his mush and not the black prostitute and none of this was real.

Using only a penlight, he sat at the kitchen table and wrote these words on top of a flattened paper bag: *Some guys think I'm tight with the Horowitz girl at Albert Hollister's ranch. I'm not. I've used up nine of the twenty-four hours they gave me. If you find this and not my body, they got me. I'm sorry for what I did to that girl. As far as the rest of it is concerned, fuck it.*

He signed his name and under it wrote his LAPD badge number. Up on the two-lane, a car slowed and then accelerated, its headlights bouncing off the trees and the mountainside that bordered the far side of the asphalt. Bill Pepper went into the yard, his Glock hanging from his hand, the wind cold on his face, a stray raindrop or two striking his skin. Farther down the shore, lights were burning in a house close to the water. The glow reflected on the waves sliding under a dock where a red canoe was tied. The sight of the occupied house and the canoe bobbing in the chop and the waves sliding on the sand cheered Bill Pepper up and made him wonder if he hadn't been too pessimistic, too hard on himself, too quick to write off the rest of life.

He turned in a full circle, his arms stretched out like a bird's wings. There were no cars on the two-lane, no one hiding in the trees, no powerboat approaching from the far side of the lake. He went back inside and turned on the kitchen light to show his absence of fear, then started in on a plate of fried chicken and deviled eggs that had been in the refrigerator all week. It was cold and delicious, and he ate it hungrily with his fingers, washing it down with milk, his melancholia finally lifting, his eye on his spinning rod in the corner. It wasn't too late to fling a red-and-white-striped Mepps in the water, he told himself. The rainbow were in close to shore, down in the weeds, hiding from the pike. They fed by the moon and, at this time of evening, would hit anything he threw at them, bending the rod's tip to the surface, stripping line off the reel. Yes, he thought, to hell with the girl, to hell with the guys who thought he knew something he didn't, and to hell with his own foolish behavior. A man had a right to catch trout at moonrise on a Friday night.

Then he heard a sound that shouldn't have been there, a hand turning the front doorknob and then releasing it, the sole of a shoe scraping on the concrete step as the person stepped onto the grass and disappeared into the shadows.

Bill Pepper picked up the Glock and went out the back door. The wind was blowing harder, shredding leaves from the branches overhead, rocking the canoe with a metronomic beat against the dock. "Who's out there?" he said.

There was no reply.

Bill Pepper walked around the side of the house into the front yard and shone his penlight on the lawn and concrete steps but could see no depressions in the grass or mud smears on the steps. He looked at the lights of the house down the shore and thought about knocking on the door, introducing himself, inviting everyone over for a drink. That would be the coward's way. He walked down to the lakeside, constantly glancing back over his shoulder, his breath wheezing in his nose. Up the slope, by the corner of the cottage, he thought he saw a figure step from behind a tree and stare straight at him. He lifted the penlight into the darkness but could see nothing except a car passing on the two-lane and the bonelike whiteness of the birch trunks in the headlights. *Calm down,* he told himself. *You're going into the DTs, that's all it is.*

That's all it is? a voice mocked him. The DTs were a *minor* consideration? He was *that* sick? Then he heard a loud thud, and this time he knew the sound was not a product of his imagination. It was heavy and solid, like a sack of grain smacking down on the roof. He lifted the beam of the penlight just as a cougar jumped from the cottage roof into a tree and, in one bound, sprang off a limb and landed on four feet in the yard.

The cougar must have been six feet from

tail to nose. Its coat was yellow and gray, and white around the mouth and on the belly, a dark streak of fur running up the nose between the eyes. Its tail flipped as though discharging the tension in its body.

"This is my place. You're trespassing," Bill Pepper said.

The cougar seemed to slink away, then turned and walked in a figure eight. It stopped and looked at Bill Pepper again, sniffing at the air.

"Go back up the mountain where you belong. Go on, now. I don't want to shoot you."

The moon broke from behind a cloud, and Bill Pepper could see the muscular smoothness of the cougar's neck and forequarters, the thickness of its feet, the ribs that looked stenciled above the sag of the belly. The cougar's whiskers were as stiff as wire. It turned and ran along the shore, leaping over a creek that fed into the lake, the whiteness of its hindquarters showing under its tail in the moonlight.

Well, what do you know? Bill Pepper said to himself.

Except his satisfaction in standing up to the cougar was short-lived. He could not explain away the doorknob turning and the sole of somebody's shoe scraping on the concrete step. And what about the figure he'd thought he saw among the trees? He walked to the front of the house and examined the ground and saw nothing that indicated anybody had been there in the last week except him.

"If anybody is out there, I'm yours for the asking," he called out. "Come and get it. I'd love to have a tête-à-tête with you."

The only sounds he heard were the wind and the husks of winter leaves tumbling across the cottage roof, perhaps a pinecone rolling down the incline. "I don't care what you do to me," he said. "Before I check out, I'll paint the bushes."

He waited in the silence, then went back in the house and clicked on all the lights, in control again, his forearms pumped. He was Bill Pepper, the scourge of East Los, the Bama Badass cruising South Central, a cigarette hanging in his mouth, the friend of street people from Adams Boulevard down to Hawthorne. He had been in the middle of the Rodney King riots and had carried a two-hundred-pound black woman out of a burning building on his back. He'd still have his badge if a queer-bait bicycle cop in West Venice hadn't hung a second DWI on him. It wasn't fair. None of it. The murder of his father, the loss of his home in Mobile, the shanty his mother and siblings had lived in on the backside of Macon. He wanted to smash his fist into the wall.

Standing at the kitchen table under the

lightbulb, he drank the last of the brandy in the bottle and stuffed the Glock back in its holster and picked up his spinning rod and went out the back door. Someone in the house down the shore had turned on *Rhapsody in Blue.* The skies were clearing, the stars were out. It was a perfect night. Except for the fact that he hadn't relieved himself in two hours and his bladder was bursting. He unzipped his trousers.

You joining ranks with the Wyatt Dixons of the world? a voice said. *Why not get yourself some Copenhagen and a Styrofoam spit cup while you're at it?*

He returned to the house and walked through the kitchen and into the narrow hallway that led to the bathroom. In under a second, his universe turned upside down.

The bone-crunching pain that exploded in the back of his head could have come from a sap or a chunk of pipe with a bonnet on it or maybe someone touching a Taser to his scalp. It didn't matter. He crashed against the wall, taking the telephone stand down with him, landing on his face, his nose bleeding. He wanted to crawl away, but his arms wouldn't work properly. A figure that smelled like rain and leaves and body heat was pulling his wrists behind him, fitting handcuffs on them, squeezing the steel tongues tightly into the flesh.

"Who are you?" Bill Pepper said.

The figure released his wrists and walked through the cottage, clicking off all the lights. The hallway dropped into total darkness. The figure closed the door to the bathroom and the kitchen and then turned Bill Pepper over and looked down at him.

"Tell me what you want," Bill Pepper said, straining to see the face. "Who sent you here? I can't fix anything unless you tell me what you want."

He heard a sound that made him think of metal snipping against metal. "No, please," he said. "I haven't done anything to deserve that. Please don't do that. Listen to me. There's no reason for this."

He stared up at the face coming closer to his own, his viscera turning to water, the music of George Gershwin disappearing inside a voice he hardly recognized as his own.

CHAPTER 8

The phone rang at six-fifteen Saturday morning. Everyone else was still asleep. I picked up the receiver and went out on the balcony and closed the door behind me. In the east, the light behind the mountains was cold and weak, hardly more than a flicker touching the bottom of the clouds. Gretchen's hot rod was parked by the creek bed, the top white with frost. The Caddy was gone. "Hello," I said.

"This is Sheriff Bisbee, Detective Robicheaux. I need to confirm some information. You know a man named Clete Purcel?"

"I've known him for forty years. He's staying with us at Albert Hollister's place."

"Right now he's staying in a jail cell in Big Fork. Do you know any reason why he'd be in the Swan Lake area?"

"Maybe he went fishing. He didn't tell me. What's he charged with?"

"He got stopped at a roadblock at twelve-fifteen this morning."

"That's not what I asked. Why are you calling me about a traffic stop in Lake County?"

"I didn't say anything about a traffic stop. He was carrying a cut-down pump in his car. He also had burglar tools in his possession, along with latex gloves, a throw-down, a blackjack, plastic ligatures, brass knuckles, and a boxful of buckshot. I almost forgot. He had some nylon fishing line with a hoop tied on the end. The kind of rig home invaders stick through a window to turn the latch."

"He's a private investigator, and he runs down bail skips for a couple of bondsmen in New Orleans."

"He told me that. Otherwise, I might have thought he was planning to break into someone's residence. He wouldn't do that, would he?"

"No."

"Glad we got that out of the way. What's the worst homicide you ever investigated?"

"I never got around to ranking them."

"You must have been a busy man. I didn't get much sleep last night. Bill Pepper had his problems, but nothing that would warrant the mess I saw in his cottage this morning. Do you read me?"

"I'm trying to be helpful. To my knowledge, Clete never met Detective Pepper."

"Then I wonder why he was at Pepper's cottage. Just passing by, I guess. Maybe you should come up here. Pepper died with a plastic bag over his head. With luck, he died of asphyxiation. The blood loss is like nothing I've ever seen. Are you starting to get the picture?"

"No, not at all," I said.

"When it's this bad, it's usually sexual. Does your friend have problems along those lines?"

"Pepper was mutilated?"

"That's one way to put it."

"You're looking at the wrong guy."

"Somebody called in a 911 and reported a maroon Cadillac convertible with a Louisiana tag leaving the crime scene."

"Who was the caller?"

"The issue is your friend, not the caller. He seems to have an extraordinary capacity for getting into trouble."

"He's the best guy I've ever known."

"Pepper was dead when Purcel left the cottage. Why didn't he report it?"

I didn't have an answer. "Ask him."

"Oh, I will."

"What did the killer do to Pepper?"

"Probably several things. I'll have to wait on the coroner's report to know for sure. His penis and testicles were in the sink. You believe in an afterlife?"

"Why do you ask?"

"I suspect Bill Pepper found his hell right here on earth," the sheriff said.

Clete had fallen asleep sitting on a bench in

a holding can somewhere on the north end of Flathead Lake. In his dream, he was a little boy and had gone with his father and mother and sisters to Pontchartrain Park for July the Fourth. It was dusk in the dream, and the sky was printed with the fireworks exploding over the lake, and he could hear the popping of rifles in the shooting gallery and the music from the carousel. His father and mother were smiling at him, and his sisters were holding hands and skipping down the board-walk, the wind smelling of salt and caramel popcorn and candied apples.

When he woke from the dream, he looked through the window and saw the pink glow in the sky and thought the neon-striped Kamikaze packed with screaming kids was teetering against the sunset, about to rip like a scythe through the air and plummet toward the ground, then rise again into the gloaming of the day. He closed and opened his eyes and looked at the peeling yellow paint on the walls, the names burned into the ceiling with cigarette lighters, the toilet where someone's vomit had dried on the rim.

The sheriff of Missoula County pulled up a chair to the barred door and sat down. He placed a yellow legal pad on his knee and studied it. "Other people will be talking to you, Mr. Purcel. But since it was a member of my department who was killed, I want the first crack at you," he said.

"Y'all towed my Caddy?"

"I think that's the least of your worries."

"Where's it parked?"

"You want to explain what you were doing at Bill Pepper's cottage?"

"I already did. To anyone who'd listen. I went there to talk with him. The back door was open. He was lying in the hallway. I didn't touch anything other than the outside doorknob. I left the inside as I'd found it. I tried to call in the 911, but I didn't have cell service. I got stopped at the roadblock five miles from Big Fork. Where'd you put my Caddy?"

"Why were you carrying burglar tools and ligatures and all those weapons in a duffel bag?"

"I'm sentimental about memorabilia."

"That's pretty amusing. You think cutting off a man's penis and testicles is amusing?"

"The guy was a dirty cop, and somebody caught up with him. But it wasn't me."

"How do you know he was a dirty cop?"

"He was compromising the investigation into the death of Angel Deer Heart in order to earn favor with her grandfather."

"So you went up to his cottage on Swan Lake to talk to him about that?"

"That and a couple of other things."

"What might the 'other things' be?"

"He and another idiot in your department made sexual remarks about my daughter in

171

front of her and others. This was right after your man kicked the shit out of Wyatt Dixon."

"When were these remarks made?"

"Why don't you ask your crime scene investigator? He was there."

"You were just looking out for your daughter's interests?"

"Wouldn't you?"

The sheriff stared at his legal pad. "Detective Pepper left a note behind. Did you know that?" he said.

"No."

"He said some people thought he had a relationship with the 'Horowitz girl.' Would that be your daughter?"

"Horowitz is my daughter's last name. Your man didn't have any 'relationship' with her."

"You know that for a fact?"

"Yeah, I do. We don't invite cockroaches into our environment."

"In the note, Detective Pepper indicated that he did something to your daughter. What would he be referring to?"

"I guess the remarks he made."

"You're telling me a man who's coming apart, who's drunk out of his mind, who's telling the world 'fuck it,' is doing all this because of some sexist remarks he made to a young woman?"

"You'd know the answer to that better than me. I never met the man."

"How did you know where his cottage was?"

"I called up a PI I know in Missoula."

The sheriff nodded, his face composed, the long white tips of his mustache hanging below his jawbone. "That's right, you were here many years ago, weren't you? You did security for Sally Dio and some other mobsters."

"That's correct."

"That was right before his plane crashed into the side of a mountain, wasn't it?"

Clete looked thoughtfully out the window. "Yeah, I think I was still around here when that happened. It was a big loss. I think a pizza parlor in Palermo shut down for fifteen minutes."

"We pulled your sheet at the NCIC, Mr. Purcel. You have a longer record than most felons. You killed a federal informant and dropped a Teamster official from a hotel window into a dry swimming pool. You and your friend Detective Robicheaux left a bunch of people dead on the bank of a bayou in Louisiana not once but twice."

"That's why we're here — to rest up."

"There's only one reason you're not being arrested. There's no trace of blood on you or your clothing or shoes or in your vehicle. That leaves me in a quandary. If you're an innocent man, why are you lying?"

"I'm not. And the reason I'm not under ar-

173

rest is so you can question me without giving me my rights."

The sheriff's face was tired, his eyes without heat or anger or any emotion that Clete could see. "This is all about your daughter, isn't it? What is it you're not telling me, Mr. Purcel? What did Bill Pepper do to your little girl?"

Wyatt Dixon was unloading three tons of sixty-pound hay bales off a flatbed at his place on the Blackfoot River when he saw the two cruisers coming up the dirt road, their tires splashing through the puddles. He was shirtless and wearing a straw hat and Wranglers tucked inside his boots, a bandana knotted around his neck. He fitted his fingers under the twine on a bale and lifted it out in front of him, his chest and arms blooming with green veins. He walked to the edge of the bed and dropped the bale into space, his gaze never leaving the cruisers. His shoulders were pink with fresh sunburn, and his back was crosshatched with scar tissue that looked like it had been laid there with a whip. A scar as thick as an earthworm ran from under his armpit and disappeared inside his leather belt. The deputies parked in the shade of the cottonwoods and approached him as a group of four, studying his half-crushed house, his barn, the trees, the bluebirds, the Appaloosas in the corral, the riffle in the middle of the stream, anything that kept them from having to look directly at Wyatt Dixon.

Wyatt removed his hat and unknotted his bandana and wiped his face and gazed at the Indian paintbrush and wild roses that grew in the grass along the riverbank. The river was deep and wide from the runoff and contained a coppery green light where the sun shone directly upon it. Wyatt put his hat back on and fingered the long red welt that ran down his side. For just a second he thought about the bull that had impaled him at the Calgary Stampede, shaking him on its horns like a piñata and goring him again on the ground, the crowd rising, the women holding their hands to their mouths.

"Howdy-doody, boys," he said.

The lead deputy had to squint into the sun to look up at Wyatt. "Know why we're here?"

"To pester people?"

"Somebody killed Bill Pepper up at Swan Lake."

"I'm totally broke up," Wyatt said.

"We'd like to have you come down to the department."

"I already been there. I didn't enjoy it too much."

"The sheriff probably wants to exclude you."

"I'll save y'all the time. Just consider me excluded."

"It's important, Wyatt."

"Not to me it ain't."

"We're just doing our job. How about hooking yourself up? It's not personal."

"Speaking of job performance, I'd rate y'all's somewhere between mediocre to piss-poor."

"Is it true you can speak dead languages?"

Wyatt blew his breath up into his face and looked at the sunlight wobbling inside the riffle on the river, then jumped down from the flatbed into the middle of the deputies. All of them stepped backward before they could check themselves. He began picking pieces of hay off his arms and chest, dropping each one into the wind. "How'd Pepper go out?" he asked.

"Hard," the lead deputy said.

"How hard?"

"Hard as it gets."

"It happened this morning?"

The deputy shook his head noncommittally. Wyatt lifted his T-shirt off the outside mirror on the driver's side of the flatbed truck. He studied his reflection in the mirror, touching at a razor nick on his jaw, then worked his shirt over his arms and head and neck. The T-shirt fitted him so tightly, it looked like latex on his skin. His eyes were empty when he looked at the deputy. "Did Pepper go out with a bag over his head?"

"I don't know all the details," the deputy said. "I can't discuss them with you, anyway."

"Did you know Angel Deer Heart?"

"Afraid not," the deputy said.

"Did you ever wonder why rich people would adopt a raggedy-ass little girl from the rez?"

"Put on the cuffs, Wyatt."

"Half of them come out of the womb with alcohol on the brain. The other half are crack babies."

"You could ask the lead investigator about all this, except he's dead."

"You ever hear Southerners talk about the 'dumbest white person' they ever met?"

"Nope."

"Most people think that's an insult to people of color. What that really means is the dumbest person on earth is a stupid white man. You can teach a horse, a dog, or even a tree frog to tap-dance before you can teach toilet training to a white man who is willfully ignorant. All colored people know that."

The deputy cupped his hand around Wyatt's upper arm. "You're a puzzle, buddy."

"Did you know y'all are living in the middle of biblical events?"

"Biblical?"

"That's what I said."

The deputy walked with him to the cruiser. "I love your accent, Wyatt. Watch your head getting in," he said.

At one-thirty P.M. on Saturday, the sheriff called me again. "You want to come down

177

here and talk to this crazy bastard?" he said.

"Excuse me?" I said.

"Most of the DIs I knew in the service were from the South. I always thought someone had pissed inside their brains when they were infants. Now I'm sure of it. I just spent twenty minutes listening to Wyatt Dixon talk about the history of the earth and the coming of the Antichrist. Did you know the world is sixty-four hundred years old?"

"He's probably psychotic. Why pay any attention to anything he says?"

"Because he had motivation to kill Detective Pepper. He's also one of the last people to see Angel Deer Heart alive."

I didn't want to remind the sheriff that he had spoken favorably of Dixon after Alafair and I had trouble with him. "Does he have an alibi for last night?"

"His neighbors across the river say there was a light on in his barn and they thought they saw him shoeing horses until after midnight."

"So he's not your guy?"

"Probably not. But he has information about the Deer Heart girl that he's not sharing."

"What kind of information?"

"He thinks she was adopted for reasons other than humanitarian ones."

"What reasons?"

"He's a little vague on that."

"Why'd you call me?" I asked.

"Because I don't know what the hell I'm dealing with. What makes it worse is that Wyatt Dixon has almost convinced me."

"Of what?"

"That there's an evil presence in our midst. That the cave behind Albert Hollister's house is the source of something that I hate to even think about."

"Don't let this guy get to you," I said.

"Come down here and tell me that after you look at Bill Pepper's face in the crime scene photos. One of his eyes looked like an eight ball. The coroner says he was alive when he was castrated. Where's the Horowitz girl?"

I looked out the window. Gretchen's pickup was parked by the guest cabin. "She didn't do this," I said.

"We talked to a homicide investigator at Miami-Dade. She was known in the trade as Caruso. You want to vouch for Caruso, Mr. Robicheaux?"

After Clete was released from the holding jail in Big Fork, he did not ask Gretchen if she'd had anything to do with the death of Bill Pepper. At the cabin, she kept waiting for him to stop talking and look directly in her face and ask the question, but he didn't. She fixed bacon and scrambled eggs and set his plate on the table and sat down across from him and waited some more. He started eating, buttering a biscuit, drinking his coffee, spearing his fork through the eggs, but he didn't ask the question.

"I went looking for you," she said.

"I figured you would," he replied.

"You didn't find Pepper, did you?"

"Not alive, I didn't."

"You think I did him?" she asked.

"Of course not."

"What makes you so sure?"

"If he'd drawn down on you or tried to attack you again, you would have blown him out of his socks. Maybe you would have broken a couple of his spokes. But you didn't have anything to do with what happened inside that cottage. Neither did I. Anyone who thinks different doesn't know anything about either of us."

"I told you what I wanted to do to him. I told you how I wanted him to suffer."

"You're like most brave people, Gretchen: too brave to know you're supposed to be afraid, and too good to understand you're incapable of doing bad."

She thought she was going to cry.

He stopped eating. "Dave and I did a lot of stuff at NOPD that we don't like to remember. We called it operating under a black flag. That's when the Contras and the Colombians were filling our cities with cocaine. But we never did anything beyond what we had to. That's the only rule there is. You do what you

180

have to, and you never hurt people unnecessarily." He started eating again.

She got up from the table and went into the bathroom and washed her face and dried it. When she came back out, he was looking at the FedEx mailer she had left on the coffee table. "What's that?" he said.

"Some Sierra Club guys got ahold of a core sample from an exploratory well drilled on the Canadian side of the frontier. I sent it to a geological lab in Austin. This stuff has the same kind of sulfurous content that's coming out of the shale-oil operation up in Alberta. Supposedly, it heats up the planet a lot faster than ordinary crude."

"Pepper left a note. Evidently, some guys scared the hell out of him. They thought maybe you were his girlfriend and you had some information that was harmful to their interests."

"Why didn't you tell me that?"

"I thought the sheriff had his ass on upside down. You think this has something to do with the documentary you're making?"

"I just got out of film school. Why should anyone be afraid of me?"

"I can't imagine," he replied.

That afternoon she took her nine-millimeter Beretta and her Airweight .38 up to the gun range behind Albert's house. The sun had already gone behind the ridge, and the trees were full of shadows and clattering with robins. Up the arroyo by the abandoned log road, she saw a flock of wild turkeys that had been down to the creek to drink before going to bed. She set up a row of coffee cans on a wood plank suspended between two rocks and clamped on her ear protectors and, from twenty yards away, aimed the Beretta with both arms extended and let off all fourteen rounds in the magazine, blowing the cans into the air and hitting them again as they rolled down the hillside, birds rising from the trees all around her.

She saw the man on horseback out of the corner of her eye but showed no recognition of his presence. She set down the Beretta on Albert's shooting table and removed the ear protectors and shook out her hair. She picked up the five-shot Airweight and flipped out the cylinder from the frame and picked the rounds one at a time from the ammunition box and plopped them into the chambers, then closed the cylinder, never glancing at the man on horseback. "What do you think you're doing here?" she said, as though speaking to herself.

"I rent pasture on the other side of the ridge. You shot the doo-doo out of them cans."

She began picking up the cans and replacing them on the plank. "What can I do for you?"

"Nothing. You already done it," he said. He stood up in the stirrups and grabbed the limb of a ponderosa and lifted himself free of the horse, his biceps swelling to the size of softballs. He was wearing a maniacal grin when he dropped to the ground, his shoulders hunched like an ape's. He caught the reins of the Appaloosa and flipped them around the lower branch of a fir tree. "You've got a fourteen-round pre-assault-weapons-ban magazine in that Beretta. That's right impressive."

"I think you're probably a pretty good guy, cowboy. But you're off your turf," she said.

"You got a mouth on you. Ain't many that speaks their mind like that."

"Does Mr. Hollister mind you riding up here?"

"He never mentioned it."

"You know who he is?"

He seemed to think about the question. "A famous writer."

"Have you tried any of his books?"

He looked into space. "I don't recall. My brain ain't always in the best of shape," he said. He was wearing a candy-striped shirt with a rolled white collar. His shirt was pressed and his needle-nosed boots spit-shined, as bright as mirrors even in the shade. "You like rodeos?"

"Sometimes."

"I furnish rough stock to a mess of them.

You like bluegrass music?"

" 'Sex, drugs, Flatt and Scruggs.' "

"There's a concert tonight at Three Mile."

"Maybe another time."

He sat on a boulder and removed his straw hat. There was a pale band of skin at the top of his forehead. When he looked at her, all she could see were his pupils. The rest of his eyes seemed made of glass. "I ain't here to bother you. You stood up for me, missy. I owe you," he said.

"You don't owe me anything. Let's be clear on that."

"If you hadn't been there, Bill Pepper would have put out my light with that Taser. I thought he was gonna dump in his britches when you called him 'bacon.' "

"You want to shoot my Airweight?"

"I'm an ex-felon. Ex-felons ain't supposed to mess with handguns."

"It's Wyatt, isn't it?"

"That's me. From Calgary to Cheyenne to Prescott to the Big Dance in Vegas and every state fair in between. I'm a rodeo man."

"I'm glad you came by, Wyatt. But I'm tied up today."

"They're gonna hang Pepper's killing on you," he said.

"Repeat that?"

"They wanted to stick me with it, but I got an alibi. They know Pepper insulted you up by that cave. Maybe they know he done even worse."

"You need to be a little more explicit."

"Bill Pepper was meaner than a radiator full of goat piss. He was mean to females in particular. You're from Florida, right?"

"What about it?"

"In my former life, I heard about you. Or at least about somebody down in Miami who sure fits your description."

"You heard what?"

"You worked for the Cubans and them New York Italians. You're flat heck on wheels, woman. If I can put it together, them sheriff's deputies can, too."

"I'll keep all this in mind."

He took a penknife from his watch pocket and pared one of his fingernails. "You don't hang out with rodeo people?" She winked at him and didn't reply. He gazed at the sunlight breaking on the tops of the trees. "Whatever you do, stay away from that cave up yonder."

"It's just a cave," she said.

"Something is loose here'bouts, something that ain't supposed to be here. I can smell it. That Indian girl that got killed?"

"I heard about it."

"Her death was over something the cops ain't figured out yet. She was from the Blackfeet rez, up somewhere east of Marias Pass. I called her Little Britches, 'cause she was such a little-bitty slip of a thing."

"You've lost me."

"You know the Younger family?"

"Not personally."

"It's got to do with them. And with that thing in the cave. I just ain't ciphered it out yet. I'm working on it."

"Why?"

" 'Cause of what got done to that little girl."

Gretchen flipped open the cylinder of her pistol and dumped the cartridges in her palm and put the cartridges and both guns and the ear protectors back in her canvas shooting bag. "Take care of yourself," she said.

"If you ever want to mess around with an older man, I'm available," he said.

"I'm not worth it. Keep your powder dry for the right girl," she replied.

He laughed under his breath. She walked down the hillside to the cabin, her gun bag looped over one shoulder, the wind scattering her chestnut hair on her cheeks and forehead. Wyatt Dixon stared after her, bareheaded, his features as chiseled as a Roman soldier's. Then he stared up at the cave, his good humor gone, his eyes containing thoughts that no rational person would ever be able to read or understand.

CHAPTER 9

On Sunday morning Molly and I went to Mass at a small church by the university. When we got back, Clete was standing on the porch of the guest cabin, waiting for me. "I found a bug," he said.

"Where?"

"Above the door to Gretchen's room."

"Have you told Albert?"

"Yeah, he said, 'What else is new?' I'm going to get a guy out here to sweep the place."

"How long do you think it's been there?"

"There's no way to tell. I'd say it's state-of-the-art. We need to stop pretending, Dave."

"About what?"

"Somebody has us in their sights. It started with somebody shooting an arrow at Alafair. Now both Gretchen and I are part of a homicide investigation. It's time we take it to these cocksuckers."

"Have any idea who these *cocksuckers* are?"

I thought he would give me a facile answer, but Clete was the most prescient cop regarding human behavior whom I ever knew. "I think we're dealing with multiple players, maybe guys with different objectives. The best place to start is with the money. Always. Come inside. I want to show you some information I dug up."

For years he had chased down bail skips for two bondsmen named Wee Willie Bimstine and Nig Rosewater. The conventional portrayal of a PI's life is a romantic and noir excursion into a world of intrigue, with wealthy female clients swathed in veils and overweight villains sweating under a fan in a saloon on the Pacific Rim. The real world of a PI, and the clientele of Willie and Nig, could be compared to the effluent running through an open sewer. Anyone who thinks otherwise knows nothing about it. Criminality and narcissism are not interchangeable terms, but they are closely related. The checkbook of a narcissist or a recidivist is always balanced, but at someone else's expense. With rare exceptions, anyone working on his second or third jolt is looking for an institutional womb. Most of them have no feeling about the pain they cause other human beings, either inside or outside the system. The culture of cruelty inside a prison makes you wonder if there is not a genetic flaw in all of us, like an embryonic lizard waiting to crack free from its shell.

Clete hated his job. The NOPD pulled his

shield in 1986, and ever since, he had tried to pretend that the loss of his career was of no consequence. Occasionally, I would see him bending over the lavatory in his office, his sleeves rolled up, his wristwatch on the edge of the basin, scrubbing Ajax into his pores, and there would be a level of regret and loss in his eyes that had nothing to do with the face Clete Purcel showed the world.

Working for Wee Willie and Nig had one advantage only: They were anachronisms, but they knew everything about everyone in the city of New Orleans, at least everyone who went against the grain or was a half-bubble off or was part of a sybaritic culture that celebrated its own profligacy.

"I told you Love Younger's daughter-in-law, Felicity Louviere, was from New Orleans, didn't I?" Clete said. "She grew up by the old Prytania Theatre. Not far from where I did. Did you know Lillian Hellmann grew up on Prytania?"

"Yeah, I did," I said, waiting for him to get to the point.

"It's the accent. That's how I knew."

"Yeah, I got that. What I don't get is why you're homing in on her and not her husband or father-in-law."

"Give me some credit, Streak. The woman's in grief. You think I'd try to put moves on her?"

I let my eyes go empty. "No," I said. *But*

189

you're a sucker for a woman who's in trouble.

"What was that?" he asked.

"I said no, you wouldn't take advantage of a woman who just lost a child, for God's sake."

He gave me a look and picked up a handful of printouts sent to him through Albert's computer by a reference librarian who worked for Willie and Nig. "Felicity Louviere's old man was Rene Louviere. Remember him?"

I remembered the name in the way you remember high school friends who never had a category, people who floated hazily on the edge of your vision and whose deeds, for good or bad, never seemed memorable. You may think of them with fondness, as compatriots with whom you shared a journey. You're sure they were good at something, but never sure exactly what. "He was in the department for a while?" I said.

"Yeah, for about three years. In community outreach, over by the Desire Project. He got canned for cutting too much slack to the local pukes. He was a nice guy. He just wasn't a cop."

In my mind's eye, I saw an indistinct image of a man who was too thin for his clothes and went a long time between haircuts and was uncomfortable with the coarseness common during morning roll call. "What became of him?"

"He was a social worker in Holy Cross and

190

got fired for giving welfare money to illegals. He ended up roughnecking in a rain forest in South America. Get this. The local Indians burned the bones of their dead relatives and mixed the ashes in the food to keep the family line going. They also shot blowguns at the Americans on the drilling rigs. Some geologists decided to do some payback and flew over the village in a single-engine plane and dropped a couple of satchel charges on them. They killed and wounded a bunch of people, including children."

He set the printouts on the breakfast table and pinched his eyes, a look of weariness if not soul sickness stealing into his face. I waited for him to go on, but he didn't.

"What is it, Clete?" I said.

"You know the drill. The motherfuckers who start wars have never heard a shot fired in anger, but they wave the flag and make speeches at Arlington and run up the body count as high as they can. I hate them, every one of them."

I knew Clete was no longer talking about events in the rain forests of Brazil or Venezuela. He was back in the Central Highlands, on the edge of a ville that stank of duck shit and stagnant water, the flame from the cannon of a Zippo track arching onto the roofs of the hooches, a mamasan pleading hysterically in a language he couldn't understand.

"Finish the story, Clete," I said.

191

His eyes came back on mine. "Rene Louviere quit his job with the oil company in protest. He went back to the States and joined a relief agency and returned to the ville the geologists had bombed. Guess what?"

"Don't tell me."

"A couple of Indians got wasted on mushrooms and chopped him into pieces."

"How did Felicity Louviere meet her husband?"

"At a Mardi Gras ball. He probably didn't tell her he got expelled from college for cheating. He's also a degenerate gambler and had a hundred-grand credit line in Vegas and Atlantic City, until his father forced him into Gamblers Anonymous. Here's the weird part: The guy supposedly has an incredible mind for figures. The reason he got comped in the casinos was because no matter how much he won, the house took it all back, plus the fillings in his teeth."

"You think Younger's people put the bug above Gretchen's door?"

"They probably know she's doing a documentary on Love Younger's shale-oil projects in Canada. But . . ."

"But what?"

"Nobody cares about the damage these guys are doing, including the Canadians. Why spend money eavesdropping on us?"

"Maybe they're hiding something that has

little or nothing to do with the environment."

"I don't know what it is, and neither does Gretchen."

"There's another possibility, Clete. I just don't like to think about it."

"The guy up at the cave?"

"Asa Surrette is the name."

"Dave, guys like this have a way of staying alive in our imagination long after they're dead. Sometimes I still see Bed-check Charlie in the middle of the afternoon. He's up on a rooftop, locking down on me through a scoped sight on a Russian rifle, just about to squeeze off a round. I feel like somebody is taking off my skin with a pair of pliers. What are the chances of Asa Surrette being the only survivor in a collision between a prison van and a gasoline truck?"

"What are the chances this guy could torture and kill people in his hometown and go undetected for two decades?"

Clete rubbed the back of his neck. "What do you know about him except he was active in his church?"

"He was an electrician and sometimes installed burglar alarms in people's homes," I replied.

He stared at me in the silence, his eyes lidless.

So far only two people gave any credence to the possibility that Asa Surrette had escaped from a gasoline-tanker explosion in West Kansas or that someone like him had stenciled the message on the cave wall. One was Alafair and the other was Wyatt Dixon, a man who proved so uncontrollable in custody that the state had tried to short-circuit his brain. I had told the sheriff not to listen to Dixon's quasi-psychotic ravings. But I was wrong. Dixon was con-wise. He had information and levels of experience that other people couldn't guess at. He was also the kind of guy you enlist in your cause if you want to win a revolution.

The discrepancy between the real world and how the world is reported by the media is enormous, and I've always believed this is why most newspeople drink too much. People like Wyatt Dixon understand how Frankenstein works and speak in metaphors that come out of their experience. Unfortunately, most of them have fried their SPAM, and their symbols and frame of reference don't make much sense to the rest of us.

I grew up in the Deep South in an era when institutional cruelty was a given. I have never met one person in normal society who would admit knowledge of the cast-iron sweatboxes on Camp A in Angola Penitentiary. Nor have I met anyone who wasn't shocked when I mentioned that there are more than a hundred convicts buried in the prison levee along the Mississippi River. Normal people will tell you they have never known a criminal, although they have sat in church pews next to slumlords, zoning board members on a pad, and defense contractors who have contributed to the death of thousands of human beings.

Here's the biggest joke of all: Wyatt Dixon was probably a genuine believer. He may not have believed in God, but no one could deny he hadn't been on a first-name basis with the devil. Maybe that's a pathetic cachet, but as Clete would say, who's perfect?

Where do you go on a Sunday if you want to find a man like Wyatt Dixon? I saw Albert working in his flower bed and asked him. "There's a holy roller meeting up on the rez this afternoon," he replied. "You might try there."

"Thanks," I said.

"What do you want with Dixon?"

"Information."

"The boy had a hard life. Don't be too rough on him."

"Dixon doesn't impress me as a victim."

"That's because you don't know anything about him. You loved your parents and your parents loved you, Dave. Dixon didn't have that kind of luck."

"You're a good man, Albert."

"That's what you think," he replied.

The holy roller meeting was held at a pavilion

on the Flathead Indian Reservation not far from the Mission Mountains. It involved what people down south call dinner on the ground and sometimes devil in the bush. At five P.M. Clete and I drove in the Caddy up a long grade through wooded hills that were a deep green from the spring rains into a valley that rose higher and higher as the road progressed toward Flathead Lake. The sky was clear and blue, and fresh snow had fallen on the tops of the Missions during the night; in the sunlight, you could see the ice on the waterfalls melting. The mountains were so massive, the rock chain they formed against the sky so vast, that you lost perspective and the forests growing up the sides resembled green velvet rather than trees. It was one of those places that seemed to reduce discussions about theology to the level of folly.

The service was almost over when Clete parked the Caddy in a pasture lined with rows of cars and pickup trucks. Someone had extended a huge vinyl canopy from the pavilion over the grass, where at least a hundred people were seated in folding chairs, listening to a minister preach into a microphone. The sunlight looked like hammered bronze on the surface of the Jocko, the wind cutting serpentine lines through the fields, the canopy ballooning and popping overhead. The work-worn faces of the congregants were like those you would expect to see in Appalachia, the eyes burning with a strange intensity, and either awe or puzzlement or vulnerability, that reminded me of the paintings of Pieter Brueghel's Flemish peasants.

The real show wasn't the preacher. When it was time to give witness, he paused and held on to the sides of the podium, lifting his chin, sucking in his cheeks, his mouth puckered, as though he were teetering on the bow of a ship bursting through the waves. "Paul and Silas bound in jail!" he called out.

"That old jailhouse reeled and rocked all night long!" the congregation shouted.

"Hebrew children in the fiery furnace all night long!" the preacher shouted.

"Lord, who will deliver poor me?" the congregation shouted back.

"There's worse bondage than the jail. It's bondage of the spirit," the preacher said. He pointed his finger into the crowd. "There's a man here gonna give witness to that, too. A man who had to be struck dumb in order to speak, and by heavens, each of you knows who I'm talking about. Come on up here, Wyatt."

"These people vote in elections," Clete whispered.

"Be quiet," I said.

Dixon faced the crowd, his eyes close-set, the sleeves of his cowboy shirt rolled above his elbows, the veins in his forearms pumped with blood. Then I witnessed the strangest transformation I had ever seen take place in a human being. He looked briefly at the canopy rippling and snapping in the wind, then his mouth went slack and his eyes rolled up into his head. He began to speak in a language I had never heard. The syllables came from deep down in the throat and sounded like wood blocks knocking. He held his arms straight out from his sides, as though about to levitate. I would like to be able to say his performance was fraudulent, nothing more than a manifestation of tent-show religious traditions that go back to colonial times. Except the glaze in his face was not self-manufactured, nor was the energy that seemed to surge through his body as though he had laid his hand on a threadbare power line. Had I been a neurologist, I probably would have concluded he was having a seizure. I was not alone in my reaction. The congregation was transfixed, some pressing their hands to their mouths in fear. When Dixon finished his testimony, if that's what it could be called, there was dead silence except for the wind popping the canopy.

Dixon balanced himself on the side of the podium, his pupils once again visible, a crooked smile on his face, like a man who was sexually exhausted and trying to recover perspective. Clete screwed a cigarette into the corner of his mouth and flipped open his Zippo.

"Are you crazy?" I said under my breath.

"You think these guys are paying any attention to us?" he replied.

"I don't care. Show some respect."

He slipped the cigarette back into his shirt pocket. "Check out the broad in the last row."

She was wearing a hat and dark glasses, but there was no mistaking the creamy white skin and the mole by her mouth and the demure posture. "What is Felicity Louviere doing here?" I said.

"Maybe she thinks Dixon was mixed up in her daughter's death."

"You see the husband anywhere?"

"He's probably getting laid."

"We don't even know the guy. Why be so critical?" I said.

"He's a piece of shit, and you know it."

We were standing at the back of the crowd. A fat woman in a print dress with lace on the sleeves turned around and stared at us. "Sorry," I said.

"Here comes our man," Clete said. "I hope you're up to dealing with this crazy bastard."

"Clete, will you stop it?" I said.

Dixon worked his way through the congregants while they folded and stacked their chairs, returning congratulations, shaking hands, even though his eyes never left our faces.

"I declare, it's Mr. Robicheaux, fresh up from the bayou," he said. "Or is it a swamp or a cesspool and such as that where you live at?"

"More like an open-air mental asylum. Is that Aramaic you were speaking?" I said.

"Some people say it's Syriac. Some says Aramaic and Syriac is the same thing. I couldn't comment, 'cause when it's over, I don't have no memory of it."

"I really dug it," Clete said. "It put me in mind of one of those Cecil B. DeMille films. You know, Charlton Heston up on the mountain shouting at the people down below in the middle of an electrical storm."

Dixon was standing six inches from my face, his head tilted to one side; he seemed to take no heed of Clete. "You been bird-dogging me, Mr. Robicheaux? You still think I'm out to hurt your daughter?"

"That's one reason I came out here. I think you got a bad rap on that."

"I declare. I'm overwhelmed."

"We have the same objective. We want to find the man who killed the Indian girl," I said.

"Who says I'm trying to find anyone?"

"Gretchen Horowitz."

"She was talking about me?"

"She said she thought you were a decent guy. Does that bother you?" I said, my control starting to slip.

"Nothing bothers me. Not when I'm in the spirit."

"That brings up an interesting question," Clete said. "If you're giving witness in a language no one can understand, and you have no memory of what you said, what's the point of giving witness?"

"Who says nobody understands it?" Dixon said.

"I got it. These guys are international linguists," Clete replied.

This time Dixon looked directly at him. "Is that your Cadillac out yonder?"

"It was when I drove it here."

"Nice ride. I hope the people driving the junkers next to it don't skin it up. Maybe that's the price of slumming."

I saw the crow's-feet at the corner of Clete's eyes flatten, the color in his face change. "Maybe you and I should walk over in those trees and talk about it," he said.

"Mr. Dixon?" I said, edging into his line of vision.

"What?" he replied, his eyes locked on Clete's.

"Why is Felicity Louviere here?"

"Who?"

"Angel Deer Heart's mother."

"How the fuck should I know?" He turned his gaze on me. "Y'all don't have no business here. This is our place. When we're here, we do things our way. I don't like people looking down their noses at my friends."

"Clete grew up in the Irish Channel, Wy-

201

att," I said. "I got this white patch in my hair from malnutrition. When I started first grade, I couldn't speak English. I respect you and your friends, and I think Clete does, too."

"What you don't seem to understand, Mr. Robicheaux, is I ain't bothered y'all or put my nose in your business. I didn't bother your daughter, and I didn't bother them cops that drug me out to Albert Hollister's place. But every time I turn around, one of y'all is in my face. It's Sunday, and we're fixing to have a community meal. All we want is to be left alone."

Clete lit his cigarette and snapped the cap closed on his Zippo. "Why don't you peddle your douche rinse somewhere else and let these poor bastards alone?" he said.

How's that for diplomacy? I gave up and walked away. "Dave, where you going?" I heard Clete say.

I was so irritated with Clete that I kept walking toward the Caddy and didn't turn around. I heard somebody walking fast behind me.

"Mr. Robicheaux," said a woman's voice.

She was a tank in her late forties, dressed in a frilly blouse and a suit with big buttons, her hair piled on her head, her face flushed and as round as a muskmelon. She had a notebook in one hand and a ballpoint in the other. For whatever reason, she seemed to be wearing amounts of perfume that could knock down a rhino. "Talk to me, please," she said.

I tried to smile. "What can I help you with?"

"I'm doing an article on the Indians and the spread of fundamentalist religion. Also on the death of that young girl," she said.

She told me her name was Bertha Phelps. She seemed agitated and breathless and out of her element. She started to write something on her notepad, then realized her pen was out of ink. "I hate these. Do you mind?" she said, looking at the Uni-ball in my shirt pocket.

"No, not at all," I replied, handing it to her.

"Was that the mother of Angel Deer Heart I saw sitting in the back row?"

"That's correct. How did you know my name?"

"I saw you in the grocery with Albert Hollister and asked someone who you were."

Though that didn't quite come together for me, I didn't pursue it. "I'm in a bit of a hurry, Ms. Phelps. What's up?"

"It's terrible what happened to that young girl. I don't understand why her mother is here listening to that man."

"Wyatt Dixon?"

"A sheriff's detective told me Dixon was the last person to see her alive."

"I'd say he's not a viable suspect."

"Why wouldn't he be?"

"I'm not qualified to comment, Ms. Phelps.

It was nice meeting you." I turned to go.

"It was just a question," she said at my back.

The Caddy was locked. I looked back at the pavilion and saw Clete talking to Felicity Louviere. I also saw Wyatt Dixon carrying a paper plate stacked with fried chicken to a picnic table. *One more try,* I told myself.

I made my way through the crowd and, without being invited, sat down next to him. He never looked up from his food. "You weren't truthful about your testimony," I said.

"I'm done talking with you," he said.

"You indicated you had no memory of it. That was a lie, wasn't it?"

His forearms rested on the edge of the table, his hands empty and poised above his plate. He kept his eyes straight ahead, the late sun catching in them like reflected firelight. "I'd be careful what I said to the wrong man."

"You're an honest-to-God believer, Wyatt. You see things out there in the world that other people don't. Does the name Asa Surrette mean anything to you?"

"Never heard of him."

"You're sure?"

"You got a hearing disorder?" he asked.

"The man who left that message in the cave was no ordinary man, was he?"

"You got it wrong."

"Got what wrong?"

204

"It wasn't no man that was up in that cave," he said.

"Want to spell that out?"

"He's goat-footed and has a stink on him that could make a skunk hide. Think I'm taking you on a snipe hunt? Ask Albert Hollister if he ain't seen presences in that arroyo behind his place. Indians and such."

"A goat-footed creature was in that cave?"

"There's a hearing specialist in Missoula I can recommend," he replied.

I decided it was time to get a lot of distance between me and Wyatt Dixon.

Chapter 10

I tried to stay mad at Clete for provoking a situation with Dixon, but I couldn't. Clete was Clete. He didn't like religious fanatics and believed most of them were self-deceived or mean-spirited and did great harm in the world. I didn't believe Wyatt Dixon fell into either of those categories. He may have been psychotic, or he may have been an unedu- cated man who'd found a form of redemp- tion among the only friends he'd ever had, blue-collar people to whom the struggle of Christ was their own story. Regardless, Dixon had said something I couldn't get out of my mind. He had mentioned Indian presences behind Albert Hollister's house.

The arroyo that led from Albert's gun range up the hillside to the logging road had been the route used by Chief Joseph and the Nez Perce after they outflanked the United States Army up on Lolo Pass and tried to escape relocation to Oklahoma Territory. Hundreds of them had filed down the arroyo in the dark, carrying their children and everything they owned on their backs. They followed Lolo Creek down to the Bitterroot River and then went south to the Big Hole, where they thought they would be safe. When the army attacked their village, the soldiers killed man, woman, and child, just as they had on the Washita and on the Marias and at Wounded Knee. It was genocide, no matter what others wanted to call it.

I asked Albert if he had ever seen anything unusual up the arroyo.

"What do you mean by 'unusual'?" he said.

"Apparitions."

"You saw something?"

"Not me. Wyatt Dixon may have," I said.

"One time at sunset, I thought I saw dark-skinned people coming over the ridge and walking down the trail through the trees. I went outside, and nobody was there. Another time, when there was heavy fog, I could hear people talking up there. I walked about fifty yards up the hillside and heard a child crying. I also found the stone head of a tomahawk. I had been over that same spot many times, but I'd never seen any artifacts there."

"What happened to Chief Joseph and his people?"

"The army put them all on cattle cars and shipped them to a mosquito-infested sinkhole in Oklahoma. What are you getting at?"

"I don't want to believe that people like

Wyatt Dixon have an accurate vision of either this world or the next."

"Did you know the word 'Kentucky' comes from a Shawnee word for 'bloody land'?"

"What's the point?"

"When you kill large numbers of people in order to steal their land, they get pissed off, and their spirits have a way of hanging around," he replied.

I wasn't up to a barrage of Albert's morbid polemics, so I went to find Clete. But he had gone off on his own and had not told anyone of his destination. I should have known a bad moon was on the rise.

The saloon where they had arranged to meet was down by the railroad tracks, in a part of town where the brick shell of a three-story nineteenth-century brothel was still standing and cowboys and Indians and bindle stiffs and rounders and bounders and midnight ramblers still knocked back doubles and chased them with pitcher beer. Clete was drinking at the far end of the bar when she entered. The front door was open to allow in the cool of the evening, and the redness of the late sun backlit her hair and the creamy texture of her shoulders and the beige skirt that swirled around her knees. He raised his hand awkwardly to indicate where he was, then tipped his shot glass to his mouth as she approached him.

"Is this place okay?" he said.

"Why wouldn't it be?"

"It gets a little rough sometimes."

"I like it here. They have a western band on Saturday nights," she replied, sitting on a stool.

"What are you drinking?"

She looked at the shot glass and the small pitcher of draft beer in front of him. She touched the condensation on the pitcher with the ball of her index finger. "A glass of this will be fine," she said.

"You like Indian culture?"

"Excuse me?"

"The way you dress and all."

"I wanted to get out of New Orleans as soon as I could. When I had the chance, I took it. Now I live out in the West. It's clean out here."

He looked out the door, then back at her. He wasn't sure what he was supposed to say. "Some people think Missoula is turning into Santa Fe."

"I wouldn't know. I've never been there. It's the model for something?"

"I've never been there, either," he replied, feeling more and more inept and wondering why he had agreed to meet her.

"There's always time," she said. She held his eyes. "Isn't that the way you look at it?"

Time for what? He ordered a draft beer for the woman and another shot for himself. He waited until the bartender had filled and set down their glasses and walked away. "You said maybe I could help you with something."

"You and your friend were talking to Dixon. He sold my daughter a bracelet before she died. Do you think he could have killed her?"

"I don't doubt he's a dangerous man."

"Dangerous to women?"

Clete was standing at the bar, one foot resting on the brass rail. In the mirror, he could see her looking at his profile, her face tilted upward. "Who am I to be judging others?" he replied.

"You looked angry when you were talking to him. I don't think you hide your feelings well. I think we're a lot alike."

"In what way?"

"You're not ashamed of your emotions."

"I don't know if I'd put it that way. I don't like criminals. Sometimes you meet a guy who's been inside and is on the square, but not too often. Anyone who's been down at least twice is probably a recidivist and will be in and out of the can the rest of his life."

"Why won't you answer my question?"

"A man who strikes a woman is a physical and moral coward. There's no exception to that rule. We call them misogynists. The simple truth is, they're cowards. Dixon is a head case and probably a lot of other things, but a coward isn't one of them. I hate admitting that."

"What is it you don't like about him?"

"I don't like reborn morons who say they understand the mind of God."

"Could he have been working with someone else?"

"He's a loner. Most rodeo people are. I got to ask you something, Miss Felicity. The Wigwam, the bar Angel was drinking in the night she died? It was full of outlaw bikers. A lot of those guys are sexual fascists and get off on smacking their women around. Dixon went to the joint for shooting a guy who murdered a prostitute. Why is everybody zeroing in on him?"

"Why were you all talking to him if he's of no importance?"

"My friend Dave thinks Dixon knows something about a guy who left a message on a cave wall behind Albert Hollister's place. Sometimes Dave reads more into something than is there." He motioned to the bartender for a refill. "Look, I'm sorry about your daughter. If I could help you, I would."

"You can't?"

"Maybe I could, but not officially."

"What's that supposed to mean?"

"I'm licensed as a PI in Louisiana. A private investigator's license has the legal value of a dog's tag. Because I chase down bail skips for a couple of bondsmen, I have extrajudicial powers that cops don't have. I can cross state lines and break down doors without warrants. I can hook up people and hold them in custody indefinitely. See, when a guy is bailed out of the can by a bondsman, he becomes property. The law lets you go after your property. You can hang the guy up like a smoked ham if you want. I'm not proud of what I do, but it's what I do."

"I want the person who killed my daughter."

"The locals will nail him sooner or later."

"Do you really believe that?"

He scratched at his cheek with three fingers. The jukebox was playing a country song, but it wasn't Hank or Lefty; it came from a new era in Nashville, one that Clete didn't understand. "The locals are like cops anywhere. They give it their best shot. The bad guys go down, but usually because they do something really stupid."

"My father was a policeman in New Orleans."

"Yeah, I knew him. He was a good guy."

He saw the recognition in her eyes. "You researched my background."

"Like I said, it's what I do." He had put on a summer suit and a blue dress shirt and his Panama hat and had shined his loafers before meeting the woman. Now he felt foolish and old and duplicitous. "I blew my career in law enforcement with booze and weed and pills and the wrong kind of women. I had a daughter out of wedlock, too. She grew up without a dad, and some bad guys did a lot of hurtful things to her. That's why I admire somebody like you who'd adopt a kid from the rez. This is great country around here, but the Indians get a bad shake."

"How well did you know him?"

"Your old man? I'd see him at roll call. That was when Dave and I walked a beat on Canal and in the Quarter, in the old days when cops signaled each other by hitting their batons on the pavement. We'd bounce the stick on the curb, and you could hear it a block away." He knew she wasn't listening and that he was making a fool out of himself.

"My father was such a good person that he took care of everybody except his family," she said.

"Beg your pardon?"

"He wasn't happy unless he was wearing sackcloth and ashes for other people's sins. He named me for Saint Felicity."

"I don't know who that is."

"She was the slave of a Roman aristocrat named Perpetua. Perpetua kept a record of the events leading up to her and Felicity's deaths in the arena. It's the only account that we have by a victim of the persecutions."

"I don't know much about that stuff. From what I remember, your dad was pretty religious."

"If that's what you call it." She pushed back his sleeve from his watch and glanced at the time. "I wonder if each one of us is allotted a certain number of days. We're here, then we're not. We look back and wonder what we've done with our lives and think about all the opportunities we let slip by. Do you ever feel like you lived your life for somebody else?"

"I was always getting in trouble. I didn't have time to think about things like that. I'm not too profound a guy."

"I think you're a much more complex man than you pretend." She rubbed her finger on the dial of his watch.

He could feel the heat in the back of his neck, a tingling sensation in his palms. He poured the remainder of his whiskey into his beer and drank it. It slid down inside him like an old friend, lighting the corners of his mind, stilling his heart, allowing him to smile as though he were not beset with a problem of conscience that, in the morning, could fasten him wrist and ankle on a medieval rack.

"I just barely made a plane to El Sal before I went down on a murder beef," he said. "My liver probably looks like a block of Swiss cheese with a skin disease. Dave is the only cop from the old days who'll hang out with me. I'm not being humble. I worked for the Mob in Vegas and Reno. I've done stuff I wouldn't tell a corpse."

"If you're thinking about my marital status,

my husband is the most corrupt, selfish man I've ever known."

"Maybe he had a good teacher." He saw the look on her face. "I'm talking about his father, Mr. Younger. He doesn't just vote against politicians he disagrees with, he smears their names."

"Caspian couldn't carry his father's briefcase."

"Why'd you marry him?"

"I was the little match girl looking through the window. I took the easy way."

Her fingers rested on the bar, inches from his hand. Her nails were tiny and clipped, the bones in her wrist as delicate as a kitten's. Whenever she lifted her eyes to his, her mouth became like a compressed flower, the black mole at the corner a reminder of how perfect her complexion was. Her blouse hung loosely from her shoulders, and he could see the sunlight from the door reflecting on the tops of her breasts. He wanted to reach out and touch the mole.

"I'm alone, Mr. Purcel," she said. "My daughter is dead. My husband is a satyr. Think ill of me if you wish. I don't apologize for what I am."

"I don't think you ought to apologize to anybody. I think you're a nice lady. Maybe you don't like New Orleans, but you don't know how beautiful your accent is. It's like a song."

"I haven't eaten supper yet. That's why I didn't want to drink a lot," she said. "Have you eaten, Mr. Purcel?"

"You want to go to the Depot? It's right down the street. We can eat on the terrace. In the evening you can see the deer up on the hills above the train tracks. I always like this time of day."

"You really worked for the Mafia?"

"Just one guy. His name was Sally Dio. Sometimes people called him Sally Deuce or Sally Ducks. Somebody put sand in the fuel tank of his airplane. He survived the crash, but he was turned into a french fry. Dave and I ran into him again a few years back."

"Where is he now?"

"Sally Dee caught the car to Jericho. That's an expression people in the life used in New Orleans years ago."

"I don't get it."

"Jericho is a dead city. If you got on the streetcar to Jericho, you weren't coming back."

Maybe, he thought, he would scare her and she would go away. She got up from the stool and pushed a strand of hair away from her eye, her profile as perfect as a miniature inside a Victorian locket. She tripped in the doorway and fell against him, then blushed and apologized and walked with him into the twilight, neither touching the other.

They did not pay attention to a man leaning against a parking meter down the street. He was smoking a pipe and gazing at the freight cars pulling out of the train yard. His hair was oiled and combed back over the tops of his ears. He puffed on his pipe and let the smoke curl out of his mouth into the breeze. He seemed to take a special pleasure in the purple cast of the hills, backdropped by a sky that was the blue of a robin's egg. He did not seem to notice Clete and the woman as they walked past him into the restaurant called the Depot.

A locomotive backed into the train yard, pushing a long row of boxcars ahead of it, the couplings clanging with such force that chaff from the boxcar floors powdered in the sun's afterglow. The man leaning against the meter tapped the bowl of his pipe on his hand, ignoring the live cinders that stuck to his skin. Then he put away his pipe and entered the restaurant through the terrace and took a seat at the bar, staring with self-satisfaction at the face he saw in the mirror.

"What are you having?" the bartender asked.

"A glass of ice water and a menu," the man said.

"You got it. Visiting?"

"Why do you think that?"

"Saw your tag through the window. How do you like Montana?"

"The state tree of Kansas is a telephone

pole," the man said. "Does that tell you something?"

Two hours earlier, Gretchen had gone up to the main house and thrown a pebble against Alafair's screen on the third floor. "Want to take a ride?" she said.

"Where to?" Alafair replied.

"A dump by the old train station."

"What for?"

"To find Clete."

"Call him on his cell."

"He turned it off. If he's doing what I think he is, he doesn't plan to turn it on again."

"Leave him alone, Gretchen. He's a grown man."

"Except he needs someone to strap a cast-iron codpiece on his stiff red-eye."

"Do you know how bad that sounds?"

"I heard him talking on the phone to Love Younger's daughter-in-law. Are you coming or not?"

They drove in Alafair's Honda to the saloon where Clete sometimes drank. Gretchen got out and went inside while Alafair waited in the car, the motor running. Gretchen came back out and got in the car and closed the door. "The bartender said he left with a woman five minutes ago."

"Gretchen, don't get mad at me. What's the harm if he's with this woman?"

"Duh, she's married? Duh, the Younger

218

family would like to turn Montana into a gravel pit?"

"Sometimes Clete drinks at the Depot."

"I thought he only drank in dumps," Gretchen said.

"It was James Crumley's hangout."

"Who?"

"The crime novelist. He passed away a few years back. Can I make a suggestion?"

"Go ahead."

Alafair pulled away from the curb. "Ease up on your old man. He thinks the world of you. He's easily hurt by what you say."

"So don't hurt your father's feelings, even if he's about to walk in front of a train?"

"You're a hard sell," Alafair said.

They drove up the street and stopped in front of the restaurant. Gretchen went inside by herself. She looked in the dining room, then went into the bar and gazed through the French doors at the people eating on the terrace. A man hunched on a stool a few feet from her had just said something about the state tree of Kansas. Through a door pane, she could see Clete sitting with a small woman at a linen-covered table under a canopy stretched over the terrace. The woman had a shawl across her shoulders. A candle flickered on the table, lighting her hair and mouth and eyes. She seemed captivated by a story Clete was telling while he drank from a tumbler of ice and whiskey and cherries and sliced oranges, both hands lifting in the air when he made a point, the ice rattling in the glass. Gretchen was breathing hard through her nose as though she had walked up a steep hill.

"Buy you a drink, legs?" asked the man hunched on the stool.

"I didn't catch that," she replied, not taking her eyes off Clete's back.

"You've got long legs, lady. I should have called you 'beautiful.' I didn't mean anything by the other name."

"Blow me," she said without looking at him. She went out on the terrace and approached Clete's table. "You shouldn't be driving," she said.

Clete and the small woman looked up. His cheeks were flushed, his eyes lit with an alcoholic shine. "Hey, Gretchen. What's the haps?" he said. "Miss Felicity, this is my daughter, Gretchen Horowitz."

"Did you hear me?" Gretchen asked.

"Hear what?" he said, grinning, squinting as though the sun were in his eyes.

"You're sloshed," she said.

"It's so nice to meet you," Felicity said.

Clete tried to hold his smile in place. He pushed out a chair. "We just ordered. Did you eat yet?"

"Yeah, by myself. After I fixed supper for both of us."

He looked confused. "We were supposed to

eat together? I must not have heard you. Is Alafair with you?"

"Yeah, I'll drive the Caddy. She'll follow us home. Let's go."

"Maybe we should do this another time, Clete," Felicity said.

"No, no," Clete said. "Sit down, Gretchen. I'll go get Alafair. Order me a refill."

Gretchen propped her palms on the table and leaned down. "What's your name again?" she said to the woman.

"Felicity Louviere."

"You're married to Caspian Younger?"

"Yes. How would you know that?"

"I'm making a documentary on your family and your oil and natural-gas explorations. You're not aware of it?"

"Somehow it escaped my attention."

"I don't like to say this, Ms. Louviere, but I think you've asked for it. You're out with a man who's not your husband after just losing your daughter. Does that seem normal to you?"

"Clete, I'd better get my car," Felicity Louviere said. "I appreciate your thoughtfulness. I hope to see you another time."

Clete pinched his temples as though the pressure of his fingers could impose a modicum of sanity on the situation. "Tell Alafair to come inside," he said. "We're going to have dinner. We're going to talk like civilized human beings. This bullshit ends, Gretchen.

Now sit down."

Gretchen felt the blood go out of her cheeks. The candle on the table seemed to brighten and change shape and shine as though burning underwater. "She looks like Mickey Mouse's twin sister," she said. "What's the matter with you?"

"Don't talk like that," Clete said.

"It's your life, Clete. Be a public fool if you want. You're really good at it," Gretchen said.

She walked toward the French doors, her eyes shiny, an electric grid printing itself all over her back. "Don't go, Gretchen," she heard him say.

She gripped the brass handle on the French doors and turned to look once more at the table. Clete had stood up and was leaning over Felicity, his hand resting on the back of her chair, as though he were comforting her. His eyes met Gretchen's. He smiled and walked toward her. Her heart was pounding so loudly, she could hardly hear his words.

"Are you all right?" he said.

"Get rid of her. Don't do this to yourself."

"There's no problem. We're just having dinner."

"You may have the right to hurt yourself, but you don't have the right to hurt others."

"You want me to leave her alone in the restaurant? A woman whose daughter might have been murdered by the same guy who was stalking Alafair?"

"She'll use you. When she's finished, she'll be fucking some other poor halfwit who thinks he's the love of her life. You make me so mad, I want to get as far away from you as I can and never come back."

People at the tables turned and stared.

"We'll talk later. I'll see you at the cabin," he said.

"You mean after you get your ashes hauled. After you come home hungover and stinking like a cathouse in Trinidad on Sunday morning."

She saw the twitch in his face, the injury in his eyes. "Okay, I messed up about supper. I got a long history of being irresponsible," he said. "You knew that when you signed on."

"That's the way you feel? A bimbo lets you scope her jugs and you dump the only family you have? That's pathetic. I hear there's a T and A bar on North Higgins. Maybe both of you can get jobs there."

She went through the French doors into the bar. It was crowded with college boys and tourists, all of whom were talking as loudly as they could. A television set was blaring, and someone was yelling whenever a soccer player on the screen kicked the ball down the field. She wanted somebody to start something with her, to step in her way, to put a hand on her, to make a pass, to comment on the anger in her face. She wanted to twist off someone's head and kick it down the sidewalk. Where was the smart-ass who had called her "legs"?

She seemed to have become invisible. She walked out the front door and got in Alafair's car.

"What happened in there?" Alafair said. "You look like someone put you in a microwave."

"Don't be clever at my expense."

"What did Clete say to you?"

"Nothing worth repeating. He's an expert at empty rhetoric. Fuck *him.*"

"We're your family, Gretchen. You need to trust people a little more."

"I told you to give it a rest, Alafair. You sound like your father."

"Clete's charity is his weakness. Manipulative women use it against him," Alafair said. "And don't be making remarks about Dave."

"Porking a bitch like Felicity Louviere is an act of charity? No wonder your family is screwed up."

Alafair drove down a brick-paved street that paralleled the train tracks. The evening star was bright and cold above the hills in the west. A solitary drop of rain struck the windshield. "I'm going to forget what you just said."

"Did I need to put this on flash cards? Clete just made a choice. He wants to get in that bitch's bread. If that hurts his daughter, too bad. His swizzle stick comes first."

Alafair pulled the Honda to the curb and cut the engine. She waited for a rusted-out Volkswagen bus and two bicyclists to pass. She started to speak, then studied a reflection in the outside mirror.

"Let's get going. I don't need any more psychoanalytical crap," Gretchen said.

"I thought I saw a guy come out of the restaurant and look at the back of my car. He's gone now."

"A guy was hitting on me in there."

"Who?"

"How would I know? The kind of guy who sits on a barstool like a vulture. Who cares? What were you going to say?"

"You have to accept Clete as he is," Alafair said. "When we take people to task for being what they are, we're deceiving ourselves. It's also pretty arrogant. We're telling others they have to be perfect in order to be our friends. It took me a long time to figure that out. You need to dial it down, Gretch."

"Oh, really?"

"Clete would lay down his life for any one of us. This stuff with the Louviere woman will pass. Clete has never grown up. He probably never will."

"How would you feel if your father put another woman ahead of his family?"

The car was quiet.

"Not too goddamn good, right?" Gretchen said.

225

"You're right," Alafair said.

"Start the car and drop me by the Caddy."

"What for?"

"I have a spare set of keys. If Clete wants to go to a motel, his punch will have to take her car, because I'm going to boost the Caddy."

"You don't take prisoners, do you?"

Gretchen didn't reply and stared out the side window into the darkness. She sniffed and dabbed her nose with her wrist.

"You're my best friend," Alafair said. "I'm sorry if I hurt your feelings. I'll drive you to Clete's car. But after that, you're on your own."

"I've always been on my own," she said. "That's what none of you have figured out. You don't know shit about what's in my head."

They were silent while Alafair circled the block and pulled to the curb by the restaurant parking lot. Gretchen got out and walked to Clete's convertible, her tote bag swinging from her shoulder. She stuck her spare key into the door lock and looked back at the street. Alafair cut her engine and walked into the parking lot. "I'll make this brief," she said. "I'll always be your friend, no matter what you say or do. Dave and Molly will always be there for you, too. But if you ever speak to me like that again, I'm going to kick your butt around the block."

CHAPTER 11

Clete sat back down at the table and drank the melt in the bottom of his tumbler, crunching the cherries and orange slices between his molars. "I shot off my mouth," he said.

"I don't know if I'm up to this kind of evening," Felicity said.

"Gretchen is a good kid. She just had the wrong idea. My body doesn't process booze the way it used to."

"Maybe you shouldn't drink."

"It doesn't quite work like that."

"You treat your daughter as if she's a child. Mature people don't throw temper tantrums in a restaurant."

"I wasn't there for her when she was growing up. She was surrounded by bad guys. I'm talking about johns and degenerates, one in particular."

"You're talking about a molester?"

"A guy who burned her all over with cigarettes when she was a toddler. He isn't around anymore." He felt her gaze rove over his face.

"What are you telling me?" she asked.

"I'm saying the guy who hurt my daughter isn't going to hurt anybody else."

"No, what are you trying to tell me about your daughter?"

"Not everybody grows up in a regular home. Gretchen's mother was a hooker. Her old man was a drunk and on a pad for the Giacano crime family in New Orleans. The old man tried to set things right and took care of the guy who hurt her. But punching somebody's ticket doesn't give back the life a pervert stole from a little girl. That's what I was trying to say."

"Maybe you're a better man than you think you are. When I said you shouldn't drink, I wasn't criticizing you. I thought maybe we would have a fine evening."

"I've got King Midas's touch in reverse. Whatever I touch turns to garbage. Excuse me, I got to go to the restroom."

He went into the men's room and relieved himself and washed his hands. The reflection he saw in the mirror could have been that of a profligate doppelgänger come to mock him. The skin around his eyes was green, his face dilated and oily with booze, the welted scar running through one eyebrow as red and swollen as an artery about to burst. There was a lipstick smear on his shirt pocket, where she had fallen against him when they were going out the door of the saloon. He washed his face in cold water, heaping it with both hands into his eyes and rubbing it on the back of his neck. He wiped his face with paper towels and combed his hair and returned to the table.

"We can cancel the order and maybe go somewhere else," Felicity said.

"I think I've blown out my doors for tonight. I've got to square things with Gretchen. You're a nice lady. I'll help you in whatever way I can, but right now I'm done."

She placed her hand on his knee. "Don't let our evening end like this."

"End like what? I'm tired. I'm running on the rims. I'm a fucking mess."

"Don't let situations and people control you, Clete. Our destiny isn't in the stars, it's in us. We can control the moment we have. That moment is now." Her fingers lingered on his knee, as light as air, one finger idly brushing the fabric. "I really like you," she said.

"Gretchen is a little girl in a woman's body. I owe her. She's my kid. She'll always be my kid."

Felicity lifted her hand and placed it on top of the table just as their food arrived. Clete stared out at the street, his jaw tightening.

"What is it?" Felicity said.

"My Caddy just went by. There it goes, down by the red light."

"I don't see it."

"There's a pickup behind it. Stay here. I'll be right back." Clete went through the bar and out the front door and looked at the parking lot. The Caddy was gone. He went back inside the bar. "Did you see a maroon Caddy convertible pull out of the lot?" he asked the bartender.

"Yeah. A guy at the bar did, too."

"I don't follow."

"A guy went out the door without paying for his drinks and sandwich. I went outside after him. He got in his truck and took off after the convertible."

"What kind of truck?"

"I don't know."

"You get the tag?"

"The guy said he was from Kansas. He made a crack at a girl who was in here. I didn't get the tag number."

"Which girl?"

"Good-looking, wearing jeans, long legs. That's the crack he made. He said she had long legs. He had a face kind of like a shoe box."

"Did he use a name?"

The bartender thought for a moment. "I heard him coming on to a college girl. He told her his name was Toto. What kind of name is that?"

Gretchen turned off the brick-paved street by

the tracks and drove aimlessly through the downtown area, unable to sort out her thoughts, her palms dry and stiff and hard to close around the steering wheel, her anger and depression like a stone in her chest. She passed the Wilma Theater and crossed the Higgins Street Bridge. Raindrops and hail were clicking on the convertible's top; down below she could see a park and a carousel and the Clark Fork boiling over the boulders along the riverbank, the flooded willows bending almost to the waterline. On the other side of the bridge, she turned onto an unlit street down by the river, the same neighborhood of brick bungalows and early-twentieth-century apartment buildings where Bill Pepper had lived.

A pickup truck that had been behind her on the bridge kept going and disappeared from her rearview mirror as soon as she turned off Higgins. She parked under a maple tree and cut the engine and dialed Alafair's number on her cell phone. "Have a drink with me at Jaker's," she said.

"Are you there now?" Alafair said.

"No, I'm down by the river. I'm sorry for all those things I said to you. I feel really bad, Alafair."

"It's not your fault. I was lecturing you."

"You always know how to handle things in an intelligent way. I don't. Sometimes I wish I were you."

"Is Clete all right?"

"He's with the Louviere woman. Maybe I should go back there. At least return his car."

"I don't think that's a good idea."

"Why not?"

"It's time to disengage and let Clete solve his own problems. Remember the story of Tom Sawyer's fence? The best way to get people to do something is to tell them they can't."

"You always make me feel good, Alafair."

"See you at Jaker's. And stop worrying about everything. Leave a message on Clete's cell and tell him where we are."

Gretchen closed her phone and cracked the window, letting in the cold air and the smell of the trees and the river. The windshield was filmed with ice crystals, a streetlamp glowing like a yellow diamond inside the maples. She started the engine and glanced in her outside mirror. A pickup truck turned out of a side street and approached the Caddy from behind, the driver slowing. In the mirror she could see two silhouettes in the front seat. Was that the same truck she had seen earlier?

She pulled open her tote bag and rested her hand on the checkered grips of the fourteen-round Beretta. The truck passed, its high beams bouncing off the trunks of the trees, lighting the bottom of the canopy. At the end of the block, it made a wide U-turn and headed toward her again, its headlights almost blinding her.

She released her safety belt and slipped the Beretta from her bag and lowered the window all the way. Though the driver's window in the truck was down, she could not make out his face. Then she saw him lift a nickel-plated snub-nosed revolver into full view and point it at her. The first round shattered the outside mirror, and the second one pocked a hole in the windshield and blew glass on her skin. She had already thrown herself sideways on the seat and popped the door handle on the passenger side. She slid off the edge of the seat onto the swale and pushed the door shut, which turned off the interior light. She positioned herself on one knee, the Beretta in her right hand, and waited. On the far side of the Caddy, she heard the truck turn around and head toward her again.

She stood up and walked into the middle of the street and extended the Beretta in front of her with both arms, her feet fifteen inches apart. The driver hesitated, windshield wipers beating furiously, milky vapor rising from the hood's surface. The passenger was attempting to work himself partway out the window to get a clear shot. She clicked off the butterfly safety and thumbed back the hammer. The driver of the pickup floored the accelerator, and the truck leaped forward and roared straight at her. Gretchen began shooting, each crack of the nine-millimeter like a splinter of glass in her right eardrum. The sleet pelted her head and stung her eyes, but she kept pulling the trigger, both feet anchored to the asphalt, the brass hulls ejecting into the darkness.

She could hear the rounds punching through the radiator and whanging off the hood and toppling through the windshield. She tried to count the rounds but couldn't keep track. One thing she was certain about: Anyone inside that truck was having a bad night.

The driver ducked down as the truck veered out of control and passed her. For just a second, in the glow of the dashboard, she saw the passenger leaning forward, staring straight at her. His cheekbone was shattered, and he was trying to hold it in place with his left hand; the blood from his wound had welled through his fingers and was running down his wrist.

She turned with the truck and began firing again. At least one round went through the back window; another hit the tailgate. She let off two more rounds, hoping to punch a hole in the gas tank. Instead, one round must have ricocheted off the asphalt and popped the left front tire, bringing it instantly down on the rim, the truck skidding against the curb. Gretchen looked down at her Beretta. The slide was locked open on an empty chamber.

She opened the driver's door of the Caddy

and leaned over the seat and retrieved a backup magazine from her bag. The driver of the pickup shoved the transmission into reverse and backed into the center of the street, burning rubber, smoke rising from the rear tires. She jammed the loaded magazine into the Beretta's frame and released the slide, chambering a round. The driver of the pickup shifted out of reverse and gave the engine all it had, the fan screeching, the radiator bleeding antifreeze, sparks gushing off the left front wheel rim, the flattened tire slicing into strips.

Gretchen didn't have a clear shot. The angle could carry it into a yard or porch or housefront. How much time had passed since the driver had fired the first round? Probably under two minutes, long enough for someone to call in a shots-fired. As the pickup wobbled down the middle of the street, Gretchen repositioned herself and lifted the Beretta so the sight was just below the rear window. Then she saw a car turn down the far end of the block, putting itself directly in her line of fire.

She lowered her weapon. Her ears felt like they were stuffed with damp cotton. She swallowed and tried to clear her ear canals with no success.

The driver of the pickup wasn't finished. Steering with one hand, he opened the passenger door and shoved his friend out on the street. The man was short and compact and dressed in heavy jeans and work boots and a long-sleeved cotton shirt. He landed on his side, hard, then struggled to his feet and lumbered down an embankment toward the river. He was holding his face with one hand, as though he had a toothache, his sleeve sodden with blood. The pickup went through the intersection at the end of the block, the bare rim clanging like a garbage can rolling down a rock road.

How much time had gone by? Three minutes, maybe three and a half, she thought. Response time would be at least ten minutes. That was just a guess. She followed the wounded man down to the water's edge. The river was blown out and full of leaves and twigs and foam and running dangerously high and fast through boulders that usually lay exposed in dry sand. Plus, the river was making a relentless humming sound, similar to a sewing machine's.

"Give it up, buddy," she called out.

For a moment she thought she saw him inside a stand of willows, watching her, maybe sighting on her face or chest. She froze and slowly squatted down behind a beached cottonwood, lowering her face so that light did not shine directly on it.

When the wind blew through the willows, all of the shapes inside it moved except one.

"Your pal screwed you. You want to take his

weight?" she said. "Bad deal, if you ask me."

She walked farther along the embankment, rocks as heavy as petrified dinosaur eggs clacking under her feet. "My name is Gretchen Horowitz. I used to blow heads for a living. That means I've got a sheet, and I won't be a credible witness against you. You can skate and say, '*Adios*, motherfuckers, I'll be in Margaritaville.' "

There was no answer from the figure. She wiped the rainwater out of her eyes with her sleeve. "Listen to me," she said. "You were probably trying to clip my old man, Clete Purcel. So you and your friend screwed up twice. Then your friend rat-fucked you on top of it. I can drive you to the ER. This is Montana. Gunfights are a family value here. Think it over."

"I already did," said a voice inside the willows. "I never saw a Hebe that didn't try to work the angle."

She knew the drill and didn't want to be there for it. Fear and desperation always took them to a precipice where they gave up hope and pulled the rip cord and leaped into space. There were memories buried in her mind that were like film clips from a documentary no one should ever have to see. But the memories were hers, not someone else's, and the characters were not from central casting. She saw herself on a boat off Islamorada on a blazing sunlit day, the ocean green and filled with patches of indigo, an Irish button man from the Jersey Shore aiming a harpoon gun at her breast. The scene shifted to Little Havana, where a gumball who'd raped the daughter of a Gambino underboss came out of a whorehouse closet shooting, wearing panties and a bra, his body covered with monkey hair. Odds were that either man would take her off at the neck. Instead, they both died with a look of disbelief she could never forget. Their prey had not only become their executioner; they had died at the hands of someone they'd always thought of as the weaker sex, a receptacle of their seed, to be used and discarded arbitrarily.

Unfortunately for her, all the weed and angel dust in Florida couldn't change the fact that of her own volition, she had become employed by the worst people in America, including some who may have been involved with the murder of John Fitzgerald Kennedy.

The man in work clothes came around the far side of the willows, knee-deep in the current, the lights from the vaudeville theater and the park across the river reflecting off the rapids behind him. His hair was black and thick and unwashed and hung in dirty strings around his face. His left hand was clenched on his cheek, pushing his lips out of shape, exposing his teeth. A dark fluid was leaking from below his rib cage, down his shirt and trouser leg. In his right hand, he held a small semi-auto, perhaps a .25 or .32. He was obviously weak from blood loss and probably had decided he would either see the sunrise from a plane window or with a DOA tag tied to his toe.

"You were stand-up. Your bud was a rat bastard," she said. "Throw your piece in the water. You can go into wit pro. There're all kinds of —"

He raised the semi-auto. "Chug this," he said.

Maybe he fired, maybe he didn't. She didn't try to think it through. She was sure her first round hit him in the forehead, the second in the throat, the third in the chest. Maybe one went long or hit him in the arm. He went straight down, as they always did. Even while he slid into the current, the back of his shirt puffing with air, his head bobbing like an apple in the chop, she couldn't stop pulling the trigger, the bullets dancing all over the water's surface. In seconds the current or a cottonwood snag took him under, and all she could hear was the incessant humming of the river.

"Shit! Shit! Shit!" she said under her breath.

Inside her head, she heard a cacophonous voice that sounded like it had risen from the bowels of a building through a heating duct: *Hi, baby doll,* it said. *Welcome back to that old-time rock and roll. It's so nice to have you back on board.*

239

■ ■ ■ ■

By Monday morning Clete Purcel didn't think much else could go wrong with his day. Not until he saw a hand-waxed, metallic-purple, chrome-plated Humvee coming up the road, splashing through the rain puddles, almost running over Albert's border collie. The Humvee turned into the driveway and stopped by the pedestrian gate to the north pasture. A slight man wearing a Mexican vest and a flowery shirt with blown sleeves and a braided cloth belt and trousers stuffed inside hand-tooled, multicolored boots came through the gate with a self-satisfied expression while he eyeballed the pasture and the low-hanging clouds and the sunshine spangling on the wet trees, as though he owned whatever he walked on.

Clete stepped out on the porch, steam rising off the tin cup he held. "What can I do for you, Mr. Younger?" he said.

"Call me Caspian. Is that your restored Cadillac under the tarp?"

"Yeah, the ravens keep downloading on it. It's a way of life with me."

"Getting dumped on?"

"Yeah, think of me as a human Dumpster. What do you want?"

"Not much. I felt obligated to tell you you're not the first."

"First what?"

Caspian Younger gazed at the sheen on the fir and pine trees on the hillsides and the clouds dissolving like smoke as the day warmed. "I understand you worked for Sally Dio in Reno and Vegas."

"I used to get comped at the Riviera. I stayed in the penthouse, right next to Frank Sinatra's old suite. The greaseballs loved it there. It was the worst shithole on the Strip. You ever stay at the Riviera?"

"I never had the pleasure. You don't like Vegas?"

"There's nothing wrong with it that a hydrogen bomb and a lot of topsoil wouldn't cure."

"Did you enjoy yourself last night, Mr. Purcel?"

"Actually, I don't remember much of what I did. I have blackouts, see? I wake up in the morning and don't have a clue about where I was or who I was with."

"Know where I met her?"

"Not interested."

"She was a ticket taker in an art theater in Metairie. I thought she was the cutest thing I had ever seen. She looked like a little teenage girl with a woman's jugs. You ever see skin like that on a woman? Or didn't you notice?"

"I met your wife in town to talk about the death of your adopted daughter. We had a drink in a bar and went to the Depot and ordered a dinner we never ate. In the meantime, your family keeps showing up in our lives. I don't see y'all as the offended party."

"She'll fuck your brains out and throw the rest of your body parts on the roadside. She fucked the governor of Louisiana right before he went to prison. The poor schmuck probably never figured out why she balled him. She collects stuffed heads. Hey, nobody complains. Felicity can have four orgasms in one night."

"If you want to talk about your wife like that, it's your business. I don't want to hear it, Mr. Younger."

"I'm a realist. I knew what she was when I married her. You go out with another guy's wife, but you're offended by profanity?"

Take a chance, Clete thought. "You know that dude who was following me and Miss Felicity around?"

"Which 'dude'?"

"Driving a pickup, Kansas plates, rectangular face, maybe, what's the gen on this guy?"

"The 'gen'?"

"Yeah, the background. You know this guy?"

"I don't know what you're talking about."

"You know what bothers me most about your visit here, Mr. Younger? You haven't made one mention of your daughter. Your wife wants to hire me to help find your daughter's killer, but you show no curiosity at all about what I might know. You don't

242

show any rage, either. Most fathers who lose a daughter to a predator don't want the guy cooled out. They want to feed him into an airplane propeller."

"I didn't raise the subject, Mr. Purcel, because I don't think you know anything. I think you're a rotund, self-deluded fellow who will bed another man's wife and pretend he's part of a noir tradition he learned about from watching too many movies. We checked you out. Wherever you go, you have the reputation of a court jester with dunce cap and bells, an alcoholic idiot who can't keep his flagpole in his pants."

"We were talking about your lack of anger or desire for revenge or even justice."

"Anger is the stuff of theater. Revenge is a science, my friend. Stay away from my wife. The first time wasn't altogether your fault. The second time won't be nice."

Clete felt his hands close and open involuntarily at his sides. "I guess you're not a listener," he said.

"And you look like you had a hard night," Caspian said. He reached out with his fingernail and ticked the lipstick smear on Clete's shirt. "I hope it's worth it. When she gets rid of a cop — and there have been other cops before you — he's usually ready to eat his gun. Can you see yourself eating your gun over a broad? Hey, I like this place. You get to stay here rent-free?"

■ ■ ■ ■

Clete went back inside the cabin, his blood pressure throbbing in his wrists, a taste like copper pennies in his mouth. Gretchen had just gotten up. "Did you know you have lipstick on your shirt?" she said.

"Thanks for pointing that out."

She looked through the window. "That's Caspian Younger. I've seen his picture. He got in your face about his wife?"

"More or less. He wanted to convince me he's a good loser. You know what it takes to be a good loser? Practice."

"What'd you say to him?" she asked.

"I told him nothing happened. I don't think he believed me." He sat down at the breakfast table and rubbed his forehead. "Let's go over a couple of things from last night. You tried to make the guy in the water give it up before you dropped him?"

"Were you in the sack with her?"

"No. And my private life is not the issue, Gretchen."

"Maybe the guy got off one round. I'm not sure. I waited till the last second before I shot him. Then I couldn't stop."

"How do you feel about it?"

She was sitting in the chair across from him. She stared at the floor, her face still lined with sleep. She was wearing pink tennis shoes without socks, and somehow they made Clete feel guilty about the childhood she'd deserved but been denied. "I'm alive, he's dead. What should I feel? I don't feel anything," she said.

"Don't lie."

"I fired on the truck in hot blood. I could have let the guy on the riverbank go. He had two holes in him. He probably would have bled out and died on the riverbank and wouldn't have floated away. We'd know who he was. I blew it."

"He was out to kill you, kid. He got what he deserved. I'm proud of you."

"I heard a voice inside my head. The voice said, 'Welcome back, baby doll,' or something like that."

Clete's eyes went away from her and looked at nothing. "Like the voice that was telling you you're back on that old-time rock and roll?" he said.

"I don't like to think in those terms anymore."

"You stood directly in front of a speeding truck and took everything they could throw at you. How many people have that kind of courage? Don't you dare blame yourself for being the noble woman you are."

"I don't need the Valium, Dad."

"Don't be smart. You belong to a special club. You paid a lot of dues to join it. Stop beating up on yourself, and don't ever mock our relationship."

Her face showed no expression and he wondered if he had said too much.

"Who were those guys? Who sent them?" she said.

"Think of it this way: At least one of them won't be back."

"I want to be a film director. I'm supposed to go over on the east side of the Divide in two days. How'd we end up in this mess?"

He didn't answer. He got an ice tray and a bottle of grape juice and a bottle of Canada Dry out of the refrigerator and filled two glasses. He dropped a lime slice in each. "This is the best drink in the world, did you know that?" he said. "You're my kid. In spite of the fact that your old man was a deadbeat and a drunk, you turned out to be the best kid on the planet. None of this other stuff means diddly-squat on a rock. You roger that?"

"You're the worst actor I've ever known," she replied. "But you're a good guy just the same. Now change your shirt, for Christ's sake."

That afternoon I was watering Albert's flowers for him when I saw Sheriff Elvis Bisbee come up the driveway in a cruiser. He walked into the yard and stood in the shade of the house, a manila envelope in his hand, a relaxed expression on his face. Clete was grilling hamburgers up on the deck, glancing over his shoulder at us, pressing a spatula down on the meat.

"I want to talk with you and your pal at the same time, Mr. Robicheaux," the sheriff said.

Clete closed the top on the barbecue and came down the steps into the shade. The wind was up, the air cool and smelling of cut grass and the water sprinklers in the yard; Albert's horses were galloping in the pasture, hooves drumming, tails flagging. It was a fine afternoon. I didn't want to be at odds with the sheriff, who seemed an admirable man.

"Last night there was a shoot-out not far from the Higgins Street Bridge," he said. "The person who called in the 911 claims a woman driving a vintage Cadillac convertible was involved. Who might that be?"

Clete's eyes showed no expression.

"Can you venture a guess, Mr. Purcel?"

Clete watched a robin light on the branch of an ornamental crab apple. "Shit happens," he replied.

"There's another interesting development. We found Gretchen Horowitz's fingerprints inside Bill Pepper's home," the sheriff said.

Clete nodded gravely. "If I had a man like that in my department, I'd pay a reward to the person who put him on the bus. If I knew where his grave was, I'd piss on it."

"We also found an abandoned pickup with a tire blown off the rim. Somebody had wiped the inside and the door handles with motor oil, so we couldn't lift any prints."

"Sounds like you've got some pretty sharp criminals around here," Clete said.

"We have our share of visiting comedians, too," the sheriff said. "Let me line this out a little more clearly so there's no misunderstanding between us. This isn't the O.K. Corral. We're not a collection of hicks. You gentlemen don't make the rules."

"We can't argue with you on that," I said.

"You don't know anything about a shooting by the bridge, Mr. Robicheaux?"

"I don't know what to tell you, sir," I replied.

"Here's how it went down, Sheriff," Clete said. "Two guys tried to smoke my daughter. One guy got away in a pickup, Kansas tags. The other guy's whereabouts are unknown. I told my daughter not to call it in because I didn't want to see her hung out to dry. Bill Pepper was a dirty cop. You know it and so do I. First time, shame on them, know what I mean?"

"You don't trust us?"

"We didn't deal the play," Clete said.

"I've got a surprise for both of you," the sheriff said. "My biggest concern isn't the shooting by the bridge. Two witnesses said your daughter acted in self-defense, Mr. Purcel. Evidently, one man was badly wounded, so I expect he'll show up one way or another.

I want you to look at some photos."

He untied the manila envelope and took out at least a dozen crime scene photographs. "The former sheriff was an obsessed man when it came to crimes against children and women. Beginning in 1995, there were a number of murders in the Northwest that seemed to bear similarities. The first one was right here in the Bitterroot Valley, followed by one in Billings, then Seeley Lake, Pocatello, and Spokane." He began placing the photos in a line on top of the stone wall by the front entrance. "There were never any forensics that would tie one homicide to another, except they were all obviously committed by a sexual deviant. I'd like both of you to study these and tell me what you see."

Crime scene photography, especially homicide, is never pleasant to look at. Defense attorneys try to suppress it as inflammatory, more so as the trial nears the sentencing phase. It's invasive in nature and seems to degrade the victims in death. Their eyes are fixed and stare at nothing; their mouths often hang open, as though they realized in their last seconds the irreparable nature of the fate imposed upon them. As you gaze at their photos, you identify with them, and for just a moment you understand the terrible nature of the crime that, in retrospect, you are being made witness to: These people, made out of the same clay as you, were not simply killed;

they were robbed of their dignity, their hope, their identity, their belief in humanity, and sometimes their religious faith. As you gaze at these photographs, you are tempted to revisit your objections to capital punishment.

Clete picked up the photos and looked at each and passed them to me. "What do you want us to say?" he asked the sheriff.

"You think these people were killed by the same guy?"

"The killer was into bondage and torture. He was big on suffocation and using plastic bags."

"What else?" the sheriff asked.

"The women's dresses have been pulled up. You or somebody else have drawn felt-tip circles on the women's legs."

"That's where the killer or killers ejaculated on them."

"Most of these bastards mark their territory," Clete said.

"In the same way at every homicide scene?" the sheriff said.

"What difference does our opinion make?" I said.

"The guy who killed Angel Deer Heart ejaculated on her."

"Where?" I said.

"On her legs."

"There was no penetration?" I said.

"None."

"Did you get a hit on the DNA?"

"We're working on it," he said.

That one didn't sound right. "You ever hear of a guy named Asa Surrette?" I asked.

"I talked to your daughter about him," the sheriff said.

"I didn't know she called you."

"I got the sense you don't agree with your daughter's perceptions about him. You think he's dead?"

"The state of Kansas says he's dead."

"What do *you* say?" the sheriff asked.

"Maybe he's out there. Maybe he was the guy who left the message in the cave. Or maybe somebody is using his MO."

"Why did you mention the cave?"

"I don't know," I lied.

"It's the biblical reference, isn't it?"

"No, evil is evil. There's enough of it in the human breast without having to ascribe it to the devil."

"I hope you're right," the sheriff said, gathering up the photos and replacing them in the envelope. "Where's your daughter, Mr. Purcel?"

"In town."

"That's convenient."

"If she has time, maybe she can give you a ring," Clete said.

"Repeat that, please?"

"Gretchen isn't the problem," Clete replied. "It's not our job to follow you guys around with a dustpan and a broom."

"Come back here, Mr. Purcel," the sheriff said. "Did you hear me? Sir, don't walk away from me."

That was exactly what Clete did, gazing up at the strips of pink cloud in the sky and at the trees bending in the wind on the hillside. I knew we were in for it.

Chapter 12

At first light Tuesday morning, Wyatt Dixon woke from a nightmare, one that left his armpits damp and turned his heart into gelatin. For Wyatt, the dream was not about the past or the present; nor did it have a beginning or an end. Instead, the dream was omnipresent in Wyatt's life, and it waited for him whenever he closed his eyes, whether day or night. In the dream, the man he grew up calling "Pap" was walking toward him barechested in his strap overalls, his skin as shriveled and bloodless as a mummy's, his bony hand knotted into a fist. "You touch your sister again, boy? Your mother seen you," Pap was saying. "Don't lie. It'll go twice as hard if you lie. You worthless little pisspot. The best part of you run down your mother's leg."

Wyatt got up and put on his jeans and went outside barefoot and shirtless into the cold morning and the mist that was a ghostly blue in the cottonwoods and as bright as silver dollars on the steel swing bridge over the river. The current was dark green and swirling in giant eddies around the boulders and beaver dams on the edges of the main channel, and wild roses were blooming along the banks. The dawn was so soft and cool and tangible, Wyatt believed he could taste it in the back of his mouth and breathe it into his lungs. He pulled a tarp off a woodpile and threw it on the grass and lay on his back with his arm over his eyes, his chest rising and falling slowly, the world once again a place of leafy trees and a breeze blowing down a canyon and German brown trout undulating in the riffle. Just that fast, Pap had gone away and become the bag of bones that someone finally dropped in a hole in a potter's field.

When Wyatt awoke, the sun had just broken above the canyon, and he could hear footsteps clanging on the steel grid of the swing bridge and the cables creaking with the tension created by weight. He sat up and saw a heavyset woman in a suit and heels trying to work her way down the slope without falling, a notebook in her hand.

Where had he seen her? At the revival on the rez?

"Could I have a word with you, Mr. Dixon?" she asked.

The breeze was at her back. He closed and opened his eyes. "What the hell is that smell?" he said, looking around.

"I guess that's my perfume."

"Who are you?"

"Bertha Phelps. I'm doing an article on charismatic religions among Native Americans."

"I was about to fix breakfast."

"I don't mind," she replied.

You don't mind what? he thought. He took her inventory. "I've seen you before."

"Could I ask you some questions?"

He broke off a blade of grass and put it in his mouth. "Whatever blows your skirt up," he replied.

She followed him into the house. He put on a long-sleeved shirt without buttoning it and started a fire in the woodstove. There was so much clutter in his kitchen that there was hardly a spot to sit down. He went into the living room and returned with a straight-back chair and set it beside her. "Take a load off," he said.

"I heard you speaking in tongues Sunday afternoon," she said.

"You were the woman talking to Mr. Robicheaux."

"That's right. Were you raised Pentecostal?"

"I didn't have *no* raising, unless that's what you call breaking corn and picking cotton from cain't-see to cain't-see."

"Would you say you found your religion through the Indians?"

"I never give it much thought."

"You had a hard life, didn't you?"

"No."

"Other people say you did."

He cracked four eggs and plopped the yolks in a skillet and set the skillet on one of the stove lids. "Maybe other people ought to mind their own goddamn business."

She leaned over her notebook to write in it. She rubbed her pen back and forth on the paper, trying to make ink come out of it. "Drat," she said.

"That's them kind Walmart sells. They're about as good for writing as tent pegs."

"I have another one in my purse," she said.

He looked at her with increasing curiosity. "You're not here to ask me about the revival, are you?"

"I'm also doing an article on the local Indians."

"You know where I saw that kind of ballpoint before?"

"You just told me. At Walmart."

"There was a cop here'bouts named Bill Pepper. He carried ballpoints just like that one in your hand. He was the kind of man who did things on the cheap. Did you happen to know Detective Pepper?"

"The name is familiar."

"While I was in his custody, I heard him talking on his phone to Love Younger. I think the good detective was on a pad for Mr. Younger."

"A what?"

"Detective Pepper was taking money on the side. That's what cops call being on a pad."

"You're saying this police officer was corrupt?"

He looked through the back window at a doe and a fawn crossing through the shadows, their hooves stenciling the damp grass. They looked back at him, flipping their tails, theirs noses twitching. "I'm saying you got something on your mind, lady, and it ain't religion."

"I wondered if you knew the murdered Indian girl."

"The Youngers sent you here?"

"No, sir, I'm here on my own."

"You from down south?" he said.

"I've lived there."

Wyatt opened the window and picked up a magazine from the drainboard and fanned his face with it.

"Does my perfume bother you?"

"I guess I've smelled worse."

She seemed to concentrate on a reply but couldn't think of one.

"If you see the Youngers, I want you to tell them something for me."

"I've already told you I don't work for them. I'm a freelance journalist."

"Right. Tell Mr. Younger I know what he can do to me if he takes a mind. But I'll leave my mark on him before we get done. He'll know when it's my ring, too."

"If you want to make threats, Mr. Dixon, you'll have to do that on your own."

"It ain't no threat."

"I think maybe I should leave."

"Suit yourself."

She stood up, then looked out the window at the deer. "There's corn on the grass," she said.

"The doe's got a hurt leg. I put it out at night for her and the fawn."

"Isn't that illegal?"

"I didn't check."

"Maybe you are a kinder man than you pretend to be, Mr. Dixon," she said. "Why are you looking at me like that?"

"You're a right handsome woman, if a little on the heavy side," he said.

"That's supposed to be a compliment?"

"I'd call it a statement of fact. You're a nice-looking lady. I get out of sorts sometime. You already ate breakfast?"

"No, I haven't."

"Stick around."

"I'm not sure for what purpose."

"My huevos rancheros ain't half bad. I got coffee and biscuits, too. There's a bowl of pineapple in the icebox I chopped up. I learned cooking in the army before they kicked me out."

"You do have manners," she said.

"You're working for Love Younger, though, ain't you?"

"I most certainly am not. I do not care for Mr. Younger. I do not care for his ilk, his progeny, or the industries he owns."

"What was that second one?"

"His offspring. They're like their father. They're notorious for their lack of morality."

He snapped the buttons into place on his cowboy shirt, the tails splaying across his narrow hips. He pulled on his boots and filled the coffeepot under the spigot, his mouth a slit, his eyes as empty as glass.

"Is there some reason you're not speaking to me now?" she asked.

"There's something you hid from me. I just ain't figured out what it is," he replied. His eyes rested on the ballpoint in her hand. "You like ham or a chunk of steak with your eggs?"

Wyatt Dixon had never been on the property of a wealthy man and had always assumed that the geographical passage from the world of those who ate potatoes and those whose bread was served on a gold plate would involve rumbling over a drawbridge and a moat, not simply driving up a maple-shaded road through an open gate and cutting his engine in front of a ten-thousand-square-foot mansion overlooking the Clark Fork of the Columbia River.

The gardens were bursting with flowers, the lawn a blue-green mixture of fescue and clover and Bermuda grass. Three men who looked like gardeners were watering the flowers and weeding the beds, hummingbirds hanging in midair above them, the sun a yellow flame through trees that grew higher than the roof.

One of the gardeners snipped a rose and set it in a bucket of water and walked toward Wyatt, sticking his cloth gloves in his back pocket, smiling behind a pair of Ray-Ban wraparounds. His hair was gold and braided in cornrows, his tanned scalp popping with perspiration. A red spider was tattooed on the back of one hand. "You the plumber?" he said.

"I look like a plumber?" Wyatt replied.

The gardener gazed up the driveway at the road and at the sunlight spangling in the canopy, his smile never leaving his mouth. His lips had no color and seemed glued on his face. "You're lost and you need directions?"

"I got a message for Mr. Love Younger. Is he home?"

The gardener took a two-way phone from a pouch on his belt. "I can ask."

Wyatt glanced at an upstairs window from which an elderly man was looking back. "Is that him yonder?" he said.

"What's your name, buddy?" the gardener said.

Wyatt pulled the walkie-talkie from the gardener's hand and pushed the talk button.

"Howdy-doody, Mr. Younger. This is Mr. Dixon. You got yourself a little-bitty teensy-weensy pissant down here deciding who talks to you and who don't. I need to have a word with you about the death of your grand-daughter. You want to come down here or not?"

"You're the rodeo man who sold her the bracelet?" a voice replied.

"Yes, sir, that would be yours truly. I sold it to her in the biker joint she didn't have no business in."

"Stay right there," the voice said.

A moment later, a man with a broad fore-head and vascular arms and a glare emerged from the front door. When Wyatt extended his hand and stepped toward him, the man with the cornrows and another gardener grabbed his upper arms, struggling to get their fingers around the entirety of his triceps.

"Let him go," Younger said.

"Thank you, kind sir. Breeding shows every time," Wyatt said, straightening a crick out of his neck. "A journalist named Bertha Phelps come to see me this morning. I think maybe she's working for you, but she says that ain't true."

"I have no idea what you're talking about," Younger said.

"The cops are trying to put your grand-daughter's murder on me. The one who tried hardest was Bill Pepper. I bet you know who he is. Or rather, who he was."

"I do."

"You were paying him?"

"Why have you come here, Mr. Dixon?"

"To find out why y'all are trying to do me in."

"I have no interest in you at all, except for the fact that you were the last person to see my granddaughter alive."

"That's a lie, Mr. Younger. Every biker in the Wigwam saw her. Except I'm the only man there what got pulled in."

Younger held his gaze on Wyatt's face. "I understand you have quite a history. You ever kill anyone, Mr. Dixon?"

"They say I busted a cap on a rapist."

"But you didn't do it?"

"I'm just telling you what they say. In prison you don't ever ask a man what he done. You ask, 'What do they *say* you did?' "

"I think you're a dangerous and violent man."

"Not no more, I ain't. Not unless people fuck with me."

"You can't use that language here," Younger said. "State your purpose or leave."

Wyatt folded his arms on his chest and looked at the Tudor-style house and the beige walls and the purple rockwork around the windows and entranceways and the flowers blooming as big as cantaloupes in the beds. "I just wondered why a man who owned all this would hire a small-town flatfoot and general loser like Bill Pepper to give grief to a man what ain't done him nothing. You must be pretty goddamn bored."

"I've done you no harm. Don't you dare say I have."

"What do you call tasing a man?"

"I don't even know what the term means."

"You have a reason for staring into my face like that?" Wyatt said.

"Where'd you grow up?"

"Northeast Texas, just south of the Red."

"You have unusual eyes."

"What's my place of birth have to do with my eyes?"

"Nothing. I have a feeling you want trouble. I don't think you'll be happy until you get it."

Wyatt peeled the paper off a lollipop and stuck the lollipop in his jaw. "There *is* one other thing you can tell me, because it's perplexed me for years. It's got to do with the unpleasant subject of incest and such. I heard this tale about a mountain boy in Kentucky who married a girl from the next hollow and learned on their wedding night she was a virgin. In the morning he sent her back to her folks. When his daddy asked him how come he kicked her out, the boy said she was a virgin. His pap said, 'You done the right thing, son. If she ain't good enough for her own family, she ain't good enough for ours, either.' Is that story true?"

"Get him out of here," Younger said.

The next day the sheriff called Albert's house. By chance I answered the phone. I wished I hadn't. "Where is the Horowitz woman?" he asked.

"I think she went to the airport early this morning," I said.

"She did what?"

"She's making a documentary," I said. "Can I help with something?"

"The abandoned truck that woman shot up is registered to an old man in a remote place in West Kansas. The locals found him in his barn yesterday. The coroner said he'd been dead for months. Where did Horowitz go?"

"I don't know. What do you want her for?"

"Last night we pulled a floater out of the Clark Fork. He was peppered with rounds from a nine-millimeter."

"The guy Gretchen shot?"

"How would I know? One in the head, one in the throat, one in the chest. Is that the way she does it? Let me share my feelings with you, Mr. Robicheaux. You guys are starting to be a real nuisance."

"Why us?"

"We didn't have this mess on our hands until you and your friends arrived."

"Run your bullshit on somebody else, Sheriff."

"What did you say?"

"Bill Pepper was a dirty cop and on a pad for Love Younger, and you didn't do anything about it. You turned over the investigation of a young girl's death to a bum. In the meantime, somebody put an electronic bug in Clete Purcel's cabin."

"When did this happen?"

"Probably a few days ago. What's the deal on the floater?"

"His name was Emile Schmitt. He was a private investigator in Fort Lauderdale and Atlantic City. He got his license yanked when he was charged with battery involving the apprehension of a female bail skip."

"How did the owner of the pickup die?"

"The decomposition was too great. The coroner couldn't be sure. There was a strand of looped fence wire close by."

"Do you believe we're dealing with Asa Surrette?" I asked.

"Why would a Kansas sex pervert and serial killer be mixed up with a PI from the East Coast?"

"Maybe they have a shared agenda."

"Like what?" the sheriff said.

"If I knew that, we wouldn't be having this conversation. What do you want me to tell Gretchen Horowitz, Sheriff?"

I could hear him breathing against the receiver. "I want her to ID the body. I want her to look at the man she killed."

"For what purpose?"

"Maybe it's time she becomes accountable for some of her deeds."

How about accountability from the society that produced her? I thought. "Clete and I will come with her to your office," I said, and hung up.

I hoped I was through with Elvis Bisbee, at least for the day. I wasn't. Five minutes later, he called back. "I didn't tell you something. There was a stink in the abandoned truck," he said. "It wasn't motor oil or dried blood or decayed food or a creel of fish somebody left under the seat. The stink didn't come from anything we could find."

"I'm not tracking you, Sheriff."

"It smelled like excrement. Like somebody had rubbed it into the upholstery. Except the lab tech couldn't find any. This guy Asa Surrette has a hard-on about your daughter, so maybe you and your family are part of the problem. Frankly, I wish you and your daughter had stayed in Louisiana."

"Yeah, and maybe you're in the wrong line of work," I said. This time I pulled the phone out of the jack.

At five-fifteen A.M., Gretchen climbed inside the two-engine plane volunteered by a Sierra Club member and took off two minutes later from the Missoula airport, rising out of the predawn darkness into a breathtaking view of

266

the mountaintops that surrounded the city, the streets below streaked with night-damp and car lights, the Clark Fork wending its way into the mystery and vastness of the American West. As the plane gained altitude and banked east toward the Grand Divide, she wondered if the pilot, a nice boy by the name of Percy Wolcott, had any idea who his passenger actually was, even though she had known him for several months. She wondered what his comfort level would be if he were privy to the thoughts and memories she could never free herself of. Would he be repelled? Would he be afraid?

He was good-looking, about twenty-five, with thick dark brown hair he had let grow long without affectation. He was a good pilot and soft-spoken and considerate. When they first met at a Sierra Club function in West Hollywood, she thought he was gay. When she decided he was heterosexual, she wondered why he didn't try to put moves on her, since most men did. Then she decided he was like two or three boys she had known in Miami who were shy and private and respectful toward women and nothing like their peers, most of whom were visceral and loud and, when they got her in the backseat, had a way of moving her hand down to their nether regions.

What a drag, she thought, realizing she had been guilty of falling into the national obsession of classifying human beings in terms of their sexual behavior. *Do Europeans and Brits do that? Nice to meet you, gay guy. Thank you, but I'm trans. How about you? You look like you might be hetero. Actually, I'm more of an across-the-board premature ejaculator, thank you very much.*

At five thousand feet, they hit turbulence that shook the plane and caused Percy to look at her in a protective and reassuring way, and in that moment, in the gentleness of his expression, she knew that her great concern was not about bigotry and obsession and the limited thinking of others; it was her fear that her friend Percy would be horrified if he knew the history of Gretchen Horowitz, that his kind validation of her would be withdrawn.

In junior college she had read an autobiographical account written by a white man who was kidnapped as a child from a sod house in Oklahoma and raised among Comanche Indians. He grew up in the shadow of Quanah Parker and participated in atrocities that were the worst she had ever seen described on a printed page. The lines she remembered in particular were the elderly frontiersman's depiction of himself as a white teenage boy, smeared with war paint and sweat and the dust of battle, a boy who, in the old man's words, "thirsted to kill" and did things that were depraved and cruel beyond comprehension. When she read the descriptions, she realized she had found a kindred spirit, one who lived with thoughts and desires that might forever separate her from the rest of the human family.

Bill Pepper had robbed her in every way possible. He had lied to her and turned her charity into a sword he drove into her breast. He had drugged her and bound her and systematically degraded her and mocked her while he did it. Then he escaped into the Great Shade at the hands of another and now lay safe in a stainless steel drawer inside a refrigerated room that smelled of formaldehyde. *Where do you put your bloodlust now?* she asked herself.

Why did people give so much importance to drug and alcohol addiction? The day you gave up dope and booze was the day you got better. The day you gave up bloodlust was the day you allowed a succubus to devour the remnants of your self-respect.

"There's coffee in a thermos and an egg sandwich in the canvas bag behind your seat," Percy said.

"I'm fine," she replied.

"I can get us into Canada today if you want," he said.

"I've got too much footage on the shale operation. In some ways, it's not effective."

He glanced sideways at her, not understanding.

"The areas that are most damaged up there are already totally destroyed," she said. "People don't see what the area used to look like. They only see it after it's been turned into a gravel pit. They're also depressed by the fact they can't do anything about it, so they don't want to look at it or think about it anymore."

"I bet you're going to be famous one day," he said.

"Why would I be famous?"

"Because you're the real thing."

"What's the real thing?"

"You think the work you do is more important than you are," he said. "Hang on. There's some weather up ahead. Once we're over Rogers Pass, we'll be in the clear."

She drifted off to sleep as the plane bounced under her, the rain spidering and flattening on the glass. When she awoke, they had just popped out of the clouds, and she saw the sharp gray peaks of mountains directly below her. They made her think of sharks clustered inside a giant saltwater pool with no bottom. "Who was that guy this morning?" Percy said.

"Which guy?"

"The one who dropped you at the airport."

"There wasn't any guy. I drove myself. My pickup is parked in the lot."

"There was an older man in the waiting

room. I thought maybe he was your father, the way he was looking at you."

"No," she said. "My father is probably still asleep at Albert Hollister's ranch. What did he look like?"

"Long face, high forehead. I don't remember. Can you get the thermos for me?"

"Think hard, Percy."

He shook his head. "I don't remember. Just a guy, about fifty-five or so. Older guys never look at you?"

"I scare them away."

"*You?* That's a laugh."

"You said I was the real thing. That's kind of you, but you're assigning me a virtue I don't have. I love movies. I've loved them all my life. I never knew why until I read an interview with Dennis Hopper. He grew up poor in a little place outside Dodge City, Kansas. All he remembered of Dodge City was the heat and the smell of the feeder lots. Every Saturday he went to town with his grandmother and sold eggs. She gave him part of the egg money to go to a cowboy movie. Hopper said the movie theater became the real world and Dodge City became the imaginary one. When he was in his teens, he went out to Hollywood. His first role was in *Rebel Without a Cause,* with James Dean. His second movie was *Giant,* with James Dean again. Not bad, huh?"

"People like you."

"What?"

"The Sierra Club people like you." Percy leaned forward, seeming to stare at a point beyond the starboard wing. "Check out the Cessna at three o'clock."

"What about it?"

"He's been with us awhile. Is anybody following you around?" His eyes crinkled.

"Maybe I upset a few people in Florida and Louisiana."

"You'll never make the cut as a villain, Gretchen. Here comes the Cessna. I didn't tell you I used to drop fire retardant for the United States Forest Service. Let's go down on the deck and see if he wants to stay with us."

They had just flown through clouds above a mountain peak into sunlight and wide vistas of patchwork wheat and cattle land. Percy took the twin-engine down the mountain's slope like a solitary leaf gliding on the wind, the plane's shadow racing across the tips of the trees. Gretchen felt as though she were dropping through an elevator shaft. Percy leveled out at the base of the mountain and began to gain altitude again, the engines straining, a barn and a white ranch house couched inside poplar trees miniaturizing as Gretchen looked out the window. "Where'd that red Cessna go?" Percy said.

"I don't know. Just don't do that again," she said.

272

"Everything's cool," he replied. He touched a religious medal that hung from a chain on his instrument panel. "What can go wrong when you have Saint Christopher with you?"

"I don't find your attitude reassuring," she said.

They flew along the edges of the Grand Divide and Glacier National Park, where the flat plains seemed to collide with the mountains. On the western end of the Blackfoot Reservation, Gretchen saw several test wells, one close to the border of the park. The plane climbed higher into the mountains and made a wide turn over Marias Pass. She could see snow packed inside the trees on the crests and the slopes, and deep down in the canyon, an emerald river that wound through boulders that were as big as houses.

She pulled open her window. "Get down as close as you can," she said.

"What are you doing?"

"Filming. That's why we're here."

"You want to fly through that canyon?"

"You've got to do something for kicks."

He blew out his breath. "I underestimated you," he said.

You can say that again, she thought.

He made another turn and headed straight at Marias Pass, dropping lower and lower, the trees standing out individually on the peaks, snow melting on rocks, a train trestle glinting above a gorge, Gretchen hanging out the window with her camera, her hair whipping in the wind.

Her face and hands were cold, her shirt was ballooning, her ears were deafened by the wind stream and the roar of the engines. None of that mattered. Through the lens of the camera, she was capturing topography whose geological age could only be guessed at. Even when the train trestle sped by and she could smell the trees and the coldness of the snow down below and see a canyon wall approaching the plane, she never took her eye from the lens.

She felt the plane lift violently, the engines shuddering, the wings stressing, as Percy took them along the edge of a cliff and over a mountain crest where the tips of the Douglas fir were probably no more than ten feet below the plane's belly. Percy turned in to the sun and flew toward the plains, his hands opening and closing on the yoke. She sat back down in the seat and shut the window. "Thanks," she said.

"Thanks?"

"Yeah, that was very nice of you."

"We came within about three seconds of pancaking into that cliff. Where have I heard that line 'You've got to do something for kicks'?"

Rebel Without a Cause."

He smiled, his expression like a young boy's. "You ever read a biography of Ernest

Hemingway?"

"Probably not."

"He used to say his third wife, Martha Gell-horn, had legs that were six feet long. That's what you look like, Gretchen. You're the most beautiful woman I've ever seen. On top of it, you're a beautiful person."

"Maybe there are some things you don't know about me. Maybe you shouldn't be telling me about your feelings."

"Gay guys hit on you all the time?"

"You're gay?"

"What did you think I am?"

"A gorgeous man." She got up on her knees and put her hand on the back of his neck and kissed him on the cheek. Then she did it again.

"Jesus Christ, Gretchen."

"What?"

"Cut it out or I'll have to stop being gay," he said.

They landed on the rez at an airstrip mowed out of a pasture, a windsock at the far end straightening in the breeze. The sky was full of dust and pollen and chaff blowing from a field where a farmer was harrowing. It was a bleak place devoid of trees or shade, the ground studded with rocks, and tangles of mustard weed were bouncing across it like jackrabbits. At the crossroads was a general store with two gas pumps in front and a col-lapsed barn in back. One of the pumps had been vandalized and was powdered with rust. Gretchen looked at the sign over the door. It said DEER HEART ONE STOP.

"You've been here before?" she said.

"A couple of times. To gas up and hire a driver."

"Deer Heart was the name of a teenage girl who was murdered outside Missoula. She was the adopted granddaughter of Love Younger."

"That bastard adopts Indian kids?"

"His son did. The one called Caspian."

"These people have enough trouble without the Youngers taking their kids. I wonder if there's a curse on this country. You ever hear of the Baker Massacre?"

"No."

"In 1870 an alcoholic army major by the name of Eugene Baker murdered two hundred and seventy Piegan Blackfeet up on the Marias River. Most of them were women and children. It was January, and the survivors were driven into freezing water or out on the plains to die. They hadn't committed a crime against anyone. I know a wildlife photographer who camped on the Marias to take some pictures at sunrise and said he heard the sounds of women and children wailing in the wind. It scared him so bad he couldn't start his truck."

"What's the story on the Deer Heart family?"

"There aren't many good stories on the rez.

Check out the jail in Browning on Saturday night."

A bell tinkled on the door when they went inside. The proprietor was an old man with steel-gray braids and blue eyes and skin that looked as soft as tallow. He said if they wanted to hire a car and a driver to tour and photograph the area, he would call his nephew, who lived a short distance away. Gretchen studied a framed photograph on the wall beside an ancient refrigerator. "Is this your family?" she asked.

"That's us, ten years back. Ain't many of us still around," the old man said. He was sitting on a stool behind the counter, surrounded by shelves of canned goods, his shoulders stooped.

In the photo, several elderly people were standing under a picnic shelter. In front were a young couple and three small children. "Is Angel Deer Heart in this picture?" Gretchen asked.

"You know Angel?" the old man said.

"Just by name. She was adopted by the Younger family, wasn't she?"

"Her mother and father were killed on the highway north of Browning. They got drunk and went straight into a truck. The children were taken by the adoption agency. Angel is the only one left."

"Pardon?" Gretchen said.

"I heard her brother and sister died of

meningitis in a hospital in Minnesota. You heard something about Angel? Is she doing okay?"

Gretchen didn't answer.

"We don't want to take a lot of your time," Percy said. "Can you call your nephew for us?"

"If you ever see her, tell her to write home and tell her great-uncle Nap how she's doing," the old man said.

Gretchen looked blankly at the canned goods on the shelves. She opened the refrigerator and took out two bottles of pop. "How much are these?" she said.

"A dollar each," he said. "Are you all right, miss?"

"I get airsick sometimes," she replied.

She and Percy went out on the porch to wait for the nephew. A grass fire was crawling up a row of brown hills in the distance. The dust and smoke had turned the sunlight into pink haze, more like evening than morning. "You really think this place is haunted?" she said.

"That's what the Indians want to believe."

"Why should they want to do that?"

"As bad as the past was, they were probably better off then," he replied.

A plane came out of nowhere and flew above the store and made a turn over the airstrip, then climbed into the smoke rising off the hills. "There's our friend in the

Cessna," she said. "I think those are Love Younger's people up there."

"Forget it. We're on the right side of history," Percy said, watching the plane grow smaller inside the smoke. He looked at her. "You don't agree?"

"The ovens at Auschwitz were full of people who were on the right side," she said.

It was almost sunset when they landed in Missoula. She was tired and dirty, her clothes smelling of smoke, her body stiff from sitting in the plane's passenger seat without enough room for her legs. Percy was going to refuel and take off for Spokane, where he was supposed to meet his partner. "Can I buy you dinner?" he said.

"I'm going to use the restroom and head home. Thanks for a great day."

"If I ever decide to cheat on my partner, could I give you a call?"

"That's not funny."

"I don't think before I speak sometimes."

"Percy?"

He waited. She looked at the youthfulness in his face, the moral clarity in his eyes, and wanted to tell him something but didn't know what.

"You worried about me?" he said.

"Sometimes I think I'm a jinx. Is your plane okay?"

"Did it seem okay when we flew through

the canyon above the Marias?"

"Take care of yourself. Call me on my cell when you get to Spokane."

"You're a worrywart," he said.

Later, on her way to use the women's room, she felt rather than saw a man standing at the corner of her vision, his eyes dissecting her. It was a sensation she could compare only with a spider crawling across her face in her sleep as she lay helpless inside a dream from which she couldn't wake. She shifted the weight of her backpack from one shoulder to the other, her expression flat, turning her head slightly to get a look at a figure silhouetted against the entranceway.

His face was shadowed by the sunlight shining through the front of the building. She pretended to study a stuffed grizzly bear in a giant showcase, its upraised paws and bared teeth looming above her. In the reflection of the glass, she watched the man walking toward the waiting room. She turned slowly and saw a late-middle-aged man about six feet, with a tapered waist and hair combed in ducktails like a 1950s hood's. He wore an unpressed white shirt and Roman sandals and black socks and a cheap brown belt and rumpled slacks with dirt on the cuffs. A tobacco pipe was stuck through one of his belt loops. For just a moment she smelled an odor that didn't belong inside an air terminal.

Then she lost sight of him in the concourse.

He had gone into either the men's room or the lounge. She walked through a crowd in front of the souvenir store and stood at the entrance to the lounge and studied the people eating at the tables or drinking at the bar or playing the video poker machines. If he was in there, she didn't see him.

She waited in front of the men's room for two minutes, then pushed the door open and went inside. A man at a urinal grinned at her. "One of us is in the wrong place," he said.

She dropped her backpack on the floor and put a hand inside her tote bag. "You see a rumpled-looking guy with a duck ass in back?"

"A what?"

"Zip up and get out."

A fat man came out of a stall, tucking in his shirt with his thumbs. "You, too," she said. "Beat it."

"Who do you think you are?" the fat man asked.

"I think there's a bad guy in one of these stalls. Now get the fuck out, unless you want to catch a stray bullet," she said.

Both men rushed out, looking over their shoulders at her. She walked the length of the stalls but saw no feet under the doors. She began kicking open each door, slamming it back against the partition, the Airweight .38 special in her right hand.

They were all empty. As she kicked open

the last stall, an odor rose into her face that made her gag.

She backed away from the stall and blew out her breath and dropped the Airweight in her tote bag just as the front door opened and a tall man in a Stetson entered the room.

"Come on in. I went in the wrong room. I'm on my way out," she said.

"No problem," he said. He cleared his throat loudly and pressed the back of his wrist against his mouth. "Good Lord!" he said.

"Tell me about it," she said. "You see a guy in Roman sandals with ducktails out there?"

"Come to think of it, I did."

"Where?"

"Going out the front. Is there something a little strange going on here?"

She went back into the concourse, expecting to see security personnel heading toward her. The concourse, the souvenir shop, the waiting area, and the lines at the counters were as they had been when she entered the restroom.

She went through the revolving door onto the sidewalk. The air was warm, the sun little more than a spark between the hills, the clouds in the west orange against a blue sky. She felt a wave of exhaustion wash through her. Was the man with the 1950s hairstyle the same one she had seen at the bar in the Depot, the same one who had tried to kill her below the Higgins Street Bridge?

Was the abominable odor in the men's room his? Was she losing her mind? She was too tired to answer her own questions. She started walking toward her pickup. Percy Wolcott's twin-engine flew overhead into the sun's afterglow, its propellers spinning with a silvery light, almost in tribute to the day. As the drone of the engines faded, she walked farther into the parking lot, the equipment in her backpack knocking against her side.

Then she heard a sound that was like dry thunder, a rumbling that had no source, a reverberation that seemed to bounce off rock walls and the trunks of trees, as though magnifying itself, refusing to be gathered into the sky.

She stared at the hills, dark with shadow on the slopes and lit from behind by clouds that were as orange as Halloween pumpkins. *Don't think those thoughts,* she told herself. *Do not look in his direction. Do not become the jinx you called yourself.*

Others in the parking lot were pointing toward the west. At what? How can you point at a sound? Before she could think about the denial in her question, she saw a fire burning inside the trees on a distant hill and a dark mushroom cloud rising from it.

She thought of the twin-engine parked unguarded on the airstrip, the elderly Indian man in the general store, perhaps asleep behind the counter; a red Cessna circling above, radioing to someone else the location of Percy's plane.

She had to sit down on the bumper of a truck, her eyes tightly shut, to keep from losing her balance.

CHAPTER 13

Thursday morning, Clete and I kept our word to the sheriff and drove Gretchen to identify the body his deputies had pulled out of the Clark Fork, west of town. It was obvious she couldn't have cared less about the name of the dead man in the drawer at the mortuary. Her eyes roved over the bluish-white sheen on his refrigerated skin and the wounds in his head and throat and chest and side without seeming to register any of it.

"You've never seen him before?" the sheriff said.

"He's the man I shot, if that's what you're asking," she replied.

"You never saw him before that?"

"No."

"You're sure?"

"Why would I say no if I meant something else?"

"He worked out of Fort Lauderdale and Atlantic City. You spent most of your life in Miami. His name was Emile Schmitt. He was a PI and bail-skip chaser. He also worked for an armored car service. You're not familiar with that name?"

"No," she said.

"But you recognize him as the man you shot and killed?"

"It was dark, but yes, I believe this is the man who tried to kill me and who I shot and killed, after giving him every chance to surrender. Is there something about the words that you don't understand?"

"You seem to have a built-in defense mechanism that kicks into gear whenever you're asked a question," the sheriff said.

"I told you what occurred. You can characterize it in any fashion you like."

"The pickup truck driven by the other man trying to kill you was stolen from a farmer in Kansas. The farmer may have been murdered. Or maybe you already know that."

"Clete and Dave told me."

"Do you believe the driver could be Asa Surrette?"

"How would I know who he is? Maybe I saw him last night in the airport."

"Would you repeat that?"

"At the airport, I might have seen a guy who tried to hit on me at the Depot. Maybe he was the guy in the stolen truck. Maybe he was following me yesterday. My friend Percy Wolcott died in his plane last night, right after dropping me at the airport. Have you been to the site yet?"

"That's the jurisdiction of the National Transportation Safety Board. Let's not change the subject. From what we could learn, Emile Schmitt's clients as a PI included several attorneys who represent the Mafia in South Florida and New Jersey. I think you knew the same people. Except you claim to have no knowledge of this man, that your life and his intersected by coincidence in a small city in western Montana."

"I'm not making a claim about anything," she said. "I'm telling you what happened. Percy's plane was parked several hours on an airstrip east of Marias Pass. The airstrip was next to a general store owned by the great-uncle of Angel Deer Heart. Think that's co-incidence, Sheriff? I think somebody put a bomb on that plane and the timer went off late."

"I'm not making the connection."

"All of this has something to do with Angel Deer Heart. But your investigation never gets beyond an ex-convict rodeo clown."

The sheriff started to speak, but Gretchen cut him off. "Bill Pepper abducted me after he violated every inch of my body he could rub his dick on. If I could have gotten to him before someone else did, I would have clicked off his switch. So would my father. We didn't have the chance. If that doesn't sit too good with you, go fuck yourself."

"You're an angry woman, Ms. Horowitz, and sometimes angry women do irrational things."

I could hear Clete breathing through his nose, almost feel the heat radiating from his body. "Sheriff, this isn't getting us anywhere," I said.

"Stay out of this, Mr. Robicheaux."

"No, sir, you're out of line," I said. "That crack was about as dumb a remark I ever heard an officer of the law make."

I could see pale spots in his face, his hand tightening on the edge of the drawer that contained the earthly remains of a man who, in death, had the significance of a doorstop. The sheriff's discomfort was obvious. He knew he was wrong, and it was not a time to crowd the batter any more than I had.

"Sheriff, you found the perpetrator's semen on the body of Angel Deer Heart," I said. "You went to the data bank for a match, right? What did you find out? Are we dealing with Asa Surrette or not?"

"The specimen got lost," he said, his face reddening.

The only sound in the room was the hum of the refrigeration.

"Bill Pepper?" I said.

"I think he was drunk. Whatever he did with the specimen, we can't find it."

"I have to ask you a question," I said. "Why did you let a man like that stay on in your department?"

"At one time he was a good cop. When his marriage went south, he started drinking. Maybe you've never had problems like that. I have. So I gave him a chance. I wish I hadn't. I apologize to Ms. Horowitz for the remark I made. But I'll be damned if I'm going to have gunfights in the streets of my city. And nobody is going to show disrespect for my office, either."

Fair enough, I thought. *He's not a bad guy. Time to boogie and leave others to their own destiny. Err on the side of charity and let disengagement become a virtue.*

"I heard Percy Wolcott's plane explode. Not crash. Explode," Gretchen said. "Forget the apology, Sheriff. Then pull your head out of your ass and do your job for a change."

If you are a parent, you know the following to be true: Even though your child has grown into adulthood, you never see the man or the woman; you see only the little boy or the little girl.

Whenever I looked at Alafair, I saw the little El Salvadoran girl I pulled from a submerged plane that went down in the salt by Southwest Pass. I saw a little girl I called Alf who wore a Donald Duck cap with a quacking bill and a T-shirt with a smiling whale named Baby Orca and tennis shoes embossed with the words LEFT and RIGHT on the respective toes. The image of that little El Salvadoran girl will always hover before me like a hologram.

Why get into that now? Because all of the events I have narrated started with an attack upon Alafair's person while she was jogging on the hill below Albert Hollister's ranch. Somehow the fact that her attacker may have been Asa Surrette had fallen through the cracks.

Did Asa Surrette survive the crash of the prison van into the gas truck, then hook up with a fellow predator and come to Montana in pursuit of Alafair? It was possible. But Emile Schmitt did not have that kind of history and had been on retainer by law firms that represented members of the Mafia. The Mob is many things, but it doesn't hire serial predators to look out for its interests.

Let me make a confession. I would like to say I became a police officer with the NOPD in order to make the world a better place. I became a cop in order to deal with a black lesion that had been growing on my brain, if not my soul, since I was a child. My parents embarked upon the worst course human beings are capable of: They destroyed their home and their family and finally themselves. If there is any greater form of loss, I do not know what it is. It stays with you every day of your life; you wake with it at dawn and carry it with you into your nocturnal hours. There is no respite or cure, and if your experience has been like mine, you have accepted that only death will separate you from the abiding sense of nothingness you wake with at the first touch of light on the horizon.

A man named Mack ruined my mother, and she helped turn my father, Big Aldous, into a sad, bewildered, raging alcoholic who once wrecked Antlers Pool Room and tore up seven Lafayette police officers with his bare fists. I had no feeling about the Vietcong or the NVA, but I put Mack's face on every enemy soldier I killed. When I came back home, I rented an apartment in the French Quarter and slept with a .45 under my pillow, a round in the chamber, not in fear but in hope that someone would try to break in.

Please forgive my obsession. My own story isn't important. The story of the human condition is. If you see your natal home destroyed, one of two things will happen: You will let the loss of your childhood continue to rob you of all happiness for the rest of your life, or you will build a family of your own, a good one, made up of people you truly love and in whose company you are genuinely happy. If you are unlucky, born under a dark star, violent men will ferret their way into the life of your family and re-create the act of theft that ruined your childhood. From that moment on, you will enter a landscape that only people who have stacked time in the Garden of Gethsemane will understand.

You will discover that the portrayal of law enforcement on television has nothing to do with reality. Chances are, you will be on your own. Perhaps you will find out that the suspected perpetrator has been released on bail without your being notified. The detective assigned to your case might do his best, but you will sense he is drowning in his workload and not always happy to see you. Your phone calls will go unanswered. You will become a nuisance and begin to talk incessantly about your personal problems, to strangers as well as friends. When you think it's all over, you may receive a taunting call from the person who raped or murdered your loved one.

Sound like an exaggeration? Dial up someone who has been there and see what he has to say.

I remember sitting naked and ninety-proof in an Orleans Parish holding cell, flexing my hand, my body running with sweat, as I watched the veins swell in my forearm while I fantasized about a man I was going to kill as soon as I was released. The target of my anger was a Mafia boss I normally referred to as a three-hundred-pound load of whale shit whose name wasn't worth remembering. I changed my mind when one of his gumballs shot my half brother, Jimmie, in the head and blinded him in one eye. That was when I decided to get back on that old-time lock-and-load rock and roll and turn a certain Mafia boss into wallpaper. At the time I thought and did these things, I was a police officer sworn to protect and serve.

Now I felt great shame at having doubted Alafair's conviction about Asa Surrette surviving the wreck of the prison van. I felt I had not only let down my daughter, I had joined the ranks of deadbeat cops who turn a cynical ear to those who need and deserve help the most.

When we returned to Albert's ranch from the mortuary, I made three calls to Kansas. The people there are among the best on earth, but bureaucracy is bureaucracy wherever you go. I've always suspected bureaucracy serves an ancillary purpose in the same way the human body absorbs an infection and prevents it from getting to the brain. Bureaucracy protects the people in charge from accountability. My efforts on the phone with the Kansas officials were beyond worthless. I was left with the impression that I had just conducted three separate conversations with a grain elevator.

I went out on the deck and sat on a chair in the sunshine, surrounded by huge pots of purple and blue and pink petunias, the wind ruffling the flowers. Molly came out and sat beside me. "Don't let it get to you," she said.

"Talking to people with CYBS?"

"What's CYBS?"

"Cover-your-butt syndrome."

"You think it's Surrette?"

"It's somebody who's pure evil."

"You think he killed Bill Pepper?"

"He didn't just kill him."

She waited for me to go on.

"You don't want to hear the details, Molly. Whoever killed Pepper was a monster. Surrette may be one of the worst serial killers in American history. He's cruel to the bone. I don't want to tell you what he did to the children he murdered."

"Don't talk about it anymore."

"I want to kill him."

"You can't carry around those kinds of thoughts. It's like drinking poison."

"It's the way I feel. If he gets his hands on Alafair, she's going to die a terrible death."

"Stop it, Dave."

I clenched my hands on my knees, stiffening my arms. In the distance, I could see Alafair's Honda coming up the dirt road, driving faster than was her custom.

"Did you hear me?" Molly said.

"I've dealt with only one other man like Surrette. Remember Legion Guidry?"

"I remember what you said about him. When he was an overseer, he sexually abused black women in the fields."

"What else did I say about him?"

"I disregarded that, Dave. I don't believe we should think of our fellow human beings in those terms, no matter how bad they are."

"I told you I thought he might be the devil. He had a smell about him like none I ever smelled on a human being."

She got up from her chair. "I love you, but I won't listen to this."

I sat for what seemed a long time in the chair without moving. When Alafair turned under the arch into the driveway, I got up and walked down the steps and across the lawn to meet her. The back of my shirt was peppered with sweat in the wind, the flowers in Albert's gardens bright with drops of water from the sprinklers. I wanted to gather Alafair in my arms and take her and Molly to a place ten thousand miles away, perhaps to an Edenic island on the Pacific Rim, like in the stories of Somerset Maugham and James Michener. But the canker in the rose is real, and Polynesian paradises long ago had been turned into cheap farms to supply the breadfruit fed to Caribbean slaves.

Alafair got out of the car and walked toward me, her fingers holding a sheet of lined yellow paper by one corner. "This was under my windshield wiper when I came out of the post office," she said.

I got my handkerchief from my pocket and took the paper from her and read it. The message had been hand-printed with a felt-tip pen, each of the letters like a block or a cube, as stiff and linear as a hieroglyph. I could hear the wind coursing through the maples and the ornamental crab apple. Molly had followed me down from the deck and was looking over my shoulder. "What is it?" she said.

"Read it," I replied, holding the letter by the corners.

"I don't need to. Just tell me what it is," she said.

"Read it," I repeated.

Her eyes followed one line into the next, the blood draining from around her mouth.

"Where are you going?" I said.

"To get that goddamn do-nothing sheriff on the telephone," she said.

I wanted to laugh or at least to smile to take the tension and angst out of the moment. But humor was not an option. That's the hold evil has upon us. There is nothing funny about the kind of evil represented by men like Asa Surrette or Legion Guidry. Charlie Manson was funny because he was so inept and cowardly, he had to use a collection of mindless vegetables to carry out his crimes. I was becoming convinced that creatures like Asa Surrette and my old antagonist Legion did not have human origins. They came from somewhere else. Where? you ask. I didn't want to think about the possibilities.

The letter read:

Dear Alafair,

It's so good to be in touch with you again. Sorry to hear about Ms. Horowitz's friend the weenie-boy who smacked into the mountain. It must be terrible knowing you're going to crash and you can't do anything about it. Oh well, he's a crispy critter now. Poor little fag. Boohoo.

Tell Ms. Horowitz she should stay out of the boys' room or someone will think she's not all girl.

Are you still interested in doing a book on me? I think there's enough material for a movie. I will tell you later who I would like to see cast in my role.

As ever,
A.

Wyatt Dixon had never been keen on picnics, at least not until Bertha Phelps called and invited him to go on one way up the Blackfoot Valley, a lovely spot she said she'd found on a drainage that flowed down through cottonwood trees into the river. When she met him at the bridge by his house, she was wearing a flowery sundress and a straw hat with a blue band and brand-new white tennis shoes that looked cute on her large feet. She was carrying a wicker basket loaded with cheese and cold cuts and potato salad and French bread from the deli, plus a half-gallon capped jar of homemade lemonade. "You put me in mind of this countrywoman who drove an ice cream truck out to the rural area where I growed up," he said. "She had apples in her cheeks and smelled like peach ice cream. I asked her once if I could hide under her dress and run off with her."

"You have a way with words, Mr. Dixon. Are you telling me you like big women? I might be too big for you."

"Ma'am?"

"You're trying to make me blush."

If she wanted to turn his head into a Mixmaster, she was doing a good job of it.

They drove in his truck up the Blackfoot Valley and crossed a wood bridge and entered a wide alluvial landscape that seemed left over from the first days of creation. Wyatt shifted into four-wheel drive and clattered over a bed of white rocks and parked up on the slope and lifted the wicker basket out of the camper shell. "I declare, Miss Bertha, there must be thirty pounds of food in here," he said.

"You're a nice gentleman in every way, Wyatt, but you must stop calling me 'miss.' We are not on the plantation," she said.

"I need to own up to something." He folded his arms and looked at the ground, a strange tingling in his wrists that he didn't understand. "I hope it don't make you mad."

"You know what the problem is? You're not used to sharing your feelings. How could anyone get mad on a lovely afternoon like this?" She gazed at a towering cliff on the far side of the river and at the thickness of the pines on the top. "In a place like this, we shouldn't have a care in the world."

"I went out to Love Younger's place and had some words with him. I asked if you worked for him. He didn't have no idea who you were. I was glad."

"Why would I be angry about that?"

"I doubted your word."

"Spread the blanket while I make our sandwiches. Tell me about your life in the rodeo."

He shook his head. "You're an educated woman. Why are you interested in a man such as myself?"

"Mine to know."

"There's people here'bouts who'd take a shithog to church before they'd invite me on a picnic. It's not adding up for me."

"Maybe I like you. Did you think of that?"

Wyatt rubbed his wrists, his facial skin as smooth and expressionless as clay, his eyes following an osprey gliding low over the river. "I don't let people use me," he said. "I just walk away from them. In the past I did a whole lot worse than that."

"Someone has taught you that a good woman would never be attracted to you," she said. "Someone did you a great wrong."

"I ain't good at this. That's a pretty dress. It looks like it come from a florist."

She was making the sandwiches on the tailgate of his truck. She turned her head toward him and smiled, her face lighting in a way that made something drop inside him. "You're one of the most interesting men I have ever met. I think one of the nicest, too."

"You got a way about you that ain't ordinary. You're a powerful woman."

"I'm not sure what you mean."

"You don't let men push you around. It's something a man senses. It's what men admire in a woman most."

"What are you trying to say?"

The river was wide and flat here, the grass tall and green on both banks of the river, the slopes heavily wooded near the base of cliffs that were gray and smooth and rose straight up into the sky. Why did he feel enclosed, almost suffocated, by either his situation or the feelings churning inside him? Behind her, he could see a white-tailed buck on the edge of the timber, the points of his antlers curled and sharp and hard-looking in the light. There was not a house or a soul in sight. He looked at Bertha, then let his eyes slide off her face. "You've been hiding something. I need to know what it is," he said.

"I thought you might be a bad man. You're not. There's a deep sense of goodness in you, that somebody tried to take away from you."

"That ain't true. Nobody's ever taken anything away from me. They know better than to try."

"You consider yourself saved, don't you?"

"I don't take nothing for granted. The state shot my head full of electricity and made me drink a bathtub-load of chemicals. Sometimes I think I hear my brain gurgling."

"Fix us some lemonade. It's so pleasant out here. When I come to a place like this, I stop thinking about all my cares and worries. Smell the wind? I bet that's what the world smelled like when this was a field of ice lilies."

"What cares and worries would a lady like you have?"

"More than you know. But you're not the source of them."

He removed his cowboy hat and set it on her head.

"Why'd you do that?" she said.

"It looks better on you than on me."

The entirety of her face seemed suffused with a pink loveliness that he never thought he would associate with a woman who had upper arms as big as hams. His hat slipped down on the corner of her eye. "Go ahead," she said.

"Go ahead what?"

"Do whatever you're fixing to do."

"I knew you were from the South." He

lifted his hat off her head and let it hang from his fingers behind her back while he kissed her on the mouth. Then he put his arms around her and did it again. She leaned back, still in his arms, and looked into his eyes, her stomach against his, her face glowing. "You feel like a stack of bricks," she said. "Or maybe a leather bag full of rocks. Did anyone ever tell you that?"

"Not recently."

"Your physique is very appealing, Mr. Dixon."

"It's mighty bright out here in the sun. Can we take our blanket over yonder in the trees?"

She blew out her breath. "Right here is lovely," she said. "Oh, my heavens, what a marvelous afternoon. Hurry, now. Don't be embarrassed. What finer place for love than the earth? That's Robert Frost."

He didn't catch that last part, but he didn't really care. Congress with Bertha Phelps was not what he'd expected. Over the years most of his relationships with women had little to do with any consideration outside his skin. This time he felt he had stepped inside a rainbow. No, that wasn't correct; it was more than that. Bertha's sexual embrace of his body was like riding a winged horse or giving himself up to a cresting wave or swimming through warm water carpeted with flowers, and all the while she kept moaning his name in his ear. A few minutes later he felt a weakness shudder through his body and a dam break in his loins, and he held her tighter, more dependently, than he'd ever held a woman in his life, his breath coming hard in his throat, his head on her breast.

Then he felt her stiffen under him and knew that something was terribly wrong. When he pushed himself up on his arms, her face was sweaty and white and disjointed with fear and surprise, her eyes fastened on someone standing directly behind him.

CHAPTER 14

He looked over his shoulder and saw not one but three men silhouetted against the sky, all wearing gloves and plastic masks that were a bright metallic gray and gave the impression of a weeping specter with a downturned mouth and cheeks pooled with shadow. One of the men was holding a police baton, a lanyard looped around his wrist. He stepped forward as though on cue and swung it across Wyatt's ear, putting his shoulder into it, snapping it like a baseball batter connecting with a fat pitch.

Wyatt suspected his eyes rolled but couldn't be sure. The trees and mountains and sky suddenly reduced themselves to a pinpoint of light inside a sea of blackness, then the pinpoint disappeared, too. Wyatt fell sideways into the grass, naked except for his unsnapped cowboy shirt, a trickle of blood sliding down his neck.

When he woke, the shadow of his truck was in the same place where it had been when he was hit with the baton, but Bertha Phelps was gone. His hands were tied behind him with rope, and his wallet and its contents were scattered on the ground. He got on his knees and worked the rope under the bumper, then rose to a squat and strained against the rope to the point where he thought his molars would break. He took a breath and tried again, this time tearing the skin off his knuckles. Suddenly, he was free and standing erect, his head throbbing, his hands bleeding. He pulled on his underwear and Wranglers and searched for his Tony Lama boots and the six-inch bone-handled Solingen clasp knife he carried. They were not there. Neither was the money in his wallet.

Who were they? Some guys fresh out of the can, maybe wiped out on crystal? These days the jails were full of guys with no class, all rut and penis and shit for brains. Where was Bertha?

The wind changed and he heard her voice up the slope, deep in the trees, and he had no doubt what the three men were doing to her.

He opened the back of the camper shell. His 1892 lever-action Winchester lay on the floor, but the shells for it were at his house. He reached into a duffel bag where he kept his camping gear and removed an army-surplus entrenching tool. The blade was locked into the straight-out position of a shovel, the edges of the blade filed clean and sharp. His gaze swept across the hillside, then he ran to the left of where the men had probably entered the trees with Bertha, the hatched scar tissue on his back as white as snow.

The floor of the forest was soft with damp grass and seepage from a spring in the hillside. To his right, inside a widely spaced stand of ponderosa lit by a solitary band of sunlight, two men were holding Bertha on her back while the third man attempted to mount her. When she tried to cry out, one man scooped a handful of dirt from the ground and poured it into her mouth.

They were still wearing their masks and apparently had not heard him coming. When they heard his bare feet running across the forest floor, they twisted their heads toward him in unison, frozen in time, like men who'd thought they possessed total control of the environment only to discover they had just locked themselves in a box with the most dangerous man they had ever met.

Wyatt's upper body was streaming sweat and stenciled with nests of veins when he struck the first blow, catching the man on top of Bertha across the back, slicing through his shirt, slinging blood through the air. He wielded the e-tool like a medieval battle-ax and didn't aim his blows or plan his attack.

The power of his swing and the level of energy and rage that went into each blow was devastating and similar in effect to a jackhammer deconstructing a plywood house. Oddly, there was little sound inside the grove of columnlike pines, other than the muffled grunts his adversaries made behind their masks whenever he hit them.

Bertha got to her feet, stumbling off balance down the hill, her backside covered with dirt and twigs and leaves and pine needles. Wyatt kicked a man in the groin and split his scalp when he doubled over, and was sure he broke a third man's ribs when he stomped him on the ground.

There was blood on the trunks of the trees. Wyatt was revolving in a circle, hitting his assailants as many times as he could, inflicting as much bone damage as possible before their superiority in numbers took its toll. One man fell out of the fight and scrambled away on his hands and knees, then rose to his feet and began running, his mask off, his long blond hair tumbling from a bandana that had come loose on his head. That was the moment when Wyatt made a critical mistake. He took time to try to see the running man's face and instead saw a hand with a rock in it swing from the corner of his vision. His eyebrow split against the bone, and he tumbled down the side of a ravine into a creek bed.

The man who had struck the blow followed

Wyatt in his slide down to the water's edge. He wore a painter's cap pulled down tightly on his scalp and a long-sleeved black shirt and tan strap overalls. The hair on his chest resembled gold wires. Wyatt was standing in the creek, his feet freezing. He had another problem. Just before he went over the side of the ravine, he felt his ankle fold under him, like a thick tuber bent back on itself.

The man in the painter's hat opened Wyatt's six-inch clasp knife and held it out from his body, blade up. "I'm gonna cut off your sack, Jack," he said, his voice echoing inside his mask.

Wyatt had dropped the e-tool at the top of the ravine. He picked up part of a cotton-wood limb from the rocks. It felt soggy and cold and foolish in his hands, the leaves dripping into the stream.

Long ago, on the yard, Wyatt had learned that real badasses didn't talk. Nor did they shave their heads and wear tats from the wrist to the armpit. Nor did they mob up with the Aryan Brotherhood. Genuine badasses curled 150 pounds, picked up five hundred on their shoulders, and did fifty push-ups while another guy sat on their backs. Their bodies radiated lethality the way hog shit radiated stink. As an old con in Huntsville once told him, silence was your greatest strength. It forced your enemies into the theater of the mind, where their fears ate them alive.

"Then we're gonna finish our date with your gash," the man in overalls said.

Wyatt didn't move. He could hear the water coursing around his feet and ankles and the cuffs of his jeans, the canopy swaying high above the ravine.

"Looks like you might have broke your ankle," the man in tan overalls said.

Had he heard the voice behind that mask before? He couldn't be sure. It was distorted, as though rising from the bottom of a stone well. Why wasn't the man carrying a piece?

"Maybe we'll call it a draw," the man said. "Maybe you learned your lesson."

Lesson about what? Wyatt thought.

"You got nothing to say?"

He blinked inside the mask. He's lost his guts. He's fixing to step backward.

"Count your blessings, Tex," the man said. "We're going to allow you to walk out of here. The broad got off easy, too. If you ask me, she majored in ugly."

When the man in strap overalls stepped backward, Wyatt whipped the cottonwood limb down on his forearm, knocking the knife from his hand onto the rocks. He swung again and missed, his ankle folding under him, a sickening pain traveling upward into his genitals and stomach. He threw himself forward and grabbed the man's legs and tried to pull him down but lost his purchase in the stream and was barely able to hang on to the man's right wrist.

The man fell backward, stomping Wyatt in the face. His gloves were cloth, the kind you would buy in a garden store. As he pulled away from Wyatt, his left glove slipped down to his knuckles, exposing the back of his hand. On it was a tattoo of a red spider. He kicked Wyatt in the side of the head and in seconds was running through the trees.

Two hours later, Wyatt was sitting on the side of an examination table in the ER at Community Medical Center, out by old Fort Missoula, his ankle wrapped, his eyebrow stitched. A plainclothes detective pulled back the curtain and stared at him. "Heard you had some bad luck today."

"You could call it that," Wyatt said. "I seen you somewhere before?"

"I don't know. Have you?"

"By that cave up behind Albert Hollister's house. Except you were in uniform. You and Detective Pepper was talking about the Horowitz woman, something about needing a board across your ass so you wouldn't fall in."

The detective was a lean and angular man with grainy skin and jet-black hair and sideburns that flared on his cheeks. He had a mustache and wore a new suit of dark fabric with blue stripes. He looked like he hadn't shaved in at least two days. "Did you recognize any of your assailants?" he asked.

"They had on masks. I need to see Miss Bertha."

"I just left her. She's fine."

"When was the last time you seen a rape victim doing fine?"

"Were they white men? Not Indian or African-American or Hispanic?"

"I don't know what they was."

"You see any identifying marks?"

"No."

"None? No tattoos, scars, that sort of thing?"

"They were buttoned up. One man had a baton."

"Like a policeman's?"

"Or an MP's. He put himself into it."

"What was it made of?"

"Wood. It had a lanyard."

"Police officers don't use that kind anymore."

"That makes me feel a whole lot better."

The detective stopped writing in his notebook. "You don't like us much, do you?"

"I learned to read lips in prison."

"I'm not quite making the connection."

"I saw you out in the hall earlier. You was telling a joke to another guy. It was about Miss Bertha."

The detective dropped his eyes to his notepad and wrote in it.

"What are you putting down?" Wyatt asked.

"That you read lips. That's quite a talent."

"What's your name?"

"Detective Jack Boyd. I don't have a business card yet. Call the department if you want to add anything to your statement."

"You took Detective Pepper's place?"

"What about it?"

"I think they got the right man for the job," Wyatt said.

Molly and I were clearing the table at sunset when she glanced out the French doors at the backyard. "Dave, come here," she said.

A man in a slouched cowboy hat was sitting atop the fence that bordered the north end of the pasture. He was drinking from a longneck, tilting it up, letting the foam slide down his throat, his boots hooked on the rail below him. He dropped the empty bottle on the grass and took a second one from the pocket of his canvas coat and twisted off the cap, then put the cap in his coat pocket. Albert's horses were gathered around a circular water tank on the other side of the fence, their tails whipping at flies. The sky was purple, hung with dark clouds that looked like torn cotton. The man on the fence looked up at the lights in the kitchen and dining area and took a long drink from his beer bottle. "That's Wyatt Dixon," I said.

"The one Alafair had the run-in with?"

"The one and only."

"Why is he here?"

"The day you figure out a guy like Dixon is the day you check yourself into rehab."

I put on a coat and walked down to the fence. The double metal gate to the pasture was creaking in the wind, the lock chain clinking softly. "You always throw your beer bottles on other people's lawns?" I said.

"I was gonna pick it up when I left." He glanced at the cabin in the south pasture. The light was on inside, and you could see Clete's rubber waders hanging upside down on the gallery. "Where's Dumbo at?"

"I'd give some thought to what I said about Clete Purcel. What happened to your eye?"

"A guy caught me with a rock. That was after him and two others attacked the woman I was with. She's at Community Hospital now."

"Who were the guys?"

"I got an idea who *one* of them was."

"You told the cops that?"

He twisted his mouth into a button. He was wearing half-top boots that looked like buckets on his feet and seemed out of character. "I come here to get your opinion on something," he said.

"Why me?"

"I checked out you and that fat-ass friend of yours. Y'all got in a shoot-out down in Louisiana and flushed the grits of some guys just like Love Younger and his crowd."

"You have reason to believe Love Younger sent these three men after you?"

"One guy had a tattoo on the back of his hand. I've seen it before."

"On somebody who works for Love Younger?"

"Here's what don't compute. I got nothing on Love Younger. He's rich and powerful, and I'm an ex-con and rough-stock supplier at state fairs. Why would I be a threat to him?"

"Who was the woman they attacked?"

"Her name is Bertha Phelps."

"The lady at the rez?"

"She probably never hurt a soul in her life. With time she may get over it. But she won't be the same. They never are."

"If I understand you correctly, these guys did everything they could to provoke you, but they managed to leave you alive, knowing what you'd probably do."

"None of them tried to pull a piece. Maybe they wasn't carrying. Maybe they just wanted to shake me up. They ain't high-end operators, that's for sure. One of them stole my cordovan Tony Lama boots."

"You think you're being set up?"

"Ever see a bullfight? Before the matador comes out, the banderilleros stick the banderillas in the bull's neck. They're like miniature harpoons. The barbs hurt like hell and get the bull into a rage. That's when he makes mistakes and gets a sword in the soft spot between the shoulder blades."

"Knowing all that, you still want to get even?"

"An eye for an eye."

"That's not what the admonition means."

"What it means is don't tread on me. I celled with a guy in Texas whose kid was murdered by a pedophile. He chain-drug him down a highway. What do you think of that?"

He took a sip from his beer, looking sideways at me, waiting for me to answer. His mind-set was one that every Southerner recognizes. Whether it's a defective element in the gene pool or an atavistic throwback to the peat bogs of Celtic Europe, it is nonetheless the family heirloom of a class of people who are not only uneducable but take pride in their ignorance and their potential for violence. If you have the opportunity, study their faces carefully in a photograph, perhaps one taken at what they call a "cross lighting," and tell me they descend from the same tree as the rest of us.

"You just conceded somebody is trying to throw you a slider. Why swing on it?" I said.

"Maybe I got tricks they don't know about. Maybe I'll call down fire and lightning on the whole bunch."

"You think you have that kind of power?"

He shook his head. "No, I ain't got no power at all. I was just talking. They done permanent harm to Miss Bertha, and they

315

got to pay for it, Mr. Robicheaux. You'd do the same. Don't be telling me you wouldn't. I know the kind of man you are. You might try to hide it, but I can see it in your eyes."

He climbed down from the fence, favoring one foot. He clasped the neck of the beer bottle with three fingers and tilted it to his mouth and drank until it was empty. Then he stuck it in one coat pocket and picked the empty off the grass and stuck it in his other pocket. He winked at me. "See, I always keep my word," he said.

I was wrong about Wyatt Dixon. If this man could be placed in a category, I had no idea what it was.

I couldn't blame Clete for what he did next. He had never done well when he left South Louisiana. Most GIs hated Vietnam and its corruption and humid weather and the stink of buffalo feces in its rice paddies. Not Clete. The banyan and palm trees, the clouds of steam rising off a rain forest, the French colonial architecture, the neon-lit backstreet bars of Saigon, a sudden downpour clicking on clusters of philodendron and banana fronds in a courtyard, the sloe-eyed girls who beckoned from a balcony, an angelus bell ringing at six A.M., all of these things could have been postcards mailed to him from the city of his birth.

For many people, New Orleans was a song

that sank beneath the waves. For Clete, New Orleans was a state of mind that would never change, a Caribbean port that practiced old-world manners, its pagan culture disguised by a thin veneer of Christianity. The dialect sounded more like Brooklyn than the South, because most of its blue-collar people were descended from Italian and Irish immigrants. The gentry often had accents like Walker Percy or Robert Penn Warren and had an iambic cadence in their speech that on occasion could turn an ordinary conversation into a sonnet.

People referred to "lunch" as "dinner." "Big-mouth bass" were "green trout." The "esplanade" was the "neutral ground." A "snowball" was always spelled as "sno'ball." The street Burgundy was pronounced as "Bur*gun*dy." "New Orleans" was pronounced as "New Or Lons" and never, under any circumstances, not even at gunpoint, "Nawlens."

Sometimes in the early-morning hours, Clete rode the St. Charles streetcar to the end of the line in Carrollton, the fog puffing in clouds from the live oaks that formed a canopy over the neutral ground. Then he rode the car back to Canal and walked through the Quarter to his office on St. Ann and never told anybody, his secretary included, where he had been.

Clete practiced a private religion and had

his own pew inside a cathedral no one else knew about. He never told others of his pain, nor would he allow himself to be treated as a victim. He hid his scars, made light of his problems, and despised those who preyed on the weak and those who championed wars but avoided fighting when it was their turn. You could say his value system was little different from that of Geoffrey Chaucer's good knight. I suspect there was a bit of Saint Francis in him as well.

I can't say exactly why he was drawn to Felicity Louviere, but I have an idea. She was diminutive and seemed never to have been exposed to a harsh light, like a nocturnal flower that needed to be protected from the sun. The black mole by her mouth seemed less an imperfection than an invitation for a man to lean down and kiss her. Her little-girl vulnerability did not fit with her robust figure and the dark and lustrous thickness of her hair and the mercurial changes in her manner, one moment grief-ridden, one moment seductive, one moment angry, perhaps because her father lost his life while trying to do good for others and left his daughter to founder.

Maybe the attraction was her accent, one you hear only in uptown New Orleans, an accent so singular and melodic that actors and actresses can seldom imitate it. Or maybe it was the fact that she was named by her father for a brave woman who died in a Roman arena.

Felicity Louviere was a mystery, and therein lay her attraction for Clete Purcel. She represented his memories of old New Orleans — alluring, profligate, addictive, filled with self-destructive impulses, her beauty as fragile as that of a white rose with a black spot on one petal. The greatest irony of Felicity's contradictions was her name. Did she, like her namesake, have the strength and resolve of a martyr? Did she have the courage of Felicity's fellow martyr, Perpetua, who pointed the sword of her executioner into her side? Or was she a deceiver, a female acolyte of the Great Whore of Babylon?

Clete got the call on his cell phone early Saturday morning, while he was eating breakfast at the McDonald's in Lolo. "Did I wake you up?" she said.

"No," he replied. "But whatever it is, I don't think it's too cool we see each other."

"I'm scared."

"About what?"

"It's Caspian. I always knew he had problems, but this is different. I can see it in his eyes. He's involved with something really bad."

"Can you be a little more specific?"

"I don't know. Maybe it has to do with gambling. He used to lose tens of thousands a night until Love made him go to Gamblers

319

Anonymous."

"What, he's flying to Vegas or something?"

"No, he's scared about something. He went to meet someone yesterday and came home drunk. Caspian never drinks."

"Who'd he meet?"

"He won't say. I heard him talking to Love in the den. He asked if there was a hell."

Clete got up from the booth and went outside with the phone. A semi was making a wide turn onto the two-lane highway that led up the long grade to Lolo Pass and the Idaho line. "My daughter had just gotten off the plane that crashed west of Missoula two days ago," he said. "The pilot was a member of the Sierra Club. My daughter is making a film about the oil companies that want to drill next to Glacier Park."

"You think the plane was sabotaged?"

"What's *your* opinion?"

"Love Younger doesn't blow up planes."

"I didn't say he did."

"Caspian? He wouldn't know a can of 3-In-One from Spindletop."

"I got the impression his father had a way of rubbing his nose in it."

"I need to see you."

He took the phone away from his ear and looked at the truck shifting down for the long pull up the grade. *Don't do it,* a voice said. *You can't help her. She married into the Younger family of her own free will.*

"Are you there?" she asked.

"Yes," he said.

"I know you have every reason to distrust me. But I'm telling you the truth. There is something truly evil happening in our lives."

"Where are you?" he asked.

"Not far. We have a camp on Sweathouse Creek."

"I got to ask you something. Your husband came to our place and said some ugly things. Did you know the governor of Louisiana, the one who went to prison?"

"I met him once at a political event. Why?"

"Your husband said you got it on with him."

"That's because my husband is paranoid and a liar."

His head was bursting. He let out his breath, widening his eyes, unable to sort out his thoughts. "He said you were a trophy hunter."

"Believe what you want. Caspian is a sick, sad man. I'm afraid, and I need help."

He hesitated, his head throbbing. "Give me directions," he said.

CHAPTER 15

The cabin was built of field stones on a whiskey-colored, tree-shaded creek at the base of the Bitterroot Mountains. The smoke from the chimney flattened in the breeze and disappeared inside the blueness of a canyon that didn't see full sunlight until midday. Sometimes there were bighorn sheep high up on the cliffs of the canyon, and in the fall, the sky would have the radiance and texture of blue silk and be filled with red and yellow leaves blowing from a place on the mountaintop that no one could see.

Clete thought about all these things as he parked the Caddy and walked up on the wood porch of the cabin and knocked, his heart beating hard.

She had a hairbrush in her hand when she opened the door. "You found it okay?" she said.

"I fish down here a lot. Dave and I fish here together. It's always cool in the summer. One time in the fall, I backpacked way up that trail and saw a moose."

Her eyes went past him, then came back on his. She touched the hair on her neck with the brush. "Your car looks like you just had it waxed."

He turned around and looked at it as though observing it for the first time, wondering if the disingenuous nature of their conversation was as embarrassing to her as it was to him. "I just got it out of the shop. It got shot up when this guy from Kansas tried to kill my daughter. You want to sit out here?"

"No, come in. What did you say? A man from Kansas?"

"He was driving a truck with a Kansas tag. Maybe he's Asa Surrette."

"The psychopath that Mr. Robicheaux's daughter interviewed in prison?"

"Yeah, he's a bad guy. You told me you were afraid. What are you afraid of?"

She looked beyond him at an old red boxcar that lay desiccated and half-filled with rotting hay inside a grove of cottonwoods. "I don't know what I'm afraid of. I feel a sense of loss I can't get rid of. I think about Angel and how she died and what the killer probably did to her before he put a plastic bag over her head. I can't get those images out of my mind. I hate my husband. I'd like to kill him."

"Why?"

"Will you come in, please?"

He stepped inside. She closed the door behind him and turned the key in an old-fashioned lock. Then she went to the windows and pulled the curtains closed.

"Who do you think is out there?" he asked.

"I can't be sure. Caspian is afraid of someone. More so than I've ever seen him. When he's afraid, he's cruel."

"To you?"

"To anyone. I never knew a coward who wasn't cruel. I had to make him bathe. No, I had to get Love to make him bathe."

"I'm losing the picture here."

"He wouldn't take a bath or get in the shower. I told him I didn't want him in our bedroom. Maybe he's depressed. When people get depressed, they behave like that, don't they?"

"Depressed over your daughter's death?"

"I don't know. I can't think." She sat down at a wood table, the hairbrush still in her hand. There was a vase of cut flowers on the table and another one on the kitchen windowsill. Her face looked freshly made up, her mouth glossy with lipstick that was too bright for her complexion, the streaks of brown in her hair full of tiny lights. "Nothing makes sense to me. Did this man Surrette kill our daughter?"

"Evidently, nobody saw her leave the Wigwam. Would she leave with somebody she didn't know?"

"She was seventeen. A girl that age has no judgment."

He sat down across from her. "Had she ever gone off with guys she didn't know?"

"I tried to talk her into going to Alateen. She wouldn't do it. Sometimes she'd come home at ten P.M. Sometimes she'd get dropped off at ten the next morning."

"Would she go off with strangers, Felicity?"

"Not to my knowledge."

"Who were her friends?"

"Druggies, boys on the make, kids who wanted access to her money."

"Was she promiscuous?"

"Today they all are," Felicity replied.

Clete looked around the cabin. The walls were pine, the floors constructed from railroad ties, the stone fireplace outfitted with steel hooks for cook pots. "What do y'all use this place for?"

"Hunting during big-game season. When Angel was younger, she had her friends out. We had ice cream parties on the bank of the stream."

"Were Caspian and your daughter close?"

"I don't know who Caspian is anymore."

"Pardon?"

"When I met him, he was a different person. He had a brilliant mind for figures. He wanted to create a high-tech company and compete in the defense industry. He borrowed a half million dollars in start-up money from Love. Then he started gambling in Vegas and Atlantic City and Puerto Rico. Here's the funny part. At the blackjack tables, he could count cards coming out of a six-deck shoe. He got banned from several casinos. Then they caught on to what he was doing."

"I don't understand. You said they caught on to him *after* he was banned."

"They realized if they let him stay at the table, he would lose everything he had won and drop ten to thirty thousand on top of it. How sick is that?"

"That's why they do it," Clete said.

"Do what?"

"That's why they gamble. They want to lose. They like to punish themselves. They want to feel there's a cosmic plot working against them. Go into the bar at the track after the seventh race. It's full of losers. They're happy as hogs rolling in slop."

She stared at him blankly. "I feel like an idiot."

"Because you never figured out your husband?"

"Because I married him."

"My ex gave our savings to an alcoholic Buddhist guru in Boulder," Clete said. "This guru made people take off their clothes at poetry readings. My ex thought he was a holy man and I was a drunk cooze hound. Unfortunately, in my case, she was right."

Felicity propped her elbow on the table and

rested her chin on her hand. For the first time since he had come into the room, she smiled. "You always talk like that to women?"

"Only the ones I trust."

Had he just said that?

"Why should you trust me?"

"Because we both grew up in the same part of New Orleans. Because everybody from Uptown knows what everybody else there is thinking. It's probably like an A.A. meeting. There's only one story in the room. We all come out of the same culture."

The fear she had described seemed to have lifted momentarily from her soul. There was a warm light in her eyes. Her hair had the tone and variations of color you see in old hand-rubbed mahogany. "When you talk, you make me feel good," she said.

"I'm an overweight former homicide roach, Miss Felicity. I'm still persona non grata at NOPD. That's like being a top sergeant in the Crotch, then getting your stripes pulled. Dave Robicheaux sobered up and got his life back. I never could pull it off. Three days without a drink, and my head turns into a concrete mixer." He could see her attention fading, the fear and concern creeping back into her face. "I got a bad habit," he said. "I start talking about myself and put everybody to sleep."

She touched the top of his hand. "No, you're a nice man. I mentioned something about Caspian that you wouldn't have a way of understanding. He asked Love if he believed in hell. Caspian has never had any interest in religion. Why would he ask Love a question like that?"

Clete shook his head. "Guilt?"

"If Caspian ever felt guilt about anything, I never saw it. He's the most selfish human being I've ever known."

The kitchen window was open, and the curtains were blowing in the breeze. They were printed with small pink roses and made Clete think of the flower bed that his mother kept behind their small house in the old Irish Channel. "I think I'd better go," he said. "I have a way of getting into trouble, Felicity. Lots of it. The kind that doesn't go away and leaves people messed up for a long time." The disappointment in her face was not feigned. He was sure of that, or at least as sure as he ever was when it came to matters of the heart. He got up to leave.

"Do what you need to do," she said.

He nodded and walked to the door and tried to turn the key in the lock.

"Here, I'll get it," she said. She twisted the key and opened the door, her shoulder brushing against his arm. She turned her face up to his. He could feel his manhood flare inside him. Her mouth was like a rose, her hair blow-dried and so thick and lovely that he wanted to tangle his fingers in it. "Clete?"

she said.

"Yeah?"

"You like me, don't you?"

"Do I? I've got a fire truck driving around inside my head."

"My daughter and my father are dead. I don't have anyone."

She let her arms hang at her sides and leaned her forehead directly into his chest, as though in total surrender to him and the level of failure that characterized her life.

One hour later, as he lay beside her, all his good intentions gone and his sexual energies exhausted, he thought about a story he had read as a boy in the old city library on St. Charles. The story was about Charlemagne and Roland on their way to Roncevaux. He wondered if they and their knights ever gave heed to the horns echoing off the canyon walls that surrounded them, or if they galloped onward through the cool blueness of the morning, beside a tea-colored stream, inside the rhythmic sweep of the wind in the trees, never realizing that the littered field began with a romantic quest, one that was as inviting and lovely and addictive as the grace to be found inside a woman's thighs.

I have never laid strong claim on rationality, in fact have often felt that its value is overrated. Let's face it, life is easier if we maintain a semblance of reasonable behavior and hide some of our eccentricities and not say more than is necessary in our dealings with others. The same applies to our actions. Why attract attention? No one takes an accordion band to a deer hunt.

Like most people, I wonder why I don't take my own advice.

The cave behind Albert's house began to bother me. Had it provided shelter to Asa Surrette? Was the perversion of Scripture on the wall of no consequence? Was it not a hijacking of a Judeo-Christian culture on which most of our ethos is based, in this instance a hijacking by a subhuman abomination who should have been hosed off the bowl thirty seconds after his birth?

I found two empty wine bottles in Albert's trash and filled them with gasoline I kept in a five-gallon can inside a steel lockbox welded to the bed of my pickup truck. I corked both bottles and carried them and the gas can up the hillside to the old logging road that traversed the mountain above Albert's house. A doe with two fawns bounced through the trees ahead of me, flicking their tails straight up, the white underside exposed.

The area around the cave entrance had remained undisturbed. Inside the overhang, I could see the message. I began heaping deadwood and leaves and pine needles and big chunks of a worm-eaten stump that was as soft and dry as rotted cork, shoving it

330

against the wall that contained the pirated lines.

I poured gasoline on the pile and set the can twenty feet from the cave opening, then lit a paper match and threw it inside the cave. The flame spread quickly over the fuel, climbing up the wall and flattening on the roof. Then I picked up the first wine bottle and flung it end over end into the fire. It broke against a fallen boulder and showered against the wall. Flames leaped from the cave, curling over the rim, scorching the overhang and singeing the grass and mushrooms that grew on top of it. I stepped back and tossed the second bottle inside. It landed on the deadwood and, seconds later, exploded from the heat rather than the impact. The fire was soon out of control, twisting in circular fashion, the flames feeding on themselves, spreading deeper into the cave, where there was probably a chimneylike opening drawing cold oxygen into the mixture of organic fuel and gasoline.

I could feel the heat on my face and arms and smell a stench that was like the odor of pack rat nests burning. I heard a sound behind me and looked over my shoulder and saw Albert laboring up the hill, sweating, his flannel shirt open on his chest, a fire extinguisher swinging from his hand. "What in the Sam Hill are you doing?" he said, out of breath.

"I thought I'd clean up the cave."

"Why didn't you napalm the whole mountain while you were at it?" He pulled the pin on the extinguisher's release lever and sprayed the rim of the cave, then the inside. Huge clouds of white smoke billowed from the opening and floated through the treetops. "You know how to do it, Dave. What's got into you?"

"I believe a genuinely evil man was up here, Albert. I believe he has no right to take language out of Scripture and deface the earth with it."

"Sit down a minute."

"What for?"

"I want to talk to you."

I wasn't up to one of Albert's philosophic sessions. He'd had chains on his ankles when he was seventeen and had belonged to the Industrial Workers of the World and had known Woody Guthrie and Cisco Houston. He'd followed the wheat harvest from the Texas Panhandle to southern Alberta and had been on a freighter that hit a mine in the Strait of Hormuz. He was a charitable and fine man, and I held him in the highest regard. There were also times when he could drive you crazy and make you want to throttle him.

"You were raised up in a superstitious culture," he said. "When you let your imagination get the best of you, you start to see the devil's hand at work in your life. The devil isn't a man, Dave."

"Then what is he?"

"Those goddamn corporations."

"I don't want to hear this."

"You're going to whether you like it or not. They bust our unions and use coolie labor in China and buy every goddamn president we elect."

"I can't take this, Albert."

"Those men who tried to kill Miss Gretchen were working for somebody. Who would that be? Satan or Love Younger?"

"A man like Younger doesn't hire hit men."

"You don't know your enemy, Dave. You never did."

"You want to translate that?"

"How'd your father die?"

"As the result of an accident. Don't be using my old man in your polemics."

He placed his hand on my shoulder. "All right, I won't. But don't hurt yourself like this. The enemy is flesh and blood, not a creature who wears a pentacle for a hat."

I took the extinguisher and finished spraying the cave and the bushes around the entrance. "Better come have a look," I said.

"What is it?" he said, getting to his feet.

"Check out the wall."

He stood at the entrance, the smoke from the ash rising into his face, his eyes watering.

"It's an aberration caused by the heat," he said.

I wanted to believe him, except in this case, I think Albert also had his doubts.

The message had probably been incised into the lichen with the point of a rock. The letters had not been cut much deeper than the moldy green patina. The intensity of the fire, augmented by two bottles of gasoline, should have burned the wall as clean as old bone. Instead, the letters were black and smoking, as though they had been seared into the stone with a branding iron.

"Don't just walk away," I said.

"I'm done with this foolishness, and I won't discuss it with you or anybody else," he replied. "Not now, not ever. You get yourself to a psychiatrist, Dave."

At dawn on Sunday, Wyatt Dixon awoke to a sound that didn't fit with either his dreams or the sounds he usually heard at daybreak. It was a sound like the pages of a book or magazine flipping in the breeze. Had he left a window open? No, the temperature had dropped last night, and he had shut and latched all of them. He sat up in bed and removed the sheathed bowie knife he kept under his pillow. He put on his jeans and limped barefoot and shirtless into the kitchen, his hair hanging in his face, his bad ankle wrapped with an elastic bandage.

She was sitting at the table, her long legs propped on a chair, reading a copy of *People,* a cup of Starbucks coffee in her hand. "What are you doing in my house?" he said.

"I didn't want to wake you, so I let myself in," Gretchen said.

"My door was dead-bolted."

"It was dead-bolted until I got a coat hanger on it. Dave Robicheaux told me about the three guys who attacked you and your friend. How is she doing?"

"She's home."

"That's not what I asked."

"They messed up her head proper."

"You recognized a tattoo on one guy's hand?"

He sat down across from her and stretched out one leg. "His glove slipped. I couldn't hear his voice good inside the mask, but I saw the tattoo, and I knew where I'd seen it before."

She waited for him to continue, but he didn't. "You look a little hobbled up," she said.

"It was a red spider. The gardener at Love Younger's place had one like it. What are you aiming to do, Miss Gretchen?"

"Cook their hash, hon. Want to come along?" she said.

The saloon on North Higgins, down by the old train station, had been through a number

335

of incarnations. For decades it was a brightly lit low-bottom watering hole where working-men and terminal alcoholics could shoot pool and play pinochle and drink pitcher beer and bulk wine and whiskey at prices that had no peer, except for the Oxford down the street, which in the 1960s charged only five cents for a glass of beer. Academic writers and flower children tried to appropriate the saloon, but their presence was transitory and cosmetic, and the core clientele remained the same — old-time bindle stiffs, gandy dancers, marginal criminals, pullers of the green chain, reservation Indians who drank up their government checks on the fourth day of the month, gypo loggers, miners from Butte and furnace stokers from Anaconda, used-up prostitutes, and the biggest group of all, one that has no categorical name other than the people for whom the phrase "born to lose" was an anthem and not an apology.

Over a long period of time, the photographs of these people were taken by an eccentric and enormously talented daytime bartender named Lee Nye, who framed and hung them on the wall in rows down the length of the saloon. By the 1990s almost all of these Depression-era people were dead and forgotten. The ownership changed and the tobacco-stained floors were replaced, the restrooms painted and remodeled, and a small restaurant was installed in back. The saloon became a cheerful and crowded place in the evenings, full of laughter and free of smoke and worry about privation and disease and mortality.

The photographs of the men and women in tattered clothes remained, their toothless mouths collapsed, their faces wrinkled with hundreds of tiny lines, their recessed eyes containing a strange kind of radiance, as though they wanted to tell us a secret they'd never had a chance to share.

On Sunday evening a man riding a new white Harley flanged with polished chrome drove up the alley behind the saloon and parked next to the brick wall and entered through the back door. The man's name was Tony Zappa. His eyes were pale and elongated, his hair braided in cornrows. He had the flat chest of a boxer and sun-browned skin as tight as latex on his frame. He did not pay attention to a chopped-down pickup truck with twin Hollywood mufflers that passed the alley and pulled to the curb just beyond the lee of the building.

A few minutes later, Gretchen Horowitz entered the saloon through the front door and went to the bar and stood next to Tony and ordered a beer. She put one foot on the brass rail and looked up at the flat-screen television on the wall. "You ever been in New Orleans?" she said.

"You talking to me?" Zappa said.

"Did you know that was Robert De Niro's

most famous line? It's from *Taxi Driver.*"

"You saying I'm copying Robert De Niro?"

"No, I asked if you'd ever been in New Orleans."

"I'm from Compton by way of Carson City. Know what I mean?"

"Not exactly."

"Compton is where you go if hell is over-crowded."

"Wednesday night is yuppie night in New Orleans," she said. "That's what this place reminds me of, except tonight is Sunday."

"You don't sound like you're from New Orleans."

"What do people from New Orleans sound like?"

"Part Italian, part boon, although I hear a lot of the boons got washed out during Katrina," he said. "You want a shot to go with that beer?"

"Long day, boss. Another time." Her attention seemed to fade. She yawned and looked up at the television screen.

"I say something wrong?"

"No, I need to get something to eat."

"I bet you wear contacts."

"You're going to tell me something about my eyes?"

"They're violet. You got reddish hair with violet eyes. It's not something you see every day."

"I was conceived in an in vitro dish. The

male donor was a package of purple Kool-Aid."

"That's pretty good."

"You took a slide on your bike?"

He gazed at her, puzzled.

"The bruises on your arms and neck. I saw you on Higgins a little while ago. You were riding a white Harley."

"You were looking at me?"

"What's the spider on your hand mean?"

"You know what Compton is like if you're white or Hispanic?"

"You're lunch meat?"

"Ever hear of the Arañas?"

"No."

"That was our gang, the Spiders. We had one rule and one rule only, and all the Crips and Bloods knew what it was: Anything they did to one of us, we did to ten of them. If a cannibal got caught in the wrong apartment building, he got a free flight off the roof."

"You look a little hyper."

"I consider myself pretty mellow."

"You get into it with somebody?"

"No. Why you asking?"

"Because you're agitated and because I saw something outside."

"Where you come from, people talk in code?"

She finished her beer and stared into space as though coming to a decision. "I don't like to mind other people's business, but you seem like a nice guy. That's your Harley in back, right?"

"What about it?" he said.

"When I walked past the alley, there was a guy out there."

"Which guy? What are you talking about?"

"A guy. He was dressed like a cowboy."

"What was he doing?"

"Looking at your hog."

"Who cares?"

"He squatted down like he was examining the engine, like it was his hog."

"Did this guy look like he's part white, part Indian? Or more like a white Indian?"

"His Wranglers were splitting on his ass. He was wearing a straw cowboy hat. A *white* Indian?"

"He had a limp, maybe?"

"I didn't stick around to see. Maybe I shouldn't have said anything."

"You wait here."

"I didn't get that."

"Wait here. I'll be back."

"How about it on the attitude?"

"I want to buy you a drink or dinner. Don't go anywhere. That's all I was saying, for Christ's sake."

Tony Zappa went out the back and returned in under five minutes. He was grinning and obviously feeling good and ready to resume the conversation. "No problem. I cranked it up. It's fine. You had me going there. How about that drink now?"

"No, thanks."

He seemed to reevaluate, as though he couldn't free himself of a self-centered fear that had probably governed his thoughts for a lifetime. "One last try. Was there anything different about this guy? Did he have weird-looking eyes, maybe a cut on his head?"

"He looked like a cowboy. I told you. You get into it with somebody?"

"No. There's a lot of riffraff around these days, that's all. How about dinner? A nice place, maybe El Cazador if you like Mexican, or Romeo's if you like Italian?"

There was a beat. "I need to take a shower and change."

"So shower and change."

"I'm at a motel on West Broadway." She gave him the name. "Know where that is?"

"You're staying there? That's a shithole."

"Tell me about it. Room nine. Give me a half hour. If I'm in the shower, the door will be unlocked."

"You never asked my name."

"You didn't ask mine," she said.

"What is it?" he asked.

"Trouble, with a capital T. You think you can handle it, Spider-Man?"

He slipped on his Ray-Bans. His incisors were white and pointy when he smiled. "I like the way you talk, mama. I promise you the ride of your life. Hey, I'm talking about on my Harley. Jesus, you're touchy."

CHAPTER 16

That same evening, I tapped on Albert's office door on the first floor in the back of the house, just past the glassed-in gun cabinets in the hallway. He kept an extraordinary collection of firearms and ordnance, most connected in some way to historical figures or events: several 1851 Navy Colt revolvers, many World War II rifles and handguns, a 1927 Thompson submachine gun with a fifty-round drum magazine, an 1873 Winchester, an AK-47 and an AR-15, disarmed hand grenades, shelves of .58-caliber minié balls and canister and grapeshot. Above his desk were other shelves stacked with bowie knives, glass telegraph transformers, Spanish wine bags, tomahawks, and framed collections of coins and Indian arrowheads and stone tools. Above his work desk, where he wrote both in longhand and on his computer, was a huge photograph of Woody Guthrie holding a guitar with THIS MACHINE KILLS FASCISTS painted on the soundboard.

He also kept a corkboard where he thumb-tacked his collection of crank and hate mail, which he received with regularity, most of it written by racists throughout the United States. The centerpiece of the display, and my favorite, was a letter written by a prisoner on death row at Huntsville State Prison in Texas. The condemned prisoner's mother had given him a copy of Albert's last novel, narrated by a fictitious former Texas Ranger. The prison censor had expurgated so many passages that the text was unreadable. The inmate attached a copy of the censor's justifications: Albert's novel promoted racial divisiveness and a disrespect for authority.

"Am I bothering you?" I asked.

He was sitting at his desk, his reading glasses on, a dozen grade sheets spread before him. "No, come in, Dave," he said, waving me in.

"What are you working on?"

"The general pain in the ass that made me quit teaching — fooling with grades and all that nonsense."

"You're retired. Why are you worrying about student grades now?"

"People I gave an incomplete to years ago finally end up doing the work and want credit for the course."

I had known some of Albert's students. They had told me about his method of teaching: He didn't have one. His classes were chaos. Often he conducted them in a saloon or, if the weather was nice, on the lawn. He didn't check the roll. He didn't give grades for assignments. As a rule, he knew the students only by their first names. He told them to forget everything they had ever learned about literature and write about what they knew and remember that in art, there were no rules. The lowest grade he ever gave anyone who completed his creative writing workshop was a B. The only text he ever used was John Neihardt's *Black Elk Speaks*. The only critic he ever respected was Wallace Stegner, not because Stegner was a scholar at Stanford but because he had been a Wobbly.

"Pack rats got into my file drawer. These grade sheets are useless," he said. "I can't find this guy's name."

I didn't want to ask him how he never noticed that pack rats were living in his office. "What are you going to do?" I said.

"Well, I can't give him an A because he turned the work in eleven years later. But he probably deserves at least a B, so that's what he's going to get."

"I'm sorry for setting a fire in the cave," I said.

"That's all right. Your heart was in the right place. I just worry about you sometimes."

Don't buy into Albert's doodah and get into it with him, I thought.

"There's a lesson you never learned," he

345

said. "Do you remember the last line of dialogue Harry Morgan speaks in *To Have and Have Not*?"

"Not offhand."

"Harry is shot up real bad on his boat and dying and can hardly talk, and he says, 'No matter how a man alone ain't got no bloody fucking chance.' "

"You're saying I'm a loner?"

"Inside you are. You have people around you, and they mean a lot to you, but inside you're always by yourself."

"You've been a loner since you were a kid," I said.

"I've been alone since Opal died, but not before. Don't ever make yourself alone, Dave. That's the big lesson. When you start to see evil forces at work in the world, you give them power they don't have."

I was sitting in a leather swivel chair by his bookcases. I looked at my shoes and wasn't sure what I should say. Albert had chain-ganged on the hard road in Florida. I didn't want to talk down to him. But he made me mad. "I saw GIs who had been hanged in trees and skinned alive. I had a marine friend from Georgia, a sergeant, who went crazy with remorse over what he saw some other guys do to a Vietnamese girl in a ville they trashed. You want to know what they did?"

"No, I don't."

I told him anyway and saw him swallow and

his eyes recede with a look of sorrow that would not go away easily. "You know that story to be true?" he asked.

"The guy who told it to me killed himself. Evil isn't an abstraction," I said.

"None of those things would have happened if we hadn't taken on the neocolonial policies of the French and the British."

"This isn't politics. Asa Surrette is out there. He's been on your property, and he tried to kill Alafair and Gretchen. How did he survive a head-on crash between a prison van and a tanker truck filled with gasoline?"

He shook his head. "I'm old, and I live by myself in a house where I hear my wife's voice talking to me. Sometimes I think it's my imagination, sometimes not. Sometimes I want to unlock my gun cabinet and join her. I don't believe in the devil, and I don't believe in Asa Surrette. The evil in our lives comes from men's greed, and the manifestation of that greed is in the corporations that cause the wars."

I loved Albert and felt bad for him. I hadn't meant to hurt him or remind him of the loss of his wife or call up the feelings of loneliness and mortality that beset all of us when we live longer than perhaps we should. A window was open, and the wind was blowing strands of his white hair on his forehead. The evening was warm and the trees on the hillside were glowing in the sunset, and there was something about the moment that made me think of traditional America and lighted houses throughout the land and family people whose only goal was to lead good lives and be with one another. As I looked at Albert's broad face and wide-set eyes and purposeful gaze, I thought of the ragtag army of Anglo-Scotch soldiers who formed up at Breed's Hill outside Boston in 1775. I realized there was someone else Albert resembled, a man who was a collector of historical firearms and who represented everything Albert despised. I kept my opinion to myself and did not tell Albert how much he reminded me of Love Younger.

The west end of Broadway in Missoula was a study in contradictions. The vista was lovely. The mountains were mauve and purple in the sunset, the river wide and braided over the rocks and rimmed along the banks with willows and cottonwoods. The street was lined on either side with bars, liquor stores, casinos, and run-down independent motels. Saturday-night knifings were not unusual; neither were sexual assaults. If you wanted to get falling-down drunk, laid and dosed with the clap, shanked or shot or just beat up, arrested, and jailed, this was the place to do it.

Tony Zappa drove around to the side of a motel by the river's edge and parked in a handicap zone not far from a green door with a tin numeral nailed on it. He took off his gloves and looked up and down the street at the bars and casinos that had turned on their neon signs, then gazed through the window of Gretchen's pickup at the rolled leather interior and the polished woodwork and high-tech gauges on the dashboard. He looked at the heavy tread on the tires and the chrome on the radiator and the moon hubcaps and the Frenched headlights and the waxed three-layer black paint job, all of which were high-end modifications that cost high-end money.

He tapped his gloves in his palm and went into the office. The clerk was a kid with zits on his forehead and thin arms wrapped with tattoos of snakes and skulls and bleeding daggers. He was glued to the screen of his laptop. On it, a naked man and woman were in full-body inverted congress.

"You know the broad in room nine?" Zappa said.

"She's a guest."

"I know she's a guest. What's her story?"

"How the fuck should I know?" the clerk replied.

"I can see this is a class joint, the kind that protects its guests' privacy. You accept food stamps?"

"I can give you a break on a coupon from *Screw* magazine," the clerk said. "You got to provide your own sheets, though."

"You're a funny guy. That boner fills out your pants nicely. Enjoy your movie." Zappa left the office and got ten steps down the sidewalk, then turned around and went back. "I'm gonna ask you this once, and I don't want a smart-ass answer. Is the girl in room nine by herself?"

"She came in by herself."

"That's not what I asked you."

"It's a single. On Sunday nights, it's twenty dollars. For two people, it's thirty dollars. She paid twenty dollars."

"Are you retarded? Answer my question. You see anybody else hanging around? A cowboy, maybe?"

"We have three kinds of guests here: shit-kickers, drunk Indians, and street people. The street people pool their money and send one person in, usually a woman. The Indians drink on the balcony and puke over the rail on the cars down below. Most of the street people were kicked out of detox."

"I didn't ask for all that information. Did you see a shitkicker in her room? A guy with a white straw hat?"

"No."

"If you're lying to me, I'll be back."

"Go fuck yourself, man."

"Tell you what. I'll be back whether you're lying or not."

Zappa went back down the sidewalk to room nine and twisted the doorknob. The door swung back slowly across the carpet. He could hear the shower running in the back-

350

ground. "All right if I come in?" he said, his eyes searching the room. "Can you hear me? I'm coming inside. Don't come out without a towel around you." The bathroom door was ajar, and the water was drumming loudly on the tin sides of the stall. "Hey, I'm inside now. I'm closing the door. I got a little weed. You mind?"

No answer.

He turned in a circle, letting his eyes adjust to the poor light and the shadows the neon sign outside created through the curtains. There was nobody else in the room. He pulled a Ziploc bag from his coat and sat down in a chair by the bed and rolled a joint and lit it, ignoring the NO SMOKING sign above the doorway. He stood up and faced the bathroom, holding down the hit, releasing it incrementally, feeling a great calm take hold in his chest for the first time that day. "What are you doing in there?"

He heard the outside door open behind him. Before he could turn around, an arm that felt as hard as angle iron clenched around his throat and squeezed his windpipe shut and almost snapped his head from his shoulders.

"Howdy-doody," Wyatt Dixon said into his ear. "Let's talk about what you boys done to my friend Miss Bertha. It's a pleasure to get together with you."

■ ■ ■ ■

Gretchen was dressed and blotting her hair with a towel when she came out of the bathroom. Tony Zappa was sitting very still in a chair, his hands duct-taped behind him, a rubber ball wedged and taped inside his mouth. His eyes were bulging, the tubes of muscle in his triceps as taut as rope. She spread the towel on top of the bedcover before she sat on it.

"We're going to keep it simple," she said. "You got stung. We win, you lose. Maybe you can walk out of here. Maybe not. That depends on what Wyatt decides and how much you cooperate. I'll be up-front with you. When I was a little girl, I knew several guys like you. I see them in my dreams and sometimes in the middle of the day. I'd like to kill them, but I can't do that because they're already dead. That makes you the surrogate, Tony. You know what the word 'surrogate' means?"

He kept his eyes on hers, not moving, the rubber ball wet in his mouth.

She pulled on a pair of latex gloves. "I'm going to take the ball out of your mouth. You're going to talk in a normal voice and answer our questions. You've got no parachute, no cavalry, no Love Younger to back you up. You thought Compton was a bad gig?

Those were your salad days, pal." She pulled the ball from his mouth and set it on the carpet and wiped her glove with a paper napkin. "Don't speak until I tell you," she said. "I know everything there is to know about you. You were in juvie and Atascadero and Lompoc. You went down once for distribution and sale to minors and once for theft from the mails. In juvie, you were repeatedly sodomized. Maybe it's not your fault you're a bucket of shit. Believe it or not, we're probably the best friends you'll ever have."

He started to speak. Dixon slapped him across the side of the head, so hard his eyes crossed and the imprint of the blow glowed on his skin. Gretchen raised her hand for Dixon to stop. "He's all right," she said.

"Leave him with me, Miss Gretchen."

"No, no, Tony wants to cooperate. He's been around the block a few times and isn't going to take somebody else's weight. Right, Tony? Whatever you did, you were ordered to do. In a way you're a soldier, just like mobbed-up guys are. Here's the *problemo* with that. From everything Wyatt and I have been able to figure out, your attack on him and his friend was meant to provoke him, not scare him off, because you know a guy like Wyatt doesn't rattle or scare off."

"It wasn't me," Zappa said.

"Wyatt saw the red spider on your hand."

"Years ago kids all over East Los wore

353

those," Zappa said. "Love Younger hires ex-felons and gives them a second chance. I know at least two other guys working for him who were Arañas."

"How'd you get bruised up?" she said.

"Fell off a ladder."

"Look at me," she said.

"What do you think I'm doing? Where else am I gonna look?"

"When is the last time you saw Asa Sur-rette?"

"Who?"

"You were wired up earlier," she said. "Why would a guy who did time in Lompoc and Atascadero be wired up in a yuppie bar on Sunday evening?"

"Because I'm not good with women. Because you got big knockers. Because you look like you could rip the ass out of an elephant. I get nervous about those things."

She pulled off her latex gloves and dropped them on the floor. "Bill Pepper drugged and sexually tortured me."

"I don't know anybody by that name."

"I believe you. You know why?"

"Because I'm telling the truth?"

"No, because you blinked after you spoke."

"I don't understand what you're saying."

"When I asked you the previous questions, you widened your eyes so you wouldn't blink. That means you were lying, Tony," she said. "We're back to square one. You remember what square one was, don't you? On square one, you were the rapist who attacked Wyatt's friend. For me, that makes you the kind of guy who deserves anything that happens to him. I don't want you to misunderstand. I'm not trying to scare you. I just want you to know what your victims feel about you and what they're capable of doing when they get the chance. Am I getting through?"

"No," he said.

"There was this mobbed-up guy named Bix Golightly who forced his cock into the mouth of a six-year-old girl on her birthday and told her he'd kill her if she ever told her mother. The little girl grew up and found this guy in New Orleans sitting behind the wheel of his van. She parked one in his forehead, one in the middle of his face, and one in his mouth. It was pretty messy. See, the shooter was using twenty-two hollow-points. They don't exit, they bounce around inside the skull. As I recall, Bix Golightly's brains were running out his nose."

Zappa's lips were gray, his elongated eyes sweeping around the room, as though an answer to his situation lay inside the shadows.

"Wyatt is not the person you need to worry about," she said. "I want to pop you and do it in pieces. I hope you keep lying. I've got a feeling you've hurt lots of women, and all of them will be cheering when we drop you in a Dumpster. Want to clear your conscience?"

"I'm a gardener. I stacked time when I was young. I got a good job in Carson City and cleaned up my act. If you know everything, check my sheet. I work for the Youngers, but I never talk to them. The old man is in his helicopter or in his library with his guns. The daughter-in-law acts like her shit don't stink and we don't exist. Caspian hands out the chores through the head groundsman."

"Let me show you something, Miss Gretchen," Wyatt said. He positioned himself in front of Tony Zappa and ripped open his shirt, popping off all the buttons. Then he tore the shirt off his shoulders and peeled it down his arms. "See that bruise on his forearm? That's where I hit him with a cottonwood limb. See that gold hair on his chest? It was sticking out of his shirt when he come at me with the knife he took off me." Dixon looked down at Zappa. "I told Miss Bertha I was gonna bring her your ears. She cried. That's the kind of lady y'all ripped the clothes off. You smiling at me, boy?"

Wyatt picked up the telephone book and swung it with both hands into Zappa's head. The chair toppled backward, Zappa falling with it hard against the floor, the back of his head thudding against the concrete beneath the carpet. He stared at the ceiling with the empty look of a man who had plunged backward to the bottom of a well. "I wasn't smiling. I wasn't doing anything," he said.

"Do to me whatever you want. I heard talk about a guy you're not gonna like meeting."

"Maybe the guy who did Bill Pepper?" Gretchen said.

"They say this guy can't die. I've heard about what he's done to some women. I hope you meet him. I hope I'm there to watch it."

Gretchen squatted on her haunches so she could look directly into Tony Zappa's face. She could smell the weed on his clothes and the beer on his breath and the deodorant layered under his armpits and the sunblock he had rubbed into his scalp and cornrows. She took her Airweight .38 special from her side pocket and flipped out the cylinder and removed four of the five rounds loaded in the chambers. "You were one of the guys who attacked Wyatt and his friend, weren't you?"

"I never saw the guy. Why should I want to attack him?"

"Earlier tonight you were worried about a cowboy with a limp and a cut on his head. That's the man you're looking at right now. How could you describe him to me if you never saw him?"

The blood drained from Tony Zappa's cheeks. Gretchen rotated the cylinder of the Airweight with her palm without looking at it, then snapped it back into the pistol's frame. "Do you know who Percy Wolcott was?"

"No."

"He was my friend. I think someone you know sabotaged his plane."

"I never heard of him."

"I had a feeling you might say that. Are you good at math?"

"What are you doing to me, lady?"

"There are five chambers in this revolver. Only one of them is loaded. On the first trigger pull, there is an eighty percent chance the hammer will come down on an unloaded chamber. To be honest with you, I don't feel good about tormenting a man whose hands are taped behind his back. I'll start the process, and maybe you'll do the right thing and our situation will be over. If not, we'll have to take it from there. You with me so far?"

"No," he said, swallowing as he spoke.

She pulled back the hammer and placed the muzzle of the Airweight against the side of her head and squeezed the trigger. Her face jerked when the hammer snapped on an empty chamber. She heard Wyatt release his breath. "Miss Gretchen, don't do that again," he said.

"It's your turn," she said to Zappa.

"Lady, don't do this to me," he said.

"The chances are one in four that the next chamber is loaded. That means you have a seventy-five percent chance of being okay. Are you following me?"

"You're going too fast."

She touched the barrel to his temple and cocked back the hammer.

"Please," he said. "You don't know everything involved. I didn't have a choice."

"About hitting a man in the head with a baton?" she said. "About gang-raping a woman? You didn't have a choice about that? You're starting to piss me off."

"Kill me. I don't care." Tears were welling in his eyes. "I saw pictures of what this guy has done. Go online. Somebody sold them to a guy who makes snuff films. Maybe it was the guy who sold them."

"What guy? What's his name?"

"I don't know. I'm a gardener!" He squeezed his eyes shut and kicked his feet and ground his teeth.

Gretchen heard the roar of a truck engine on the other side of the wall, followed by someone pounding on the door and shouting: "Hey, asshole! Your Harley is being towed! Come outside and see *how* it's being towed!"

Gretchen pulled back the curtain and looked outside. The clerk had backed up a wrecker to the handicap zone and attached a steel hook and cable around the Harley and hoisted it into the air so it was hanging at an angle, upside down, the handlebars and gas tank and engine partially on the concrete parking pad.

"Did you hear me, shit-breath?" the clerk

shouted, pounding the door again. "I want to thank you for helping me quit this job! Put your plunger back in your pants and watch the show!"

The clerk climbed into the cab of the wrecker and shifted into gear and clanked forward into the street, dragging the Harley over the curb and banging it against a light pole. Then he gave the wrecker the gas and roared down Broadway, the Harley bouncing end over end, skittering off a fireplug, metal screeching, sparks geysering in the dark as he made a wide turn at the intersection.

Gretchen and Wyatt were standing at the window, dumbfounded, the curtain peeled back. "I don't believe this," she said.

"This ain't too good, Miss Gretchen," Wyatt said.

The reversal of their situation was not over. Behind them, Tony Zappa picked himself up from the floor, wobbled once or twice, and charged through the side window, smashing through the curtain and glass, the chair on his back, landing on the gravel slope behind the building. Upon impact, the chair splintered into sticks, and in seconds he was running across the rocks along the river's edge, his wrists still taped behind him, his ripped shirt streaming in rags.

"Time to get out of Dodge, Wyatt," she said.

"I got to tell you something, Miss Gretchen. I don't like what you done, snapping the gun at your head like that. It froze my heart up. You shouldn't ought to do that, even if you was pretending. You was pretending, right?"

"Not exactly," she said. "You're a good fellow, Wyatt. Come on, I'll buy you dinner."

His face resembled a clay sculpture, his glasslike eyes absent of any emotion she could detect. She held her eyes on his. "Something wrong?" she asked.

"That smile of yours, it's the light of the world," he said. "You got the prettiest smile in the history of smiles, woman."

CHAPTER 17

Growing up in the old Irish Channel, down by Tchoupitoulas, Clete Purcel heard older boys and men share their knowledge about the opposite sex. He heard the same wisdom in the Marine Corps and from fellow cops and any number of newsmen and barroom personalities and frequenters of pool rooms and sports parlors. All spoke with authority about the rewards and perils of romance and gave the listener the sense that they had women of every stripe at their disposal. These great authorities on sexual relationships knew every detail about the joys of copulation as well as some of the pitfalls, which they reduced to the cynical and succinct statements that entertain the readers of pulp fiction and please those who have the thinking powers of earthworms. Here are a few bits of bedroom wisdom passed by these wise and worldly men:

1) Don't go to bed with a woman who

has more problems than you.

2) Divorcées and widows can't get enough.

3) Catholic girls are better in the sack because they're full of guilt and stay on rock and roll right down to the finish line.

4) Black women have more powerful libidos than white women and are always eager to get it on with white men.

5) Old ladies make outstanding mistresses because they are not only mature but their parts are tender and they are ever so grateful (this observation was made by Benjamin Franklin).

This is the counsel that millions of men and boys have heard and probably on occasion taken seriously. Once in a long while, inside a late-night bar or the cab of a long-haul semi or a foxhole when trip flares are floating down over a piece of third-world moonscape, you might hear a cautionary word connected to reality. Someone who has strayed from his marital vows, or betrayed his lover's trust, or destroyed his family or someone else's, will describe to you in painful detail the nightmare that can be yours if you make one wrongheaded decision.

If the errant lover or husband is willing to

tell you everything, he will confess his naïveté. He will say he had no idea how many lives would be affected by his decision. He will acknowledge that none of the players was either all good or all bad but were little more than children. This is not a welcome revelation for those men who wish to feel that the cuckold precipitated his own fate or that he was saving the adulterous wife from an abusive marriage or that he was lured into the situation. It's no fun to discover you've been swindled. It's even worse when you discover that the swindler is you.

Clete arranged to meet Felicity at the stone cabin on Sweathouse Creek Sunday evening and got there before she did. The sun was gone, and the air was cold and smelled of the creek and the lichen on the stone walls of the canyon. When she arrived, she was wearing a long dark dress with tiny white flowers and a white lace hem, and a knitted white sweater and a tiny hat like a woman from the early twentieth century would wear. Her hand was shaking when she turned the key in the plated lock on the door.

"Are you okay?" he asked when they were inside.

"I'm not sure," she said. "We just made our first visit to Angel's grave. Something happened that really bothers me. Caspian cried. I've never seen him do that."

"That's the way people behave in those

situations," he replied. Those situations? They were talking about the murder of a child. What was he saying?

"Caspian never shows his feelings," she said. "He always has this little smile on his face, like he knows something you don't."

"The reason I wanted to talk to you, Felicity —"

"You don't have to tell me. It's written all over you. You made a mistake. I'm a nice lady and deserve better. We have to be mature people about this and be objective and say good-bye. Blah, blah, blah. Usually, men choose a restaurant to say these things so the woman can't yell and throw things."

"I wasn't going to say that. I was going to tell you how much I like you, and like being with you, and like the way you talk and carry yourself. You're grieving over your daughter, and a guy like me seems like a safe harbor for a little while. I don't want to hurt you, that's all. You don't know my history. Dave and I put some guys down real hard. They're not coming back."

"Why did you want to meet?"

"Because I want to know why you haven't split from your husband. Or maybe I wondered if you want to split with him now. I'm not good at figuring things out sometimes."

She sat down on a cloth-covered couch by the far wall. Through the window behind her, Clete could see the limbs of a cottonwood thrashing in the wind and the flicker of lightning on the canyon wall. "When I married Caspian, I was a good girl. I was mad at my father for going to South America and getting himself killed. I strayed sometimes, but I felt sorry about it later and tried to do right. Caspian said he loved me and he'd never slept with another woman. I didn't believe him, but after a while I thought he was telling the truth. Caspian's money could have bought him any woman he wanted, but the only love he cared about was the one he couldn't have — the love of his father."

"I can relate to that," Clete said. "Except you got to grow up and stop resenting people for what they did to you when you were a kid. You got a drink?"

"Are you talking about me resenting my father? Is that why we're out here?"

"No, I just need a drink. What do you have?"

"There's some Bacardi and Coca-Cola in the refrigerator. Why don't you lay off it for a while?"

"I don't feel like laying off it. Go on with what you were saying."

"Oh, Clete, I feel like such a fool when I talk this way," she said, putting her hands in her lap and lowering her head. "I told you I was angry at my father, but the truth is, I loved him and I was proud of the name he gave me and I wanted to be brave like the woman who died in the arena. I used to go to church and try to be charitable toward people, and I thought marrying Caspian would be wonderful and we'd live in all the magical places we talked about. I slept around and I was selfish, and any criticism others make of me is justified. What bothers me most about Angel's death is that she's dead and I'm alive."

Clete was putting ice and four inches of rum in a glass of Coca-Cola, trying to concentrate on what she was saying. From the kitchen, he could not see her face, but her tone had changed — it held a plaintive element that was making him feel worse and worse. A storm had moved out of the south end of the Bitterroot Valley, and he could feel the barometer dropping and the air turning colder outside.

"Are you listening?" she said. "I always thought about death, even when I was a little girl. Then I met Caspian and thought we'd live in Hawaii or Malibu or Martha's Vineyard. He asked me to sign a prenuptial agreement and said it was because of his father and his father's distrustful and stingy ways. I should have known better, I guess. We were happy, even though I couldn't have children. I thought, after we adopted Angel, we'd be a real family. That's not how it turned out."

"That's why you adopted her?"

"No, it was Caspian's idea. That's when I

thought he had a kinder and more loving side. It's what I thought today when he cried at her grave."

Clete took a long drink. He was standing in the kitchen under the light fixture, unable to take the glass from his mouth, his shadow like a pool of ink around his feet. He drank until the glass was almost empty, wishing he could melt and seep through the cracks in the floor and disappear into the wind and rain starting to streak the windows. A bolt of lightning struck somewhere up on the mountain, the rocks and ponderosas and larch trees in the canyon trembling yellow and gray and shadowing against the canyon walls.

"You regret getting involved with me?" he asked.

"No, not at all. Sit down next to me. Please."

"I got to have a refill."

"No one can drink that much alcohol."

"I can. I've made a lifetime study of it. Did you ever try to leave him?"

"And go where?"

"To the state employment office, if nowhere else."

"I haven't explained myself very well. I was always afraid of death. When people left me, I felt as though I'd died. It was like being inside a dark house that didn't have any doors. You ever felt that way?"

"You've heard about the Serenity Prayer,

right? I use the short version: 'Fuck it.' "

"Except it doesn't work that well, does it?"

"When that doesn't, this does," he said, lifting his glass.

"Sit down."

"I'd better go. I thought we'd talk things out. You already said it all. You got feelings for your husband. The guy lost his daughter. I'm sorry for any harm I've caused y'all."

"You sit down, Clete, and sit down now. Please don't be hard on yourself. You still don't understand."

He sat down next to her, his knees turned toward her, his weight sinking deep into the cushions. "Understand what?"

She picked up his left hand in both of hers. "When you made love to me, I felt like I had gone off the planet. I haven't felt like that in years. I felt like I was seventeen again. I felt like the world was brand-new."

"I'm old, Felicity. I don't delude myself. Once in a while a guy like me gets lucky. I know my limitations."

"I want you. That's what I'm trying to say. I feel sorry for Caspian, but I want you."

"You can do better."

"I want you, not somebody else. You appreciate a woman. You're respectful. You're loving. You think that's lost on me? Take off your coat."

"I don't want to," he said.

"You spilled your drink on it. If you get

stopped, the police will think you're drunk. I'll clean it for you."

He stood up and removed his seersucker coat and laid it on the coffee table. She looked at the shoulder rig he was wearing and at the snub-nosed blue-back .38 he carried in a nylon holster. "Why do you need that?" she asked.

"Because not to carry it is to say I believe in the world. I don't believe in the world, at least not the one I've seen. I don't like authority, either. Anyone who wants to control other people is out to fuck you over. So I carry my own authority."

She took his coat into the kitchen and ran cold water over the rum-and-Coke stain, then blotted it with a paper towel and put it on a hanger. She went into the living room and stood in front of him, backlit by the electricity flickering outside. "Is my conduct embarrassing to you?" she said.

"What conduct?" he asked, looking up at her.

"This."

He looked away, then back. "You're beautiful."

"You don't think I'm an adventuress or a Judas?"

"A guy with my record can't judge anybody."

"You do like me, don't you? I don't look too old or heavy and wrinkled?"

"You're not any of those things. You're like New Orleans, Felicity. You're an orchid in a garden that never saw sunshine."

Her mouth parted. "No one ever said anything like that to me."

"You're every man's dream. Give yourself some credit."

She spread her knees and knelt on his thighs and held his head against her breasts and kissed his hair. "Oh, Clete," she said. "Don't go away from me. Not now, not ever."

He didn't know what to say or do. He closed his eyes and saw an image deep in his mind that made no sense. He saw his father's milk truck driving away from him, the melted ice draining over the back bumper, swinging in a thick, dirty spray on the street.

On Monday afternoon I looked through the upstairs window and saw three cruisers pull up in front of the north pasture, and one deputy get out and unchain the vehicle gate. The three cruisers went inside the pasture, and the deputy chained the gate behind them. The vehicles drove through the grass and came to a stop thirty yards from Clete's cabin.

Earlier in the day, Albert Hollister had dumped and scrubbed out and refilled the water tank by the barn. The horses were drinking out of it when Sheriff Elvis Bisbee and two uniformed deputies and a man in a suit stepped from the vehicles and fanned out and approached the cabin, each with the heel of his hand resting on the butt of his sidearm. The horses backed away from the tank, their skin twitching the way it does when they're attacked by blowflies.

By the time I got downstairs and out the front door, I could see two deputies shaking down Gretchen against a cruiser, running their hands under her arms and inside her thighs. Clete was arguing with Bisbee, up close and personal, his face red, his hands barely held in check at his sides, like a ball-player getting into the face of an umpire.

I went through the pedestrian gate, past the horses and the barn. "Hold on," I said.

The sheriff turned around. So did the plainclothes. I realized he was the uniformed deputy who had ridiculed Gretchen.

"No, sir, Mr. Robicheaux," the sheriff said.

"No, sir, what?" I replied.

"This time you back off."

"What's she charged with?" I asked.

"Put it in the plural," he replied.

"You want me to tell him?" the plainclothes said.

"What's your name?" I said.

"Detective Jack Boyd."

"Sheriff, this is the same guy who called Miss Gretchen 'butch' up on the hillside," I said.

"Then she can file a complaint," he replied.

"I asked you what she's charged with."

"How about vandalizing a motel room?" said the sheriff. "How about kidnapping and assault and battery? How about conspiracy to commit kidnapping? Her partner in this is Wyatt Dixon. How do you like that?"

"Who'd they kidnap?" I said.

"A guy named Anthony Zappa," the sheriff said. "Know the name? He worked for Love Younger."

Behind him, the two uniformed deputies were hooking up Gretchen. Her shoulders looked wide and stiff against her shirt, her midriff showing.

"That's ridiculous. She's not a kidnapper or someone who vandalizes motels," I said.

"She only kills them?"

"You're talking about the guy on the river, the one who shot at her from a pickup truck? That was self-defense."

"Yesterday evening Zappa was taped to a chair in a motel on West Broadway. He bailed through a window, probably because he was being tortured. In the meantime, the clerk chained up his Harley and dragged it down the street and left it burning in the middle of an intersection. When I asked if you knew Anthony Zappa's name, I used the past tense."

"He's dead?" I said.

"He was when we found his body up Rattlesnake Creek this morning."

"She was with me last night," Clete said.

"Where?" the sheriff said.

"Here, at the cabin," Clete replied.

"It's funny you say that," the sheriff said. "Detective Boyd came out here when we first got the report on the motel incident. Except your Cadillac was gone, and so was her pickup. Where were you, Mr. Purcel?" Clete started to speak. The sheriff raised his hand. "You lie to me again, you're going downtown, too," he said.

The deputies were putting Gretchen behind the wire-mesh screen in a cruiser, her wrists cuffed behind her.

"You're charging her with homicide?" I said. I saw his eyes waver, his confidence slip. "What are you not telling us?" I asked.

"What makes you think we need to tell you anything?" Jack Boyd said.

"I'm asking you for the same information you give out to the news media," I said.

"You're not the news media," he replied.

I looked at the sheriff and waited.

"Take her in," he said to Boyd.

"Yes, sir," Boyd said. "Sheriff, I made a joke to Bill Pepper. I didn't mean for the girl to hear it. I was wrong. I hope that clears up the matter once and for all."

"All right, Jack. I'll see you back at the department."

"Yes, sir."

"Miss Gretchen is not a 'girl,' buddy," I

said. "That's a term you guys can't seem to lose. I also think you guys have a way of keeping your distance from Love Younger. Don't feel bad. I grew up in the same kind of environment. People with money got a free pass on just about everything, sometimes including homicide."

"It doesn't work that way here," the detective said. His black hair was shiny, his eyes liquid and iniquitous, his sideburns flaring like grease pencil on his cheeks. Inside his narrow-cut suit coat, he wore a white snap-button shirt with silver stripes in it. I could hear the wind channeling in the trees and the horses nickering by the barn. There was something wrong with the procedure, the way Bisbee and the detective were going about it, the circuitous nature of their conversation. And the sheriff knew that I knew.

"What was the weapon?" I said.

"That's not your business," the detective said.

I looked at the sheriff again.

"You heard Detective Boyd," he said.

"You don't have a warrant for the cabin, do you?" I said.

His eyes were empty, the white tips of his mustache lifting in the breeze.

"What was the weapon?" I repeated. Clete was staring at me now.

"Did you hear what the sheriff said? Butt out," the detective said.

I waited for the sheriff to speak. He put a cigarette in his mouth but didn't light it. "Put her in the interview room when you get back to the department," he said to the detective. "I'll wrap up things here."

"If any of your people hurt my daughter, you're going to wish your mother used a better diaphragm," Clete said.

"You're about to find yourself under arrest, Mr. Purcel," the sheriff said.

"Try it. See what happens if one of these guys puts his hands on me."

The detective and one of the uniformed deputies drove away, Gretchen leaning forward on the backseat, her wrists cuffed behind her. When she twisted her head and looked through the rear window, I thought of a balloon snipped loose from its string, floating away in the wind stream.

"The judge wouldn't give you a warrant for the cabin, would he?" I said to the sheriff.

"We're still in the early stages of the investigation," he said. "You made a remark about the integrity of my department. I want you to take that back."

"I think the problem is yours, sir, not mine."

He lit his cigarette and puffed on it thoughtfully, the smoke drifting from under the brim of his hat, his pale blue eyes fixed on the horses. "Did you know Albert Hollister did time on a Florida chain gang?"

I didn't know what he was getting at, but it

wasn't good. "Albert makes no secret about his jail time. He was a kid. He wasn't a criminal, either."

"So how'd he end up on a chain gang?"

I didn't want to pursue it. "How did Zappa die?" I asked.

"He was shot to death. Two in the head, one in the mouth. Sound like the signature of anyone you know?"

"What caliber?" I said.

"Approximately forty-four."

"Approximately?" I said.

"The ballistics on this one will probably remain uncertain."

"What the hell are you talking about?" I said.

"There are no striations in the ball," he said.

"The *ball*?" I said.

"All three projectiles were fired from a weapon with no rifling in the barrel."

"Like a cap-and-ball pistol or a smoothbore musket?"

"Like one that Albert Hollister might have in his gun cabinet," he replied. "One he might have given to Gretchen Horowitz."

"Or like one that Love Younger might own?" I said. "It's funny how his name keeps getting pushed out of the conversation."

"Use your common sense, Mr. Robicheaux. Do you believe Love Younger is a killer?"

It was pointless to argue with Bisbee's mind-set or his frame of reference. Would historians call John D. Rockefeller a murderer because his goons killed women and children at the Ludlow Massacre? Did the Du Pont family have blood splatter on their shoes? Was dropping a five-hundred-pound bomb marked "occupant" a questionable act? What greater authority is there than ignorance?

"I've got to ask you one more question, Sheriff," I said. "Why would you promote a man like Boyd to detective grade?"

"He passed the test. He claims to be Indian, so I have to deal with affirmative action. Also, I didn't have anybody else, and it's a temporary appointment. Anything else?"

"Yeah, you've got the wrong person in custody, and I think you know it," I replied.

"I'll hate myself later for saying this," he said. "I know I will. It will eat my lunch. But I have to do it, so please accept my apology in advance. I can't stomach you two guys. I look at you and get mad. I wish you'd go back home and drown in the mosquitoes or whatever it is you grow down there. I don't know why I have these feelings. There's just something about you that really pisses me off."

Bail was to be set for Gretchen early Tuesday morning. Clete and I drove to town and ate breakfast in a café across from the courthouse and waited on a bondsman Clete knew. Clete had lied when he told Elvis Bisbee he was with Gretchen the night Anthony Zappa was shot to death. I had not been able to bring myself to ask him where he actually was. The waitress set down our order and refilled our coffee cups and went away. Clete dipped a biscuit in a bowl of milk gravy and bit into it. So far all he'd told me was that Gretchen and Dixon had gone after Zappa because he was one of the men who'd attacked Dixon and his girlfriend on the Blackfoot River.

"Where'd you go Sunday night?" I asked.

He kept chewing, his gaze fixed on a group of homeless people sitting under the trees on the courthouse lawn. "I think some of those homeless guys are Rainbows," he said. "They used to follow the Grateful Dead around. When I came back from Vietnam, I got stoned in Oakland with the Merry Pranksters. At least the girl I woke up with said she was a Merry Prankster. She introduced me to Hunter Thompson. I ever tell you that?"

Clete had gone into his old mode of slipping the punch and talking about every subject on earth except the one at hand. "You were with Felicity Louviere Sunday night?"

"What do you want me to say? I'm getting it on with a married woman? I can't keep it in my pants?"

"You tell me."

"I went to meet her at the stone cabin the Youngers own on Sweathouse Creek. I went to tell her I'd made a mistake, that I didn't want to hurt her and maybe not her husband, either. I went there to tell her I was wrong."

"What happened?"

He had put down his biscuit and was staring at his plate. "She said she and her husband had just visited their daughter's grave. She said he was full of grief. She said maybe he wasn't such a bad guy after all."

"That should have been it, right? I mean, she was admitting the mistake, and so were you. That's all people can do."

"It didn't work out that way. She said she'd fallen in love with me and she didn't want me to go away. She didn't care if I was old or fat or a drunk or a guy who's done some stuff he won't ever talk about."

"You got it on with her?"

"Why don't you put it up there on the blackboard so the customers can read about my sex life while they check out the daily special?"

"Clete, what are you doing?"

"Getting my daughter out of the can. I thought that's why we came to town."

"I didn't mean to sound judgmental."

"Except you are judgmental, and it makes me feel like somebody poured liquid pig flop in my shoes."

"Is she going to leave her husband?"

"We didn't talk about that."

"This is going to tear you up, partner."

"What am I supposed to do about it? Rip out my genitalia? Kill myself?"

"Bail out of it."

"That's why I met with her at the cabin Sunday night. Except things didn't work out as planned. I didn't get home till two in the morning."

I started to tell him I didn't need any more details, then realized how cruel that would be. Across the street, the homeless people were out on the sidewalk sailing a Frisbee. "We've been in worse trouble," I said.

"When?" he asked.

"Gretchen didn't do Zappa. That's all we have to keep in mind right now. We get her out of jail, and we get rid of this bogus murder beef," I said.

"How?"

"I saw an antique Winchester inside the camper shell on Wyatt Dixon's truck. It looked like an 1892, the one with the elevator sight. It wouldn't be unlikely for him to own a couple of smoothbore black-powder pieces. Montana has a primitive weapons big-game season that opens in the early fall. It's the kind of gig Dixon would be up for."

"You think Dixon capped Zappa?"

"He told me an eye for an eye. I think he meant it."

"I got something else bothering me, Dave. You think Gretchen might have a thing for Dixon?"

"She has better judgment," I replied.

"But it's a possibility?"

"Give her some credit." I tried to sound convincing. I doubted if anyone knew what went on inside the head of Gretchen Horowitz.

"This is a crock, isn't it?" Clete said.

"We need to get to the heart of the problem. Elvis Bisbee isn't going to be much help."

"Asa Surrette is at the center of it all?"

"Yeah, the guy who probably wants to do things to Alafair that most people can't imagine. I can't sleep thinking about it. We've got to put this guy out of business."

"To what degree?"

When I didn't reply, he picked up his fork and started eating. His food had grown cold; he was chewing and swallowing it as he would cardboard. He drank a glass of water and looked at me, his face round and flat. "Answer my question, Dave. How do we play this one?"

"We wipe him off the planet," I said.

"That's more like it, big mon."

No, it wasn't. Grandiosity is always the mark of fear and uncertainty, and as soon as I'd spoken those words, I knew they would come back to mock me.

CHAPTER 18

Asa Surrette was officially dead, even though he had left a note under Alafair's windshield wiper outside the Lolo post office. I wanted to be angry at the authorities in Kansas and also at the FBI for concluding that he had died in the collision of the prison van with the tanker truck. Unfortunately, I had been guilty of the same obtuseness when Alafair told me she was sure Surrette was stalking her.

After we returned from the jail with Gretchen, I sat down with a legal pad and a felt-tip pen by our bedroom window and began writing down as many details as I could about Surrette. Any detective who has investigated serial killings, or any psychiatrist who has spent time interviewing psychopaths such as the cousins Angelo Buono, Jr., and Kenneth Bianchi or the satanist Richard Ramirez or the BTK killer, Dennis Rader, will be the first to tell you that behavioral science tends to fall apart when you probe the souls of men like these. It's not unlike an attempt to fathom the origins of the universe. At a certain point, the laws of science lose their applicability.

When it came to motivation, misogyny was often in the mix. So was pedophilia. These two forms of psychosis did not explain the level of violence and savagery the perpetrators inflicted on their victims. I have my speculations, although they are founded on personal experience and not the results of any study I'm aware of. I have known many cruel people in my life. Their cruelty, in my opinion, was the mask for their fear. It's that simple.

We all agree that anyone who is cruel to animals is a moral and physical coward and undeserving of the air he breathes. This same person, however, has a way of working himself into a position of authority over others, often children, even though all the warning signs are there. I've never understood our collective unwillingness to question the authority of a predator who happens to acquire a badge or an insignia or a clerical collar or who carries a whistle on a lanyard around his neck. Without our sanction, these pitiful excuses for human beings would wither and die like amphibians gasping for oxygen and water on the surface of Mars.

The motivations of a psychopath are almost irrelevant in an investigation. Psychoanalytical speculation about a moral imbecile makes for great entertainment, but it doesn't put a net over anyone, and you do yourself no favor by trying to place yourself inside his head. The methodology of the psychopath is a different issue, one that frequently proves to be his undoing. In all probability, the perpetrator's pattern will repeat itself, primarily because he's a narcissist and thinks his method, if it has worked once, is fail-safe; second, the psychopath is not interested in the hunt but, rather, in assaulting and murdering his prey, unlike a professional thief, who is usually a pragmatist and considers theft an occupation and not a personal attack upon his victim.

Asa Surrette's pattern in Kansas was not imaginative. He used his job as an electrician to enter the victim's home and lie in wait. He bound and tortured and suffocated most of his victims and ejaculated on the women and girls but did not penetrate them. He posed them and took trophies home — purses, underwear, costume jewelry, wedding rings, driver's licenses. If he took money from the crime scene, it was coincidental.

I had created two columns on my legal pad, one detailing the characteristics of Surrette's crimes and the other a list of his jobs, the uniforms he might have worn, his travels, and his known friends.

I compared the information I had written

on the legal pad with what I knew about his crimes in Montana, if indeed Asa Surrette was the same man who had shot an arrow at Alafair and left the message on the cave wall and murdered Angel Deer Heart and Bill Pepper and perhaps the pilot whose twin-engine Cessna had exploded west of Missoula.

The murders in Wichita were aimed at women and girls with whom he had no known prior contact. Was the same true of Angel Deer Heart? Why would a seventeen-year-old girl leave a biker nightclub full of music and excitement and go off with a seedy old man who had the social appeal of a soiled litter box?

Unless she knew him.

There was another troubling issue. To anyone's knowledge, with the exception of the farmer from whom he possibly stole a truck, Surrette had never attacked a lone male. If Surrette was our man, why would he go after Bill Pepper in the cottage up at Swan Lake, and why would he sexually mutilate him?

I had only one answer: Surrette had planted the bug in Clete's cabin and learned that Pepper had kidnapped and sexually abused Gretchen Horowitz. He murdered Pepper, knowing there was a good chance Clete or Gretchen would be blamed for his death.

Why go to all this trouble to do injury to

Clete and Gretchen, neither of whom had done him any harm? It wasn't adding up. Also, what was Surrette living on?

Crime is about money, sex, or power. I had a feeling all three were involved with our visitor from the land of the Yellow Brick Road. As I stared down at my legal pad, I realized there was one element missing from all the forensic evidence gathered by authorities during the twenty-year period Surrette had been torturing and murdering people. He had not left messages with biblical or messianic overtones. Even when he called the authorities or the news media to tell them where they could find a body, he made no grandiose claims. Where and when had he taken on his new persona? In prison? Or had the transformation not been of his choosing?

Some people in A.A. say a recovering drunk should not go inside his own head without an escort. I was beginning to think they were right.

I went into Alafair's room. She had worked all night on her new novel and had eaten breakfast while the sky was dark, then had gone to bed. She was sleeping on her side, her long black hair scattered on her face, her mouth slightly parted. She had grown into a tall and lithe young woman who spoke with a South Louisiana accent and whose posture was always erect and whose eye was clear and whose sense of principle governed every aspect of her life. Even in sleep, an aura of peace and strength seemed to radiate from her face. The window was open, and up the hillside I could see the darkness of the pines and cedars and fir trees, and I knew that inside the deep shade on the hillside was the tiger William Blake had written about, burning brightly in the forests of the night, his brain dipped from a furnace and forged with a hammer and chain. The tiger was Asa Surrette, the bane of us all, the trees lighting when he padded through the undergrowth, his guttural sounds a prelude of things to come.

Where are you, sir? How brave and fearsome would you be on a level playing field? Do you swell with pride when you remember the child you hung from a pipe in a basement? I wonder how well you would fare if you were faced with the prospect of eating eight rounds from a 1911-model .45 auto?

Alafair's eyes opened and looked into mine. She lifted herself on one elbow and pushed her hair over her forehead. "Is everything all right?" she asked.

"It's fine," I replied.

"That look on your face."

"Let's stay close together until this stuff with Surrette is over."

"I'm not afraid of him. I wish he would come around."

388

"Caution and fear aren't the same thing."

"You don't know him, Dave. I do. He's a frightened, pathetic little man."

I pulled up a chair next to her bed. "So was Hitler," I said. "Don't underestimate the power of evil. Sometimes I think it finds a vessel to operate in, then discards it and moves on."

"I think you're giving Surrette too much credit."

"About fifteen years ago, a twenty-one-year-old kid broke into a home in the Blackfoot Valley and tied up the husband and wife in chairs and butchered them alive. The husband had a seventh-degree black belt in karate. When the kid was awaiting execution in Deer Lodge, some inmates got out of lockdown and took over the cell house for three days. The kid killed or helped kill five more people. On the day of his execution, he had to be awakened from a sound sleep."

Alafair went into the bathroom and washed her face and came back out. "Want to go back to Louisiana?"

I didn't answer.

"Of course not," she said. "Because we don't run away from problems. That's what you always taught me. And we never allow ourselves to be afraid. You said it over and over when I was growing up."

"I didn't say close your eyes to reality."

"Where's Gretchen?" she said.

"At the cabin with Clete."

"None of this is her fault. Don't put it on her, Dave."

"I haven't," I said.

"You were thinking about it."

"She's a lightning rod, Alf."

"Let's get something straight, Pops. I'm the one who stoked up Asa Surrette, not Gretchen."

"It's not all about you. He has other reasons for being here. I just don't know what they are."

She put her hand on the back of my neck and squeezed. "You worry too much. We'll get through this. What is it Clete always says? Good guys *über alles*?" She took her hand away from my neck. "You're hot as a stove. You have a fever?"

"Like you say, I worry too much," I replied.

He had his hair barbered by a stylist and his suit dry-cleaned and pressed and checked into a motel under the name of Reverend Geta Noonen, way up a long mountainous slope next to a river, almost to Idaho, in an area where people still lived up the drainages and off the computer. Inside his room, he threw away his pipe and tobacco and dyed and blow-dried his hair a sandy blond and, for twenty minutes, used a brush and washrag in the shower to scrub the smell of nicotine off his skin and nails. He shaved his chest and armpits, pared and clipped his nails, and layered his body with deodorant.

When he was tempted to retrieve his pipe from the wastebasket and core it out and refill it with the dark mix of imported tobaccos he had loved for years, he put a piece of licorice in his mouth and sucked it into a tiny lump and did push-ups in front of the television and then ate another piece until the craving passed. He showered again and kept the cold water on his face and head and shoulders so long that he was numb all over and had no desire other than to get warm and to put hot food in his stomach.

Yes, he could do it, he told himself. The sacrifice of his only vice was small compared to the reward that awaited him west of Lolo, on the ranch owned by Albert Hollister. He took a print shirt from a box of eighteen he had bought at Costco and put it on with his beige suit and a pair of new loafers and looked into the mirror. Clean-shaven and blond, he hardly recognized himself. He looked like an aging sportsman, a sun-bleached fellow strolling along a beach in the Florida Keys, his mouth effeminate in an appealing way, the palm trees lifting against a lavender sky, a woman at an outside bar glancing up at him.

Not bad, he thought.

He ate supper at the counter in the café attached to the motel. Through the back window, he could see the river flowing long and straight out of the hills, the rocks protruding from the riffle, the surface dark and glistening with the last rays of a red sun. A man in hip waders was fly-casting in the shallows, working the nylon line into a figure eight above his head and laying the fly onto the riffle as gently as a butterfly descending on a leaf. Except the man who had registered as the Reverend Geta Noonen was not interested in fly-fishing. He could see a swing set on the motel lawn, down by the water, and a little girl throwing rocks in the current while the mother watched. He put a forkful of meat loaf in his mouth, blowing air on it as he chewed, as though it were too hot to swallow.

"The food okay?" the waitress asked. She was young and uncertain, her bones as fragile as a bird's. Her pink uniform was splattered on one side with either grease or dishwater, and she kept looking away from the man's face as she waited for him to answer.

"It's perfect," he said.

"I thought it might be too hot. I put it in the micro because you were in the washroom."

"You have a nice place here."

"It's out of the way, but we like it," she said, refilling his coffee cup, her face filling with pleasure because the customer had complimented the place where she worked.

"It's a family-type diner. That's the best

kind. I bet it's American-owned," he said.

"Yes, sir, it is."

He gazed out the window, his eyes sleepy and warm with sentiment. "Salt of the earth," he said.

"Pardon?"

"I was talking about those people out there. Mother and child. That's the salt of the earth."

"You talk like a preacher."

"That's because I am."

"Which church?"

"The big one, the one that doesn't have a name."

She seemed to think a moment. "Meaning Jesus doesn't belong to just one denomination?"

"That pretty much says it all. Watch yourself."

"Sir?"

"You're about to spill that hot coffee on your foot."

"I know better than that."

"I bet you do. I bet you know plenty."

"Beg your pardon?"

"About the restaurant business and public relations. About the people who come in here. You're a good judge of people, I bet."

"I can tell the good ones from the bad ones."

"Which am I?"

"You're a preacher, aren't you? That speaks

for itself, doesn't it?"

"You better be careful. I might run off with you. If my daughter had grown up, I bet she'd be like you."

"You lost your daughter?"

"It was a long time ago. You have a sweet face, just like she did."

She blushed and was about to reply when another customer came through the front door and tapped on the counter for his order to go. "Excuse me," she said. "I better get back to work."

As she walked away, she did not see the change of expression in the face of the man who called himself the Reverend Geta Noonen. He set down his fork and looked at it with deliberation, then picked up his coffee and drank from it and stared at his reflection. By the time he set the cup back in the saucer, his expression was once again benign and ordinary, his attention focused on his meal, his eyes drifting back to the scene behind the motel, where the mother was pushing her daughter back and forth on the swing.

He put a two-dollar tip on the counter and waited until the waitress was in the vicinity of the cash register before he got up to pay his check.

"I forgot to ask if you wanted any pie," she said. "We have peach cobbler that's good. The cherry pie isn't bad, either."

"I never pass up cherry pie. What time do you close?"

"Ten. I usually don't work this late. I'm filling in for somebody else. In the morning I have to come in early and open up. I don't mind, though."

"You belong to a church?"

"I go at Christmas and Easter."

"I'll wager they know you're there, too."

"I don't understand."

"I didn't mean to be too personal a moment ago. But I need to tell you something. You have an aura. Certain people have it. I think you're one of them."

Her eyes filmed, and there was a visible lump in her throat when she looked back at him.

He walked out of the café into the night, the stars like a spray of white diamonds from one horizon to the other, the highway that led to Lookout Pass climbing higher and higher into the mountains, where the headlights of the great trucks driving into Idaho tunneled up into the darkness, then dipped down on the far side of the grade and seemed to disappear into a bowl of ink.

Reverend Noonen walked onto the lawn where the mother had been swinging her little girl. The swing was empty, the chains clinking slightly in the breeze. The man glanced at his wristwatch and looked back at the lighted windows of the café, inside which the young waitress was wiping off the counter, bending over it, scrubbing the rag hard on the surface where some of his spilled food had dried. He worked a toothpick between his teeth while he watched her, then heard voices from the parking lot and realized the mother and her child were moving their suitcases from a battered van into a room at the back of the motel, in an unlighted area where no other guests seemed to be staying.

The woman was struggling with a suitcase while the little girl was climbing through the side door of the van, trying to pull out a sack of groceries that had already started to split apart, her rear end pointed out. The man removed the toothpick from his mouth and let it drop from his hand onto the grass, then walked into the parking lot. "My heavens, let me help you with that," he said.

"Thank goodness," the mother said. "I've had enough problems today without this. Our room is just over there. This is very kind of you."

In the morning he rose with the sun and showered again and put on fresh clothes and ordered a big breakfast in the café. The owner was doing double duty, running the cash register and carrying plates from the serving window to the counter and the tables.

"Where's the little lady who was working here last night?" said the man who called

396

himself Reverend Geta Noonen.

"That's Rhonda."

"Where might she be?"

"She didn't show up this morning."

"She has a glow about her. Sorry, what was that you said?"

"She didn't come in. It's not like her." The owner looked out the window at the highway, where the sun was shining on a rock slide. The rocks were jagged and sharp-edged, and some had bounced out on the shoulder of the asphalt. The owner frowned as he looked at the broken rock on the roadside.

"Maybe she's sick," said the man sitting at the counter.

"She didn't answer her phone," the owner said.

"Does she have folks here'bouts?"

"Not really. She lives way up a dirt road by Lookout Pass. I've always told her she should move into town."

"I bet she had car trouble. Her cell phone wouldn't work out here, would it?"

"I called the sheriff. He's sending a cruiser. You want more coffee?" the owner said.

"Maybe a piece of that cherry pie to go. I guess every man should be allowed one vice."

"What's that you say?"

"I've got an addiction to desserts. I can't get enough. Especially cherry pie."

"I know what you mean."

"I doubt it."

"Come again?" the owner said.

"Nobody likes pie and cobbler and chocolate cake and jelly roll doughnuts as much as me. I don't gain weight, but I can sure put it down. I hope the lady is all right. She seemed like a sweet thing."

The owner turned around and looked at the shelf where he kept his pastries. "Sorry, the cherry pie is all gone."

"I'll have some the next time I'm by. I like it here. You've got a nice class of people."

The owner began picking up the dirty dishes from the counter and didn't look up again until the man had left. He dialed the number of his missing employee and let the phone ring for two minutes before he hung up. Because he didn't know what else to do, he went outside into the harshness of the sunlight and looked up and down the highway, waiting for her car or a sheriff's cruiser to appear. Then he crossed the four-lane and began kicking the fallen rock off the edge of the road back onto the shoulder.

Geta Noonen loaded his suitcase into the used SUV he had just purchased and drove slowly out onto the highway, the gravel that was impacted in his tire treads clicking as loudly as studs on the asphalt. He passed the owner and tapped on the horn and stuck his arm out the window to wave good-bye. The owner waved back and continued to clean the broken rock out of the traffic lane, lest someone run over it and have an accident.

The morning was bright and cool when Geta Noonen drove into Missoula and went into a hardware and farm-supply store and came out with four hundred dollars in boxed and bagged purchases. After he had covered them with a tarp in the backseat of the SUV, he drove downtown and found a parking spot under the Higgins Street Bridge, one hour in advance of the Out to Lunch concert held weekly in the park by the Clark Fork. He slipped on a pair of aviator glasses and bought an ice cream cone from a vendor and strolled along the river walkway, pausing on an observation deck that allowed him an unobstructed view of the children riding the hand-carved wooden horses on the carousel and the kayakers practicing their maneuvers in the rapids by the bank.

As the sun rose into the center of the sky, he took up a position by a concrete abutment in the shade of the bridge and watched the cars filling the lot. When he sighted a rusted compact with two teenage girls in it, he folded his arms over his chest and gazed at the riverbank and the crowd filing under the bridge to the concert. The two girls locked their vehicle and walked through the man's line of vision without noticing that he was watching their every move.

He strolled close to their car, then placed

his hands on his hips and looked up at the sky and the mountains that ringed the city, like a tourist on his first day inside the state. He stooped over as though picking up a coin from the asphalt and sliced the air valve off one tire, then another. After the tires collapsed on the rims, he inserted the knife blade into the soft folds of rubber and sawed through the cord so they could not be repaired. He folded the knife in his palm and dropped it in his pants pocket and watched the concert from the back of the crowd, his eyes fastened on the two teenage girls.

At 1:05 P.M. the girls returned to their rusted compact and stared in shock at the slashed tires.

"I saw a couple of bad-looking kids hanging around your car," the man said. "When I walked over, they took off. I got here too late, I guess."

The girls were obviously sisters, perhaps two years apart, with blue eyes and blond hair that was almost gold. The older girl had lost her baby fat and was at least three inches taller than her sister. "Why would anyone do this to us?" she said.

"Guess it's the way a lot of kids are being raised up today," the man said. "I'd offer to change your tire, but you've got two flats and probably only one spare. Is there somebody you can call?"

"Nobody's home," the younger girl said.

"Where are your folks?"

"Our mother works at the Goodwill," the older girl said. "Our father drives part-time for a trucking company. He's in Spokane today. He'll be home tonight. He's a minister. We have assembly at our house on Wednesday nights."

"I'm Reverend Geta Noonen. Call your mother and ask if it's all right if I drive you two home," the man said.

"There's no point in worrying her."

"I tell you what. I'll put your spare on, and we'll take the other rim to the tire store and get the tire replaced. Then we'll come back here and put it on, and you'll be on your way."

"I have to be at work at the Dairy Queen at three-thirty. I can't think. I don't have any money, either," the older girl said.

"I'll pay for it, and you can pay me back later."

"What does a tire cost?" she asked.

When he told her, she looked as though she were about to cry.

"Look, don't worry about it," he said. "Take my cell phone and tell your mother what's happened. We'll drop the rim at the tire store, and I'll drive both of you home. I'll take you to work, if need be, or I'll take you to pick up your new tire. We'll handle it together. There's no problem that can't be solved. Whereabouts do you live?"

"Out Highway 12, west of Lolo."

"You'll have to give me directions. Now call your mother and tell her everything is okay."

"I don't know how to thank you."

"You don't owe me anything. You're giving me a chance to practice a little of what I preach," he said.

Forty-five minutes later, he turned off Highway 12 onto a dirt road and headed up a gulch between wooded hills that were scarred by logging roads from the days of the clear-cuts. "It's sure pretty out this way. Do you know if there are any rentals hereabouts?" he said.

"We rent out a room sometimes," the older girl said.

"I just need a place to come and go, and a small storage area," he said. "I'm a traveling minister, kind of like the old-time saddle preachers, except I don't have a saddle."

"You want me to ask my mother?"

"I'd appreciate it. I wouldn't be any trouble. Say, that's a big ranch up there."

"That's Mr. Hollister's place. He's a writer. Three of his books have been made into movies."

The man pushed the sun visor across the driver's window as he drove past the archway over Albert Hollister's driveway and did not look at the rock-and-log house up on the bench or glance in the direction of the barn or the horses in the north pasture.

"Imagine that, a man who makes movies tucked away here in the backcountry. This life is sure full of surprises," he said. "Is that your house in that green hollow at the end of the road? If you ask me, you have yourselves a regular paradise up here. It'd suit me to a T."

CHAPTER 19

I have always loved and welcomed the rain, even though sometimes the spirits of the dead visit me inside it. During the summer, when I was a child, no matter how hot the weather was, there was a shower almost every afternoon at three o'clock. The southern horizon would be piled with storm clouds that resembled overripe plums, and within minutes you would feel the barometer plunge and see the oak trees become a deeper green and the light become the color of brass. You could smell the salt in the wind and an odor that was like watermelon that had burst open on a hot sidewalk. Suddenly, the wind would shift and the oak trees would come to life, leaves swirling and Spanish moss straightening on the limbs. Just before the first raindrops fell, Bayou Teche would be dimpled by bream rising to feed on the surface. No more than a minute later, the rain would pour down in buckets, and the surface of the Teche would dance with a hazy yellow glow that looked more like mist than rain.

For me, the rain was always a friend. I think that is true of almost all children. They seem to understand its baptismal nature, the fashion in which it absolves and cleanses and restores the earth. The most wonderful aspect of the rain was its cessation. After no longer than a half hour, the sun would come out, the air would be cool and fresh, the four o'clocks would be opening in the shade, and that evening there would be a baseball game in City Park. The rain was part of a testimony that assured us the summer was somehow eternal, that even the coming of the darkness could be held back by the heat lightning that flickered through the heavens after sunset.

The rain also brought me visitors who convinced me the dead never let go of this world. After my father, Big Aldous, died out on the salt, I would see him inside the rain, standing up to his knees in the surf, his hard hat tilted sideways on his head. When he saw the alarm in my face, he would give me a thumbs-up to indicate that death wasn't a big challenge. I saw members of my platoon crossing a stream in the monsoon season, the rain bouncing on their steel pots and sliding off their ponchos, the mortal wounds they had sustained glowing as brightly as Communion wafers.

The person who contacted me most often in the rain was my murdered wife, Annie, who usually called during an electric storm to assure me she was all right, always apologizing for the heavy static on the line. Don't ever let anyone tell you this is all there is. They're lying. The dead are out there. Anyone who swears otherwise has never stayed up late in a summer storm and listened to their voices.

The rain drummed on Albert's fireproof roof through Wednesday night and into the early-morning hours until it quit at dawn and left the pastures pooled with water and the trees smoking with fog. When I looked out our bedroom window on the third floor, I saw an animal emerge from the woods on the north end of the property and step through the wire back fence and enter the pasture. I thought it was a coyote, one of several that came onto the property in the early hours to dig pocket gophers out of their burrows. Then I realized the color was wrong. Its fur was black, flecked with silver, its shoulders heavy, its step quick and assured, its muzzle pointed straight ahead and not at the ground. The horses in the pasture were going crazy. I realized I was looking at a wolf, perhaps the leader of a pack that had come in from the Idaho wilderness west of Albert's ranch.

I put on my coat and half-topped boots and went downstairs and removed Albert's scoped '03 Springfield from his gun cabinet. I also scooped up a handful of .30-06 cartridges and dropped them in my coat pocket. Albert was drinking coffee in the kitchen, dressed in pajamas and slippers and a robe. "Where are you going with my rifle?" he said.

"There's a wolf in the north pasture," I said. "It's after your horses."

"We've never had wolves."

"You do now."

"Don't shoot it."

"You want to take care of it?" I said, offering him the rifle.

"I'll be down in a minute."

I could hear the horses whinnying and their hooves thudding on the sod and splashing through water. I went through the mudroom and out the garage door and ran toward the pedestrian gate in the north pasture. The horses were in full panic, running in circles, corkscrewing, kicking blindly behind them. The wolf was moving through the grass in a half crouch, increasing its speed, its jaw hanging loose. I pressed five rounds into the Springfield's magazine and locked down the bolt. Inside the gate, I passed the barn and, on the far side, saw the wolf splash through a pool of water, drops of mud splattering its muzzle and forequarters. I twisted my left arm through the leather sling on the rifle and threw the stock to my shoulder and swung the crosshairs of the telescopic sight on the wolf's rib cage.

The wolf seemed to sense that a new factor

had entered the equation. I saw it look directly at me, its nose black and wet and filled with tiny lines, the nostrils dilating. I moved the sight four feet in front of the wolf and squeezed off a round. Fire jumped from the muzzle, and the loud *carrack* echoed off the hillsides. I saw a jet of mud and water fly in the air.

The wolf went back under the fence, the wire twanging on the steel stakes, a fence clip popping loose. I thought the wolf would keep moving, but I was mistaken. It went up the slope and disappeared behind a boulder, then reappeared next to a cedar tree and stared at me. I put the sight right on its face. There was a gray scar below one eye and another scar on its chest. On the front right paw was an area almost entirely clean of fur, as though the animal had stripped off its skin in a trap.

I ejected the spent cartridge and pushed another forward in the chamber and locked down the bolt. I moved the crosshairs to the base of the boulder and fired. The round was a soft-nose, and it flattened into the rock and powdered the air with a dirty mix of lichen and rock dust.

The wolf bounded through the trees and up the hill. I worked the bolt again and fired one more round for good measure and heard it strike a hard surface and whine across an arroyo with a diminishing sound like the tremolo in a banjo string.

"Did you hurt it?" Albert said behind me. He had pulled his trousers on over his pajamas and was wearing rubber boots and a flopbrim Australian hat.

"No. I didn't try to."

"I'm glad. They're protected, unless you or your livestock are in danger."

"Your livestock *are* in danger."

"I'm glad you didn't shoot it, regardless. Come inside and have some coffee."

"You never had trouble with wolves?"

"No. It's probably operating by itself. I doubt it'll come back."

"In my opinion, that's wishful thinking. That wolf is not afraid. He knows there's food here."

"It's nature's way."

"If that wolf had its way, it would have grabbed one of your horses by its face, pulled it down on the ground, and ripped out its throat."

"I guess that's possible."

This is not a rational discussion. Don't say anything else, I told myself.

The creek bed in the pasture was swollen with rainwater and running brown and fast over the banks in the grass, the cottonwoods dripping, the clouds of fog in the fir and pine trees so white and thick that we couldn't see the tops of the hills.

"I wish you hadn't shot toward the end of the pasture, Dave," Albert said. "There's a house inside that box canyon."

"I know where it is. My angle was such that even if the bullet ricocheted, it would have gone into the hillside. I exposed no one to risk when I took those shots."

"Let's not talk about it anymore."

"You want me to walk down there and knock on the door? I'd be happy to do that."

"I said forget it. I'm sure they're fine."

Albert really knew how to plant the harpoon. "Who lives there?" I asked.

"A part-time preacher and his wife and two teenage daughters," he replied. "I'll talk to them later, in case they wonder why we were shooting down here."

I ejected the spent cartridge from the chamber into the mud, and the rounds from the magazine, and did not bother to pick up the unfired rounds. I think I stepped on them and pressed them into the mud. I closed the bolt and handed Albert his rifle. "The next time I try to save your horses from a predator, please reload this and shoot me, and after you've shot me, please shoot yourself. The world will be better off all the way around."

"What set you off?" he asked.

Clete had made a lifetime practice of not arguing with fate. He had also accepted the harsh reality that most experience, whether good or bad, comes at a price. Was a hangover worth the experience of the previous night?

Rarely if ever, he would probably reply, though he repeated the same behavior over and over. Was falling in love worth the cost? He didn't have to dwell on the answer to that one. Life had no value if it didn't contain love.

Was there any worse fate than not loving another and not being loved in turn? If the color gray could be applied to an emotional condition, it was a life without affection or human warmth. The absence of love ensured depression, resentment of self, feelings of guilt and fear and hostility, and an inexplicable sense of personal failure that tainted every relationship and social situation. If you wished to destroy a person, at least in Clete's opinion, you only needed to teach him that he was not acceptable in the eyes of God or his fellow man.

These were the lessons he had to learn as a child in order to survive. He didn't talk about the dues he'd paid, and he considered self-pity the bane of the human race. The downside of his stoicism was the emotional isolation it imposed upon him.

On Thursday morning Clete arranged to meet Felicity Louviere in downtown Missoula. He thought they would visit a fly and tackle shop or perhaps investigate the antique and secondhand stores by the railroad tracks, or just enjoy the weather, the way other couples did. And that was what they did, under a blue sunlit sky that seemed to stretch infinitely over the horizon. At noon they ended up at a grocery store and deli that had been open since the late nineteenth century. They ordered salads and cold drinks and sandwiches bulging with sliced meat and cheese and lettuce and tomatoes, and found a table outside, under the canvas awning flapping in the breeze. The lampposts were hung with ventilated steel baskets that overflowed with petunias; bicyclists in spandex togs powered through the traffic; the mountains and hills surrounding the town were green from the spring rains, the air as pure and clean as wind blowing off a glacier.

There was only one problem: Clete had brought his own rain cloud with him, and he didn't know how to make it go away without paying a price that so far he had not been willing to pay.

She ducked her head until she made his eyes meet hers. "You're deep in thought," she said.

"It's my kid. I think she's getting a bad deal."

"With the sheriff?"

"People are trying to kill her, but she gets rousted. I'd call that a bad deal. This guy who ended up with a pistol ball in his head? What's-his-name?"

"Tony Zappa. He was part of Love's grounds crew."

"That's not all he was. When he wasn't clipping hedges, he was raping the girlfriend of this character Wyatt Dixon."

"I didn't know him, Clete. Love hires exfelons. I think that's how he convinces himself all the other things he does don't matter."

"What other things?"

"Political intrigue. Despoiling the environment. Bribing Arabs. Whatever works. He grew up in a dirt-floor shack and thinks of the world as a shark tank."

"Because guys like him are in it, that's why."

"What are you trying to tell me?"

"Somebody wants my daughter dead. She's making a documentary that exposes some of Love Younger's enterprises. What conclusion should I come to? In the meantime, this nutcase from Kansas is out there somewhere, and he's probably got connections to the Younger family."

"That's not what you're really trying to say, is it?"

Her hand rested on her plastic cup. There was moisture on the balls of her fingers, and he wanted to reach over and clasp her hand in his and warm it and protect her. But from what?

"I owe my kid," he said. "Her father let her down. That's me. Now I got a chance to make it right. I got the feeling I'm not doing a very good job of it."

"Maybe you'd be doing a better job if you

let go of me?"

She was wearing a peasant dress and a beret and tennis shoes and a thin jade necklace. She looked outrageous and mysterious, like an orphan girl who had wandered out of a nineteenth-century novel into the world of the rich and famous. Or was that simply an identity she had manufactured in order to turn a burnt-out bail-skip chaser into a sock puppet? If she was looking for a guy to use, why him? If you wanted a thoroughbred, you didn't go to an elephant farm.

"I asked you a question, Clete. Do you want me to disappear from your life?" she said.

"Don't say that." The canvas awning swelled in the wind, popping loose from the aluminum frame that held it in place. The sunlight was blinding. "I care about you. I don't want to let go of you. But I can't forget that you're married." His face reddened when he realized how loud his voice was.

"You just noticed that I'm married? Somehow that got lost in your mental Rolodex?"

"You don't want to leave him when he's in mourning. I understand that," he said. "But it doesn't make me feel too good."

She covered his hand with hers. "You haven't done anything wrong. If anybody has done wrong, it's me. I married Caspian because he was rich. I tried to convince myself otherwise, but that's why I did it. It's not his fault, it's not yours, it's not Love Younger's, it's not my father's, it's mine."

"What are we going to do, kid?"

"I look like a kid to you?"

"Yeah, you do. I'm old, you're young. You're a gift that guys who look like me don't receive too often."

The color in her eyes deepened, and her face seemed to grow small and more vulnerable. He was sweating, even though the wind was cool; the sun seemed to be burning a hole through the top of his head. "We can go away," she said. "Maybe for just a little while. Or maybe forever."

"Go where?" he said.

"A friend of mine lets me use her ranch outside Reno. Her mother was an actress in western movies. It's like going back to America in the 1940s. The view is wonderful. In the early mornings, you can smell the sage and flowers that only open at night. We could have such a grand time together."

"I got to take care of my daughter. I got to help Dave."

"It doesn't matter. You'll always be my big guy."

"Let's go somewhere. I mean now. Maybe the DoubleTree on the river."

"I can't. I told Love I'd go with him to visit Angel's grave. He's not doing very well."

"He was close to your daughter?"

"In his way. He's a private man and doesn't

show his feelings. He thinks of the world as his enemy. His real tragedy is he tries to control the people he loves most, and he destroys them one at a time."

"Why didn't you eighty-six this bunch a long time ago?" Clete said.

"Greed, selfishness, anger, because my father's ideals were more important to him than I was. Take your pick." She rose from her chair with her purse. "I've got to go. Caspian was suspicious when I left."

"I hate that word. It makes me feel like a bucket of shit."

"I'm sorry for using it."

"Meet me tonight," he said.

"I think bad things are going to happen to both of us, Clete."

"In what way?"

"What's the expression? 'Our fate lies not in the stars but in ourselves.' No matter what happens, I'll always love and respect you. I wish we had met years ago." Then she walked away.

He felt as though all the oxygen had been sucked out of his chest. He stared at her back as she walked to the end of the block, her dress swishing on her hips, her beret tilted on the side of her head. In seconds she was gone, like an apparition that had never been part of his life. He looked emptily at the street and took out his wallet to leave a tip on the table. That was when he saw Caspian Younger stepping into the intersection, after the traffic signal had turned red, crossing the street without looking at the cars, his face knotted with the rage of the cuckold or that of a dangerous drunk who had decided to sail across the Abyss.

As Caspian threaded his way through the people on the sidewalk, Clete could see the weakness in his chin, the petty and childlike look of injury around the mouth, the flaccid and tubular arms that had probably never picked up heavy weights or split wood with an ax, the hands that were incapable of becoming fists that could deliver a blow stronger than a mosquito bite. Caspian Younger had been one who was always shoved down in line, or stuffed headfirst into a toilet bowl in the boys' room, or bailed out of trouble by his father and treated as an infant by his mother; he was one of those whose dreams were filled with bullies at whom he flailed his fists while they laughed in his face. He was also the kind who would pull a .25 auto from his pocket and park one between your eyes before you ever saw it coming.

Clete remained seated, raising one hand gently, avoiding eye contact. "Whoa," he said.

"I warned you before," Caspian said.

"You got a right to be mad, Mr. Younger. But not here. We can talk about it somewhere else."

"I'll decide that."

"Yes, sir. That's your right. But no good will come out of this. I say let it slide for now. I'll stay out of your way."

"You're balling my wife and you dare lecture me? Where did she go?"

"Sorry, I don't know."

"She's meeting you at a motel? Don't tell me she isn't. I know her pattern."

"Time to turn the volume down, Mr. Younger."

"Really? How's this?" He picked up Clete's iced tea and threw it in his face.

"I might do the same thing if I was in your shoes," Clete said. He took out his handkerchief and wiped his face. "Maybe I'd do worse. None of this is on your wife. If there's one person responsible, you're looking at him. But I'm asking you to call it quits."

"Stand up."

"No, I won't do that. I'll get up and leave after you're gone. In the meantime, I'm sorry for the harm I've caused you."

"I'm overwhelmed at your humility. Is this hers? Must be. Her whorehouse-purple lipstick is on it," Caspian said. He picked up Felicity's plastic cup of Coca-Cola and poured it slowly on top of Clete's head, the crushed ice sliding down his forehead and face onto his shirt and shoulders.

Clete wiped his hair and face again. "She's a good woman," he said. "I think you're a lucky man."

"You're just going to sit there, in front of all these people, and not defend yourself? Stand up. I'm not afraid of you."

"You don't have any reason to be," Clete said. "I'm leaving now. Stay away from me. Don't take your anger out on your wife. If you do, you'll be walking around on stumps."

He put on his porkpie hat and walked down the street toward his Caddy, his pale blue sport coat striped with tea and Coca-Cola and grains of melting ice, everyone at the other tables too embarrassed to look directly at him.

Two hours later, he called me from the only saloon in Lolo, a biker hangout, one often crowded during the summer, particularly in the run-up to Sturgis. "Come on down. I'll buy you a lime and soda," he said.

I could hear music and a clatter of pool balls in the background. "You sound like you're half in the bag."

"My mind is crystal-clear. That's my problem. When my mind is clear, I go into clinical depression."

"Come back to the cabin, Clete."

"No, I dig it here, big mon. Right now I'm watching this fat slob with an earring through his eyebrow shoot nine ball." He took the phone away from his ear. "Yeah, I'm talking about you. That last shot was a rocket. You're beautiful, man. I've never doubted the genetic superiority of the white race."

"Are you crazy?" I said.

"When did I ever claim to be normal? Are you coming down here or not?"

"Did something happen between you and Felicity Louviere?"

"Dave, I feel like killing myself. I've never felt worse in my life."

How's that for getting a jump-start on the evening? I got in my pickup and drove down to the saloon. Two rows of motorcycles were parked outside. Clete was standing at the far end of the bar by himself, a longneck Bud and three full jiggers of whiskey in front of him. The bartender stopped me. "You know the guy down there?"

"That's Clete Purcel. He's an old friend. My name is Dave Robicheaux. I'm a cop," I said. "He's a PI. He doesn't mean any harm."

"He needs to go home and take a nap. Maybe start the day over."

"I'll see what I can do."

"The guys at the pool table paid for those three whiskies and the Budweiser. They were all in Afghanistan or Iraq."

"There won't be any trouble," I said.

I ordered a Dr Pepper and carried it down to the end of the bar. The back of Clete's neck looked oily and red and pocked with acne scars in the neon glow of the beer sign on the log wall. His coat was folded on top of the bar, with his porkpie hat placed crown-down on it. "What's the haps, noble mon?" he said.

"You called me on your cell phone."

"I did? What did I say?"

"You don't remember?"

He squeezed his eyes shut and opened them and looked into space. "I feel like my brain has been soaked in a septic tank."

"Did Felicity Louviere cut you loose?"

"You know how to turn a phrase, Streak."

"You were talking about killing yourself. What am I supposed to say?"

He told me everything that happened at the outdoor table under the awning, on a breezy day in early summer, in the midst of an alpine environment that you would consider the perfect backdrop for star-crossed lovers. When he told me what Caspian had done, I had to drop my eyes and clear my throat and pick up my glass of Dr Pepper and cracked ice and cherries and orange slices, and drink from it and pretend that nothing Clete had told me was that serious in nature. At the same time, I wanted to tear Caspian Younger apart.

"I think you did the right thing," I said.

"Right thing in what way?"

"Walking away. Taking the heat for his wife. You don't lower yourself to the level of a guy like that."

"That's not what I was asking."

"Then what's the question?"

"You know what the question is."

"You mean is a certain someone trying to do a mind-fuck on you?"

"In a word, yeah," he said.

"How would I know?"

"You're smarter about women than I am."

"I say blow it off. Let go of her."

"She bothers me. I can't get her out of my head."

"You don't think you deserve a good woman's love. That's the real problem, Clete. That has always been the problem."

"Quit it," he replied. He tipped one of the shot glasses to his mouth and drank it down, then upended the Bud and swallowed for a long time, until foam ran down the inside of the bottle's neck into his throat. He set the bottle on the bar, the alcohol glowing in his cheeks. "Somehow Surrette is a player in all this, isn't he? With Angel Deer Heart, with Caspian Younger, and maybe with the old man."

"Take it to the bank."

"Remember Randy's Record Shop? Randy would come on the air at midnight and say, 'Hang on, chil'en. We're coming to you direct from Gatlinburg.' Then he'd kick off the show with 'Swanee River Boogie' by Albert Ammons. It was great back then, wasn't it?"

"You bet," I said, avoiding his eyes and the chemically induced glow in his face.

"Maybe it's still the top of the sixth," he

said. "You think?"

"Why not," I said, falling into the old lie that both of us told ourselves.

He looked at the two remaining whiskies on the bar, then put on his porkpie hat and his stained sport coat and laid his big arm heavily across my shoulders and walked with me through the front door and out into the sunlight.

"You think she meant that about running off to a ranch in Reno?" he said.

This time I had nothing more to say.

That evening after supper, Alafair and Albert and I watched the network and the local news. The lead story locally was about a twenty-six-year-old single woman who had failed to show up at the café where she worked as a waitress on Interstate 90, east of Lookout Pass. Her name was Rhonda Fayhee. Her automobile was found parked in front of her small frame house, the keys in the ignition. All the windows and doors in the house were locked and the doors deadbolted from the inside. Her purse and wallet were on the dining room table. Her three cats were inside the house, their water bowls half full. Dry cat food was scattered on a piece of newspaper someone had spread on the kitchen floor.

On camera, a sheriff's detective said the pink uniform she had probably worn to work the previous night had been washed in a sink and put on a coat hanger in the bathroom. Anyone with knowledge about her whereabouts was asked to call the Mineral County Sheriff's Department.

CHAPTER 20

Wyatt Dixon was sitting in the living room of
Bertha Phelps's apartment, ten floors above
the old vaudeville theater called the Wilma,
with a magnificent view of the bandstand and
the merry-go-round in the park and the river
that flowed high and roiling through the city.
The light was fading in the sky, and he could
see stars high above the pink and lavender
afterglow on the rim of the mountains far to
the west. Wyatt's mind was not on the view.
When he looked up at Bertha's silhouette as
she watered her window plants, he felt the
same conflict of emotions that had always
beset him whenever he placed his trust in
others.

For most of Wyatt's life, survival had meant
war, and the rules of engagement had remained the same: If you wanted women, you
had to fly the flag; if you wanted the respect
of men, you never showed fear, and when
provoked, you rattled only once.

Bertha Phelps was an ongoing riddle he

couldn't figure out. She was an educated and intelligent countrywoman who seemed to genuinely like him and accept him, and smelled like a floral delivery truck on a hot day. She also had sand. After the attack, she called a women's crisis hotline and made an appointment with a psychotherapist, as though contracting a pest exterminator to rid her house of termites. As soon as she was released from the hospital, she insisted that she and Wyatt immediately go to bed to prove she wasn't snakebit. He had the feeling Bertha Phelps had an aggressive side that she herself wasn't aware of; the kind of woman who'd slap the hat off your head if you didn't remove it in the house on your own. Any man who said he wasn't attracted to the Calamity Janes of the world was a damn liar.

Bertha was staring at the television screen. "Listen to this, Wyatt," she said.

A sheriff's detective was being interviewed in front of a frame house sheathed with asbestos shingles up by Lookout Pass. The tenant, a woman named Rhonda Fayhee, had gone missing, not unlike a Hutterite woman who had gone for a walk outside St. Regis two months ago and hadn't been seen since.

In the background, Wyatt could see a parked Mazda and a side yard with wash hanging on a line. A uniformed deputy was crossing the grass with a pet cage in his hand. The local anchorwoman came back on the screen and said that investigators could not account for the fact that the windows were locked and the doors bolted from inside.

"This ain't the first time he's done this," Wyatt said. "He's what's called a house creep."

"Who is?" Bertha said.

"The guy who snatched her. It's like the ship in the bottle, except the house is the bottle."

"I'm sure that makes sense to you, but it doesn't to me."

"The guy dead-bolted the door, then went out a window and used a rig to slip the latch from the outside. The newslady said the animals was watered and fed. The guy who done this is a stage director. He gives the cops plenty to study on. It makes him feel powerful. In the meantime, the woman is probably going through hell, if she ain't already dead."

"How do you know all this?"

"I knew men in Huntsville pen the devil wouldn't let wash his socks."

"Do you think it's him?"

"The guy who killed Angel Deer Heart? Yeah, I do."

She sat down next to him, the couch sinking under her. "I have to tell you something. Both the city police and the sheriff's department interviewed me. They wanted to know if you owned any cap-and-ball weapons."

"What'd you tell them?"

"I don't even know what cap-and-ball means."

"Black-powder firearms. Somebody put three lead balls in a man who worked for Love Younger. The cops want to put it on me. Except I don't own no cap-and-ball guns."

"The man who was killed is one of the men who attacked us, isn't he?"

"No doubt about it."

"He was kidnapped and tortured in a motel. That's what the paper said."

"I wouldn't call it torture."

"You were there?"

"Yes, ma'am."

"I don't want you doing things like that, Wyatt."

"He was a son of a bitch and deserved a whole lot worse than what he got."

"You can't do those kinds of things in my name."

"I done it in my own name."

She placed her hand on his forehead and smoothed back his hair. His eyes never changed expression. "I have to confess something to you," she said.

"What's that?"

"I think you'll be very disappointed in me."

"No, I won't."

"You don't know what I'm about to say."

"I got my suspicions."

"Like what?"

"Those trashy ballpoint pens you was using, you didn't get them from Walmart, did you?"

He saw her swallow. "No, I didn't."

"You knew that no-good detective Bill Pepper."

"I did. I knew him very well."

"Out in Los Angeles, when he was with the LAPD?"

"Before that," she said.

"You're saying you were sexually involved with him?"

"He was my brother."

Wyatt's colorless eyes showed no reaction, but the blood in his head seemed to go somewhere else and leave helium in its place.

"So you thought it was me who done him in, carved him up with a knife and such? Thought you'd get next to me and maybe do some payback? Is that what you thought, Bertha?"

"I didn't know you. Then I learned you're incapable of doing something like that."

"You don't know what I'm capable of doing. You didn't get to know me before the state turned my head into a pinball machine and made me drink all them chemical cocktails. Maybe the man I used to be is hiding in the weeds. Ever give that some thought?"

"Remember when I saw the corn on your lawn?"

"What about it?"

"You were putting out feed for the injured

doe and her fawn. I knew then I was wrong about you and that you were a kind man."

"Maybe I knew that was exactly what you'd think. Maybe I did that for show. I got two sets of cops trying to put me back inside. I don't need a Jezebel in my life."

"I know I've hurt you deeply."

"For somebody to hurt me, they got to mean something to me in the first place," he said, rising from the couch.

"Please don't say that, Wyatt."

"I already did," he replied.

Three seconds later, he was out the door, the window at the end of the corridor lit by dry lightning, a sound like a windstorm roaring in his ears.

Friday morning he woke early at his place up the Blackfoot River and put on a western-cut suit and buffed his boots and took a new Stetson from a hatbox in the back of his closet. He sorted through a drawer full of Indian and western jewelry and broken watches and rabbit-foot key rings and found an honorary sheriff's badge that a barmaid in Prescott, Arizona, had given him years ago. He found an empty wallet and fitted the badge onto one side and slipped a photo ID he had gotten at the Houston livestock show into the celluloid compartment on the other side. An hour later, he pulled into the parking lot of the café on I-90 where Rhonda Fayhee had been employed.

"Howdy-doody. The name is Wyatt Dixon," he said to the owner, opening his improvised badge holder. "I'd like to talk to you about the Fayhee lady."

The owner was squirting a hose on the roof of the café to rinse off the ash drifting down from a fire that was burning out of control on the mountainside. He tried to study the badge, but Wyatt put it back in his coat pocket. "I've already told the sheriff's department everything I know," the owner replied.

"I'm running at it from a different angle," Wyatt said. "I think the man who grabbed her was a little different from your normal motel guests and the regular customers at your café."

"What do you mean, 'different'? What makes you think one of my guests or customers abducted her?"

"I don't think I said that. Maybe you weren't listening. Maybe somebody followed her from work to her house."

The owner's eyes wandered over Wyatt's face. "Let me turn off my hose."

"What I'm really asking you is whether Ms. Fayhee would talk in a personal way with just anybody. Would she tell a trucker or a low-rider or a husband on the make where she lived or what time she got off work?"

"No, she's not that kind of girl."

"That's my point. Do you remember her

431

talking to an older man, maybe well dressed, with a comb-over, or a man who might own a big ranch, or maybe a family-type man?"

"Somebody she'd trust?" the owner said.

"Good, we're on the right track."

"That could be lots of people. Where'd you say you're from?"

"Missoula. I told you."

"You don't sound like you're from around here."

"*I* ain't the issue. Did you have a guest here who might impress a young gal that's tired of guys who are always trying to get in her bread?"

"Who the hell are you?"

"What do you care? I'm assisting the state. Try to imagine what that girl might be going through while we're out here talking and squirting a garden hose on the rooftop."

"There was a minister here. He was a nice fellow. I saw him helping a lady unload her vehicle and carry her things inside."

"Where's his church at?"

"He didn't say. I remember Rhonda asking him. He said his church was the big one that didn't have a name."

"Which means he probably got his ordination off the Internet. What'd he look like?"

"His hair was kind of blond, like he'd been out in the sun a lot. He was clean-looking. He said he'd lost his daughter."

"You got his name and tag number inside?"

"He paid cash, so I didn't bother with the tag. I remember his name, though. I'd never heard it before. Reverend Geta Noonen. I said that was quite a name. He said, 'You can't ever tell who's going to wander in from the storm.'"

"Remember what he was driving?"

"A gray SUV. Maybe a Blazer. It had some rust on one side. Who is he?"

Wyatt looked at the fire burning on the mountainside and the ash that floated like black thread out of the sky. "Maybe he's just another rounder scamming a dollar or two out of ignorant people," he replied. "Or maybe he's just a guy that likes to get into a young girl's panties."

"I don't like the way you talk."

"Did you smell a peculiar odor in the room he slept in?" Wyatt asked.

The owner bit down on his lower lip.

"You think that fire up on the hillside is hot?" Wyatt said. "If you see that guy again, ask him what 'hot' is."

The changing of the seasons in Louisiana — the changes taking place in the earth, if you wish — were predictable and followed the rules of cause and effect, regardless if the results were good or bad. Hurricanes brought floods; tornadoes destroyed towns; and tidal waves destroyed seawalls. The footprint of the Industrial Age was there in the form of

433

canals that channeled millions of gallons of saline into freshwater marsh and poisoned the root system that bound the wetlands together.

Montana was different. Friday evening at sunset, I sat on the deck with Albert and Molly and Alafair and watched dry lightning strike in three places on a distant ridge. In under fifteen minutes, I saw three narrow columns of black smoke rising from the woods, straight up into a windless pink-tinted sky. The spring had been long and cold, with more than average rainfall, and snow was packed deep inside the trees on the peaks of the Bitterroots. How could a green forest, one damp with snowmelt, be set ablaze so easily?

"Because we've been in a drought since 1990," Albert said. He was drinking Scotch and soda, more of it than he should. "Because insects kill more trees than wildfires do. The drought arrives first, then the pine beetles. Dry lightning provides the ignition. There're places over in Idaho that look like they were sprayed with Agent Orange."

"I think I'll take a walk. How about you?" I said to Molly and Alafair.

"Maybe Albert might like to go," Molly said.

"Dave thinks I rain on parades," Albert said.

"He does not," Molly said.

"Go on. I'm going to fix another drink," he said.

We walked down the long drive and under the arch onto the road. The temperature was dropping, the sun's afterglow fading beyond the mountains.

"Why didn't you invite Albert to come along?" Molly asked.

"He's in one of his moods. I didn't want to get into an argument with him."

"This is the third anniversary of his wife's death."

"I didn't know that."

"He told me this afternoon."

"I'll go back."

"No, he'll be all right. Don't let him think we feel sorry for him."

"No, I was wrong. I'm not going to drop it," I said.

I walked back up the driveway. The valley was almost completely dark. I could hear the chain tinkling on the gate and the horses nickering and bolting in the north pasture. The wind had come up and was blowing in the cottonwoods by the creek bed, but I couldn't smell smoke or detect any other cause that might agitate the horses.

When I reached the top of the driveway, I saw the flashlight beam bouncing along the ground behind Albert's office. "What are you doing?" I said.

Albert pointed the flashlight beam below

the windows that ran along the back of the house. "I thought I saw a man out here," he said.

"When?"

"Two minutes ago." He walked closer to me, shining his light up into the trees on the hillside. I could smell the Scotch on his breath and the heat trapped in his flannel shirt.

"Where did he go?" I asked.

"When I came outside, there was nobody here."

"Sometimes the wind makes shadows on the grass," I said.

"I never saw a shadow run. Take a look at this."

He pointed the light down at an area between the lilac bushes and a bathroom window. I could see two funnel-shaped tracks stenciled deeply into the compost.

"Those look like they belong to a dog or a coyote," I said.

"No, they're too big."

"A wolf?" I said.

"Yeah, I think that's Brother Wolf's prints, all right." He moved his light around the base of the lilacs and out onto the belt of lawn between the house and the hillside. "Here's the problem. There're only two of them."

"Say again?"

"Two paw prints. They're three inches deep in the soil. You can see the points of the nails.

There was a heavy animal here. But it left only two impressions. How is that possible, unless it was standing up? Besides, I didn't see an animal out here. I saw a man."

"Maybe it's time to cork the jug for the evening," I said.

"Don't you be talking down to me like that, Dave." He swept the flashlight beam across the tree trunks, illuminating boulders that were half buried in the soil. "I always said this was bloody ground. Why is it we think we can destroy a whole race of people and not pay a price for it?"

"*We* didn't do it."

"Like hell." He clicked off the light. "I'm going inside. It's cold out here."

I didn't believe in wolves that stood on their hind legs to look through bathroom windows, any more than I believed in Wyatt Dixon's claim that a goat-footed creature out of a medieval book on demonology had taken up residence in the cave behind Albert's house. At least that's what I told myself. Regardless, I couldn't sleep that night. In this case, the source of my insomnia was simple: I feared for Alafair's life.

On the late-night news, there had been a follow-up story on the waitress who had gone missing. A silver bracelet with her name inscribed inside it had been found by a fisherman on a flat rock in the middle of the St.

Regis River. There was no explanation as to how it had gotten there.

In my opinion, the abduction was the work of Asa Surrette. He had placed one of his trophies on the rock to confound his pursuers. He was one of those serial predators who controlled both his victims and his adversaries by stoking their imaginations, leading them up a cul-de-sac, making them resent themselves for their powerlessness and the suffering he brought into their lives. Surrette wanted to instill as much pain as possible in the friends and family of the victim. Until her body was discovered, they would get no rest, find no peace, and be tormented by every dark possibility imaginable each time they closed their eyes.

While Asa Surrette was doing this kind of damage to other people, Love Younger and his family lived in wealth and splendor and dealt with problems like the temperature of their bathwater and the noise the gardener was making with the Weed Eater. I'm aware that all of us reach the same denouement, that we return to dust and our teeth are sown in the field by the farmer's plow, but that is poor solace when you look into your daughter's face and try to guess at the fate a man like Asa Surrette might be planning for her.

I fell asleep around four-thirty in the morning and woke at seven. Molly was still asleep. I got dressed and went down to Clete's cabin and woke him up. "What's going on?" he said.

"I need Felicity Louviere's cell phone number."

"What for?"

"Because I don't have Love Younger's number, and I need to talk to him."

"I'll call her for you."

"No, I'll do it."

"She doesn't know you real well. She thinks you don't like her."

"I don't. I think she's screwing up your life."

"You remember those fireworks we called devil chasers? They'd ricochet all over the place and go nowhere. We'd stick them up people's tailpipes on neckers' row at the drive-in. That's exactly what you remind me of."

"Are you going to give me her number or not?"

He was sitting on the side of the bed, the covers pulled across his lap, his face full of sleep. Gretchen's bedroom door was closed. He threw his cell phone to me. "It's in my contacts," he said.

I drove down to the foot of the road to get service, then dialed Felicity Louviere's number.

"Clete, you shouldn't call me at home," she said.

"It's not Clete. It's Dave Robicheaux. I'd like to speak with Love Younger, please."

"About what?"

"About none of your business, Ms. Louviere. Would you mind putting him on?"

"I'll ask him. You don't have to get snippy about it."

"You'll ask him?" I said it again. *"You'll ask him?"*

"My sympathies to your family," she said.

She must have been gone two minutes. Then I heard her talking and someone else taking the phone from her hand. "Love Younger," a man's voice said.

"I need to speak with you, sir, man-to-man, at your home or some other place of your choosing," I said.

"Regarding what, Mr. Robicheaux?"

"Asa Surrette may have been on Albert Hollister's property last night."

"What evidence do you have?"

"We can talk about that in person."

"One of my employees, Tony Zappa, was murdered. Your friend's daughter, Gretchen Horowitz, is a suspect in his death. Why should I be speaking with you at all on any subject?"

"Number one, the charge against Gretchen Horowitz is not only fraudulent but unprosecutable and will be dropped, and both the sheriff and the district attorney's office know it. Second, the man you refer to as your employee was a rapist."

"Tony had a troubled life. But I've yet to see any proof that he committed a crime of any kind while he was in my employ."

"You ever hear of Jack Abbott? He wrote a book titled *In the Belly of the Beast.* Norman Mailer was deeply moved by it and helped get Abbott out of the Utah state pen. Abbott paid back the favor by shanking a twenty-one-year-old waiter to death."

"I never read Norman Mailer and have no interest in him. I think I'm going to terminate this call, Mr. Robicheaux."

"Your granddaughter was probably abducted and killed by Surrette. I don't want my daughter to suffer the same fate. Surrette has a passionate hatred of her and will probably do worse to her than he did to your granddaughter. Frankly, I suspect you're a genuine son of a bitch, Mr. Younger. That said, you're obviously a man who cares about his own and understands the nature of loss. If you won't agree to meet with me, I'll come out to your house, and we'll take it from there."

There was a silence. "I'm hosting a barbecue on my ranch out on Highway 12 at one o'clock," he said. "I'll give you fifteen minutes in private. Then you can leave or stay and eat. I don't care which. You will not make demands of me again. Do you understand me on this?"

"I look forward to our conversation," I replied.

He broke the connection. I turned off the

cell phone and drove back to the house. When Alafair came down for breakfast, I asked if she wanted to go to a barbecue.

"Whose?" she asked.

"Love Younger's."

"He called up and invited you to his barbecue?"

"Not quite."

"Will Miss Piss Pot of 1981 be there?"

"You're talking about Felicity Louviere? I didn't know y'all had met."

"I haven't. I saw her downtown. Gretchen pointed her out. She carries her nose in the air, literally. She looks like an actress trying to impersonate a world-class bitch."

"How about it on the language?"

"Yeah, I'd like to go to the barbecue. Quit protecting Felicity Louviere. She's an opportunistic bitch, and you know it."

After Alafair ate, she went back upstairs to revise a scene she had written in the middle of the night. There was a haze on the south pasture, as though it were powdered with green pollen; a fawn and its mother were licking a salt block by the water tank. I went into the backyard and looked for the tracks in the flower bed outside the bathroom window. They were still there, deep and sharply defined, even though the sprinklers were on. In the daylight I could also see where several branches had been broken on the lilac bushes, at a height much greater than that of a wolf or a coyote. How could a large, heavy, four-footed creature leave only two impressions in the bed? And what had broken the lilac branches?

I wished I had dropped the wolf in the north pasture when I had the opportunity, permit or not.

Alafair came back downstairs dressed in jeans, alpine hiking shoes with big lugs, and a blue denim shirt with white piping and, embroidered on the back, a huge silver American eagle clutching a clawful of arrows. "Are you sure you want to go out there, Dave?"

"It's Saturday. God is in His heaven, and all is right with the world," I said.

"I'm sorry I called the Louviere woman names," she said.

"Maybe she deserves them," I replied. "Come on. What can go wrong at a barbecue on a fine day like this?"

CHAPTER 21

Love Younger's ranch was located twenty miles west on the two-lane highway that gradually ascended over Lolo Pass into the Idaho wilderness. The countryside was riparian and lush and green from the spring rains, the leaves of the cottonwoods along Lolo Creek flickering in the breeze, the lilacs and wild roses blooming, the wheel lines filling the air with an iridescent mist. There were Angus and longhorns and Holsteins belly-deep in the grass down by the creek, and horse farms with Morgans and Thoroughbreds and Appaloosas and Foxtrotters outside breeding barns you expect to see in Kentucky but not in the West. It was one of those rare places that commercialization and urban sprawl had skipped over, and I wondered how many of Younger's guests — who drove modest vehicles, the bumpers glued with patriotic stickers — believed that they could ever own a ranch in a setting like this; or did they concede that they would always be visitors? I wondered if this was their notion of the American Dream. Or were they like the many who wanted only to touch the hem of a powerful man's garment, to not only be healed but to elude mortality?

Their cars and trucks were lined up at the entrance for a half mile, all with their turn signals blinking in unison. The arch over the drive was made of historical branding irons and great links of iron chain welded together, all of it supported by two columns of white stones. There was no admission price for the barbecue, no proof of invitation required, except an indication that everyone entering the ranch was of one mind and believed the hallowed spirit of the minutemen dwelled in their midst. The guests of Love Younger came in large numbers, trusting and glad of heart, their children riding in the beds of pickup trucks, all of them filled with joy and expectation as they entered an environment that seemed an extension of a magical kingdom.

Large-bodied men wearing western clothes and Stetsons and sunglasses and boots looked in each car entering the property, but only to welcome the drivers and passengers and point out the best parking spots. There was no need for a martial or police presence on Love Younger's ranch. A country band was playing on a stage carpentered out of newly milled pine; children rocketed into the air inside the bouncy houses; the smell of drawn beer and barbecued chicken and sliced sirloin and roasted pig was mouthwatering. Could any event be grander or more American than a visit to the ranch of an egalitarian billionaire, a patriarch who was of them and for them and who, with a wave of his hand, could wipe away their doubts and fears?

Pennants and flags of every kind flew from tent poles all over a pasture that had been cleaned of animal droppings. The ambience could be compared with the celebratory nature of a medieval fair. It needed only jugglers and flutists and jesters in sock caps and bells and pointy shoes. The elements in the Everyman plays and the caricatures in the tarot deck were everywhere. Death had lost its sting and been driven from the field, and virtue and good deeds and courage and folk wisdom had triumphed over evil. Unfortunately, the medieval morality play required a villain. Who or what might fit the role?

"Check out the art on the T-shirts some of these guys are wearing," Alafair said. "I think they're ramping up for a firefight in the mall."

"Lower your voice," I said.

"They think we're admiring them."

"I mean it, Alf. Don't get things started."

"Don't worry about me," she said. "Look out there on the road."

Thirty-five years ago Clete Purcel had assigned himself the role of my guardian angel, and he wasn't about to resign the job now.

His hand-waxed vintage Caddy, the top down, was in the line of vehicles working its way under the arch.

"This is one Clete needs to stay out of," I said.

"Don't take your anxieties out on me, Dave."

"How did he know we'd be here?"

"He called up to the house and asked what we were doing today. What should I have said?"

"Great. Keep him occupied. I'm going to find Love Younger."

An oversize pickup truck, with smoked windows and huge cleated tires, pulled into a parking spot not far from where we were standing. "How do you like this guy's bumper sticker?" Alafair said.

"Don't say anything. It's their turf. They have the right to do whatever they want here."

"So do the patients in a mental asylum."

The sticker read DA BRO GOTTA GO.

"There's Younger coming out of the house," Alafair said. "Who's the guy with him?"

"Take a guess."

"The son who poured Coke all over Clete's head?"

"I'll be back in fifteen minutes. Then we're leaving."

"Clete just headed for the beer tent."

I had the feeling that not only was our situation starting to unravel but Alafair had decided to go with the flow and enjoy it. I left her standing under a canopy and cut off Love Younger and Caspian between the ranch house and the crowd. "You promised me fifteen minutes," I said.

His eyes were sky blue, his face flushed and soft-looking as a baby's, loose strands of his white hair moving in the breeze. "Step inside the house with me," he said.

"Get rid of him, Daddy," Caspian said. "He's here to cause trouble. It's written all over him. He's a drunk and a cooze hound."

"Go find your wife," his father said.

"She's just over there someplace. She's fine."

"Did you hear me?" the older man said.

I saw Caspian's scalp constrict visibly. He looked like a child who had been struck in the face by a trusted parent.

"I don't think you need me here. I think I'll take a drive into town," he said.

"Goddammit, son, for once just do what I ask. It's time to act like the husband of your wife and the father of your dead child," Younger said. His face softened. He squeezed his son's shoulder. "Come on, boy. Buck up and get us a table. I'll be along directly."

As Caspian walked away, a flatbed truck turned off the highway and drove under the arch. Several people began pointing, then a ripple of laughter spread through the crowd that quickly turned into collective joy. On the back of the truck, boomed down with chains, were two portable toilets with the name of our current president and the words WHITE HOUSE spray-painted on them. Both toilets had been shot full of holes.

Love Younger's gaze remained on his son. Then he turned back to me. "You coming?" he said.

The ranch house was constructed of tear-down lumber that was probably a century old, the rusted impressions of iron bolts and steel spikes and bits of chain deliberately left in the wood. The exterior of the house was cosmetic and had nothing to do with the interior. The lighting was turned on and off by voice command; the faucets and sinks in the kitchen were gold-plated. The living room had a fireplace the size of a Volkswagen; there was an elevator in the hallway that evidently accessed a parking garage under the house.

Through the kitchen window, I could see people lining up at the serving tables. "That's my daughter in front of the cold-drink tent," I said. "I pulled her out of a submerged plane when she was five years old."

"Yes?"

"I don't plan on losing her to Asa Surrette."

He didn't seem to hear me. He rolled up his sleeves in front of the sink and turned on the water and began soaping his hands and forearms, scrubbing them as a surgeon might. He squeezed a disinfectant on his hands and ran cold water up and down his arms, then dried them with paper towels and stuffed the towels in a waste can under the sink.

"So you don't plan on losing your daughter?" he said. "What should I make of a statement like that, Mr. Robicheaux?"

"I think you're one of those who have ears that don't hear and eyes that don't see."

"I see. That's your mission here? Carrying your spiritual wisdom to the halt and the lame?"

"Your employee, the rapist, was killed with three forty-four-caliber balls. Why would somebody use a nineteenth-century firearm to commit a murder?"

"I've talked to the sheriff about that. He says Dixon is still under the microscope on that."

"Dixon is not your man. I think the forty-four was used to point suspicion at him and perhaps you."

"I don't mean this offensively, but I would gladly pay double my taxes if people like you and Albert Hollister could be paid not to think."

"I want to tell you something else about my daughter. She survived a massacre in her village in El Salvador. She was kidnapped at age eight by an evil man who thought he could terrify her. She bit the hell out of him. I saw her kidnapper eat six soft-nosed rounds from a three-fifty-seven. The wounds looked like flowers bursting from his shirt. The last round virtually eviscerated him. I enjoyed watching him blown apart. I wished I had done it instead of someone else. What does that suggest to you?"

"That you're an obsessed and sick man."

"Here's the point. Booze probably burned up fifteen or twenty years of my longevity. That means I don't have a lot to lose. I think you've been getting a free pass with the sheriff's department. You're either in total denial about your situation, or you're aiding and abetting a killer."

"How dare you."

"You have resources that even the federal government doesn't have. Why aren't your people looking for the man who killed your granddaughter?"

"Why do you think I'm not looking for him?"

"Because you seem uninformed. Surrette did it. The question is why and how. She was in a saloon full of outlaw bikers. Then, puff, she was gone."

"I'm not convinced this man exists."

"He tortured and killed people in his hometown for two decades, under the noses of the FBI. You don't think he could escape a wrecked jail van and be killing people in this area? How about the waitress who disappeared up by Lookout Pass?"

"I didn't hear about that."

"Which means none of your investigators bothered to look into it. Or they didn't tell you about it."

His gaze went away from mine. When he looked at me again, the confidence was not in his face. "What happened to the waitress?"

"She didn't show up for work. Her house was locked and dead-bolted from the inside. Her bracelet was placed on a rock in the middle of the St. Regis River. It's all part of Surrette's pattern. He feeds on attention and the confusion and angst he instills in others."

"What does the sheriff in Mineral County say?"

"The sheriff will do everything he can. If Surrette is the abductor, that won't be enough. Does it strike you as ironic that I have to explain these things to you, sir?"

He didn't answer. He kept staring at me inquisitively, the way a clinician might.

"Do you want to ask me something?" I said.

"I'm trying to figure out what you're after."

I couldn't believe his statement. "I told you. I'm afraid it didn't do much good."

"Earlier you called me a son of a bitch. I don't hold that against you, because you were speaking honestly about your feelings. But I think you have an agenda. You resent others for their wealth. Everywhere you look, you see plots and conspiracies at work, corporations destroying the planet, robbing the poor, that sort of thing, and you never realize these things you think you see are a reflection of your own failure."

"Mr. Younger, if I harbor resentment toward anyone, it's toward myself. I couldn't prevent my daughter from interviewing Surrette in prison and writing articles about him that exposed him to a capital conviction. He won't rest until he kills her."

"You told her not to do it?"

"That's correct."

"Then it's on her."

I wondered what it must have been like to grow up in a home governed by the value system of Love Younger.

I heard someone knock tentatively on the kitchen door. Through the glass, I saw a blond man in shades. Caspian was standing behind him, raising up on his toes to see inside the house. Love Younger opened the door. "What do you want, Kyle?" he said.

"Caspian thought I ought to see if you needed any help."

"I don't."

"Yes, sir. I'll be right outside."

Younger shut the door but continued to look through the glass at his son's back. "I never get over it," he said.

"Sir?" I said.

"When I look at Caspian, I always see the little boy, not the man. I don't know if you've had that experience. He was always a little-bitty chap tagging along after the others.

453

He'd have his elbows poked out, like a rooster that wants to fight. When he was about nine or ten, I took him to visit the hollow where I grew up. The kids there went barefoot in the snow and were meaner than spit on a church wall. Caspian wanted to pretend he was as tough as these poor little ragamuffins. He'd say 'ain't' and 'he don't' and talk about putting on his 'britches' in the morning. He loved to say 'britches.' "

The content of our conversation had flown away, along with any apparent awareness on his part of who I was. He continued to stare through the glass, his hands on his hips. Then he shook his head and turned to me as though addressing an old friend. "Smart at figures and dumb as a turnip about everything else. Where did I go wrong with that poor boy?" he said.

"When I look at Alafair, all I see is the little girl. I guess that's what I came out here to tell you," I said.

There are moments when our common humanity allows us to see into the souls of our worst adversaries. I wanted to believe this was one of them. It wasn't.

"Well, I guess I started this saccharine introspection," he said. "Now that you've accomplished your objective, Mr. Robicheaux, you can be on your way."

Any illusions I had about Love Younger were gone. I realized that I had the same importance to him as any number of service-people who swam in and out of his ken every day.

I walked outside onto the lawn, into the breeze and the popping of flags and pennants atop the canvas tents and canopies. The guests of Love Younger were not bad people. They worked hard and loved their country and were fiercely self-reliant. They didn't apologize for their values or their belief systems, and their physical courage was unquestionable. My quarrel was with the illusion into which I felt they had been lured. I had thought earlier that the gathering at the Younger ranch was akin to a medieval festival. It was no such thing. Love Younger was not an ideologue. Politics had nothing to do with the energies that drove him. His invitation to his ranch was a charade, a mask for the design of a willful and imperious man who had spent a lifetime controlling and destroying the people he loved most.

Why my lack of charity? Because the security man named Kyle, who did the bidding of his master, was staring at me from behind his sunglasses with far more interest than casual curiosity. His khakis were belted high up on his hips, his long-sleeved shirt snap-buttoned at the wrists. His body English did not serve him well: His arms were folded, an unconscious mechanism that often indicates repressed hostility or retention of information the individual takes pride in not sharing. It was his boots that caught my attention. They were cordovan, and from the stiffness in his trouser legs, I guessed they were stovepipes. Perhaps Tony Lamas.

I walked toward him. Caspian stood at his side, inserting a pinch of Copenhagen inside his cheek. "I was admiring your footwear," I said.

"I bet one day you'll have a pair of your own," Kyle said.

"Are they Lamas?"

"Justins."

"I'd like to have a look at them. Would you mind?" I said.

He laughed to himself and turned his face into the breeze. His hair was long, over his collar, stiff with gel. He looked back at me. There was something wrong with his eyes. He seemed to gaze at two objects simultaneously, or to be thinking about something that had nothing to do with the subject at hand. "Can I help you find a table?"

In the background I could see Alafair and Clete watching us from under a canopy. Clete held a foaming beer cup in one hand and a huge barbecue beef sandwich in the other. "No, thanks. My daughter and a friend are with me," I said. "I'd still like to have a look at your boots, though."

Kyle smiled at nothing and lifted the toe of one boot off the ground, the heel anchored on the grass. "They're first-class. I recommend them," he said. "Anything else?"

"You look like you've got a nasty cut under that bandage on your neck."

"You got that right. My girlfriend is a biter. She's a screamer, too. But what are you gonna do?"

"I bet your Justins are hand-tooled. Can you let me see the tops?"

Kyle looked at Caspian Younger, grinning. "Buddy, you're a case," he said.

"A lot of people tell me that. You know what a short-eyes is?"

He looked thoughtfully into space. "A pygmy?"

"That's a guy who's gone down for molestation of a child. A guy with a short-eyes in his jacket has a hard time inside. My suspicion is that most child molesters are capable of gang rape as well. What's your opinion on that? Did you know any gang rapists inside?"

"Kyle answers to me," Caspian said. "If you have a beef with him, talk to me about it."

A *beef*? I wondered which movie he had learned the term from. "You and your father give jobs to former felons. I thought Kyle might know something about rapists and child molesters."

"Why'd you come here? Was it because of what I did to your friend over there?" Caspian said.

"Clete? No. He did tell me about your

throwing a cupful of Coca-Cola in his face, but I think he's written it off."

"That's because he knows he's out of his depth," Caspian said.

"Do you have any idea how fortunate you are, Mr. Younger?" I asked.

"Before you give me a speech about how dangerous your pal is, let me explain something to you. I gave him a warning the first time he messed with my wife. I told him it wasn't his fault. I also told him not to do it again."

He had a point. Clete was sleeping with another man's wife, a situation that gives the philanderer little claim to the high ground. I guess I should have walked away. Except I could not forget a detail from Wyatt Dixon's account about the assault on him and his girlfriend by three masked men on the Blackfoot River.

"I have compulsions, Kyle," I said. "I get something in my head, and it just won't let go. With me, it's your boots. I'd also like to know more about your history. You see, I know you've been up the road. You don't like cops, you're a wiseass, and you think you're smarter than other people. That's a profile of about ninety-eight percent of the people inside the system. My guess is you don't like women, and the reason for that is they don't like you."

"What's gonna make you happy?" Kyle

said. "You want to get thrown out or beat up? There's something about me that gives you a hard-on? You're too old for it, man."

It was none of the above. I was not sure what I felt toward Caspian and Love Younger and the employee named Kyle. They may have been the catalyst for the strange physiological and emotional change taking place inside me, but they were not the source. The change always started with a twitch under one eye, as though I were losing control of my facial muscles. Then I would experience a popping sound in my ears, one that was so severe I could not hear what others around me were saying. I would see their mouths opening and closing, but none of their words would be audible. I guess a therapist could call the syndrome a chemical assault on the brain, the same kind that supposedly occurs when a suicide goes off a roof or paints the ceiling by placing a shotgun under his chin. In my case, the inside of my head would fill with a whirring noise that arrived in advance of a red-black rush of color and heat that I can compare only to gasoline and oil igniting inside a confined space.

When those things happened in the sequence I described, I became someone else. I did not simply want to punish my adversary, I wanted to kill him. It gets worse. I did not want to kill him with a weapon, I wanted to do it with my bare hands. I wanted to break the bones in his face with my fists, to knock his teeth down his throat, crush his thorax, and leave him gasping for breath as I rose splattered with blood from the damage I had inflicted upon him.

When I told others these things, I saw a level of sadness and pity and fear in their eyes that made me vow to never again discuss the succubus that has lived inside me most of my life.

Over Kyle's shoulder, I saw Clete and Alafair walking toward us, Clete pausing only long enough to place his sandwich and beer cup on a picnic table. He had polished his shoes and put on a suit for the occasion. His eyes were clear, the gin roses gone from his complexion, his porkpie hat at a jaunty angle. When Clete was off the dirty boogie, he looked almost as youthful and handsome as when he and I walked a beat in the Quarter.

"How's your corn dog hanging, Casp?" he said, swinging his arm through the air, slapping Caspian Younger between the shoulder blades with such force that he almost knocked him down.

"It's under control here, Clete," I said.

"I grok what you're saying," he replied, easing himself between me and Kyle, his eyes sweeping the crowd, not looking at any of us. "I grok this whole place. I grok the food. I grok the people."

"You do what?" Kyle said.

Clete's gaze was still on the crowd. "Is Dave right, Caspian? Is everybody copacetic here?" he said.

"If you're looking for her, she's inside," Caspian replied, arching his back from the blow Clete had delivered. "Why don't you go talk to her, then get the fuck out of here?"

"*Who's* inside?" Clete said.

"You know who. She's going to stay inside, too," Caspian said.

"You got a trophy room in there, heads on the walls, stuffed cougars crouched on the beams, that kind of thing?" Clete said. "I get the feeling I'm standing in the middle of an ammo dump."

Clete was like the baseball manager who comes out of the dugout, his hands stuffed in his back pockets, and starts yelling harmlessly at the umpire to take the heat off one of his players. In this instance, he had intervened in a situation on my behalf and perhaps saved me from getting hurt. But now he was testing the edges of the envelope.

"Go ahead," Caspian said.

"Go ahead, what?" Clete said.

"Do what you're thinking about and see what happens. I think you're a lard ass and you've got a Vienna sausage for a penis. At least that's what Felicity says. Yeah, you got it, she made her big confession. All sins are forgiven. I called a couple of guys in Tahoe. They say Sally Ducks kept you around for laughs and let you polish his car or clean his toilet, I don't remember which. They say when Sally Dee met you, you were one cut above queer bait on the Strip."

"Here's the rest of the story: Sally Ducks got french-fried in his own grease, along with everybody else on his airplane," Clete said.

Kyle removed a two-way phone from his pants pocket.

"Put it away," Clete said. "Alafair and Dave and I are going back to our table. After I finish my beer and sandwich, we'll motivate on down the road."

"You're gonna do *what*?" Caspian said.

"Motivate. It's from Chuck Berry, asshole," Alafair said. She pushed past Clete and pointed in Caspian's face. "Say one more word like that to Clete, and I'm going to rip you apart, you little twerp."

How do you pull the plug on a situation like this?

"I came here to speak with Mr. Younger, and I did," I said. "That's it. We're gone."

I started walking as though our departure were a done deal. Alafair and Clete hesitated, then caught up with me.

"You're just going to walk away?" Clete said.

"I appreciate what you did back there," I replied. "Now we're going home."

"What was all that about, anyway?" Alafair asked.

"One of the men who attacked Wyatt Dixon and his girlfriend stole his Tony Lama boots. He said they were cordovan, just like the ones this guy Kyle is wearing."

"He's wearing Lamas?" Clete asked.

"He said they were Justins. He wouldn't show them to me."

"Why didn't you tell me?" Clete said. "Hang loose."

He turned around and headed straight for a tent where Kyle was standing by himself, lighting a cigarette, both hands cupped around the burning match. His eyes lifted above the flame as Clete came toward him. He flicked away the match and removed the cigarette from his lips and blew a stream of smoke into the air.

"Hey, I forgot to tell you something," Clete said.

"I can't wait to find out what that is."

"You know what the Eleventh Commandment in New Orleans is?"

"Tell me, blimpo."

"Don't try to put the slide on the Bobbsey Twins from Homicide."

"The who?"

"I knew you'd say that. Take off your boots."

"Tell you what, I'll let you shine them," Kyle said. He lifted his cigarette to his mouth and took a puff. "While you're down there, you can cop my stick."

Clete stared at his reflection in Kyle's

sunglasses. The image was anatomically distorted, the head small, the body elephantine, the skin amber-tinted, like those of a miniaturized man trapped inside a beer bottle. "The sign out there says For Staff Only," he said. "You want to pollute the place reserved for your fellow employees?" Clete pulled the cigarette from Kyle's mouth and flipped it out on the grass. Then he dropped the flap on the front of the tent.

"Buddy, you just don't learn," Kyle said.

"Pull up your pants leg."

"Enough with the boots. They're *boots.* What the fuck is with you?"

"There's no chance you and your buds tore the clothes off a woman up the Blackfoot and poured dirt in her mouth, is there? Right before two of you held her down and the third guy climbed on top of her?"

"You and your friend got a serious thinking disorder." Kyle started out of the tent, but Clete stepped in his way.

"I want your boots."

"If you haven't noticed, there's maybe five hundred people out there. A lot of them are my friends."

"You're right," Clete said. "Forget everything I said, and let's see if we can't find another way."

Clete cupped his left hand behind Kyle's neck, almost as if consoling him, then drove his right fist into the man's stomach, the blow sinking so deep that Kyle's upper body jacked forward and his mouth formed into a cone, as though he wanted to speak but couldn't, the blood draining from his cheeks.

Clete pushed him onto the ground, stepped on one of his ankles, and twisted the boot off his other foot. He looked at the label inside. "That's what I call really low-rent. You steal the boots off a guy like Wyatt Dixon? He's probably got hoof-and-mouth disease. Did you get his socks, too?"

He stuck the boot under his coat and walked out of the tent onto the fairway. Kyle stumbled after him, thrashing his way through the tent flap. He slipped on the grass and fell down again, gasping for air.

"The guy's having a seizure!" Clete shouted, his face dilated with feigned alarm. "Get an ambulance!" He pushed his way through the crowd, not looking back.

"What happened?" I said.

"I've got one of his boots. It's a Tony Lama," he said.

"What did you do?" Alafair said.

"I think the guy fell down and got the wind knocked out of him. Don't run. Everything is copacetic." He glanced over his shoulder. "I take that back. Haul ass!"

CHAPTER 22

Sunday morning Wyatt Dixon was lying shirt-less and in his socks in a hammock strung between two cottonwoods, down by the water's edge, in front of his house on the Blackfoot. When he heard somebody clang-ing across the steel swing bridge, he didn't know if the sound was real or if a junkyard was rolling around in his head. He picked up his pint of mint-flavored sloe gin and took a sip and gargled with it, then swallowed. With one eye closed, he watched a slender man with a jet-black mustache and flared side-burns approach him. The man was carrying a paper sack.

"Do you know some people say a law dog has a smell that don't wash off?" Wyatt said. "They say it's like trying to launder the stink out of shit."

"You're a hard man to find, Dixon."

"Not if you come to the place I happen to be at. You can call me Mr. Dixon."

"Your neighbors say you've been drunk for

the last couple of days."

"I cain't necessarily say one way or the other. I have these empty spaces in my memory, kind of like holes in rat cheese. My neighbors are still giving out news bulletins on me, huh?"

"You remember me?"

"Jack Something. I know it's not Jack Shit. Wait a minute, it's coming. You replaced Detective Pepper. The name is Jack Boyd. Or do you like Jack Shit better?"

The detective lifted his finger at the pint bottle balanced on Wyatt's chest. "I always heard that stuff tasted like mouthwash with turpentine poured in it."

"It does. That's why I drink it."

"I went by your girlfriend's apartment. Bertha Phelps is still your girlfriend, right?"

"We're in a holding pattern."

The detective gazed at the river. It was wide and green and veined with froth from a beaver dam upstream. "You must have your women trained. I wish I knew the trick."

"About what?"

"Training women. You use Viagra?"

Wyatt screwed the cap on his gin bottle and set it down in the grass. He looked at the detective with one eye. "I'm having a little trouble focusing on the direction of your conversation."

"She accused the department of trying to put you back inside. From what she says,

467

you're an innocent man. In fact, you hung the moon. What's your secret? That's what I'm saying."

"Secret about what?"

"Lighting up a woman's inner self. You don't ride them hard and put them away wet, I guess. I thought that was the cowboy way."

Wyatt sat up in the hammock and rested his sock feet on the grass. "I don't know as I care for the way you're talking about Miss Bertha."

The detective turned the paper bag upside down and let the contents slip loose and fall on the ground. "Ever see that before?"

"It's a boot."

"It's a Tony Lama boot. You claimed the men who attacked you stole your Tony Lama boots. They were cordovan. So is this."

"It ain't mine."

"How do you know?"

"It's too small. I'll show you." Wyatt picked up the boot and felt for the label inside. "This one is a ten and a half. I wear a twelve."

"Your feet don't look like a twelve to me."

Wyatt pointed to a pair of suede half-top boots in the grass. "Check them out."

"You could be wearing those because you have an ACE bandage on your ankle."

"I wear them because my feet are a size twelve. If that was my boot, I'd take it and ask you where the other one was at. But it ain't mine."

Wyatt's face remained empty of expression. He looked at his nails, then up through the cottonwoods at the sky, seemingly uninterested in the origins of the boot. The detective handed him a photo lineup with six mug shots. "You ever see any of these men?"

Wyatt studied the photos. "I've seen this guy here in the middle."

"Are you positive?"

"Absolutely."

"Where?"

"At the fairgrounds or a powwow."

"When?"

"Last summer. Up at the Indian rodeo on the rez."

"That's interesting, because he died in Deer Lodge ten years ago. I reread the report, Dixon. You said one of your attackers had long blond hair. He lost his mask, and his bandana came loose from his head. That's when you saw his hair. You must have seen at least part of his face."

"That was at the same time I got hit upside the head with a rock."

The detective tapped his finger on the mug shot of a man whose eyes seemed mismatched, as though they had been transplanted from two separate faces. "Did you ever see this man?"

"No. Who is he?"

"Kyle Schumacher. He did three years in California for statutory rape."

"Where'd you get the boot?"

"If it's not yours, you don't need to worry about it. On second thought, I guess it won't hurt anything. A PI from New Orleans brought it in."

Wyatt watched a wood duck bob down the middle of the riffle. "Y'all hear anything else about that waitress who disappeared up by Lookout Pass?"

"What about her?"

"You don't think the same guy who killed Angel Deer Heart might have kidnapped the waitress?"

"There's no evidence linking the two cases."

"I'm trying to track your logic, Detective. The stuff you ain't been able to find somehow proves there ain't no relationship between the two cases?"

"Maybe you ought to apply for a job with the sheriff's department in Mineral County. You could conduct your own investigation."

"I'll think about it."

The detective picked up the boot and replaced it in the sack. "I thought we might have our man," he said. "Too bad."

"Are you supposed to give away the name of a suspect in a photo lineup?"

"What difference does it make? You said he's not our guy."

Wyatt picked up his gin bottle from the grass and flipped it in the air and caught it. "You said something about me riding a woman hard and putting her away wet. Was you talking about Miss Bertha or not?"

There was a long silence. "It was just a joke."

"A joke about Miss Bertha?"

The detective's throat bladed with color. "I wasn't talking about any woman in particular," he said. "No, I wasn't saying anything about her."

"That's what I thought," Wyatt said.

It was evening before Wyatt Dixon worked up the courage to go see Bertha Phelps. He rode the elevator up to her apartment overlooking the Clark Fork and knocked. When she opened the door, it was hooked on the chain. He saw her nostrils swell. "Have you been drinking?" she said.

"I was. I ain't now."

"Is that detective out there?"

"No. He come to my house, though. You want me to go away?"

"I just don't like to see you hurt yourself. If you want to know the truth, I've been awfully worried." She slid the chain and opened the door. "I didn't think you were a drinking man."

"I ain't. At least not the hard stuff."

"You sit down at the table. I'm going to fix you a cup of coffee and a plate of lasagna. I called you three times. Why didn't you answer?"

"I was out of sorts. I get that way sometimes."

"Because I deceived you?"

"That plainclothes detective said you spoke
up for me."

"Why wouldn't I?"

"Did you know there's people that's not
capable of doing wrong, at least not deliberately?" he said.

"You fixing to give me a compliment? If
you are, don't. I don't care for flattery, Wyatt."

"You're one of them kind, Miss Bertha.
You're a good lady with a big heart."

"Don't be calling me 'miss' anymore, either."

He sat down at the table by the window.
There were children riding the wooden
horses on the carousel, each of them leaning
far out of the saddle to grab the brass ring
that guaranteed them a free ride. "Did you
study history in college?" he asked.

"I went to business school. I'm not as
highly educated as you think."

"I'm looking for a preacher who calls hisself Geta Noonen. I couldn't find nobody by
that name on the Internet. You ever hear the
name Geta before?"

"Not that I recall."

"I did a Google search on it. There was a
Roman emperor with that name. He was the
brother of a guy named Caracalla."

"I don't understand what we're talking

about." She took a plate of lasagna out of the microwave with a dish towel and carried it to the table. "Start eating. You need to start taking a whole lot better care of yourself."

"When this guy Caracalla wasn't building baths, he was killing people, including his brother Geta."

"Why are you looking for this preacher?"

"I think maybe he kidnapped that waitress up by the Idaho line. I don't believe he's a preacher. I think he's somebody who comes from a place people don't want to study on."

"Those are the shadows of the heart speaking. It's part of our upbringing that we have to get rid of, Wyatt."

"I didn't learn about evil in a church house. I learned about it from my fellow man."

"That's because you never knew love. You have to forget those years in prison and forgive the people who hurt you."

"I ain't real big on the latter."

"It'll happen one day down the road. Then your life will change. In the meantime, just be the man you are."

"That preacher may be the man who killed your brother."

She brought him a cup of coffee and sat down across the table from him. Through the window, he could hear the music from the carousel. "I don't want to talk about that anymore," she said. "I want to let go of all the evil in the world and never have it in my life again."

"Why would a phony preacher choose the name of a Roman emperor?"

"You mustn't drink anymore," she said.

"I won't."

"Please don't go out and do something you'll regret." When he didn't reply, she said, "Are you going to answer me?"

He put the tines of his fork through a piece of lasagna and placed it in his mouth, gazing out the window at the redness of the sun on the river and the way the children kept grabbing at the brass ring, no matter how many times their outstretched fingers went flying past it.

The day was cooling, the leaves scudding along the concrete walkways, more like fall than summer. Wyatt felt a chill in his body that he couldn't explain. "I never make plans. Nobody knows what's gonna happen tomorrow. So there ain't no use in planning for it. That's the way I see it."

"You can choose to be the person you want, can't you?"

"What some call revenge, I call justice."

"They're not the same."

"Is this food Italian?"

"Don't hurt me any more than you have. Don't you seek revenge in my name."

"I ain't meant to hurt you, Bertha. You ever been on a carousel?"

"When I was a child."

"Let's go down there and take a ride in those big seats for adults. Then we'll go for ice cream," he said.

"If that's what you want," she replied.

"See the sky? It looks like it's raining way out there on the edge of the world, like you could sail right into it and leave all your cares behind. That's what I'd like to do one day, with you at my side. Just sail right off the edge of the earth into the rain."

That same evening Gretchen Horowitz lay on her stomach in front of Albert's television set, on the bottom floor of the house, and watched a DVD of the cable series *The Borgias.* She watched it for three hours. Albert came downstairs from the kitchen with a cup of cocoa and a plate of graham crackers. "I thought you might like these," he said.

"Pardon?" she said, not taking her eyes from the screen.

"I'll put them down here," he replied, and turned to go.

She paused the show with the remote. "That's nice of you," she said.

"What do you like most about that series?"

"It reminds me of *The Godfather.* I think *The Godfather* is the best movie ever made. Every scene is a short story that can stand by itself."

"Really?" he said.

She turned on her side and looked up at

him. "See, *The Godfather* is not about the Mob. It's about Elizabethan tragedy. Have you ever met anybody in the Mob?"

"I don't recall anyone introducing himself to me that way. Do they hand out business cards?"

She ignored his joke. "Most of them are dumb and smell like hair oil and garlic. My mother used to be the house prostitute in three hotels on Miami Beach. She did the Arabs for a while, then went back to screwing the greaseballs. On balance, I think the greaseballs were the bigger challenge. I think that's why she got out of the life."

Albert stared at her as though the floor were tilting under his feet.

"Did I say something wrong?" she asked.

"No, not at all."

"Did you watch *The Sopranos*?"

"A little bit."

"That's what the Mob is really like. The only honest work they can do is recycling garbage. Here's the deal about that series. It's not tragedy. *The Godfather* is. You know why people kept watching *The Sopranos*?"

"No."

"They wanted to see Tony Soprano find redemption. Too bad. Tony murdered his nephew and turned out to be a dumb shit who didn't want redemption. I think the creators of *The Sopranos* did a number on their audience. Do you know what John

Huston always told his people? 'Respect your audience.' "

"Your ideas are interesting," Albert said.

"That's what people say when they're grossed out and don't know how to exit a social situation."

He sat down, his hands propped on his knees, and looked at the frozen image on the television screen of Pope Alexander VI burning his archenemy alive. "You know what the hard road in Florida was?"

"A chain gang?"

"I spent a half year on one. I also did some time in a parish prison in Louisiana. Of all the boys I knew inside, I'd say only two or three of them were sociopaths. The rest of them could have led good lives if somebody had cared about them."

"Why are you telling me this?"

"No reason. I think you're an artist. I think you have a great future ahead of you."

"How much of my history are you aware of, Mr. Hollister?"

"I don't care about your past or anyone else's. The past is nothing more than a decaying memory. Clete and Dave and his family think highly of you. That's good enough for me. You tried to help Wyatt Dixon when he was tormented by that detective. *That's* your history, *that's* the woman you are. Don't ever let other people tell you different. If they do, it's for one reason only."

477

"What?" she said, looking at him in a different way.

"They want you to lose."

"I appreciate that," she said.

"Advice is cheap," he said. He climbed back up the stairs, silhouetted against the kitchen light, one hand on the rail, his shoulders and back as round and hard-looking as a stone arch.

She turned off the television and went outside into the twilight to check an infrared trail camera she had strapped to a tree trunk behind the house. The camera had a camouflaged housing that could be left for days or weeks or even months to capture images of wildlife passing through a stand of timber. The only technological downside was its inability to distinguish the movement of animals from the wind blowing through the trees and underbrush, causing the lens to click every fifteen seconds, until both the batteries and the space on the memory card were used up.

Gretchen loosened the canvas strap on the tree trunk and slid the camera out and used the viewing screen to click through the images on the memory card. She saw an elk with one eye pushed against the lens, a skunk, a flock of wild turkeys dropping from a tree, a cougar cub, and a black bear. Then a man.

Or what she thought was a man. The figure was erect, moving uphill, the head twisted away from the lens as though the figure had just heard a sound down below. The next photo had been taken fifteen seconds later. In it, the figure was deep inside the second growth and the black shade that fell on the mountain immediately after sunset, its dimensions impossible to estimate. She looked at the date and time the two frames had been taken. The figure had passed in front of the camera ten minutes earlier.

She showed no reaction. She slid the camera back inside its housing and notched the strap into the tree bark and walked downhill to the cabin. The temperature seemed to drop without warning or transition, and she tried to remember if there had been mention of a cold front on the weather report. She removed a flashlight from a kitchen drawer, took her Airweight .38 from under her mattress, and put on a coat and a shapeless cowboy hat. When she returned to the hillside, the light had gone from the sky, the moon was rising, and she could barely make out the abandoned logging road that ran beneath the cave where Asa Surrette might have camped.

She held the flashlight at eye level with her left hand, the Airweight in her right, and stepped onto the logging road. The air was dense and smelled of woodsmoke from a neighbor's chimney. Down below she could see the lights inside Albert's house and the shadows of the lilac bushes moving on the lawn. The wind shifted and began blowing out of the north, puffing the metal roof on the barn, scattering pine needles on the forest floor, filling the air with the cool smell of oxygen and humus and stone and lichen and toadstools that never see sunlight. She moved the flashlight beam through the trees that grew above the road and the cave. Where were the turkeys? Every night at sunset the entire flock, fifteen or so, went down to the creek in the north pasture and drank, then went back up the hill and roosted in tree limbs or around the trunks.

Her eyes were watering in the wind. Then she smelled an odor that was like humus but much stronger, as though its presence were heavier than the wind, as though it were ubiquitous and had settled into the stone and the tree trunks and the ground and the pine needles that carpeted the slope. Some people said that was what a griz smelled like. A griz stank of the deer it killed and buried by its den in the autumn and the deer it ate and defecated after it awoke in the spring. It stank of rut and the excrement it slept in, the blood that had dried on its muzzle, the fish it had swatted out of a stream and devoured, guts and all. The odor she smelled now was all these things and so thick she thought she might swoon.

"Are you there?" she said into the wind.

Her chest rose and fell as she waited for a

response. She closed her eyes and opened them. *Nothing is out there,* she told herself.

Hi, baby doll. You've been kicking some serious ass, haven't you? a voice said.

Her breath caught in her throat.

You're more like me than you think. Remember how their eyes beg? You can do anything you want with them. You have power that no one else of the earth has.

"I'm nothing like you, you motherfucker," she said.

Sticks and stones.

"Where are you?"

Inside your head. In your thoughts. In all the secret places you try to hide who you really are. You can never get to me unless you kill yourself.

"You don't know me."

You're not a person, Gretchen. You're a condition. You enjoy killing. It's like an orgasm or your first experience with China white. Once you taste of forbidden fruit, the addiction never goes away.

"You're not there."

Keep telling yourself that, little girl.

"Show me your face."

This time there was no answer. She was sweating inside her clothes. She approached the mouth of the cave, then stopped and tried to breathe as slowly as possible. She stepped in front of the opening, the flashlight shining

481

inside, the Airweight pointed straight out in front of her. She could see the scorch marks of a fire on the walls and the ceiling, and the fresh droppings of bats and pack rats on the ledges and in the ash, but no sign of human habitation. The odor inside the overhang made her think of a dead incinerator in winter.

She backed out of the cave, into the wind, and clicked off the flashlight. "If you're Asa Surrette, give me a sign," she said.

She counted off five seconds, then ten, then twenty. She felt as though someone had looped a piece of baling wire around her head and inserted a stick in it and was twisting it tighter and tighter.

"I'm stronger than you," she said. "So is Alafair and so is Albert Hollister and so is my father. You murder children."

The moon was high enough to light the tips of the trees, and she began to walk farther up the logging road, her eyes on the parklike slope of the hill. She thought she saw an animal running through the timber, just below the crest, its black fur threaded with silver. Its shoulders and forequarters were sinuous and heavily muscled, and it thudded solidly against the earth when it jumped over a broken tree, never interrupting its stride or momentum.

Was it the wolf Albert had seen? If it was, it had shown no interest in her. She put away her flashlight and turned in a circle, pointing the Airweight in front of her. The voice had gone from inside her head, if that was where it had come from. The only sounds she heard now were the wind coursing through the canopy and a pinecone or two toppling down the hillside.

Had she become delusional? Weren't voices among the first indicators of schizophrenia? Or was her conscience taunting her? Was the Gretchen whom Albert spoke of nothing more than an invention, a cosmetic alter ego that allowed her to remain functional while she continued to shed the blood of others and take secret delight in it?

She turned and began to descend the hill. A pebble or tiny pinecone struck the brim of her hat. She looked back up the slope just as a second object, no larger than the first, struck her cheek.

Thirty yards up the hill, she saw the shape of a man on a deer trail. He was standing stock-still, like a jogger who had paused to rest in his ascent. She could not make out his face in the dark. She pulled her hat down on her brow and lowered her face so it would not reflect light, then began walking slowly up the road, to a place where a deer trail intersected it and she could climb to the crest without taking her eyes off the man, who had not moved.

She walked ten yards up the slope, breathing through her nose, trying to ignore the hammering of her heart. Then she heard rather than saw the figure break for higher ground, running hard, tree branches slashing against his body, a body that was flesh and blood and not that of a lamia or a specter.

She began running up the trail after him. He went around a corner and zigzagged through the trees, heading north, toward the far end of the valley, at the same time gaining elevation until he was almost to the crest of the ridge.

If he reached the top of the ridge, he would silhouette against the sky and she would have a clear shot at him. But what if the voice she had heard was imaginary? What if the running man was one of the homeless who sometimes wandered in from the two-lane?

The air was thinner and colder and suffused with smoke that hung in the trees and burned her lungs. The deer trail became serpentine, dropping through a gully and winding through brush as coarse as wire. He was standing at the head of the trail, looking back. Then she saw him break for the crest and stop again and turn and spread his arms against the sky, as though creating a mockery of a crucified man.

She ran faster, heedless of the sharp rocks and broken branches on the trail, her eyes locked on the man.

A snowshoe rabbit burst from the undergrowth and darted in front of her, triggering a spring-loaded saw-toothed steel bear trap that had been staked down with a chain and pin in the middle of the trail. The jaws of the trap sprang with such tension that the trap seemed to rise from the ground, virtually severing the rabbit's hind legs. Gretchen was crying when she reached down and tried to free it from the trap.

The man on the ridge cupped his hands around his mouth. "You're lucky, little girl," he said. "I had a delightful experience planned for you and me."

She stood erect and raised the Airweight with both hands, sighting on the silhouette, her chest heaving with exertion and the inhalation of smoke, her cheeks hot with tears. "Suck on this, you miserable fuck," she said.

Even as she heard the solitary *pop* of the report and felt the recoil against her palms, she knew the angle was bad and the shot had gone wide and high. When she lowered the revolver, the figure was gone, probably down the other side of the ridge. She knelt next to the rabbit and stroked its head and ears. "I'm sorry, little guy," she said. "You saved my life. If there's a heaven, that's where you're going."

She stayed with the rabbit until it died, then buried it and walked down the hill in the dark, a taste like ashes in her mouth.

CHAPTER 23

After having his boot twisted off his foot in front of half of Montana, Kyle Schumacher decided he would ease out of the scut work for the Younger family for a few days and spend a little vacation time up on Flathead Lake, among the cherry orchards and sailboat slips and waterside saloons.

He wasn't running away from anything. Kyle Schumacher had done hard time with badasses from East Los and blacks who were half cannibal. Kyle had never run from anybody. He just needed a little R & R to get his head together. What was wrong with that?

He had acquired a taste for tequila and Dos Equis when he was a heavy-equipment operator down in Calexico. That was just after he had finished a three-bit as a nonpaying guest of the California Graybar hotel chain. Unfortunately, he had acquired a taste for other things as well, coke and Afghan skunk and an occasional injection of China white between the toes, to be exact. The real high in Kyle's life was geographic. Reno and Vegas were the playgrounds where the party never ended and lucre and sensuality were virtues, not vices. For Kyle, the light radiating upward from the casinos into a summer sky took on a peculiar theological overtone, a testimony to the possibility that modernity and self-indulgence might be a stay against the hand of death.

The only downside in his life was the conviction that followed him wherever he went. Registering in a new city as a sex offender was like undressing in the middle of a county courthouse. The alternative, not registering, was a ticket back to the slams. What was the old saw? You do the crime, you stack the time? What a laugh. When you went down on a sex beef, you did life, with a two-by-four kicked up your chubbies. So he'd signed on with the Youngers. It was a safe berth. What was wrong with that?

His favorite saloon and casino in the vicinity was on the north end of Flathead Lake, up in the high country, on the road to Whitefish, where the movie stars and the Eurotrash hung out. It wasn't Vegas or Reno, but it had its moments, particularly when a sweet thing was still at the bar at closing time. He knocked back a shot of tequila and sucked on a salted lime and gazed through the saloon window at the immensity of the lake. It was twenty-four miles long, the biggest body of water west of the Mississippi, rimmed by mountains that were part of a glacial chain. This was the place he needed to be, a place where he could stop thinking about all the events that had happened in Missoula, events that were not of his manufacture and that he had been unfairly pulled into. Like the business with the boot. Did the PI take it to Wyatt Dixon? Kyle did not like to think about the prospect of dealing with Wyatt Dixon.

The clock on the wall said 1:46 A.M. The last time he looked, the clock said 11:14. What happened to the interlude? Maybe the clock was broken or the bartender had messed with it. "Hit me again," he said.

"Yeah, but this is last call, Kyle," the bartender said.

"So line 'em up. We can shoot the breeze while you shut down."

"Can't do it," the bartender said. He tipped the spout on the tequila bottle into Kyle's shot glass. "How about one on the house?"

"I look like I can't buy my own drinks?" Kyle replied.

A couple went out the front door and started their automobile. The bartender began rinsing glasses in an aluminum sink. The interior of the saloon was paneled with lacquered yellow pine and seemed to exude a honeyed glow from the green-shaded lamps hung on the walls. The ambience created a sense of warmth and belonging that Kyle did not want to let go of.

"Give me a couple of Dos Equis to go," Kyle said.

"You drank the last one."

"Then give me any import you got."

"You staying up here with that Mexican gal?"

"Who says I'm staying with anybody?"

"I thought you had a girlfriend up here."

"I don't remember saying that. Did somebody tell you that? Is this some kind of information center?"

"What do I know?" the bartender replied.

"That's a good attitude."

The bartender propped his arms on the bar and looked toward the front door and seemed to concentrate on what he should say next. His head resembled a white bowling ball with dents in it. A nest of blue veins was pulsing in one temple. He glanced at his wristwatch. "I forgot. That clock is slow. Happy motoring."

Kyle walked outside and got in his truck. The sky was as black as India ink and blanketed with stars, the cherry orchards on the shore and up the hillsides in full leaf, swelling with wind. Why should he be worried? No one knew where he was. He had told Caspian he might head down to Elko and shoot some craps and chill out. Caspian didn't like it? Too bad. Kyle hadn't signed on for that boot gig in front of all those people. Neither had he signed on for getting into a shit storm with a psychotic cowboy who had a body that looked like skin stretched on spring steel.

As he drove down the narrow two-lane toward the cottage on the hillside where the Mexican woman lived, he could not rid himself of the fear eating a hole in his stomach. He wanted to roll a fatty and get stoned and get laid and disappear inside a safe place where he didn't have to think about Wyatt Dixon and all the other issues that came with working for the Youngers. Then it would be daylight and he could score some coke or hang out in a bar and sip drinks on the deck through the day and figure out an answer to his situation. He fished his stash out of the glove box and held it up to the light. There was only a thin band of seeds and stems at the bottom of the Ziploc. Great. He held the bag out the window and felt the wind rip it from his hand.

He felt under the seat for his .357 Mag and inadvertently touched the baton he always carried to iron out differences in traffic situations. He had forgotten about the baton. How dumb could he be? He shuddered at the thought of Dixon finding it under the seat and stuffing it down his throat as payback for the lick Kyle had laid on him. He rolled down the window and flung the baton into the darkness and heard a sound like glass breaking. This couldn't be happening. Nobody's luck was this bad.

He turned up the dirt road that led through five acres of cherry trees to a cottage where an overweight Mexican woman with two children waited for him, convinced he would keep his promise and marry her that summer and get her a green card.

The light was on in the kitchen. The wind was blowing hard off the lake, bending the cherry trees that grew in tiers from the top of the slope down to the road. The mountain peaks looked as sharp-edged as sheared tin against an electric storm building in the west. Kyle saw someone get up from the kitchen table and look through the blinds and then go away from the window. Was that Rosa? If so, why didn't she come to the door? What if Dixon was inside?

Kyle turned off the interior light before he got out of the truck. He removed the .357 from under the seat and snugged it inside the back of his jeans. *Get a grip,* he told himself. So what if Dixon was inside? Kyle had been in Tracey before he took a fall on the statutory beef, which involved getting it on with a sixteen-year-old runaway who turned out to be a cop's daughter. Three years hard time for doing a good deed. How bad does it get? He did the three-bit straight up and went out max time and survived the black and Hispanic gangs in Quentin without joining the AB. He pumped iron and stacked his own time and didn't get in anybody's face. He

491

even earned a degree of respect out on the yard. Could Dixon say the same? From what Kyle had heard, the state had melted Dixon's brain with chemicals and electroshock treatments, and he thought he was a player in that end-of-times bullshit you hear about on late-night radio in the San Joaquin Valley. How nuts does it get?

By the time he reached the back steps of the cottage, he felt a sense of indignation and self-righteousness that almost relieved him of his fear. Time to concentrate on getting his ashes hauled. Rosa wasn't half bad in the sack. Through the pane in the kitchen door, he saw a shadow on the wall, not far from the stove. He put his right hand behind him and gripped the checkered handles of the .357 and opened the door.

"Where you been?" the Mexican woman said. She wore an apron splattered with tomato sauce and held a wooden spoon. There was a half-eaten birthday cake on the table. "You said you was gonna be back at seven."

"I had engine trouble. Was anybody here?"

"Yeah, me and the kids, waiting on you, you piece of shit. I tole the minister I'm tired of it. He said we was living in sin. I tole him he was right."

"What minister?"

"What do you care? It's Miguel's birthday. He waited up."

"I forgot."

"Get out," she said.

"Say that about the minister again. Did he have red hair and a Texas accent?"

She studied his face. "Somebody after you? I hope they are. You're a *cobard.* That means 'coward.' A *gusano,* a yellow worm."

"Shut your mouth," Kyle replied.

She picked up a pan of tomato sauce from the stove and threw it in his face, almost blinding him. He stumbled down the steps into the driveway, his eyes staring out of a red mask. She slammed the door and shot the bolt.

He couldn't believe how his life had changed in under two minutes. His hair and face and clothes were dripping with tomato sauce, his suitcase was locked in the house, and he was shivering in a cold wind blowing off a lake that offered no safe harbor for the likes of Kyle Schumacher. And he was absolutely convinced that the most frightening man he had ever encountered, a man whose face was as mindless as a Halloween pumpkin's, had just missed catching him at Rosa's cottage.

He thought about heading for British Columbia, except his passport was in his suitcase and his suitcase was locked in the house. This was a plot. It had to be. He picked up a brick and flung it through the kitchen window. "What did this minister look

493

like?" he yelled.

"Chinga tu madre, maricón!" she shouted back.

He got in his truck and roared down the dirt road and fishtailed onto the Eastside Highway. Immediately, his engine began lurching and backfiring. He hit the brake and shifted into neutral and pumped the accelerator until the engine caught and started firing on all eight cylinders again, then sped down the two-lane in the dark, toward Polson, the storm clouds on the far side of the lake flickering as though strings of damp firecrackers were popping silently inside them.

There was not a soul on the highway. The stars had dimmed, and the lake was as black as an enormous pool of prehistoric oil. His engine was running hot and making a sound like the cylinders were firing out of sync. What was wrong? He'd had a tune-up only last week. Polson was at least fifteen miles down the road. He had to take control of his emotions and think. He had his .357. He had two hundred dollars and the credit cards in his wallet. He could check into a motel and come back to the cottage in the morning and reason with Rosa. She wanted a green card, didn't she? He had always been nice to her kids, hadn't he? So he forgot the boy's birthday, for Christ's sake. It wasn't like he didn't have a couple of problems on his mind.

Why didn't she try a little empathy for a change?

Before he could continue his litany of grief, his engine backfired with enough force to blow out the muffler. Then the engine died, and all the warning icons lit up on his dashboard. When he pulled to the side of the road, he was surrounded by trees that had been planted to shield the house below from view. Polson was ten miles away, and the wind was cold and blowing at over twenty knots.

He looked in the rearview mirror and saw a truck approaching from the north, its high beams on. Was it a pickup with a camper shell inserted in the bed? An orange pickup, like Wyatt Dixon's? No, it was a wrecker. He could see the boom and winch mounted on the rear. *What a break,* he told himself.

He got out on the asphalt and began waving his arms. The driver of the wrecker slowed and hit his emergency flashers and eased onto the shoulder. Kyle heard him open his door and step out of the cab, forgetting to click off his high beams. "Hey, I'm about to go blind here," Kyle said.

"Sorry," the driver said. He dimmed the lights. "I have to back around to hook you up. You want to go to the dealership in Polson?"

Kyle closed his eyes and saw red circles that seemed to have been burned onto the backs of the lids. "Yeah, that would be great," he said. "You just cruising by?"

The driver of the wrecker had wide shoulders and wore a rumpled suit and a baseball cap and tennis shoes. He seemed to be smiling. "I work irregular hours," he said.

"I'd like to get to a motel and get some sleep. Can we get on the road?"

"You got to sign a form. Step back here, if you would."

"Can we do that in town? It's cold out there. I don't have a coat. I also have tomato sauce all over me. I'm not having the best day of my life."

"You have to sign a release before I hook you up. It's for the insurance company." The driver took a clipboard off the seat of the wrecker and handed it to Kyle, along with a pen from his shirt pocket. "Right there on the bottom line," he said.

Kyle coughed, deep down in his throat. "What's that smell?"

"I ran over a hog north of Big Fork."

"It must have been rolling in shit before you hit it. You wear a suit when you work?"

"I went from vespers straight to the job and didn't have time to change. I'm a minister, too."

Was this the mystery man? "You didn't happen to visit Rosa Segovia earlier, did you?"

"Don't know the lady. Please sign."

Kyle scribbled his name on the form and handed back the clipboard.

"Thanks," the driver said. "Take your keys out of the ignition. Company rules again. People leave the ignition on and sometimes start electrical fires."

Kyle began walking back to his truck. In the headlights of the wrecker, he noticed a bib of white granules at the bottom of the flap that covered the cap on his gas tank. As he rubbed his fingers on the granules, he heard a brief rattling sound behind him, like a hard wooden object scraping against a steel surface. He turned around just as the driver swung a sawed-off pool cue into the side of his head, knocking him to one knee in the middle of the road. The driver hit him again, this time across the back of the head. He was on all fours like a dog, unable to speak, blood leaking down the side of his face.

"Get up," the driver said. "That's it, you can do it. Let's walk behind my truck and get rigged up, then we'll be toggling on down the road."

Why are you doing this? Kyle wanted to say. But the words wouldn't come. The driver had done something to his throat or his voice box, and the words dissolved into paste and ran over his lip and down his chin. His wrists were fastened behind him with ligatures of some kind, and a looped steel cable had been dropped over his head and fitted around his neck. He heard the driver stripping cable off the spool, putting more slack in it. *Don't do this,* Kyle wanted to say.

"I know all your thoughts," the driver said. "They won't help you. Nothing will. When you die, you won't know why. You've lived your life for no purpose, and you'll be mourned by no one. Those will be your last thoughts. Then all breath and light will leave your body, and you'll descend into a black hole with no memory of ever having lived."

The driver kicked Kyle's feet out from under him. Kyle struck the road's surface with his face. He could taste the blood in his mouth and smell the tar and oil and even the day's heat in the asphalt. His concerns about the cold wind had disappeared. He wanted to remain where he was for the rest of his life.

The driver got in the wrecker and drove away, accelerating gradually until he was doing sixty, gliding into the curves as his cargo swung from side to side on the asphalt, caroming off tree trunks and road signs like a surfboard out of control.

Sheriff Elvis Bisbee called me at three-thirty P.M. Tuesday. "We've got Wyatt Dixon in custody," he said. "He's not under arrest, so he hasn't been Mirandized. He says he'll talk to us but only if you're here."

"Why me?"

"Ask him."

"Why'd you bring him in?"

498

"Call it littering."

"Is that some kind of insider joke?"

"Not if your name is Kyle Schumacher. His body parts were scattered for two miles along the Eastside Highway next to Flathead Lake. Come on down and I'll show you a few photos. We're at the jail."

"Who's 'we'?"

"Me and Detective Boyd."

"Can I bring Clete Purcel?"

"Are you serious?"

Forty-five minutes later, I parked in front of the old courthouse in downtown Missoula. Wyatt Dixon was being held in a holding cell on the second floor. Elvis Bisbee and Jack Boyd walked with me to the cell. Dixon was sitting on a wood bench against the wall, asleep, his chin on his chest. He was wearing a T-shirt that showed Geronimo and three other Apaches, each holding a rifle. The inscription read: HOMELAND SECURITY — FIGHTING TERRORISM SINCE 1492.

The detective unlocked the cell and kicked the toe of Dixon's boot. "Wake up," he said.

Dixon lifted his head. "You caught me on my sore foot, Detective," he said. "Is it dinnertime yet?"

"Mr. Robicheaux is here," the sheriff said.

"Howdy-doody," Dixon said.

"Why'd you want me here, Wyatt?" I said.

"Because you're a believer, and they ain't."

"A believer in what?" I said.

"What's out there," he said. "You might be a college man, but me and you see the world the same way. You know what's behind all this trouble, and it ain't a bunch of lame-brains that work for Love Younger."

"You've got a couple of strikes against you, Wyatt," I said. "You had a grievance against Kyle Schumacher. Second, he was dragged to death."

"It ain't no skin off my ass."

Boyd looked at me. "See, he's a comedian. He's always thinking. Isn't that right, comedian?"

"You told me your cell partner in Texas chain-drug a man down a road," I said.

"Yeah, I did tell you that, didn't I? That probably wasn't too smart."

"Detective Boyd also showed you a mug shot of Schumacher in a photo lineup," I said. "The next thing we know, Schumacher is dead."

"Detective Boyd not only showed me a photo, he gave me Schumacher's name. Up until that time, I'd never heard of him."

"You're lying," Boyd said.

"What reason would I have to lie?"

"Because you were out to get the guys who jumped you and your girlfriend, and you have no alibi," Boyd said.

"I slept on Miss Bertha's couch last night. I wasn't nowhere near Flathead Lake."

"Why didn't you say that?" the sheriff asked.

"Because Detective Boyd wants me back in the pen or wants me to go after the Youngers. It's one or the other. I ain't sure which."

"Is Detective Boyd part of a conspiracy?" the sheriff asked.

"He thinks I had something to do with cutting up Bill Pepper. How come y'all don't have no leads on that waitress that was abducted up by Lookout Pass? The man who drug Schumacher down the Eastside Highway is the same man who grabbed the waitress. Ask Mr. Robicheaux."

The sheriff and the detective looked at me. "In my opinion, it's Asa Surrette," I said.

"You *know* that?" Boyd said.

"No," I replied. "The pattern is his. The agenda is his. But I cannot say with certainty that the perpetrator is Asa Surrette. I was expressing an opinion."

"Why don't you call up the sheriff in Mineral County?" Boyd said.

"I don't have any authority here. My concern is my daughter. Her name seems to get lost in the mix."

"We're sorry about that," Boyd said. "Two men who worked for Love Younger are dead, but we'll drop everything and get back on your daughter's case. Let's see. She *thinks* somebody shot an arrow at her? That's some earthshaking shit, Robicheaux."

501

"Are we done here?" I said to the sheriff.

"No. Walk outside with me," he replied.

"What do you want me to do, Sheriff?" Boyd said.

"Go to my office and stay there."

"Sir?" Boyd said.

The sheriff and I went through the side door of the building onto the courthouse lawn. The flowers were blooming in the gardens along the walkways, the maples darkening with shadow against the western sun. "What is Surrette going to do next?" he asked.

"Cause as much injury and suffering as possible."

"You think the waitress is alive?"

"No."

"Why not?"

"Surrette doesn't take chances. And he's afraid of his victims."

"I don't follow you."

"All serial killers are cowards. They want their victims to remain terrified. They don't want their victims to see the frightened child living inside them."

"Where's the Horowitz woman?" he said.

"At Albert Hollister's place."

"No matter how this shakes out, I think she should move on."

"Somebody tried to bait her into a spring-loaded bear trap."

"I don't believe that."

502

"That's why she didn't report it," I said.

"Dixon called you a believer," the sheriff said. "What did he mean?"

"Who knows what goes on in the mind of a guy like that?"

"I think you do. I think you and he are of one mind. That's what bothers me about you," he said.

I drove back to Lolo. The sky was blue and ribbed with strips of pink cloud above the mountain peaks in the west, but I couldn't get my mind off the abducted waitress. If she was dead, Asa Surrette would be seeking a new victim soon. He had tried and failed with Gretchen. Would Alafair be next? I couldn't bear thinking about it.

CHAPTER 24

The morning after Gretchen's life had been saved by the snowshoe rabbit, she climbed to the top of the ridge and tried to track the man who had mocked and almost killed her. She found broken branches in the under-growth, skid marks where he probably slid down a trail, and the muddy print of a hiking shoe on a flat rock. Down below, she could see the fenced pasture that Wyatt Dixon rented for his horses. To the south, toward the two-lane that led over Lolo Pass, she could find no sign that anyone had passed through the foliage or rock slides or the damp areas where springs leaked out of the hillside. To the north, there was an escarpment that only a desperate person would try to scale. Where had the man on the ridge gone?

There was another possibility: What if he hadn't gone anywhere? Maybe he had doubled back on his trail and was hiding in the woods in another cave. There were only two or three houses north of Albert's ranch, all of them located in a natural cul-de-sac formed by cliffs and steep-sided hills that no one would try to climb in the dark.

She decided to retrace her own tracks and start her search all over again. She began by returning to the place where she had almost been caught in the saw-toothed jaws of the bear trap. The trap and the chain and the steel pin that had anchored it were gone.

She turned in a circle and stared at the dust floating in the shafts of sunlight that shone through the canopy. "You out there, bubba?" she called out. "You had plenty to say last night! Let's have a chat!"

She heard her voice echo off the hillside.

"You're not going to let a woman run you off, are you?"

Nothing.

Now it was Tuesday, and she had no evidence to prove that anyone had tried to maim or kill her on the hillside behind Albert's house. That afternoon, she packed her gym bag and drove to the health club on the highway between Lolo and Missoula, unaware that she was about to face her oldest nemesis, namely, her fear that disobeying her instincts and placing her trust in others would lead invariably to betrayal and manipulation.

She dressed in a pair of sweatpants and a sports bra and running shoes and a Marine

Corps utility cap and did three miles on the indoor track, up on the second floor. Then she went into an alcove on the edge of the track and slipped on a pair of gloves with dowels inside them and started in on the heavy bag, hitting it so hard, it bounced on the suspension chain and swung into the wall. After every fourth blow, she twisted her body and delivered a kick to the bag that made such a loud *whap* that people running on the track turned and stared, almost in alarm.

She pulled off her gloves and wiped her face and neck with a sweat towel, then loaded an audiobook into her iPod and went to work on the speed bag. She started out hitting doubles, two blows with one fist, two blows with the other. After fifteen minutes, she switched to singles, creating a bicycle-like motion, allowing one fist to follow the other without interruption, the bag thundering off the rebound board. All the while, she counted her strokes under her breath, making bare-knuckle contact with the leather sixty times in forty seconds. The bag looked like a black blur thudding off the board.

She went to the water fountain and took a long drink and walked back to the alcove just as a runner came around the bend in the track. The runner was a short woman with very pale skin and black moles on her shoulders. Her hair was thick and sweaty and held a dark luster and streaks of brown. Her face was heated from running, her breath coming short in her chest. She slowed to a stop when she recognized Gretchen. "How do you do?" she said.

Gretchen removed her earbuds and paused her iPod. "I'm fine, Ms. Louviere," she said.

"I could hear you hitting that bag all the way on the other side of the track. I didn't know it was you."

"I come here a couple of days a week," Gretchen said. To occupy her hands, she rubbed her knuckles and the skinned places along her palms. Down below, she could see a heavyset man named Tim who had been crippled and whose speech had been permanently impaired in a motorcycle accident. He was known for his personal courage and his determination to be self-reliant. He was wheeling himself slowly across the basketball court.

"Would you like to go downstairs and have a glass of iced tea with me?" Felicity asked.

"I have to be somewhere."

"I don't blame you for not liking me, Ms. Horowitz. I do blame you for not giving me a chance."

"Chance to do what?"

"Perhaps to explain some things. To apologize."

"People are what they do, not what they say."

"I see."

"You're married, Ms. Louviere. That fact won't go away. My father wakes up every morning with his head in a vise."

"I'm sorry."

Gretchen tapped the speed bag with the flat of her fist and watched it swing back and forth on the swivel. "I'd better get back to my workout."

"What are you listening to?"

"*The Big Sky,* by A. B. Guthrie."

"That's a grand book."

Gretchen tapped again on the bag, hitting it in a slow rhythm on the second rebound. "Did you see *Shane*?"

"With Alan Ladd and Jean Arthur and Van Heflin."

"Guthrie wrote the screenplay. It's supposed to be the best western ever made. Except it's not a western, it's a Judeo-Greek tragedy. Shane doesn't have a last or first name. He's just Shane. He comes out of nowhere and never explains his origins. In the last scene, he disappears into a chain of mountains you can hardly see. Brandon de-Wilde played the little boy who runs after him and keeps shouting Shane's name because he knows the Messiah has gone away. Nobody ever forgets that scene. I wake up thinking about it in the middle of the night."

"Where did you learn all this?"

"At the movie theater. You know why the cattle barons in the film hate Shane? It's because he doesn't want or need what they have."

Felicity's eyes went away from Gretchen's. "Are you trying to tell me something?"

"No, not at all. How did you know Jean Arthur and Van Heflin costarred with Alan Ladd?"

"I was a ticket taker at an art theater."

"I'm doing my second documentary. My first one made Sundance. I think I might get enough financing from France to do a period film, an adaptation of a novel about Shiloh."

"Why go to France for financing?"

"American producers are afraid to risk their money on historical pieces. Did you see *Cold Mountain*? It was one of the best films ever made about the Civil War, but it bombed. The rest of the world is fascinated with American history. We're not." Gretchen tapped the bag. "I've got to get back to my workout."

"You're an interesting woman, Ms. Horowitz."

"Who played the role of Jack Wilson, the hired gun?" Gretchen asked.

"Jack Palance," Felicity said.

"How about Stonewall Torrey, the guy he kills?"

"Elisha Cook, Jr."

"Did you know that in the scene when Stonewall gets shot, he was harnessed to a cable and jerked backward by an automobile?"

"No, I didn't know that. I suspect most people don't."

"Let go of my old man, Ms. Louviere. He's a good guy. His problem is, he's not as tough as he thinks, and he gets hurt real easy."

"Ask him what he wants to do and then tell me," Felicity said. "That way, all three of us will know."

Five minutes later, Gretchen glanced through the window at the health club's parking lot. The crippled man named Tim had been working his chair down the sloped concrete walkway to the spot where he was picked up each day by a specially equipped vehicle. His hand had slipped on the wheel of his chair, and the chair had spun out of control on the incline and tipped sideways, throwing him on the concrete. No one else was in the parking lot. Felicity Louviere stopped her Audi and left it with the engine running and the driver's door open while she tried to lift Tim by herself and get him back in the chair. When he fell again, she cradled his head in her lap, both of her knees bleeding, while she waved frantically at the entrance to the building.

Gretchen was no longer thinking about Felicity Louviere. She had figured out a way to put Asa Surrette in a vise. She drove downtown and placed notices in the personal columns of the city newspaper and two independent publications.

I woke at five Wednesday morning. A heavy fog had settled in the trees and on the north and south pastures, and I could hear Albert's horses blowing inside it. I fell back asleep and dreamed I was in our home on Bayou Teche in New Iberia. It was late fall, and I could see the fog puffing in thick clouds out of the cypress and live oaks and pecan trees and flooded bamboo and elephant ears that grew along the banks. Then I saw myself walking in the mist to the drawbridge at Burke Street and gazing at the long band of amber light that ran down the center of the bayou, all the way to the next drawbridge, the live oaks forming a tunnel that made me think somehow of a birth canal. However, there was nothing celebratory about my perception. The back lawns of the houses along the bayou were blooming with chrysanthemums, not with the flowers of spring, and I could smell gas on the wind and the odor of ponded water and pecan husks and leaves that had yellowed and turned black with mold.

The scene changed, and I saw an image that woke me as though someone had struck me on the cheek. I sat on the side of the mattress, my hands on my knees, my throat dry. I had seen myself enter an old tin boat shed on Bayou Teche, its outside purple with rust, strung with wisps of Spanish moss that had blown off the trees. The wind was rattling the roof and walls of the shed, stressing the metal against the joists. When I stepped inside, the door slammed behind me, and I was surrounded by darkness, left to feel blindly along the walls, the coldness of the water rising into my face. There was no exit anywhere.

Molly put her hand on my back. "Did you have a bad dream?"

"It's nothing. I'm all right."

"You called out your mother's name."

"I did? She wasn't in the dream."

"You said, 'Alafair Mae Guillory.' "

"That was her maiden name. She'd use it when she got mad at my father. She'd say, 'I'm Alafair Mae Guillory, me.' "

"I wish I had known her. She must have been a fine woman."

"An evil man corrupted her. The things that happened to her later weren't her fault."

I went into the bathroom and got dressed. I didn't want to talk anymore about the dream. I knew what it meant, and I knew why and in what circumstances men cried out for their mothers. "Let's have breakfast and take Clete fishing," I said.

"Now?" she said.

"Is there any better time?" I replied.

It was not a sentimental act. At a certain age,

you realize the greatest loss you can experience is a theft you perpetrate upon yourself — the waste of days given us. Is there any more piercing remorse than the realization that a person has thrown away the potential that resides in every sunrise?

Alafair chose to stay at the house and work on her novel, and Clete and Molly and I drove in my truck to a spot on the Blackfoot River not far from Colonel Lindbergh's old ranch. It is difficult to describe what the Blackfoot is like, because many of its natural qualities seem to have theological overtones. Maybe that's why the Indians considered it a holy place. After the spring runoff, the water is blue-green and swift and cold and running in long riffles through boulders that stay half-submerged year round. The canyons are steep-sided and topped with fir and ponderosa and larch trees that turn gold in the fall. If you listen carefully, you notice the rocks under the stream knocking against one another and making a murmuring sound, as though talking to themselves or us.

The boulders along the banks are huge and often baked white and sometimes printed with the scales of hellgrammites. Many of the boulders are flat-topped and are wonderful to walk out on so you can fly-cast and create a wide-looping figure eight over your head and not hang your fly in the trees. Wild roses grow along the banks, as well as bushes and

513

leafy vines that turn orange and scarlet and apricot and plum in the autumn. When the wind comes up the canyon, leaves and pine needles balloon into the air, as though the entirety of the environment is in reality a single organism that creates its own rebirth and obeys its own rules and takes no heed of man's presence.

The greatest oddity on the river is the quality of light. It doesn't come from above. There is a mossy green-gold glow that seems to emanate from the table rocks that plate the river bottom, and the trout drifting back and forth in the riffle are backlit by it.

Molly and Clete and I built a fire from driftwood and made cowboy coffee and melted a stick of butter in a skillet and browned ham-and-onion sandwiches that we added strips of cheese and bacon to. After the sun had climbed above the rim of the canyon, the first flies rose from the bushes along the banks and hovered in the spray above the riffle. We waded into water up to our hips and fished a pool behind a beaver dam where both rainbows and cutthroats were hitting anything we threw at them. They hit with the same fervor you see in trout when the first mayflies hatch. They rise quickly out of the shadows, rolling the fly, slapping their tails on the surface, then running with it for the bottom of a pool, your rod arching and throbbing in your palm. All of the worries and concerns that plague us on a daily basis seem to dissolve and disappear, like smoke, inside this sun-spangled canyon deep in the heart of Blackfoot country.

Jim Bridger and Andrew Henry and Will Sublette had been here, and Hugh Glass, who later crawled a hundred miles to the Missouri Breaks after he was mauled by a grizzly on the Milk River, and Lewis and Clark and Sacagawea and the black man named York, who was the delight of the Indians because he could walk on his hands. To me, this was a magical land, watched over by ancient spirits, a reminder of the admonition in Ecclesiastes that the race is not to the swift or the proud and that the earth abideth forever.

We worked our way upstream a half mile from the truck, and while Molly collected rocks, Clete and I began casting on a long blue-green undulating ribbon of trout water bordered on one side by a pebble beach with no brush and, on the other side, a grassy bank full of grasshoppers that fell regularly into the stream and brought the browns and the bulls to the top of the pools.

Clete was ahead of me, his right arm lifting the fly neatly and cleanly from the riffle before it could be pulled under by the current. His hand would stop at twelve o'clock high, and with his wrist, he would create a slow elliptical pattern over his head, drying the fly, filling the air with a swishing sound that was almost musical.

Then I heard his cell phone ring. He reeled in his line and hooked his fly in the cork handle of his rod and waded to shore. I couldn't hear his conversation over the stream, but I saw the concern in his face and the way he turned his back to me and kept glancing over his shoulder, as though he wanted to conceal the intrusion of the outside world on this perfect stretch of river we had stumbled upon.

That was when I saw something that later seemed too much for coincidence. At least five canine animals were running through the trees on the far bank. At first I thought they were coyotes. But as a rule, coyotes are loners and don't run in packs. Unlike wolves, they sniff the ground, not the wind, in search of rabbit trails and pocket gophers and chipmunk dens. The canines running through the trees were dark, their ears pointed forward, their heads erect, their tails thick and bushy. The humps on three of them were silver-tipped. I had no doubt they were wolves.

I saw Clete close his phone and put it in his pocket. I walked up on the beach, water squishing out of my tennis shoes. "Was that Gretchen?" I asked.

"How'd you know?"

"The look on your face. You don't hide your emotions well. Did Surrette come back?"

"The National Transportation Safety Board issued its report on the crash of the Sierra Club plane. There was an explosion inside the cabin. It was probably a bomb."

"How did it get on the plane?"

"Gretchen said she and the pilot left it parked by a general store on the edge of the Blackfoot rez. The guy who runs the store is a relative of Angel Deer Heart."

"Gretchen thinks the Indians are involved in blowing up a plane?"

"No, she thinks somebody connected with the Youngers planted the bomb while she and the pilot were taking photographs up the road."

"Maybe the bomb was put on there earlier," I said.

"She says the cabin was clean when she got on at Missoula. At least as far as she could tell."

"How is Gretchen taking it?"

"The pilot was her friend. How do you think she's taking it?"

"Let's go back to town," I said.

"I didn't mean to sound sharp."

"We had a good time. Let's get Molly and head home."

He looked across the river into the trees. He pointed. "Do you see what I'm seeing?"

"They're wolves."

"I never heard of wolves on the Blackfoot.

Are they part of that reintroduction program?"

"I don't know, Clete. I'm not sure about anything anymore."

We walked back down the river, over rocks that were as white as eggs, the trees ruffling on either side of the canyon. A blue rubber raft full of revelers floated past us, all of them toasting us with their beer cans, their faces happy and pink with sunburn. I wanted never to let go of this place. We walked around a bend and saw Molly coming toward us, her mouth moving, her words lost in the wind. Behind her, I could see my truck parked up on the bench, the sun hammering like a heliograph on the windshield.

"What's wrong?" I asked.

"I walked down below the bend to collect some pieces of driftwood. I didn't lock the truck. You'd better look inside."

"What is it?" I said.

"See for yourself. I didn't touch anything."

I took off my fly vest and set it down on the rocks and laid my fly rod on top of it. As I approached the truck, I could see a pair of blue women's panties hanging from the rearview mirror. There was no movement in the trees, no sign of tire tracks other than mine on the access road, nobody on the bank of the river except Molly and Clete. I opened the passenger door and removed the panties from the mirror. There were specks of dried blood near the elastic band. Clete had been standing behind me. He removed a small pair of binoculars from the canvas rucksack he always carried on fishing trips, and began scanning the woods, then the far bank.

"Maybe it was some college kids playing a prank," he said. "A bunch of them kayak through here."

Someone had placed a Montana driver's license on the dashboard. I picked it up by the edges and looked at the laminated photo of a young woman. She was pretty and seemed pleased to be photographed. There was a bright prospect in her eyes, a glow about her.

"Who's it belong to?" Clete asked.

"Rhonda Fayhee."

"Who?"

"The waitress who went missing up by Lookout Pass."

"That son of a bitch was here?"

"Get Elvis Bisbee on the horn and tell him what we've got."

"Bisbee is a boob. I'd rather deal with Fart, Barf, and Itch. At least they don't wear mustaches that look like rope."

"The FBI had twenty years to pinch this guy. It took Wichita PD to do it."

"How'd he get in and out of here without us seeing him?" he said, punching in a 911 call with his thumb.

I didn't want to think about the wolves in

the trees on the far side of the river or the wolf that was probably living somewhere behind Albert's house. The theater of the mind was Surrette's ally. But I had no doubt he had been here and left two of his trophies for us to find. I also felt that he represented a level of evil far greater in dimension and cunning than the machinations of one individual. I have interviewed condemned inmates on death row in Louisiana, Mississippi, and Texas. My experience with each of them was the same. I believed they were not only dysfunctional but irreparably impaired. They were either schizophrenic or had fetal alcohol syndrome or had been neurologically damaged by severe beatings as children. Normality had never been an option in their lives. And there was no theological side to the story.

Surrette was different. Men of his ilk wish to re-create the world in their image. The evil they do is of a kind we never erase from memory. I knew I would never forget the image of the woman's blood-spotted undergarment hanging from my rearview mirror. Nor would I ever be able to explain how a man could take pride in torturing to death an innocent young woman in the flower of her life. I wanted to confront Surrette and make him accountable, not simply for his crimes but for his existence. I think I know why Himmler and other Nazi war criminals killed themselves. They ensured their own immortality by denying us knowledge of who they really were. If I caught Asa Surrette, I was determined that he would tell us his secrets and his origins, even if the rule book got tossed over the gunwale.

Clete closed his cell phone.

"What did they say?" I asked.

"They're sending a couple of lab guys out. We shouldn't touch anything," he replied. He stuck an unlit cigarette in his mouth and gazed across the river. "This one really bothers me, Dave."

"Join the club."

Before he spoke again, he checked to see if Molly was within earshot. "When we get this guy, he's going into a wood chipper. We're on the same wavelength about this, right?"

"I made a mistake earlier," I said.

"About what?"

"I should have listened to Wyatt Dixon."

"Are you crazy?"

"That's the point. I'm not, and neither are you. Dixon is. He probably sees a netherworld others can't. This one doesn't have a zip code, Clete. Surrette is the real deal."

I thought Clete was going to dismiss me. He didn't. His face became empty of expression, as though he had lost the thread in our conversation. He leaned over and picked up a handful of rocks and began throwing them in the river, watching them make big plopping holes in the riffle. Then he said, "If I get back to New Orleans, I'm never going to leave."

Gretchen's notice in the personals read:

Dear friend from the Yellow Brick Road,
     I was impressed. I'm a filmmaker. My first documentary screened at Sundance. I think you and I could work together on a biopic. I've already got the financing. Someone told me you have an unpublished novel. You know how to contact me. It's your call.
                    The munchkin from the ridge,
                                        G.H.

"How'd you think up something like this?" Clete said when she told him what she had done.

"All predators troll. Even when they're inactive or in prison, they troll."

"That's not the issue."

"He let Alafair interview him in prison because he thought she was going to write a book about him. He took creative writing courses at Wichita State and wrote a novel based on himself. He thinks he's an intellectual and a great artist."

"You should have talked to me first."

"I need approval?" she said.

"The guy tried to kill you with a bear trap. Your life was saved by a rabbit."

"I get you. I'm so inept, I'd be dead except for the intervention of an animal."

"I didn't mean it that way."

"Surrette is a narcissist, Clete. Believe me, he'll swallow the bait. Hollywood is a drug. Its sharpest critics are fascinated by it. Otherwise they wouldn't be talking about it all the time."

"He outsmarted the cops for twenty years, Gretchen. He survived a collision with a gas truck. Dave thinks Surrette may come from somewhere else. He didn't say it exactly that way, but that's what he's thinking."

"How about taking the mashed potatoes out of your mouth?"

"Years back we went up against a guy named Legion Guidry. He was an overseer on a plantation in Iberia Parish." Clete shook his head as though deciding whether he should revisit the experience. "I think maybe this guy wasn't human. I try to forget about him. I get the heebie-jeebies when I start thinking too much about stuff like that."

They were sitting on the front porch of the cabin. It was Friday, the beginning of a fine weekend, and Gretchen could see the mist from the sprinklers in Albert's yard blowing on the flower beds and the patches of clover in the fescue. It was the kind of summer day that lacked only the smell of mowed grass to be perfect. "What stuff?" she said.

"I don't want to talk about it."

"Don't leave me hanging like this."

"Dave believed Legion Guidry worked for the devil. I didn't want to hear it. I grew up listening to stuff like that. But Dave and I never could explain a lot of the things Guidry did or the power he seemed to have over people."

"You guys got him, right? Doesn't that tell you something? He was flesh and blood."

"It wasn't us. He was hit by lightning. He ran into a swamp with bullets flying around him. Then lightning hit the woods. The coroner and some deputies found his body floating in a bay with a bunch of dead pigs."

Clete had been drinking a can of warm beer. He picked it up, then looked at it as though he didn't know where it had come from. He set it back down and stared into space.

"Are you all right?" she said.

"Yeah, I'm fine. I don't like to go inside my own head sometimes."

"Wichita PD nailed Surrette," she said. "He wasn't the criminal genius of the century."

"He sent them a floppy disk that could be traced to his employer's computer. He made the disk on a Saturday, when no one else was in the office. I think he deliberately screwed up."

"What for?"

"He wasn't getting enough attention. He wanted to stand up in court, in front of the families, and describe in detail what he did to his victims. He was happier than a hog rolling in shit."

"Both you and Dave are letting this guy get to you. There's one way you deal with a guy like Surrette. You put more holes in him than he can put plugs in. It's that simple." He turned in his chair. She saw the sadness in his eyes. "Don't look at me that way," she said.

"That's the stuff shank artists in the joint say," he replied. "You get that kind of language out of your vocabulary."

"What I'm saying is the guy's no supervillain. He's not from the Abyss," she said. "You've been around the worst of the worst. You know they all go down."

"I took money from the Giacanos and worked for Sally Dee. They were bad guys, but they didn't come close to Legion Guidry. This is what you're choosing not to hear. Dave is right about Surrette. How does he come and go on Albert's property? How'd he disappear after he almost killed you with a bear trap?"

"Are we working together or not?" she asked.

"I'll always back your play. You know that."

"Sometimes I'm not sure."

"Don't ever say that to me again," he said.

"Why do you talk to me like that?"

"Because sometimes I feel like it."

"You really know how to treat a girl, Clete. Fuck you," she said.

CHAPTER 25

Albert came down to the cabin Saturday morning and told Gretchen someone had left a message for her on his answering machine. The call was not from Asa Surrette but from a woman who sounded as though she were reading a prepared statement. "This is for Gretchen Horowitz from her friend up on the ridge," the female voice said. "You're correct about me having written a novel. Maybe Mr. Hollister might like to read it sometime. He might even like it. I would also like to talk with you about the biopic. Will Alafair be working on the project? Take care of yourself, munchkin. I think you and I might have great fun together."

The woman gave a number and broke the connection. Gretchen jotted down the number and turned around. Unbeknownst to her, Albert had been standing two feet behind her. "What was that about?" he said.

"A project I'm working on," she replied.

"We need to understand something, Miss

Gretchen. I don't impose my way on others. But my name was used in that message. I want to know what this is about."

"Asa Surrette," she replied.

"You're going to bait him out of his hole, are you?"

"If I can."

"What are you going to do when you catch up with him?"

"That's up to him."

"You have a gift. It comes from a source outside of yourself. It was given to you for a reason, and eventually, that reason will manifest in your life. Don't let the world taint it or take it from you. Men like Surrette despise you for the talent and intelligence that were given to you for a higher purpose."

"I doubt if a guy like that dwells on the arts and humanities, Mr. Hollister."

"You're wrong. The Surrettes of the world despise you because the Creator gave you the gift and not them."

"Surrette has always operated in rural areas that lack sophisticated law enforcement," she said. "That means he's an amateur and he'll slip up."

"Don't bet on it," he replied.

Without telling Clete, Gretchen drove down the road to the two-lane highway, where she could get cell service, and dialed the number the woman had left on Albert's machine. She believed the number belonged to a stolen phone and that Surrette probably paid someone to leave the message for him. The question was who would pick up on the other end. She didn't have to wait long to find out.

"Is that you, Gretchen?" a man's voice said.

"It sure is."

"Did you tell the police I contacted you?"

"I'm not a big friend of the cops."

"I understand you were a bad girl in Florida."

"Not so much. Think you'd like to make a movie with me?"

"Ever hear of a guy named Bix Golightly?" he asked.

"I've heard the name."

"Bix Golightly from New Orleans?"

"What about him?" she said.

"He got three in his face, sitting in his vehicle, in the what-do-you-call-it, the Big Easy."

"Not true. It was across the river in Algiers."

"There're no flies on you," he said.

"How would you know about Bix Golightly?"

"Your reputation gets around. Maybe you have fans you don't know about."

"Do you mind if I call you Asa?"

"Call me the Tin Man. How is Alafair?"

"She worries you might be mad at her."

"I'd love to get together with both of you. I

have some very good ideas. For many years I lived inside my head and thought about things I would like to do with others."

"What kinds of ideas?"

"Maybe I shouldn't tell you. I have a feeling you get embarrassed about sexual matters. I never knew a tomboy who wasn't a prude at heart."

"I'm a filmmaker. I live in West Hollywood. Does that sound like a prude?"

"I like your legs. Alafair's figure is lovely but not as interesting as yours."

"Are you trying to tell me you want to get it on?"

"You *are* a bad girl."

"Where can we meet?" she asked.

"Let me get back to you on that. I've been busy of late."

"With the guy who got dragged down the highway by Flathead Lake?"

"The simpleminded ones aren't much fun."

"The waitress up at Lookout Pass? Was that you?"

"Lookout Pass? Let me think." He made a bubbling sound, as though flipping his index finger up and down on his lips. "I'm not sure where that is. There's one thing I wanted to ask you."

"Go ahead," she said.

"When you eased Golightly into the next world, you enjoyed it, didn't you? It wasn't just a job. You love the rush. Your loins buzz with it, like a nest of bees. No, that's not well said. It's a wet lick on an ice cream cone."

She tried to keep her voice empty of emotion. "I think we can make a successful film together," she said.

"I got a little close to home, didn't I?"

"Unauthorized photos from your crime scenes were posted on the Internet. Did you take those?"

"Maybe. How did you like them?"

"I can teach you about film. I have friends at Creative Artists. They can help us in lots of ways."

"You sound a little weakhearted," he said. "Be advised that Alafair must be on board, our centerpiece, so to speak. Give me your cell number. I have a couple of commitments that need to be wrapped up, but you and I will have our date."

She gave him her number and closed her phone. After he hung up, she opened the door of her truck and vomited into the road.

Gretchen drove up to Albert's house and told Alafair of the conversation.

"You're sure it's him? You actually had this bastard on the line?" Alafair said.

Gretchen was sitting by Alafair's writing desk on the third floor of Albert's house, her shoulders rounded. She looked out the window, not wanting to say the things she had to say. "He's after you. It's obviously an obsession."

"That's not exactly a big revelation," Alafair said.

"He was hinting he would meet with me. But only if you're on board, as he puts it." A pool of heat seemed to shimmer and go out of shape on the barn's metal roof. "I didn't say anything to discourage him."

"Without asking me, you were making deals with this asshole? Deals that include me?"

"I admire you. You're everything I'd like to be. I wouldn't let anyone hurt you. I'd kill them if they tried to hurt you."

"What do you think this guy has been trying to do? You think you're going to outsmart him?"

"I have experience other people don't."

"Did you ever read 'Young Goodman Brown' by Nathaniel Hawthorne?"

"No."

"It was made into a film. Goodman Brown thought he could stroll with the devil in a midnight woods and outwit him. His wife was named Faith. He ended up losing not only his wife but his soul."

Gretchen began writing on a piece of typewriter paper. "Who did the film?" she asked.

Alafair pulled the sheet of paper away from her and tore it in half and threw the pieces in the wastebasket. "Are you out of your mind? This isn't about movies. It's about evil. How did Surrette know about Bix Golightly?"

"I haven't figured that out."

"Think about it. There are only two ways he could know, Gretchen. He's either mobbed up, or he's privy to a world we can't guess at."

"No. The Mob uses pros. They're businessmen."

"So where does he get this omniscient knowledge?"

"You're saying he has special powers?"

"I'm saying we ought to go to the cops." Alafair put her hand on Gretchen's back. "Your muscles are as hard as iron. I worry about you."

"I'm doing fine."

"You're the sister I never had, Gretchen." She touched Gretchen's hair.

"Surrette put a bomb in Percy Wolcott's plane. Percy was one of the gentlest people I ever knew," Gretchen said. "His body was burned beyond recognition. I think Surrette did it. I'm going to saw him apart."

Alafair gazed at the manuscript basket on her desk. It was half-filled with typed sheets. "What do you want me to do?" she asked.

"Surrette has plenty of money. Where does it come from? We also want to check out Felicity Louviere's background. Her husband says she was the town pump. She says her father left her to founder while he went off to be a professional good guy among the Indians in South America."

"So what?" Alafair said.

"She doesn't add up. Clete is easily taken in by bad women. Because he follows his schlong doesn't mean the rest of us have to."

"I can't believe you just said that."

"There's one other thing. You can't tell your father or Clete about this."

"That doesn't sound too good."

"Are you in or out?" Gretchen said.

On North Higgins, next to a saloon that had not closed its doors since 1891, was a newsstand and tobacco store that carried pulps and tabloids and magazines of every stripe. A man wearing two-tone shoes and a rain hat and aviator glasses and a loose-fitting tan suit and an open-collar blue shirt with white stripes came through the front door and began looking at the magazines on the rack, flipping through a few pages and replacing the magazine sloppily on the rack when he found nothing of interest in it. Or he simply let it fall to the floor, the pages splaying by his foot, while he reached for another magazine.

Two teenage girls with blond hair that was almost gold had gotten out of his SUV to watch a street guitarist playing on the corner. Then they window-shopped and walked out of the clerk's line of sight, but the man in the tan suit seemed to pay little attention to them. He had the air of a beachcomber or a quasi-dissolute figure prowling the backstreet dens of an Oriental city in a 1940s film noir. He picked up a copy of *Hustler,* occasionally wetting a finger as he turned the pages, tilting the magazine sideways to get a better view of the artwork inside.

The clerk was a zit-faced kid whose skinny arms were tattooed from wrist to armpit with images of snakes and skeletal heads and bloody knives. He was sitting on a stool behind the counter, eyeballing the customer in the tan suit, a matchstick flipping up and down between his teeth. "I just started this job. I'd like to keep it," he said.

"Yeah?" the customer said.

"How about not wrecking the magazine rack?"

"Why do you carry this trash?"

"Because horny old geeks come in here and buy it?"

"I like that new way of talking you kids have. You end every sentence like it's a question."

"I don't think you get it. *I'm* not the issue."

The customer went on reading, his eyes crinkling at the corners.

"How about picking up the magazines off the floor, man?" the clerk said.

"You shouldn't sell this junk."

"Then why are you looking at it?"

The customer kept reading, never raising

his eyes. "What's your name?"

The clerk hesitated before he spoke. "Seymour Little."

"That's perfect."

The clerk made a snuffing sound down in his nose. "You step in dog shit or something?"

The customer lifted his eyes from the magazine. "Repeat that?"

"There's a funny smell in the air."

"You're saying the funny smell is me?"

"No, I was just wondering."

"But you were wondering if it was me that smelled like dog shit?"

"No, I lost my job at the motel. I'm just trying to get a fresh start."

"Yeah, you worked at a fleabag on West Broadway, didn't you? You got fired because you dragged somebody's Harley down the street."

"How'd you know that?"

"You made some ink. You're a celebrity."

"No, I didn't."

"I say you did. But you should take your mind off world events, Seymour. You think you can do that?"

"Yes, sir."

The customer took a hundred-dollar bill and a folded piece of paper out of his shirt pocket and placed them on the counter. "I want you to walk down to the pharmacy and pick up a prescription for me. There're several other items you'll have to get off the shelf."

"I can't leave here."

"I'll fill in for you."

"What the fuck is with you, man?"

"I say and you do. That's not hard to understand, is it? You shouldn't wise off to the wrong people, Seymour."

The clerk unfolded the piece of paper and read it. "You want me to shop for tampons?"

"You need to be back here in thirteen minutes. Don't make me come after you."

"Are you nuts?"

"Run along now."

"Thirteen minutes? Not twelve or fourteen?"

"Look into my face. Tell me what you see there. Don't look away. Look straight into my eyes. Do you have any doubt what might happen to you if you don't do what I say?"

"I'm sorry. I don't want trouble. Hey, man, I was just doing my job. What the fuck?"

There was a long pause. "I was having a little fun with you. I saw you drag that motorcycle down the street."

"Why do you keep looking at me like that?"

"Like what?"

"With that smile on your face."

"Your tats. You want people to think you've been inside. But you haven't. You couldn't cut it inside, Seymour. First night in the shower, the wolves would make lamb chops out of you. They would have you sizzling in the pan like a lump of butter."

"Why are you doing this?"

"I'm helping you so you won't shoot off your mouth to the wrong man again. You'll always remember this moment. No matter how long you live, you'll remember me. When you think you've changed, that you're strong and all this is behind you, you'll have a dream about me and realize I'll always be inside your head. Run along now. Everything will be shipshape when you get back. Do you mind if I get myself a soda?"

The clerk went to the pharmacy and returned in under thirteen minutes, his face chastened, his skin as dry and bloodless as paper. He looked as though half of what he used to be had been left outside the store. "Can I ask you something?" he said.

"Go ahead," the customer replied.

"The girls in your SUV, are those your daughters?"

"I'm their godfather. Why do you ask?"

"Why do you need all that OxyContin?"

"I'm pimping them out." The man waited, then his face split into a grin. "You never know when a guy is ribbing you, do you? Enjoy the rest of your day, Seymour. Take consolation in the fact that you're a part of history. You just don't know it yet."

As the customer drove away with the two teenage girls, the clerk memorized the tag

538

number and wrote it in pencil on the counter. Then he picked up the telephone and dialed 911. As soon as he had completed the third digit, he hung up and rubbed the tag number out of the wood with the heel of his hand, a lump as big as a walnut protruding from his throat.

Why do people in A.A. claim they pay the biggest membership dues in the world? That's easy. Early in life, you set out to deconstruct everything good you thought you'd turn out to be. When you're finished doing that, you foul your blood, piss your brains into the street, trade off your tomorrows, destroy your family, betray your friends, court suicide on a daily basis, and become an object of ridicule and contempt in the eyes of your fellow man. That's for openers. The rest of the dance card involves detox, jail, padded cells, and finally, the cemetery. If you want your soul shot out of a cannon, or you want to enter a period of agitated depression and psychoneurotic anxiety known as a Gethsemane Experience, untreated alcoholism is a surefire way to get there.

The big surprise at your first A.A. meeting is the apparent normalcy of the people in the room. They come from every socioeconomic background imaginable. The only thing most of them have in common is the neurosis that has governed their lives. The meeting I attended on Monday night was held on the second floor of a Methodist church, across from a high school in a maple-lined neighborhood reminiscent of an earlier time. The woman seated next to me was a Lutheran minister. The woman on the other side of me was a former middle-school teacher who had been molested as a child and had seduced two of her male students. The man leading the meeting was a housepainter who had been a door gunner in Vietnam and had killed innocent people in a free-fire zone (in his words, "just to watch them die"). The kid who came in late during the recitation of the Serenity Prayer and plunked down next to me in a whoosh of nicotine was the first to speak when the moderator opened up the meeting.

"My name is Seymour, alcoholic addict," he said.

"Hi, Seymour!" everyone said.

He carried his wallet on a chain and wore a long-sleeved flannel shirt, even though the evening was warm. He wore jeans stitched with guitars on the back pockets and cowboy boots that looked made of plastic. There was an oily shine on his forehead, and his voice sounded like a guitar string wound on a wood peg to the point of breaking.

"The subject I got tonight is people who try to take a dump inside your head, and after a while you don't know if it's them who's the

540

problem or you," he said. "What I'm saying is there was this guy who came into the place where I work, and he had this stink on him like dog shit, and when I said something about it, he told me I had shot off my mouth to the wrong guy and he was gonna teach me a lesson.

"He told me to look into his face. No, he said look into his eyes. He really made me afraid. My sponsor says I haven't owned up on the Fifth Step and I got a lot of buried guilt that bounces off other people and comes back on me. It makes me want to drink and use. I thought about going out and copping tonight, but I came to a meeting instead. Maybe all this is just my imagination working, right?"

Everyone thought he was finished and had started into a collective "Thanks, Seymour" when he waved his hands at the air and began talking again. "See, he made me go down to a pharmacy and pick up his prescriptions for him and shop for women's stuff, a guy I never saw before, I mean a guy who took pleasure in telling me what a pitiful loser I was. Maybe that's what I am. I don't know, man, but I feel like walking out on the fucking railway track. Know what he said when he was going out the door? 'Hey, tell your friends you met the Tin Man.' Who's the fucking Tin Man?"

Others tried to help him by telling their stories, but it was obvious that Seymour had packed his bag and moved into a dark space inside his head that no one else could enter. After the meeting ended, I put my hand on his shoulder. "My name is Dave Robicheaux," I said. "You got a minute?"

"You a cop?"

"What makes you think that?" I said, smiling.

"I've seen you at another meeting. You wear a sport coat and keep your hands at your sides. Cops never let you know what they're thinking. I'm right, huh?"

"Yeah, how about we go outside?" I said.

"I'm not feeling too good right now. Maybe I should head home."

"The guy in your store is from Kansas. He's a bad dude. And we need to talk."

He looked out the window at the sun descending beyond the mountains in the west. "Mind if I smoke?"

"No," I lied.

We sat on the steps of the church in the twilight. The streetlamps had come on, and the maple trees along the sidewalks contained a green luminescence that reminded me of the subdued yet brilliant colors you see in a van Gogh painting. He pulled a cigarette out of the pack in his shirt pocket and stuck it in his mouth and struck a paper match and tried to cup it in his palms, but he was shaking so badly, he dropped the match on the concrete. "I feel like I'm jonesing," he said.

"I think you're a stand-up guy, Seymour. It takes guts to talk about your problems in a roomful of people, many of them strangers. Did this guy in your store have a name besides Tin Man?"

"No, just a stink. It's like he left shit prints all over the place. I had to wipe down everything he touched with Lysol."

I didn't want to see him get wired up again, so I changed the subject. "You're not too warm in that shirt?"

"I was trying to hide my tats."

"You were in the system?"

"No. The guy called me a fraud. I think he's probably right. I didn't earn my ink. I wanted people to think I was a badass. I even got the meeting off track tonight. We're supposed to talk about using and drinking, not about problems with old geeks who read porn magazines. I feel awful."

"He wants to infect others with his sickness, partner. Don't let him get inside your head. You're a good guy. You keep remembering that."

"When I looked into his eyes, it really scared me, man. It was like looking into a cave that didn't have a bottom."

"Did he give you any indication where he might be living?"

"No. He had two girls with him. He was driving a gray SUV."

"Do you remember the tag?"

"I wrote it down, then erased it."

"Do you remember any part of it?"

"No. It was a Montana plate. That's all I know. He said he was the godfather of the two girls. You've had some kind of run-in with him?"

"I think he tried to kill my daughter. If we're talking about the same man, his name is Asa Surrette. He's tortured and killed eight people."

"Jesus," he said. "Maybe that's why he had those girls with him. You think they're runaways? I wonder if that's why he had all the dope."

"What dope?"

"The OxyContin. He had another prescription, too. I think it was for sleeping pills or downers."

"What were the other items he made you buy?"

"Tampons, toothpaste, fingernail clippers, dental floss, women's deodorant, Pepto-Bismol."

"He didn't say who these things were for?"

"He wasn't someone you ask a lot of questions. He said I was part of history. What'd he mean by that? What the fuck does history have to do with any of this?"

"Nothing," I said.

"OxyContin is as close to heroin as legal dope gets. He's gonna cook the Oxy and shoot those girls up, isn't he? That's how he's gonna get in their pants."

"He masturbates on his victims after he strangles them. That's the guy who was in your store, Seymour. You treat your encounter with him as you would a sickness. You let go of it forever. He has nothing to do with your life. You have a lot of friends in that room upstairs. You keep remembering who you are, a likable guy who's doing the best he can. You got me on that?"

"Yes, sir."

I wrote my cell number on the back of my departmental business card and gave it to him. When I got up to go, he remained on the steps, staring up at me, not speaking.

"Tell you what, how about a hamburger and a cup of coffee?" I said.

"I think I can handle that," he replied.

The real significance of my conversation with him did not hit me until four the next morning. I sat up in bed, numb, my ears ringing with a sense of urgency that seemed to have no origin. I went into the bathroom and turned on the light and propped my arms on the lavatory, trying to reconstruct the dream I'd just had. In it, I saw a girl locked inside a giant plastic bubble, her hands pressed against the side, her cries inaudible, her oxygen supply running out.

I looked in the mirror and saw Molly standing behind me. "Did you have a nightmare?"

she said.

"She's alive," I said.

"Who's alive?"

"The girl who was abducted up by Lookout Pass," I replied.

CHAPTER 26

I was in Elvis Bisbee's office by nine that morning. I told him of my chance meeting with Seymour Little. He made notes on a legal pad while I spoke. "Okay, we'll talk with this kid and check out the pharmacy," he said. "Thanks for coming in."

"I've already been to the pharmacy. The prescriptions were phoned in by a scrip doctor in Whitefish. I called his office. He's somewhere in Canada and not expected back for a while."

"*You* went to the pharmacy?"

"That's right."

"What makes you think you can come here from out of state and conduct your own investigation?"

"I'm sorry you don't approve."

He set down his pen and stared out the window at the trees and the war memorial on the courthouse lawn. "Mind telling why the pharmacist shared his information with you?"

"I showed him my badge."

"You explained to him you were from the state of Louisiana and you had no legal authority here?"

"That didn't seem to be a problem for him."

He remained motionless in his swivel chair. The tips of his mustache were as white as ash. The clarity in his blue eyes made me think of an empty, sunlit sky. He was one of those whose decency and sense of honor were not an issue. A less patient man would have been far more severe in his attitude toward Clete and Gretchen Horowitz and me. Elvis Bisbee believed the world was a rational place and that procedure in many ways was an end in itself. Without his kind, we probably would have chaos. However, there is a caveat to that kind of thinking. Those who are rapacious and prey upon the weak and who would undo the system are not bound by procedure, and they take great delight in the presence of those who are.

"Rhonda Fayhee is alive, Sheriff. I don't think we have a lot of time," I said. "I was almost sure Surrette had killed her. He has never kept his victims alive, except to torture them. This time he decided to do it differently."

"Why?"

"He doesn't telegraph his pitch. He hides it in his glove or behind his thigh."

"Why are you so sure it's Surrette?"

"Because he's getting better and better at what he does. He could have picked up the prescriptions himself. Instead, he used and degraded a kid who looks like a sack of broken Popsicle sticks. He also knew the kid would report him and we'd figure out the girl is still alive. Except we have no idea where she is or what she's going through while we're wasting time in your office."

"Waste of time, is it?"

I got up from the chair. "Surrette is about to send us something. They all do. I don't know what it will be. I don't even want to think about it. But that's what he's going to do. Something is troubling me about our conversation, Sheriff."

"Don't hold back."

"You're an intelligent man. I think you already know all these things. Surrette is here for the long haul, and your department isn't equipped to deal with him. So it becomes a whole lot easier to swat at flies rather than admit you've got a real monster in your midst. I don't blame you for being impotent about your situation. I do blame you for pretending to be ignorant of it."

He picked up the pen from his desk and balanced it on one end, then on the other, and finally let it topple onto the blotter. "Good-bye, Mr. Robicheaux. If you have any other information for me, phone it in. I make this request of you because I would like you to stay the hell out of my office for a very long time."

When she was little, Alafair could never hide secrets. Her emotions immediately showed on her face, with a transparency that was like looking through glass. She used to get into raging confrontations with Batist, the elderly black man who worked at our bait shop and boat dock. The issue was always the same: Tripod, her pet raccoon, who had only three legs but was a master burglar when it came to breaking into Batist's stock of energy bars and fried pies. In one instance, I looked down the slope from our old home and saw Alafair racing from the bait shop with Tripod cradled in her arms and Batist in full pursuit, a broomstick cocked over his head. She powered up the slope through the pecan trees and live oaks and streaked past me into the house, Tripod's tail flopping like a spring.

"What happened down there?" I said.

"Batist is mean! I hate him!"

"You shouldn't talk about Batist like that, Alafair. Did Tripod do something that got him upset?"

"He didn't do anything. Batist said he was going to cook him in a pot. I hope he falls in the water and gets hit by a boat. Why doesn't he take his smelly cigars and go home?"

"Can you explain why Tripod has chocolate on his paws and all over his mouth?"

Her face was as round as a plate, her bangs hanging in her eyes. She looked sideways. "He probably found a candy bar on the dock."

"Yeah, a lot of people throw their candy bars on the dock. Did you notice that Tripod's stomach looks like a balloon full of water?"

"He was going to hurt Tripod, Dave. You didn't see his face."

"Batist can't read or write, but he takes great pride in the work he does for us. When Tripod tears up the counter, Batist feels like he's let us down. You and Tripod have to see things from his point of view."

Her face crumpled and she began to cry. When I tried to pat her on the head, she ran out the back door, slamming it as hard as she could, Tripod bouncing in her arms.

She had a horse named Tex that I let her ride only when I was close by. While my wife, Annie, and I were gone one afternoon, Alafair put on Tex's bridle and bit and used the slat fence to climb up on his back. She was wearing her Baby Orca T-shirt and the Donald Duck cap with a quacking bill that we had bought at Disney World. For whatever reason, she decided to start quacking the bill. Tex responded by pitching her end over end into our tomato plants. When we returned from town, Alafair had dirt in her hair and a scrape on the side of her face, but she refused to tell us what had happened. I looked through the side window and saw Tex standing by the shed, his reins hanging in the dirt.

"Did you ride Tex while we were gone?" I asked.

She squinted as though she couldn't quite recall the event. "Maybe for a little bit. Yeah, I think I did."

"You fell off?"

"No, he went up in the air and threw me over his head!"

"Okay, so let's not do that again. What if you had been knocked unconscious?" I said.

She shut her eyes, tears leaking down both cheeks.

"What's wrong, little guy?" I said. "It's not that bad. Just don't do it again."

"You said the tomatoes are for the black people. Now I smushed them, and they're not going to have anything to eat, and everybody is going to get mad at me," she said.

Many years down the road, the same little girl was still in my life, no different in my mind from when we lived in an idyllic world south of New Iberia. When I returned from the courthouse in Missoula, I went into the kitchen to fix a sandwich. Through the window, I could see Alafair watering the potted petunias and geraniums on the deck with a sprinkler can. She swept the can back and forth over the flowers, hitting the deck as often as the pots. Then she refilled it and started watering the pots a second time. "Did you water last night?" I said through the screen. "Your catch saucers are overflowing."

"Oh, I didn't see that. Sorry," she said, setting down the can.

"You want something to eat?"

"No, I'm fine."

She gazed at the lawn and at the horses drinking from the tank in the south pasture and at two chipmunks eating the shells that had spilled from the bird feeder.

"Something on your mind?" I said.

She turned and looked me full in the face. "What kind of morning have you had?"

"Sheriff Bisbee indicated he didn't need to see me in his office for a long time."

"Can you come out here?"

"I'm fixing lunch. Come inside."

"I think I'd rather not be in a confined space right now."

I opened the sliding screen door and sat down at a table with a ceramic top that Albert had bought in Mexico.

"Gretchen made contact with Asa Surrette," Alafair said.

I nodded, keeping my expression blank. "When?"

"Saturday."

I watched the shadows of clouds moving across the pasture and up the hillsides and over the fir and larch and cedar trees on the ridges. I looked at the sun and felt a pain that was like a laser burning through my retinas. "This happened three days ago?"

"She ran a notice in the personals. She told Clete about it."

"But not about Surrette calling?"

"No, she hasn't told him about that."

"Is there any reason you've kept this information from me?"

"I waited for Gretchen to tell y'all. I made a mistake."

"You didn't think you could trust me?"

"Dave, we can't be sure she actually talked to Surrette. Any crank could have read her notice in the paper."

"Stop it."

She had one hand resting on the deck rail, as though the wind were affecting her balance. "You didn't want me to go to Kansas and interview him. I wouldn't listen to you. I'm to blame for a lot of what's happened."

"I don't know if I want to hear this, Alafair."

"I have another problem," she said. "After I met Surrette, I wrote articles that were meant to inflame the reader. I wanted to see him sent to the injection table. No, that's not accurate. I wanted to see him boiled in his own grease."

"That's what he deserves," I said.

"Using journalistic advantage to promote someone's execution doesn't make me feel very good, even if the subject is a sorry sack of shit."

"You wanted to cap him yourself?"

"I could shoot Surrette and take a nap after I did it."

"Don't give power away to a man like that. Don't ever let him taint you with his poison."

"I didn't want you going after him, Dave. You're shot to hell. You just won't admit it."

I rubbed my face. "You remember your Baby Orca T-shirt?"

"Don't change the subject," she said.

"I still have it in my footlocker, along with your Donald Duck cap and your Baby Squanto books and your tennis shoes with 'Left' and 'Right' embossed on the toes."

She waited for me to go on.

"That's all I was going to say," I said. "I get your cap and T-shirt and your books and your tennis shoes out of the footlocker and I look at them and then I put them away. I'll probably do that every three or four days for the rest of my life. That's the way it is, little guy."

I went back inside and made lunch for both of us.

It's called an M-1 thumb. If you get one, it's usually during the cleaning of the sweetheart of all World War II infantry weapons, a lovely creation by John Garand that the Imperial Japanese and the Third Reich had not planned to deal with. Had it not been for the M-1, the ground war in Europe and the Pacific theater may have worked out differently. It was a marvelous yet simple piece of engineering, its peep-sight accuracy and rapid-fire punch and knockdown power without peer. It took only seconds after the bolt locked open for the boogie-woogie boys from Company B to thumb another eight-round clip into the magazine.

With Albert's permission, I unlocked one of his gun cabinets and removed his M-1 and a bandolier heavy with .30-06 clips and went up to the shooting range with them. I pulled back the bolt and wiped down the barrel and stock and peep sights and magazine and receiver. I eased my thumb down on the trip mechanism that released the bolt, the heel of my hand anchored on the operating-rod handle, and rolled my thumb and hand free before the bolt slammed home. The M-1 weighed over ten pounds and felt heavy in my hands, but in a reassuring way; its aim was not affected by wind or inclement weather or tall grass or underbrush scraping against the stock and barrel. Every inch of the M-1 was devoted to practicality and efficiency, even the tubular insertions in the butt where you could carry a cleaning rod and barrel swabs and a bore brush. It didn't jam; it was easy to tear down. You couldn't have a better friend in snow or tropical rain.

For the ultimate improvised gun-range target, Albert had placed a World War II salvaged tank turret on a mound of dirt against the hillside. It was tall and cylindrical and dark brown with rust and had a viewing slit in the top. It resembled the helmet worn by Crusader knights. I knelt on one knee, perhaps forty yards from the target, opened the bolt on the M-1, and pushed a clip loaded with armor-piercing rounds into the magazine. I sent the bolt home, wrapped my left forearm in the sling, aimed through the peep sight, and began firing. I saw rust powder in the air and the scoured streaks on the sides of the turret where the rounds didn't impact dead-on, then the holes in the center where the rounds punched through the steel and out the other side.

After I fired the eighth round, the bolt locked open and the clip ejected with the *ping* that anyone who has fired an M-1 associates with it. I removed the plugs from my ears and gazed at the tank turret and tried to imagine what the same rounds would have done to the head of a human being, in this instance the head of Asa Surrette.

Why such a dark speculation?

Just before removing Albert's rifle from his gun cabinet, I had once again accessed the photographs of Surrette that could be found on the Internet. I discovered two posts I hadn't seen. One contained photographs, probably taken by a news photographer at Surrette's crime scenes in Wichita. These are of a kind you do not want to see, not now, not ever. The second post included a photo of a typed letter Surrette sent the Wichita Police Department, one xeroxed on a copy machine in the WSU library. In the letter, he described in detail every moment of his victims' torment, the degree of pain they suffered, and their pleas for mercy. He said the latter brought him a rush he had never thought possible.

I had known sociopaths and sadists in the army and in Vietnam. I had known them in law enforcement and in prisons and in lockdown units where they awaited execution. But Surrette's letter was the cruelest use of language I had ever read. My advice is that no person of goodwill should ever read this man's words, thereby giving a second life to his deeds.

Albert had let me appropriate his M-1, and I not only planned to hang on to it, I planned to use it. Maybe these were foolish and vain thoughts, but sometimes our own self-assurances are our only means of dealing with problems that are far greater than their social remedies. Sometimes, at least in your head, you have to link arms with Doc Holliday and the Earp boys and stroll on down to the O.K. Corral and chat up the Clantons in a way they understand.

I took the M-1 and the bandolier of clips to our room and put them in the closet, then picked up the telephone and made a call I didn't want to make, primarily because I knew it would be a total waste of time.

I was rerouted a couple of times, but finally, I was connected to a special agent at the FBI named James Martini. "I've heard of you," he said.

"You have?" I said.

"Apparently, you and your friend Purcel have quite a history with us down in Louisiana."

"Is that good or bad?"

"How can we be of help?" he replied.

"I think Asa Surrette, the killer from Kansas, is alive and well. I also think he kidnapped the waitress Rhonda Fayhee from her home by Lookout Pass."

"You got that scoped out pretty good?"

"No, not at all. I have no investigative power or legal authority in the state of Montana. That's why I called you. I think Rhonda Fayhee is alive."

"How is it you know that?"

I told him about my conversation with Seymour Little. I told him about the female items and the prescriptions for OxyContin and downers Seymour had been forced to pick up at the pharmacy by a man who trailed a fecal odor into the newsstand.

"Why do you conclude the prescriptions are being used to sedate the waitress?"

"Surrette is a trophy hunter. He's about to send us one."

"A lot of people say Surrette is dead."

"He's been on the property where we're currently living. He left a message on the wall of a cave behind the house."

"What did it say?"

"It was a grandiose statement based on an excerpt from the Bible."

"Could you take a photograph of that and e-mail it to me?"

"I burned it."

"You set lots of fires in caves, do you?"

I could feel my pulse beating in my throat.

"You there?" he said.

"It was an impulsive moment."

"Really? An aunt of the missing woman received a postcard from the missing woman yesterday. It was postmarked Boise, Idaho. The handwriting seems to be hers."

"You're wrong, sir."

"We'll try to blunder through and see what happens," he replied.

"Tell you what," I said. "Forget I called. We'll update you if we come across any information we think you should have."

"You'll do *what*?" he said.

I hung up, feeling foolish and vain and ultimately old, even for my years. Also, I had not told him about Gretchen Horowitz's possible contact with Surrette. Why? I thought his agency wanted to hang her out to dry and I would be giving them the ammunition to do it. If they went after Gretchen for obstruction, of which she may have been guilty, they might take Alafair for good measure. What about the waitress named Rhonda Fayhee? I couldn't get her off my mind. I called Special Agent James Martini back. "Someone I know may have established contact with Surrette," I said. "This individual ran a notice in the personals and got a response from a guy who sounds like Surrette."

"You mean you heard his voice?"

"No, *I* have not heard his voice. My daughter, Alafair, interviewed him in a Kansas prison. I think he has tried to kill her. I think he'll try again. That's why I have a personal stake in the investigation."

"What's the name of the person who made contact with the guy you think is Surrette?"

My head was pounding, the veins in my wrists throbbing. "Gretchen Horowitz," I said.

"She's a friend of yours?"

"You could say that."

"Believe me, if I meet you in person, I'll have a lot to say to you," he replied.

I went to Alafair's room and told her what I had just done. She looked at me for a long time. The window was open, and I could hear the leaves of last winter scudding dryly across the driveway. "I don't know what to say, Dave," she said. "Do you want to tell Gretchen or should I?"

"I will."

"Why did you do it?"

"Rhonda Fayhee's life is in the balance."

"How about Gretchen's?"

"Gretchen has choices. The waitress doesn't," I said.

She had been working on her manuscript with a blue pencil, deleting adjectives that were not in the predicate form, compressing sentences, paring the dialogue down to the bone until there wasn't a rattle in a single line. She set her pencil at the top of a page and stared out the window. A brief sun shower had just blown through the valley, and a rainbow had descended out of the clouds into the middle of the north pasture, where the horses were standing under a clump of cottonwoods. "I know you've acted in conscience," she said. "But I feel emptier than I think I've ever felt. I want to go away and be alone for a long while. It's not your fault, so you don't need to say anything more. As a great favor, please don't say anything to me at all. I'll be in your debt."

She got up from her chair and walked downstairs and out the door. I heard her car start and drive away. When I looked at the pasture again, the rainbow had dissolved into a poisonous patch of henbane as quickly as it had formed.

I am sure there are those who would dismiss Gretchen Horowitz as a sociopath. Her body count would indicate that. However, she was a complex human being, and I suspected that more than one person lived inside her skin. Sigmund Freud borrowed most of his clinical terminology from the ancient Greeks, who possessed a cultural insight into the foibles of human behavior like no civilization before or since. If I've learned anything at all from my years, it's the simple lesson that human beings are always more complicated, brave, long-suffering, and, ultimately, heroic than we ever guessed, and that none of us completely understands another, no matter how intimate we are with them.

I put the face of the pimp named Mack on the enemy soldiers I killed in Vietnam. What if I had not gone to Vietnam? Would I have found another way to release my rage upon other surrogates here in the United States? As a police officer, yes.

Gretchen drove up the dirt road at five that afternoon. She parked her pickup beside the north pasture and started walking toward the pedestrian gate. From the yard I could see Clete in front of their cabin, barbecuing a pork roast on the grill, fanning the smoke out of his face. I headed Gretchen off before she could go through the gate. "I have to talk to you," I said.

She turned toward me. As always, there was a martial element in her body language, an intensity in her eyes, that you did not want to directly confront. She was holding a manila envelope in her right hand. "What is it?" she said.

"I dimed you with the feds."

"About what?"

"Your contact with Asa Surrette."

"Alafair told you I talked with him?"

"I wouldn't have called them, Gretchen, but I think Rhonda Fayhee may still be alive."

"So you're telling me I might get picked up for obstruction or even aiding and abetting?"

"It's a possibility."

"Now you want absolution? That's what this is about?"

"I didn't have a choice," I said.

"Yeah, you did. You could have talked to me first. While the local jokers were figuring out ways to put away me or Wyatt Dixon, Alafair and I did some research on Felicity Louviere."

"What did you find out?"

"Her mother died in Mandeville. Insanity evidently runs in the family. Felicity was known as anybody's punch before Caspian Younger met her. You know what else we found out?"

"Sorry, I don't."

"She got involved with some rural black people whose neighborhoods were being used as sludge ponds for petrochemical waste. She tried to stop a tanker truck from dumping a load in an open pit in St. James Parish and was almost run over."

"What are you trying to tell me?"

"What's it sound like? For all I know, she's a schizoid. But I think better of her than I did. We also found out that Love Younger kept fuck pads in Atlantic City and Vegas and Puerto Rico, in the same casino hotels where his son had six-figure credit lines."

"He's not the oil industry's answer to Cotton Mather?"

She stepped closer to me, her chest rising and falling, her shirt pulled tight on her shoulders. "I don't like people fucking me over, Dave. And I think that's what you did."

"If you'd squared with your father and me, we wouldn't have this problem."

"What makes you think I *didn't* square with him?"

I looked past her shoulder at Clete flipping the roast with a fork on the grill, his face happy at the prospect of having his daughter home and the possibility of inviting his friends to dinner. "I believe you did what you thought was right, Miss Gretchen," I said. "I apologize if I've caused you harm."

She puffed out one cheek and tapped the heel of her fist on the fence rail. "I was parked down at Harvest Foods. I'd left my window partly down. When I came outside, this had been dropped on the seat."

She removed an eight-by-ten photograph from the manila folder and handed it to me.

It was probably taken without a flash. The interior of the room was gray, the walls concrete and without windows, like those in a basement. The lighting was poor. A woman dressed only in her undergarments was bound in a chair, a gag tied across her mouth. The eyes had been razored out of the photo, creating the effect of a mask, making any positive identification of the woman impossible.

"Here's the note that came with it," Gretchen said. "It's a Xerox. You can bet it and the photo and the envelope are clean."

Regardless, I held the sheet of paper by the edges. The note was typed, unlike the one sent by Surrette to Alafair after she interviewed him in prison. If the sender was Surrette, he was a smart man. There was no way to compare the notes. Even the dashes between the sentences had been replaced with conventional punctuation. It read:

Dear Munchkin,

I have already started casting our film. I think this lady is perfect for the role of "the sacrificial queen," don't you? We can add others as we go. You have no idea how many "volunteers" are out there and how easily recruited they can be. Please bring your equipment to our first meeting and we'll get started immediately. We'll have some cherry pie.

Sincerely,
Your biggest fan,
A.

"This has to go to the sheriff and the FBI," I said.

"That's what he wants me to do," she replied.

"How do you figure that?"

"Because Surrette will disappear and I'll look like an idiot. In the meantime, we'll go crazy thinking about what he's doing to that girl."

"I'll go with you to the federal building in Missoula."

"You can take the note and the photograph, Dave, and do whatever you want with them."

She unhitched the chain on the gate and started through it.

"You're the beloved daughter of my oldest and best friend, Miss Gretchen," I said. "Do you believe I would deliberately hurt either of you? Do you honestly believe that?"

She rechained the gate and didn't look back. I might as well have been speaking to the wind.

CHAPTER 27

On Wednesday, Wyatt Dixon was building a sweat lodge in his side yard with stones from the river, hauling them bare-chested uphill in a wheelbarrow, when he saw a chauffeured black Chrysler pull off the highway and park by the entrance to the steel footbridge on the opposite bank. Love Younger got out of the backseat and began walking across the bridge, his rubber-booted feet clanging on the grid, a straw creel hung from one shoulder, a split-bamboo fly rod in his right hand, a cork sun helmet on his head.

He stepped off the bridge and walked down to the water's edge, where Wyatt was lifting a large stone into the wheelbarrow. "You mind if I fish along the front of your property?" he asked.

"Montana law allows you to go through anybody's land, long as you're within the flood line of the river," Wyatt said.

"I heard there's a deep hole under the bridge here. They say it's full of German browns."

"Have at it," Wyatt said. He sat high up on the bank, a long-stemmed weed between his teeth, his straw hat slanted down on his forehead, and watched the older man wade into the water and thread his nylon leader through the eyelet of a woolly worm. *What's really on your mind, old man?* he thought.

Wyatt could not reconcile the proportions of the older man with his wealth and status. Love Younger had the neck of a bull and the hands of a bricklayer. The few rich people Wyatt had known did not resemble Love Younger. Did Younger come up the hard way, racking pipe and wrestling a drill bit in the oil field? Or had someone bequeathed him money, a rich wife, maybe? Wyatt did not believe that great wealth came to people through hard work. If that were true, almost everyone would be rich.

He got to his feet. "You won't catch none like that," he said.

"Oh?" Younger said, turning around in the water, the current cutting across his knees.

"You have to face the opposite bank and throw the woolly worm at eleven o'clock from you. Then you let your line billow out in a big bell. As your worm sinks, it'll swing past you and straighten the line. That's when the hackle on your worm will start pulsing. By that time the line will be at two o'clock and the worm will be drifting right above the bottom. Them browns will flat tear it up. The best time is in the fall, when they spawn. They'll knock the rod plumb out of your hand."

Wyatt knew Younger was not listening, and he wondered why he was going to such lengths to explain a fishing technique to a man who probably cared little or nothing about it.

"I see you're an expert," Younger said, wading out of the stream. "Can I sit down?"

"Suit yourself."

"I'd like to buy that acreage you have behind Albert Hollister's place."

"It's owned by the Nature Conservancy. I lease the grazing rights."

Younger's eyes dropped to Wyatt's shoulders and back. "Where'd you get those scars, boy?"

"On the circuit. Before that, my pap give them out free."

"He was a harsh disciplinarian?"

"He couldn't spell the goddamn word."

Younger opened his straw creel and took out a bottle of dark German beer. "You want one?" he said.

"No, thanks."

"You look like you're part Indian. Your profile, I mean."

"That's what people tell me. I ain't."

"What'd your folks do?"

"Chopped cotton and broke corn. My pap

taught me how to put dirt clods in the bag when we weighed in. Sometimes my mother cleaned at a motel on the highway, at least when they was still drilling there'bouts."

"My father made shine and transported it up to Detroit," Younger said. "I was fifteen before we had a wood floor. Your pap wasn't much good, huh?"

"I don't know what he was. I don't study on it no more."

Younger gazed at the mountains that bordered the river and at the cottonwoods that grew along the banks, their boughs swelling in the breeze. "You've got yourself a fine place here," he said.

Wyatt popped a pimple on the top of his shoulder and didn't reply. He wiped his fingers on his jeans.

"Name your price."

"I ain't got one. That's 'cause it ain't for sale."

"You sound like a man who's at peace."

"Peace is what you get in the graveyard, Mr. Younger."

"I get you mad about something?"

Wyatt pulled the weed out of his mouth and flipped it down the bank. "I went up to your place to tell you Bill Pepper was trying to put your granddaughter's death on me. You had me thrown off the property. Now you cain't wait to give me a suitcase full of cash."

"Maybe we have a lot in common, boy."

"I don't like nobody calling me that."

"I had a son like you. He had no fear. He was an aviator."

"What happened to him?"

"He crashed in a desert and died of thirst. Another son died in a car wreck. I had my daughter lobotomized."

Wyatt didn't reply. He could feel the older man's eyes on the side of his face.

"In ancient times, you would have been a gladiator, Mr. Dixon."

"I think I'll stick to rodeoing."

"It's been an honor talking to you," Younger said. He put one hand on Wyatt's shoulder and got to his feet. His hand felt like sandpaper on Wyatt's skin. "What became of your folks?"

"I ain't sure. I got these blank spots in my head. I see people walk in and out of my dreams, like they're trying to tell me something. These are people I used to know. But I cain't remember what happened to them or who they are. I get the feeling they're dead and they don't like staying under the ground."

Wyatt stared at the river for a long time and listened to the humming sound the current made through the hollowed-out places under the bank. A cloud had covered the sun, and there was an impenetrable luster on the water's surface, as though the light that lived in the rocks and the sand on the bottom had died and the world had become a colder and more threatening place. When he looked up, he realized Love Younger had mounted the suspension bridge and was walking toward the opposite side, indifferent to the bridge's bouncing motion or the rapids below. Wyatt tried to remember what he had said to Love Younger that might have driven him back across the river, but the words were already gone from his memory, along with the images of the people who spoke to him in his dreams and that rarely gave him rest.

Felicity Louviere had asked Clete to meet her that evening at the Café Firenze, a lovely buff-colored restaurant on a side road in the Bitterroot Valley, set among aspens and poplar trees, backdropped by the Sapphire Mountains in the east and the gigantic outline of the Bitterroots in the west. Clete shined his shoes and laid out his clothes on the bed and shaved in the shower stall and stayed under the hot water until his skin glowed. Then he put on his beige slacks and tasseled loafers and a blue shirt with a lavender tie and the sport coat that he wore to the track in New Orleans. The perfection of the evening, the pink sky, the distant smell of rain, a flicker of electricity in a cloud, reminded him of springtime in Louisiana, when he was young and the season seemed eternal and all of his expectations were within inches of his grasp.

He arrived early at the restaurant and ordered a glass of red wine at a table by a window. He saw her turn off the highway in the fading twilight and come down the county road and park her Audi by a row of poplar trees. She put on a pair of dark glasses before she came into the restaurant.

When he stood up to hold out her chair, he saw the red abrasions at the corner of one eye and the bruise on her jaw that she had covered with foundation. "Did your husband do that?" he said.

"I told him I'm leaving. The prenup is a hundred thousand. I'm going out to Nevada with it." She took a sip from his wineglass and smiled in a self-mocking way. "Want to roll the dice under the stars?"

"He beat you up?"

"Who cares? He's a child."

"I care."

"He's taken to drinking absinthe. It makes him go crazy sometimes. He's a scheming, cruel little man, but nobody forced me to marry him. Now I'm going to unmarry him and do something with my life. You don't want to come along?"

"I can't think straight right now, Felicity. My daughter still has this bogus murder beef against her. It'll go away, but in the meantime, I can't just take off."

She picked up the menu and stared at it without seeming to see it. "Can we order?"

she asked.

He took the menu from her and set it on the tablecloth. "You want to get married out there?"

"I'm not divorced yet."

"You want to or not? You ever spend time around Austin, Nevada?"

"No," she said.

"It's seven thousand feet up in the clouds. It's like going back a hundred years. People play poker twenty-four hours a day. The river is so cold, the rainbow trout have a purple stripe down their sides. I could seriously dig a lifestyle like that."

"You're serious?" she said.

"I've got addictive issues. I'm no bargain."

"I've got to make up for some wrong choices I've made, Clete. I haven't thought it all out yet."

"Get away from that kind of thinking. The past is the past. Why spend your time sticking thumbtacks in your head?"

"I married into wealth, and I did it for selfish reasons. Somehow I feel I'm responsible for Angel's death. If I'd been a better mother, she wouldn't have been drinking at the biker saloon."

"Her presence in that saloon didn't have anything to do with her death. The issue was money. In almost every homicide, the issue is sex or money."

Felicity's brow wrinkled. "Angel didn't have

any money. Not of her own."

"This crap is all about money. I'm not sure how, but that's the issue. Or most of it, anyway."

"Your marriage offer is very generous. There's another problem. Caspian is jealous and vindictive. He knows people who can hurt you."

Clete looked out the window. "Are you expecting him?"

"Here? No, I'm not. He doesn't know where I am. Unless he heard me on the phone."

Clete took his cell phone from his coat pocket. "He and another guy just pulled into the lot. You said he goes crazy sometimes. Does he ever carry a weapon?"

"I'm not sure," she replied.

"Who's the other guy?"

She looked through the window. "He used to be with the sheriff's department. Caspian just hired him as his new security chief. His name is Boyd."

Albert called me into the kitchen and said Clete was on the line.

"I'm with Felicity at Café Firenze in Florence," Clete said. "I think I might need backup or a witness."

"For what?"

"Caspian Younger and a dude who used to be a sheriff's deputy are sitting on the other side of the room. Younger beat up Felicity earlier today. I think maybe it's a setup."

"Who's the ex-deputy?"

"Boyd."

"He was one of the guys who gave Gretchen a bad time up by the cave. What are they doing right now?"

"Ordering. It's a setup, Streak. I can smell it."

"Do you have your piece?"

"It makes Felicity nervous. I left it at the cabin."

The little settlement of Florence was on the four-lane, ten miles south of Lolo. When I pulled into the parking lot, the summer light was still high in the sky, the mountains massive and purple with shadow against the western horizon. I went directly to Clete and Felicity Louviere's table without looking in Caspian Younger's direction.

"He's packing," Clete said.

"Who?" I said.

"The ex-deputy. When he got up to go to the restroom, I saw his clip-on. It's probably a twenty-five."

I pulled up a chair and asked the waiter to bring me a cup of coffee. Clete and Felicity Louviere were already eating. She hadn't spoken or even acknowledged my presence. I could not see through her dark glasses and had no idea whether she was looking at me or not. She ate in small bites, as though the food were tasteless or a forbidden pleasure. I had no idea what went on in her head or if she was part of a plot to take Clete Purcel off the board.

"It's nice to see you again," I said.

"I'm glad you feel that way," she said.

How do you respond to a statement like that? "You miss New Orleans sometimes?" I said.

"My memories of New Orleans are more bad than good. I suspect that's my fault. But no, I don't miss it."

I saw the blank look in Clete's face. I ordered a bowl of minestrone. Across the room, Caspian Younger and Jack Boyd were eating silently, without expression. Caspian's right leg was jiggling up and down.

"I'm going into the can," Clete said. "If one of those guys follows me, it's going down."

"Sure you want to play it out here?" I said.

"I've got to use the can. What am I supposed to do? Hold it all the way back to Lolo?" he replied.

After he had left the table, Felicity Louviere looked up from her food and said, "You don't approve of me, do you?"

"I like you just fine," I replied. "But I don't like the fact that you're married, and I don't like what you're doing to Clete."

"I don't blame you," she replied. She resumed eating, tilting her head back down.

"Why don't you cut him loose?"

"I already have. I'm leaving my husband. Watch out for the father."

"Why should I be worried about Love Younger?"

"He's sentimental, and like most sentimental people, he's unaware of his own cruelty. He has great guilt for what he's done to his family. If you cross him, he'll destroy you."

I looked over at Caspian Younger's table. Neither he nor the former detective seemed to have taken notice of Clete's trip to the restroom. Maybe Clete had been unduly alarmed and the evening would pass uneventfully, I thought. The tables were set with flowers, the tablecloths immaculate. Music was playing in the background, and families at the other tables were breaking loaves of fresh bread and dividing platters of spaghetti and meatballs. I wanted to put aside all the violence and rage and self-destructiveness that had characterized my life and Clete's and join in the festive mood. I had even come to like Felicity Louviere, and I wondered if he and she could start a new life, one that would preempt the denouement he and I had courted for decades.

Clete returned to the table without incident. "How about we eat up and go somewhere else?" I said.

"I need another drink. How about you, Felicity?" Clete said.

"I wouldn't mind," she said.

"We can get a drink down the road," I said.

"You worry too much, Streak," Clete said.

I felt like getting back into my truck and leaving them to their own devices. Felicity looked at my face. "He's right. We should go, Clete," she said.

Clete paid the check, and the three of us walked outside together. "Sorry I got you out here for no reason," Clete said.

"Maybe they were going to pop you in the lot. Maybe my being here discouraged them."

It was apparent that Clete had already moved on. "We thought we'd take a drive farther down in the valley, maybe talk some things out," he said.

Back on the horizontal bop, I thought. But it was Clete's gig, and I needed to leave it alone. "See y'all around," I said.

They left Felicity's Audi in the parking lot and drove down to the four-lane in the Caddy and turned south toward Stevensville. Behind me, I heard the front door of the restaurant open and the voice of Caspian Younger talking to Jack Boyd. Neither looked in my direction. They got into Younger's vehicle and drove away. They, too, turned south, not back toward Missoula.

I followed Younger and Boyd farther down into the Bitterroot Valley. Outside Stevensville, they passed a semi and gave it the gas and left me stuck behind a slow car blocking the left lane. When I was able to pass, their

580

vehicle was nowhere in sight. I made a U-turn and headed back in the opposite direction. Then I saw a filling station and convenience store by the Stevensville exit and Clete's Caddy parked at one of the pumps. Caspian Younger had pulled into the parking area on the side of the store. I swung my truck off the four-lane.

Everyone in law enforcement is aware of the following lesson: You don't get nailed in a firefight with the bad guys. The bad guys usually give it up when they're confronted with an assault team made up of former SEALs and marines and paratroopers. When you go up against a barricaded suspect — usually a mental case who's determined to write his name on the wall with his own blood or the blood of his hostages — the bad guy gets isolated and gassed, and if that doesn't work, he gets hosed.

When a police officer is killed, it's usually in the most innocuous of circumstances, such as a noise complaint. The responding officer walks up some rickety back stairs attached to a tenement, where a man and his wife, both of them drunk, are fighting in the kitchen. Maybe the officer is at the end of his watch, tired, resigned to ennui, careless, his cautionary instincts dulled by fatigue. Before he can even speak, the husband stumbles out on the porch in his undershirt and fires a gun point-blank into the officer's face.

Here's another scenario, the kind you can't foresee or do anything about. A taillight up ahead is flickering on and off. The problem is probably a loose wire or bulb, something that can be fixed in ten minutes at a truck stop. You protect and serve in a state that permits people to own and drive motor vehicles whose windows are smoked the color of charcoal. Maybe the same state allows the driver to carry a loaded handgun in the glove box or under the seat. The officer approaches the driver's door with no knowledge of who or what is waiting for him inside the vehicle. Emotionally, it's like stepping out on a high wire while blindfolded. An incautious moment, a slip in judgment, a mistaken extension of trust, that's all it takes. You're not in Shitsville. You're dead.

Clete had gotten out of the Caddy and inserted the gas nozzle in his tank, the blue fluorescence of the lighting overhead shining on his car and the concrete pad. Felicity was sitting in the passenger seat, looking straight ahead. Caspian and Jack Boyd walked toward Clete, Caspian in front, his jaw hooked like a barracuda's.

"You can't say I didn't warn you," he said.

"About what?" Clete said.

"Putting your dick where it doesn't belong."

Clete looked down at his fly. "No, it's right where it's supposed to be."

I parked by the air pump and stepped out

582

on the concrete. I saw Jack Boyd look back at me, then at Caspian and Clete. I started walking toward the rear of the Caddy, unarmed and certain that Clete was about to be shot. The gas pump had done an automatic shutoff, but Clete squeezed the trigger on the handle and restarted the flow, glancing at the stars above the mountains, his face serene.

"You think you're a comedian?" Caspian said. "You hump a broad who's thirty years younger than you, and you think you're hot shit? Adultery is a virtue in New Orleans? That's what you think?"

"It's time for you guys to beat feet," Clete replied.

"Look at me."

"I am. Remember the guy in the Charles Atlas ads? The ninety-pound weakling who was always getting sand kicked in his face? I look at you and think about that ad from forty years ago. It's a nostalgic moment."

"You're a fun guy. I like you. I can see why she likes you, too," Caspian said. "But dildos are dildos. I hope it's been worth it."

Clete removed the nozzle from the tank and began to screw the gas cap back on the funnel, his expression flat, his eyes neutral. One of the fluorescent tubes above the gas island had shorted and started buzzing, like a wasp trapped inside a crawl space. Caspian leaned forward, within six inches of Clete's ear, and spat on him.

Clete finished screwing the cap back on the gas tank, his green eyes as dispassionate as marbles. He pulled two paper towels from a dispenser and wiped the spittle from his cheek and ear and hair and dropped the towels into a trash barrel. Felicity opened the passenger door on the Caddy and stepped outside. "Can't you leave us alone, Caspian?" she said. "You've gotten everything you wanted. Why do you want to go on hurting people?"

Caspian grinned at Clete. "Did you go downtown with her?" he said. "I have a feeling that's one reason she's kept you around. The bigger they are, the easier they are to control."

"You guys win," Clete said.

"Win what?" Caspian asked.

"You guys have got your way. Y'all are a whole lot smarter than me. What can I do?"

"Sorry, I don't understand Sanskrit," Caspian said.

"Really?" Clete said. "See how this translates." He kicked Jack Boyd so hard in the groin that his face turned beet-red, then eggplant, as he went down on his knees, both hands clenched to his privates, his mouth locking open with pain that was so intense, no sound came out of his throat.

The roundhouse that caught Caspian lifted him into the air and sent him crashing into the side of the Caddy. Clete turned his attention back to Jack Boyd and kicked him in the face and stomped his head with the sole of his loafer, breaking his lips and nose and teeth. When Caspian tried to get up, Clete grabbed him by the back of the shirt and drove his face down on the Caddy's fin, then whipped his head into a gas pump again and again, finally flinging him to the concrete.

He wasn't finished. He ripped a small automatic from Boyd's clip-on holster and released the magazine and threw it into the darkness, then ejected the round in the chamber and threw the gun on the roof of the convenience store. "Where's your drop, asshole?" he said.

Boyd was trying to sit erect, coughing teeth and blood on his shirt.

"Clete, stop it! Please!" Felicity said. "Please don't hit them anymore!"

"See this?" Clete said to Felicity, jerking up Boyd's trouser leg. "It's called a throw-down. He was going to pop me. Maybe you, too."

He pulled the small revolver from the Velcro-strapped holster and flipped out the cylinder and shook the five .22 rounds from the chambers into Boyd's face. The revolver was rust-pitted, the bluing on the cylinder worn, the sight filed off, the wood grips wrapped with electrician's tape that was inverted, sticky side out. Clete shoved the revolver into Boyd's mouth and hammered it down with the heel of his hand.

"We're done, Cletus. Back away," I said.

"They were going to take both of us out, Streak. These guys need special handling. Yes, indeedy they do. You ever see a ville trashed with Zippo tracks, boys? You can't believe what ran out of the hooches."

At that moment I knew Clete had gone into a separate time zone, one where reason and morality held no sway and psychosis was the standard. He drenched both men with gasoline, spraying it in their faces and mouths and eyes. He fished his lighter out of his pocket. "Nobody does a number on the Bobbsey Twins from Homicide. You got that? Show me you understand, or you're going to be a pair of human pinwheels."

"Clete, don't!" Felicity begged. "This isn't you. No matter what they've done, you can't do this."

"Listen to her," I said. "It's over. Look at them. They're pitiful. They'll never forget this night as long as they live."

I put my hand over the lighter and squeezed, splaying his fingers and thumb. He stared at me woodenly. I saw the glaze go out of his eyes, the heat leave his face, like the glow of a hot coal dying inside its own ashes.

"They knew I was kidding," he said. "No big deal. Right? You boys copacetic down there? How about a soda?"

Through the window of the convenience store, I saw a clerk dialing the phone and talking into the receiver, his mouth moving rapidly.

"We're in Ravalli County," I said. "I don't want to explain this to the locals."

I started toward the pickup. I thought we were done. Then I heard Caspian get to his feet and stumble against the pumps, grabbing the trash barrel for support, gasoline and blood running down his face, his broken lips twisted into a grin. He started to speak, then had to spit and begin again. "Neither one of you has any idea what this is about, do you?" he said. "Know why that is? You're the little people, but you're too stupid to realize it. Ask Felicity what kind of guy my father is. She ought to know. He fucked her. Now they're both going to fuck you, just like they both fucked me."

He started laughing, sliding down the side of the pump like a scarecrow collapsing on its own sticks.

CHAPTER 28

The sun hadn't risen above the mountain when Gretchen woke the next morning. The inside of the cabin was cold, and when she washed her face, the water was like ice on her skin. Clete had just lit the woodstove, and she could see the fire through the slits in the stove's grate, the condensation on the iron shrinking and disappearing into wisps of steam. She pulled aside the curtain on the kitchen window and looked at the fog on the pasture and the snow flurries blowing out of the darkness, as white and fluttering as moths trapped inside a closet.

She had not remembered the dream she was having when she woke, but as she looked at the outside world, she knew the man who had fingers with lights on the tips but no face had come to visit her again.

"Albert left a message on the door. An FBI agent wants you to call him," Clete said. "Dave took the photo of the missing waitress to them."

"I'm not sure it was Surrette who put it on my truck seat. I'm not sure the photo is of the waitress, either."

"What are you trying to do, Gretchen? Get yourself killed or sent to prison? You want to go down for obstruction? Stop fooling yourself."

"I want to cap Surrette."

"You made a conscious choice to leave the life. Don't let this guy change that."

"I don't know how many times I have to say this to you: I was never in the life."

"What do you call it?"

"Getting even."

"Are you going to talk to the FBI agent?"

"Would *you*?" she replied. She raised her eyebrows in the silence, her hair hanging in her eyes. "That's what I thought. I'm going to have breakfast in town."

She drove down the dirt road to the two-lane and ate at McDonald's in Lolo. Through the window, she could see the sunlight climbing up a huge sloping hillside covered with Douglas fir, as though the sunrise were involved in a contest of wills with the forces that ruled the night. She knew these were foolish thoughts, but she woke with them almost every day of her life. The man whose fingertips glowed with fire and who leaned down over her crib and touched her skin would always be with her. She wanted to tell Clete these things, but he had started talking about the federal agent and the photo of a girl taken in a basement, a girl wearing only her undergarments, a girl with a gag in her mouth, her ribs stenciled against her sides, her identity robbed by someone who had razored the eyes from the photo.

Gretchen knew that any number of psychiatrists would conclude she had conflated Asa Surrette with the man whose fingertips had burned her body from head to foot, or with the man named Bix Golightly who had sodomized her on her sixth birthday. *What if I did?* she heard herself ask the imaginary psychiatrists she often held conversations with. Abusers were all cut out of the same cloth. In her opinion, they all deserved the same fate. There was nothing complex about any of them. They were craven, and they delighted in the satisfaction of their own needs at the expense of others. Asa Surrette was the embodiment of every misogynist and predator she had known. How he had been allowed to kill people for twenty years in his hometown was beyond her. Was it wrong that she wanted to track him down and force him to the edge of the abyss that had been created for men of his ilk?

In her experience, the only men who understood the level of pain undergone by a female rape victim were men who had been molested or raped themselves. Most of them did not talk about it, and most of them lived lives of quiet desperation and took their feelings of guilt and shame to the grave. Did they deserve an avenger? *What a stupid question,* she thought. Was she it? No, she was simply a survivor. Her abusers had made her a victim, and in doing so, they had made her powerless. The day she stopped being a victim was the day her abusers began to learn the meaning of fear.

Her cell phone vibrated on the tabletop; the words BLOCKED CALL appeared on the screen. She drank a sip of orange juice to ensure that there would be no obstruction in her throat when she answered. She opened the phone and placed it to her ear. "This is Gretchen," she said.

"Good morning, munchkin."

"I'm not keen on assigning other people nicknames."

"I won't do that anymore. Promise."

"Can I call you Asa?"

"Who?"

"If we're going to work together, we have to be honest about who we are."

"Did you give the photo to the FBI?"

Don't get caught in a lie, a voice said. "*I* didn't," she replied.

"But someone did?"

"I can't control what other people do."

"That's a good answer, Gretchen. The more contact I have with you, the more I feel we belong together."

She waited for him to continue, but he didn't. "A biopic is a challenge, Asa. The story line has to be authentic. Simultaneously, it has to conform to the rules of drama. These are things you and I have to work out as a team."

"You wouldn't patronize me, would you? I studied creative writing and read Aristotle's *Poetics*. Why do you keep calling me Asa?"

"Because you're a famous man. Anonymity is the pretense of the weak."

"Oh, I like that."

"We have to meet. It's imperative."

Again he went silent.

"Are you there?" she said.

"Go to her house."

"Whose?"

"You know whose. Up by Lookout Pass. There's a flowerpot on the back porch. You'll find something interesting under the pot. I put it there at daybreak, just for you."

"You shouldn't jerk me around."

"I'm smarter than that. I've done a lifetime study of people. I know their secret fears and their desire for forbidden fruit. I see the weaknesses they try to hide from others. You're different. You're strong in the same way I am."

"Thank you," she said.

"What is your opinion of the cowboy?"

"Which cowboy?"

"The one who might be a player in our film."

"Are you talking about Wyatt Dixon?"

"Is that his name? Have a nice drive up to Lookout Pass."

"No, what are you telling me about Dixon?"

"Nothing. Someone doesn't like him, that's all. I thought we might cast him. There's a tautness about him that I'd like to investigate. They all break, you know. It's like a dam bursting. I can't tell you how pleasurable that moment can be."

She wadded up a napkin and pressed it to her mouth, her stomach roiling. "I want to ask a favor of you," she said.

"Anything."

"Don't hurt the waitress."

"You're a tease," he said. The connection went dead.

Gretchen drove up the long grade that led to Lookout Pass and the high mountains that often disappeared into the clouds on the Idaho border. During the night, a storm had come down from Canada and left the sky dark at sunrise and the tops of the trees stiff with snow that had frozen on the branches. She turned off the highway, snow flurries spinning off the hillsides into her windshield, and followed a dirt road to the small frame house where Rhonda Fayhee had lived.

The house was isolated, a cracker box in

the midst of a windswept landscape that didn't seem intended for human habitation. She parked in back and stood in the yard and gazed at the rock slides that bled down the sides of the mountains, the thin stands of pine that could barely find root, the sharpness of the peaks and crags, as though they had never been affected by the erosive forces of wind and water. Higher up, on an old logging road, someone had gouged a gravel pit into the side of the mountain, leaving an environmental wound that, in these surroundings, seemed natural.

She knew Surrette could be anywhere, watching her with binoculars or framing her inside the crosshairs of a telescopic sight. The storm clouds rolling across the mountaintops were bluish-black and forked with electricity, and she heard thunder boom in a distant canyon. She realized her skin was prickling, even though the cold usually did not bother her, and she got her canvas coat off the truck seat and tied a bandana on her head.

Like most people with meager incomes who live up the drainages in the high country, Rhonda Fayhee had winterized her house by nailing sheets of clear plastic over the windows. Now the plastic, along with the yellow crime scene tape, was broken and flapping in the wind. On the back step was a large ceramic pot with half a dirt ring next to the drain dish. Gretchen set the pot and the dish on the grass and picked up a conventional envelope with a sheet of folded paper inside. On it was a map drawn with a felt-tip pen that showed the house, the dirt road, a mountain two miles away, and a place designated as "old mine."

The note at the bottom read, *I'm not jerking you around — You mustn't say that about me again — Go see the mine — You'll like what you find — Our cast is growing, even though our cast members don't know it yet.*

The slash-mark calligraphy was the same as in the letter Surrette had written to Alafair after she interviewed him in prison. Surrette was either getting careless or starting to accept Gretchen as a kindred spirit. His allusion to their conversation indicated he had written the note that morning. She was convinced he was somewhere up on a hillside, wetting his lips, enjoying the fact that his words were reaching inside her, stirring her imagination, while he watched from afar. She forced herself not to look up and got back in the pickup and drove up the road toward a mountain furrowed with slag and carpeted with miles of trees that had been denuded by a forest fire.

She turned off her engine in front of the mine and got out of the truck and stuck her Airweight .38 in her back pocket. The wind was colder and drier and smelled like ash or charred wood or smoke from an incinerator on a winter day. In her left hand, she carried a flashlight that used a six-volt battery. Down below, she could see Rhonda Fayhee's house and the tiny lot on which it had been built and the dirt road winding away into the distance. She could see the vast emptiness in which one young, thin-boned poor woman had lived and struggled and eked out an existence until the day she met Asa Surrette. Gretchen walked up to the mine's entrance and shone the light inside.

It didn't go deep into the mountain. It probably was dug during the Depression, when the West was filled with unemployed men who saw a vein of quartz in an outcropping of metamorphic rock and knew that gold and silver were often wedged inside the same seam. She moved the flashlight beam along the floor and against the walls. At least half a dozen photographs were taped to the walls, all of them eight-by-ten, all of them showing a bound woman with a drawstring cloth bag over her head. In two photos, the woman was in an embryonic position on a rock floor, a blanket pulled over her. In another photo, she was sitting upright, the bag on her head, wrists tied behind her, knees drawn up, bare ankles showing above tennis shoes.

On a flat rock at the back of the mine was a bubble-wrapped thumb drive. The note on it read, *She was here the first night — No one thought to look — It's like the other places where I've hunted on the game reserve — What do you think of the images — I think a before-and-after presentation of our subjects will give the film more shock value — I can't wait to work with you, Gretchen.*

When Gretchen got back to the cabin on Albert's ranch, she inserted the thumb drive into her laptop. The scene taking place on the screen was no longer than a minute. The lens had been pointed through a leafy, sun-dappled bower on the bank of a creek. A man and woman were broiling frankfurters on a grill, backs to the lens. A girl was turning somersaults in the background. Another girl was watching her. They were both blond. The lens never focused on their faces.

Just before the clip ended, a hand placed a note in front of the lens. The note read, *If they only knew.*

"You'd better come in here and look at this, Clete," Gretchen said. She replayed the video while he looked over her shoulder.

"Where'd you get this?" he said.

"From Asa Surrette."

"Are you kidding?"

"He left it for me in a mine by the Idaho border. Do you recognize anybody on the screen?"

"No. Who are they?"

"His next victims. I called the FBI and the

597

sheriff's department in Mineral County. I suspect the feds will be out here soon. Give them the thumb drive and tell them to go fuck themselves."

"Where are you going?"

"To find Wyatt Dixon," she replied.

"What for?"

"I think Surrette is after him."

"Why is Surrette interested in Dixon?"

"I don't know," she said. "Nobody in his right mind would want Wyatt Dixon as an enemy."

"Last night I bruised up Caspian Younger and Jack Boyd a little bit. I think Younger was setting me up."

"This was over his wife?"

Clete ignored the question. "Boyd was carrying a drop," he said. "There's something else I should mention."

"What?" she asked.

"Felicity and I might get married. One thing bothers me, though: Her husband says she got it on with the old man."

"With Love Younger?"

"That's what he said."

"What did *she* say?"

"What she always says: Her husband is a liar. I believe her. I think."

"Nobody can get in this much trouble," she said.

"I was trying to be straight with you. I wanted to bust up Jack Boyd worse than I did. It wasn't because he was out to clip me, either. He called you 'butch' up by the cave, and his friend Bill Pepper kidnapped and assaulted you. So I made sure he'll be taking his nutrients through a straw for a while. If I see him again, I may finish the job."

She opened a tin of Altoids and placed one on her tongue. "What am I going to do with you?" she said.

"Nothing. I'm your father. It's the other way around. You need to understand that, Gretchen."

"You're an absolute mess," she said. She stood up on her toes and kissed him on the forehead. "Don't let the feds throw you a slider. They'd like to jam both of us."

The rodeo and county fairgrounds were midway down in the Bitterroot Valley. All week an army of carnival people had been erecting the Ferris wheel, the Kamikaze, the Tilt-A-Whirl, the Zipper, the pirate ship, the fun house, the merry-go-round, planes that swung on cables, and a miniature train that ran on a looping track never over five feet from the ground. The sun was still high in the western sky when Wyatt returned from a concession trailer and sat down at a table under a cottonwood beside Bertha Phelps, a paper plate loaded with chili dogs in each hand. Indians wearing beaded costumes strung with feathers and tinkling with bells walked past them to a huge open-sided tent where the snake dance was about to begin. Wyatt popped open two cans of Pepsi and set them on the table.

"You know what rodeo people call Christmastime?" he asked.

"No, I don't. But I know you'll tell me," she replied.

"Christmastime is the two weeks before and after the Fourth of July," he said. "That's when all the prize money gets won."

"You're not going to put on greasepaint, are you?"

"I might."

"The years take their toll on all of us, Wyatt. You should think about that."

"I say ride it to the buzzer. I say don't give an inch."

She put her hand on his.

"What?" he said.

"Nothing," she replied. "You're just a special kind of man, that's all."

The breeze came up, and the leaves in the cottonwood tree seemed to take on a life of their own and flicker faster than the eye could record their movement. Their sound reminded Wyatt of a matchbook cover in the spokes of a bicycle wheel. He started in on his chili dogs, then stopped and stared at the mountains in the west. In minutes the sun had become a reddish-purple melt above a canyon already dark with shadow. He stared at the sun until his eyes watered and he saw a woman separate herself from its radiance and walk toward him in silhouette, her chestnut hair blowing on her cheeks, her legs longer than was natural, her posture like that of a man.

"Is something wrong?" Bertha asked.

"I get these lapses in my head. Time goes by, and I don't have no memory of where it went or what I done. My head gets like it was before I drank all them chemical cocktails. It's been happening to me of late, and it gives me feelings of anxiety I don't have no name for."

"You've been right here," she said. "With me. There's nothing to worry about."

"You see yonder?"

"See what?"

"The woman walking out of the sun. She's coming straight to our table. I already know what she's gonna say and why she's here. How come her words are already in my head?"

"The sun is too bright. I can't see her. Wyatt, you're not making sense."

"She's been sent."

"You're scaring me."

"Her name is Gretchen Horowitz. She's come to tell me about *him*. I knew it was gonna happen."

"I can't follow what you're saying. Let's eat our food. Don't pay attention to that woman or these crazy thoughts. Pick up your fork and eat."

"People don't want to believe he's here. That Lou'sana detective, Robicheaux, he knows it, too. So does the woman. He did your brother in. Stop pretending, Bertha."

"You were raised among primitive and violent people. The superstition and fear they taught you is not your fault. But you cannot let their poison continue to cause injury in your life. Are you listening to me, Wyatt Dixon?"

He stood up from his folding chair. He was wearing garters on his sleeves, his gold-and-silver national championship buckle, a spur with a tiny rowel on one boot, and an oversize cowboy shirt that wouldn't bind when he rode a horse. He was wearing all the things that told him who he was and who he was not. Except now these things seemed to mean nothing at all.

Gretchen Horowitz stepped out of the sun's brilliance so Bertha Phelps and Wyatt could see her clearly. Behind her, the Kamikaze rose into the air, teetering against the sky as the teenagers inside the wire cage screamed in delight, then rushed toward the earth. "Hello, cowboy," she said. "I won't take but a minute."

"I know why you're here," he replied. "This here is Miss Bertha. I ain't sure I want to get involved."

602

"Asa Surrette says someone wants to see you hurt. I think he means to do it himself," she said. "You know who Surrette is, don't you?"

"It don't matter what he calls hisself. His real name is in the Book of Revelation."

"No, it isn't. He's a serial killer from Kansas. He's not a mythological figure. He's a sack of garbage. He killed Angel Deer Heart, and he may try to kill you."

"Don't you be telling him these things," Bertha said. "Who are you to come here and do this? You should be ashamed of yourself."

Gretchen looked at the heavyset woman, then back at Wyatt Dixon. "Do you know any reason the Younger family might hold a grudge against you? Caspian Younger in particular?"

"I could say their kind don't like working people, and I got in their face. But that ain't it."

"Miss, please leave," Bertha said.

"It's all right," Wyatt said. "Miss Gretchen is just doing what she thinks is right. He was using the name Geta Noonen when he grabbed the waitress."

"How do you know this?" Gretchen asked.

"I did some investigating on my own."

"Have you told anyone?"

"The state of Montana shot my head full of electricity. You think they're gonna ask me for advice in catching serial killers? Besides, that ain't what he is."

"He's the beast in the Bible?"

"No, he's probably an acolyte, a lesser angel in the bunch that got thrown down to hell."

"I've had all this that I can listen to," Bertha said, getting up from the table. "You get out of here and leave us alone."

"I'm sorry for upsetting you," Gretchen said.

"Love Younger come out to my place and fished off my bank," Wyatt said. "He asked about my folks. He asked if I was part Indian. What the hell would he care about my folks?"

"Watch your back, Wyatt. Good-bye, Ms. Phelps," Gretchen said.

Wyatt watched Gretchen walk through a field of parked cars, her red shirt and chestnut hair seeming to blur and merge with the molten intensity of the sun. He pushed aside his food and removed a whetstone and a large sheathed bowie knife from a rucksack by his foot. The knife had a white handle and a nickel-plated guard. He began sliding the blade up and down the length of the whetstone, his eyes fixed on a spot three inches in front of his face.

"Why are you doing that?" Bertha asked.

"I'm gonna wear it in the snake dance."

"Why are you sharpening it?"

"I used to do this when I was a little boy. I'd take my bicycle way out in the woods, along with my pocketknife and a piece of soap rock I dug from a riverbed. That's when I learned not everybody has the same clock. I'd disappear and go somewhere I wouldn't have no memory of later, then come back and still be sharpening my pocketknife."

"You mustn't talk about these things anymore," she said. "We need to go on a trip, maybe to Denver. We could stay at the Brown Palace. The Sundance Kid and Butch Cassidy stayed there. Did you know that?"

"I think some things are starting to catch up with me, Bertha. In my dreams, there's something I ain't supposed to see. I got a feeling what it is."

"Don't talk about it. Let go of the past."

"Something happened when I was about fifteen. I can almost see it, like it's hiding right around a corner. You know what all this is about?"

"No, and I don't want to hear it," she said, her voice starting to break.

"I picked the wrong goddamn parents," he said. "Either that or they picked the wrong kid to use a horse quirt on."

CHAPTER 29

The room reverend Geta Noonen had rented was located on the second floor of an old frame house at the far end of the hollow, below a slit in the mountains through which he could see the evening star from his window. Geta, as his host family called him, had a backstairs entrance and his own bathroom with an old-fashioned claw-footed bathtub. There was a nostalgic element about his new home, a hint of the agrarian Midwest and the immigrant farm families who plowed the prairies and planted the land with Russian wheat. Everything about the house reminded him of the world in which he had grown up: the glider on the front porch, the linoleum floor in the bathroom, the freeze cracks in the paint around the window, the stamped tin ceiling, a stovepipe hole in the wall patched with an aluminum pie plate. The upstairs echoed with the sounds of the teenage girls running through the hallways, slamming doors, giggling about the boys who called them on the phone, not unlike the way his sisters had carried on during adolescence. Geta thought of all these things with great fondness until he began to remember other things that had occurred in the foster home west of Omaha, a house in which one room always stayed locked and no one ever asked what was beyond the door.

It was not a time to reflect upon these matters. The world moved on and so did he. As he soaked in the tub, his chin barely above the gray patina of soap that covered the surface, he could see the sun setting beyond trees that grew out of the rocks, its orange glow as bright as a burnished shield hung on a castle wall. No, it was not a shield, he told himself. It was a celestial talisman, a source of enormous natural heat and energy that was about to be transferred into the hands of a man the world had too long taken for granted.

Many a night he had studied the heavens through a cell window and had seen his destiny as clearly as he saw the Milky Way, a shower of white glass on black velvet trailing into infinity, not unlike the magical light that he sometimes felt radiating from his palms.

The greatest gift he possessed and that others did not was recognition. He saw a universe that was not expanding but contracting, a vortex at the center sucking all of creation into its maw. The goal of the physical universe was the reverse of what everyone thought. Its goal was annihilation. What could equal nothingness in terms of perfection? Those who could accept such conclusions became the captains of their souls, the masters of their fate, the puppeteers who looked down from above at the stick figures jiggling on the ends of strings.

Did he cause pain in the world? So what? Moses executed hundreds if not thousands; during the Great War, the kings of Europe dined on pheasant while sending hundreds of thousands to their deaths. No one dwelled upon the damage a boot print did to an anthill. The strong not only prevailed over the weak, they deliberately freed themselves from the restraints of morality. In so doing, they became weightless, able to float loose from their earthly moorings. It wasn't a complex idea.

He shut his eyes and slipped deeper into the water, luxuriating in its warmth, his hands clasped on the tub's rim, his phallus floating to the top of the water. Half of the upstairs had been ceded to him by the family, along with keys to the back entrance and the bathroom. He kept the bathroom door locked whenever he was not using it, in part so no one else would see the photos he had taped to the walls, in part to conceal the odor he left twice a day clinging to the sides of the tub, the bar of soap he used, the brush he scrubbed his skin with, the towel he wiped under his armpits.

The problem was a parasite, he was sure, one he had ingested by eating off a dirty plate in prison. It had laid its eggs in his viscera and cycled its way through his system and hidden in his glands, filling his clothes with an odor that made people move away from him in elevators and on public transportation. He was not the only victim. A blind inmate who had murdered his wife and children and stayed in twenty-three-hour lockdown had the same syndrome. So did a pederast who worked in the prison laundry. The prison psychiatrist said the problem was caused by either an obstructed bowel or food poisoning, and the odor associated with it was only natural; he said it would pass. When the psychiatrist excused himself to use the restroom, Geta spit in his coffee cup.

Now he drained the tub and washed himself again, this time with ice-cold water, sealing his pores, then sprayed his body with deodorant. He dressed in clean slacks and a white shirt and combed his bleached hair straight back in the mirror. He had lost weight and browned his skin and added bulk to his upper arms by splitting firewood in the sun, taking ten years off his appearance. Maybe it would be a good evening to do a little trolling downtown, visit a college bar or two. Just for fun. Nothing serious. A test of his powers. His own kind of catch-and-release program.

He smiled at his sense of humor.

All the photos on the walls had been shot with a zoom lens after he decided to reopen his career in western Montana. Of the twenty photos, eight of them contained a diminutive yet buxom middle-aged woman who affected the dress and indifferent air of a 1960s flower child.

He touched one of the photos with his fingertips, then breathed on it as if trying to fog a windowpane. He stroked her face and hair and wet his index finger and drew a damp line across her throat and another one across her eyes and another one across her ribs. There was a whirring sound in his ears, like the hum of a crowd in a giant stadium, the sun boiling down directly overhead. He thought he heard the cry of wild beasts, a rattling of chains, an iron grille sliding open, the crowd roaring. He could have sworn he smelled the raw odor of blood and hot sand and the sweaty stench of people held captive in underground rooms.

He patted the photo affectionately, his cheeks dimpled with a suppressed smile. *Our time is almost at hand,* he thought. *It will be a grand event announced by trumpets and dwarfs beating drums and a costumed Chiron waiting to dance around the dead and soldiers thumping the shafts of their spears on stone.*

He began to experience a sense of arousal

so intense that he had to close his eyes and open his mouth, as though he were on an airplane that had lost altitude in the midst of an electric storm.

Through the door, he heard the two girls hurrying down the wood stairs and out the front of the house, their father telling them to be home early. Geta went back to his bedroom and bolted the door behind him, then took four clear plastic wardrobe bags from his footlocker and laid them on the bed. *Yes, be home early, my little ones,* he thought. *And you, Mommy and Daddy, enjoy your menial, insignificant lives while you can. Your embryonic sacs await you.*

He was startled by a knock on the door. "Who is it?" he said.

"It's me," the wife said. "Will you join us for coffee and dessert?"

He thought for a moment. "Are you having cherry pie?" he asked through the door.

"Why, how did you know?"

"The season for cherry picking is upon us," he replied. "I'll be along in just a minute. It's so nice of you to invite me."

I slept until seven A.M. Friday and woke with no memories of my dreams or even of having gotten up during the night. I woke with a clarity of mind that seems to come less and less frequently as we grow older, maybe because the memory bank is full or because

611

our childhood fears are unresolved in the unconscious. Regardless, I came to a realization that had eluded me prior to that morning — namely, that Asa Surrette, a man I had never seen, had threaded his way into all our lives and divided us among ourselves.

I had alienated both Alafair and Gretchen by going to the FBI and placing Gretchen in their bomb sights. I suspected the discord and distrust was exactly what Surrette wanted. The great irony in combating evil people is the fact that any proximity you have to them always leaves you soiled, a little diminished, a little less sure about your fellow man. It's theft by osmosis.

After I brushed my teeth and shaved, I went downstairs and fixed two cups of coffee and hot milk, then took them to Alafair's bedroom. She was awake in bed, lying on her side, gazing out the window at a yearling and its mother playing with one of Albert's colts, racing up and down the pasture.

Alafair looked over her shoulder at me. "What's up, doc?" she said.

I pulled a chair up to her bed and handed her one of the coffee cups. "The only lasting lesson I've learned in life is that nothing counts except family and friends," I said. "When you get to the end of the road, money, success, fame, power, all of the things we kill each other for, fade into insignificance. The joke is, it's usually too late to make use of that knowledge."

She sat up, her back against a pillow, her long black hair touching her shoulders. "I never doubted what was in your heart," she said.

"We've all done the best we could in dealing with Surrette," I said. "He wins if we become angry and distrustful with one another."

"I started all this when I interviewed him."

"That's good of you to say, but I don't think that's where it started. Surrette didn't follow us from Louisiana to Albert's place. He was already here."

"But why?"

"Maybe it has to do with the Youngers. Maybe not. He shot an arrow at you on the ridge behind the house. He left his message in the cave behind the house. He set a bear trap for Gretchen behind the house. He seems to take an enormous interest in this particular stretch of terrain."

"Albert?" she said.

"Surrette fancies himself an intellectual and a writer. Albert is both, and notorious for his radical political views. Maybe that has something to do with it."

Alafair drank the rest of her coffee and put on a robe. "Gretchen and I did some background checking on Angel Deer Heart's family," she said. "Her parents were killed in an automobile accident. The three children were sent to an orphans' home in Minnesota. Angel's brother and sister died during an outbreak of meningitis. That's when Angel was adopted by Caspian Younger and Felicity Louviere. You with me so far?"

"Go ahead," I said.

"The family owned a hundred acres between the rez and the boundary of Glacier National Park. The Deer Heart land isn't far from where several exploratory wells have been drilled."

"What happened to the land?"

"It was put in a trust for the children. It doesn't have much agricultural value, but the family held on to the mineral rights."

"Who owns it now?"

"Angel Deer Heart would have inherited the land on her eighteenth birthday."

I looked at her blankly. "So it goes to whom?"

"Take a wild guess."

"Caspian Younger and his wife?"

"No, just Caspian. Isn't that lovely?"

"How'd you find out all this?" I asked.

"Gretchen hired two reference librarians. Both of them are retired and in their eighties. They asked if ten dollars an hour would be too much to charge," she said.

I couldn't concentrate. I did not like Caspian Younger. I had known many like him, raised in an insular environment, protected from the suffering and pain and toil of the masses, effete and vain and incapable of understanding privation. But the implication was hard to accept.

"You think Caspian knows Surrette?"

"We couldn't find any evidence to that effect. After Surrette got out of the navy, he did security for some casinos. Atlantic City and Reno and Vegas were second homes for Caspian as well as his father. Gretchen told you the father kept fuck pads in several places, didn't she?"

"How about it on the language?"

"When will you stop moralizing at my expense?"

"I'm serious. It sounds terrible. You can't imagine how bad that word sounds when it comes out of your mouth."

"Not someone else's?"

Don't take the bait, I thought. I also knew, with a great sense of relief, that our relationship was back to normal. "I'm going to fix breakfast for you and Molly. You coming?" I said.

"You didn't answer my question."

"You'll always be my little girl, whether you like it or not."

"You'll never change," she said. "That's why I love you, Pops."

Gretchen woke at sunrise and looked out her window. Normally, at this time of day, the horses were grazing by the wheel line, where the grass was taller. Instead, they were in a grove of aspens up by the road, their heads and necks extended over the rail fence, eating carrots a woman was feeding them from a sack. Gretchen put on jeans and a jacket and her half-topped suede boots and walked into the trees.

"Clete's still asleep, if that's who you're looking for," she said.

"I was just taking a drive. I stopped at the grocery in Lolo and bought these for the horses," Felicity Louviere said. "Does anyone mind if I feed them?"

Her face held no color or expression. Even her voice was toneless. She made Gretchen think of someone who wanted to offer condolences or amends at a funeral but arrived too late and found the church empty.

"You want me to wake Clete?" Gretchen said.

"No. He said you were in contact with Asa Surrette. Is that true?"

"I've been in contact with a guy who might be him. But I can't swear to it."

"He has the waitress with him?"

"I don't know. Can I help you, Ms. Louviere? You don't look well."

"You've actually talked to this man?"

"He's called me on my cell phone."

"Did he say anything about Angel?"

"No. I think you should come inside." Gretchen stepped between two of the horses and

616

took the bag of carrots. "You shouldn't give treats to horses with your fingers. You let them take it from the flat of your hand so they won't accidentally bite you."

"Thank you."

"Did something happen that you want to talk about?"

"I shouldn't have bothered you. What time is it? There's no light in this valley until after nine, is there? Or is it dark most of the time? It seems Montana is like that. Often dark."

"I'm going to the health club in a few minutes," Gretchen said. "Why don't you come with me?"

"That's very nice of you, but I've probably already bothered you enough."

"Ms. Louviere, I don't have great experience in these things, but I think you're blaming yourself for something that happened recently, or something you just found out about. Is it related to your daughter's death?" The hollowness in Felicity's eyes was such that Gretchen could hardly look at them. "I know Clete would like to see you," Gretchen said. "Stay awhile. We can have breakfast together."

"Maybe another time. Thank you, Ms. Horowitz. I think you're a nice woman." Felicity got into her Audi and drove away.

Gretchen went back into the cabin, packed her workout bag, and went to the health club, thinking that her strange encounter with

Felicity Louviere was over. Early on in her life, she had come to believe that the differences in human beings were not of great magnitude and had more to do with appearance than motivation. The exception was the difference between the sick and the well. Some people glowed with sunshine and health; others seemed stricken in body and spirit, as though they had walked through an invisible cobweb and their pores could not breathe.

Three hours later, when Gretchen emerged from the dressing room at the health club, her skin ruddy, her hair damp from her shower, she was convinced that Felicity Louviere carried a form of perdition with her wherever she went.

Felicity was standing by the registration desk, her bag on her shoulder, oblivious to the club members who had to step around her to swipe their membership cards. Gretchen put a hand on her shoulder. "Let's have a bagel and some cream cheese," she said.

"I'd like that," Felicity said. "Is Clete with you?"

"He's at the ranch. It's just you and me. I'll put in our order. Sit down over there on the sofa, and we'll talk."

After Gretchen had ordered, she checked her phone for messages, then sat down next to Felicity in a quiet area by the fireplace.

"I have to confide in somebody," Felicity

said. "I feel worse than I've ever felt in my life. I don't want to burden or hurt Clete any more than I have."

"What is it?"

"My husband left his financial statement from Vanguard on his desk. In four months, he's made withdrawals of eighty-five thousand dollars from his money-market account. I thought maybe he was gambling again. I looked at the accounting book he keeps in the bottom of his desk. He enters every expenditure and deposit and transaction in ink and never puts information in a computer. The Vanguard withdrawals were there. Beside each of them were the initials A.S."

"Asa Surrette?"

"That's what I asked him. He went into a rage."

"Why would he be paying Surrette?" Gretchen asked.

Felicity stared into Gretchen's face without replying. Felicity had put on no makeup; her lips were cracked.

"Surrette is blackmailing him?" Gretchen said.

"I think he paid Surrette to murder our daughter. I think I shut my eyes to what he did. I think I'm responsible for my daughter's death."

"You mustn't say that," Gretchen said. "You had nothing to do with your daughter's death. Where's your husband now?"

"I don't know. He's frightened. He was drunk last night, and I saw him doing lines on a mirror this morning. I don't think he's bathed in days. He hates Clete and he hates Dave Robicheaux. He killed our daughter. The man I have slept with for years killed Angel."

"Regardless of what may or may not have happened, you're not responsible. Do you understand me?"

"There's something else. I think I've seen him. Twice, maybe three times."

"Seen who?"

"*Him,* the man who killed Angel. He had a camera with a zoom lens. I looked at the photographs of him that are posted on the Internet. He's lost weight since he went to prison in Kansas, but I'm almost sure it was him."

"Did you tell your husband?"

"Yes. It terrified him."

"I'm not sure what you're saying. He fears for your safety?"

"He fears Surrette will take both of us. Ms. Horowitz, you've been very patient. But I know what I have done, or what I have failed to do. I didn't protect Angel. I'm partly at fault for her death. I'll never forgive myself."

One of the club's employees held up the heated bagels on a plate so Gretchen could see them, then set the plate on the counter.

"I'll be right back," Gretchen said. She

charged the bagels to her account, then picked up the plate and returned to the sofa. Felicity had disappeared. Gretchen's hobo bag lay on the coffee table, the drawstring pulled loose. She rummaged through it. Her cell phone was gone. Through the glass doors, she watched Felicity's Audi drive away.

Alafair was sitting in the passenger seat of Gretchen's pickup when they turned off the Higgins Street Bridge and parked down by the river, next to the old train station that had become the national headquarters of a conservation group founded by Teddy Roosevelt.

Six hours had passed since Felicity had stolen Gretchen's cell phone.

"Are you sure you want to do this?" Alafair asked.

"Love Younger is one of the most powerful men in the United States," Gretchen said. "You think he doesn't know what's going on in his own family?"

"I doubt he does."

"You can say that with a straight face?" Gretchen said. She cut the engine. The river was high, slate-green, coursing over the submerged boulders close to the banks.

"Younger probably used Cronus as a role model," Alafair said.

"Who?"

"The Greek god who ate his children,"

Alafair said.

"I don't care about Younger's children. They were born rich. They had choices. I was wrong about Felicity Louviere. She wants to punish herself, and I think she's going to use Asa Surrette to do it."

"She's not innocent in all this, Gretchen."

"Are you coming with me or not?"

"I'm your friend, aren't I?"

Gretchen hooked the strap of her hobo bag over her shoulder, but did not get out of the truck. The refurbished train station looked like an orange fortress and had the clean lines of an architectural work of art. It was located at the base of a hill that sloped abruptly down to the river. At the top of the hill was the maple-lined street where Bill Pepper had lived and where he had drugged and sexually assaulted her. "You're more than a friend," she said.

"You don't need to say any more."

"I'll say what I feel like. You know what you mean to me, Alafair?"

"Sometimes it's better not to be too specific about feelings."

"What did you think I was going to say?"

"I'm not quite sure."

"You're everything I want to become. You're educated and smart and beautiful. You stand up to people without having to threaten them. I sleep with a gun. You can walk away from situations that make me want to tear people apart."

"I don't know if that's always a virtue."

"You've published a novel. You were Phi Beta Kappa at Reed. You had a four-point average at Stanford Law. Everybody in New Iberia respects you."

"People respect you, too, Gretchen."

"Because they fear me. They know I have blood on my hands. You know what's even worse?"

Alafair shook her head, her eyes lowered, not wanting to hear more.

"I'm glad they know," Gretchen said. "I want them to know what blood smells like. I want them to know what it's like to live with the kind of anger that can make you kill people. You know how I feel today, even though I think I've changed? I wish I could dig up every person who ever hurt me and kill them all over again. What do you think of me now, Alafair?"

"I love you. You're one of the best people I've ever known. I'd do anything for you."

Gretchen grasped her by the back of the neck and kissed her on the mouth. "You rip me up, girl," she said.

Then she got out of the pickup and started toward the train station, her bag swinging from her shoulder. Alafair stared through the windshield at the river and at the water sliding over the boulders and eddying in deep pools that were dark with shadow and strung with foam. Her face was tingling as though it had been stung by bees. She let out her breath and blinked and followed Gretchen inside.

A meeting was under way in a spacious room hung with rustic paintings containing scenes from America's national parks. Perhaps ten men were seated at a long hardwood table set with a silver service and a decanter and glasses and a silver bowl with red flowers floating in the water. Love and Caspian Younger were seated at the head of the table. A well-dressed man with gray hair was in the midst of introducing Love Younger to the group. He was a pleasant-looking man whose manner was deferential and whose sentiments seemed genuine. He had probably labored for hours on his introductory remarks.

"Mr. Younger formed an early and protective attachment to the woods and rivers and streams and mountains of his East Kentucky home," he said. "The cabin in which he was born was not far from the Revolutionary fort built on the Cumberland River by Daniel Boone. His ties to American history, however, are not simply geographical in nature. He's a descendant of Tecumseh, the great Shawnee leader, and proud of his relationship to Cole Younger, who fought for his beliefs during the Civil War and was admired by both friend and foe. Mr. Younger's donation of ten thousand acres to the Conservancy is not only an act of great generosity but of vision."

The gray-haired man turned to Love Younger and continued, "I cannot tell you how appreciative we are of your support. Your investment in wind and solar power has set an example for everyone committed to finding a better way to supply energy for the twenty-first century. You've demonstrated that the rancher and the sportsman and the conservationist and the industrialist can work together for the common good. It's a great honor to have you here today, sir."

Love Younger studied the tumbler of whiskey in his hand, tilting the glass slightly, as though more praise had been given him than was his due. He rose from his chair. "The honor is mine," he said. "You gentlemen have invested a lifetime in a higher cause. I have not. People such as me are bystanders. Tecumseh was a man with a noble vision, one far greater than mine has been. Cole Younger led a violent life but became a Christian before his death. He was a business partner in the operation of a traveling Wild West show with Frank James. The two men were not cut out of the same cloth. I say this not to judge or condemn Frank James but to remind myself of the biblical admonition that many are invited and yet only a few are chosen. I believe my ancestor redeemed himself. The donation I make to your cause is my small attempt at righting some wrong choices in my own life." Younger raised his whiskey glass. "Here's to each and every one of you," he said, and drank it to the bottom. Only then did he seem to notice Alafair and Gretchen standing in the doorway. "Would you ladies like to come in?" he asked.

"That's Robicheaux's daughter," Caspian said, looking up from his chair at his father's side. There was an ugly scab across the bridge of his nose from the beating Clete had given him, and a bruise couched like a tiny blue-black mouse under one eye.

Alafair waited for Gretchen to answer, then said, "We can speak with you later, Mr. Younger."

"No, if you have something to say to me, do it now," Love Younger replied.

"Your son is being blackmailed by Asa Surrette," Gretchen said. "Your granddaughter's death might make your son an independently wealthy man. I'm saying your son may have paid Asa Surrette to kill your granddaughter."

"Who sent you here?" Younger said.

"No one. I called your office and was told this is where I could find you. I think your daughter-in-law is in danger, Mr. Younger," Gretchen said. "I think she may be trying to contact Surrette."

The gray-haired man leaned toward Younger. "I'm sorry about this, Mr. Younger. I'll take care of it," he said.

Younger placed his hand on the man's

shoulder so he couldn't rise from his chair, his gaze never leaving Gretchen's face. "Felicity is trying to contact this killer?" he said.

"She thinks she's responsible for Angel's death," Gretchen replied.

"And out of goodwill, you've come here to discuss my family's personal tragedy in public? You use my granddaughter's first name as though you knew her?"

"Maybe you'd rather see your daughter-in-law dead?" Gretchen said.

"I know all about you. You're a contract killer from Miami. I think you're working with Albert Hollister to blacken my name in any way you can."

"I came here to prevent your daughter-in-law from being killed. I don't see you as a victim, Mr. Younger."

The other men at the table were silent, without expression, hands motionless on the tabletop. One man cleared his throat, then picked up his water glass and drank from it and set it down as quietly as he could.

"I think you ladies have come here to cause a scene and to further the agenda of Albert Hollister and the ecoterrorists who are his proxies," Younger said.

"I've told you the truth," Gretchen said. "I think your son has done everything in his power to provoke Wyatt Dixon into harming you. Why would he want to do that, Mr.

Younger? Dixon said you were out on his property. Why do you and your son have all this interest in a rodeo cowboy?"

Love Younger looked at the other men at the table. "My apologies, gentlemen," he said. "My family has been through a difficult ordeal. I'm sorry that you've been witness. I'm sure we'll see one another again soon. Thank you again for allowing me to participate in your mission. I think you're a fine group of men."

"We feel the same about you, Mr. Younger," one of the seated men said.

"I have to say something else," Gretchen said. "You're educated and wealthy and have knowledge about foreign governments that only intelligence agencies have access to. But you use your education and experience to deceive people who never had your advantages. I'm not talking about these men here; I'm talking about people who never had a break. You exploit their trust and patriotism and inspire as much fear in them as possible. Tell me, Mr. Younger, do you know of any viler form of human behavior?"

The only sound in the room was the wind blowing through the trees behind the train station.

"Come on, Caspian," Younger said to his son. "We've taken up too much of these gentlemen's time."

"I'm sorry I had to disrupt your meeting,"

Gretchen said to the men at the table. "I admire the work you do. If I could have talked to Mr. Younger somewhere else, I would have."

She walked outside, leaving Alafair behind, the back of her neck as red as a sunburn.

"Is there something you wanted to say, Ms. Robicheaux?" Love Younger asked.

"Yeah, you got off easy," Alafair replied. "Your son is mixed up with Asa Surrette, a man who ejaculates on the bodies of the little girls he tortures and murders, the same guy who murdered your foster granddaughter. You're a real piece of work. I've known some scum in my time, but you take the cake."

"You can't talk to me like that," he said, his face quivering.

"I just did," she replied.

Alafair caught up with Gretchen outside. "Where are you going?" she said.

"I think I'll drown myself."

"I'm proud of you," Alafair said.

"For what?"

"What you said in there. The way you talked to those guys when you left."

"What about it?"

"They know courage and integrity when they see it. They can't say it to Love Younger, but they respected what you did. It was in every one of their faces."

"Are you telling me the truth?"

"You shouldn't ask me that. I've never lied to you," Alafair said.

"Care to explain why you're looking at me like that?"

"Your smile," Alafair said.

CHAPTER 30

From the moment Felicity Louviere stole Gretchen Horowitz's cell phone, she knew that her life had changed and that she would never be the same again. She also knew that nothing from her past life could possibly prepare her for the ordeal that lay ahead. As she drove away from the health club, there was a well of fear in her breast that seemed to have no bottom. At the red light, she looked at the impassive faces of the drivers in other cars, as though these strangers, whom she never would have noticed under ordinary circumstances, might know an alternative to her situation and somehow remove her from the scorched ruins that her life had become.

Her hands were small and powerless and without sensation on the steering wheel. She felt that a poisonous vapor had invaded her chest and attacked her organs and that nothing short of death was worse than living in her current state of mind. She drove through town, barely aware of the traffic around her, going through a yellow light without seeing it, ending up in a park on the north side of Missoula, not sure how she got there.

She turned off her engine down by the creek, in the shade of trees, and didn't pick up calls. The creek was as clear as glass and rippling over rocks that were orange and green and gray-blue, but she could take no pleasure in the pastoral quality of the scene. She had never felt more alone in her life, except on the day when she realized her father had abandoned her to seek martyrdom in a South American jungle. For the first time since she last saw him, she understood the burden he must have carried to his death. The guilt over the killing of the Indians by the men he worked with must have been so great, he could have no peace until he atoned for them and himself. He did this, she was sure, in order to be the father he wanted his daughter to have.

She had never thought about her father in that way. That he'd chosen to travel the path up to Golgotha's summit on her account.

Gray spots, like motes of dust, were swimming before her eyes. She opened the windows to let fresh air in the car and was surprised at how cold the weather had turned, even though the equinox was at hand. She got out and saw snow flurries spinning in the sunlight, sparkling in the branches of the trees that lined the stream. Her stomach was sick, her skin clammy; she could not remember when she had felt this light-headed. When she closed her eyes, the earth seemed to tilt under her feet. Gretchen's cell phone vibrated on the dashboard. She reached back in the car and looked at the screen. The call was blocked.

"Hello?" she said.

"Who's this?" a man's voice said.

"If you called for Gretchen Horowitz, she's not available."

"So I'll talk to you. What's your name?"

"Felicity Louviere."

There was a pause. "Caspian Younger's wife?"

"Yes."

"This is a surprise."

"You're Asa Surrette?"

"Surrette is dead. Burned up in a big puff of smoke. That's what the state police in Kansas say."

"You were photographing me."

"I'm casting a movie. You might be in it. Where's Gretchen?"

"Gone away."

"To a bar mitzvah?"

"I don't know where she went."

"The weather has taken quite a turn. The snow is falling on the creek while the sun is shining. It looks like cotton floating on the water, doesn't it? Maybe the devil is beating his wife."

She turned in a circle, her heart pounding. She saw no one. On the far side of the creek, an SUV was parked by a picnic shelter. No one seemed to be inside it. The SUV was either painted with primer or it was black and powdered with white dust. "Is the girl alive?" she said.

"Who?"

"The waitress."

"Could be. I can check. Want me to do that and call you back?"

"I want to take her place."

"You're a bag of tricks, aren't you?"

"I can see you," she lied.

"What?"

"You heard me."

"If we get together, I might have to wash out your mouth with soap."

"Are you afraid of me?"

"Of you? How silly."

"You murdered my daughter. Are you afraid to look me in the face and admit that? Are you the frightened little man the authorities say you are?"

"The authorities? What are the *authorities*? Stupid and uneducated people who would be on welfare if they didn't have uniforms. Maybe you should watch what you say."

Her knees felt weak. She sat down behind the steering wheel, the door open, the wind like a cold burn on her brow. She could hear herself breathing inside the confines of the car. "Is the girl hurt badly? What have you done to her?"

"Maybe I'm a kinder man than you think. Maybe I have a side that others don't know about. You think you're going to set me up?"

"I don't want to live," she said.

"Say that again."

"You'll be doing me a favor if you take my life. But you're not up to it. You're what they say you are."

"What do they say?"

"You were in a foster home. There was a room where someone was kept locked up. Or where the children were forced to go when they were bad. What happened in that room? Were you sodomized? Did you have to kneel all night on grains of rice? Were you told you were unclean and unacceptable in the eyes of God? My mother was declared insane. Maybe I can understand what happened to you as a child."

"Somebody put that on the Internet. It's a lie. Those things never happened," he said.

"Then why are you so afraid of me? Did you plan to kill me from afar?"

"Who says I was planning any such thing?"

"I think my husband paid you to kill my daughter. That means I was next."

"Your husband does what I tell him. Don't provoke me." His voice sharpened. "Believe me, you do not want to provoke me, you little bitch."

"I saw the pictures of the people you suffocated."

"You want that for yourself? I can arrange it. I would love to do that for you."

"I think you're all talk. I think you're scum. Call me back when you can speak in an intelligent manner."

He was starting to shout when she closed the phone.

A moment later, she saw someone enter the SUV through the passenger side and drive away, scouring divots of grass out of the lawn, the exhaust trailing off like pieces of dirty string.

An hour later, at the Younger compound on the promontory above the Clark Fork, the cell phone Felicity had taken from Gretchen's purse vibrated on top of her dresser. She picked it up and placed it to her ear. The French doors on the balcony were open, and she could see the pink and blue blooms on the hydrangeas by the carriage house. She thought of New Orleans and the Garden District and the way the tenderest of flowers opened in the shade, as though defying the coming of the night or the passing of the season. "Did you mean what you said?" the voice asked.

"Yes," she replied.

"Wait on my instructions. Tell no one about our conversation. If you do, I'll put Rhonda's tit in a wringer and let you listen. You'll never get those sounds out of your head. You still there?"

"Yes," she said.

"We'll see if you're up to this. Have a nice day."

After he hung up, Felicity sat down slowly in a chair, as though afraid that something inside her would break. Then she began to weep. When she looked up, her husband was standing in the doorway, blocking out the sunlight, his face veiled with shadow. He was eating a bowl of ice cream mixed with pineapple syrup and appeared to be savoring the cold before he swallowed each spoonful. "PMS time again?" he said. "That stands for 'piss, moan, and snivel.'"

"You did it, didn't you?"

"Did what?"

"Paid Surrette to kill Angel."

"Your mother was crazy. So are you."

"Why did you do it, Caspian?"

"I didn't pay anybody to do anything. I've been trafficking in cocaine. Large amounts of it."

"What?"

"I quit going to G.A. and put my toe back in the water. I dropped a half mil in Vegas alone. The vig was two points a week. I hooked up with some guys in Mexico City. They stiffed me on the deal."

"So you had Angel murdered?"

637

"I didn't."

"What are you telling me? You make no sense."

He walked to the French doors and gazed out at the lawn and the potted citrus and bottlebrush trees on the terrace and the roll of the mountains in the distance. "When I first saw you at the art theater, I thought you were the most beautiful girl I had ever seen. What happened to us, Felicity?"

"Nothing," she replied. "People don't change. They grow into what they always were."

At six that evening, Clete came up to Albert's house and knocked on the front door with the flat of his fist. Albert got up from the dining table and opened the door. "Is this a raid?" he asked.

Clete's face was flushed, as though he had been out in the sun or drinking all afternoon. "Where's Dave?"

"Eating," Albert replied.

"Can I come in?"

"You're not going to start a fistfight, are you?" Albert said.

"What are you talking about?" Clete said.

"You look like somebody put a burr under your blanket," Albert said. "You want a plate?"

"Felicity doesn't pick up her phone," Clete said to me, ignoring Albert. "I think Surrette

638

has her."

Molly and Alafair had stopped eating. "Clete, I don't want to hear about that woman," Molly said.

"You want to take a ride?" Clete said, his eyes on me.

"Where?" I said.

"To Love Younger's," Clete said.

"No, he doesn't," Molly said. "I mean it, Clete. Don't bring that woman's troubles into our lives."

"Five minutes ago this was my home," Albert said. "Do you people carry a fight with you every place you go?"

"I'll be right back," I said. I walked out into the yard with Clete. The sun had dipped behind the ridge, and in the shadows, I could feel the temperature dropping, the dampness rising from the grass and flower beds. "I know you're worried, but think about what you just said," I told him. "Felicity Louviere is an intelligent woman. She's not going to deliberately put herself in the hands of a depraved man."

"You don't know her," he said. "Maybe she wants to suffer. Maybe she wants to cancel his ticket. But she always leaves her cell phone on for me. Now I go directly to voice mail."

"Then let her live with her own choices."

"That's a chickenshit thing to say."

"I meant let her pop him if she can. What

she may be doing is not any crazier than what Gretchen has been doing."

"You want to nail Surrette or not?"

"He tried to kill Alafair, Clete. What do you think?"

"You're not hearing me. My point is, we're smarter than this guy. Money is involved, but it's not the issue. It's personal, and it's coming out of the Younger family. It also involves Wyatt Dixon. And I've got another suspicion."

"What?"

"Maybe it's off-the-wall."

"Say it."

"I wonder if Albert has something to do with it. He has a way of bringing people out of the woodwork."

"I've thought the same thing."

We looked at each other. I walked up on the porch and opened the door slightly. "Albert, could you step out here, please?" I said.

He came outside and closed the door behind him. He was wearing a heavy cotton shirt and corduroy trousers with a wide leather belt outside the loops and sandals with rope soles, the way a Spanish peasant might. He was smiling, his small blue eyes buried inside his face.

"Is there any reason Asa Surrette would want to do you harm?" I said.

"Maybe he doesn't like my books."

"Any other reason?" I said.

"Maybe he didn't like my film adaptations. No one did."

"This isn't funny," Clete said.

"That's what the producers said when they lost their shirts."

"Think," I said. "Did you ever have contact with this guy? Or anyone who could have been him?"

"I don't think he'd be someone I'd forget. I spent four weeks in Wichita and loved the people there. I didn't have a negative experience with anyone. They're the best people I've ever met. What I've never understood is why they live in Kansas."

"You were in Wichita?" I said.

"I was writer-in-residence in their MFA program. I taught a three-hour seminar one night a week for a month. They were all nice young people. You're barking up the wrong stump, Dave."

"What year?" I said.

"The winter term of 1979."

"Surrette was a student at Wichita State University then."

"Not in my class, he wasn't."

"How do you know?" Clete asked.

"I still have my grade sheets. I checked them. He's not on there."

"Was anyone auditing the class, sitting in without formally enrolling?" I said.

"Two or three people came and went. I never checked roll."

"Surrette told Alafair he had a creative writing professor who claimed to be a friend of Leicester Hemingway."

Albert's eyes had been fixed on the north pasture and the horses drinking at the tank. They came back on mine. "He did?"

"Surrette accused this creative professor of name-dropping," I said. "He seemed to bear him great resentment."

"I knew Les many years," Albert said. "I fished with him in the Keys and visited his home in Bimini. He always said he was going to start up his own country on an island off Bimini. It was going to be a republic made up of writers and artists and jai-alai players and musicians. He even had a flag."

"Surrette said this professor wouldn't read his short story to the class," I said. "Do you remember anything like that?"

Albert's gaze roved around the yard, as though he saw realities in the shadows that no one else did. He was breathing hard through his nose, his mouth pinched. "I don't recall the exact content of the story, but I thought it was an assault on the sensibilities rather than an attempt at fiction. It was genuinely offensive. He was older than the others. I think I told him it was too mature a story for some of the younger people in the seminar. He seemed to take it well enough, at least as I recall. Maybe we're talking about a different fellow."

"Surrette also said he wrote a note on the evaluation, something to the effect that he understood your objection to a story about boys chewing on each other's weenies."

I saw the color drain from Albert's face. He started to speak, then looked up at the hillside and the dark conical shapes of the trees that hid the cave where Asa Surrette had camped. "I'll be," he said.

"It was Surrette?" I said.

"How does the expression go? There's no fool like an old fool?" he said.

On Saturday, Wyatt Dixon emerged from his Airstream trailer at the fairgrounds and flexed his shoulders in appreciation of the summer evening and the salmon-colored sky and the neon ambience of the amusement rides and game booths and concession stands that had defined his youth and were, in his opinion, as much a stained-glass work of art as any fashioned from stone by medieval guildsmen. He had put on his puff-sleeved sky-blue shirt with red stars on the shoulders, his championship buckle, and his soft lavender red-fringed butterfly chaps and a Stetson that fit tightly on his head, down low on the brow, one that didn't fly off with the first bounce out of the bucking chute. The summer light was trapped high in the sky, as though it had no other place to go, the breeze balmy and redolent of meat fires. What finer place was there?

If only Bertha would close her mouth for a little while. "You're too old for it," she said, following him out the door onto the apron of grass where they had dropped the trailer. "Do you want to be a quadriplegic? Do you want to wear a drip bag under your clothes for the rest of your life?"

"I rode Bodacious to the buzzer, woman," he replied. "There ain't many can say that. We used to call him the widow-maker. I rode him into a tube steak. What do you think of that?"

"Call me 'woman' again, and I'm going to slap you cross-eyed."

"Bertha, I'm not exaggerating, blood is leaking out of my ears."

"Where are you going?"

"To get a brain transplant."

"*Please,* Wyatt."

"I got the message. Even though I am near deaf, by God, I got the message."

"You won't ride?"

"I don't think I said that. You want some cotton candy or a tater pig?"

"No, I do not. I want you to act like a reasonable human being."

"There ain't no fun in that."

She threw a slipper at his head.

Oh, well, he'd known worse, he consoled himself. When he was seventeen, he'd married a Mexican woman who used to blow flaming kerosene out of her mouth in a carnival. Or at least he *thought* he'd married her. The two of them had eaten enough peyote buttons to start a cactus farm and had woken up on top of a bus loaded with stoned hippies on their way to San Luis Potosi. He remembered a ceremony conducted by an Indian shaman dressed in feathers; he was almost sure of that. But maybe the ceremony was a funeral, because somebody had dropped a wooden casket off a mountainside, and Wyatt had seen it bounce and break apart on the rocks. Or maybe the fire-eater was in the casket. Or maybe that was her mother. It was somebody, for sure.

He had decided long ago that memory and reliving the good times weren't all they were cracked up to be. Anyway, Bertha Phelps was a good woman. The problem was, she was too good. She worried about him day and night and made love like it was about to be outlawed, sometimes leaving him worn out in the morning and afraid she would corner him in the bedroom by midafternoon.

He bought her a tater pig whether she wanted it or not, and a great big fluffy cone of cotton candy for himself. He heard the announcer on the loudspeaker in the box above the bucking chutes tell the crowd to stand up for "The Star-Spangled Banner." Through an aisle lined with game booths, he saw a familiar figure walking toward him, followed by three men wearing suits and shades.

Wyatt was not up for another session with a billionaire oilman who just wou dn't let it alone, whatever "it" was. Wyatt had never given much thought to rich people; he'd always assumed they had the same vices and compulsions as everyone else but were a whole lot smarter about hiding them. He didn't care what they were, as long as they tended to their own business, which was buying politicians and making sure the toilets flushed and the cops got paid off, and nobody told him what he could and couldn't do.

Too late.

"I just want a couple of minutes," Love Younger said.

"Not a good idea," Wyatt said.

"Come on, sit down, son. Let me have my say, and I'll be gone."

They were standing on a grassy spot under a birch tree by the bingo concession, the grandstand not far away, buzzing with noise. "Is that Jack Shit with you?"

"That's Jack Boyd."

"What happened to him?" Wyatt asked.

"Excuse me, I have to rest a minute," Younger said, easing himself down at one of the plank tables. "Age is a clever thief. It takes a little from you each day, so you're not aware of your loss until it's irreversible."

Wyatt could hear the announcer in the

grandstands trading jokes with one of the rodeo clowns. "Tell me what you're after and be done with it," he said, and sat down at the table.

"My granddaughter is dead," Younger said. "My daughter-in-law has disappeared, and my son is dissolute and perhaps in a dangerous state of mind."

"What's that got to do with me?" Wyatt asked.

"Be patient. I'm trying to set some things straight without causing unnecessary harm to anyone. Have you seen my son?"

"I wouldn't know what he looks like. What the hell is this?"

"What would you do if a great amount of money came into your hands?" Younger asked.

"I'd ask what the trade-off was, 'cause ain't nothing comes free. Second of all, I'd probably say kiss my ass, 'cause I ain't interested in what other people own."

"Then you're a rare man."

"You didn't answer my question about Jack Shit."

"A man named Clete Purcel attacked him."

"You let Louisiana Fats knock you around?" Wyatt said to Boyd.

"Listen to me, son," Younger said.

"Take your goddamn hand off me. Don't be calling me 'son' again, either."

"The fates have not been kind to you. I

want to correct that if I can. Do you understand what I'm trying to say?"

"No, I got no idea. I'm getting pretty tired of it, too. How come you always got guys like this around? People that's been inside or belong there?"

"I try to give other men a second chance. Pap, why did he beat you? Why did he have such animus toward you?"

"Ani-what?"

"You're part Shawnee Indian, boy. It's in your profile. Your people were trash, but you're a warrior. Look at my hands, look at yours. Those are hands that could break down a brick wall. How do you think you ended up the man you are? You think your genes came from your worthless father or your whore of a mother? Was it the nigger in the woodpile?"

"You get the fuck away from me, old man," Wyatt said.

He threw his cotton candy and Bertha's tater pig in a garbage barrel and walked behind the bucking chutes, a sound like fireworks popping in his head. He squatted in the sawdust and began buckling on his spurs.

"You're not up, Wyatt," a cowboy said.

"Hell I ain't."

"I'm just doing my job."

Wyatt lifted his eyes to the cowboy's face. "Do I got to say it again?"

He climbed on top of the chute while his horse was loaded, then eased down on its back, hooking his left palm through the braided suitcase handle on the bucking rig. Like most rough stock, the horse was almost feral, walleyed, jerking up its head, its body quivering with fear and rage at the confines of the chute, knocking against the wood sides, trying to kick itself free of the flank strap.

Wyatt fixed his hat and steadied himself. "Outside!" he said.

He was once again borne aloft, his legs up, his body springing backward almost to the croup, the rowels of his spurs slashing down, the twelve hundred pounds of gelding thudding so hard into the sod that Wyatt thought his sphincter had been broken and he was about to urinate into his athletic supporter. He'd drawn Buster's Boogie, a hot-wired gelding that had crippled a rider for life at the Russian River Rodeo in California. Buster's Boogie sunfished twice, then corkscrewed and twisted sideways unexpectedly, all within three seconds. Wyatt saw the grandstand begin rotating around him, then the bucking chutes, then the Ferris wheel, then the greased faces of the clowns by the rubber barrel, as though he were stationary and the entire world, even the stars embroidered on the pink sky, had all become part of a giant Tilt-A-Whirl that had gone out of control and was doing things that had never happened to him before.

He felt the gelding explode under him with renewed energy, prying Wyatt's clamped legs loose from its sides, flinging him high in the air, his shoulders and back still hunched in a rider's position, the suitcase handle slipping beyond his reach, the ground suddenly coming up like a fist, the blat of the eight-second buzzer coming too late, almost like a pent-up mockery that had never been allowed to express itself.

He heard the thud when he struck the sod, then all sound went out of his head, as though he had been plunged deep underwater, his lungs collapsing like punctured balloons, his eardrums about to burst. He saw the pickup rider coming hard toward him, swinging down from the stirrup, a paramedic running with a first-aid bag, the crowd rising in unison, their faces filled with pity and sorrow.

I'm all right, he wanted to say. *I just got the wind knocked out of me. There ain't no problem down here. Just let me get on my feet. Anybody seen my hat? Why y'all looking at me like that? Have I done gone and messed myself?*

His shirt was wet. He clutched it in his fingers and pulled it loose from his belt and saw the starlike wound where his championship silver buckle had punched a hole in his stomach, releasing a fluid that felt more like water than blood.

Then he saw Bertha Phelps running toward him, her breasts bouncing inside her oversize dress, her body haloed by the electric lights and humidity and dust and desiccated manure in the arena. He wanted to ask her if someone had just played a terrible joke on him. The kind Pap might play, if he were still alive and full of meanness, ready to work mischief in the world in any fashion he could.

CHAPTER 31

Asa Surrette called again at noon on Saturday and told her where to park her car. "I'll be watching you," he said. "If everything meets my approval, you'll be given a sign."

"I need to see the girl," Felicity said.

"You will. She'll be glad to see you. She hasn't seen a human face in some time."

"What do you mean?" Felicity asked.

"You're a foolish woman," he replied.

She was sitting on the edge of her bed. She closed her eyes, shutting out the light from the French doors, and tried to think. What was he saying? "She hasn't seen your face?"

"She hasn't heard my voice, either. At least not since somebody came in the back door of her little house up by Lookout Pass. What do you think of that?"

"I'm not interested in your games."

"You have a strange way of showing it," he replied. "I have reservations about you. You wouldn't try to trick me, would you?"

"Why did you kill my daughter?"

"Who says I did? From what I've read, it's an unsolved crime."

"Tell me where to go or I'll hang up."

"You know where the Alberton Gorge is?" he said. "Get off at the Cyr exit. Cross the river and go four miles north on the dirt road, then wait."

After he broke the connection, she called Clete Purcel and got his voice mail. "Clete, I'm not sure if I'll ever see you again," she said. "There's a good chance you'll never know what became of me. I want you to know that none of this is your fault. I also want to apologize to Gretchen for stealing her cell phone. You're a lovely man. I wish we had met years ago in New Orleans. It's not really such a bad place. We could have had great fun there."

She stood up from the bedside, her palms dry and stiff, the skin around her fingernails split and painful whenever she touched a hard surface. In the silence, she could hear the pine needles sifting across the roof in the wind, scattering in the sunlight onto the balcony. The house seemed to swell with the wind, the joists and walls creaking in the silence. She had no idea where Caspian was. Maybe he was drunk; maybe he was with his father. Her footsteps were as loud as a pendulum knocking inside a wood clock as she walked down the stairs and into Love's den. She opened one of the toolboxes on his worktable and lifted out a leather punch that he used sometimes when he made a holster for one of his antique revolvers. It was sharp at the tip and mounted on a T-shaped wood handle. She lifted her dress and taped it inside her thigh, then walked outside and got in her Audi and drove away. The sun had passed its high point, and the shadows of the poplars that lined the road looked as sharp-edged as spear points on the asphalt.

At 1:48 P.M. Clete came up to the main house. I was sitting on the deck by myself, Albert's potted petunias in full bloom all around me. It was a fine day, the kind that, at a certain age, you do not let go of easily. When I looked at Clete's face, I knew that whatever plans I'd had for the afternoon were about to change. He played Felicity's message. "She knows where Surrette is," he said. "She's going to meet him."

"That's hard to believe."

"You don't know her. She loved her daughter. She thinks she closed her eyes to what her husband was doing."

"Maybe she plans to kill Surrette."

"That's not like her. Surrette has out-smarted us, Dave. He'll kill Felicity and the waitress, too."

"I don't think that's the way it's going down. He has something else planned. I think he'll let the waitress go."

"Why?"

"To show his power. He decides who lives and who dies. He also proves he's not governed by compulsion. Look, Clete, Felicity Louviere may be suicidal. She's going to let Surrette do it for her."

"She's risking her life to help somebody else. Why don't you show a little respect?"

I had been drinking a glass of iced tea with a twist of lemon. I wished I had not come to Montana. I wished I had the authority and power and latitude that my badge in Louisiana gave me. I also wished I had the option of operating under a black flag and going after Surrette with a chain saw.

"I'm trying to figure out what we can do," I said. "I think we should contact the sheriff or the feds."

"They're not going to believe us. We're on our own."

"We should start with Caspian Younger."

"I kicked the shit out of him. He laughed at me," he said.

"Who do you know in Vegas and Atlantic City?"

"Lowlifes and warmed-over greaseballs who wouldn't piss on me if I was burning to death."

"Dial them up."

"Talking to those guys is like drinking out of a spittoon."

I set down my iced tea and looked at it.

"He's going to kill her, isn't he?" Clete said.

I lowered my eyes and didn't reply. The twist of lemon in my glass made me think of a yellow worm couched inside the ice, the canker inside the rose, the inalterable fact that you cannot hide from evil.

Felicity Louviere followed the instructions and drove through the tiny settlement of Alberton. She exited not far from a railroad track and crossed the Clark Fork and continued up a dirt road into an unpopulated area of wooded hills and outcroppings of gray rock that resembled the knuckle bones of prehistoric animals. Rain clouds had moved across the sun, dropping the countryside into shadow. She turned on the car heater, even though the dashboard told her the temperature outside was sixty-seven degrees. When the odometer indicated she had traveled exactly four miles from the bridge, she pulled to a wide spot in the road, next to a hill that sloped up into lodgepole and ponderosa pine and black snags left over from an old burn.

She cut the engine and stepped out into the wind, her ears popping slightly with the gain in elevation. *What's that sound?* She turned in a circle and saw no other vehicle but thought she heard the throaty rumble of twin exhausts, a sound she associated with 1950s films about hot rods, or one she'd heard in the parking lot at the health club.

She suspected that her caller was watching her through binoculars and that her wait would be a long one. The air smelled of night damp and the outcroppings of rock that seldom saw sunlight and were freckled with lichen.

He surprised her. No more than three minutes passed before she saw a figure inside the trees up on the hillside, just below a switchback logging road left over from the days of clear-cutting. He took a white handkerchief from his pocket and held it in the air. There was nothing histrionic in the gesture. He didn't wave it; he simply held it, showing his control over the situation.

She walked to the front of the Audi and stared up the hill, the wind blowing her hair over her face. The figure turned and walked back in the shadows, then reemerged with a woman wearing shorts and a T-shirt; a drawstring bag had been pulled over her head, and her wrists were fastened behind her.

Felicity began walking up the hill, her eyes lowered, stepping carefully over the holes burrowed between the rocks by pocket gophers and badgers. The sun had disappeared from the sky entirely, and she felt as though a cold wind were blowing through her soul. *Give me strength, give me strength, give me strength,* a voice chanted in her head.

She heard the rumble of the twin exhausts again, echoing in a canyon, trailing away into the trees. She was forty yards from the man on the hill and could see his wide shoulders and the tropical shirt that he wore inside a cheap tan suit. He held his captive by the arm with his right hand and began cupping the fingers of his left, indicating that Felicity should keep walking toward him.

"You have to let her go first," she said.

He stared at her without replying. Behind him, up on the logging road, Felicity could see a gray SUV, a spray of rust on one side. "I've done what you asked," she said. "Release the young woman and I'll go with you."

A smile tugged at the corner of his mouth. He walked the woman thirty feet away, upwind from where he had been standing. He eased her into a sitting position on top of a fallen tree trunk and returned. The bound woman was out of earshot. Still he did not speak. He turned up his palms as though they glowed with spiritual grace.

"She's never heard your voice or seen your face?" Felicity said.

He shook his head, his grin in place.

"You're Asa Surrette," she said. "You're older than your pictures, a little more coarse. Your hair is dyed, but you're him."

"Nice to meet you in person. Please get in my vehicle. I'm looking forward to our association."

"You had all of this planned."

"Of course."

"Why do you want me?"

"I think we knew each other in another life. I knew it when I first saw you from afar. I could smell the heat in the sand and the ring of swords on copper shields. I could hear a crowd roaring. Sound familiar?"

"What you're describing are the symptoms of schizophrenia."

"Could be. But as Charles Dickens wrote, 'It's a mad, mad world, Master Copperfield.' " Then he seemed to hear the twin exhausts, too. "You didn't try to get clever on me, did you?"

"If I'd wanted to do that, I would have called the FBI."

"I suspect that's true. Well, let's leave Rhonda to find her way out of here and toggle on down the road."

"I have to use the bathroom."

"You *are* a strange duck, aren't you?"

"Do you mind turning around?"

"You're cute," he said.

She kept her eyes on his, her expression flat.

"Go ahead. I'll just step up here a little ways," he said.

She squatted in the leaves and pine needles, her back to him, her dress spread. She reached between her legs and pulled Love Younger's leather punch from the tape on her thigh.

"Finished?" he said.

"Yes," she replied, standing erect.

He extended his hand, leaning forward, his eyes merry. "You're very pretty. A nice little package."

She let him take her left hand in his. "Is the place we're going very far?" she asked.

"What do you care? I've got you, you little whore."

"Asa?"

"What do you want?" he replied.

"Here's something for you," she said.

The T-shaped handle of the leather punch was snugged tightly against her palm when she drove it into his face, the point sinking cleanly through his cheek, her knuckles touching his skin. When she pulled the shaft free, his eyes were popping, and blood was spurting from his mouth. On the edge of her vision, she saw the waitress trying to walk downhill, the cloth bag still over her head. Felicity drove the leather punch at his throat.

He knocked it aside and struck her with his fist. The blow exploded against her eyebrow and the bridge of her nose, tearing something loose inside her, blurring the trees. As she rolled down the slope, she could smell the drowsy odor of leaves and pine needles and the raw damp ground, and she wanted to crawl inside a cocoon and remain there in the coolness of the afternoon and the sway-ing of the trees for the rest of her life, secure in the knowledge that she had done all she could and her ordeal was over.

That was when he lifted her to her knees, his clothes exuding an eye-watering fecal stench, the bloody drool from his mouth matting in her hair. She blacked out as he dragged her up the slope toward his vehicle, hardly aware of the grinding sounds that issued from his throat or the fingers that sank like talons into her skin.

Gretchen Horowitz had followed Felicity's Audi from Missoula and lost sight of it after taking the exit by the Alberton Gorge. She made a wrong choice at a fork and ended up in a blind canyon, then had to retrace her route, and only through dumb luck did she see the Audi a hundred yards away, parked in a bare spot by the side of the road.

Wherever she traveled, she kept several weapons in a long steel box welded to the floor behind the seat, one of which was a scoped K-98 German Mauser. She left the truck in a grove of pine trees, the rifle slung on her shoulder, and crossed the dirt road and worked her way uphill until she caught sight of Felicity Louviere standing below a switchback. Felicity was looking up at a figure who stood in the shadows. Gretchen unslung the rifle and dropped to one knee behind a boulder, gazing through the telescopic lens at the bizarre scene on the hillside.

A bound woman with a cloth bag over her

head was sitting on a log, wearing only a T-shirt and shorts, her knees skinned. Gretchen moved the lens from the bound woman to Felicity. She unlocked the bolt on the Mauser and slid it back, then eased an eight-millimeter soft-nosed round into the chamber, locking down the bolt soundlessly with the heel of her hand.

The K-98 had never failed her. It was amazingly light for its size and era, deadly accurate at long range, even with iron sights, the bolt action as fluid and smooth as water. She had no doubt that the third person was Asa Surrette. But the light was bad, his outline dissolving into the shadows when Gretchen tried to lock him inside the crosshairs of the scope.

Then he stepped forward, extending his hand. His unshaved cheeks and the prune-line furrows in his throat and his boxlike head came into focus inside the lens. She took a breath, releasing it slowly, her finger tightening inside the trigger guard. In under a half second, the eight-millimeter round would strike home with almost no trajectory, coring through the brow, flattening inside the brain, cutting his motors, extinguishing all light from his eyes, before he ever heard the report echoing through the hills.

It didn't happen. Felicity decided to take matters into her own hands and attack Surrette with a tool of some kind, and she made a mess of it.

Gretchen took her finger from the trigger guard, her right eye focused through the scope, and watched the situation come apart.

Take the shot, she heard a voice say.

I'll hit Felicity, she answered.

Do it. She screwed things up.

My head hurts. I can't think. Just shut the fuck up.

She saw Surrette hit Felicity, and she tightened the stock against her shoulder again, sure that this time she had a clean shot. She didn't. Surrette grabbed Felicity as he would a slab of beef and wrestled her to his vehicle, blood leaking from his mouth. He opened the driver's door and began stuffing her inside, at the same time driving his right fist into her ribs and the side of her head.

He's going to kill her, the voice said. *Do it while there's still time. Have you grown weak?*

I don't have the right to risk someone else's life.

You want to feel good about yourself at the woman's expense?

If you were in the SUV with Surrette, what would you want me to do?

Take the shot.

I see. Just spit into the wind and see what happens? Oh, I hit you in the brisket? Sorry about that.

Take the shot, Gretchen.

You're not inside the vehicle. You're one of those who like to use terms like "collateral damage."

He'll torture her to death. Try to imagine the level of pain she'll suffer in just one minute. Then multiply that by several hours.

I can't do it.

Take the shot now, bitch, or stop pretending you're a player. Sign up with the titty-baby brigade and burn candles for the person you could have saved.

Gretchen rose to her feet, lifting the rifle, trying to refocus on the target and catch the exact moment when Surrette's image stood out in clear relief, separate from Felicity Louviere's, framed forever inside the crosshairs, his face about to dissolve like a photograph curling over a flame.

Surrette slammed the door and turned and looked back down the slope. The sun had just broken from behind a cloud, and he had probably seen the glint on her scope. He appeared puzzled rather than alarmed, as though no one had the right to intrude upon what was clearly his province.

Eat this, Gretchen thought.

Just as she squeezed the trigger, she saw Felicity Louviere raise her bloodied head directly behind Asa Surrette's.

The round ticked the top of the steering

wheel, an inch from Surrette's hand, and pocked a hole the size of a nickel through the windshield, powdering the dashboard with splinters of glass. He floored the accelerator, the tires spinning on the slick logging road, and bounced over the apex of the switchback and down the far side. Felicity Louviere was thrown against the passenger door by the SUV's momentum, her hair in her eyes, her face swollen and bleeding.

"You told Gretchen Horowitz we were out here?" he said.

"What does it matter?" Felicity replied. "She'll hunt you down for the rodent you are. She'll make you beg."

"Not like you will. Wait till you see what I have planned."

She was losing consciousness and talking at the same time. Surrette hit chuckhole after chuckhole, bouncing in the seat, looking sideways at her, his safety strap not snapped in place. "What are you mumbling about?" he asked.

"He is risen," she replied.

He hit the brake and skidded to a stop. He lifted himself up on one knee in the seat and began beating her in the face with both fists, as though his rage could never be sated.

Gretchen worked her way up the slope, through the tree trunks, carrying the Mauser at port arms. The bound woman had tripped over a log and fallen to the ground. Her bare legs were smeared with dirt and leaves and deer droppings and tiny twigs; a mewing sound came from the cloth bag cinched under her chin.

"Hey, it's okay. You're safe," Gretchen said, kneeling beside her, propping the rifle on the log. "Surrette is gone. I'm here to help you."

She placed a hand on the woman's shoulder and felt her shiver as though she had been touched with a piece of dry ice. "My name is Gretchen Horowitz," she said. "I'm going to remove the bag from your head now, then cut the tape on your wrists. Don't be afraid."

The woman did not reply. Gretchen loosened the drawstring and slipped the bag from her face. The woman stared into Gretchen's eyes with the expression of an infant just emerging from its mother's womb.

"What's your name?" Gretchen asked.

"Rhonda. My name is Rhonda Fayhee. I live up by Lookout Pass. I work in the café. I went home from work. I don't know what happened to me."

"Many people have been looking for you, Rhonda. They're all your friends. The whole world is on your side." She opened her pocketknife and cut the tape on Rhonda Fayhee's wrists.

"Who kidnapped me?" Rhonda asked.

"You don't know?"

"I never saw anyone. I felt the needles

someone put in me. Somebody fed me, too. A man did. The same one who put his —" She couldn't finish.

"It's all right," Gretchen said. "I'm going to take you to the hospital in Missoula."

"I don't want to go there."

Gretchen sat down next to her. "Why don't you want to go to the hospital?"

"He did things to me."

"We're going to fix him for that. I promise you," Gretchen said.

"I want someone to kill him."

Gretchen put her arm around Rhonda and kissed her on the cheek. "You're going to be all right," she said. "Not all at once but with time. Do you hear me? All of this will pass. None of it is your fault. All of the things that were done to you happened outside of you and have nothing to do with your soul or who you are."

"He had a smell. It will never go away."

"Yes, it will. I promise. Terrible things were done to me when I was a child, and also when I was an adult. But I'm still here. I'm here for you, too. Are you listening, Rhonda? I give you my word: We're going to blow up this guy's shit." She pressed Rhonda Fayhee's head against her breast and kissed her hair. "We've got to go now," she said.

"Not yet."

"He has another hostage, Rhonda. She traded herself for you. Her name is Felicity

Louviere."

"I don't know anyone by that name. Who is she?"

I don't know. I'm not sure anyone does.

Gretchen did not share her thoughts and simply said, "We don't have any phone service here. Let me help you up. There you go. Just put one foot after the other. See? You're doing fine."

Gretchen did not return to Albert's ranch until almost dark. The news media cooperated with the sheriff's department and released a minimum amount of information about the rescue of Rhonda Fayhee, to avoid telling Surrette that he'd been identified as her kidnapper. However, the redacted story was troubling on another level. There was no mention that Felicity Louviere had been abducted.

I still had Love Younger's unlisted number. I called it at 10:17 P.M. I thought he might screen the call, but he didn't. When he picked up, I was treated to another instance of his irritability. "Why have you called my home?" he said.

"I suspect by now you know that Surrette has abducted your daughter-in-law," I said.

"Why is that your business?"

"Where's your son?"

"You're probably the most presumptuous man I've ever met, Mr. Robicheaux."

"Sir, what in the name of suffering God is wrong with you? This isn't about me or you. It's about Felicity Louviere and my daughter, Alafair. It's also about Gretchen Horowitz, who was almost killed by Asa Surrette."

"Yes, the same woman who shot at him and may have wounded my daughter-in-law."

He was a master at deflecting any reasonable form of redress for a problem that involved his agenda and his pride. Or in this instance, his profligate son. I asked again if he knew Caspian's whereabouts.

"I have no idea," he said. His voice had dropped in register. "He's drinking or using drugs. He's been gone all day. Why do you torment us so?"

"Every perp I ever met feigned the role of victim, Mr. Younger. A role like that is unworthy of you."

I did not expect what he said next. "My son may have become deranged. He's always been frightened, ever since he was a little boy. Caspian, Caspian, my poor son Caspian. What else can I say, sir? His sins are mine. It's I who planted the seeds of doubt and self-hatred in him. Do you know what it's like for a father to accept the fact he has ruined his son, Mr. Robicheaux? Do you have any idea what that is like?"

"Why would Surrette kidnap Felicity Louviere? Why would she be of interest to him?

669

Is he working with Caspian?"

The line went dead.

CHAPTER 32

Clete had made several calls to people he knew in Vegas and Reno and Atlantic City and had found out little he didn't already know about Caspian Younger. He tapped into another resource, a notorious New Orleans attorney by the name of Philo Wineburger, also known as Whiplash Wineburger. No one could say Whiplash was low-bottom, because Whiplash had no bottom. Over many years, he had fronted points for porn vendors in Baton Rouge and Miami, helped keep cock-fighting legal in Louisiana, and represented not only the Mob but a Nicaraguan drug lord named Julio Segura, right up until the day Clete and I blew Julio apart in the backseat of his Cadillac.

My favorite story about Whiplash involved his indignation at his divorce hearing when his wife described walking in on him while he was in the sack with the maid. When the judge asked Whiplash what he had to say in his defense, he answered, "I'm no snob, Your

Honor!"

Clete came up to the main house early Sunday morning. He was carrying a yellow legal pad, the top two pages filled with ink. He asked me to sit out back of the house, where we could be alone. He looked like he had just showered and shaved and put on fresh clothes and was in charge of his day, but I knew he had gotten little if any sleep the previous night.

"Here's what I got," he said. "After Caspian's father killed his credit lines at all the big casinos, he ran up a six-figure tab with a couple of shylocks in Miami, then couldn't make the vig. So he borrowed more from some guys in Brooklyn, not telling them he was on the hook with these other guys in Miami. This time he invested the money in a big coke transfer. Ever hear of La Familia Michoacana?"

"In Mexico?" I said.

"Yeah, they're meth addicts and religious crazoids," Clete said. "They cut off people's heads and leave them on curbsides with cigarettes hanging out of their mouths. According to Whiplash, Younger financed a two-hundred-grand shipment of coke that was supposed to go through a tunnel under the border somewhere around Mexicali. It gets even better. The shylocks bundled up a bunch of queer with real bills and passed it on to Caspian, who used it to pay the Mexicans.

Can you imagine paying those guys with counterfeit? They were going to take his skin off."

"How'd he get out of it?" I said.

"His father bailed him out and got him in G.A. again, but it didn't do any good. He went right back to Vegas for more of the same. Get this: The shylocks told Whiplash they didn't like dealing with Caspian because they didn't trust Felicity."

"Why not?"

"She was honest. These guys consider honesty a character defect," he said.

"Did Wineburger know anything about Surrette?"

"He didn't know the name, but he said Caspian had the reputation for being an easy mark and for hanging around weird people. I think the tail has been wagging the dog on this one."

I waited for Clete to continue. He set down his legal pad and propped his hands on his knees and watched two white-tailed does and a fawn walking along a trail through the trees. Wildflowers were growing inside the shade, and the deer began grazing, indifferent to our presence. "I can't take this, Dave," he said. "I think about Felicity in the hands of that guy, and I start to go crazy."

"We'll get her back." I placed my hand on his shoulder. It felt like a chunk of concrete. "Did you hear me?"

"Where do you think he took her?" he asked.

"A place with a basement."

He lowered his head and shut his eyes. "I'm going to find Caspian Younger. If he doesn't tell me where Surrette is, I'm going to do some things I've never done. There won't be anything left of him."

"You want to let Surrette make you over in his image?"

The back of his neck was flaming, his chest rising and falling. I could smell the heat in his clothes.

"She made a choice, Clete. Maybe we have to honor it."

"That's sick," he replied.

"You said it yourself — she was willing to risk her life to save the waitress. In her way, maybe she's making up for her daughter's death. Guilt is a luxury we don't have time for, partner."

"I wish I'd run off with her to Nevada."

"She's still married. That's not your way," I said.

"That didn't stop me from getting it on with her."

When others show levels of courage that seem beyond our own capabilities, we feel reduced in stature and are left wondering if a spiritual component is missing from our makeup. I once saw a black-and-white photograph of a Jewish mother walking with her daughter to a shower room in a Nazi death camp. The mother was holding the little girl's hand. The weather was obviously cold; they were wearing cloth coats and scarves tied on their heads. They were flanked on either side by barbed wire and surrounded by other children filing into the same room, inside a concrete building somewhere in eastern Poland. No other adults, except the Nazi guards, were present in the photograph.

There was no cutline on the photo that would explain the incongruity of the mother among all the children. The viewer could come to only one conclusion: She had asked to die with her daughter. The white sock on the little girl's left foot had slipped down on her ankle. I have never been able to forget that image, nor the courage that the mother had shown in refusing to abandon her child, even at the cost of her own life.

It's my belief that the great heroes in our midst are the ones we never notice. I believed Felicity Louviere was one of them.

"Let's pull out all the stops," I said. "If we have to paint the trees, fuck it. At our age, what's to lose?"

That afternoon Wyatt Dixon drove his pickup to the Younger compound and parked in front. The grounds were empty, and he could see no movement inside the house. His 1892 Winchester rested in the gun rack behind his head. He sat in the silence, trying to organize his thoughts, the taped bandage on his stomach as flat as cardboard under his shirt. He thought he could hear voices in the backyard and smell smoke from meat cooking on an open fire. He stepped out on the driveway and felt the earth shift under him, the stitches in his stomach drawing tight against the muscles like a zipper catching on skin.

He walked around the side of the house and through a border of wood-tubbed bougainvillea and citrus and bottlebrush and Hong Kong orchid trees. He saw Love Younger sitting in a canvas chair by a picnic table, the sunlight dappling his face. Younger was wearing alpine shorts and sandals and a print shirt open on his chest. A decanter of whiskey and a silver bowl full of crushed ice had been placed in the middle of the table, along with a tray of picked shrimp. Jack Boyd was sitting across from him, his long legs out in front of him, his ankles crossed. Both men looked at Wyatt with an alcoholic warmth in their faces, although neither man spoke.

"At the fairgrounds, you said something about my folks that I didn't quite catch. Or maybe the words got knocked out of my head when Buster's Boogie put me in the dirt. Can you refresh me?"

Younger looked genuinely puzzled. "Whatever we were talking about, it's flown away."

"You was saying something about white trash and the nigger in the woodpile. You was talking about making me a rich man."

"I see. You're here about money?"

"No, I'm here 'cause I don't like the way you was talking about my folks."

"I owe you an apology," Younger said. "I thought you were someone else. What did you say your mother's name was?"

"I didn't."

"Would you mind telling me now?"

"It was Irma Jean. Her maiden name was Holliday. Her people was from Georgia."

"Like Doc Holliday, the tubercular dentist?" Younger said.

"I wouldn't know."

"That's interesting. Your name is Wyatt. Maybe that's more than coincidence."

"You was calling us white trash?"

"No, I was saying you're a man among men. I was saying we probably have many things in common."

Wyatt gazed at the flower gardens and the fruit trees in the shade, and at the hand-waxed cars parked by the carriage house. "I can see our lifestyles are six of one and a half dozen of the other."

Younger picked a sprig of mint out of a bowl and put it in his glass, then refilled it with whiskey and fresh ice. He did not invite Wyatt to join them. Wyatt watched Love Younger raise his glass and drink, his throat moving smoothly, as though he were drinking beer rather than whiskey. The stitched wound in Wyatt's abdomen began to throb against the pressure of his belt buckle.

"Is there anything else?" Younger asked.

"Is there a reason your son has a hard-on for me, or is he just a nasty little termite by nature?"

"I'd appreciate it if you didn't use that kind of language while you're on my property."

"Where's he at?"

"Taking a nap. He won't be seeing you."

"Directly, he will, one way or another."

"Would you clarify that?" Younger said.

"He sent them men who attacked me and Miss Bertha. I don't know why, but he done it."

Younger put one sandaled foot up on the redwood bench. "Let's talk another time. It's such a fine day. Why cloud the sky when you don't have to?"

"The name Irma Jean don't mean nothing to you?"

"Afraid not." Younger took a sip from his glass and set it down on the table. He scratched at the edge of his eye with his fingertip. "It's rude to stare in another man's face."

"I can always tell when a man's lying."

"No man calls me a liar, Mr. Dixon."

"It's the other way around."

"You'll have to explain that."

"The name Irma Jean didn't ring no bells for you. If you'd known my mother, her memory would have been tattooed inside your pecker. Tell your son and Jack Shit here to forget they ever heard my name."

Wyatt began walking back toward his truck, his day a little more intact. When he walked through the border of bougainvillea and ornamental trees, he heard either Boyd or Younger laugh behind him. He wasn't sure at what. What he heard was not the laugh but its undisguised level of irreverence and ridicule. When he turned and looked through the branches of the trees, Younger was leaning toward Boyd like a man who had come down from the heights to share a private joke with one of his minions.

Because the two men were upwind from Wyatt, they obviously assumed he could not hear their words. Unfortunately for them, he didn't have to.

I even told Jack Shit yonder I could read lips, he thought. *Mr. Younger, if you're so goddamn smart, how come you surround yourself with people who cain't blow their noses for fear of losing a couple of brain cells?*

He read each of Younger's words like a bubble rising in the air, popping softly in the breeze. Then the words became a sentence, and the sentence continued into another sentence, and the sentences became a paragraph, and the paragraph became a knife blade that seemed to work its way through Wyatt's abdomen into his scrotum.

I lived three months in a motel when we were drilling in East Texas, Younger said. *Every third night, I fucked this cleaning girl named Josie something. An ass on her as big as a bed pillow. About a year later, I got a card from her saying I'd fathered her child. I tore it up and figured any number of men could have knocked her up, but from time to time it would bother me. I'd always carried my own water and paid my debts, including taking care of a woods colt or two. Finally, I had some private detectives look into it, and I thought Dixon might have been the product of my misplaced seed. But he's not, thank God. He's just run-of-the-mill rodeo trash and probably psychotic to boot.*

What happened to the cleaning gal? Jack Boyd asked.

I'm not sure, really. One of the detectives said she and her husband may have been murdered. I wasn't interested in the details. One of the detectives thought Dixon could have been Josie's kid. Who knows? Nits all look alike. Anyway, Dixon's mother was named Irma Jean. Case closed.

Too bad about the girl.

You're right about that. She was the best piece of ass I ever had.

■ ■ ■ ■

At noon on Sunday, Clete told me he was going to the sheriff's home, then to Love Younger's compound. I didn't argue. Felicity was in the hands of a bestial man, and Clete was powerless to do anything about it. I believe the strongest, most suffering people on earth are those whose family members are abducted by monsters, and who never see their loved ones again. If there is any worse fate that can be visited upon human beings, I don't know what it could be.

I was up on the hillside when Clete returned at 3:17 P.M. and parked by the garage. His face looked thinner somehow, as though he hadn't eaten in a couple of days. I walked down the hill to meet him. "How'd it go?" I said.

"Younger was half-sloshed and cooking out," he replied. "There were three or four other guys drinking in the backyard with him. I asked him what kind of day he thought his daughter-in-law was having. You know what that arrogant cocksucker said? 'She's in the Lord's hands.' "

"When did you eat last?"

"I don't remember. What were you doing up on the hill?"

"Trying to figure out how Surrette came and went with such ease on Albert's property."

"If Felicity dies, I'm going to smoke Love Younger. I'm going to smoke his son, too."

"What else did Younger say?"

"Nothing. He's an ice cube. Here's what's crazy: On the way up to his house, I thought I passed Wyatt Dixon."

"Why would Dixon be at Younger's place?"

"Maybe he knows something we don't. I went to the sheriff's home and asked why Felicity's abduction wasn't on the news. He says he and the feds want to force Surrette to make contact with the media."

"That's not a bad idea."

"I think it sucks. You know why Love Younger is so relaxed? Surrette is getting rid of a big problem for him. Felicity knows Caspian was behind Angel Deer Heart's homicide. Surrette is going to wipe the slate clean. I need a drink."

Before I could answer, I saw a compact car coming up the road. The female driver looked too large for the vehicle. She turned under the arch and came up the driveway, braking at the last moment, almost running over Clete's foot. She got out of the car, looking around as though not sure where she was. The density of her perfume made me think of magnolia blossoms opening on a hot night in the confines of a courtyard.

"You're the fat one who gave Wyatt trouble," she said to Clete.

"How you doin', Miss Bertha?" I said. "Can I help you?"

"*You* can. He can't," she replied, pointing to Clete.

"Is something going on with Wyatt?" I asked.

"Yes, and I'm very frightened about it. I need to talk with you, Mr. Robicheaux. Does this man have to be here?"

"Yes, he does," I said.

"I'll be at the cabin," Clete said.

"No, stay here," I said. "Miss Bertha, Clete is on our side. The good guys need to stick together. Did Wyatt go see Love Younger today?"

"How did you know?"

"Clete was out there, too."

"Wyatt reads lips. Love Younger was telling an ugly story to an ex–county detective, a man who worked with my brother. It was about Wyatt's mother. Mr. Younger was bragging on seducing a cleaning girl in a motel years ago. Earlier he had asked Wyatt for the name of his mother. Wyatt told her it was Irma Jean. Mr. Younger told the detective that wasn't the same woman he seduced."

"I'm not sure what you're saying, Miss Bertha," I said.

"Mr. Younger said the cleaning girl's name was Josie, so that meant she wasn't Wyatt's mother, and Wyatt couldn't possibly be his son. What Mr. Younger didn't know was that

Wyatt's mother was Josie Irma Jean Holliday. She used the name Josie at work, but to her family, she was always Irma Jean."

"Love Younger is Wyatt's father?" I said incredulously.

"His mother was working in the motel when Younger's company was drilling not far from Wyatt's home."

"You're saying Wyatt feels betrayed or rejected?"

"Have you seen his back? That's what his stepfather did to him. He was punished every day of his life for his mother's infidelity. *Rejected?* Where did you get such a stupid word?"

"Can I talk with him?" I asked.

"I don't know where he's gone. I thought he might be here."

"Why here?" I said.

"He respects you."

"What for?"

"He says you two are alike, that you see things that aren't there. He also says you have blood on your hands that no one knows about. That isn't true, is it?"

"No," I said. "It isn't."

Clete leaned against his Caddy and lit a cigarette with his Zippo, the smoke breaking apart in the wind, his green eyes dulled over, locked on mine. He removed a piece of tobacco from his tongue and flicked it off his fingertip. I could see his shoulder holster and snub-nosed .38 under his seersucker coat. How many times had he and I operated under a black flag?

"Wyatt left the house with his bowie knife," she said. "He has that old rifle in his truck, too. I have to find him."

"If you see him, tell him to keep his mouth shut about the Bobbsey Twins from Homicide," Clete said.

"I don't like your tone," Bertha said.

"Few people do," Clete replied.

She turned back to me. "You have to help him, Mr. Robicheaux. He's tortured by what Love Younger has done to his life. He also has uninformed religious attitudes that were taught to him as a child. Wyatt has both too little and too much knowledge about certain things. And he's confused by the name this killer may have been using."

"You mean Asa Surrette?" I said.

"Who else would I be talking about? Wyatt did his own investigation into the disappearance of the waitress. He said the killer was using the name of a Roman emperor."

"As an alias?" I said.

"He was calling himself Reverend Geta Noonen."

I had heard the name Geta in a historical context, but I couldn't place it offhand.

"He was the brother of Caracalla," she said. "He was a cruel man, just like his brother. The two of them gave the Christians a terrible time."

Clete was staring at me, the connections coming together in his eyes. "This has to be bullshit, Dave. Right? It's bullshit, and she knows it. I'm not buying into this. These people need to pack their heads in dry ice and ship them somewhere."

"Mr. Purcel, how would you like a punch in the face?" Bertha Phelps said. "You just take your big rear end down to the cabin and stay there, because you are starting to make me angry."

"Do you know who Saint Felicity was, Miss Bertha?" I said.

"No," she replied. "Who was she?"

"She died at the hands of the emperor Geta in a Carthaginian arena."

"I'm not up to this," Clete said. He got into his Caddy and backed down the driveway and onto the dirt road, then continued to back up until he was at the vehicle gate on the north pasture, as though eating the road and the entire world's irrationality with the rear bumper of his car.

A moment later, an electric-blue SUV with smoked windows and dealer's tags passed by the arch over Albert's driveway, headed toward the end of the hollow, the sun's reflection wobbling like a pool of yellow fire on the rear window.

"If something happens to my man, you two are to blame," Bertha Phelps said. "I may have to take care of this situation myself. Then I'll be back."

Asa Surrette parked his newly purchased SUV in front of the house at the end of the hollow, then went inside, his overnight bag on his shoulder. The nostalgia he'd experienced at moving into a home reminiscent of rural Kansas had been replaced by a growing irritability that he couldn't compartmentalize. Maybe it was the dusty baseboards and the bare lightbulbs and the dirt ingrained in the floors and thread-worn carpets; they were not only realistic reminders of his natal home, they conjured up other images for him as well: treeless horizons, winds that blew at forty knots in twenty-below weather, Titan missiles sleeping in their silos under the wheat, the nightly mold-spore report on the local news.

His landlady didn't help matters. She was Dutch or Swedish and had a loud voice and a North Dakota accent that hurt his ears. Her chirping evangelical rhetoric caused him to flutter his eyelids uncontrollably, not unlike a survivor of an artillery barrage.

He entered the house by way of the back steps, hoping to avoid her. Before he could make it to his bedroom, he heard a toilet flush and her feet pounding up the stairs. "Oh, there you are!" she said.

He stopped in the hallway. "Yes, *here* is

where I am," he replied.

She didn't catch his annoyance. "Oh, my, what happened to your face?" she said, her fingers rising to her mouth.

"I walked into a nail."

"My heavens. I hope you got a tetanus shot," she said. Her hair was bleached and frizzed and resembled a wig. She wore bright coral-red lipstick and foundation that stiffened the fuzz on her cheeks and caused it to glow like whiskers against the light. "If you get lockjaw, you'll have to take your food through a straw. Did you already get a shot? If you haven't, you should."

"I heard you. I'm fine."

She looked past him into the driveway. "It looks like someone got himself a new SUV. You bought it in Polson?"

"What makes you think I got it there?"

"The dealer's tag," she said. "When I was a little girl, I'd memorize license numbers. That's how I learned math. Did you say you got a shot?"

"I bought it from somebody who bought it in Polson."

"Not to worry," she said. "Geta, next time would you call?"

"Call about what?"

"You didn't come home yesterday. We were worried."

"I had to tie up a problem or two. That's the nature of my work."

"I see. Well, next time I'm sure you'll remember to call. You look tired. Maybe you should take a nap."

"I don't need a nap."

"Like Scripture says, we must always be alert. But as a minister, you already know that. You ran into a nail? How awful."

"I'm going into my room now."

"By the way, we're going to be painting the upstairs. We'll need to move you into the cubby for a few days."

"What's the cubby?"

"It's in the basement. It's only temporary. There's a window and a toilet. You can come upstairs to bathe."

"That's not convenient for me."

"Beg your pardon?" she said.

"I don't live in basements. I'm not a bat."

She sniffed the air and made a face. "What's that smell?" she said.

"I don't know. I don't smell anything."

"It's very strong. Check the bottom of your shoes."

He could hear himself breathing, his irritability climbing like a tarantula up his spinal cord. Her mouth made him think of a plumber's helper, one smeared with lipstick. "Who's home?" he said.

"Ralph's splitting wood. The girls went to the movies. Why do you want to know?"

"I thought we'd have a meeting of the minds."

"You're acting strangely. I think I should have a look at your cheek. You may already have an infection. Are you running a fever?"

"Don't touch me."

"Well, I never."

"Do you have some baling wire?"

"Ralph probably has some in the shed."

"Yes, folksy hinterland people would always have some baling wire lying around, wouldn't they? Ralphie splinters the wood, and then you cord it up for the winter. That's what folksy salt-of-the-earth people do."

"What has gotten into you?" she said.

"A little of this, a little of that," he said, dipping his hand into his overnight bag. "Mostly, I just don't like the way you look. Or the way you talk. Or your stupid expression."

He lifted up a .22 auto outfitted with a suppressor and popped a solitary round through the middle of her forehead, the hole no bigger than the circumference of an eraser on a wood pencil. She went straight down on the floor in a heap, like a puppet whose strings had been released by the puppeteer. That was how they always went down when they weren't expecting it. Not like in the movies, when the shooting victim flew backward through a glass window.

He studied her surprised expression and the pool of blood forming on the floor, then put away the semi-auto and picked up the brass and stepped out on the landing. "Hey, Ralph!" he called down. "Can you bring some baling wire up here? The wife wants you to help hang something."

The husband snicked his ax into the stump and gazed up at the landing, squinting against the sunlight. "Be there in a jiff, Geta. We wondered where you were," he said. "I told the wife not to worry, you were doing the Lord's work. Glad you're back home safe and sound."

CHAPTER 33

After Bertha Phelps drove away, Clete went down to the cabin, and I went back up on the hill, trying to retrace the route Asa Surrette used to get on and off Albert's property. It was 3:48 P.M. and shady and cool inside the trees, but on the opposite side of the valley, I could see harebells and asters and paintbrush and mock orange and sunflowers and bee balm on the hillsides, where the grass was green and tall and the trees were few because of the thin soil layer. Then I saw Clete laboring up the grade toward me, his porkpie hat on, a bottle of Jack Daniel's in his right hand, his shoulders as heavy-looking as a bag of rocks.

"I thought you could use some company," he said, sweating, his breath coming hard. He sat down on a boulder and wiped his brow. "I guess I still haven't acclimated to the thin air."

"Maybe you ought to put the hooch away today," I said.

Mistake.

He pulled the cork and upended the bottle, one eye fixed on my face. "See, no problem. The world hasn't ended," he said. "Marse Daniel never lets me down."

"Who are you kidding?"

"I told you, I needed a drink. So I took one. I think my liver is shot. I take one hit and it's like mainlining. That means I drink less." He waited for me to argue with him, but I didn't. "What do you think you're going to find up here?" he asked.

"The last time Surrette was on the hill, he tried to lead Gretchen into a bear trap," I said. "I followed his trail over the crest to the far side. His tracks led to a rock outcropping, then disappeared. He had to go south to get to the highway. There are two or three deer trails that would have taken him there, but his tracks weren't on them. I don't get it."

"What if he headed north?"

"He'd end up in a blind canyon. It was night. He would have to climb out of it in the dark. Where would his vehicle be?"

"What's in the canyon?"

"Three or four houses. People Albert knows," I replied.

Clete took another hit off the bottle. I could see a chain of tiny air bubbles sliding up the neck as he drank. He set the bottle on his leg. "I shouldn't do this in front of you. But I'm not doing too good today, and I need it."

"It doesn't bother me."

"Not at all?" he said.

"Maybe a little. Like a thought that's buried in the unconscious. Like an old girlfriend winking at you on the street corner."

"That bad?"

"It comes and goes. I don't think about it as often; I dream about it. The dreams are always nightmares. Sometimes I can't wake myself up, and I walk around thinking I'm drunk."

"How often do you dream about it?"

"Every third night, about four A.M."

"All these years?"

"Except when I was back on the dirty boogie. Then I didn't have to dream. My life was a nightmare twenty-four hours a day," I said.

He stared through the trees into the sunlight. Down below, Albert was watering the grass. I could hear birds singing and chipmunks clattering in the rocks. I thought of all the days Clete and I had hiked through woods to get to an isolated pond in the Atchafalaya Basin. I thought about diving the wreck of a German sub that drifted up and down the Louisiana coast, and knocking down ducks inside a blind on Whiskey Bay, and trolling for marlin south of Key Largo, the bait bouncing in our wake. I thought of all the Cubans and Cajuns and Texas fisherpeople we had known along the southern rim of the United States, and the open-air oyster bars we had eaten in and the boats on which we had hauled tarpons as thick as logs over the gunwales. What is the sum total of a man's life? I knew the answer, and it wasn't complicated. At the bottom of the ninth, you count up the people you love, both friends and family, and you add their names to the fine places you've been and the good things you've done, and you have it.

Clete stood up and dusted off the seat of his trousers. "Let's hike on up a bit higher," he said.

"Where's Gretchen?"

"I wish I knew. When it comes to her old trade, she's a loner. She said something I hadn't thought about. That Surrette is going to come apart."

"Why?" I asked.

"She's known guys like him, guys the Mob took out. She said they're all anal-retentives. They've got a master plan. When it doesn't work out, their world goes to shit."

"What's Surrette's master plan?"

"Breaking Felicity."

I didn't look at his face. The implication in his voice was enough. I heard him lift the bottle again, the whiskey sloshing inside the neck.

"Sometimes you have to keep an empty space in your head and not let the wrong thoughts get in it," I said.

"That's why I drink this. It's why I need a

little slack sometimes, noble mon," he said.

I heard him take another hit and squeak the cork tight in the bottle.

We walked up the hill, me in front, angling toward the crest in a northwesterly direction. The new grass was coming up between the winter thatch, and in places where a spring had leaked down the slope, I could see the sharply defined tracks of deer and at least one canine.

"Is that a wolf track?" Clete said.

"I think it is."

"That's another thing that's weird," he said. "Surrette comes and goes and doesn't seem to give the wolves any thought."

"They're brothers-in-arms?"

"I didn't say that. Don't pretend it's not weird, though. I don't feel easy out here unless I've got my piece."

"He's a sociopath. He thinks the universe can't go on without him."

Clete pointed down the slope at a depression where a large animal, probably a bear, had been digging grubs. The soil was black and loamy and burrowed out from under a log. Inside the dirt and the disturbed leaves and pine needles, I could see a rusty length of chain. I worked my way down the slope and jerked on the chain until the bear trap on the other end pulled free from the ground.

"That's the one he almost got Gretchen with?" Clete said.

I ran my thumb along the teeth on the two half-moon steel bands that had sprung tightly together. "Yeah, this is probably it."

"You think he buried it because his prints are on it?" Clete said.

"There's a good chance. Or he planned to come back and get it."

Clete looked toward the north, the trees swaying overhead. A hawk was drifting on the wind stream, its feathers ruffling. "Surrette is closer to us than we think."

"Or he was," I replied.

"Maybe we should start knocking on some doors," he said.

I followed him down the hill, dragging the bear trap through the thatch and detritus on the forest floor, the chain as cold and damp as a serpent in my palm.

Gretchen once read an autobiographical work titled *Something About a Soldier,* written by a Miami novelist named Charles Willeford. At age thirteen, in the bottom of the Depression, the author ran away from an orphanage and rode the rods all over the American West. Three years later, he enlisted in the horse cavalry and was stationed in the Philippines and at Schofield Barracks in Hawaii. In his account, Willeford talked about certain individuals for whom there were no lines. Some of them were fellow enlisted men, twenty-year-olds who looked him straight in the face and said, never blinking, "There are no lines." They were talking about sexual intercourse with Filipino children.

The lesson Willeford took away from the experience was simple: There are always lines. No matter how bad it gets, at Normandy or in the Hürtgen Forest or at Arnhem, where he commanded a tank, there are lines. Under a black flag, inside the belly of the beast, in a man-made hell like Auschwitz, there are still lines, and the day you say otherwise is the day something flies out of your breast and does not return.

Gretchen had read Willeford's autobiography two weeks before she popped Bix Golightly. For years she had created different scenarios in anticipation of catching up with him one day. She had convinced herself that a man who would sodomize a six-year-old girl deserved anything that happened to him.

She took the contract without fee and flew to New Orleans and followed him around the city for two days. On the third night, he crossed the bridge into Algiers and parked on a deserted side street. She could see every detail of his face as she approached his vehicle — the scar tissue in his eyebrows, the bonelike forehead, the Mongolian eyes, the crooked bridge of his nose, the flat profile from the punches he had taken at Angola and in the ring. He was smoking a perfumed cigarette and at first showed no particular interest in her presence. Then he recognized her as the contract hitter he knew only as Caruso, an almost mythic figure with obscure origins in Miami's Little Havana. He may not have made the connection between Caruso and the little girl whose life he had ruined, but he knew that the intersection of his life with Caruso's on this backstreet not far from the oily water of the Mississippi was not coincidence and that the last page on his calendar was about to be ripped off.

He began talking to her through the window as though they were old friends, his words spilling out nonsensically, his breath rife with funk. She never spoke. She watched him as she would a hamster racing around inside a glass box. She thought of popping him in the neck and pulling him out on the asphalt, where she would finish the job. She didn't. There were always lines.

She squeezed off three rounds, so fast that Golightly never knew what hit him. The side of his head slapped the steering wheel, his mouth dropped open, his eyes stared at a garbage can on the opposite curb as though it were the most interesting object on earth.

Then she spat on his corpse, indifferent to the possibilities of DNA analysis, and walked away.

Now she was troubled again by Charles Willeford's anecdotal admonition regarding lines. She had talked for forty-five minutes at the hospital with Rhonda Fayhee and had concluded that the simple and innocent girl would live with nightmares the rest of her life. Fortunately, she had been sedated so heavily by Surrette that she did not remember some of the things he probably did to her.

During the captivity, the bag had stayed on Rhonda's head, and she never saw her surroundings. Nevertheless, she remembered details that were unmistakable: the smell of damp stone or brick, a faint glow of sunlight through a window at dawn, a sound like the chuck of waves against a boathouse or a beach.

She also thought she'd heard a plane, the motors gunning during takeoff, the sound muffled by wind blowing in trees that were thickly leafed and grew side by side. There was another detail, one that seemed out of context, surreal, one that a drowning person might remember if he had been sucked into a whirlpool while people chatted on dry land a few feet away. Rhonda was sure she heard people singing while she was being loaded into a vehicle. The words she heard just before the door slammed shut were "Life is like a mountain railroad, with an engineer that's brave."

Later, Gretchen Googled the lyrics and discovered they were part of a hymn often sung in southern churches.

Where was Rhonda Fayhee held prisoner?

In all probability, it was the same place Felicity Louviere was being held now.

"Rhonda, do you think there was an airstrip close by? Did you hear planes coming in overhead?" Gretchen asked.

The girl said the sound of the plane had been down below somewhere.

"Below the level of the basement?" Gretchen asked.

"Yes," the girl replied. "It droned a long time before it took off. It sounded like it was turning. It made a fluttering sound."

The details about the place of captivity did not fit together.

For Gretchen, the answer to the riddle probably lay with Caspian Younger, a man whose whole life had been one of entitlement, a man who may have been complicit in the murder of his adopted daughter. Should lines be an issue? Should a man like Caspian Younger be protected from accountability while his wife was tortured to death? *What a stupid question to ask,* Gretchen thought.

She drove to the Younger compound, expecting to be confronted with security personnel who would do everything in their power to turn her away. That's what should have happened. Instead, she would learn that the Younger family drama was not the stuff of *Macbeth* or *Oedipus Rex* or King Arthur and Mordred or the horns blowing along the road to Roncevaux. Rather, it was the same material to be found in soap opera, as sordid and saccharine and petty as the behavior of the players in any work of pathos. The portrayal of the patrician protagonist and his tragic descent from grace made for lovely entertainment, but it seldom had anything to do with reality.

Gretchen parked her truck in front of the Younger compound and walked down the flagstones to the front door. The only vehicle she could see was a faded compact parked by the carriage house. It had dents in one fender and silver duct tape wrapped around a broken side mirror. The yard was empty, the heavy oak door ajar. She could hear voices inside and a sound like someone diving off a springboard into a swimming pool. With the tips of her fingers, she eased the door wider and walked through the foyer into the living room. Down a hallway, she could see Caspian Younger in swim trunks and a bathrobe, standing by French doors that gave onto a patio. He was pouring from a bottle of Cold Duck into a wineglass. He was unshaved and his robe was open, the mat of hair on his bony chest glistening with water. In the background, a girl not over nineteen climbed out of the pool, her bikini clinging to her body with little more density than wet Kleenex. Jack Boyd put his cigar in an ashtray on top of a glass table and handed her a towel.

Caspian took a sip from his wineglass, his

gaze roving over Gretchen's face and throat and breasts. "You again," he said.

"You look like you're pretty busted up over your wife's abduction," she said.

"I have no control over Felicity's fate. She goes her own way. I go mine. You should know that by this time," he replied.

"Where's your father?"

"I'm not sure. Out and about, I guess. It's what he does best," he replied. "He's never been a homebody. Do you know I can read your thoughts?"

"I doubt that."

"Try this. You think I know where Felicity is. You're going to do horrible things to me until I tell you."

"How's it feel?" she asked.

"How does what feel?"

"To be controlled by a guy like Surrette. The man who suffocated your daughter."

He brushed at one eye as though a lash had caught in the lid. He was standing by a black granite–topped wet bar. A piece of stationery containing a note written in flowing blue calligraphy was positioned neatly under a paperweight on the granite.

"I know about your illegitimate birth, Ms. Horowitz," he said. "I know that your mother was a whore and a heroin addict, and I know that you've murdered people for hire. So I'm going to share some things with you that might help you to understand a situation I've

703

lived with most of my life." He picked up the piece of stationery from the wet bar. The paper was thick, the color of French-vanilla ice cream. A family coat of arms was embossed delicately in the grain. "I'll give you the highlights," he said. "I took a nap earlier, and when I woke up, I discovered that my father had decided to tell me of his fear that Wyatt Dixon was his son. This is something I'd known for many years, primarily because my father has screwed women all over the world and used to brag about it. In his note, he said he has proof that Dixon is not his son, and for that he is thankful. He also says I am his only surviving son and that he loves me. Isn't that sweet? It's a bit like my father drinking a glass of champagne and pissing it into a cup, then handing it to me to drink." He paused and studied her face, perhaps waiting to see what effect his words would have. "A little too complex?" he said. "To explain: If Dixon were my father's offspring, his affections might be divided. Isn't that a grand compliment to receive? You get it now?"

"What kind of day do you think your wife is having?" Gretchen asked.

"I've had that kind of guilt heaped on me all my life, Ms. Horowitz. You still didn't get the gist of my story, did you? I thought the Mob hired intelligent people to do the kind of work you do."

"I got in through affirmative action," she replied.

"My father got it all wrong. Wyatt Dixon *is* his bastard son. His girlfriend was here and told me. Dixon is my half brother. That's a little hard to deal with. How would you like to find out your half sister is the bride of Dracula?"

"Bertha Phelps was here?" Gretchen said.

"An hour ago. I sent her down the road with a kick in her fat rump. I suspect she ran back to her cowboy."

"You kicked Wyatt Dixon's girlfriend in the butt?"

"I'm about to do it to you, too. And I'll do it to him if he comes around here again."

"You're going to do a beat-down on Wyatt Dixon?"

"There're ways," he replied. "What are you doing?"

She stepped out on the patio. The girl in the bikini was sitting in a deck chair, taking a hit off a pair of roach clips. "What's your name, honey?" Gretchen asked.

"Dora," the girl said.

"You need to hit the road, Dora. My father beat the shit out of these two assholes. I may have to do the same. You don't want to be here when that happens."

The girl looked at Jack Boyd. He smiled and shook his head. "She's a kidder," he said.

"This guy was fired from the Missoula

County Sheriff's Department because he's a dirty cop," Gretchen said. "His bud was a geek named Bill Pepper who liked to tie up girls and rub his penis on them. A serial killer named Asa Surrette emasculated Pepper up at Swan Lake. Surrette is buds with Caspian Younger. That's the kind of people you're hanging out with."

The girl looked at Jack Boyd again, this time clearly frightened.

"Don't pay attention to her," Boyd said. He was still smiling. "I was in a car accident. She makes movies. Ask her."

"Good-bye, Dora," Gretchen said.

Dora glanced at Jack Boyd, then at Gretchen. She pulled on a pair of sandals, picked up her beach bag, and walked hurriedly through the side yard to her car, her buttocks jiggling.

"Why don't you give Caspian a break?" Boyd said.

"Where is Surrette?" Gretchen said.

"You think I know that?" Boyd said.

"I hope one of you does."

"Or it's going to get rough?" Boyd said.

"I'll handle this, Jack," Caspian said, stepping out on the patio, setting aside his wineglass. "Ms. Horowitz, I don't want to be unkind, but would you please go away? You and your father and Mr. Robicheaux and his daughter have been a constant nuisance. Mr. Boyd and I could have had your father arrested for aggravated assault, but we didn't. Know why? Because that's not my way. With one phone call, I could have your father ground into fish chum. He would disappear without a trace, other than a bloody skim floating on Flathead Lake."

"You're connected in Vegas?"

"I know some of the same people you do. Except they listen to me because I have money," he said. "You won't change anything. I made some mistakes. There's no way to undo them. What's done is done."

"You're going to give me Surrette. On this one, there are no lines."

His eyes shifted sideways, as though he were processing her words. "I'm sure that makes sense to you. It's lost on me."

She glanced at her watch. "Your window of opportunity is closing," she said.

"I'll walk you to your truck. You're a film-maker. Maybe I can help you later. I know a number of people in the industry." He fitted his hand around her upper arm and squeezed it tentatively. "Nice. You lift weights?"

Jack Boyd was grinning lasciviously.

Gretchen wet her bottom lip before she spoke. "I was never good at communication skills. A psychologist told me that. He suggested I try what he called 'massage therapy.' He was going to do it for me in his off hours. For free."

Caspian was standing beside her as he

clutched her arm. Without removing his hand, he stepped in front of her, looking warmly into her face. His eyes were pale blue and didn't seem to belong inside the graininess of his face, like blond hair on a Mexican. He had a weak chin and a nose that was both sharp and small. She had seen toy men like him on the French Riviera. They seemed like caricatures of nineteenth-century aristocracy whose bloodline had run out. Gretchen wondered what life would have been like for Caspian Younger in the kinds of public schools she had attended in Miami and Brooklyn.

"I told you I could read your thoughts," he said, sinking his fingers a little deeper into her upper arm, a flicker of lust and anticipation lighting on his mouth. "Be a good girl. Don't do something rash. If you'd like to stay and have a good time, I'd say all sins are forgiven, including your father's."

Jack Boyd's grin would not go away. "I wouldn't argue with sloppy seconds," he said.

"You're asking me to get it on?"

Caspian raised his eyebrows and smiled. "You can tell me about your documentaries."

"Can I ask you a question before we go any further?" she said. "Do you really believe you can go up against a guy like Wyatt Dixon?"

"It's what's under the hood that counts," he said. "I'll let you have a test drive upstairs."

He worked his thumb deeper into the

muscle of her arm, inching his fingers up on her shoulder, kneading the flesh along her collarbone, his mouth coming closer to hers.

Her reaction was not emotional, nor could it be described as vengeful. She didn't consider it of much consequence and wondered that either man could have expected a different outcome.

"What do you say, babycakes?" Caspian asked.

"Say about what?"

"Going upstairs. You've got beautiful arms," he said. "If the Venus de Milo had arms, they'd look like yours."

"That's a great come-on line. If I ever go trans, I think I'll give it a try."

"Are we on or not?" Jack Boyd said.

"You sure you guys want to do this?" she asked.

"Say the word," Caspian said.

"What the fuck," she replied.

"You won't regret it," Caspian said.

"But you will," she said.

She ripped her elbow into Jack Boyd's face and drove her fist between Caspian's eyes. Then she pulled her blackjack from her side pocket and whipped it across the back of Boyd's head and backstroked it across Caspian's jaw, knocking the spittle from his mouth. She hit him on the collarbone and the points of his shoulders and shoved him through the open French doors onto the floor. Behind her, she heard Jack Boyd trying to rise to his feet. "Run," she said.

"Do what?" Jack Boyd replied, barely supporting himself on the back of a chair. She brought the blackjack down on top of his hand. He cradled his arm against his chest, the color draining from his face.

"Run! Don't come back. You're finished here."

She stepped toward him. He bolted through the yard, looking back once, knocking the concrete bowl of a birdbath off its pedestal. She turned to Caspian Younger and slid a pair of needle-nosed pliers from her back pocket. He was sitting up on the floor, pressing his palm against his mouth, looking at the thick red smear on his hand. She got down on one knee. "Do you know what I'm about to do to you?" she asked.

"I don't know where Surrette is," he said.

"Where do you want me to start?"

"Start what?"

"Pulling off your parts."

"Please. I didn't have a choice. He's not human. You may think he is, but he's not. He's what he says he is."

"So what is he?"

"I don't know."

She bent down closer to him, the pliers extended in front of her. His eyes were tightly shut. *There are always lines,* she heard a voice say.

He was probably telling the truth, she told herself. If he gave up Surrette, the feds would take him off the board, and no matter how the legal implications played out, Caspian Younger would be free of the man who had probably extorted him for years.

There was a problem, and it didn't have to do with Surrette. Caspian had said he didn't know where his father was. This was after his father had left him a note of endearment, one that should have made him conclude he was of some value to someone. Would he have brought a teenage girl onto the property, with the intent of debauching her, if he had no idea of his father's whereabouts or the approximate time of his return?

She touched the point of the pliers to his cheek, just below his eye. "Where did your father go? You do not want to give me the wrong answer."

"He has a place on Sweathouse Creek. He goes there because it reminds him of growing up in East Kentucky. Clouds of fog in the hollows and all that hillbilly crap he's so fond of."

"You brought the girl here and didn't worry about him coming back unexpectedly?"

"She just came here to swim."

"You told Bertha Phelps where he was, didn't you?"

"No," he replied, clearly forcing himself not to blink.

"You know what a professional liar never does?" she said. "Blink. His eyelids stay stitched to his forehead. It's a sure tell every time."

"I survived, just like you. You know the edge I got on Wyatt Dixon? I don't care whether I live or die."

"Dixon is like your father. He's a self-made man. I don't think you're anything at all. You're a condition, not a man. I feel sorry for you."

"Tell me that when I take a shit on your chest, because that's what I'm going to do when I get out of here."

She tapped him lightly on the tip of the nose with the pliers, then stood up. "Go wash your face. Come around me again for any reason, and I'll blow your head off."

She went out the front door and left it open behind her. There were squirrels playing overhead in the trees. She watched them for a moment, then started her pickup and drove away. She tried to think of all the things he had just said to her. Two words stood out in bold relief and were not in harmony with his self-congratulatory statements about being mobbed up in Vegas. What were the words?

Flathead Lake? Why that choice of location for his metaphor about getting rid of Clete Purcel?

CHAPTER 34

It was 4:48 P.M. when Clete and I starting knocking on doors at the end of the hollow, up the road from Albert's ranch. The first place we stopped was a remodeled barn that a young couple from California had rented for the summer. They said they taught at Berkeley and knew Albert and his work and sometimes hiked along the ridge above his house but hadn't seen any other hikers there. They were nice people and invited us in for coffee. I did not want to tell them that Surrette was somewhere in the neighborhood. "Do you all have children?" I asked.

"No, we don't," the husband replied, trying not to show offense at the personal nature of the question. "Can you tell me what you guys are looking for?"

"A man named Asa Surrette has been around here. He's a serial killer who escaped from a prison van in Kansas," I said. "He may be long gone, or he may be close by. Have you seen any vehicles that don't belong here? Or somebody up in the rocks above your house?"

The wife looked at the husband, then they both shook their heads. "This is a little disturbing," the husband said. "Nobody else has told us about a serial killer."

"He's the guy who abducted the waitress up by Lookout Pass," Clete said.

"There's a minister who lives in that two-story house with the cedar trees in front," the wife said. "He has his congregation there on Sunday mornings and Wednesday evenings. His name is Ralph, I think."

"Did you see anybody unusual over there?" I asked.

They shook their heads again. "Sometimes after their services, they throw a football back and forth in the yard," the wife said. "I saw Ralph chopping wood earlier. I think his church friends come and go. This serial killer is probably gone by now, isn't he?"

"Probably," I replied.

"By the way, I saw the girls' car pull into the driveway earlier. I'm pretty sure some-body's home," she said.

I wrote my cell number on the back of my departmental business card and left it with the couple.

Clete and I knocked on the doors of two more houses in the hollow with the same results. The four houses in the natural cul-de-sac were spaced a considerable distance apart, all of them set in the shadows of the mountains, and the people in the houses apparently had amiable but not close relationships. In effect, it was a community where insularity came with the property deed.

Our last stop was at the minister's house. An old Toyota Corolla was parked in the driveway and a Bronco in the garage. The window shades were down, the front door shut. The glider on the porch rotated slightly on its chains in a mild breeze blowing down the canyon.

"It doesn't look like anybody is home," Clete said.

I looked at my watch. "Maybe they're eating dinner," I said.

I tapped on the door. I could hear no sound inside. I tried again. Nothing. I tried to turn the doorknob. It was locked. "Let's walk around back," I said.

We went through the side yard. The shades on the dining room windows were pulled halfway down. There were no place settings on the table or any sign of movement in the house. In the backyard, there was a pole shed attached to the side of an old barn where firewood had been stacked neatly against the barn wall. The grass was scattered with freshly split chunks of pinewood; the woodcutter's ax had been left embedded on the rim of the chopping stump, the handle at a stiff forty-five-degree angle. Clete looked up at the sky. A bank of thunderheads had moved across the sun. "You'd think a guy this neat would want to get his wood under the shed before it rained," he said.

He went up the back steps and banged on the door. No response. He held up one hand to keep the reflection off the glass and attempted to see inside. Then he went up the rear stairs to the second floor and tried the door and pressed his ear against the glass. "I can't hear a thing," he said. He went around the side of the house and came back. "Maybe they went off somewhere."

I wished I had asked one of the neighbors how many vehicles the minister's family owned. "Could be. But the Bronco is in the garage. This doesn't look like a three-car family."

"What do you want to do?" Clete said.

I glanced at my cell phone. No service. A cat walked around the corner of the house and watched us. Its water and food bowls were empty. I stared at the house. Its quiet and dark interior was of such intensity that I could hear a ringing sound in my head. "There's something wrong in that house," I said. "Break the glass."

Clete knocked out a pane in the kitchen door with a brick and reached inside and opened the door, his shoes crunching on top of the shattered glass. I followed him through the mudroom into the kitchen. The oven had been left on, and the heat was enough to peel the wallpaper. Clete turned off the propane and took his .38 snub from his shoulder holster, letting it hang from his right hand, the muzzle pointed at the floor. The only sound in the house was the scraping of a tree limb on the eave.

"This is Clete Purcel and Dave Robicheaux," he called into the dining room. "I'm a private investigator, and Dave is a sheriff's detective from Louisiana. We're visiting at Albert Hollister's place down the road. We think there might be a problem in this house."

His words echoed through the downstairs. We started moving through the house, Clete in front, his .38 held up at a right angle. We opened the closet doors and the door to a bedroom and the door to a pantry and a laundry room. Nothing appeared to be disturbed. Clete started up the stairs one step at a time, his gaze fastened on the landing, his left hand on the banister. His back looked as wide as a whale's, the fabric of his coat stretching across his spine.

On the left side of the landing was another bedroom, its door open, the bed made, raindrops clicking on the windowpane. I went inside the bedroom and looked in the closet. It was full of clothes that probably belonged to a teenage girl. I came back out on the landing. Neither Clete nor I spoke. He opened the bathroom door and winced. I could smell the fecal odor without going inside. If I hadn't known better, I would have concluded someone had just used the toilet.

There were no towels on the racks, no toilet paper on the spindle. An incense bowl rested on top of a dirty-clothes hamper. Clete felt the bathroom walls and rubbed his fingertips with his thumb. It was obvious someone had used adhesive tape of some kind to hang up pictures or pieces of paper all over the walls. I tried the door on the right side of the landing. It swung back from the jamb, revealing a small room furnished with a chest of drawers and a narrow bed without sheets or a mattress cover. On the floor was a dust-free rectangle where a footlocker might have rested. Clete turned in a circle and lifted his arms to show his puzzlement.

We left the bedroom and closed the door behind us. Clete flicked on the light above the landing. The oak floor had been wiped clean in the center, but there were tiny hairlike traces of a dark substance between two boards. I squatted down and rubbed my handkerchief along the grain, then held up the handkerchief for Clete to see. I returned to the bathroom, holding my breath against the odor, removed the incense bowl, and opened the hamper. I had found the towels that were pulled off the racks. I tilted the hamper so Clete could see inside. He silently mouthed, *The basement.*

We went back downstairs and through the hallway. When I opened the door to the basement, I smelled an odor that was like night damp and mildew and perhaps a leak from a sewage line, but nothing you wouldn't expect in a basement that seldom saw sunlight. We waited at the open door for at least ten seconds, listening. Then I felt for the wall switch and clicked it on, flooding the basement with the harsh illumination of three bare lightbulbs. This time I went first. We had to lower our heads when we passed under some water and heating pipes; we found ourselves standing in the midst of what seemed a conventional setting beneath an early-twentieth-century farmhouse. There was a propane-fed furnace that had rusted out along the floor, a keg of nails and a wheelbarrow full of broken bricks shoved in a corner, two cardboard boxes filled with Christmas-tree ornaments and strings of colored lights under a window whose wood frame had rotted. Clete turned around and peered through the shadows at something no human being ever wants to see, an image that no amount of experience can prepare you for. "Mother of God," he said.

The two figures had been put in transparent garment bags, and the bags hung with baling wire from a rafter. The weight had stretched the bags into the shape and wispy texture of cocoons. One of the figures was a woman. Her hair was pressed in a bloody tangle against the plastic. She was probably dead when she went into the bag. The other figure was a man. His wrists were crisscrossed behind him with duct tape. One eye was half-lidded, the other popping from the socket. His mouth was attached to the plastic like a suction cup.

Clete walked to the corner of the basement and retched, his big arms propped against the wall, hiding his face from me, the smell of whiskey rising from the concrete.

The rain shower had already stopped when the first sheriff's cruiser arrived, followed by the paramedics, the crime scene techs, the coroner, the sheriff, and the FBI special agent I'd had words with earlier, James Martini. He went down in the basement for five minutes. When he came back, his tie was pulled loose and his face had a winded look, although he was a trim, muscular man in his late thirties who probably worked out regularly. He seemed unsure of what he wanted to say. "Who got sick down there?" he asked.

"My friend Clete Purcel."

He nodded, looking around, his gaze focused on nothing. "You ever work one like this before? Down in Louisiana?"

"Not exactly."

"Why is Surrette prowling this ridge?" he asked.

"Part of it has to do with Albert Hollister."

"The writer?"

"He owns a ranch just down the road. He was Asa Surrette's creative writing professor at Wichita State University in 1979. Surrette has a grievance against him, something about an objectionable short story he turned in."

"That's a new one."

"A guy like this doesn't need much of an excuse."

"Your daughter interviewed Surrette in prison and got him stoked up?"

"That's close enough. Right now I'd like to keep her alive."

"You don't think we're doing our job?"

"He means to kill her if he can. Surrette should have been gutted, salted, and tacked to a fence post years ago. That didn't happen."

"The Bureau is at fault?" he said.

"One time I pulled over a drunk driver, then let him go because he had no priors and was two blocks from his house. Three hours later, he killed his wife."

"The Bureau had limited reach on Surrette's crimes in Kansas," he replied.

He was a company man and he wasn't going to concede a point. I didn't blame him for it. I had a feeling he wasn't dealing well with the scene in the basement. No normal person would. The day you are not bothered by certain things you witness as a police officer is the day you need to turn in your shield. Martini removed a notebook from his coat pocket and opened it. He was a nice-looking man, with high cheekbones and a flush to his cheeks and a crew cut that had started to recede. He seemed to study the notebook, then gave up the pretense.

"I don't blame you for your feelings," he said. "I have a teenage daughter. I don't think I could handle it if she were abducted by a predator. I don't know how any parent does."

"You're sure the two girls are with him?" I said.

"The older one, Kate, was scheduled to be at work at Dairy Queen at six. She didn't show up. Lavern was supposed to go to a birthday party this evening. There're some messages for her on the phone. Truth is, we don't have a clue about this guy's where-abouts. Why do you think he didn't kill the girls inside, when he had the chance?"

"A friend of mine thinks he's going into meltdown and planning to take it out on the girls."

"Why's he going into meltdown?"

"Felicity Louviere is stronger than he is, and he knows it."

Clete Purcel was talking to a sheriff's detective by a cruiser. The agent watched him curiously. "I think you guys are operating as vigilantes, Detective Robicheaux," he said. "I think you plan to cool out Surrette."

"That's news to me."

"A guy with the AG's office in New Orleans says Clete Purcel may have poured liquid Drano down a Nazi war criminal's throat."

"I wouldn't believe everything I hear down there," I replied.

"The guy says you were probably there when it happened."

"Some days I think I have Alzheimer's."

"Maybe you ought to see a doc. Take Purcel with you."

"What for?"

"There's blood in his barf," he said. "Maybe he drank some of that Drano himself."

At eight-fifteen that evening, Gretchen Horowitz went up to Alafair's bedroom. Alafair was working at her desk, wearing jeans and loafers without socks and a man's long-sleeved khaki shirt. Shadows had already started to fall on the pasture and the barn, and the crests of the hills had taken on a golden glow in the sunset. "I was wondering where you were," Alafair said.

Gretchen sat down on the edge of the bed. "I had a visit with Caspian Younger."

"Did Dave tell you what happened at the house up the road?"

"Clete told me. I need to talk to you about something."

"You know about the abduction of the two

girls? They used to feed carrots to Albert's horses."

"Yeah, I heard all about it, Alafair. Did you hear what I said? I've got to talk with you."

Alafair set down the sheet she had been working on and took off her glasses. "You need to rein it in, Gretchen."

"I did a beat-down on Caspian Younger and that ex-detective Jack Boyd."

"Clete already tore them up."

"I thought a second helping wouldn't hurt. My head is bursting. Will you please listen to me?"

"Yes, please *tell* me, whatever it is."

"You don't have to get bent out of shape. Rhonda Fayhee told me she was kept in a basement of some kind. She could hear water lapping against a boat or a dock or a beach. She also heard an airplane taking off and landing, but it was below the level of the window. She heard wind through a lot of trees close by. Here's the last part: Not far away, people were singing a hymn of some kind. Rhonda remembered the words 'Life is like a mountain railroad, with an engineer that's brave.' "

"Those details don't go together very well," Alafair said. "The plane was beneath the level of the window?"

"She could hear water chucking at the same time."

"She was on a hillside by a lake, one big

enough for an amphibian?"

"That's what I would think," Gretchen said. "A lake that has a lot of trees on the shore."

"There are lakes all over this area. Over in Idaho, too."

"She said the wind made a rushing sound in the trees, like they grew everywhere and were thick with leaves."

"An orchard?" Alafair said.

"Yeah, an orchard," Gretchen said. "It's cherry-picking season. Where would that put us?"

"Flathead Lake?" Alafair said.

"I'm glad you said that."

"Why?"

"Because Caspian was bragging about his contacts in Vegas. He said he could have Clete shredded into fish chum. He said there would be nothing left of Clete except a bloody skim floating on Flathead Lake. What does Flathead Lake have to do with Vegas?"

"He had the lake associated with Surrette's previous involvement with the casinos?"

"It's a possibility," Gretchen said.

"It's more than that," Alafair said.

"There's something else. Caspian Younger told Bertha Phelps where his father was."

"You lost me," Alafair said.

"Wyatt Dixon is Love Younger's illegitimate son. His stepfather treated him terribly. Who do you think Dixon blames?"

"Dixon is going to do something about it?"

Alafair said.

"Maybe."

"You're wondering if you should warn Love Younger?"

"Yeah, I am. What would you do if you were me?" Gretchen asked.

"It's their grief."

"That simple?"

"Wyatt Dixon can take care of himself. Love Younger is a professional son of a bitch and would be the first to tell you that."

Gretchen stood up. "Want to take a ride up to the lake?"

"Let me tell Dave," Alafair replied.

Wyatt Dixon was standing shirtless and barefoot in his kitchen up on the Blackfoot, a ring of fire glowing around one of the lids on his woodstove, where he had set his coffeepot to boil. Through the side window, he could see the boughs of the cottonwoods swelling in the wind down by the riverbank, the trout starting to rise and dimple the riffle under the steel swing bridge. Through the screen, he could smell the evening as though it were a living presence, the purple and yellow flowers in his yard and the dark green wetness of the fescue part of a song that was never supposed to die. Except he could feel things ending, coming apart at the center, and he didn't know why.

"You went up to Younger's place, didn't

you?" Wyatt said.

"I was looking for you. I didn't know where you were," Bertha said.

"Was the old man there?"

"No, he was not."

"That twat of a son was, though, wasn't he?"

She looked away, her eyes full of injury.

"He did something to you?"

"I won't lie about it."

"He put his hand on you?"

"I said I wouldn't lie about it, but that doesn't mean we should fall into his trap," she replied. "I hate the Youngers. I hate what they've done to you."

"Tell me what he did, Bertha."

"I was going out the door. He kicked me. He laughed when he did it, too."

The coffee had started to boil. Wyatt removed the top from the pot and fitted his palm through the handle. He lifted the pot to his mouth and drank, his face as expressionless as a leather mask, his pupils like dead flies trapped in glass. "Where did he kick you?"

"In the behind."

He looked into space and drank again from the pot, his lips gray from the heat. "He told you where the old man was at?"

"Don't ask me questions you already know the answers to."

"I just want to know where Love Younger is at."

"So you can do exactly what Caspian Younger wants you to?"

He set the coffeepot back on the stove. There was a red stripe across his palm. "Hear it?" he said.

"Hear what?"

"A train. Up on the railroad bed."

"Those tracks were torn up decades ago. There's nothing there except the cliff and an empty rail bed."

"I heard it a-blowing down the line, whistling through a canyon."

"That's the wind."

"No, ma'am, it ain't. I been hearing that whistle all my life. He's at Sweathouse Creek, ain't he?"

"How'd you know?"

"I followed him there once. Love Younger ain't that smart. He sired the likes of me, ain't he?"

He slipped on his boots and stuck his sheathed bowie knife in the back pocket of his Wranglers, then pulled on a long-sleeved snap-button shirt and walked through the clutter of his living room and out the front door.

"I'm coming," she said. "You're not going without me."

He turned and looked at her. Her expression was disjointed, her anatomical construction seeming to disintegrate as she approached, like a digital figure collapsing into a pile of dots. He pushed at his temple with his thumb until his vision seemed to correct itself.

"We're in this together," she said. She took hold of his right arm with both hands and clutched it tighter than anyone had ever held him in his life. "We'll never be apart again. If I have to go with you to the grave, Wyatt Dixon, you hear what I'm saying to you? Don't you ever try to leave me."

Love Younger stood behind his cabin on Sweathouse Creek and stared up at the canyon walls. There were boulders in the canyon the size of a two-story house, even bigger, all of them surrounded by towering trees that grew cheek by jowl against the stone. He could see bighorn sheep up on a ledge, one that was no more than two feet wide. They were working their way toward the summit of the mountain while tiny rocks rilled down from their hooves, over the lip of the trail, falling at least four hundred feet onto the canopy of cottonwoods that grew along the banks of the creek. A slip, a miscalculation, a weak spot in the stone that split under their weight, and they would plummet to their deaths. Yet they never hesitated or showed fear, as though knowledge of the topography had been wired into them. Love

Younger wondered why humankind did not feel the same kind of security. The sun was west of the Bitterroots now, and the air in the canyon had turned cold, and the magenta coloration above the top of the canyon was fading to a dark shade of blue that made him think of a curtain being closed on a stage.

He had taken a black-powder revolver to shoot at targets he picked out randomly along the creek — a wet rock dancing with spray, a wild rose hanging on a green stem over the current, a cedar stump that had decayed into pulp the color of rust. He aimed at all three of these targets but could not bring himself to pull the trigger. There was a stillness inside the entrance of the canyon that felt almost holy. He raised his eyes to the ledge and realized the bighorn sheep had disappeared inside a low-hanging cloud, as though the mountain had provided sanctuary from either his gaze or his firearm. Was that his role in the world? The harbinger of destruction? The twentieth century's representative of a petro-chemical empire staining the ground with the greasy imprint of his shoes?

Maybe this was not a good time to be alone, he told himself. But what merit was there in a man's life if he had to fear solitude? Love Younger had created jobs for hundreds of thousands of workers all over the globe. His pipelines and drilling platforms delivered the oil and natural gas on which the entirety of the industrial world depended. Did any rational person believe he wanted to pollute the earth and incur environmental lawsuits that could cost his companies billions of dollars? Love Younger was a fair man. No one could say he wasn't. The enemy was poverty, not refineries. How many environmentalists had worn clothes sewn from Purina feed sacks when they were children?

For Love Younger, depression was another term for self-pity. He had only one problem: He could not reason himself out of the black box he found himself inside. What was the truth about his life? The truth was, he woke every morning with a bête noire that he crowded out of his mind with sums and debits and concerns about the Saudi bench price on the barrel of oil in the same way a drunkard fills himself with whiskey to avoid acknowledging the catastrophe he has made of his life. The story of Love Younger was simple. He had committed the worst crime of which an ordinary human being was capable: He had destroyed his family.

He set down the heavy Navy Colt .44 on a spool table and waded into the creek. The coldness ran over the tops of his shoes and into his socks with a brittleness that reminded him of drawing water with a bucket from the stream that ran through Snakey Hollow, Kentucky, the place of his birth. As he stared at the long silvery ribbon winding through the canyon, he realized the gleam on the surface he had taken for granted was dying, as though the light were being drawn up through the trees and the canyon walls by the heavens, a shutting down of the day that was more an act of theft than a natural phenomenon.

He wondered what would happen if he began wading up the creek into the crack in the mountains that gave onto the great Idaho wilderness, disappearing inside its gathering shadows, crunching on the soft bed of sand and coppery pebbles that had been polished as bright as pennies. Could he keep going all the way to the top of the Bitterroots, where the snowmelt formed chains of lakes surrounded with miles of velvet greenery on which deer and elk and moose grazed in the sunrise?

Like the deerslayers of pre-Revolutionary America, could he walk all the way to the Missouri Breaks and follow the tributaries and the riparian paths of Indians to the inception point of the Mississippi, then find his way to Louisville and west through the bluegrass to the edge of the Cumberlands? Would his birthplace be changed significantly? Would there be a ragged child there who resembled another impoverished Kentucky child, one born during the first administration of Herbert Hoover? Was there some way to go back in time and undo his mistakes and set a straight path that would make his legacy acceptable in the eyes of others?

He knew these were foolish and vain thoughts, but if a man were contrite of heart, would not a merciful Creator make an exception and return, if only in token fashion, the children who had chosen either physical or spiritual death rather than live under the dominion of their father?

He walked farther up the creek, into a pool up to his knees, where the current was so cold that his shinbones felt as though they had been beaten with wood mallets. Holding on to a tree branch, he kept going deeper into the canyon, pulling himself along the edges of the current until he was up to his thighs and had no feeling at all beneath the dark wet line across his fly. He wondered if this would not be a bad way to go. He would simply keep walking up the creek into deeper and deeper pools until his entire body was numb and he was subsumed by the woods and the wild roses on the banks and the mist boiling at the bottom of a waterfall. *Be my rod and staff,* he thought.

The words angered him. *Am I becoming one of the herd, the nitwits who roll in sawdust at camp meetings and dip their hands in boxes of copperheads? Get ahold of yourself.*

He stepped out of the creek, water draining from his trouser cuffs onto the bank, the wind blowing as cold as an icicle through his thin shirt. He had thought his way through his problems and done what he could. The only concern that nagged at the edge of his conscience was his daughter-in-law, Felicity Louviere. But she was not a Younger. She was the offspring of a professional do-gooder and, from what he'd heard, a profligate working-class girl who had decided to enrich herself by marrying his pitiful son. Her fate had nothing to do with him.

He began walking back down the bank toward the cabin. He could hear bats flying by his head, their leathery wings throbbing, and he remembered how they had frightened him when he was a little boy, at dusk, when the hollow turned into a winter set, no matter what the season. Now he gave them no thought whatsoever, although he was sure some of them were rabid, just as they had been in Snakey Hollow. Why didn't he fear them? The answer to the question was not complex. A king did not die from the bite of a rodent.

He went back inside with his .44 cap-and-ball revolver and hung it in a holster on the back of a wicker chair. Then he went outside again and gathered an armful of wood he had split and stacked under a pole shed. He thought he saw a pickup truck, one with a camper mounted on the bed, wending its way out of the dusk toward him, its headlights jiggling with a strange blue-stained white radiance that Love Younger associated with fairy tales more than he did with motorized vehicles.

Fornicators have to go somewhere, he thought. *In the barn or the woods or on top of a corn-shuck pallet. Nothing will ever stop them from mating and pumping out legions of the same mentally defective creatures the world never seems to tire of. Well, have at it. I hope you have better luck with the product of your misspent seed than I did.*

He started a fire in the stone fireplace. As he stood in its heat, steam rose from his wet khakis, and he felt a sense of tranquillity he hadn't experienced in years. From down below, he heard a vehicle clank across the cattle guard. Was it the fornicators? Or perhaps Caspian's ex-convict security people coming to tell him that Felicity Louviere had been released by the predator from Kansas? He didn't care one way or another.

Love Younger walked to the door, a bourbon and branch water in his hand. He started to turn the doorknob, then paused and glanced over his shoulder at the blue-black walnut-handled thumb-buster hanging from the back of the chair. *What a fine weapon,* he thought. *Kicks like a jackhammer and, in the dark, throws out a six-inch muzzle flash that would make the devil jump. One hundred and fifty-two years old and deadly as the day of its manufacture.* He clicked on the porch light without unlocking the door and pulled aside the window curtain. An orange pickup with a chrome grille was just turning off the dirt road onto Younger's property. A man wearing a starch-white cowboy hat was behind the wheel, his left arm propped on the window, a purple garter snugged around his upper arm. The man in the white hat drove to within fifty feet of the cabin and cut the engine.

Dixon again, Younger thought. *So it's about money after all. They claim they don't want it. They love Jesus and country and their mothers. But it's always about money and then more money, and if they could, they'd all get naked and wallow in it in the middle of a Walmart. Okay, Mr. Dixon, maybe it's time you heard a wrathful voice, since you seem to understand no other kind.*

Love Younger set down his tumbler and pulled open the door, his irritability overriding caution. He was staring straight into the high beams of the truck, his eyes tearing and blind to what might be taking place in the truck's cab.

"Begone, Wyatt Dixon," he said. "Disappear into the primeval soup that bred you, and never let the name of my family issue from your lips."

The wind had dropped, and he thought he

could hear the heat of the engine ticking under the hood.

CHAPTER 35

At 8:47 P.M. the phone rang in the kitchen. Molly picked it up. I could hear a man talking on the other end. Molly cut him off. "Sheriff, why don't you just do your job and stop bothering us?" she said. "I don't want to hurt your feelings, but you're a genuine test of Christian charity, if not a pain in the ass."

Then she handed the phone to me. *Great start,* I thought.

"Can I help you?" I said.

"Agent Martini thinks you and Purcel are concealing information from us," the sheriff said.

Only minutes earlier, Alafair had told me of Gretchen's speculations on the whereabouts of Asa Surrette. "Why would he think that?" I asked.

"Surrette was living within a quarter mile of Albert Hollister's house, but you had no suspicions that he was there. Is that correct?"

"Yes."

"The agent doesn't believe that."

"If I thought Surrette was living up the road, why wouldn't I tell you or the FBI?"

"Because you wanted to bust a cap on him yourself."

"That's ridiculous."

He was silent a moment. "Maybe it is. Here's the second reason for my call. A short while ago Wyatt Dixon caused a disturbance at the truck stop in Lolo. He tried to put air in his tires, but the hose was leaking, and he lost ten pounds of pressure on a tire that was already low. He pulled the clerk over the counter and threw him into a stack of oil cans."

"Why are you telling me this?" I said, growing more uncomfortable.

"Because beating up on clerks isn't Dixon's style. A woman, probably Bertha Phelps, was with him. You have any idea what they might be up to?"

"Dixon knows he's Love Younger's illegitimate son. He may be going to Younger's cabin on Sweathouse Creek."

"How long have you known this?"

"My daughter just told me. She found out from a third party. But all of what I've told you is speculation, Sheriff. How about easing up a little bit?"

"I'll be honest with you, Mr. Robicheaux. Before this is over, I think you're going to be charged."

"With what?"

"I'll check with the district attorney and get back to you. By the way, he was stationed at Fort Polk and hates the state of Louisiana."

"It's not for everybody."

"Is there anything else you've concealed from this office?" he said.

"Surrette may be on Flathead Lake. Somewhere around an orchard, close to the water. Maybe there's an amphibian close by. I'm going up there in a few minutes."

"You're not going to do a goddamn thing, Mr. Robicheaux. I can't express how angry you make me —"

Molly pulled the receiver from my hand and put it to her ear. "Listen, you simpleton," she said. "My husband has dedicated his life to law enforcement. He doesn't need a tobacco-chewing pinhead lecturing him on legal protocol. My husband was also in the shit. Do you know what that means? He's the recipient of the Silver Star and two Purple Hearts. Do not call here again unless you have something worthwhile to say. If you try to harass him again in any way, you'll hear from me." She slammed down the phone, her cheeks flaming.

"I don't think he chews tobacco," I said.

"Whatever," she said.

Wyatt turned off the engine but left the headlights on. There was a silver skull on the tip of his key chain, hollow-eyed and buffed

740

smooth, like old pewter, and it swung back and forth under the dash. When it stopped, he popped it with his thumb and index finger. There was no other sound inside the cab. He looked out the side window and saw lights in the sky.

"You still haven't told me what you plan to do," Bertha said.

"Maybe I'll kill me an old man. I ain't decided yet."

"It won't be prison this time. They'll execute you."

He reached behind him and took the vintage Winchester from the rack and placed the butt on the floorboards, the barrel resting against the seat. He clicked a switch on the headliner that would prevent the interior light from turning on when he opened the door. "This one ain't gonna make the jail," he said. "No matter how it plays out."

"You're breaking my heart, Wyatt."

"There's three thousand dollars taped in envelopes under my dresser drawers. There's a quart jar of silver dollars buried under the rosebush in the flower bed. In my footlocker, you'll find my championship buckle and a Nazi dagger with a pearl handle that's got a ruby swastika set in it. You listening to me?"

"Let it go."

"It ain't me that's doing all this. Time's done run out. When that happens, people ain't got no say in things."

"We can just drive away. Leave the nasty old man to himself."

"I saw some pictures in my mind this evening I ain't told you about. I would have told you before, but I didn't know they was there."

"Pictures of what?"

"Something that happened in a piney woods. It was summertime and real hot inside the trees, so hot I couldn't hardly breathe. I could smell sap running out of the bark. I never been inside a woods that smelled that raw, like the smell that comes off a buzz saw when you run a fresh-cut pine through it. Pap and my mother was there, looking at me. From the ground, I mean. They was both looking up into my face."

"What are you telling me?" she asked, her voice starting to slip.

"I ain't sure. I told them to get up, but there wasn't no doubt they was dead. Somebody made sure of that. In the pictures in my head, I'm fifteen. That's when I left home for Big D, riding on a side-door Pullman. I always knew I was gonna get on that train again. It's been waiting for me all these years."

He pushed down the door handle and started to get out, his right hand clutching the 1892 Winchester. His sheathed bowie knife rested on the dashboard. She held him by the arm. "We have a special thing between us," she said. "Don't let this man take that away."

"I'm gonna fix it so he don't ever hurt nobody again, Bertha. What happens after that ain't in my hands."

"They'll crush us, Wyatt. You know why? Because you're too good for them. They hate and fear a brave man. You don't know you're essentially good, so you keep giving away your power."

The front door of the cabin opened. Love Younger stood in the doorway, squinting into the brilliance of the pickup's high beams. "Begone, Wyatt Dixon," he called out, his teeth baring in the headlights.

Wyatt was no longer listening to the thespian rhetoric of Love Younger. Bertha Phelps reached up on the dashboard and clutched his bowie knife. The blade was thick across the top and eleven inches long, the nickel-plated guard bigger than her cupped hand. "You stay here. Don't you dare try to stop me," she said.

"What do you think you're doing?"

"Saving you from yourself. Paying a debt. Bringing judgment on the wicked. Call it anything you want. But it's going to be over."

She climbed out of the cab, her big rump sliding off the seat, carrying her cloud of perfume with her, the blade still sheathed in its beaded Indian scabbard.

■ ■ ■ ■

Love Younger raised his hand against the glare of the headlights. His eyes were burning, his tear ducts streaming. He brushed at his cheeks with the back of his wrist, almost like a child recovering from an unfair reprimand. The air seemed lit with an oily iridescence that he could reach out and touch. "Who comes there?" he said, feeling like one of the grandiose characters he discovered in the medieval romances carried to the hollow by the bookmobile.

He smelled her before he saw her. The odor made him think of flowers on a warm night. Where had he smelled it before? Down south somewhere, perhaps in the tidewater country, a place where moss-hung oaks and palm trees both grew in profusion and the glory of a failed nation clinked and popped on a flagpole at every sunrise. Then he saw her and the reality that she represented.

He did not know who she was, but he quickly recognized the rage that lived in her face. He had seen it many times over the years and factored it in as part of the long gloomy march from Eden into the land of Canaan. Women were cursed with childbearing and scullery and the back of a man's hand and the wanton breath of a drunkard against the cheek in the middle of the night. Until modern times, many of them died while giving birth, or were haggard and exhausted at forty, with tattered memories of the expectations they had brought to their beds on their wedding night. He had always considered it their misfortune and none of his own.

She flung the sheath off the knife she held in her right hand, the blade as bright and honed as an Arthurian sword pulled from stone.

"You corrupted and destroyed my brother," she said. "His death is on you, not on the serial killer. Now you're fixing to take my man."

"Your brother? What brother?" he said. In his confusion, he tried to answer his own question. The faceless men he had destroyed were too numerous to count. He saw the knife blade rise to eye level, out of the headlights' glare, and wondered how someone he had never met could hate him so much.

"Your dress is purple," he said.

She drove the knife into his chest. He felt its point reach deep inside him, cutting through tendon and muscle, searching out the source of the blood that pounded in his temples and wrists when he was angered, now probing the outer edges of the heart, the steel tip going deeper each time the muscle swelled and receded. Her face was no more than three inches from his, her mouth a tight seam, her eyes burrowing into his, as she forced the knife deeper inside, pinching off the flow of light into his brain, stilling the fury and mire of veins and heart's blood that, for a lifetime, had fed his thoughts and given him the libidinal power of a lion and allowed him to build a business empire that thrilled him as would the jingle of sabers and spurs.

He felt himself slip off her knife blade and fall backward through the open door of the cabin. He could see the Colt revolver hanging on the back of the wicker chair and wondered if he could crawl across the floor and reach up to the holster and pull it loose and raise it and cock the hammer in a last effort to save his life.

"What do you care if I wear purple?" she asked.

It befits royalty and should be worn even by the king's executioner, he tried to say. The words would not leave his throat.

He rolled on his side and tried to crawl toward the chair. Or was he watching himself and the woman from someplace in the rafters, as though he had left his body? He couldn't be sure. He felt her tangle her fingers in his hair and pull his head back, stretching his throat tight, her shadow falling across him like a headsman's.

"Where do you think you're going, Buster Brown?" she said. "I'm not through with you. This is for Bill Pepper."

■ ■ ■ ■

After my aborted conversation with the sheriff, I asked Albert for permission to borrow his M-1.

"What for?" he asked.

"There's a chance we can find Surrette. Gretchen thinks he might be holed up in a place down by the water."

"The lake is twenty-four miles long," he said.

"I won't be able to sleep tonight, thinking about the two girls he took from the minister's house."

He handed me the key to one of the gun cabinets in the hallway. "There's a bandolier full of clips in the drawer under the glass doors. Dave?"

"Yes?"

"Know the worst thing about age? You start thinking you've seen it all, no different from the way you looked at the world when you were seventeen. All this started with me. I brought Surrette here."

"You're wrong about that. All this started when Surrette was born," I said.

"Take care of yourself, boy. Take care of Clete, too," he said.

There was finality in his voice that bothered me. Maybe it was resignation on his part. With the passage of time, we wish to feel we can find the answers to all our problems, but sometimes there are no answers. The minister and his wife had been murdered in their home a short distance from Albert's ranch. The daughters were in the hands of a fiend. And there was nothing we could do about it. How do you resign yourself to a situation like that? The answer is, you don't. You arm yourself with a World War II infantry weapon and a canvas bandolier stuffed with eight-round clips, at least one clip loaded with armor-piercing rounds, and drive up to an enormous alpine watershed in the hope that you can find a psychopath who had outwitted all of us, and by "us," I mean every decent person who wants to see the earth scrubbed clean of men like Asa Surrette.

He had changed all of us. He had taken over our thinking processes, invaded our dreams, and set us against one another. His evil would live on long after he was gone. To dismiss him as a transitory aberration was a denial of reality. Surrette left his thumbprint on the soul in the same way that a stone can leave a bruise buried deep inside the soft tissue of your foot. In the meantime, all we could do was try to save others. In this instance, Felicity Louviere and the two girls from up the road. If I had to, I would knock on every door along the shore of Flathead Lake.

I slung the M-1 and the bandolier over my

shoulder and was almost out the door when the kitchen phone rang again. Molly picked it up, then removed it from her ear and looked at me. "Guess who?" she said.

"Hello?" I said.

"You know where Sweathouse Creek is?" the sheriff said.

"West of Victor?"

"I want you and Purcel here. *Now.* Got it?"

"No, I don't *got* it at all."

"Some rock climbers called in the 911. I want you to see what they found."

"Doesn't Love Younger have a place up there?"

"Past tense. Either get your ass up here or I'll have you charged as an accessory, Mr. Robicheaux. I give you my word on that," he replied. "Tell Purcel the same. I'm sick of you guys."

I truly wanted to abandon all restraint and tell him to go fuck himself, but he didn't give me the chance.

I doubted we had incurred a level of legal jeopardy that would allow the sheriff to charge us as accessories in a crime, but Clete and I did as he asked and drove south on Highway 93 to the little tree-lined town of Victor, couched against a backdrop of jagged blue-gray mountains whose peaks stay veined with snow through most of the summer. It had been a long day for the sheriff, and I didn't blame him for his exasperation. The investigative process taking place in front of Love Younger's cabin was one that was altogether too familiar. Law enforcement agencies don't prevent crimes; they arrive in their aftermath. In this instance, the aftermath was one that I think Love Younger never would have anticipated as his fate. Even though I did not like him, when I looked through the doorway, I silently said a prayer that his end had come more quickly than it probably had.

"Watch where you step," the sheriff said. He glanced out the door. "You, too, Purcel. Get in here."

"What's the point in bringing us down here?" Clete said.

"You guys knew Dixon and the woman were on their way to do harm to Mr. Younger, but you didn't inform us until I got ahold of you," the sheriff said. He stepped aside to let a crime scene tech photograph the body on the floor. "How do you like it? Use your phone to take a picture if you like."

"I think I'll go sit in Dave's truck. You mind?" Clete said.

"Is that a revolver under your coat?"

"It's a thirty-eight special. Old-school," Clete said, peeling back his jacket to expose his holster and shoulder rig.

"Do you have a concealed weapons permit?"

"I don't remember," Clete said. "With all

respect, Sheriff, we didn't have squat to do with this. You guys were chugging pud for Love Younger long before we came to Missoula. Don't put your problems on us."

"What did you say?" the sheriff asked.

"You got a weapon, Sheriff?" I asked. "Any forensics that put it on Wyatt Dixon?"

"Not yet," he replied, his eyes leaving Clete's face. "I think whoever did it sat in that stuffed chair over there and wiped the blood on that towel on the floor. I want you to smell something."

"I don't think we can be of any help here," I replied.

"Just hold your water," he said. He walked to the chair and pulled a fringed coverlet off the back and held it up to me. "The place smelled like a perfume factory when we got here. Take a whiff. Recognize it?"

"No," I lied. "I don't."

"It smells like orange blossoms or magnolia to me," he said. "My wife is the expert on flowers. What about you, Mr. Purcel? Does this awaken any memories in you?"

"Sorry, I've got a head cold," Clete replied. He pointed at a leather jacket someone had used to cover a round object on the floor. "Is that the rest of him?"

"Yeah, it is," the sheriff said. "I want both of you to see it." He leaned over and picked up the leather jacket by one sleeve, pulling it loose from the blood that had congealed in

Love Younger's hair. "You guys had no idea Wyatt would do something like this? A man who evidently believed the Youngers sent rapists after his girlfriend?"

Clete nodded as though agreeing with a profound truth. "The VC did that sometimes," he said. "A guy who was genuinely medevac in my recon group did it, too. By 'medevac,' I mean he was nuts, you dig? He rolled a head into a fire where we were cooking a pig. It scared the shit out of us. Then we all laughed. I didn't take any pics, or I'd show you one."

"I want both of you out of my sight," the sheriff said.

Clete's face looked poached in the artificial light, his green eyes neutral and unblinking, puffing air with one cheek and then the other, like a man gargling with mouthwash. The scar that ran through his eyebrow resembled a strip of welted rubber on a bicycle tire. "One of your guys just stepped in Younger's blood," he said. "Too bad Bill Pepper and Jack Boyd aren't still on the job."

Tell me Clete didn't know how to do it.

We drove through Missoula and into the Jocko Valley and onto the Salish Indian reservation. We passed under a pedestrian bridge that had been created out of stone and dirt and trees for big-game animals, and through the tangle of shrubbery and birch trees planted along the retaining wall, I could see the multipointed racks of half a dozen elk crossing right above us.

"One day you and I will come up here and stay at the campground on the Jocko and fish for a week, then head on up to British Columbia," Clete said. "A guy was telling me you can take a dozen twenty-inch cutthroat trout a day on the Elk River. You don't even have to rent a canoe. You can catch a dozen lunkers right off the bank."

"That sounds great, Clete."

"See, you drive into Fernie, and you're into mountains even bigger than these. It's like being in Switzerland, I guess. You could go to meetings. I could do a little roadwork and lighten up on the flack juice and get my weight down. We eighty-six all these bozos. What do you think?"

"Sure," I said. "When we get things squared away here, I'll talk it over with Molly."

"Gretchen and Alf might want to go, too," he said. "Canada is the country of the future. See, places like British Columbia and Alberta give you the chance to start your life over. They do things in a smart way up there."

It would have served no purpose for me to mention the Canadian exploration for shale oil that was destroying whole mountain ranges. Clete had transported himself into a brighter tomorrow in order to avoid thinking about the things we had seen today. If we were lucky, we'd make the trip to Fernie one day, but I knew he would never stop drinking, nor stop eating large amounts of cream and butter and fried food. If we had another season or two to run, we would probably involve ourselves in the same situations we had seen today. If you're wired a certain way, you'll always be in motion, clicking to your own rhythm, all of it in four-four time, avoiding convention and predictability and control as you would a sickness, the whole world waiting for you like an enormous dance pavilion lit by colored lights and surrounded with palm trees. I'm not talking about the dirty boogie. The music of the spheres is right outside your bedroom window. It just comes packaged on a strange CD sometimes.

I checked in with Alafair on my cell phone. "Where are you, kid?" I said.

"What's with the 'kid' stuff again?" she replied.

"That's the way I always talk to my broads," I said.

"Well, lose it, Pops," she said. "We're up by Yellow Bay. The lead on the amphibian plane isn't much help. So far we've seen four of them, spread out all over the lake. There might be more north of us."

"Don't do anything else until we get up there, okay? Let's meet in Polson and start over."

"The clock is running out for those girls, Dave."

The evening star was twinkling in the west. Even though their great bulk was dark with shadow, the Mission Mountains were lit on the tops by streaks of gold that probably reflected off the clouds after the sunset. The world was indeed a glorious place, well worth fighting for. But what kind of place was it for two innocent girls whose parents had been murdered and who were perhaps entombed in a basement, at the mercy of a monster, while the rest of the world passed them by?

"We're on our way," I said. "I love you, Little Squanto."

That had been her nickname when she was a small child. It was borrowed from the Baby Squanto Indian books she had loved, and I seldom used it today. I closed the phone so as not to embarrass her any worse than I already had.

We drove through Ronan and past the Salish Kootenai College and entered Polson, located at the southern tip of Flathead Lake. Alafair and Gretchen were waiting for us by the side of a Dairy Queen that had closed for the night. I could see the great blackness of the lake and a white amphibian moored by an island, rocking in the chop, the cherry trees on the slopes along the lakeshore alive with wind and the flicker of heat lightning. It was part of the chain of glaciers that had slid down into Montana aeons ago, scouring out lakes that contained mountain peaks a few feet under the hull of your boat, as though you were floating through the heavens rather than on top of a lake.

I mention these things for one reason: The setting did not seem coincidental. The topography was primeval. It had been the playground of dinosaurs and mastodons. Some archaeologists believed there had been people here who antedated the Indians, or at least the ones who migrated from Asia across the Bering Strait. Had we somehow allowed Asa Surrette to entice us into a backdrop containing a seminal story encoded in our collective unconscious? Was he hoping to rewrite the final act? The idea sounded fanciful. However, there was a nagging question: Why would a psychopath from Kansas name himself Geta unless he was acutely aware of the name's historical implications and wanted to reach back in time and gather the sand from a Carthaginian arena and throw it in our faces?

Alafair and Gretchen got out of the chopped-down pickup and walked toward us when we pulled into the lot. "Molly is pissed," Alafair said.

"What's wrong?" I said.

"You bagged out and left her," she said.

"I told her where we were going."

"That doesn't cut it, Dave. She was getting her coat, and y'all drove off. She and Albert are on their way."

"Don't tell me that."

"She said she called the FBI and the sheriff. She was in fine form."

"Why didn't she call me?" I said.

"Because she's so pissed off, she's afraid of what she might say?"

"Why'd you bring this?" Gretchen said. She was standing by the bed of my pickup.

"Bring what?" I said.

She lifted up a rusted chain. "The bear trap Surrette almost lured me into," she said.

I looked at Clete.

"I put it in there," he said. "You never know."

"Know what?" I asked.

"When you might need one." He stared out at the black luminosity of the lake, his fatigue and powerlessness clearly greater than any hope he had for the rescue of Felicity Louviere and the two teenage girls.

CHAPTER 36

Asa Surrette did not like electricity. During winter, in the home where he was born, static electricity was always nestled in the house, in the rugs ingrained with dust, on the surface of doorknobs and refrigerator handles and pipes in the cellar, in the touch of another human being's hand. It was symptomatic of a harsh and unforgiving land, of winter winds that could sand the paint off a water tower, of horizons that seemed to blend into infinity.

Nor did he like electricity in the heavens, when it crawled silently through the clouds, flaring in yellow pools that leaped chainlike all the way to the earth's rim, as though there were powers and spirits at work in the natural world that he could never control or understand. He sat in a straight-back chair on the first floor of a two-story stone house that had belonged to a California woman who no longer needed it. That was how he remembered her. She was the California woman who no longer needed things, not even her name. Now he sat in the almost bare living room of her former house, gazing at the light show in the sky, thinking about what he should do next, his fingers hooked under his thighs, his sandy-blond hair hanging in his eyes, a scab the size of a dime glued on his cheek.

He could hear no sound from the basement. He slipped off his loafers and pressed his feet flat against the floor, wondering if he would feel any movement from below or the vibrations of a voice, even a whisper, through the wood. It wasn't impossible. Not for him, it wasn't. When he was in twenty-three-hour lockdown, he had come to believe he possessed not only a third eye but sensory powers that went far beyond the skills blind people developed out of necessity. That said, he had to keep his ego in check. His IQ and the classics he had read and his study of people and their weaknesses gave him a tremendous sense of confidence in his dealings with others but made him vulnerable. Excess confidence could lead him into entanglements with women, all of whom carried elements in their emotional metabolism that were like a drug.

Women were devious and alluring by nature, the sirens who waited on the rocks, their breasts bare, beckoning with their pale arms for the ship to sail just a little closer, through the froth of a wine-dark sea, their teeth white and their lips opening like purple flowers.

He did not like these images. They alarmed and attracted him at the same time, not unlike the smell of opium burning, or the smell of men in a steam room, or the happy cries of children playing in a park. Each of these things was a thorn inside a rose, and when he tried to think through the connections, nothing made any sense, and he felt a sense of anger and impotence that made his nails cut into his palms.

He was having other problems: his posture in a straight-back chair and the way he unconsciously gripped its undersided. The prison psychiatrist had latched on to that one — after he caught Asa Surrette spitting in his coffee cup when he stepped out the door for a minute. He said Surrette's body language indicated the residual stress and anger and rebellion characteristic of people who went through severe toilet training. The psychiatrist became enthused by his own rhetoric and began to riff on the subject, enjoying himself immensely. "Some adult children of dysfunctional parents, people such as you, Asa, were probably strapped down for hours, usually by the mother. Do you have any memories of her giving you enemas? You don't need to repress those memories anymore. Are you feeling anger about these things? You can be honest here. Oh, excuse me, you're not angry? Then why is your face so heated? Did your mommy reward you when you went poo-poo?"

Asa Surrette decided he might return to Kansas and visit his old friend the psychiatrist when this Montana situation was resolved. Maybe fix him a cup of coffee he wouldn't forget.

Right now he had to unload ten bags of crushed ice, each weighing thirty pounds, from the Mercedes SUV that the California woman didn't need anymore. The Mercedes was parked in the garage, down by the lake. And the woman from California was parked three feet under the dirt in the cherry trees next to the garage, may that loudmouth tub of lard rest in peace.

Few people realized how easy it was to take others under your sway. A kind word at the supermarket, a tip of the hat, a show of sympathy at a funeral or after a 12-step meeting, that's all it took if the situation was right and the target was trusting and needy.

Introspection was a luxury he could not afford at the moment, and the foibles of the *folk* had nothing to do with the problems dropped on him by Felicity Louviere. She was slipping away from him, about to be saved by mortality, the very weapon he had always held over the heads of his victims. She'd even thanked him for her pain. How sick was *that*?

He stood up in the bareness of the room. Even though the house was built of stone, it seemed to swell with the force of the wind sweeping down from the mountains to the north. *I'm your master and unto me your knee will bend,* he heard himself saying. *I have powers you cannot imagine. I can reach into the grave and extract your soul and make you my handmaiden for eternity. The choice will be mine, not yours. You will not reject me. Do you not understand that, you stupid woman?*

He realized he was grinding his molars. His words seemed pretentious and self-mocking. "Damn her to hell," he said under his breath, and wondered if anyone had heard the fear in his voice.

We started up Eastside Highway and stopped at eleven P.M. down by the shore. We woke up people, confused most of them, and probably frightened some. It was late, and I could not blame them for their reaction. We had no legal authority there, and the implications of our questions were not the kind anyone would want to deal with on a Sunday night. Flathead Lake and its environs were supposed to be a safe harbor from the problems in the rest of the country. The residents kept looking beyond us into the darkness, unsure who we were and yet fearful that we were telling them the truth. How do you explain to people who are basically good and trusting that their lives are predicated on an enormous presumption, namely, that the justice system works and that evil people will be prevented from coming into their lives?

Surrette could be dismissed as a psychological monstrosity whose mother would have been better off raising a gerbil. Here's the rub: He's not the only one. If you've ever been inside, either as a correctional officer or as an inmate, you know what "con-wise" means. The majority of people who stack time, male and female, are not different from the rest of us. They have families and work histories and skilled trades and are surprisingly patriotic. Some of them have remarkable levels of personal courage and are stand-up in an environment that would break a lesser man or woman. Most of them are also screwups. In other words, they belong to the family of man, even if only on its outer edges.

But ask anyone who has been inside about the bunch in permanent lockdown. These are the ones who scare you, even when they're draped with waist and leg chains, and they scare you because looking into their eyes assures you they love evil for its own sake. Talk to the trusties who mop the floors in the lockdown unit and wheel the food cart from cell to cell. They do not make eye contact. Nor do the correctional personnel who sometimes have to enter a cell with body and face shields and cans of pepper spray and sometimes, like anyone who has witnessed a state execution, need to stop at a bar before going home that night.

Here is the most bothersome part about the men in permanent lockdown: They can hear each other's thoughts. They network; they exchange kites with pieces of string the way pen pals might; they share stories that could have been invented by a medieval inquisitor. They're shunned and reviled by the rest of the prison population, but among themselves, they rejoice in their iniquity. Check out the video of Richard Speck getting stoned in a cell with some of his buds, his naked breasts enlarged by hormones, while he makes a joke about the nurses he raped and murdered.

Halfway up the lake, my cell phone chimed. It was Molly.

"I'm sorry we took off," I said. "I thought you understood that the sheriff wanted to see us before we headed up to Flathead Lake."

"Do you think I'm going to allow my family to expose themselves to risk without my being there?" she replied. "Is that what you think of me, Dave?"

"No, I don't."

"Then why did you leave me behind?"

In my frustration, I took the phone away from my ear, then replaced it. "Maybe I didn't want you to see something."

"Like *what*?" she said.

"Maybe Surrette's not going to be around much longer."

"I don't like what you're suggesting."

"That's the way it is."

"No, it is not. We don't do things that way."

"Where are you?" I asked.

"We just passed a marina. I didn't catch the name. There's a house down the slope with a couple of junk cars in the yard. There's a shed with an auto repair sign on it."

I had no idea where she was.

"Let me call you back," she said.

"No, listen to me —"

She broke the connection. I tired to redial, but we had gone around a curve on a high spot above the water and had lost service.

"She'll be all right," Clete said.

"Albert is with her."

Clete scratched his cheek. "I guess that's a little different."

I was trying to concentrate. I had missed a detail in Molly's conversation. What was it?

Clete put his hand on the wheel. "Watch where you're going. There's an eighty-foot drop on the other side of that rail."

"The wrecker," I said.

"What wrecker?"

"See if you can get the sheriff on the phone," I said.

"Are you kidding? I can't stomach that guy."

"For once, don't argue, Clete," I said. "Can you do that? I know it's hard. But try. I'm sure you can do it if you work on it."

"Who lit *your* fuse?"

A tractor-trailer rig passed us in the other direction, then a truck pulling a camper and what looked like a Cherokee. Up ahead, I saw Gretchen's brake lights go on. I followed her to the bottom of the grade and into a parking area by a guardrail overlooking the water. It was almost midnight, and the heat lightning had drained from the clouds and disappeared in a dying flicker beyond the mountains. Small waves were capping on the lake, slapping the beach with the dull regularity of a metronome.

Gretchen stepped out of her pickup. "Did you recognize the guy in the Cherokee?" she said.

"I didn't pay any attention," I said.

"I think it was Jack Boyd," she replied.

"Are you sure about that?"

"I should be. I kicked his ass today," she said.

"I got the sheriff on the line," Clete said.

Felicity's eyes had been bound when he laid her down on the bedsprings and secured her hands and feet to the four bedposts. She assumed the electric current came from a wall socket, but she could not be sure. The first jolt knocked her unconscious. When he threw

766

water on her and shocked her again, she heard a grinding sound inside her head that could have been a generator or the vibration of the bedstead against the concrete floor.

There were interludes when he went away, stomping as he climbed the wooden stairs, not unlike a resentful child. While he was gone, she drifted in and out of consciousness and experienced dreams or hallucinations she could not separate from reality. He had gagged her and left a window open, probably to clear the air of the sweaty odor that seemed painted on the basement walls. At first she thought she heard the wind blowing through a copse of thickly leafed trees; then she realized the sounds were not leaves rustling together but the voices of human beings, many of them talking at once, creating a drone that made her think of a beehive.

The cotton pads taped over her eyes admitted no light, but she believed she could see tropical plants and flowers and palms, and she wondered if her ordeal had not bought her passage to the place where her father had died among the Indians in South America.

All her anger toward her father had disappeared. She wanted to reach out and touch his fingers and tell him that her life had not been bad after his death. She wanted to tell him that she had gotten by on her own, and she was proud of the sacrifice he had made for others, and that as long as he was in the basement with her, no harm would come to either of them.

Then she realized she was not in touch with her father. Instead, she was in an arid country where date palms grew along the roadways and the stone in the amphitheater was hot enough to scald the hands of the spectators in the noonday sun, and the only shade was over the box where Roman nobility sat.

Her warders had been Nubians who were so black, there was a purple shine on their skin. They herded her and her companions with spears from the dungeon below the seats into the brilliance of the day, and only then did she smell the blood that had dried in the sand and see the array of executioners with trident and flagellum and gladius and a metal-sheathed instrument she had not seen before.

They're going to scrape you first, a voice whispered close to her ear. *Then you'll be given a chance to reconsider. A flick of incense on the fire, and you're free.*

I won't do it, she answered.

Many of the others have. Are you too proud? Do you think you're special?

Yes.

Don't mock me. I can hurt you very badly.

I want to die.

Not really. You think you're better than others. Your pride wants to live. You'll beg. I guarantee it. Here's another little reminder of reality.

She knew the pain had driven her mad. She didn't care. The next shock was so great, it seemed to rattle the entire room.

I took the cell phone from Clete's hand. The moon was down, and the lake looked as dark as oil. "What are you guys into now?" the sheriff said.

"The gumball who was killed up here, what's-his-name, he was dragged by a wrecker?" I said.

"The gumball? You're talking about Kyle Schumacher?"

"I don't remember his name. He was down on a child molestation beef of some kind in California."

"What about him?"

"He was dragged by a wrecker, wasn't he?"

"We're not sure. There was only one witness, a man driving back from a bar. He was pie-eyed when he called 911."

"Did you find the vehicle that dragged him?"

"The sheriff there checked out a place where the killer may have boosted it."

"The killer?" I said.

"Okay, *Surrette*. If he boosted it, he returned it. So we're not sure."

"Thanks," I said.

"Thanks? That's it?"

"Yeah, that's it. We didn't mean to cause

769

you trouble, Sheriff. You got any idea where Jack Boyd might be?"

"What's he got to do with this?"

"Gretchen Horowitz thinks she just saw him go by in a Cherokee. Is that what he drives?"

"As a matter of fact, he does."

"We'll be in touch," I said.

"You guys covered up for Bertha Phelps."

"I didn't get that."

"Her perfume. Both you and Purcel smelled it. It's her logo. You lied about it. I won't forget that, Mr. Robicheaux."

"I think Love Younger got what he deserved. I hope Dixon and Bertha Phelps get away."

"You've got some damn nerve."

"Not really. On my best day, I've never earned more than a C-minus at anything," I said.

My last statement probably didn't make much sense to him, but I couldn't have cared less. I folded the phone and handed it back to Clete.

"Where to?" he asked.

"Molly said she passed a mechanic's shed and some junk cars south of here. Maybe the mechanic has a wrecker service. Maybe that was the wrecker that tore pieces off Kyle Schumacher for two miles down the highway."

"Sounds like a long shot, Dave," Clete said.

"Surrette got the wrecker from somewhere.

If not here, where?"

Clete pinched his eyes with his thumb and forefinger and peered down the road. It was completely dark. He looked at the luminous dial on his wristwatch. "What's keeping Molly and Albert?" he said.

They were driving in Albert's diesel truck, one so caked in mud that no license plate or logo was visible. It was the same truck that a number of hunters wanted to put a bullet hole in after he began chain-dragging logs across public roads to block access to the national forest. As he came down a long grade through an unlit area, he ran over a large chunk of rock that had fallen from the hillside. It wedged under the frame, scouring sparks off the asphalt. Albert pulled onto the shoulder.

A Jeep Cherokee approached from the opposite direction, the driver not bothering to dim his high beams, slowing down to look into Albert's face as he passed. Then the Cherokee's brake lights went on, and the driver began to back up.

The driver was a dark-complected man. His face was bruised, and there was a strip of white tape across the bridge of his nose. "What the fuck are *you* doing here?" he said.

"Not much. Trying to avoid some of the riffraff that's floated into the state," Albert replied.

Another man was sitting in the passenger seat. He was wearing a black polyethylene raincoat. He leaned forward to get a clear look at Albert. "I asked you a question," the driver said.

"I know you did. I also know who you are. You were fired from your department. Your name is Boyd."

"Maybe you know more than you should," Boyd said. "Maybe you never learned how to keep your nose out of other people's business."

"That's because he's a smart guy," the passenger said. "A college professor. I've seen him."

"This is Terry," Jack Boyd said. "You don't want to meet him."

"Let's go," Molly whispered.

But the transmission was jammed. Albert tried to back up to free it and heard something clank loudly and vibrate through the undercarriage.

"Did I say you could go somewhere?" Boyd said.

"I'll have a look at the problem," Terry said.

"See? You get to meet Terry after all," Jack Boyd said.

Terry got out of the Cherokee and walked to Albert's window. His raincoat was flapping like torn vinyl in the wind. He had a small, tight face and tiny eyes and wore no hat. The hair on his head looked like wheatgrass growing on white stone. "You've been down on the water, snooping around, bothering family people when they're trying to sleep?"

"You need some breath mints, son," Albert said.

"Step out of your truck. You, too, lady."

Albert opened his cell phone. Terry slapped it from his hand. He was wearing a jersey and a pair of navy blue workout pants under his raincoat. He reached into his waistband and lifted a .25-caliber semi-auto into view and rested it on the windowsill. He looked back down the road, his expression relaxed, drumming with his left hand on his wrist. He smiled into Albert's face. "All quiet on the Western Front," he said. "I read books, too. I read one of yours, Professor. I think you should stick to teaching."

"Give me the title and your name and address, and I'll make sure the publisher sends you a refund," Albert said.

"I already wiped my ass with it," Terry said. "Get in the back of the Jeep."

"You'll last about thirty seconds with my husband," Molly said.

Terry was still smiling when he walked to the other side of the truck and dragged Molly from the passenger door, flinging her onto the gravel, the .25 auto tucked inside his waistband again. "I look forward to meeting your husband. But right now it's just me and you. So please don't give me a bad time."

■ ■ ■ ■

Asa Surrette took the gag from Felicity's mouth and the tape and cotton pads from her eyes. He fitted his hand gently under her chin and moved her head back and forth. "Are you awake?" he said.

She wasn't sure. Maybe she was dreaming. She had heard a rattling or cascading sound in the basement, like ice being poured into a large receptacle. She had also heard the girls whimpering. Now there was no sound in the room except the steady breathing of Asa Surrette, drawing air into his lungs like an asthmatic and savoring it as long as he could and releasing it only because he was forced to.

"I taped over the window," he said. "I'm going to turn on the light now. Don't let it hurt your eyes." He pulled a beaded chain on a lightbulb. "See? I put a leaf bag across the window. That way the sunrise won't bother you, and you can rest up, get some extra shut-eye, so to speak."

"Where are the girls?" she said.

"Right over there. They're fine. You know you can't get away from me, don't you? The girls are not really part of the relationship between you and me."

"I'm going to die soon. Then what will you do?"

"Keep you. Over there in the bathtub full of ice. You'll always be mine. At least until I decide to dispose of you. No one will ever know what became of you."

She closed her eyes against the glare of the electric bulb. "You were in my dream."

"I'm flattered."

"You were standing inside a conduit that led through a cloud, blocking the ascent of others. Then you were flung into a place that had no bottom."

"If I were you, I'd be careful about what I say."

"Everyone felt sorry for you. But after you were gone, no one remembered or cared. You weren't worth hating."

He fitted his hand over her mouth, squeezing her cheekbones. "You will not speak to me like this."

"People are coming for you. They're going to put an end to your misery," she said.

"They'd better not find me."

She turned her head. She could see the two girls in a corner. They were inside a wire cage of some kind, the bottom padded with a quilt. "The girls called you Geta," she said.

"That's a name I sometimes use. I think you know why."

"Yes, you have delusions of grandeur."

He went to strike her, then withdrew his hand. A vehicle had just come up the driveway and stopped close to the house, the vibration of its engine coursing through the basement wall.

I called Molly on her cell phone, but it went directly to voice mail. We drove south along the lakeshore, with Alafair and Gretchen behind us. Almost all the houses on the lake were dark. We went over a rise and down the other side and saw an auto repair sign on a shed near some junker cars. There was a cottage close by, the lights off. I turned my truck's spotlight on the yard. The lawn was uncut, the front porch of the cottage blown with leaves and pieces of newspaper, the screen door flapping. I moved the beam across the property until it fell upon a blue wrecker parked by a barn.

"Looks like nobody has been there for a while," Clete said. "Surrette might have taken this wrecker because he knew it wouldn't be missed. Maybe he's holed up not far away."

I thought Clete was right. The problem was, I couldn't stop thinking about Molly and Albert. I didn't have Albert's cell number; I wasn't sure he had one. I tried Molly again. No luck. Clete knew what I was thinking.

"Dave, Gretchen can't be sure that was Jack Boyd in the Cherokee," he said. "Besides, what are the chances of Boyd recognizing Albert and Molly on the highway?"

"Then where did they go?"

"Maybe they saw something on a side road

and pulled off."

"Why would she turn off her cell phone?"

"She probably lost service. This is a lousy area for cell phones."

We were on the shoulder of the road, looking down over the tops of cherry trees at the shadows playing on the cottage and the mechanic's shed. The moon had come out from behind the clouds, and farther down the shore, I could see a two-story house constructed of what appeared to be yellowish-gray stone. There was a marina by the lake and a number of sailboats rocking in their berths. I looked in the rearview mirror. Gretchen and Alafair were parked behind us, the engine running.

"I've got to find Molly," I said.

"Okay, big mon," he said. "Let's go do that."

CHAPTER 37

Asa Surrette climbed the stairs to the first floor and looked out the side window at the driveway. He couldn't believe his eyes. He jerked open the side door. "Have you lost your goddamn mind?" he said.

Jack Boyd and one of Caspian Younger's security men were herding Albert and a woman inside. "They were onto you, Asa," Boyd said.

"What do you mean, they were 'onto' me?"

"Why else would they be here?"

"A thousand reasons, you stupid shit. Do you realize what you've done?"

"It was a judgment call," Boyd said.

"What happened to *her*?" Surrette said.

"She fell on the gravel when Terry was helping her out of their truck."

"That's your name? *Terry?*"

"It was when I woke up this morning."

"Who am I?" Surrette said.

Terry flexed his neck. "I'm not big on names. I hear you're a guy who leaves a big footprint."

"You don't know the half of it," Surrette said.

"Where do you want these two?" Terry said.

Surrette could hardly contain himself. "Where do I want them? I want them on the moon. But that can't happen, because you've brought them into my house." He looked into Albert Hollister's face. "Remember me? Wichita State University, 1979?"

"Hard to say. I remember a pervert in my seminar who wrote a short story that was artless and filled with misspellings. Was that your work?"

"Love Younger is dead," Boyd said.

Surrette looked at him, blinking, not sure what he'd heard.

"Somebody cut off his head. It was probably Wyatt Dixon," Boyd said. "It was on the news."

"Where's Caspian?"

"Probably cleaning out his old man's accounts," Boyd said.

Surrette's lips were crimped, his eyes busy with thought, his breathing loud enough to echo in the room.

"Think your meal ticket is about to blow Dodge?" Boyd said.

"What's that?"

"Nothing," Boyd replied.

"Where's Wyatt Dixon?" Surrette said.

"How would I know?" Boyd said. "Who

cares? The guy's nuts."

"He knows who I am," Surrette said.

"Everybody knows who you are. What are you talking about?" Boyd said. "Oh, he knows about your mission or whatever? That biblical crap on the cave wall?"

"Take them down to the basement," Surrette said, breathing through his nose.

Molly was sitting in a chair by the door. She clutched a wadded tissue speckled with blood. "My name is Molly Robicheaux," she said. "I saw the death squads at work in Guatemala and El Salvador."

"Is that supposed to mean something to me?" Surrette asked.

"They had your eyes," she said. "They always smelled of alcohol when they came into the village. They never spoke in any voice except a loud one. They chose their enemies carefully — innocent villagers who had no weapons. You remind me of them."

"Take them downstairs, Jack, and don't try to think," Surrette said. The heat seemed to go out of his face. He smiled. "No judgment calls."

"Sure," Boyd said. "I'm with you all the way. You know that."

"What do you want me to do?" Terry said.

"I'll tell you when I'm ready. In the meantime, there's no need for you to speak."

Albert looked at Boyd and Terry. "I got a question for you fellows," he said. "Do y'all think this man is going to let you walk away so you can extort him down the road?"

"Asa is a kidder. He knows who his friends are," Boyd said. "You bet on the wrong horse, old-timer."

There was a beat. Terry was silent, his concentration turned inward, as though he were examining a flyspeck inside his head.

"Right, Asa?" Jack Boyd said. "Mr. Hollister shouldn't be placing any bets in Vegas, should he? You got any snacks in the refrigerator? I'm starving."

We drove back up the two-lane, slowing at the driveways that led down to the houses on the lake or up the hillsides through the cherry orchards. We went over a rise and down a long grade into an unlit area where there were no houses and the shoreline was dense with trees and underbrush. In my high beams, I saw a large rock partially broken on the asphalt. It looked like it had been dragged under a vehicle.

"That wasn't there when we went up the road earlier," I said.

"No, it wasn't," Clete said. "Pull over."

I drove around the rock and parked on the north side of it. Gretchen and Alafair pulled in behind me. Up ahead was a dirt road that cut back up the hillside and disappeared inside trees tangled with vines and shrubbery. "Did you guys see this rock earlier?" I said.

"No, it wasn't here," Alafair said. She picked it up and set it on the shoulder. "Somebody ran over it. See the powdered spot about ten yards back?"

I took a flashlight from the glove box and walked to a dirt road that angled back up the hill. Stenciled in the dirt were the fresh tire tracks of a heavy vehicle. I shone the flashlight's beam on a bend about forty yards up the grade. At first I saw only the trees and their shadows moving in the wind; then the beam reflected off a bright surface, perhaps a bumper or a windshield or a strip of chrome.

I walked up the incline. The behemoth-like outline of Albert's diesel rig, sheathed in dried mud, was unmistakable. Whoever had left it there had backed it up and parked it with the engine pointed downhill. "Up here!" I shouted at the others.

There was nothing in the cab, no keys in the ignition, no signs of a struggle. But I knew my wife. She was not only intelligent and brave, she never went with the flow. I opened both doors of the cab and searched under the seats and behind them and in the glove box. I knew that somewhere, somehow, Molly had left me a message.

"Call it in, Clete," I said.

"You know what those cocksuckers are going to say, don't you?" he replied.

"Yeah, I do, but call it in anyway," I said, feeling down in the seats.

"It'll take at least a half hour for them to get a guy out here. Then he'll tell us to file a missing persons report."

"I know that. Just make the call," I said.

"Then wait for somebody to show up? I say fuck that."

I took out my cell phone and started to punch in 911.

"All right, I'll do it," Clete said, walking off with his phone to his ear.

I had found nothing in the cab. My heart was beating, my eyes stinging with moisture even though the night was cool. *Where are you, Molly?* I thought. I stood erect and closed the passenger door. *Where could she have left a clue? It's there someplace, I know it, I know it, I know it.* I turned in a circle. *On the truck itself,* I thought. I shone the flashlight on the door. There it was, right in front of me, two initials on the outside panel. She had probably hung her arm out the window and used her thumb to furrow the letter J, then the letter B, in the muddy splatter that had dried on the panel.

"You were right about Jack Boyd, Gretchen," I said. "He's got them. How bad did you work him over?"

"I did as much damage to him as I could in the time that I had," she answered, holding

783

her eyes on mine.

And Molly will pay the price, I thought.

"Did you say something?" she asked.

"No," I said.

"They can't be far away, Dave," Alafair said.

I wasn't so sure. Maybe Boyd or Surrette had a boat. Maybe Boyd had gotten past us on a dirt road up the hill. Maybe he had changed vehicles. We needed the state authorities. We needed roadblocks. We needed a police helicopter with a searchlight. We needed all the things I would have had access to as a police officer in the state of Louisiana. Our credibility with the locals was zero.

I had more information in my head than I could think about. Surrette was holed up in a place that had a basement. It was within earshot of a bay where amphibians landed and took off. Someone had held a revival or prayer meeting not far away. But where? The area was full of fruit pickers in the summertime, and they brought their hymnbooks and open-air churches and came and went with the wind.

"The marina," I said.

"Yeah?" Clete said, flexing his right hand at his side.

"Rich guys own sailboats. They also own amphibians."

"They don't necessarily own both," he replied.

"The marina has a bar. It's a small one.

784

But it stays open until two," I said.

"How do you know?" he asked.

Because it's what I think about all the time. "I saw it when Alafair and I were waterskiing once," I replied.

It didn't take us long to get to the marina, but we were running out of options and time. I wished I hadn't alienated Sheriff Elvis Bisbee. I wished I had not contended with Alafair when she said Surrette had survived the collision of the jail van and the gasoline truck. I wished I had accepted Wyatt Dixon's belief that Surrette represented a mindless form of evil that seemed to have neither genetic nor environmental origins. I wished I were not so powerless with adversaries like the Youngers and others whose imperious vision of the earth is seldom challenged.

Did I learn anything from sorting through the history of our relationship with Asa Surrette? No, not at all. At a certain point, I would come to a personal conclusion about who he was or who he wasn't, but it would not be one that I would share. Why is that? Because some things are unknowable, such as the origins of evil.

In the meantime, I wanted to see Surrette and his minions body-bagged and dumped ignominiously in a potter's field.

There were light poles on the docks at the marina, and moths swarmed around them and sometimes dropped in the water. Most of the sailboats in the slips were dark, their hulls rocking, their mooring ropes tensing against the chop. The bar had a counter with six stools, and a table where a chessboard had been set up. The bartender looked at his watch when we walked in. He was young and tan, wearing a yellow muscle shirt, probably a swimmer rather than a weight lifter. MYSTERIOUS GALAXY BOOKSTORE, SAN DIEGO, CA was printed on the back of his shirt. "I was going to close a little early tonight," he said.

"Know a guy named Jack Boyd?" I said.

"He keeps a boat here?" he said.

"I doubt it."

"I don't think I know him. What's the deal?"

"Any pontoon planes land around here?" Clete said.

"Some Hollywood guys flew in for the weekend. They left this morning."

"You know about the guy who got dragged down the Eastside Highway?" Clete asked.

"Who doesn't?"

"We're looking for the guy who did it."

The bartender looked past us at Gretchen and Alafair. "I don't want to be rude, but I don't think you guys are cops, and I don't know why you're asking me questions."

I opened my shield. "My name is Dave Robicheaux. I'm a sheriff's detective in New Iberia, Louisiana. This is Clete Purcel. He's a private investigator there. This is my daugh-

786

ter, Alafair, and her friend Gretchen. We'd appreciate any information you can give us."

There are two pieces of advice I've received in my life that I have never forgotten. The first came from a line sergeant who had been at Heartbreak Ridge. My third day in Vietnam, I was ordered to go down a night trail deep inside Indian country and set up an ambush. It was a night trail that was probably salted with Chinese toe-poppers or 105 duds strung with trip wires. The sergeant read the fear and uncertainty in my face the way you read contour lines on a topography map. "Here's the key, Loot," he said. "You never think or talk about it before you do it, and you don't think or talk about it after it's over."

The other piece of advice came from a corrupt and thoroughly worthless Teamster official in Baton Rouge, a man whose voice box had been eaten away by cigarettes and whiskey. He said, "It ain't about money, Robicheaux. It's about respect. That's what every workingman and -woman on this planet wants. Anybody don't know that should have a telephone pole kicked up his ass."

I gazed up the slope at the orchards blowing in the wind and the two-story house constructed of yellowish-gray stone slabs and the mechanic's shed and several concrete trailer pads that seemed to be no longer in use.

"Who lives in the stone house?" I asked.

"A lady from Malibu," the bartender said. "Or she *did* own it. She used to come in here and stay late, know what I mean?"

"Where is she now?"

"I heard she went back to her husband or something. A lot of California people come out here but don't stay. We call it the Banana Belt of Montana, but ten-below weather is a hard sell."

"This isn't ten-below weather," Clete said.

"The lady had problems. She'd go off with guys I wouldn't want to hang with."

"Which guys?"

"Guys on the make, guys trolling for older women," he said. "Anybody who's in a bar at two A.M. has a problem. Know what the problem is?"

"He doesn't have a home or family to go to," I said.

Outside the window, I could see the moths fluttering in the electric glow of the light poles and dropping into the water, their paperlike wings dissolving in the black shine of the waves. I could feel my energies draining, my concentration slipping.

"Can I fix you guys something?" the bartender said.

"Do you ever have any revivals or outdoor prayer meetings hereabouts?" I said.

"Funny you ask," he said. "Some of the migrants have gatherings at that old trailer park there."

"They're Hispanic?" I said.

"Maybe the ones who have Saturday-night vespers are. But there's a bluegrass bunch that really rocks. In winter, I play in a band in La Jolla. I'd like to take a couple of those guys with me."

I waited, giving him no lead, avoiding any hint of what I wanted to hear him say. I heard Alafair and Gretchen step closer to the counter. "They're pretty good, huh?" I said.

"When they sing 'The Old Rugged Cross,' it'd make an atheist weep."

I nodded.

"You know the old union song 'A Miner's Life Is Like a Sailor's'?"

"I do," I said.

"It comes from a song titled 'Life Is Like a Mountain Railway.' These guys can really do it."

"Son of a bitch," Clete said.

"What did you say?" the bartender asked.

"Not you, buddy," Clete said. He jabbed his finger at the air, indicating the darkened two-story house down the shore. "That's got to be it, Streak," he said. "We take these motherfuckers off at the neck, and we do it now. No thinking about it, no looking back. Full-throttle and fuck it, right?"

"Roger that," I said.

"Who are you guys?" the bartender said.

"The Bobbsey Twins from Homicide," Clete said. "You didn't know that?"

"The *what*?" the bartender said.

"Hey, handsome?" Gretchen said.

"What?" the bartender said.

"You're a nice guy," she said. "You've done your part. We've got it covered. We'll take care of the phone calls. Okay?"

"Yeah, I guess," he said.

"I like your muscle tone. Maybe I'll check back with you later. Keep a good thought," she said. She winked at him.

He looked at her with his mouth open.

Molly and Albert were sitting on the basement floor, their wrists tied behind them with wire twisted around a water pipe. Against the far wall, Molly could see a woman spread-eagled on a box spring, a sheet draped over her body. Behind a boiler, two girls were sitting in a wire cage. They were huddled against each other, their knees drawn up before them. Next to the cage was a ladder extending through a trapdoor in the ceiling. In another corner, she could hear Jack Boyd pouring liquid from a big white plastic jug into one of two washtubs set side by side. When he finished, he set the empty jug on the floor and took another one from a wall shelf. Boyd appeared to be holding his breath while he poured, his face pinched against the acidic stench.

Asa Surrette had come down the stairs twice to look at the woman on the box spring, placing his fingers on her throat to feel her pulse, staring into her face for a long time before returning to the first floor.

Terry came down the wood steps and watched Jack Boyd filling the second washtub. He glanced over his shoulder at Molly and Albert, then looked at Boyd. "Your man up there has a frontal lobe missing," he said.

"Tell me something I don't know," Boyd replied.

"He just told me what we're doing."

"You want to give me a hand here?"

"I got sinus problems." Terry gazed into the shadows behind the boiler. "Jesus Christ, there're some kids in a cage back there."

"Get with the program, Terry. Surrette has his own universe. One day he'll disappear inside it. In the meantime, keep the lines simple."

Terry lowered his voice and hunched his shoulders, as stupid people do when they don't want others to hear them. "He told me to get the electric saw out of the closet."

"Why don't you say it a little louder so everybody can hear?"

"If I wanted to join the meat cutters' union, I'd move to Chicago."

"You bounce a woman off the gravel on her face and all of a sudden you have standards?"

Terry poked a finger into Jack Boyd's back. "Hey," he said.

"Hey, what?"

"Watch your mouth."

Boyd replaced the cap on the empty jug and set it on the floor. "I know your concerns. I'm about to bail myself. Right now we got to do the smart thing. What happens here is on these other people. It might make your stomach churn, but you got to man up sometimes and do what's necessary and then let it go. Got it?"

"He said the woman on the bed is his. He's gonna put her in ice?"

"He's a little weird about Ms. Louviere."

"Ms.?"

"She's a class act."

"Were you on a pad for the Youngers? That's how you ended up working for a geek?"

"I got fired for doing my job. Now it's time for you to do yours," Boyd said.

"They inject in this state."

"It's ten grand a pop for the adults."

"What about the kids?"

"They're not our business."

"My end is ten large for each?"

"You heard me."

Terry rubbed the back of his neck, looking sideways at Molly and Albert. "When do I get paid?" he said.

"No later than noon."

Terry opened a closet door and clicked on the light. Molly saw at least three semi-automatic weapons propped in the corner.

She also saw what appeared to be an armored vest hanging on a wood peg. Terry stood on his tiptoes and removed something from the top shelf. Then he clicked off the light so she could not see what was in his hand.

Clete and I drove from the marina to the two-lane, then south to the next driveway, the one that led down to the auto repair shed and through an orchard to the yellowish-gray house that, in the moonlight and the enhancement of the shadows, seemed to contain the bulk and imperial mystery of an ancient castle. Alafair and Gretchen were right behind us. Our headlights were off. The sky had cleared, and the stars were sharply white above the jagged ridge of the mountains to the north. I felt an ominous sense that I couldn't define, as though all of us were sliding off a precipice. It was not unlike the dream that psychiatrists refer to as a world destruction fantasy, a dream that I had over and over as a child. Clete was bent forward in the passenger seat, staring through the windshield at the house, his jaw flexing.

"I thought I saw a light on the first floor," he said. "It was on, then it went off. Maybe it was a reflection off the lake."

"You see any vehicles?" I asked.

"I can't tell. The cherry trees are in the way. How do you want to play it?"

It was a good question. "We need to confirm we've got the right house," I said.

"He's in there, Dave. I can smell that guy through the walls."

I stopped the truck and cut the engine. Gretchen did the same. The wind was out of the west, and I could hear it rustling loudly through the cherry trees. I could also hear waves lapping on the shore, and I could almost hear the echoes of migrant farmworkers singing an ode about a legendary engineer taking his train through the Blue Ridge and Smoky mountains to a place beyond the stars. All the clues to Surrette's location fitted the place. The only question was whether we should call the sheriff's department.

Clete read my thoughts. "Don't do it," he said. "It will take them two hours or more to pull a team together. They'll either get here too late or screw it up."

Both of us knew that was not the reason for his objection. Clete had decided that Surrette and anyone working with him were DOA. In case I doubted that, he added, "You cut their motors and they go straight down, dead before their knees hit the ground. Bad guys lose; hostages come home. End of story. Listen to me on this, Streak. Molly's and Albert's lives depend on us, not on anyone else."

I heard a popping sound and realized someone was firing bottle rockets over the lake. Alafair walked up to my window. "What's the holdup?" she said.

"This is one we can't make a mistake on," I said. I dropped my eyes to her right hand. "Where'd you get the Beretta?"

"It's Gretchen's. Let's get on it, Dave. You've never met this guy. I have. He needs ten seconds to ruin the life of a human being. Think about that."

I got out of the pickup with Albert's M-1 rifle and the bandolier stuffed full of .30-06 clips. Clete stepped out on the other side, bareheaded, his hair blowing on his forehead. There was an innocence in his face that made me think of the little boy going to the rich lady's house in the Garden District, expecting ice cream and cake and discovering he had been invited there as an object of pity, one of many tattered children whom in reality the rich lady would not touch unless she were wearing dress gloves. He opened the cast-iron toolbox welded to the bed of my pickup and removed a pair of wire cutters and a crowbar. Gretchen came up behind us, an AR-15 hanging over her shoulder, a pair of binoculars in her right hand.

"Did you all see a light inside?" she asked.

"A few minutes ago," Clete said.

"Where?"

"On the first floor, maybe in the living room."

"For just an instant I saw a light at ground level, like somebody had pulled back a curtain on a basement window," she said.

"Hear me out before we start busting down doors. I think Felicity Louviere is dead. Maybe the girls, too. With luck, Molly and Albert are still alive. This is what I think will happen when we go in: Surrette will kill everybody in his proximity, then himself. He's a coward, and he'll die a coward's death at the expense of everyone else."

"What's the alternative?" I asked.

"There isn't one," she said. "I just thought you might like to know what we're looking at."

We walked four abreast down the driveway while someone on a boat or an island in the middle of the lake continued to fire rockets into the sky, all of them bursting into giant tentacles of pink foam high above the vastness of the lake.

I spoke earlier of advice that I had received from others and always remembered. Now I heard a nameless voice repeating an admonition that I had pushed aside, a premise that almost all investigative law enforcement officers never forget. *Crime is about money, sex, or power. If you have the money, you can buy the sex and power. So follow the money.*

The other admonition I had forgotten was from my old friend the line sergeant: *Don't let them get behind you.*

CHAPTER 38

The combination of fear and fatigue and the bruises and cuts on her face had worked like a cancer on Molly's spirit. No matter how hard she tried to hold her head erect, her eyes kept closing and her chin sinking to her chest. She could feel herself slipping away, as though she were dissolving inside warm water, the breakdown of her body becoming its own anodyne, as though a voice were whispering that it was no sin to let the soul depart from the body and be on its way.

Asa Surrette had gone back upstairs, leaving Jack Boyd and Terry in charge.

"Do you fellows know what a fall partner is?" Molly heard Albert say.

"Queer bait on the stroll in October?" Boyd said.

"The guy you get pinched with," Terry said.

"Surrette never had a fall partner," Albert said.

"Meaning he works alone?" Terry said. "What else is new?"

"He's not that smart," Albert said. "But when it's over, he's the only guy left standing. What's that tell you?"

"I know where you're going with that," Terry said. "Look, go out with some dignity, old-timer. Don't start turning dials on the wrong guy and treating other people like they're simpletons."

There was a popping sound, high in the sky. Terry climbed on a chair below the window that was taped over with a black leaf bag. He peeled the bag from the corner of the glass and peered out.

"What do you think you're doing?" Boyd said.

"That noise. It's people shooting off fireworks over the lake."

"Tape up that window!" Boyd said.

"All right, don't shit your pants. I don't want to hurt your feelings, Jack, but I think you're out of your depth. You should stick to taking bribes."

Surrette opened the upstairs door and came down the steps. "What's going on down here? What were you doing on that chair?"

"People are shooting fireworks on the lake," Terry said. "I'm a little tired of the way I'm being talked to, here. I'd like to finish this up and get paid and be on my way, if you don't mind too much. I don't like that stuff with the kids, either."

Surrette approached, his formless suit loose

on his body, his Roman sandals scudding on the concrete floor, a malevolent glow in his face. He took a coil of clothesline from his coat pocket. It seemed to drop like a white snake from his palm as he pressed it into Terry's hand. "So show me what you can do," he said.

"The broad and the old guy?"

"Yeah, you up to it?" Surrette said.

"I'll handle my end."

"Sure you will," Surrette said. "Go ahead, get started."

"The woman on the bed? She keeps moaning," Terry said.

"That's about to end. You dropped the rope. Pick it up."

Terry shook his head. "I'm going back to Reno."

"Walking, are you?" Surrette said.

"I'm saying include me out. I'm DDD on this. Deaf, dumb, and don't know. I got no issue with you. I got no issue with these people. You don't owe me anything. I'm gone. Okay?"

"No, not okay," Surrette said. "Let me show you how it's done. You might develop a taste for it." He walked to the bed and took a switchblade from his coat pocket. He pushed the release button. The blade, seven inches long with the wavy blue-and-white glimmer of an icicle, sprang to life in his hand. Felicity opened her eyes.

"It's time, is it?" she said.

"Maybe," he said.

"Go ahead."

"You really want me to?"

"I do. Untie my hand, please."

"What?"

"I'll help you. You mustn't be afraid."

"*I* shouldn't be afraid?"

"Please. Just release my right hand."

"So you can do what?"

"Touch you."

His mouth moved as though he wanted to smile. "You have things a little turned around."

Her right wrist pulled against the rope. "Please," she said.

"All right, your highness," he said. He gripped the rope and sliced it in half. "Now what?"

She fitted her fingers around his wrist and guided the blade to her breast. "Push it in," she said. "Make it quick."

"Asa! Listen to that noise out there!" Boyd said.

"What noise?" Surrette said.

"Like thousands of people roaring in a stadium," Boyd said.

"That's the wind," Surrette said. "Storms come off the lake almost every night here. The wind makes a roaring sound through the orchards."

"You hear *that*? You call it wind? What the

fuck is it, man?" Terry said.

"I don't hear anything," Surrette said.

"I'm out of here," Terry said.

Surrette started to reply. Then somebody began tapping on the window glass, the one he had blacked out with a leaf bag.

"Can you hear me, Mr. Surrette?" a voice said. "It's Alafair Robicheaux. How have you been? We've surrounded your house and cut your phone line. No police are on their way. The people with me plan to do you great physical injury, but we will not bother your friends. If you release your prisoners, you can live. Otherwise you will die, and probably not at once. Tell us what you want to do."

Surrette's face went white, like a prune that had never seen light, his eyes brightening, his nostrils swelling like a feral animal's.

Alafair remained crouched on one side of the basement window, listening for a response. She stood up and stepped away from the window.

"Could you hear anything?" I asked.

"I think I heard Surrette talking. Maybe Jack Boyd, too. There may be another guy down there, too."

"Did you hear Molly or Albert?" I asked.

She shook her head, her eyes not meeting mine.

Clete had positioned himself at the rear of the house; Gretchen was in the front yard. I signaled to both of them. Clete picked up a scrolled-iron chair from the patio and threw it through the French doors, then broke two windows in back with stones the size of grapefruit that he had picked up from the rock garden. Seconds later, Gretchen flung a flowerpot through the picture window in the living room. Alafair and I moved around to the back of the house, staying close to the walls so no one on the second floor would have an easy shot. There was no sound or sign of movement inside the house.

"I hate to admit this, Dave, but this one has me creeped out," Clete said.

"Why?"

"None of it makes sense. It's like a story written for us by somebody else. Felicity turns herself over to this sick fuck, and now Molly and Albert and those girls are in his hands. One guy can't have this much power and do this much damage."

"Hitler did."

"Bad comparison. They were just waiting for the right guy to come along and tell them it was okay to turn people into bars of soap. Let's call for backup."

"Do it," I said.

He opened his cell phone. "No service," he said.

"Good. He doesn't have any, either," I said. "I don't think Surrette will do too well on his own. You want the M-1?"

He pulled his .38 from his shoulder holster. "No," he said. "Streak, even if he puts a bullet through my brain, I'm going to kill him. But if this is my last gig, I want you to make me a promise. Take care of Gretchen. She doesn't realize how talented and smart she is. She got a crummy deal from the day she came out of the womb, and it's because her old man was a drunk and a bum."

"Don't ever say that, Clete. At least not around me," I said. I could see the pain in his eyes, and I knew he didn't understand what I was telling him. "You're one of the best people on earth," I said. "No daughter could have a better father. You saved Gretchen's life, and you saved my life and Molly's. You changed the lives of dozens of people, maybe hundreds. Don't you ever speak badly of yourself."

His eyes were shiny, his face dilated. "Let's blow up their shit."

"A big ten-four on that," I replied.

Clete kicked the back door once, twice, and on the third try, he splintered the wood from the hinges and the dead bolt and knocked the door in on the kitchen floor. Alafair came in behind us. In the living room I could hear Gretchen raking the glass out of a window frame with a hard object before she stepped inside.

The first floor was completely dark. Through the window, I could see the shadows of the trees moving on the lawn, and waves from the lake sliding up on the lighted sand by the marina. I kept hearing the sergeant's voice inside my head: *Their sappers are the best, Loot. They beat the French with the shovel, not the gun. They're behind you, Loot. They're coming through the grass.*

I felt like someone was pulling off my skin, the way you feel when someone is pointing a gun at you and you're unarmed. Clete was in front of me. He froze and cocked one fist in the air. He turned and pointed two fingers at his eyes, then at a hallway door that was partially ajar.

I couldn't concentrate on what he was telling me. I knew our vulnerability did not lie in the basement; it was behind us. *You follow the money,* I thought. *It's been about money from the beginning. Surrette got rid of Caspian Younger's daughter so Caspian could appropriate the oil lands she would inherit from a trust fund left by her parents. Surrette got rich by killing Angel Deer Heart, and Caspian got free of his father's control.*

I had no doubt that Asa Surrette and Caspian Younger were joined at the hip. I placed my hand on Clete's shoulder. He turned and stared into my face, the lines at the corners of his eyes stretched flat. "We have to take them now," I whispered. "Our back door's open."

Wrong choice of words. He shook his head, indicating that he didn't understand.

"Caspian Younger just inherited his father's empire," I whispered. "He's coming. Maybe he wants to cool out Surrette, too."

"Caspian is a punk. I don't buy it," Clete said.

"He's a *greedy* punk," I replied.

Gretchen approached the door in the hallway from the opposite direction, the AR-15 at port arms, a thirty-round and twenty-round magazine jungle-clipped together and inserted in the rifle's frame. She moved between us and the door. She cupped one hand on the back of Clete's neck and pulled his ear close to her mouth. "I think I heard something upstairs. I'm not sure," she said. "Watch your ass. I'm going down. If I get hit, don't stop. Go over me and clear the basement."

"No," I said to her.

She smiled at me, then opened the door wider with her foot and eased her way down the stairs — fearless, beautiful — a warm odor like flowers brushing past me in the dark.

In only one or two instances have I seen a firefight portrayed realistically in a motion picture. The reason for that artistic failure is simple. The experience is chaotic and terrifying, and the sequence of events is irrational and has no order that you can remember with

any degree of clarity. There is nothing dignified about it. The participants leap around
like the shadows of stick figures dancing on a
cave wall. The instinct to live often overrides
morality and humanity, and any sense of the
former self disappears into a vortex of fear,
pain, and sometimes explosions akin in
volume and heat to train engines colliding
and blowing apart.

Later, images will come aborning in your
sleep that you cannot deal with during your
waking hours: shooting a man who is trying
to surrender; firing an automatic weapon
until the barrel is almost translucent and your
hands are shaking so badly you can't reload;
lying paralyzed on your back in the mud
while a medic straddles your hips as a lover
might, trying to close a sucking chest wound
with a cellophane wrapper from a package of
cigarettes.

It's that intense and that fast, all of it ir-
reversibly installed in your unconscious. To
relive it and try to reason your way out of it
is like trying to reason yourself out of sexual
desire or an addiction to opiates.

The first bursts came from somewhere in
the corner of the basement and chewed away
part of the wall and the ceiling. Then I saw
Gretchen begin firing, squeezing off the
magazine of .223 rounds at a rate of three or
four rounds a second, the brass shell casings
jacking into the light, bouncing on the con-

crete floor.

For Molly, the gunfire within the confines of the basement was deafening and impacted on her skull like a jackhammer. Terry had armed himself first and started shooting at the top of the stairs from behind a concrete pillar. Molly thought she saw Gretchen Horowitz on the steps, firing a semi-automatic rifle, her upper body in shadow, the rounds ricocheting off the pillar, the air filling with dust from the chipped concrete. Albert was trying to raise himself to his knees, the wire rimming his wrists with blood.

Jack Boyd had hidden behind the bedstead, his fingers hooked into the box spring; he was peering over Felicity Louviere's prone body, his face terrified. "I'm unarmed! I'm not part of this!" he cried. "I was working undercover! You're gonna hurt innocent people down here!"

Albert tore one hand from the wire, then began freeing his other wrist. The air was thick with smoke and dust, the bare bulbs on the ceiling jiggling in their sockets. Asa Surrette crawled on his hands and knees to the closet and pulled a semi-automatic rifle with a short barrel and a black stock out on the floor. He reached inside again and pulled out an armored vest and a box of rounds and another rifle and two banana-shaped magazines. He still wore his suit coat and sandals and a pale yellow shirt with long-tailed birds on it, like a man who had just gotten off a plane from Hawaii. "Shut your mouth, Jack, and get in the fight," he said. He slid one of the rifles across the floor.

"Don't listen to what he says!" Jack Boyd shouted at the stairs. "Ask Caspian! I was trying to help!"

"You lying little shit, get in the fight or die now," Surrette said.

Jack Boyd crouched lower behind the box spring, his mouth trembling, his flared sideburns powdered with pieces of brick mortar. "Ask *her*," he said. "I tried to be kind to her. I respected her. She'll tell you that. I'm going to come out now. Don't shoot."

Surrette was on one knee. He began firing at the stairs while Terry reloaded, the rounds splintering wood out of the ceiling, caroming off the stone walls and whanging against the boiler. Surrette rose to his feet and bolted across the basement, smashing the bulbs in their sockets, dropping the room into darkness. "Thought it would be easy, did you?" he said. "You have no idea of the power that lives within me."

Molly would have sworn that the voice she heard was not Surrette's, that it was disembodied and had no human source and rose out of a fetid well that had no bottom.

"Defy me, will you?" Surrette said. "See how you feel one hour from now about the choices you've made. Look upon my works, ye mighty, and despair!"

Gretchen backed out of the staircase. The bolt on her AR-15 had locked open on an empty chamber. She dropped the jungle-clipped magazine from the frame and inverted it and reloaded with the second magazine. She snapped the bolt shut. "Did you hear that guy?" she said.

"Don't be taken in. It's his death song," I said.

Down below, we could hear someone moving about and shell casings rolling across the concrete.

"I'm going outside to get a shot through the window," she said.

"Did you hear that?" Alafair said.

"Hear what?" I asked.

"Upstairs," she replied. She shone a pen-light on the ceiling. "Somebody's up there."

"I heard it, too," Clete said. "I'm going up there. Alafair, go down to the marina and use the landline to call the sheriff's department."

"The marina's closed," she said.

Clete went into the living room. The floor was bare, and I could hear his shoes on the hardwood, then the creak of a banister when he mounted the stairs.

"Can you hear me, Mr. Boyd?" I called into the basement.

There was no answer.

"You can walk out of this, partner," I said. "Maybe it's as you say — you were trying to bring in Surrette and get your badge back. Don't take his fall."

"Dave!" Molly said. "Somebody else is in the house! Asa Surrette is a fiend. Kill him!"

"When this is over, I'm going to take my time with you, bitch," Surrette said.

When Clete reached the landing, he saw two doors on either side, a third directly before him, and an alcove that gave onto a balcony overlooking the lake. He paused, not moving, listening, pointing his .38 snub-nosed revolver in front of him with both hands. He opened the door on his right and let it swing back toward the wall while he aimed into the gloom. There was nothing inside except an exercise machine. He stepped back onto the landing, a board squeaking under his weight, and opened the second door. He could see a toilet bowl, a sink, and a bathtub with a shower curtain. He peeled back the curtain, looking over his shoulder through the open door.

There was water in the bottom of the tub and a layer of grit on the sides. He went back on the landing and eased his way along the wall until he could reach the third door without stepping in front of it. He twisted the knob and gently pushed the door open.

"My name is Clete Purcel. I'm a PI from

New Orleans," he said. "I don't know who you are, but our issue is with Asa Surrette, not anybody else. If you've got a piece on you, slide it out here and let me know who you are."

An odor that was like body grease and moldy towels and unwashed hair and sewage struck Clete's face with such force that he gagged and had to cover his mouth with his hand.

"Are you a prisoner here?" he asked.

He heard a voice that sounded like someone forming words in his throat without being able to hold the syllables together.

"Who are you, buddy?" Clete said. "Are you hurt?"

There was no answer. Clete eased closer to the doorframe, his .38 lowered, his shoulder and arm pressed flat against the wall. Inside the room, he could hear someone breathing with a clotted hoarseness that made him think of a wounded animal cornered in its lair.

"You heard all that shooting down below," he said. "That means other people will be here soon, including paramedics. Everything is going to be okay. Come on out, podjo."

He counted to ten, his throat drying up, his eyes stinging with perspiration. "You want a flash grenade in there? They can really mess up your ears. Come on, bud, this is a pain in the ass for both of us."

811

Whoever was in the room was not going to cooperate. Was this how it was going to end, confronting a barricaded suspect, someone he had never seen or against whom he held no grievance? Clete took a breath and gripped the .38 with both hands, his back and massive shoulders pressed tightly against the wall. *Showtime, motherfucker,* he thought. Then he swung himself into the doorway, his arms stretched straight out in front of him, his snub-nose aimed in the face of a man who had the physical proportions of a steroid addict, whose wide-set eyes and long upper lip were the classic signs of fetal alcohol syndrome, whose cheeks were covered with a soft simian pad of hair, whose mouth was twisted out of shape as though made of rubber.

"Throw it away," Clete said. "You've got no reason to be afraid. We can help you. Surrette has killed lots of people, and he has to pay for it. Guys like you and me are just doing our job. Whatever your problem is, we can fix it. Put down your weapon and back away from it."

He knew how it was going to play out, no different from a filmstrip that had snapped in half and was spinning out of control on the reel. He saw himself and the impaired man caught forever in a series of black-and-white fragments that Clete would never be able to scrub from his dreams. The impaired man pointed a single-barrel .410 shotgun pistol at Clete's chest.

Clete began firing, not counting the number of rounds he squeezed off, his ears ringing, the man going straight down on his knees, looking up at Clete. Clete kept pulling the trigger, the cylinder turning, the hammer snapping dryly on spent cartridges, both hands shaking even after his target had slumped sideways on the floor.

Clete hit the light switch. The dead man's mouth was hanging open, the overhead light shining into it. "Good God," he said, his stomach turning.

He leaned against the wall, his eyes shut, his head exploding with sound and color, wondering who he was or who he had become and at the lengths he would go in order to stay alive.

Clete came downstairs; his green eyes were the only color in his face. He paused and dumped his spent cartridges in his palm, then clinked them into his coat pocket, as though walking around inside a dream.

"What happened up there?" I said.

"I killed a guy. He had a four-ten pistol," he replied. "I tried to make him put it down. He was making sounds like he was trying to talk, and I shot him."

"Who was he?" I said.

"I never saw him before. Dave, his tongue

was cut out. I smoked a guy who couldn't talk. Maybe he was retarded. I don't know what he was."

"Slow it down. Are you sure what you saw?"

"You think I could make something like that up? He must be some guy who works for Surrette. Maybe there are more like him on the property, like some kind of cult."

"You've got to keep it together, partner," I said. "There's nothing supernatural about Surrette. Psychopaths network."

But Clete's mind was obviously concentrated on the image of the man who had died in front of his revolver, and he was not interested in hearing anything I had to say.

"I tried to go down in the basement twice but got kicked back up the stairs," I said. "Someone is in the corner with a semi-auto and a high-capacity magazine."

"Where's Alafair?" he asked.

"Outside with Gretchen."

"What are they waiting on?"

"I don't know, Clete. What are they supposed to do? Spray the basement through the window?"

"Maybe the guy upstairs was trying to tell me something. Maybe he didn't understand what I said to him. I started shooting and couldn't stop."

"Listen to me. The program is simple. We get all the innocent people out of here, and we dust the rest. That's it."

"I think we blew it. I think this one is coming apart on us."

"Wrong."

Either Alafair or Gretchen broke the glass and the taped vinyl leaf bag out of the basement window, sending all of it crashing to the floor.

"I'm going down," Clete said. "I'm going to take out these fuckers or lose it here."

And that's what he did.

CHAPTER 39

I followed him down the steps into the darkness. The air was damp and smelled of burned gunpowder and water that had stagnated in a drain. There was another odor, too, the one I had smelled outside the cave behind Albert's house. Again and again, even moments ago, I had denied to others the possibility that Asa Surrette was larger than the sum of his parts. His grandiose rhetoric was pirated from the Bible and even from Percy Shelley. His arrogance and narcissism reminded me of Freud's statement about the practicing alcoholic: "Ah, yes, his highness the child." Yet I could not explain the fecal stench exuding from his glands; the level of cruelty he imposed on others; the fact that he murdered children in cold blood and felt no remorse; and finally, his ability to recruit others to his cause, convincing them they could profit by the association and walk away from it unscathed.

Nathaniel Hawthorne and Herman Melville and André Schwarz-Bart, the French-Jewish writer who lost his family at Auschwitz, had all asked the same question and never found an answer, or at least one I knew of. Could I expect more of myself? I wanted to forget Surrette and think of Shakespeare's famous words in *The Tempest*. How does the passage go? *We are such stuff as dreams are made on, and our little life is rounded with a sleep.* The poignancy of the line calls up compassion and humility. The words of Surrette suggest a dark complexity that befouls the mind as soon as we try to address it. I think that is where his power came from. We undid ourselves in trying to fathom a mystery that was not a mystery at all.

As I descended into the basement, into its rank odor of sweat and urine and human torment, I realized that the die was cast for all of us, and speculation was of little value in dealing with evil. We try to protect the innocent and punish the wicked and don't do a very good job of either. Ultimately, we adopt the methods of our adversaries and grease them off the earth and change nothing.

These were the same thoughts I had when I went down a night trail salted with Chinese toe-poppers almost fifty years ago. If my old friend the line sergeant were still alive, I wondered what he would have to say. I suspected he would tell me that the biggest illusion in our lives is the belief that we have control over anything.

We reached the bottom of the stairs without a shot being fired. Clete and I were crouched low, shell casings and powdered brick and concrete and broken glass from the lightbulbs crunching under our shoes. I could make out a stooped figure to our right, close to the wall. "Albert, is that you?" I whispered.

He didn't answer. He was working the wire loose from Molly's wrists. He waved one hand at me, gesturing for me to approach. I worked my way across the basement and propped the M-1 against the wall, then got down on my knees and unwrapped the rest of the wire from Molly's wrists. I hugged her head against my chest and pressed my face against her hair. Both of her hands were squeezed tight on my forearm. I could feel the heat in her body and the hardness in her back and the hum of her blood when I touched the nape of her neck.

"At least one of them went up a ladder," Albert whispered. "Maybe two of them did."

"How many were down here?" I asked.

"Surrette, Boyd, and a guy named Terry," he said. "Boyd is the weak sister. Terry is the guy who opened up on y'all."

"You saw no one else?"

"We heard Surrette talking to somebody upstairs, somebody whose voice was impaired," Albert said. "Surrette was yelling at him."

"What about Caspian?" I said.

"He's not here," Albert said.

"The girls are in a cage, Dave," Molly said. "The ladder is on the other side of the cage."

"Where's Felicity Louviere?"

"On a bed against the far wall," Albert said.

"Is she alive?" I asked.

"I don't know," he replied. "She was in a lot of pain."

"He did terrible things to her, Dave," Molly said. "This man isn't human."

I got to my feet and picked up the M-1. I tried to think what Surrette would do under the present circumstances. He was a survivor of the most cynical kind. If a plane were going down and there was only one parachute on board, Surrette would have it strapped on his back. I suspected that Boyd and Terry and the impaired man Clete killed had never guessed that Surrette probably used countless people just like them, flicking them away as he would a hangnail once they served their purpose.

From what Albert had said, at least one man was still in the basement. Who would it be? Certainly not Surrette and probably not Jack Boyd.

I moved away from the wall and tapped Clete on the shoulder, then pointed toward the concrete pillar. He began inching toward the far side of the basement and the bed where Felicity Louviere was tied.

"Hey, Terry," I said. "This is Dave Robicheaux. I'm a sheriff's detective in Louisiana. Let's talk about your prospects."

There was a pause. Then he surprised me. "Go ahead," he said.

"You can give it up and cooperate with us or become potted meat here and now. What did you do to my wife's face?"

"That was an accident," he replied.

"Beating up women is an accident?"

"She fell. What the fuck, man? Am I my sister's keeper or what?"

"Slide your piece out here and live to fight another day."

"I sprung a leak. I don't think I've got another day."

"You're hit?"

I could make out his shadow and hear him moving, his shoes scraping on the concrete, as though he were pushing himself into a more comfortable position against the wall.

"An ambulance will be out here soon," I said.

"Spare me the crap, slick. There's no cell service, and you cut the telephone line. Nobody's coming. In case you haven't been listening, somebody has been setting off fireworks on the lake for the last half hour. We're just part of the fun."

"You sound like a smart guy," I said. "Why not do the smart thing now? The sunrise can be pretty nice. Why throw it away?"

"I was a jigger on the biggest armored-car score in the history of Boston. I didn't do scut work for people like Surrette. I'm not going down on a kidnapping and sexual assault beef." The finality in his tone was unmistakable.

I tried again. "It's always the first inning," I said. "Ask yourself what's the better choice, a hospital bed at St. Pat's or the DOA club."

"My full name is Terry McCarthy. Thanks for the dance, slick," he said. "My family lives in Haverhill, Mass. I'd like to get shipped back there."

He worked his back up the wall until he was standing, a Bushmaster semi-auto propped on his hip. His thigh and one arm were wet with blood, his teeth white in the glow through the broken window. He started toward me, dragging one foot, hefting up the Bushmaster so he could level it at me and Molly and Albert. I aimed the M-1 at the middle of his face so the round would destroy his motor control and send him straight to the floor before he could squeeze off a round. Terry McCarthy was grinning, as though he had demonstrated a victory of will over the powers of his executioner. I did not want to shoot him. Like many of his kind, he showed a degree of dignity at the end of the line that made you wonder if things could have been different for him. I squinted through the M-1's peep sight and tightened my finger inside the trigger guard.

That was when Gretchen Horowitz snapped off three rounds through the window, just like that, and blew his skullcap all over the floor.

Clete used his pocketknife to cut the ropes binding Felicity's hands and feet. Then he wrapped her in the sheet on her body and picked her up and carried her up the stairs and through the smashed French doors into the night. Her left arm was around his neck, her head on his shoulder. He could feel her breathing on his chest. "We're getting you out of here, kid," he said. "But I got to know who else is on the grounds."

"I don't know," she whispered.

"Dave thinks Caspian is a player."

"No, he's afraid of his father. Caspian deserted me, but he won't do anything to me."

"Caspian's father is dead," Clete said.

"Love is dead?" she said.

"That's safe to say. Wyatt Dixon or his girlfriend or both of them cut off his head."

"I don't believe that."

"You think a guy like that can't die? He was a bum, just like his son." Clete set her down inside Gretchen's pickup truck and brushed her hair away from her eyes. "You know the difference between rich guys and people like us? They get to make the rules, and we don't. They screw down and marry up, and the rest of us just get fucked."

Even in her pain, he saw her smile. He reclined the seat slightly so she could be more comfortable. There were smudges of blood and grease on the sheet wherever it made contact with her skin. "What did Surrette do to you, Felicity?" he asked.

"Everything," she said.

"Do you know where he might have gone?"

"He's here," she replied. "He won't leave. He thinks he'll prevail over all of you. That's what he calls it, 'prevailing.' He thinks that's his destiny."

Alafair and Gretchen had walked up behind Clete. "Why are we his enemies?" Gretchen asked.

"He's psychotic. He says the earth must be conquered by prevailing over its ordinary people. He says the leaders aren't important. They can always be bought."

"Watch Felicity for me," Clete said.

"Where are you going?" Gretchen said.

"To break every bone in this guy's body," he replied.

I found a piece of pipe on the floor behind the boiler and pried the lock off the cage where the girls were held. Both of them had the haunted expression that I have seen only twice in my life, once in army footage taken of the Dachau inmates on the day of their liberation, and a second time in Vietnam, when I looked into the faces of people who had survived the snake-and-nape bombing of their village.

I slung the M-1 on my shoulder and climbed the ladder that Surrette and Jack Boyd had used to escape the basement. It protruded through a trapdoor into a pantry just off the kitchen; the trapdoor looked like it had been sawed and hinged recently. I went through the first floor of the house, then climbed the stairs and searched the same rooms Clete had searched. Surrette and Boyd were gone. But where? We hadn't heard a vehicle drive away or any sound of a motorized boat on the lake.

I went out on a balcony that allowed a fine view of the grounds and the work sheds and the cherry trees, heavy with fruit. I realized a surreal phenomenon had taken place while we were in the basement, one that seemed to have no cause. I had heard about the northern lights, although I was never sure what they were. I also had been in parts of the world — the Bermuda Triangle and a similar nautical area off the coast of Japan — where the laws of physics didn't always apply and electromagnetic influences seemed to have their way with compasses and gyroscopes and radar and even the creation of whirlpools and tidal waves.

This was different. The moon had disappeared, either behind a mountain peak or in a bank of thunderheads pushing down from British Columbia. By all odds, the lake and the mountains that surrounded it should have been submerged in darkness. That was not what happened. There was a ubiquitous glow from the other side of the mountains. It was cobalt blue and seemed to emanate from the land into the sky, rather than the other way around. The lake itself, which was vast and deep and, even in July, cold enough to pucker your skin, was absolutely black and yet brimming with nocturnal radiance.

I wondered if my fatigue and adrenaline and revulsion had impaired both my senses and my ability to think. I was convinced that was not the case. I'm also convinced that all the events I was about to see and participate in happened just as I will describe them. I have never set much store in psychological stability or what we refer to as normalcy. I don't believe the world is a rational place; nor do I believe that either science or the study of metaphysics can explain any of the great mysteries. I have always fled the presence of those who claim they know the truth about anything. I agree with George Bernard Shaw's statement that we learn little or nothing from rational people, because rational people adapt themselves to the world and, consequently, are seldom visionary.

I went downstairs holding the M-1 at port

arms and walked through the French doors into the yard. The lights were off at the marina, but the hulls of the sailboats in their slips were white and sleek in the chop, rocking softly against the rubber tires hung from the mooring posts. Had not at least one person inside a cabin on one of those boats been alarmed by the gunfire and used a landline to call in a 911? Perhaps they had. Or perhaps no one was in the boats. Or perhaps they couldn't have cared less.

I saw Clete walking toward me, Gretchen's jungle-clipped AR-15 slung over his right shoulder. "Where are Molly and Albert?" he asked.

"With the girls on the back steps. Molly was opening up some canned food," I replied.

He nodded and looked around, his eyes sweeping the lakeshore and the shadows by the work sheds and the cherry trees puffing in the wind. "It's cold," he said. "None of them have wraps."

"You want to pack it in?"

"Surrette is still out here. If we leave, he skates. Let Molly and Albert take Felicity and the girls to the hospital in Polson."

"I don't like them being on the highway by themselves," I said.

"You've got a point."

"Let's search the sheds and the orchards and the cottage where the wrecker is parked," I said.

He nodded again, then I saw his expression change as he gazed up the slope toward the two-lane. "Fuck," he said.

Three sets of headlights were coming down the grade from the southern end of the lake. The first vehicle slowed and turned into the driveway that led down to the two-story stone house. The other two turned with it. None of the vehicles had emergency flashers. The drivers cut their headlights before they reached the stone house. In seconds, the three vehicles had disappeared among the work sheds and orchards.

"You were right," Clete said. "It's Caspian Younger. He's about to inherit billions, and we're the only thing standing in his way. How did we let these motherfuckers get behind us?"

Because I didn't listen to my old friend the line sergeant, I thought.

"What do you want to do, Streak?"

"Like you said."

"What did I say?"

"Blow up their shit," I replied.

Clete and I began walking toward the work sheds that were located on the far side of two cherry orchards that sloped from the two-lane down to the water's edge. The bandolier of .30-06 clips clinked softly against my back. He was carrying the AR-15 with his right hand wrapped in the pistol grip, the butt against his hip. "I've got a bad feeling about this place, Streak."

"Why?"

"I don't know how to put it. It's ancient country. It's like it's full of ghosts, like we stumbled into something a lot bigger than us."

"Don't think that way. A perp is a perp. Like you always said, bust them or dust them. We're the good guys; they're not."

"Sounds good. Except you know better," he said. "Surrette is the real deal, Dave."

"What do you mean?"

"A guy you can't put a label on. A guy who was allowed to go on killing people for over twenty years. How'd we get into this shit? Why us? It's like we didn't have a choice, like we were supposed to meet up with this guy."

I did not want to dwell on the implications. Clete was not one given to extravagant rhetoric. The fact that he had said what he said made my breath come short in my chest.

We continued through the orchard, fifteen feet apart. The first shed was a long weathered building shaped like a boxcar, with a peaked, shingled roof. Through the trees, I could see two SUVs and a Chrysler parked on a gravel roadway. Eight or nine men had gathered by the car. Both Clete and I sank to one knee and remained motionless inside the orchard, the branches waving above us, shadows shifting back and forth on our bodies.

The wind is the enemy of every infiltrator in a wooded area; when it blows, everything moves except the infiltrator. The other enemy is the reflection of light on your face. Clete and I lowered our heads and stared at the ground. We could hear one man addressing the others. There was no mistaking the imperious tone and its implicit sense of entitlement and authority. I'm sure that in Caspian Younger's mind he was not only a leader of men with the bodies of gladiators whose lives had been characterized by hardship and the violent ethos of mercenaries; he was also their brother-in-arms and knew their needs and commanded their respect. I am sure that Caspian Younger believed he was a man among men.

As I looked at his Australian flop hat, and the cargo pants tucked into his fur-lined suede boots, and the long-sleeved flannel shirt and quilted vest, and his arms that were like pipe cleaners, I wondered if he had any idea at all of the ridiculous figure he cut. His subordinates probably laughed at him behind his back. His hands were on his hips as if he were a senior officer addressing his troops. We could hear every word he said.

"Listen up, you guys. You are now in my employ as licensed private investigators and security personnel," he said. "We are stopping a crime in progress. We are rescuing two innocent teenage girls. I believe my wife is already dead. Before the sun rises, everyone on this property except the two girls may be dead also. That is not our intention, but that is probably what will happen."

Up on the highway, a pair of headlights came over the rise and descended the grade, the high beams tunneling through the darkness between the orchards and the slope of the mountain. Caspian was disconcerted for only a moment. "No matter what else happens, there is one man who will not leave this property. That man is Asa Surrette," he said. "The men who take him out will divide a twenty-thousand-dollar credit line in Las Vegas. I want him blown apart. Does everyone understand?"

The wind dropped and the night was still. A pickup truck on the highway was slowing as it came down the grade, as though the driver were looking for a turnoff. The pickup passed under a light pole that had been left on over a cherry stand. The truck was painted metallic orange; a camper shell was snugged into the bed.

"One other thing," Caspian said. "There's a fat guy out here named Purcel. He's a disgraced cop from New Orleans who abused my wife. I want him alive. You can put some holes in him, but he doesn't do the big exit before I have a chat with him. Are there any questions?"

"What if some IPs go down?" one man asked.

"Innocent persons?" Caspian said. "There are no innocent persons. That's why people get baptized. You didn't know that? You break eggs to make an omelet. One baby dies, another lives. A whole society is destroyed when one of us steps on an anthill. A hundred thousand die to control the benchmark price on a barrel of oil. That's how the world operates. We didn't make the rules. Any other questions?"

He was smiling. I wondered what Clete was thinking. I also wondered how an execrable creature like Caspian Younger, whose sneer and arrogance were like none I had ever seen, could be given the power to make decisions about the life and death of other people.

"All right, start your sweep," he said. "If in doubt, take it out."

"That truck up on the highway?" one man said.

"What about it?" Caspian asked.

"It just stopped and turned around."

Clete Purcel's night vision was not of an ordinary kind. He did not see the external world more clearly than anyone else during the nocturnal hours, nor did he see it with any less clarity; he simply saw it in a different fashion. After his return from Southeast Asia, he realized that a fundamental change had taken place inside his neurological makeup. The change was not one he understood, at least not until he read an article in a town-and-country magazine about the way horses see the world. According to the article, horses have two visual screens in their heads and watch both simultaneously.

Unlike the horse, Clete did not have two screens in his head; he had two transmitters, and they contended for space on a single screen. Any number of triggers could send him back in time and click on a live feed from the years 1966 to 1968 and force him to watch scenes from a horror show that never had a good ending.

He had not moved or even raised his eyelids while Caspian addressed his men. Inside his head, he saw a valley swirling with elephant grass that was never green but always gray or yellow or brown, as though the land had been systemically poisoned and could not follow the dictates of the season. At the far end of the valley were hills that had the softly contoured shape of a woman's breasts, and in order to reach them, he had to follow the banks of a muddy stream coated with mosquitoes and strung with the feces of water buffalo. The only sounds in the valley were the sucking noises of his boots in the mud and the thropping of helicopters in a sky the color of brass. Even though Clete was now crouched inside a fruit orchard on an alpine lake, he could smell the jungle rot in his feet and the body stink in his utilities and feel sweat running down his sides like lines of black ants.

"A couple of you guys check out that truck and tell the guy to mind his own business," Clete heard Caspian say.

"I've seen that truck," one man said. "You know who that is?"

"No, I don't," Caspian said. "That's why I told you to check him out."

"He's a shitkicker," the same man said. "You know, what's-his-name."

"Have I hired a bunch of morons?" Caspian said.

"We're on it, Mr. Younger," another man said.

"The guy has a squirrel cage for a brain," the first man said. "I can't remember his name."

"Then be quiet and go find out who he is."

Three rockets zipped from an island in the lake and popped overhead in a shower of blue and pink and white foam, lighting the orchard like a pistol flare.

"Behind you, Mr. Younger," one of Caspian's men said, pointing at the cherry trees.

That was when they all cut loose.

They had seen Clete but not me. At least six or seven were firing in his direction, the bullets ripping through the trees, cutting branches and raining black cherries on the ground. I was still on one knee. I raised the M-1 to my shoulder and aimed through the peep sight and began shooting. I had never fired an M-1 at a human target. The first man I hit was running for the edge of the shed, trying to position himself so he could choose his shots as his compatriots took the brunt of our fire. I saw red flowers bloom on the back of his shirt while his body jacked forward and struck the shed wall.

Another man had set up behind the fender of the Chrysler and was firing a semi-auto that had a suppressor and an extended magazine, not aiming and probably not counting rounds. Each shot sounded like compressed air released from a bottle of carbonated water. Because the suppressor lowered the bullet's velocity, the rounds that went past my ear made a whirring sound, like a boomerang whipping through the air. My first shot hit the headlight and blew glass into his face. The second whanged off the top of the fender and hit the shed wall. The third went home and knocked him loose from the car and onto the ground, where he remained with his feet pulled up in a fetal position.

The bolt locked open on an empty chamber, and I heard the tinny sound of the clip ejecting. I pushed another into the breech and released the bolt and began firing again, the stock recoiling solidly into my shoulder with each shot. I saw Clete Purcel coming toward me, bent low, holding his hip, as though he had walked into the sharp corner of a tabletop. His face was pale, his eyes bigger than they should have been. He sank down next to me. I gathered up the sling of his rifle and slung it on my shoulder. "How bad are you hurt?" I said.

"I think it went on through. Maybe it clipped a bone," he said. A bloodstain was spreading through his shirt. "More of them are headed our way."

"No, there were only eight or nine besides Younger. I got at least two of them."

"I saw them coming down the slope. I didn't imagine it."

I shook my head. "That's not possible," I replied. "There's nobody else up that slope. Keep it simple, Cletus. Younger is an amateur, and so are the guys who work for him. He's down to a few men."

"I know what I saw." He took his .38 from his holster. "Get going. I'll slow them up."

"That's not going to happen, Clete. Get up."

"I'm too dizzy. That son of a bitch really whacked me."

I got to my feet and pulled him up with me, working his big arm over my shoulder. "You're going with me, or we're going out together. If we can make it to the driveway, we'll spray the orchard and have Gretchen and Alf on their flanks. We'll cut them to pieces."

His eyes closed and opened again, as though he were unsure where he was. "Let's rock," he said.

We moved through the trees, the cherries hitting our faces, the tree branches like whips against our skin. Then I heard the report of a rifle from the yard of the stone house and heard a bullet zip through the trees and smack against the shed, followed by a second and a third shot, and I realized Gretchen was putting down covering fire for us with the bolt-action Mauser she carried in her pickup. "See?" I said. "We're going to make it. Just put one foot after another. It's easy. Like Rudyard Kipling said about going up Khyber Pass, you do it one bloody foot at a time."

I could feel Clete's knees starting to sag. "I need to rest," he whispered. "Let me go, Dave. I'll be all right. I've just got to sit down and rest for a while. I've never felt this tired."

CHAPTER 40

Clete sat in a grassy depression in the lawn of the stone house, a swale that probably operated as a drain during the spring runoff. He stared back at the orchard and the wind in the tops of the trees. In his mind's eye, he was back in the valley that led to the hills resembling a woman's breasts. It was sunset in the valley, and in the gathering dusk, he began the ascent of the first hill in a series he would have to traverse before he could slip off his pack and his rifle and his steel pot and lie down and sleep in a dry hole free of mosquitoes and snakes and dream about a Eurasian girl who lived on a sampan by the shore of the China Sea.

He never saw the stick grenade that arced end over end out of the shadows and bounced off a tree trunk and exploded five feet from him and killed two other marines and blew Clete down the hillside. Nor was he able to reason his way through the events taking place around him — the automatic-weapons fire that looked like flashes from an electric power line dancing in the darkness, somebody yelling for the blooker, the *throp* of helicopter blades, and the rattle of a Gatling gun that was ripping foliage and geysers of dirt out of the hillside.

Everything taking place around him no longer seemed his concern, because he knew he was about to die. The sensation was not as he had imagined it. He felt as though he were being drawn back through a tunnel, one that was translucent and pink and blue, a place he had been before. It was the birth canal, he was sure of that, and on the other end of it, he thought he could see a warm and lighted presence that should have been his birthright but had been denied him during his time on earth.

Then the face of a navy corpsman was looking into his. "Don't go dinky-dow on me," the corpsman said. "Hang on to your ass. We're going for the ride of your life. Then you're the fuck out of here, man. We're talking about the Golden Gate in '68. Just stay with me."

The corpsman wiped Clete's face and pulled loose his flak vest, then rolled him onto a poncho liner and dragged him like a human sled all the way to the bottom of the hill.

Clete lay on his back inside the swale and looked up at the stars. He could hear Gretchen shooting and smell the grass and the fertilizer in a flower bed and the cold that seemed to be blowing down from a snowfield high up in the mountains.

"We never made it back from over there," he said. "We thought we did, but they body-bagged us and forgot to tell us about it. They stole our lives, Dave."

Then he rolled on his side and vomited in the grass.

I wiped his mouth with my handkerchief and brushed the hair out of his eyes. "You can't leave me, Clete," I said.

"Who said I am?"

"You were talking out of your head," I said. "Vietnam is yesterday's box score. Forget Vietnam and everything that happened over there."

"I was talking about 'Nam? I don't think I was. I was having a dream, that's all."

"We have to go, partner. Can you make it?"

"Go where?"

"To hook up with Gretchen and Alf. We need to nail these guys as they come out of the orchard. We still have Surrette to deal with."

He widened his eyes as though trying to bring the world back into focus. "Dave, I know I dropped at least three of those ass-holes. This is what you're not hearing. There are a lot more of them than you think. I saw them coming through the grass."

"There's no grass out there, Clete. You're losing it. Come on, get up!"

He pulled the AR-15 off my shoulder and tried to stand, then fell sideways, like a drunk. "I think I'm a couple of quarts down."

"That's okay. You're doing fine," I said. I got his arm over my shoulders again and hooked one hand under the back of his belt and pulled him up. "We've been in a lot worse shape than this."

"When?"

I couldn't think of the instance. We headed across the lawn into the shadow of the stone house. I could see Gretchen and Alafair coming toward us. In the background, the lake was green-black, the rocks in the shallows illuminated with a strange light that had no source, the wind blowing whitecaps onto the shore, each as defined as a brushstroke in an oil painting.

"Things are happening here that aren't real, Dave," Clete said. "It scares the hell out of me."

"We don't have anything to be afraid of," I said.

I think he tried to laugh. I held him tighter, pulling up on his belt, my knees starting to fail.

Gretchen was holding the Mauser bolt-action with one hand across her shoulder. She grabbed Clete's other arm. "Let's get him into your truck," she said.

"Screw that," Clete said.

"Do what I tell you, big boy," she said.

"We're cut off, Dave," Alafair said. "They've got a couple of vehicles parked across the drive."

"Is there anybody in those sailboats?" I said.

"I couldn't raise anyone. I went down there twice," she said. "Somebody cut the phone line to the bar."

"Surrette?" I said.

"I don't know. What do you want to do?" she said.

"Did y'all see an orange pickup on the road, one with a camper in the bed?" I said.

"We saw some headlights stop on the road," Gretchen said. "You think that's Wyatt Dixon's truck?"

"I guess he doesn't own the only orange pickup in West Montana," I said.

"We have too many hurt people here. We've got to get off the dime," she said.

"We're in a box," I said. "That's the long and short of it. Our advantage is that they have to come to us. We've also put a dent in their numbers."

"How many of them are there?" Alafair asked.

"No more than a handful," I said.

Clete was sitting on the bumper of Gretchen's truck, bent forward, his head down.

"Wrong," he said without looking up.

"Clete saw more men than I did," I said.

"Dave, look!" Alafair said, pointing up the slope.

I don't know where they came from. I could see flashlights moving down the slope on either side of the property. I had no idea who they were or how they got there, if they worked for Caspian Younger or not. I was no longer sure that anything I saw was there.

"Give me the AR-15," Clete said, his head on his chest. "I dropped my piece on the lawn."

Gretchen squeezed my arm tightly, her face close to mine. "Time to bust some caps, Dave. We'll figure all this out later," she said. She picked up the AR-15 and left Clete the Mauser.

She was right. We were outnumbered, cut off from the highway, and flanked, with the lake at our back.

"Come on, Dave, call it," Gretchen said.

I could see Molly and Albert and the two girls on the back steps of the house, and I could see Felicity Louviere sleeping in the front seat of Gretchen's pickup. Clete could hardly move. Blood had run from his side all the way to the knee of his trousers. I felt at a total loss.

"Take it to them," I said.

"Do what?" Alafair said.

"We go right down the middle," I said. "If

Caspian Younger wants a fight, let's give it to him."

By anyone's reckoning, it was a foolish idea, perhaps one that had its origins in medieval romance or Henry V's address to his troops before the siege at Agincourt. But there are times when the probability of death in your life is so great that you step across a line and no longer fear it. I believe that was what happened to us as we stood close by a glacial lake where dinosaurs and mastodons once fed and played among the buttercups and ice lilies.

We left Clete with Felicity Louviere and walked three abreast across the lawn, Alafair and Gretchen and I, each of us bearing down on Caspian Younger, who had just emerged with his men from the cherry orchard.

Like most cowards, he had not anticipated our response. He could have opened fire on us or ordered his men to do so, but he knew they were all watching him, expecting him to be more than the posturing figure who wore the quilted vest of the hunter and used the martial rhetoric of a drill instructor. He stood awkwardly in front of his men, the breeze tousling his hair. A blue-black revolver with white handles hung from his right hand. It was probably a collectible, the kind a publicity-oriented army officer with political aspirations might wear in a shoulder holster.

"Well, what do we have here?" he said.

"Keep working on it. You'll figure it out," I replied.

"Is this the defining moment for you and your little team, Mr. Robicheaux?"

"You tell me, Mr. Younger. You're the guy who turned his wife over to the tender mercies of a sadist like Asa Surrette, the same man who murdered your daughter," I said.

"Like always, you've got it wrong," he said.

"He suffocated her with a plastic bag and ejaculated on her legs," I said. "She was seventeen. Maybe she called out your name when she begged for help."

His whiskers looked like dirty smudges on his cheeks and chin. His eyes shifted sideways when he saw that he was caught between allowing me to speak and ordering his men to shoot in order to stop me from revealing his failure as a father and husband and finally as a human being. I held the M-1 at port arms, the safety off; no matter how things played out, I was determined to spike his cannon before I went down.

"I get it," he said. "This is your finest hour. The egalitarian philosopher delivering his grand speech to the multitudes. Unfortunately, the role doesn't serve you well. We've researched every aspect of your life, Mr. Robicheaux. We have your psychiatric records, your pitiful statements about your dependency on your whore of a mother, your sexual history in Manila and Yokohama, the possibility of a homoerotic relationship with your fat friend, your constant whining about all the injustices visited on the miserable piece of swamp you grew up in. The fact that you take others to task for their mistakes has established new standards in hypocrisy."

"The problem for you, Mr. Younger, is that after I'm dead and gone, you'll still be you," I said. "You'll wake up every morning knowing that your half brother is Wyatt Dixon, and on his worst day, he could stuff you in a matchbox with his thumb. By the way, how'd a loser like you convince all these guys to work for you? Do they know you had your daughter killed so you could inherit her estate? If you'd do that to her, what will you do to them?"

"You're looking at your executioner, Mr. Robicheaux," he said. "Want to add anything to your final words?"

"Yeah, you're going with me," I said.

"No matter what happens, I'm instructing my men to enjoy themselves with Horowitz and your daughter one piece at a time. They're going to be busy girls. Let that be your last thought, Mr. Robicheaux. I think we should get the festivities started now, so you can watch what you've wrought. I understand Horowitz has already pulled a train or two, so she might enjoy it."

"Fuck you, you little pimp," Alafair said.

"Copy that," Gretchen said.

The three of us knew our time had run out,

and our flippancy was a denial of the fate that awaited us. We'd rolled the dice and lost. *So this is where it all ends,* I thought. *All our dreams and hopes become as naught, and evil men are allowed to hang their lanterns on our tombstones. What greater folly is there?*

I swallowed and looked at the ground, then raised my head. I knew if I swung the muzzle of the M-1 in front of me and began squeezing off rounds, I might put a couple of serious holes in Caspian Younger. Chances were I would not. Too many weapons were pointed at me. I suspected I had about three or four seconds to live.

I saw an electrical flash in the clouds. It seemed to leap into the sky from a snowfield cupped between two mountains and ripple through the heavens all the way to the horizon. In that brief moment, I saw a figure standing atop the peaked roof of the work shed, like a human lightning rod waiting to be struck. I was too far away to make out his features, but I was sure I saw his starched-brim cowboy hat and wide shoulders and tapered hips and thighs stuffed into tight-fitting Wranglers.

I saw the rifle, too. It was a long-barrel lever-action repeater, and I guessed it was the 1892 Winchester with an elevator sight that Wyatt Dixon carried in the camper shell on the back of his truck.

The shooter fired only once. The round was likely soft-nosed, with a notched cross hammer-tapped into the lead for good measure. When it struck the back of Caspian Younger's skull, it left a hole no bigger than the tip of your little finger but blew his forehead apart like an exploding watermelon. He fell forward into a spruce tree, stone dead, his throat catching in a fork, his knees striking the ground simultaneously.

The lightning died in the sky, and the roof of the shed receded into a blue-black darkness that seemed to be spreading from the lake across the entirety of the valley. The men who had been standing on either side of Caspian Younger moved away from his body, staring at it dumbly, glancing back at the orchard and the shed and the mountaintops, as jagged and sharp as scissored tin against the sky.

I tried to make out their faces. Were they mercenaries, adventurers, or jailhouse riffraff? They seemed to have no more depth or singularity than a computer-generated illusion. "We've got no grievance against you guys," I said. "The way I see it, Younger got what he deserved. How about we call it square?"

No one moved or spoke.

"There's another way to look at it," I said. "That was probably Wyatt Dixon on the roof. If you've been around these parts, you know his reputation. Who needs grief with a dude like that? Wyatt gives insanity a bad name."

I saw them start stepping back from us, like people withdrawing from a presence they truly fear, not because of their experience with it but because of an atavistic instinct that goes back before recorded time.

Then I realized my terrible mistake.

Surrette never left the house, I thought.

Clete was still sitting on the bumper of the truck, nauseated, his head spinning from blood loss. He was looking at his feet and the shine of his blood on the tops of his loafers, his eyes half-lidded.

"Got you, fat boy," a voice said.

Clete raised his eyes and looked straight ahead. He felt the muzzle of a handgun touch his ear. "Is that you, Boyd?" he asked.

"Surprised?"

"What happened to the light?" Clete asked.

"What light?"

"The northern lights or whatever it was. That's you, huh, Jack? You're still hanging around?"

"We never left, you idiot. We snookered you good." He pushed the gun tighter into Clete's ear. With the other hand, he picked up the Mauser bolt-action and hung it over his shoulder. "I'd say you're in a lot of trouble."

"Yep, that's true," Clete said.

"What do you think dying is gonna be like?"

"I'll let you know."

"You should have been a clown on one of those kid shows. You could be Captain Animal, an old pervert loitering around the kiddie park."

"It's a thought," Clete said.

"You think I won't pop you?"

"Not unless Surrette tells you to. You're like me: You'll always be a dirty cop, wherever you go. I've got a PI badge. You've got Surrette. For the rest of your life, you won't take a dump without his permission."

"I can leave him anytime I want."

Clete turned his head slowly, trying to concentrate on Jack Boyd's face. "If you do anything to Molly and Albert and the girls, I'm going to hurt you."

"*You're* going to hurt *me*?"

"Take it to the bank."

"You're a laugh a minute," Boyd said.

"That's me," Clete replied.

Jack Boyd walked toward the front of the house, the German rifle slung upside down on his shoulder, his trousers tucked inside the tops of his hand-tooled boots. Involuntarily, Clete's head fell on his chest, his eyes shutting, his shoulders slumping. For a moment, he thought he was going to fall on the grass. He forced himself to his feet and walked toward the back of Gretchen's pickup, the stars burning coldly in a sky that looked like purple velvet. He reached inside the truck bed and felt along the sides until his fingers touched the tip of a steel chain.

The odor from behind me was unmistakable. I turned and looked into the face of Asa Surrette. He was wearing a bulletproof vest and carrying a Bushmaster semi-automatic rifle. "We finally meet," he said. He touched the muzzle of the Bushmaster to the back of Alafair's head. "Lay your weapons down, please."

"Don't do it, Dave," Alafair said.

Surrette winked at me. "Humor me," he said.

"You got it," I said. I set the M-1 down on the grass. Gretchen lay her AR-15 down and pushed it away with her foot.

"Do as he says, Alafair," I said.

She was carrying a cut-down Browning twelve-gauge that Gretchen had given her. She squatted slowly and placed it on the grass, then stood up. She gazed at Surrette a long time. "We saw what you did to Felicity," she said.

"It was what she wanted. Have you been publishing any more magazine articles?" he said.

"No, I published a novel. What about you?" she said. "Has Creative Artists or William Morris been trying to get in touch with you?"

"Oh, you're good," he said.

"I looked through the house. Where were you?" I said.

"In the attic. The one place you didn't look."

"Pretty slick," I said. "Who are these guys?"

"You don't know?" he asked.

I shook my head.

"I'll rephrase my question," he said. "You've haven't figured out yet who I am? You're that slow on the uptake?"

"Your entire life has been characterized by mediocrity," I said. "You got busted because you were stupid enough to believe the cops when they told you the floppy disk you sent them couldn't be traced."

His smile never wavered. He stepped closer to me. The odor that rose from his body made me choke. "Breathing problem?" he said.

"Yeah," I said. "I've never been around anything like it."

Jack Boyd came out of the darkness, carrying the Mauser upside down on its sling.

"Where's Clete Purcel?" I said.

"Relaxing, I suppose," Boyd said.

"You didn't finish them?" Surrette said.

"You didn't tell me to," Boyd replied.

"I'll deal with you in a minute," Surrette said.

"What do you mean, you'll deal with me?"

Surrette looked at me and Gretchen and Alafair. "Get on your knees," he said.

"Sorry," I said.

"I can put you there if you wish," he said.

"Have you ever seen someone shot through both kneecaps? Would Daddy like to see his daughter shot through her kneecaps? Tell me now."

"Kiss my ass," Alafair said.

"Don't worry," he said. "I have something special in mind for you. I'm going to turn you into an artistic masterpiece. Unfortunately, you won't be able to see the notoriety that my artwork draws, even though you'll be the centerpiece."

"Look at me, Surrette," I said.

"Look at you? Why should I? Do you think you can condescend to me and give me commands at a moment like this? You're truly a foolish man, Mr. Robicheaux."

"You're right about that," I said, holding my eyes on his. "But at least I never wrote a short story that was so bad, the professor wouldn't allow it to be read in front of the class."

I saw his chest rising and falling and his eyes narrowing and the blood draining from around his mouth. He raised a finger in the middle of my face. "You listen —" he began.

That was as far as he got. Clete Purcel lumbered out of the darkness, holding the bear trap by a handle welded to the bottom of the frame, the jaws cocked. He swung it down on top of Asa Surrette's head like an inverted skillet, the trigger impacting on Surrette's skull. The jaws snapped shut on Surrette's ears, mashing them into his scalp. Surrette dropped the Bushmaster and whirled in a circle, fighting to pull the trap from his head, his teeth grinding, blood running down his neck into his shirt collar, the tether chain hanging down his back like a Chinese pigtail.

I picked up the M-1 and shot Jack Boyd to death and then followed Asa Surrette down the slope toward the water. I suspect his pain was terrible. I also suspect that his suffering didn't begin to approach what he had inflicted on his victims for over two decades. He was silhouetted against the starlight on the lake, trying to force the trap off his head with the heels of his hands. As he stumbled onto the dock, I aimed through the M-1's peep sight and let off three rounds.

He showed no reaction. I was tempted to believe that Surrette was indeed demonic and not human and consequently impervious to bullets. Then I remembered the vest he was wearing, and I reloaded with a clip of armor-piercing ammunition and began shooting again.

He was on the dock when I hit him with the first round. I saw his shoulder jerk and his feet stumble. I fired again and heard a round clang off the steel trap. Another round tore into the side of the vest and caught him in the rib cage. But I have to hand it to him. He was still standing when I stepped onto the dock.

I would be dishonest if I said my actions at that point were driven simply by the passion and heat of the moment. I would also be inaccurate if I said I made a conscious decision about the immediate fate of Asa Surrette. I created a blank space in my mind where I thought of absolutely nothing except the faces of the innocent people whom this man had tortured and killed. In particular, I saw the faces of children. Inside that space, I pulled the trigger over and over until the bolt locked open and the clip *ping*ed into the darkness. I'm convinced that not one round went wide or high and that he ate every one before he fell off the end of the dock.

Only one thing bothers me. I thought he would go straight down into the depths of the lake with the weight of the bear trap. Instead, I saw him roll on his back, his clothes — even the armored vest — ballooning with air. He looked up into my face and grinned, the jaws of the trap embedded an inch into his skull. Only then did the lake close over his head. I wondered if Asa Surrette didn't get the last laugh.

I heard Clete behind me. "You'd better sit down," I said, taking him by the arm.

"Where's Surrette?" he said.

"Down there," I said, motioning at the water. "He was grinning when he went under. I don't understand it. I punched holes all over him."

"Yeah?" he said. "Right there?"

"That's the spot."

Clete propped himself against a dock post and unzipped his fly. I saw a golden stream arch onto the water's surface. "Wow, does that feel good," he said, his face filled with release as he tilted it up at the sky. "Look at the stars. You ever see a more beautiful place? Lordy, Lordy, Streak, I think I'm about to pass out."

I placed my arm around his waist, and together we limped up the slope, a couple of vintage low-riders left over from another era, in the season the Indians called the moon of popping cherries, in a magical land that charmed and beguiled the senses and made one wonder if divinity did not indeed hide just on the other side of the tangible world.

Epilogue

Even in retrospect, I cannot say with any exactitude what occurred on the lake that fateful summer night in 2012. I can tell you what I believe happened. I have never bought into the notion that time is linear, in the same way I feel that straight lines are a superimposition on the natural world and contravene the impetus that drives it. All matter aspires to roundness and symmetry, in the same way that the seasons are cyclical and that God in His way slays Himself with every leaf that flies. In other words, inside eternity, the alpha and the omega meet and end at the same place. I guess a simpler way of saying it is that things are often not as they appear.

Most people would conclude that the past cannot be changed. I'm not sure about that. Felicity Louviere changed her life by somehow taking on the historical role of a slave girl who died in the Carthaginian arena in the early third century. I guess that seems like an absurd premise until we consider the possibility that the dead are always with us, beckoning from the shade, reminding us that we're actors in the same drama they have already lived and that they can help us with our lives if we will only let them.

Who were the other men on the grounds the morning Asa Surrette died? I don't know. The only bodies the authorities found at sunrise were the ones we shot. I have two theories about the shadowy figures who came out of the darkness and then disappeared. They could have been part of a larger group, perhaps international mercenaries in the pay of a global corporation run by the business partners of Love Younger. But who would believe such a wild speculation? A second possibility might have more credibility. Men like Caspian Younger and his father are always among us. They do not take power; we give it to them. The armies of the night are faceless and mindless and the modern equivalent of Visigoths, but when they have a leader, their time in history rolls around again.

Surrette appropriated the name of Caracalla's brother. Surrette was not a demon; he was a worm. The irony was that he appropriated the name of a worm and wasn't aware of it.

Clete Purcel was amazingly resilient. His wounds healed during the summer and early fall, and by October we were able to go up to British Columbia and fish the Elk River, then continue up to Banff and Lake Louise, in the heart of the Canadian Rockies. Molly and Albert and Alafair and Gretchen came with us, and each morning we ate breakfast together on a terrace overlooking gardens filled with flowers against a backdrop of the biggest, bluest mountains I have ever seen. We didn't talk about the events of the summer, or the blood we had shed, or the death of Asa Surrette and Love Younger and his son Caspian. It was autumn, a time when it's better to let the wind winnow the chaff on a granary floor. To dwell upon the evil that men do gives second life to their deeds and lionizes poseurs and nonentities who will never be more than historical asterisks.

When Clete and I hiked above Lake Louise, he had to sit down and catch his breath because of the thin air and the steepness of the grade. As always, he gave no credence to the seriousness of his physical and psychological wounds; he treated the world as a giant playground where misfortune became a problem only if you allowed it to be one. But as we sat in the dappled shade of the pines and cedar trees, looking down at the milky green waters of Lake Louise and the gold poppies in full bloom, I saw in his shirt pocket the letter he had received that morning at the hotel, and I knew where his thoughts had gone.

"Felicity is in South America, huh?" I said.

"Yep, that's what she said," he replied. "Working with the Indians like her old man did."

"She'll be back one day."

"No, she won't. When her kind go away, they go away."

"Did you know I got a card from Wyatt Dixon? He didn't sign it, but I know it was from him."

"Don't mention that guy to me, Dave."

"Okay, I won't."

He unwrapped a piece of peppermint candy and put it in his mouth and sucked on it. "So what'd he say?"

" 'Tell Miss Gretchen good luck with her moviemaking.' "

"That's it?"

"That's it," I said. "Ready?"

"I'd like to just sit here awhile. The lake looks like a giant green teardrop at the foot of that snowfield. I've never seen flowers that gold," he said.

"I think you're right."

"Dave?" he said.

"What's up?"

"You think we've done okay with our lives? You think the good outweighs the bad?"

"That's the way I'd read it." I cupped my hand on his shoulder. "Let me know when you're ready, and we'll finish our stroll and take everyone to lunch. It's a grand day for it."

"Roger that, big mon," he replied.

We got up and hiked the rest of the way to the log teahouse on top of the mountain, the trees so thick and tall on either side of us that they seemed to touch the clouds, more like the pillars of heaven than earthly trees.

ABOUT THE AUTHOR

James Lee Burke is the author of thirty-two novels and two short story collections, including such *New York Times* bestsellers as *Creole Belle, The Glass Rainbow, Swan Peak, The Tin Roof Blowdown,* and *Feast Day of Fools.* He lives in Missoula, Montana.